Alpha Kings

A Billionaire Alpha Male
Romance Collection

Alison Reid

Alpha Kings - A Billionaire Alpha Male Romance Collection

by Alison Reid

This is a work of fiction. Names, characters, businesses, places, events, and incidents are either the products of the author's imagination or used in a fictitious manner. Any resemblance to actual persons, living or dead, or actual events is purely coincidental.

ISBN: 978-1-7644837-0-4

Independently published

Introduction to…

Alpha Kings

A Billionaire Alpha Male

Romance Collection

Welcome to **Alpha Kings**—a collection of powerful billionaire romances featuring commanding heroes, emotionally charged love stories, and women strong enough to challenge the men who rule their worlds.

Each novel in this collection is a complete standalone romance, previously published individually, and written in the spirit of classic Mills & Boon with a modern edge. You'll find dominant alpha heroes, enemies-to-lovers tension, forced proximity, and deeply emotional journeys that prove even the most powerful men are vulnerable to love.

Inside these pages are stories of obsession and redemption, revenge and forgiveness, and love that refuses to be controlled. There is no cheating, and every story delivers a guaranteed happily-ever-after.

Whether you're discovering these characters for the first time or returning to familiar favourites, **Alpha Kings** invites you to sink into a binge-worthy collection where passion runs deep and love is always worth the fight.

Enjoy the journey.

Table of Contents

Falling for the Billionaire

Alison Reid

A complete standalone romance

Previously published individually

Chapter One

The heir to Kaliah Island, Julian Kingsley—broad-shouldered, dark-haired, tall—was the kind of man whose presence made people forget what they'd been about to say. Handsome, some whispered too handsome, in that way that stole breath and composure from anyone who looked too long.

Beside him, the middle-aged politician lifted his glass appreciatively. "Beautiful island you've got here." His grin broadened, eyes dancing. "The beaches are glorious, and your home—magnificent."

Julian's mouth curved, polite and faintly amused. "We do take pride in our beaches," he replied, his voice smooth as the island breeze. With the ease of a man who'd spent his life navigating power, he guided the conversation seamlessly toward global economics.

A flicker of movement near the doorway pulled his attention. Towering above most of his guests, Julian caught the newcomer's eye. He gave the slightest narrowing of his gaze, a barely perceptible tilt of his chin—nothing anyone in the bustling cocktail party would notice, but more than enough for his head of security. The man slipped silently out of the room moments later.

Ten minutes passed before Julian excused himself from the politician—having conveniently introduced him to an American entrepreneur—and began making his way across the room. He paused at intervals, exchanging pleasantries, allowing handshakes and brief conversations to slow his progress.

These social-meets-strategic gatherings were never his preferred way to spend an evening. But as heir to Kaliah Island—the richest jewel in the Pacific, the only place on earth where blue diamonds were coaxed from the earth like pieces of captured starlight—they were unavoidable.

Hosting tonight's event in his parents' stately mansion had been a calculated choice, and a successful one. More than one guest had already praised the home's elegance, its weight of history, its quiet, old-world grandeur. The place radiated exactly what he needed it to: stability, legacy, the unmistakable aura of a dynasty built to endure.

Just outside the door, Julian's head of security straightened as he approached.

"What happened?" Julian asked, his tone clipped and low.

"I saw Miss Harrison—" Sam corrected himself quickly, "I mean, Mrs. Riordan—walking down the road. Staggering. I stopped to check on her." His voice dropped into a rapid whisper. "She collapsed right in front of me. Completely out. So, I took her to your home."

Julian's expression didn't shift—all chiselled control and unyielding calm—but something tightened in the silence between his breaths.

"Is she conscious now?"

"No. She still hasn't come to. I called the doctor. He wasn't there when I left her, but…" Sam swallowed. "I thought you'd want to know."

"You did the right thing," Julian said quietly. He glanced at his watch, assessing, calculating. "I'll wrap this up within the hour."

A bright, overly enthusiastic voice sliced through the tension.

"Julian—there you are!"

Sam watched his employer turn toward the doorway where an insipid blonde hovered, expectant smile in place. Julian offered her that smile—the one polished over years, charming enough to soften tempers, dissolve suspicion, and win cooperation with barely a word.

He'd once used that very smile to quell a tantrum-throwing four-year-old nephew in seconds—a feat that had earned him near-mythic status in the family.

But anyone who mistook Julian Kingsley for a pampered, idle heir learned quickly how wrong they were.

Behind those sharply cut features lay a mind as cool, incisive, and formidable as tempered steel—strategic enough to move global markets and disciplined enough to wield power with surgical precision. In the rarefied circles of high finance and international diplomacy, Julian's name carried a weight that belied his age. His reputation already stood shoulder to shoulder with that of his father, the legendary Graham Kingsley—the man who quietly but unmistakably held the reins of this breathtaking, impossibly wealthy island.

Sam discreetly averted his gaze as the woman murmured something to Julian. His employer's reply came low and measured, each word wrapped in cool civility—polite enough to appease, firm enough to draw a line she pretended not to see.

She laughed lightly, undeterred, and brushed a quick kiss against his cheek before gliding back into the room, her perfume lingering in her wake.

Julian watched her go, expression unreadable. Then, without turning, he said quietly, "Make sure no one talks."

Aurelia Carmichael heard voices—low, blurred, drifting in and out like echoes carried on a distant tide. She had surfaced before, she was almost certain of it, but only for seconds at a time—just long enough to feel the world tilt before she slipped back into the dark, whether into sleep or unconsciousness she couldn't tell.

But this time, she didn't fall away.

Through a pounding headache and a thirst so sharp it felt like sandpaper in her throat, she strained to separate the voices. Both women—one Australian, familiar in cadence. The other had a soft island lilt unmistakably native to Kaliah Island.

"…dehydrated, and it looks like she hasn't eaten much either. She should be all right now that the drip's in, but she will need monitoring for a few days."

The woman's tone was calm but threaded with quiet urgency.

Aurelia tried to force her eyes open, but her lashes felt heavy, stuck, as though someone had pressed weights onto them.

"She's coming to," the woman said, catching the faint flutter.

An arm eased around Aurelia's shoulders, lifting her just enough for a straw to be guided to her lips.

"Jessica, here—water. Just small sips to start."

Jessica?

The name drifted through her hazy mind, catching briefly before slipping away again. She didn't have the strength to question it. She drank greedily, the cool water sliding down her parched throat, spreading blessed relief through her fevered body.

When the straw was pulled away, she croaked a weak, rasping protest, only to be met with a firm, measured reply. "Not too much at once. Just slowly. You're on a drip, so you'll feel better soon." The words were soothing, but her throat ached too much to respond properly, and her lips pressed together in a futile attempt to speak.

A subtle shift at the door stirred the air—a presence had arrived. The woman overseeing her recovery turned toward it with a small, knowing smile. "Ah, Julian. As always, your timing is impeccable. She has just woken up."

Aurelia strained against the heaviness in her eyelids, forcing them open, and met a pair of steel-grey eyes—sharp, direct, and unyielding—framed by chiselled features that were almost impossibly striking. There was something disquietingly familiar about him, though she couldn't place it, and the sudden intensity of his scrutiny made her stomach twist in a mixture of fear and recognition.

The inspection was thorough, invasive, like he could read the very thoughts she hadn't spoken, and for a moment her breath caught. Then, just as abruptly, he turned away, dismissive, as if whatever had drawn him in had lost interest. "This isn't Jessica," he said, his tone curt but not unkind, carrying a weight that demanded acknowledgment.

She registered the voice, rich and textured, resonant with an authority that made her pulse stutter. She had heard people speak of dark, commanding voices before, but experiencing one firsthand was different—like polished bronze, smooth yet imposing, a sound that seemed to mark boundaries without even trying. Even in her weakened state, it made her keenly aware of how small and fragile she felt in his presence.

Summoning the sliver of strength left in her trembling body, she rasped a whisper, her voice barely audible. "My name is… Aurelia."

He paused, as though the sound of her name was a revelation, and for a fleeting instant, his expression softened—just enough for her to glimpse a shadow of curiosity beneath the steel-grey storm of his gaze.

No response. She closed her eyes briefly, letting the heaviness of exhaustion press against her, then added in a weary, almost tentative voice, "Aurelia Carmichael."

The water had cleared her fogged mind just enough to think. This was clearly a case of mistaken identity—but for whom? Who had she been confused with? Bits of memory surfaced: walking along the sun-scorched road toward the beach, each step a monumental effort under the crushing weight of sickness and fatigue… and then the sudden screech of tires, a car pulling up beside her, its arrival abrupt, alarming.

The silence in the room pressed in on her, heavy and unsettling. Frowning, she forced her eyes open and met Julian's expressionless face. His cold, metallic gaze sliced through the fragile veil of her composure like a sword through silk, sharp and precise.

"And I'm Julian Kingsley," he said evenly, his voice calm, measured, as though this were some ordinary social introduction rather than a charged, electric moment suspended in time.

"Hello," she muttered, relief washing through her as she let her lashes drift closed again, willing the room's tension away, if only briefly.

Julian felt a flicker of something—curiosity, yes, but also a sharper, more visceral pull— stir beneath his usual, impenetrable composure. Up close, she bore little resemblance to Jessica, save for one arresting detail: the hair. Long, unevenly cut, a fierce, untamed blaze of colour that framed her pale face like wildfire. It was unmistakably natural, unpolished—nothing of Jessica's immaculate, salon-perfect sheen.

Her features were neat, almost classically balanced—she would photograph beautifully—but she lacked Jessica's curated, intentional glamour. And yet… something in her struck him with far more force than perfection ever had. An unbidden spark flared low in his chest, an involuntary awareness that unsettled him.

Her mouth did not help matters. Full, quietly sensuous, shaped with a kind of accidental temptation. There ought to be laws against mouths like that—curves designed to draw the eye, to coax the imagination into dangerous territory.

Then her lashes lifted again, unveiling eyes he hadn't been prepared for—limpid blue, the colour of dawn breaking over a restless sea, framed by naturally dark lashes untouched by cosmetics. They met his without hesitation, clear and startlingly unguarded, reading him with unnerving precision. For a breath, he felt exposed in a way he hadn't experienced in years.

A faint frown tugged at her narrow, dark brows before she inclined her square chin in a tiny, almost regal nod—deliberate, self-possessed, utterly unassuming.

And just like that, Julian Kingsley—who intimidated presidents, outmanoeuvred rivals, and never blinked first—felt something inside him shift. Something he couldn't yet name.

"Thank you," she said, her voice quiet but unmistakably clear. Then, as if the effort had drained the last reserves of her strength, she slipped back into the safe haven of sleep.

Julian remained where he was, studying her with the same unblinking intensity. For all her fragility, there was something untouchable about her, a quiet defiance, a spark he couldn't name—but one that would not be ignored.

The doctor rubbed her forehead with a quick, tired motion that spoke of too many long shifts. "I'll organise an ambulance — although with this bloody flu epidemic the hospital's full." She let the sentence hang, then added, as if to lighten the load of bad news, "By the way, the Simmons baby is on the mend."

"Thank God for that." Julian's austere features relaxed into a brief, unexpectedly genuine smile that reached his eyes and vanished almost as soon as it appeared. It was a small, human thing — startling in a face used to containment and control.

The doctor glanced down at the woman on the bed, at the smear of dried salt along her cheek and the tumble of red-gold hair fanned over the pillow. "I could put Miss Carmichael in with the general admissions—"

"She can stay here, if that's medically okay." Julian decided in a heartbeat, the words clipped, practical. There was no asking for permission — only a quiet assertion that the decision had been made.

The doctor's brows lifted at the suddenness of it. "Well… no clinical objection, provided the drip is supervised and replenished. A nurse can manage the IV and take bloods to monitor hydration and electrolytes. But she's going to be weak for several days, possibly longer." She tapped a pen against the clipboard as if punctuating the warning.

Julian watched the still, uncommunicative face framed by that wild, provocative hair. Despite the sensuous mouth and the impulsive tumble of colour, there was an undercurrent of something tighter — disciplined, like a contained ember. He found himself noting details with the clinical precision of a man who rarely wasted thought: the slight hollows beneath her cheekbones, the set of her jaw even in sleep. He turned to Sam. "Did she have a bag?"

Sam nodded toward the worn black handbag sitting on the chest at the foot of the bed. The room smelled faintly of frangipanis and the ocean breeze that had followed them in from the veranda; the bag looked out of place there, its shabby leather scuffed and careworn. "There."

"See if there's any ID and find out where she's staying." Julian's voice was flat, businesslike. He met the doctor again. "Can you arrange a nurse? One who understands discretion." There was an implication in that last word — not a request for secrecy so much as a reminder of expectations.

The doctor, Australian, with the easy, world-weary patience of someone practised in Kaliah Island's peculiarities and the Kingsley's demands, gave a small, knowing smile. "Of course. My staff know the value of discretion. One nurse is off at the moment, and she would jump at the extra money. I will send her." Her tone was half apology, half reassurance.

"Thanks." Julian turned, his movement economical, precise. Once he and Sam left the room, Julian lowered his voice until it was a clipped whisper, all edges. "Go through the bag. Get whatever ID you can and trace Aurelia Carmichael. Do a full background check — tonight."

Sam's jaw tightened; he understood the subtext. On an island this size, with a family history like the Kingsley's a name could unravel into cash registers and phone trees in minutes. He already had his phone in hand. Julian stared back at the closed door of the room as if he could see through it, then turned and walked away with the controlled urgency of a man who refused to be surprised.

When Aurelia woke again, a soft glow seeped through her closed eyelids—instinct told her it was daylight. For a few moments, she lay still, letting her senses gather slowly like scattered puzzle pieces. Nearby, a dove cooed plaintively, its gentle song threading through the warm morning air, underscored by the whisper of palm fronds swaying lazily in a teasing breeze. A delicate fragrance drifted toward her—vanilla, sweet and comforting, mingled with something richer, darker, and more exotic—transporting her, for a fleeting heartbeat, back to her mother's kitchen, where warmth and quiet love had always lingered in the air.

Here, the scent was different—seductive, opulent almost, a heady mixture of polished wood, faint citrus, and the subtle musk of sunlight on fabric. It made her chest tighten, a mixture of curiosity and unease stirring in her stomach.

Her eyelids remained heavy, weighted with exhaustion, but she knew where she was: Kaliah Island. And yet instead of the rough, unforgiving ground she had endured for three nights, she lay on something impossibly soft, cushioned, wrapped in sheets that smelled faintly of lavender and fresh linen. Carefully, she forced her lids open just enough to take in her surroundings.

Despite the tropical perfumes, she had expected the starkness of a hospital ward, with its clinical austerity, sharp smells, and antiseptic scent she had long learned to dread. But this—this was different. A bedroom, modern and spacious, airy enough that the morning light pooled across polished floors. Filmy curtains billowed gently at the windows, and stained wooden shutters were pushed back against walls painted pale, serene shades of cream and sand. Everything was carefully arranged, calm and ordered, yet suffused with an understated elegance.

She glanced down at herself. She wasn't wearing a hospital gown. Apart from a pair of simple briefs, she wore only a t-shirt—but not one of her own. Heat prickled at her cheeks as a sudden stab of humiliation surged through her, tears pricking at the corners of her eyes. Someone had dressed her. Someone had touched her belongings. Someone had decided what she would wear.

What was she doing here?

Her throat tightened as panic and confusion battled with the lingering fog of sleep. The room felt at once safe and alien, luxurious yet foreign, and Aurelia realised she had no answers—only questions.

The room's cool, restrained elegance breathed an understated luxury that both intrigued and intimidated her. Every surface seemed carefully curated—sleek black lacquer, pale walls, and pale wooden shutters catching the morning light in soft patterns. A pot of orchids perched on a long black dressing table, their blooms a riot of scarlet, crimson, and gold, demanded attention. They carried all the untamed allure of the tropics, exotic yet deliberate, a reminder that beauty here could be both fragile and fierce. On one wall hung a magnificent panel of tapa cloth, the stylised patterns in earthy tans and burnished bronze evoking the Pacific's timeless spirit, whispering of centuries of history and culture that she had only glimpsed in travel books.

Dizzy, Aurelia closed her eyes again, trying to steady her racing thoughts, but the image of the man she had seen swam unbidden into her mind—strong, autocratic, utterly compelling. He had stood beside her bed like a sentinel, tall, powerfully built, every inch the embodiment of control. His gaze had been clinical, unsparing, assessing, and somehow stripping away all her defences in a single, cold sweep.

Was he the owner? The man with the steel-grey eyes and that unforgettable voice, smooth and commanding, that had made her pulse stutter despite herself?

Despite the sun pouring lazily through the curtains, a shiver ran down her spine as she recalled that perfectly sculpted mouth—strong, confident, and almost cruelly attractive. Every feature had radiated authority, a subtle warning, and a promise all at once, leaving her both unsettled and inexplicably drawn.

Her mind groped for a name, catching only a fragment: "Kingsley," he had said.

The name stirred something familiar. Everyone in the Pacific knew the Kingsley's—the family who ruled Kaliah Island like lords of a forgotten kingdom. The patriarch, Graham Kingsley, had married a Kiwi, and their children, especially the only son and heir apparent, were fixtures in Australian women's magazines, their lives chronicled in glossy spreads and tabloid gossip. Glamour, power, wealth—everything about them spoke of a life entirely removed from her own, yet now she was here, in their world, and it was terrifying and exhilarating in equal measure.

Aurelia pressed her hand to her chest, feeling the rapid beat of her pulse, and realised that fear, fascination, and curiosity all coiled together in a knot she could not unravel. She had survived three nights on the rough, sun-baked earth—but surviving this world, this man, would require a different kind of strength altogether.

A sudden sound at the door jerked her head around. Pain knifed through her skull as the room lurched, tilting grotesquely before her eyes. A dizzy moan slipped from her throat. Foolish move. She squeezed her eyes shut and sank back onto the pillow, willing the wave of nausea to retreat before it swallowed her whole.

Footsteps crossed the floor—light but purposeful. A woman in a crisp nurse's uniform swept into view, her presence brisk yet reassuring, every movement carrying the confidence of someone accustomed to emergencies. "Oh, you're awake at last! How are you feeling this morning?" Her voice was warm and steady, a gentle anchor amid Aurelia's swirling disorientation.

"Much better, thank you." The words scraped out rough and hoarse, startling her with how small and frail she sounded. She swallowed hard, trying to ease the dryness clawing at her throat, then let her eyes fall closed again, grateful for even the faintest relief the darkness offered. So, this was a hospital—though nothing about it matched the sterile, fluorescent-lit facilities she had learned to dread. This place felt... upscale. Calmer. Softer around the edges. Maybe a private clinic, she thought vaguely, her mind drifting in and out as though suspended between waking and dream.

"Here, drink this."

Before Aurelia could muster a protest, a firm but gentle arm slid behind her back, lifting her just enough to bring a straw to her lips. This time, she drank slowly, carefully, letting the cool water soothe her parched throat without the frantic desperation she had felt the night before.

"You've been on a drip to rehydrate you," the nurse explained, her tone softening into something almost maternal. "And you certainly look much better than last night. You have been through a lot."

The kindness in her voice pierced Aurelia more sharply than pain. Exhaustion, relief, and the faintest flicker of fear tangled inside her as she clung to the straw, drinking in small, shaky sips—each one a reminder that she was alive, safe... and still had no idea where she truly was or why.

Just as Aurelia was finishing the water, the door opened again. She didn't have to look up to know who it was—the atmosphere shifted, charged in an instant, as though the room itself drew a deeper breath. The man entered with an ease that was almost dangerous, effortlessly commanding the space without a single overt gesture. Power clung to him like a second skin.

Aurelia's gaze tracked him with ragged, involuntary interest. It helped, she thought dazedly, that even his casual clothes—tailored to perfection despite their simplicity—fit his tall, lean frame as though sculpted directly onto him. A plain T-shirt and board shorts should have diminished the effect. Instead, they only underscored the primal, unsettling magnetism he exuded.

Julian. That was his name—the heir to this island paradise, to its wealth, its influence, its secrets.

Aurelia stiffened instinctively, setting her jaw as though bracing for impact. She had seen his photograph in magazines and newspapers, glossy images of a man shaped by privilege and old power. But a photograph could never have captured the sheer intensity of him. His face was the sort a fantasy illustrator might sketch for a dark prince—arrogant, uncompromising, honed by a ruthless bone structure and bronzed skin that spoke of a life lived close to the sun and the sea.

He crossed the room in a few unhurried strides and looked down at her. The smile he gave her was swift, dazzling in its ease, and it hit her like a physical blow—unexpectedly intimate, sending a tiny cold ripple down her spine. It was the kind of smile that carried layers: humour, genuine concern... and a flicker of something dangerously seductive, something he likely did not even realise he was offering.

Yes, she thought, her eyes narrowing as she studied him, Julian Kingsley was every bit as dangerous as he looked.

"You're looking much better," he said in that deep, resonant voice that filled the room, sliding over her skin in a way she wasn't prepared for. "Breakfast is on its way. Do you feel well enough to answer a few questions?"

"Of course," she managed, though her voice came out thin and uncertain. "Thank you. I—I don't remember much... what happened exactly..." The words tangled, faltered, and dissolved into silence.

Julian turned slightly and spoke to the nurse in the smooth, liquid Polynesian tongue of the island—a language so melodic, so warm, that it seemed to soothe the very air around them. The nurse nodded, her expression respectful, and slipped quietly from the room, her departure soft as a whisper.

Leaving Aurelia alone with him.

Alone with the man who, even in silence, seemed to take up all the space, all the light, all the air—leaving her unsure whether the tremor sliding through her was fear... or something far more treacherous. Her pulse fluttered unevenly as the door clicked closed behind the nurse, sealing her into the room with Julian Kingsley.

He stood over her, tall and immovable, his hooded eyes dark and unreadable beneath the strong, uncompromising lines of his face. The contrast between those eyes and the enigmatic half-smile tugging at his mouth was dangerously compelling.

"You fainted on the road," he said in a neutral tone, as though delivering a report rather than speaking to a woman he'd carried out of the sweltering heat. "My driver happened to be passing. He brought you here."

Aurelia frowned, a delicate crease forming between her brows as she forced herself to meet that piercing stare. "Why here?" she asked quietly. Her voice sounded steadier than she felt.

Julian resisted the urge to shrug. She wasn't the sort to swallow a polished lie—he could already tell that. And though he admired the wary intelligence in her eyes, he wasn't about to confess that for one disorienting moment he'd believed she was Jessica, the woman he'd shared a brief, complicated affair with two years earlier. Some truths served no one when spoken too soon.

This morning, a faint wash of pink warmed Aurelia's cheeks, softening the weariness still etched into her features. It made her look almost luminous. Her vibrant blue eyes, framed by thick dark lashes, seemed too large for her pale, delicate face. And that mouth—full, beautifully shaped—was made for far more than polite gratitude. With a little colour in her cheeks, a fresh haircut to restore the wild beauty of her hair, she would be striking. Impossibly striking. The thought rose in him before he could push it aside, sparked by an involuntary masculine appreciation that annoyed him with its persistence.

"Because the house was closer than the hospital," he said at last, pre-empting the next question gathering on her lips. "You stayed here overnight because the hospital is small and reserved for real emergencies. We are in the middle of a severe flu epidemic, and although you probably feel dreadful, you are not seriously ill—just dehydrated and exhausted."

But she didn't look convinced. He saw it immediately—the lingering scepticism flickering in her eyes, the faint tightening of her mouth, the polite, guarded tilt of her head.

"Thank you so much," she said, voice tight with resolve, "but I have to go."

And in that single sentence, Julian caught a truth he hadn't expected: Aurelia Carmichael might be fragile in body, weak from exhaustion and hunger—but the woman beneath that frailty possessed a spine forged from tempered steel.

"Why?" His tone was deliberately blunt, bordering on cruel. "So, you can return to sleeping on the beach? That's illegal on this island." His eyes narrowed, slicing clean through what remained of her composure. "Tell me—how did you get through Immigration without proof of accommodation?"

A faint flush climbed her cheeks—soft, vulnerable, painfully revealing—before draining away entirely, leaving her cheekbones too sharp against her pale, drawn skin. The realization hit him like a physical blow: she hadn't just been sleeping rough; she'd been starving. His chest tightened with a surge of anger—protective, irrational, unwelcome—but impossible to ignore.

Even so, she did not wilt. She held his gaze with a steadiness that startled him, that demanded he see her as more than the fragile stranger he'd found unconscious on his property.

"I had a holiday cottage booked," she said, her voice steady but edged with buried hurt. "But when I arrived, it turned out the person who arranged the trip—" She paused, swallowing hard as something sharp and private flickered through her eyes. "—got the dates wrong. The cottage was already occupied."

"So why not find another place to stay?" Julian asked, the cool bite of impatience sharpening each syllable.

Aurelia loathed that she blushed so easily. It made her look timid, breakable— everything she refused to be. She certainly wasn't going to confess to Julian Kingsley— the island prince with eyes like judgment and ice—that her mother had arranged this holiday shortly before dying. That this trip was supposed to be a fragile lifeline, a quiet place for her grief to breathe. That she had boarded the plane clinging to the smallest hope of healing.

Pride straightened her spine. She forced her gaze to hold steady, even as heat crept up her throat. "I don't have enough money," she said softly, the admission scraping raw against her dignity.

One black brow arched—an elegant, cutting gesture sharpened by years of authority. "And it never occurred to you to ask for help? Anyone's?"

She shook her head, then winced as a spike of dizziness narrowed her vision. Shame prickled along her skin. It should have occurred to her. She'd discovered her ticket home was non-refundable, learned there were no earlier flights available, and had convinced herself she could endure. That here—on a warm, idyllic island—sleeping rough might not be terrible. For a while, it hadn't been. Until the heat, dehydration, and creeping illness began to unravel her strength thread by fragile thread.

Julian's voice, when it came, was quiet. But it held no mercy.

"You had no money in your bag. None at all." A pause. His gaze sharpened, cool as a blade. "And where are your clothes?"

The question dropped between them like a stone—cold, unyielding—stripping away the last of her flimsy defences.

Aurelia didn't answer. Her gaze slipped downward to the sunlit pattern shimmering across the polished floorboards, as if the light itself might offer her refuge. A place to hide her humiliation, her foolishness, the vulnerability she had fought so hard not to reveal.

But silence stretched and stretched, taut as wire, as Julian waited—unyielding, unmoving—demanding the truth she could no longer conceal.

Chapter Two

When she still said nothing, his tone sharpened—not loud but edged with unyielding authority.

"Aurelia, what happened to your money and your luggage? I assume you had both when you arrived?"

She opened her eyes slowly, the dull throb at her temples pulsing in time with her exhaustion. "I had—have—a pack," she said, and even she heard the fragile quaver in her voice. "I took it with me when I went to the market to buy food. I put it on the ground to get my money out, and someone came up and offered me a lei made of frangipani flowers—actually slipped it over my head while the stall owner was weighing my fruit."

His frown deepened instantly, shadows carving sharper lines across his brow. "So, you were distracted by the pretty lei, and when you turned around, your pack was gone?"

Her eyes flashed, indignation sparking through the fog of exhaustion. "I didn't buy it," she snapped softly. "But yes—that's what happened." She caught the flicker of doubt in his expression and added, defensive, wounded, "I only looked away for a second."

His thick black brows pulled tight over his nose, darkening his already severe features. "A second is all it takes."

A pause—long enough to make her feel foolish. Then, more quietly but no less insistent:

"When did this happen?"

Her mind slogged through the memories, each thought heavy, as though wading through mud. "About three days ago, I think," she said hesitantly.

"And did you go to the police?"

"Yes." Bitterness tinged her voice. "They were as helpful as they could be, but no one saw anything. They did find the pack behind one of the stalls."

"Empty?"

Heat surged up her neck, humiliation thickening her throat. She nodded. "Except for my passport and airline tickets."

He made a dismissive gesture—impatience tempered by reluctant understanding. "Those aren't worth anything here. You didn't tell the police your full circumstances?"

"No." The word came out clipped, edged with irritation as she turned her head away. She couldn't bear the intensity of his gaze—too sharp, too invasive, too knowing.

"You didn't think to call your credit card company?"

"I don't have a credit card." The retort slipped out too quickly, too defensively— revealing not just pride and poverty but the raw shame of a woman who had run out of ways to hold herself together.

Silence followed, heavy and charged. Julian's gaze rested on her—assessing, calculating, and something else she refused to interpret.

His expression didn't soften, but it shifted, becoming quieter, more deliberate. His scrutiny felt scalpel-sharp, every question placed with surgical precision.

"Where do you live in Australia, Miss Carmichael?"

"In Strahan," she replied crisply, forcing steadiness she did not feel. "A small town on the west coast of Tasmania." She added the extra detail like armour—structure, order, control—something she could hold onto. Then, refusing to flinch beneath his gaze, she asked,

"Why?"

"I'm just seeing if the facts match your story," he said matter-of-factly, eyes unwavering.

Aurelia swallowed hard, forcing down the swirl of emotions threatening to spill over. She lifted her chin, meeting his unyielding gaze with a glare that carried the weight of every fear and frustration she had carried for days. "I'm telling you the truth," she said evenly, almost defiantly.

He nodded slowly, deliberate in every movement. "I'm sorry to be so rough on you." His voice was calm, measured—so effortlessly controlled that the tension coiling in her chest felt even more suffocating by contrast.

"I'll take that for granted," she shot back, the edge in her tone unmistakable.

A subtle tilt of his head, a quick, knowing grin, and suddenly her stomach knotted, a flicker of disorientation mingling with the rapid flutter of her pulse. Even in her exhausted, vulnerable state, she couldn't ignore it.

"So," he said lightly, brushing off the weight of his earlier interrogation as if it were nothing, "I needn't stress it. You're Aurelia Carmichael, from Australia, twenty-five years old—and a Capricorn, I noticed from your birth date."

His smile was sharp, predatory even, but it was the tone of his voice that truly unsettled her—smooth, deep, carrying an authority that allowed no contradiction, no hesitation.

She forced her throat to obey, swallowing hard before managing a curt reply: "I didn't know men were interested in star signs."

He chuckled softly, a low, wry sound that tugged at the corner of his lips in a way that made her pulse stutter. "I have two sisters," he said, the tone lightening briefly, almost mischievous, before snapping back into the commanding precision she had come to recognise. "So, I've learned a thing or two about women—and astrology."

Aurelia blinked, caught between exasperation, admiration, and a subtle, unwelcome pull of fascination she was determined to ignore. He was infuriating—and yet impossible to dismiss.

Then his expression darkened, intensity sharpening his features and making her pulse jump. "I have placed your passport and airline tickets in my safe, where they'll be completely secure. I am sorry you've had such a rough time." His words were formal, measured—but the quiet weight beneath them carried unspoken authority, leaving no room for argument.

"Kaliah Island is usually safe," he continued, gaze locking on hers with uncanny precision. "But like anywhere, there are a few untrustworthy souls. The police believe your pack was likely stolen by another tourist—possibly someone who ran out of money. They also recovered the lei from another stall. If it had been a local, someone would have noticed—or recognised the culprit."

He paused, letting the silence stretch just long enough for her nerves to coil tighter, before shifting his focus back to her. "Can you sit up without help?" His voice was calm, precise, controlled—but every word carried the subtle weight of command.

Aurelia blinked, startled. "What?"

"You're still thirsty," he said, looping a firm yet gentle arm around her shoulders, easing her upright against the pillows.

Close and impossibly solid, Julian was overwhelming. Her chest constricted at the contact, a flutter she fought to suppress. He radiated authority, control, and something more unsettling—an almost magnetic presence that made it impossible to focus on anything else. Another pillow slid behind her back, and she stiffened, caught between caution and a tension she couldn't name.

"It's all right," he murmured, soothing yet unwavering. "Blink a couple of times, then open your eyes slowly."

There was something grounding in his voice, a steady pulse she could cling to. Even as she obeyed, she couldn't ignore the way his proximity set her pulse racing.

He handed her a glass of water. "Sip this slowly. Breakfast will be here soon, and after that, the nurse will help you shower."

"No—wait," she whispered, voice trembling under the weight of his piercing gaze. Confidence evaporated. "I can't stay here," she admitted, softer than intended.

Julian's brows drew together, severe, unyielding. "You're not able to look after yourself. Dehydration can be deadly if not properly monitored. You're still very much not out of the woods. Finding other accommodation isn't an option—not now. And sleeping on the beach is out of the question."

She met his stare, fierce and unrelenting, and felt heat coil in her chest—a mixture of frustration, defiance, and an awareness she loathed to admit. "You can't want me to stay here," she whispered, voice shaking.

"Don't be foolish," he said sharply, cutting through her resistance. "You'll be far less trouble if you stay here and are properly cared for. The staff already manage children on oxygen—hospital personnel do not need anyone else in danger unless absolutely necessary."

Aurelia's heart hammered. Julian Kingsley stood over her like a force she could neither ignore nor resist, his dominance unspoken yet palpable, leaving her trembling with the realisation that survival—and something far more dangerous—was tied to staying exactly where he wanted her.

"I—thank you," she said haltingly, raising the glass to her lips as if it could shield her from the intensity of his presence. "I think."

"You have nothing to thank me for," Julian replied evenly, measured, almost cold. "If you had acted sensibly when you realised your plans had gone awry, you wouldn't be in this situation. Here on Kaliah Island, we do not allow people to starve on our beaches."

She bit back a retort, but it slipped out anyway. "No doubt because it doesn't look good in the newspapers."

Julian's expression remained unreadable, composed, every line radiating authority, but there was a dry, sardonic undertone as he responded: "If it makes you feel better, yes, partly. We guard the island's reputation zealously—which is why freeloaders and would-be beachcombers are not encouraged. But common humanity plays a part too. This situation is not your fault, so the least I can do is help."

He turned toward the door, and for a fleeting heartbeat, Aurelia caught a glimpse of something softer in his posture before he moved away. She bit her lip, struggling against the tremors coursing through her—shivers of exhaustion, fear, and something she couldn't name. She had thought she'd shed all her tears before leaving on this ill-fated holiday, yet now, drained of adrenaline and confronted with the raw reality of her helplessness, her emotions spun beyond her control.

Julian paused just outside the doorway he had closed behind him, and for the first time, a subtle tension crossed his features—brief, almost imperceptible, yet unmistakable. He did not like the way his body had reacted to their brief contact. That small, unavoidable touch had stirred something unsettling: a potent mixture of protectiveness, frustration, and an almost physical ache at the loss of control. He prided himself on command, on predicting outcomes, on managing everything in his meticulously ordered world. And yet Aurelia—shaken, defiant, fragile—had left a residue he could not simply dismiss.

His jaw tightened, fists clenching lightly at his sides as he forced himself to focus. He would not let it show. Not here. Not to her. Still, even as he moved down the corridor, he felt the echo of her presence lingering behind him—a magnetic pull that irritated and intrigued in equal measure, a complication he neither welcomed nor could entirely deny.

The return of the nurse with a tray of cereal and tropical fruit was a small but welcome relief.

She set it carefully on Aurelia's knees, arranging each dish with a practiced hand. "Eat it all," she said cheerfully. "The doctor said you need to replenish your strength. Why didn't you ask for food if you couldn't buy it? No islander would have let you go hungry—and there's more than enough to go around."

Her tone was kindly meant, but Aurelia felt a surge of defensiveness. On this island, it seemed, everyone had an opinion about her. "I had enough to eat, mostly," she said, her voice sharper than intended.

The nurse raised an eyebrow but didn't take offence. "Doesn't look like it. What I want to know," she said, leaning slightly closer with genuine curiosity, "is how you managed to hide from everyone while sleeping on the beach. The islanders usually know exactly what's happening in their own areas—you'd have been spotted on any of the resort beaches."

Aurelia felt herself flush, the heat creeping up her neck. "I found a tiny bay with only two houses in it," she admitted. "Both seemed empty—holiday houses, I think."

"About a kilometre away on the road back to town?" the nurse asked.

Aurelia nodded, avoiding her gaze. "No one seemed to live there."

"It's owned by a family who are in Australia for a wedding," the nurse explained. "They'll be back in a couple of days, so you'd have been found eventually."

"I slept under a big tree," Aurelia added quickly, shifting the focus. "Even if anyone was on the beach at night, they wouldn't have seen me." Then, trying to reclaim some normalcy, she glanced at the tray. "This looks delicious. Thank you."

"Coffee or tea?" the nurse asked.

The thought of coffee made her stomach roil. "Tea, please." Then, on impulse, she added, "Where am I?"

The nurse's eyes widened slightly at the question. "You've seen photos of the Kingsley house, haven't you? The old mansion?"

Unconsciously, Aurelia hoped—foolishly, she thought—that this was just a new wing built onto the old plantation-style house. Perhaps Julian's mother might appear at any moment, and she would be able to explain everything. The realisation that she was in Julian's house instead sent a strange mix of panic and… something else she didn't name, curling through her chest.

The nurse, oblivious to Aurelia's inner turmoil, continued in a chatty, matter-of-fact tone. "Julian had this one built a couple of years ago after he returned from overseas. He decided he needed his own place. We'd hoped he might be getting married, but it doesn't look like that's going to happen anytime soon."

Aurelia blinked, letting the words sink in. Julian's own home. Modern, private, unmistakably his. Her pulse quickened, a mixture of awe, unease, and something she couldn't yet name stirring with every beat. Even the faintest awareness of his presence seemed to linger in the air around her, a magnetic tension she both resisted and could not ignore.

Realising she was drifting into idle speculation, the nurse smiled and shifted back to practicality. "Eat up everything! Then you can have a proper shower. I've brought you a wrap to wear, and a nightgown—something a bit nicer than Julian's tee-shirt."

Aurelia's cheeks flamed. The thought of being clothed in her host's shirt now felt somehow indulgent, almost decadent. She glanced down, reluctant to admit how strangely intimate it had seemed.

"Where did you get the wrap and nightgown?" she asked, curiosity mixed with lingering embarrassment.

"The housekeeper gave me the money," the nurse replied. "So, I suppose it was from Julian."

Aurelia's mind went immediately to repayment. She vowed silently to return the favour, no matter how long it might take. Yet when she found the courage to thank him in person, Julian's reply was brisk and matter of fact: "Don't worry about that now. Concentrate on eating, sleeping, and drinking."

That day settled into a quiet rhythm that carried through the following days. Each morning, she was allowed up for progressively longer periods, though the nurse and, later, the doctor kept a close watch during their evening visits. The routine, though gentle, was strict, designed to restore strength—and it left Aurelia with the uneasy sense that Julian's presence, though often unseen, lingered in every corner of the house, shaping the pace of her recovery as surely as the care of the staff.

Julian came in twice a day, and each time, he brought with him that undeniable charge, a vital energy that seemed to sweep through the room the moment he entered. Every nerve in Aurelia's body hummed to life; her senses sharpened as though she had been living in a fogged stupor until that instant. Just seeing him—even without a word—left her simultaneously exhilarated and unsettled.

The rest of the day passed in quieter routines. She read obsessively, discovering that Julian possessed a surprisingly vast and well-curated library. He had even asked her tastes and, with the faintest hint of amusement in his tone, chose a book for her each day. She also watched local television and videos, lingering over scenes of the island that seemed almost cruel in their beauty, and she gazed wistfully at the lush garden visible through her windows.

Her body, however, remained fragile. She was too wobbly on her feet to entertain the thought of venturing outside. Yet the days stretched long, and to her own shock, she found herself thinking far too much about Julian—the way he moved, the sound of his voice, the commanding presence that never seemed to leave a room. She hated how eagerly she awaited his morning and evening visits, and the awareness made her both guilty and strangely alive.

One morning, when she was allowed up, the nurse arrived carrying an armful of brightly coloured fabric.

"Sulu," she said warmly. "My daughter sent these along for you."

"They're beautiful," Aurelia murmured, eyeing the folds of fabric, "but I can't wear your daughter's clothes."

The nurse chuckled patiently. "They're not clothes—they're just material. She's got dozens of them. Here, watch—just drape it around you and tuck it in. Hold your arms out."

Feeling both embarrassed and awkward, Aurelia hesitated, then obeyed. The nurse's hands were deft, guiding her through the folds, showing how to tuck and twist the fine cotton until it sat securely.

"Won't it come undone?" she asked doubtfully.

"Not unless it gets rough handling," the nurse said cheerfully. "Our girls wear them all the time—even swim in them. Now, watch while I show you how to fasten it again."

Once satisfied, the nurse added another bundle. "I've brought some underwear too—Julian told me to buy what you needed. I even found the right bra in one of the shops in town!"

Aurelia accepted it with a polite, tight-lipped, "Thank you," feeling her pride battered yet again.

Under the nurse's watchful eye, she showered, then wrapped herself in the sulu. It was cool and silky against her skin, a gentle contrast to the oppressive heat of the day.

"Go and see how you look while I get you a cup of tea," the nurse instructed.

Warily, Aurelia approached the mirror. The sulu was surprisingly flattering, modest above the chest, falling loosely to her knees, yet showing enough pale skin to feel airy and freeing. She tugged at the folds self-consciously, noting how it moved with her rather than clinging.

Her thoughts flicked involuntarily to Julian. *How would he see her in it? Would he notice the difference from the tee-shirt she'd been wearing?*

"He probably wouldn't even notice," she muttered under her breath, a mix of irritation and self-conscious defiance curling in her chest. She certainly hoped he wouldn't notice—or care—that she wasn't wearing a bra beneath it.

The mirror reflected a woman both vulnerable and subtly bold, and for the first time since arriving, Aurelia felt a flicker of confidence mingled with her lingering unease— a sensation she couldn't quite untangle, yet one she knew would not easily fade.

The next evening, the doctor leaned back in her chair and said, "Right, you don't need me anymore. You're fully recovered from the dehydration, but I'm not too happy about your general health." She paused, as though inviting Aurelia to speak freely.

Tonelessly, Aurelia replied, "My mother died a while ago—I nursed her until she went. I am fine. Thank you for everything you've done for me."

Dr King's eyes, unexpectedly sharp and attentive, studied her for a moment before she waved the thanks aside. "Just doing my job. How long was your mother ill?"

"Five years," Aurelia answered quietly.

The doctor nodded slowly. "And you looked after her all that time?"

"Towards the end, she spent quite a bit of time in the hospice," Aurelia said evenly, keeping her voice carefully neutral.

"I see. Well, when you go home, see your own doctor. You've been under considerable stress, and this last little episode on the island certainly hasn't helped. Talk to him and see what he can do for you."

"I'm fine," Aurelia said automatically, her tone brittle. *What could anyone prescribe for grief?*

The pleasant Australian doctor tilted her head, shrewd. "Your mother had the right idea—she knew you'd be exhausted and that you'd need a complete change of circumstances to get the full benefit of any holiday. Dehydration and heat exhaustion certainly played a part in your collapse, but there was more to it than that. Nursing someone you love is exhausting in more ways than the physical. I don't think you should go home until you're fully rested."

"How long will that be?" Aurelia asked cautiously.

Dr King smiled faintly. "At least a week," she said noncommittally.

"Two days," Aurelia said firmly. When the doctor lifted her brows, she added quickly, "I have a non-refundable ticket, and it has to be used then."

Dr King frowned thoughtfully. "I see. While you're here, stay in the shade, use sunscreen and moisturiser—the tropical sun is merciless. And keep drinking at least every half hour."

Aurelia could manage that. But now, fully recovered, she realised the pressing question: *where would she spend the next two days until she could go home?*

That night, she relayed the doctor's advice to Julian.

"Now you're worrying about it," he said, a half-smile tugging at his lips.

In spite of herself, Aurelia felt a flutter of surrender at the curve of that smile. A warmth blossomed in her chest, and to her own astonishment, she realised how sharply aware she was of her body, the sensitive peaks of her breasts tightening under her thin sulu. She hoped desperately it wasn't as obvious to him as it was to her.

"Thank you very much for your kindness," she murmured, trying to steady her voice. "If I can get a lift into town—"

"Don't be silly," he interrupted, rising to his full height. His gaze was cool, calculating, and yet oddly speculative. "It will be dark soon." He paused, as though weighing something private and unreadable. "Have a good night's sleep. Tomorrow, you're going to be allowed outside."

"I'm so looking forward to that," she said, her apprehensions momentarily swept aside by the thought of moving freely again. A spark of excitement ran through her, mingling with relief, and the promise of independence made her feel—at least for the moment—light and capable.

Chapter Three

He didn't come to see her the next morning, and to her surprise, the absence hurt more than she expected. Flustered by the intensity of the feeling, she dressed carefully in a pair of white linen trousers and a loose cotton shirt—both the right size—and spread sunscreen meticulously over every inch of exposed skin. The nurse handed her a wide-brimmed hat, which she accepted with a small, reluctant nod.

When she asked whose clothes they had been, she was told firmly, "They're new. Julian bought them." The finality of the statement pricked her pride, but she swallowed the chagrin. She would pay him back, she vowed silently, however long it took.

Her spirits, however, were too buoyant to brood over matters she could not control. Stepping onto the private terrace outside her room, she sank into a lounger and picked up the local newspaper, attempting to anchor herself in something ordinary.

Until now, she had only glimpsed the garden from indoors. She had expected a riot of tropical colours, and there was indeed vibrancy, but it was the discipline of the design— the careful shaping, the gradations of green and gold, the restrained bursts of bright red—that truly struck her. Whoever tended this garden commanded it as precisely as its owner must command his life. Like Julian, she thought, her pulse skipping at the thought—did anything ever disturb his cool, self-contained confidence?

A flutter of warmth swept through her at the notion, unbidden and startling. An odd twist of sensation—heat, longing, and something more elusive—coiled low in her stomach. Blushing, she forced herself to concentrate on her surroundings. Everything— the choice of plants, the sculpted furniture, even the tray laid out for her on the terrace—was a tableau of wealth and taste, the kind that belonged in glossy magazines dedicated to the lives of the very rich.

"You should be enjoying this," she chastised herself. Living in tropical luxury, even briefly, was an experience unlikely to recur.

Dutifully, she worked her way through the newspaper, starting with the hard-hitting local news. She lingered over the summary of a Pacific-wide conference Julian had presided over, grappling with over-fishing policies. Guiltily, she let her gaze linger on a photograph of him: stern, commanding, impossibly handsome. Even in print, he radiated authority.

"High society indeed," she murmured aloud, turning to the foreign section.

The headline screamed, "Model Leaves Husband of Six Months," and she tried to read about turmoil in the Common Market but gave up almost immediately. She set the paper aside, letting the warm sun on her skin ground her in the present. Even still slightly wobbly from recent weakness, it was a pleasure simply to be outside, inhaling the fragrance of foliage and sun-warmed earth.

Yet the pressing problem remained: what would she do until she left Kaliah Island? Overnight she had ignored the issue, but now reality pressed in. No money, no clothes, no home. And she certainly couldn't stay here.

Almost certainly, Julian would be relieved to see her leave; she had no claim on him, no right to intrude. The problem demanded a solution, but for the next several fruitless minutes, her mind churned and yielded nothing.

"Oh, Mum," she whispered, her voice tight as tears threatened.

She squared her jaw, a flicker of stubborn determination taking hold. No, she would not dissolve into a puddle. She owed her mother the effort of salvaging what she could of this situation.

Opening her eyes, she allowed the calm of the garden to settle around her, deliberately storing up its beauty. Her gaze followed a long border where tree ferns created a soft, leafy canopy over a planting of peace lilies, their white flowers hovering like doves above the glossy foliage. At the far end, a single splash of crimson—bright, vivid, almost audacious against the green—caught her eye.

"It's probably just a hibiscus," she murmured to herself.

Her mother had loved them, plucking blooms to scatter on the table, delighting in their frilly, ephemeral perfection. Aurelia's throat tightened at the memory, a mix of longing and nostalgia constricting her chest.

Determined to distract herself, she rose and stepped into the heat, padding barefoot along the terrace and into the garden, intent on discovering that elusive splash of colour. The warmth of the sun and the scent of tropical flowers surrounded her, coaxing her senses awake and forcing her focus outward, if only for a little while.

Halfway across the terrace, voices drifted from somewhere nearby, pulling Aurelia's attention. Two men were walking along the lawn, their figures outlined against the sunlit greenery. Her heart stuttered violently at the sight of Julian, tall and lean, his presence immediately recognisable even from a distance. She barely registered the other man, yet the impact of Julian's gaze—steady, piercing, unsettling—made her feel foolishly exposed. For a fleeting, irrational moment, she wished she had stayed put in the privacy of her own patio.

But turning back now would be worse—suspicious, awkward, like someone casing the place. She squared her shoulders, forced herself to step toward the creeper adorned with its riot of crimson blooms, and focused on the flowers. They were stunning, but she could barely enjoy them; her thoughts were trapped in the pull of Julian's presence. With a reluctant sigh, she turned back and hurried to the chair, the movement sudden enough to make her legs ache and head spin.

A sharp intake of breath preceded his voice. "Are you all right?"

Her heart jumped again, nearly slamming against her ribs. She swallowed hard. "I—I'm fine," she said, her voice thin, almost brittle.

He stopped in front of her, his face too handsome, too commanding, framed by that dark intensity that made it impossible not to respond. "You're white as a sheet," he said bluntly. "Didn't the doctor tell you to take things easily?"

Aurelia bristled inwardly, but she forced herself to suppress the irritation that rose like smoke. "Don't you ever stop asking questions?"

"Once I've got the answers," he said, lowering himself into the chair opposite her. His gaze swept over her, analytical and unyielding. "I saw you walking across the lawn. Was it too far?"

"I might have taken it too fast," she admitted, forcing a faint smile to soften the defensiveness in her tone. "I feel like a wimp."

"Dehydration isn't something to be taken lightly," he said without compromise. "And in the tropics, it's too easy to forget to drink enough."

Aurelia bit her lip, half in acknowledgment, half in frustration. "I'm making up for it now. Apparently, I have to drink every half-hour."

"Make sure you do. And if you must move about, take things slowly." His tone was imperious, almost brusque, and she felt herself bristle—but reluctantly acknowledged he was right. Both he and the nurse had her best interests in mind. And the doctor, too.

"Yes, sir," she murmured, watching helplessly as the corners of his mouth lifted into that infuriatingly potent smile. Her chest tightened unexpectedly, and she added, forcing her voice to remain steady, "The funny thing is—I felt pretty good until a few minutes before I—well, fainted so melodramatically in front of your car."

"It wasn't anything as easily dealt with as a faint," he said with brutal precision. "You collapsed."

"Yes, well, I'm better now," she said, sitting up straighter, squaring her shoulders, and tightening her jaw. "Thank you so much for everything you've done. I'll find some other accommodation—"

"Don't be silly." His drawl was slow, deliberate, and shaded with amusement, the thick lashes over his eyes casting a shadow that made her flush. "I've checked. The cottage is booked solid for another month. You have no money, and as Dr King wants you under observation, I told her you'd stay here as my guest until you return to Australia."

"No!" Her voice cracked, her pulse hammering in her ears.

"You needn't look at me as though I've made you an indecent proposition," he said lightly, though the amused glint in his eyes made her squirm. "It's simply the best way to handle the situation."

A fugitive flush crept over her cheeks. "I couldn't possibly impose on you," she said stiffly, her tone far too formal for the tremor in her voice.

"You're not going back to sleeping on the beach," he said, blunt and uncompromising. "In fact, you're not going anywhere for a while. On the doctor's recommendation, I've cancelled your return ticket."

Aurelia's eyes widened in shock, a mix of indignation and disbelief. "You—she—had no right to do that!" she sputtered, words tumbling out in a rush, her hands clenching in helpless frustration.

Julian leaned back slightly, a faint smirk tugging at his mouth. "I have every right to make sure you survive your holiday, Miss Carmichael," he said evenly, as if the audacity of her reaction amused him more than it alarmed.

Her throat tightened. She wanted to argue, to storm away, to reclaim some shred of independence—but every instinct told her that defiance in the face of him would accomplish nothing. Her pulse hammered, her mind spun, and she realised, with a disconcerting honesty, that the island, the house—and Julian Kingsley—had more hold over her than she cared to admit.

"Dr King said that not only were you suffering from dehydration, but that you're exhausted, run-down, and very close—she suspects—to burning out. She doesn't want to see you travel for at least a week, possibly a fortnight."

"A fortnight!" Her brain scrambled, jumbled thoughts tangling with a rising, unbidden panic. She felt an odd flutter in her chest, almost a physical jolt, and her fingers unconsciously gripped the edge of the chair. Julian's calm, almost arrogantly assured expression only made her pulse thrum faster, leaving her mentally stammering and awkwardly aware of the warmth pooling in her cheeks.

"Do you have a home to go to in Australia?"

Aurelia glared at him, mute for a moment, aware of a sudden tension coiling low in her stomach. "I… I have a room in a boarding house," she said, her voice tight and clipped, as if trying to keep her trembling under control. The image of the small, stifling space made her shoulders stiffen.

Julian's brow lifted, just enough to convey ironic surprise. "So exactly what were you planning to do once you returned to Australia?"

Her throat tightened. The plan had been simple: a temporary job, a chance to regroup, a way to breathe again—but spoken aloud, it sounded fragile, even ridiculous in his presence. The nearness of him—the taut lines of his jaw, the subtle scent of him carried on the warm breeze—made her pulse race.

Ruthlessly, Julian pressed his advantage. "Dr King doesn't feel confident about your going back unless you have support waiting for you in Australia. Do you?"

Aurelia's lips pressed together; she wouldn't lie, but she also wouldn't confess her isolation. She shifted slightly, feeling heat creep up her neck, her body responding to the intensity of his scrutiny despite herself.

"No friends to ensure you're all right?" he pressed, voice even but incisive.

Her stomach knotted. No one close—but she wouldn't say it. She averted her gaze, trying to ignore the almost magnetic pull of his presence, the way her body seemed to react without permission.

Julian's mouth curved into a faint, sardonic smile. "Of course, I can't keep you here if you don't want to stay. So, I'll organise a private room in the hospital until Dr King says you're fit to travel. You could return to Australia in the family's private jet—"

"No, don't be ridiculous!" she blurted, pressing her palms to her flushed cheeks. Her pulse fluttered like wings in her chest. "I don't want a hospital room—not when all the staff are needed for sick people. And I certainly don't want to use your private jet!"

"I'm merely outlining your options," he said smoothly, the faint lift of an eyebrow drawing another spike of heat across her skin.

She took her hands away and asked desperately, "Surely there's somewhere else I can stay?"

"Not in your present state." He paused, letting the words settle like a weight on her shoulders. "Look, you won't be imposing on me at all. My staff manage the house— they do the actual work. Staying here reassures both Dr King and me that you're eating, drinking, and resting properly."

Aurelia swallowed hard, aware of a tightening in her chest and the way her palms had grown slightly clammy. Her pride bristled, but reason crept in, hesitant and unyielding. "I don't know…"

"And when you're fully on your feet, I'll lend you enough money to see out your holiday—"

"No." She cut him off, her voice firmer than she felt. She lifted her chin, squared her shoulders, and felt the subtle flutter of nerves that always seemed to accompany his nearness. "I can't afford to repay you."

His gaze lingered, dark and penetrating, and she felt it slide over her, seeing through the careful armour she'd tried to construct. "Do you want to tell me about it?"

"No," she said, calmer now, though aware of a strange heat rising in her chest, a flutter at the back of her knees, and the tight coil of unease curling in her stomach. There was no way out; she had to accept. "Now that you've cancelled my flight, there is no alternative but to accept your offer. I'll try not to get in your way, and if there's anything I can do to repay you, I will."

The words sounded hollow even as she said them—*what could she possibly do, penniless and stranded, to repay him?* Yet her pride demanded she make the offer.

He didn't answer immediately, and the silence stretched, heavy and deliberate. Startled, she looked up and found him watching her—grey eyes like burnished steel, cool, penetrating, appraising. The intensity was almost physical, pressing against her senses, stirring something reckless deep inside that made her pulse race.

And then she realised, with a sudden, horrified jolt, what she'd just said.

Surely, he doesn't think—? Surely, he can't—?

Her cheeks flamed, hot and insistent. She stammered, words tumbling over themselves. "I don't mean—that is, I'm not offering—"

"Yourself?" His voice was low, deliberate, and the single word hung in the air like a spark.

Aurelia's blush deepened. "Yes. I mean… no, I'm not—" She faltered, wishing the floor would open up beneath her.

Then, unexpectedly, he laughed—a rich, warm sound that shattered the tension and sent a tiny tremor of relief through her. "I'm sorry," he said, the intensity vanishing as quickly as it had appeared. "I was teasing. Probably just as well you didn't have brothers—they'd have made your life a misery."

"I'd have learned to deal with them," she returned, tartly, though the blush lingered, stubborn and infuriating.

He grinned, that rare, easy tilt of his mouth. "Probably." He glanced across the lawn, voice lightening. "Ah, here's Litia with lunch. I suggest we discuss the state of the world while we eat and drink, and then you should probably go back inside. Dr King was very firm—no overexertion, and as little sun as possible."

Litia appeared, a large, comfortable-looking woman who regarded Aurelia closely when Julian introduced her as the housekeeper. There was something in that gaze that made Aurelia tense, but the big woman relaxed into a warm smile and extended her hand in a hearty shake.

"On Kaliah Island, we introduce staff," Julian explained after Litia left. "Here everyone is related, and they can usually tell you exactly how."

"That must be lovely," Aurelia said quietly, a twinge of longing in her voice.

"You sound as though you don't have much close family," he observed.

She shifted, uncomfortable. "A father in New Zealand," she admitted, "and at least one half-sibling. No one else."

The corners of his sculpted mouth lifted in a wry smile. "Relatives have a vested interest in every aspect of your life, and an opinion on everything you do."

Aurelia remembered the nurse's comment about Julian's house suggesting a marriage. "I suppose there are disadvantages to everything, but that seems minor compared to the advantages. How did everyone get to be related?"

He told her the story of the ancestor who had landed on Kaliah Island to find it nearly depopulated by disease brought by Europeans, and of the forced marriage to the sole surviving child of the paramount chief's family. His narrative wove together brutality and moments of unexpected kindness, painting a portrait both vivid and compelling. Aurelia listened, enthralled, the sunlight shifting across the terrace and glinting in the garden, yet all she could focus on was his voice, calm yet insistent, commanding attention.

Finally, he said, "I have to go out in a few minutes, but we'll meet for a drink before dinner."

He rose with effortless authority, and Aurelia's eyes tracked him, suddenly aware once more of his height, his lean, powerful frame, and the way he moved—like a predator at the top of the food chain, controlled, lithe, and utterly self-possessed. The sight made her stomach tighten again, a mixture of apprehension and a reluctant admiration she could not name aloud.

She took a deep breath and stood, forcing herself upright, spine stiff, shoulders back, determined to appear steady. But the moment she took her first step; she misjudged the distance and stumbled against the leg of her chair.

Like the predator she had compared him to earlier, Julian was instantly at her side, his hand clamping onto her arm with a strength that both steadied and unnerved her. He was impossibly close—warm, solid, radiating effortless power. The brush of his hand against her bare skin made a shiver run down her spine, igniting something she couldn't name, a pull she wanted to deny. She wanted to lean against him, to let him anchor her, to let his strength seep into her…

Alarm bells blared in her mind. *Get out of here! Now!*

Her legs, traitorous, refused to obey, and she flinched, trying to step back. A soft gasp of dismay escaped her as she realised, she could barely move.

"I think probably the best way to do this is for me to carry you," Julian said, calm, judicial. Before she could protest, he lifted her as easily as if she weighed nothing, the movement fluid, controlled, terrifyingly powerful. His body was warm and taut against hers, muscles sliding under his shirt with a predator's grace, each movement precise, commanding.

She wanted to tell him to put her down, but fatigue swept over her in waves, dulling her resistance. For the first time since her father had abandoned them, since her mother had grown frail, she felt utterly safe in a way that made her chest ache. Her mind fuzzed, almost grateful, surrendering to the sensation of being carried.

"I'm fine," she blurted, but her voice lacked conviction.

He didn't set her down until they reached the bed. When he did, she noticed how tall he was, how broad-shouldered, how every line of his lean, sculpted body hinted at power, at a strength that could not easily be resisted. Even casually standing there, he seemed to command the air around him, his presence filling the room as though the space had been built for him alone.

"Rest until later in the afternoon," he ordered, eyes locked on hers, sharp and unwavering. "And in case you feel like doing something stupid—walking out, for instance—the staff know you're staying. You wouldn't get far."

Incredulously, Aurelia lifted her head from the pillow to meet his gaze. "I hope you're not insinuating that I'm a prisoner here."

"I'm not insinuating anything," he replied, calm and unreadable, those grey eyes like steel, assessing her, measuring her resolve. "I'm telling you the staff know you're not fit to leave, so they won't let you. Only a Capricorn would call that being taken prisoner."

"I'll bet you're a Scorpio," she said irritably.

"You're an astrologer?" His voice carried a hint of cynicism, low, smooth, yet imbued with authority.

"No, but I know a Scorpio when I meet one. You all have that innate arrogance."

He laughed, a rich, deep sound that rolled across the room like distant thunder. "I draw the line at you telling me I share some genetic traits with one-twelfth of the population. My mother says it's a Kingsley characteristic."

"She should know," Aurelia replied crisply, her pride intact despite the closeness of the man before her.

Julian found himself oddly admiring her. According to the files Sam had compiled, she was penniless, with no prospects and a future uncertain. Yet even while still recovering, she radiated defiance—a fierce, quiet pride that contrasted sharply with the loose, fiery waves of her red-gold hair. The juxtaposition of strength and vulnerability drew him in, tugging at a part of him he had no intention of acknowledging.

"Are your parents here?" she asked, her voice distant, careful.

Julian noticed the almost imperceptible heat in her tone, the way it wavered despite her attempt at detachment. It hit him unexpectedly, stirring a reaction he immediately scolded himself for. "No," he said, voice clipped, masking the irritation at the stirrings in his body he had no right to feel. "They're holidaying in the Caribbean. If they were here, you would have been staying with them."

Aurelia felt the weight of his words pressing down, a mixture of authority and subtle dominance that left her feeling simultaneously chastened and keenly aware of his physical presence—broad chest, taut arms, sculpted frame, effortless height. He was a man built to move through the world like a force of nature, and in this moment, she couldn't deny the effect he had on her—both unsettling and magnetic.

She straightened, determined to appear unaffected, but the flush rising to her cheeks betrayed her awareness: Julian Kingsley was every bit as imposing, every bit as dangerously attractive, as she had feared—and as she had been inexplicably drawn to from the moment she first saw him.

When he finally left, Aurelia's mind swirled with the memory of how it had felt to be held in his arms. Against his solid, commanding frame, she had felt… right, in a way that terrified her. Her heart still thudded at the recollection, a mix of heat, awe, and that strange, fluttering awareness of her own vulnerability.

Julian, meanwhile, walked away with an unfamiliar tightness in his chest. The memory of her small, fragile weight against him lingered, the soft warmth of her body pressing close, and a reaction he hadn't felt for years—or perhaps ever—flickered uncomfortably to life. He needed to stop thinking about it. She was a guest here. Vulnerable. Exposed. And utterly off-limits.

Yet try as he might to banish the thought, the image of her in his arms clung stubbornly to his mind, a reminder that some forces were harder to control than even he, Julian Kingsley, could command.

Chapter Four

Once he'd gone, Aurelia had been sure her roiling emotions would prevent any rest, yet the supremely comfortable bed claimed her with voracious speed, lulling her into a deep, untroubled sleep.

She woke to the seductive cooing of doves, their tranquil notes drifting lazily on the drowsy air. Tropical scents—heady, sweet, and threaded with the pervasive perfume of vanilla—drifted in from the garden, prompting a long, slow sigh and a wavering smile. Not since before her mother's condition had worsened a year ago had she slept this soundly.

How strange, she thought, listening to the muted roar of the waves on the reef. Despite everything—her prickly reactions to her arrogant host, the hardships of living rough— she could sleep as deeply as she had in her childhood, when the world had been bright, seamless, and untroubled. If this was the fabled spell of the Pacific, she was completely under its charm.

Yawning, feeling much more human, she rose and showered in the white-tiled bathroom with its wooden shutters, sprays of orchids, and an air of restrained opulence. Each droplet of water seemed to wash away not only the night's sleep but the lingering tension in her body.

Now, she thought, what on earth am I going to wear if I have to stay here for another week? Even if, by some miracle, her pack turned up intact, she had nothing suitable. Her sundresses, shorts, and the few tops she owned were old, faded, and shaped for a woman who had not spent the last years caring for someone else.

A soft tap at the door swivelled her around.

But of course, it wasn't Julian Kingsley. Instead, Litia, in a sulu of bold scarlet and deep blue, said briskly, "Julian would like it if he could join you on the terrace outside in half an hour, miss. I'll collect you then."

Aurelia watched the door close and thought, with resigned awareness, that this was definitely an order. And yet, even as she acknowledged it, her heart fluttered erratically, a slow, sensuous warmth coiling through her veins like a subtle drug.

She glowered at her reflection, wishing she had surrendered to the temptation of those sexy little silk tee-shirts she'd seen in the market. Cheap as they were, they had still been beyond her reach—and even if she had bought one, it would likely have been stolen like everything else. Tee-shirts weren't for her anyway. Her mother had always said she had an Edwardian hourglass figure: a small waist emphasised by maternal hips and breasts that were slightly too full for the rest of her. Tee-shirts clung and made her feel conspicuous.

At least the outfit she wore now suited her. Whoever had chosen it had understood colour: the soft camel silk complemented her bright hair and pale skin beautifully. After one last defiant glance at her neat, unassuming reflection, she tucked a stray strand of hair back into place, just as the housekeeper tapped at the door.

However, it was Julian who now stood in the corridor, not Litia. "If I give you an arm, do you think you could manage the few yards to another terrace?" His expression was noncommittal, though the faint lift at one corner of his mouth hinted at unspoken amusement.

Aurelia's heart gave one of those peculiar, startling jumps. "Of course," she said brightly, forcing herself to focus on the magnificent portrait at the end of the hallway—an elegant woman in her thirties.

"My great-grandmother," Julian said, following her gaze. "She was French."

No wonder she radiated that sleek, effortless chic. "She looks fascinating."

"She was." His tone softened, tinged with affectionate reminiscence, and for a fleeting moment, Aurelia caught the faintest glimpse of something profoundly human behind the intimidating, magnetic man she had come to know.

There were resemblances—the midnight-black hair, the effortless sense of style. Julian's shirt mirrored the steel-grey of his eyes, and his trousers were tailored to showcase long, powerful legs. But where had that boldly chiselled face come from, the magnificent bone structure that lent him an almost intimidating authority? Coupled with a lithely powerful body, it was the kind of presence that left women—Aurelia included— breathless and slightly unmoored.

So, the rapid thud of her heartbeat in her ears made perfect sense, as did the creeping warmth in her cheeks when he offered her a lazy, knowing smile after settling her into a chair on the terrace, the horizon ablaze with the sunset over the lagoon.

"You look infinitely more yourself," he said gravely.

"I must have looked pretty dreadful before," she countered, her blue eyes glinting with playful defiance.

"Exhaustion has that effect," he agreed, his tone calm, controlled. "According to Dr King, a little alcohol would be permissible if suitably diluted. I could offer a very weak gin and tonic if you wish."

"I'd prefer something non-alcoholic and not too sweet. Fruit juice will be fine."

"We have plenty of fruit juice." He poured her a glass, the golden liquid catching the last rays of sunlight.

Aurelia sipped gratefully. "Delicious. Perfect."

"I'm glad. It's Litia's secret recipe—pineapple, papaya, mango, and a few spices she refuses to reveal."

"Vanilla, perhaps?" she ventured, noticing the subtle, pervasive scent in the air.

"The whole house smells of it?" he asked, intrigued.

"The whole house, yes."

"The whole island, actually," he corrected. "We cultivate it for export. The conditions here are perfect for it to thrive."

A dove alighted nearby on the lush grass, its white plumage vivid against the deep green, startling in its contrast. Aurelia let out a long, soft sigh. "This is beautiful," she whispered, mesmerised by the flaming sun dipping into the sea.

As the golden disc sank, Julian spoke of the fabled green flash, a rare tropical phenomenon.

"So, it's only ever seen at sunset?" she asked, captivated.

"Even then, conditions must be perfect. No one truly knows why it appears."

"It sounds… magical," she murmured. "Have you ever seen it?"

"A couple of times," he replied, his voice almost reflective.

Twilight fell swiftly, darkness creeping from the east, and Julian rose to light candles on the table. Their soft glow danced across the terrace, washing gold over the dark planes of his face. A strange, sudden sensation—a fierce, thrilling hunger—shot through her, and Aurelia found herself startled by the intensity of it. She knew she was attracted to him, but this was something sharper, more urgent, and utterly consuming.

Fortunately, he remained oblivious. They talked easily, lightly, about trivialities—the sort of refined, effortless conversation Julian seemed to master. Aurelia welcomed it; she had spent the past year immersed in medical discussions and practicalities, and the ease of idle conversation was a balm. She found herself relaxing, laughing softly, even as she realised over the drink that he was learning more about her than she might have expected.

Until she mentioned her mother.

Then her voice faltered; tears stung behind her eyes, and she clutched the glass of water he had poured for her as a fragile shield.

"I'm sorry," Julian said quietly, his tone low but steady.

"It's all right." She set the glass down and drew in a shuddering breath, forcing herself to regain composure. He made no move to rush her, no impatience in his presence—just a quiet attentiveness that made the vulnerability in her chest feel less like exposure and more like being understood.

Eventually, her words came out brittle, tight with grief. "It's just that… she died about six weeks ago, after five long years battling a progressive illness. She organised this holiday and even paid for it before she passed… she used to worry about me, worried I wouldn't have any fun." Her throat tightened. "She'd have been horrified if she knew the travel agency got the dates wrong."

"She'd probably have been even more horrified if she knew you'd planned to tough it out on the beach," he said grimly.

Aurelia's eyes narrowed indignantly. "I did not sleep on the beach. I had a comfortable little nest under some bushes nearby. I felt perfectly safe."

"You were lucky," he replied, his voice sharp with concern. "We work damned hard to keep the island safe, but we can't control everything—or everyone, unfortunately. Once you lost your money, you should have realised your position was untenable. People can survive without food longer than they think, but it was reckless to emulate that when it wasn't necessary. Any islander would have given you something to eat."

"I was managing," she protested, her voice steadier now. "I ate fruit from the trees along the road. I only fainted—"

"Collapsed," he interjected, his tone uncompromising.

"I only fainted," she repeated, sharper this time, "because I'd walked too far in the heat and stupidly forgot to refill my water bottle." Then, a sudden memory struck her. "Who is Jessica?"

His brows drew together briefly, the frown vanishing almost as quickly as it appeared, replaced by a smooth, easy tone. "She is a friend of mine. Why do you ask?"

"When I woke, I thought you called me Jessica… No—someone else did." She searched her memory aloud, piecing it together. "You said, 'This is not Jessica.' But that's who your man thought I was, and that's why he brought me here. I had completely forgotten until now."

"He brought you here because the hospital is over a half-hour drive, and he was worried," Julian said evenly. "I wasn't home at the time, but when you didn't regain consciousness, the staff called Dr King. By the time I returned, she'd checked you over and fixed your drip. If you'd collapsed in front of the car without that intervention, you could have become dangerously ill. Most people underestimate how much water they need in the tropics."

Soberly, Aurelia nodded. "I understand now, truly. It is not an experience I want to repeat." She met his gaze, voice quieter. "And I don't think I have ever properly thanked you for taking me in. I am… truly grateful."

"It's not necessary," he interrupted curtly, rising to his feet. "And you're looking smoky-eyed—time to get some rest."

Of course, she acquiesced, letting herself be guided by his calm authority. It wasn't until the edge of sleep began to claim her, pulling her down into its velvety haze, that she realised one crucial thing: Julian had said nothing about the mysterious Jessica—the woman she apparently resembled closely enough that almost everyone in the house had assumed that was who she was. Except for Julian, who had known immediately that she wasn't.

His lover?

Almost certainly, she decided, as a flush of warmth spread through her at the thought. That commanding presence wasn't just authority—it carried a subtle, magnetic sexuality. And somehow, without ever being overt or forward, he radiated a quiet promise: any woman who encountered him would instinctively understand that he was a man who could be… unforgettable.

As sleep finally pulled her under, that unsettling, tantalising thought lingered at the edges of her mind.

Julian set the receiver down and swore under his breath in a quick, clipped blend of Polynesian and English. His fists tightened; for a moment he simply stood and stared into the night, the terrace lights burning like distant stars and the sea beyond a black, indifferent surface. His mind was already racing, assembling possibilities, and discarding most of them as implausible.

Five minutes later he lifted the phone again. On the line, Sam — his head of security — sounded relaxed, the murmur of convivial voices and clinking glasses drifting behind him. Julian cut through it. "Sorry to interrupt. I've just had word from a contact in Germany — Eddie Riordan's disappeared. And yesterday morning I was interviewed by a Common Market journalist who happened to leave the house at the same time Miss Carmichael crossed the lawn. Her hair was very much in evidence."

There was a beat of silence, then Sam's tone tightened. "So, Mrs Riordan is in danger."

"Possibly." Julian's voice was flat with controlled irritation. "There are reasons he might be trying to hide — their breakup's gone global, and if he wants to reconcile with Jessica, the last thing he needs is paparazzi on his heels."

"What do you want me to do?"

Julian took a breath. "I don't know yet." He thought of Jessica — spoiled, dramatic, prone to shaping facts to fit her version — and of the research Sam had already fed him: nothing corroborating her story. "We can't ignore her either. Alert immigration. Ask them to flag any bookings in Riordan's name. Get your best man ready to tail him if he shows up."

"If he turns up with false papers?"

"Then he's probably careless; he'll assume a small island equals lax scrutiny. Let him think he's slipped the net but have him watched closely."

Sam's voice carried a hint of grim satisfaction. "We've got a decoy ready that should convince him he's made a terrible mistake coming here."

Julian's jaw tightened at the implication. He thought of Aurelia — of the fragile, bewildered woman who'd been in his house for days. The idea of her being used as bait sent an unwelcome shiver down his spine. "Absolutely not," he said, short and sharp. "Miss Carmichael has nothing to do with this. Keep digging into Riordan's background. Exhaust the contacts. If you find anything that gives weight to Jessica's allegations, or if Riordan is on the island, extract both Jessica and Ms Carmichael quietly and immediately. If the wife's story is true, he's dangerous."

Sam pushed, conservative and pragmatic. "So, we watch only?"

"For now." Julian's voice hardened. "And Sam — send your wife to town tomorrow. Get a complete wardrobe for Ms Carmichael. Everything. She needs clothes, underwear, shoes — the lot." He rattled off sizes with the curt precision of a man used to decisions being obeyed.

"Understood," Sam said. "Anything else?"

"Yes. Keep me informed. Every ten minutes if necessary. And put your best man on traffic cams; if Riordan tries to come in by road, I want eyes on him before he reaches the beach." Julian cut the connection and let the handset rest in his palm, his fingers tightening as the image of Aurelia — small, fragile in his arms days before — intruded again. He didn't like the way thinking of her interfered with his clarity. He would have to protect her, he realised with a cold certainty, even if it meant moving faster and harder than usual.

Aurelia turned away from the mirror with a grimace. In the past few days, she had spent entirely too much time scrutinising her reflection—an act she normally avoided. But this morning, before Julian left the house, he had sent a note via the housekeeper asking her to join him for lunch on the terrace. And since Litia had whisked away the shirt and trousers she'd worn previously— "For cleaning, miss"—Aurelia was left with no choice but to wear another sulu.

It showed too much skin, she thought critically. The colours—orange-red mingled with periwinkle-blue and a bold, clear purple—felt shockingly flamboyant. Yet somehow they brought colour to her cheeks and light to her face, while harmonising rather than clashing with her vivid hair. Perhaps the earthy tans and greens she'd always worn had been wrong for her pale, luminous colouring.

Or perhaps it was the spell of the tropics, coaxing her into colour, warmth, and life.

When Julian greeted her, she saw his gaze sweep from her face to her breasts in one swift, unapologetic appraisal. He didn't ogle—Julian Kingsley would never need to— but she had no doubt he approved. Heat fountained up from some previously inviolate place within her, sending a tightening through her breasts that made her breath hitch.

Clinging to her fragile composure, she sat and said lightly, "Litia persuaded me to wear this. I hadn't realised how cool they were."

Yes—that was acceptable. Her voice was steady, her tone breezy. Only the faint pink on her cheeks betrayed her. Nothing less than a shroud would hide that, she thought miserably, wishing she hadn't inherited her mother's tendency to colour at the slightest provocation.

Everything felt sharper today. Her senses hummed with a strange vitality—she was acutely aware of Julian seated opposite her, of the soft caress of air on her skin, of the sun warming her shoulders, of the intoxicating scent of flowers drifting from the garden. Rest, food, water—she supposed tartly—were a potent combination. She felt more alive than she had in years.

"Would you like coffee?" he asked. When she nodded, he added, "Could you pour for me? Black."

"Of course," she said brightly. "Scorpios always have black coffee. It goes with the sign."

Julian watched her hands as she poured—slim, graceful hands, elegant even in their simplest movements. They did inconvenient things to him, summoning reckless images that had no place at a civilised lunch—images of those hands sliding slowly over his skin, touching with that same restrained delicacy…

He had spent half his life being pursued by women, and women, he knew, rarely hid their interest well. Many were drawn to the Kingsley name, but he wasn't oblivious to the fact that his face and body held their own appeal.

And he recognised the subtle signs in Aurelia—the heightened colour, the quickened breath, the dart of her lashes—even though she gave him no deliberate signals at all. *A ploy? An attempt at aloofness to pique his interest?* He didn't think so. But it succeeded all the same.

His attention was caught—sharply, unexpectedly. Beyond the sympathy he felt for her recent ordeal, he simply wanted to know more about her.

Coolly, he said, "I must apologise for being remiss. It's been a busy few days, but now the conference is over things will return to something resembling normal. And as you can't continue walking around in borrowed sulus, I've arranged for a local boutique owner to bring clothes here this afternoon. Choose whatever you wish."

Aurelia stared at him; uncertain she'd heard correctly. Outrage warred with a demoralising flicker of pleasure. She lifted her gaze to his—those hooded iron-grey eyes, steady and unreadable. "You didn't have to do that," she said stiffly. "I can organise my own wardrobe."

"Relax. I'm not criticising your clothes or your taste," he said with infuriating calm, before adding, with lethal accuracy, "But how are you going to organise a wardrobe without money?"

He looked faintly amused, but Aurelia sensed the steel behind the coolness.

Well—she was stubborn, as her mother had often said. "If you lend me a small amount, I can buy sarongs from the market. They're not expensive, and they're all I need. Then I can return these to the nurse's daughter."

"Don't worry about the cost," he said. "You must know I've more money than I can sensibly use. Think of it as redressing the balance a bit."

Blue sparks lit her eyes. "Redressing what balance? I don't want anything more from you—you've already done too much. In fact, I feel well enough to go home now."

"Did Dr King say so?"

She hesitated. "No," she muttered, aware he could read her thoughts as clearly as if she'd spoken them aloud. "Clearly she has no hesitation in breaking patient confidentiality."

Julian's shoulders lifted in a distinctly Gallic shrug—a gesture she suddenly recognised from the portrait of his French great-grandmother. "I already knew most of it and guessed the rest," he drawled. "And if staying here galls you so much, you can earn your keep."

She froze. "How?" The word was sharp enough to cut.

"Not the way you're thinking," he said, a hint of hauteur in his tone. "I've never had to pay for sex, and I don't intend to start now."

Aurelia had always thought the expression wanting the ground to swallow you was melodramatic. Now she understood it with painful clarity. Humiliation washed over her in a hot wave; if the floor had cracked open at her feet she'd have leapt straight into the abyss.

Scarlet-faced, she managed, "I didn't think of anything like that until you… made it obvious what you thought I meant."

Before she tied herself in further knots, she drew in a shaky breath and forced herself on. "I understand now that you didn't mean it that way, but I'm afraid I don't have any skills to pay for my board."

"Let's get one thing perfectly clear," he said, his gaze hardening to metal. "I don't expect you to pay for anything. My offhand comment meant only that I'm in a bind—and if you're willing, you can help."

"I'd like to," she said softly. "You've been very kind to me, and I'm not ungrateful."

"I don't want your gratitude," he said, cool and aloof, a boundary sliding cleanly between them. "The situation is unusual. An old friend of my father's is arriving soon, bringing his granddaughter. Jasmine is young, very pretty, and I like her—but she's developed a massive crush on me. It's becoming embarrassing."

"They usually are—to both the crusher and the crushee," Aurelia said tartly. Inwardly, she doubted this was anything new for him.

"This one is edging into something uncomfortably close to stalking. I just read an interview she gave to a fashion magazine—she implied we're engaged, and that I'm waiting for her to 'grow up.'"

Rapidly reassessing the girl, Aurelia asked, "How old is she?"

"Nineteen. She's a model."

"I'm surprised. I'd have thought you could handle a situation like this easily."

"Normally, yes." His voice hardened. "But her grandfather is old. It would hurt him if my lawyers sent a cease-and-desist letter or if I went public with a denial. And I like the girl. I don't want to humiliate her."

"Someone must have given her the idea that you were in love with her."

"Not I," he said flatly.

Aurelia believed him. With all the women he could have, it seemed unlikely he'd choose someone barely nineteen. "So… how exactly do you think I can help?"

He looked at her, expression unreadable, and said, "You've been staying here for several days. It might reinforce to her that I'm not interested in her as wife material if she believes we're lovers."

"Lovers?" Her voice shot up an octave, half-squeak, half-gasp.

He rose, taking her hand and bringing her up with him. "Lovers," he repeated calmly, a cynical smile tugging at his mouth. "As in sharing a bed."

"As in being your mistress?" Her heart pounded so loudly she could barely hear her own words. She couldn't look away from his eyes—gunmetal grey, unwavering, and disturbingly warm.

"Mistress?" he echoed, with a faintly mocking lift of one brow. "That's an old-fashioned word."

Still holding her hand, he lifted his other and traced the outline of her mouth with one long, sure fingertip.

The touch was pure fire—white-hot lightning through her veins, a fever blooming beneath her skin.

"No," he went on, voice dropping to something deep and textured. "Apart from that erotic mouth, you're not mistress material. Jasmine is far more sophisticated. A mistress she could handle. But I want her to believe we're in love—that this is serious."

His knowledgeable fingertip smoothed along her cheekbone, soft and devastating. Aurelia struggled to gather her scattered thoughts. "If she's so sophisticated she'll know... she'll know..."

"What will she know?" His voice was amused, and when she lifted her lashes she caught him watching her mouth—intently, hungrily.

A jolt shot through her, hot and electric. "That... I'm not the right sort of person for you."

It was almost impossible to form coherent sentences under that gaze—under that touch. His voice was a dark velvet thread, his eyes hypnotic, and the slow, deliberate caress along her skin sank right into her core.

"I mean..." she whispered, fighting for sense, "I'm not the kind of woman you'd be attracted to. I blush all the time—my skin shows every emotion—"

Realising she was babbling, she bit off her words. *Pull away,* she told herself fiercely. *Step back. He's only holding one hand—he'll let you go...*

But Julian's gaze darkened—an unmistakable flare of male desire.

"You're wrong," he said softly. "I find you very attractive. Surely you know that?"

His voice slid over her like warm honey.

"Your skin is like silk... and those blushes you hate?"

His eyes burned into hers.

"They're charming."

He released her hand, but before she could seize the moment to leap backward, he framed her face between his palms and smiled down at her.

Even through the dazed fog of his nearness, Aurelia recognised what he was doing—wielding charm and masculine charisma like a weapon, using that devastating presence to persuade her. She should have been angry. She should have recoiled, resisted.

But his smile struck her like a bolt of heat—erotic in its simplicity, its power. It zinged through her with electric clarity, straight to the hidden, aching places she didn't want to acknowledge.

Then, abruptly, he stepped back. He dropped his hands as if he, too, needed distance. A faint, betraying flush touched his cheekbones—confirmation that his reaction to her had not been entirely one-sided, however physical, or inconvenient it might have been for him.

"Trust me," he said quietly, the steel returning to his voice. "If you agree to this, they will believe we are in love. The men in my family marry for love. And this," he added with pragmatic calm, "is the least painful—and probably the only acceptable—way for Jasmine to realise that her hopes are nothing more than fairy gold."

Aurelia hesitated. "Will she be upset?"

His broad shoulders lifted in a brief, resigned shrug. "Almost certainly—a little," he conceded. "But better a short disappointment now than years wasted believing in something that was never real. Or worse, a public embarrassment when I eventually make my disinterest clear."

"I suppose so."

Every instinct for self-preservation shrieked don't do this, but her better nature—foolish, generous, and gratefully indebted—won out. "Very well," she said softly. "I'll do it."

One way, at least, to repay him for everything he'd done.

And she'd be quite safe; she told herself fiercely. You couldn't fall in love so quickly. You needed time. Familiarity. And even then, love could be nothing more than illusion—she knew that far too well.

This would be a brief fantasy; a pretend life lived under tropical skies. Then she'd return home to reality—with no regrets.

Julian didn't gush or overwhelm her with thanks. His smile was ironic, a little crooked. "Thank you," he said simply. "Treat the clothes as part of your role. To solidify things, I'm hosting a dinner party for twenty tonight. Don't look so terrified— I'm not expecting you to play hostess—"

"Which is just as well," she cut in with feeling. "I have never hosted a dinner party in my life. Do I have to be there? We don't need to fool your friends—I can have dinner in my room."

"Like a Victorian governess?" He gave a dry lift of one brow. "Your presence here hasn't gone unnoticed, Aurelia. And of course, if anyone asks where you are, I can always share your sad little story."

She drew in a shocked breath between her teeth. "You fight dirty," she whispered. "I'll be completely out of my depth, and you know it. I know you're trying to be kind but—"

Julian barked a short, amused laugh. "I'm not, and you know that. I simply dislike watching people sabotage themselves. It's a remarkably pointless pastime."

His tone shifted, gentling—not warmer, but fairer. "You don't need to come to the dinner party. But I think you'd enjoy it—just as I'm sure you'll enjoy the day we plan to spend out on the lagoon tomorrow."

She flushed. "I'm being ungrateful... aren't I?"

Julian studied her, something unreadable flickering in the depths of those iron-grey eyes. He'd always chosen women who were polished, worldly, certain of their desirability. Aurelia was none of those things. She was proud, easily embarrassed, unexpectedly fiery, and entirely unaware of her own sensual appeal.

Fresh. Charming. A temptation he should not be entertaining.

Her mouth—a soft, lush curve—promised things he had no business imagining.

He forced the thought away.

Coolly, he said, "I told you; I don't want gratitude. And if you're wondering whether I expect any... overt displays of affection, you can put that fear to rest. I'm not so crass."

His gaze flicked briefly to her mouth—far too knowingly.

"Tonight is merely a test run. You might find it easier to step into the role when Jasmine and her grandfather are not yet here."

Chapter Five

Aurelia looked up into Julian's tough, formidable face. *What am I doing?* she thought, panic fluttering in her chest like a trapped bird.

But her voice—steady only by sheer force of will—said, "Very well, I'll come. I just hope nothing goes wrong."

"Nothing can," he replied with that infuriating, effortless self-confidence. He glanced at the watch strapped to his lean, tanned wrist. "Can you be ready to look at some clothes in half an hour?"

"I—yes."

Of course she could be ready. She had nothing else to do. Yet she felt a deep, instinctive reluctance coil low in her stomach.

She spent most of that half-hour questioning her sanity. *Why had she agreed to such a ridiculous plan?* A sense of obligation carried to lunatic extremes, she decided grimly. Panic flickered again, bright, and sharp. But Julian had taken her in when she'd been helpless. He had ensured her care, her safety, even her dignity. The least she could do was help him in return.

When Litia arrived to escort her to one of the guest bedrooms, Aurelia followed, nerves tight as piano wire.

A rack of clothing stood waiting—beautiful, colourful, luxurious. Beside it stood a woman in a high-end sulu… and Julian.

Her stomach dropped. *Did he expect her to parade in front of him like some model on display?* Shame crawled over her skin at the mere thought. She opened her mouth to object, but the words shrivelled when she met his level, commanding gaze.

"Thank you, Litia," he said easily. He waited for the housekeeper to withdraw before introducing the boutique owner. Then—with welcome tact—added, "I'll leave you to try the clothes."

Relief flooded her. She nodded quickly.

When he'd gone, the boutique owner surveyed Aurelia with a practised, appreciative eye. "He had the size right—and the colours. Clear and warm to suit your astonishing skin and hair. That boy's got a good eye."

"Boy?" Aurelia echoed faintly.

The older woman grinned. "I've known him since he was tearing around the village in a faded lavalava with the other children. He might be nearly thirty, but to me he'll always be a wild kid. Now—let's see what you like."

Left to her own devices, Aurelia would have chosen the muted earth-tones she'd always worn, colours that allowed her to fade quietly into the background. But in the crisp, vivid hues the boutique owner urged her into, she saw at once what Julian had already realised: peach tones warmed her complexion; peridot greens made her eyes glow like gemstones.

They had a polite battle over quantity.

"This is enough," Aurelia insisted firmly, indicating a modest selection.

The woman frowned. "You'll need more than that. The tropics are hard on clothes."

"I can manage," Aurelia repeated.

Labels whispered luxury. Fabrics shimmered with artisanship. The extras—lingerie, shoes, hats—were items she would never have bought in her normal life. Her throat tightened.

The boutique owner softened. "One more suggestion? Your hair is glorious, but the style isn't doing it justice. I have a friend who cuts like a genius. She can come this afternoon—free of charge, as a favour to Julian."

Tactful phrasing, but the meaning was clear: *Your hair needs help.*

Aurelia hesitated. She usually wore it tied back, trimming it herself with scissors in front of a mirror. The idea of a stranger touching it made her uneasy.

The woman gently pressed on. "Julian is... well, Pacific royalty, in a way. He's no snob—he has enough confidence not to care about appearances—but others will judge by high standards. And forgive me... you're not like his usual friends."

She paused delicately over the last word.

Aurelia mustered a smile. "You're right. Yes... please ask her to come."

The woman looked as though she wanted to say more, but a knock sounded. Litia reappeared.

"Mr Julian would like to see you, miss."

In his sleek, high-tech office, Julian sat at his desk, expression composed. "We need to talk."

Her heart jumped. "All right. But—I've arranged for a haircut in a couple of hours."

"Good." His gaze drifted over the bright fall of her hair with a sensual appreciation that made her skin tighten. "Don't let her take too much off."

Then, abruptly: "Do you ride?"

The shift in tone—from heated male appraisal to polite conversation—made her blink. "Yes, although it's been years since I've been on a horse."

"It's like swimming. You never forget. Do you feel well enough?"

"I'd love to," she said—and meant it. Her spirits soared unexpectedly.

He smiled. "Good. Change into trousers and I'll collect you in ten minutes. Make sure you wear a hat that won't fall off."

Half an hour later, Aurelia drew in a deep, shivering breath, letting the warm tropical air fill her lungs. They were riding through a papaya plantation, the large, oval fruits dangling in heavy green clusters against slender trunks. The sun blazed overhead, yet the horses seemed perfectly at ease; Aurelia noted only a faint sheen of sweat along her chestnut mare's withers. The animal moved with a spirited energy that made the ride exhilarating rather than exhausting.

"Tell me about yourself," Julian said, his voice casual yet carrying that quiet authority she couldn't ignore. "Where did you grow up?"

"Strahan," she replied, keeping her tone light. "A little town on a tiny harbour in Tasmania."

He gave a small, approving nod. "And what career did you take up?"

"I spent a year at the University of Tasmania," she said.

Julian's presence unsettled her more than she wanted to admit. He wore well-worn riding trousers that clung to his heavily muscled thighs like a second skin, and a blue shirt rolled up to reveal forearms tanned the colour of teak. Aurelia's heart had performed a couple of erratic somersaults when he'd swung effortlessly onto the black gelding and, in one fluid motion, had helped her into the saddle, his hands firm at her waist.

Those seconds of close contact had left her oddly giddy, her body still humming with a vitality she hadn't felt in years. She tried to tell herself it was merely dehydration—or perhaps the exhilaration of the ride—but the flush in her skin and the quickening of her pulse suggested otherwise.

"What degree?" he asked, his gaze appraising yet discreet, checking her confidence and composure.

"Arts," she replied. "I wanted to do history… and I'll finish it one day."

His brows lifted ever so slightly. "I see. Did your mother's illness interrupt your studies?"

She swallowed. "Yes. When she could no longer look after herself, I went home to care for her."

"That's tough. Did you have anyone to help?"

"No. My parents divorced when I was ten."

"Are you in contact with your father?"

"No," she said, briefly, then wondered if she should have prevaricated. She hardly knew Julian, aside from the snippets she'd read in newspapers and magazines.

She flicked a quick glance at him. The line of his profile was uncompromising, angular, and severe. He looked like a man who commanded the world itself—confident, unshakable, born to authority. A man entirely at ease with women and the power he had over them. She'd seen his name linked to half a dozen glamorous women, all of them moving in circles that made the paparazzi salivate. And then there was Jasmine— a young model, already infatuated with him.

Aurelia's pulse picked up. In spite of what he had told her, she doubted he would find her—Aurelia Carmichael, from tiny Strahan, Australia—particularly fascinating.

And yet, she wanted him to care about more than her appearance. Even imagining that possibility made her heart beat faster. Her knowledge of men was painfully thin; the past year had been spent on worry and caretaking, not social pursuits. This—this ride, this closeness—was thrilling and terrifying all at once.

She was still a virgin, for heaven's sake—for all she knew, the only twenty-five-year-old virgin in the Pacific Basin. And yet, here she was, hurtling headfirst into a situation that made her pulse flutter and her thoughts reel. Too late for second thoughts, she told herself grimly. She'd agreed to this charade, and she would see it through.

Hurriedly, she said, "My father forced me to choose between him and my mother. He lives in New Zealand now."

"Some men don't deserve families." His voice was quiet, almost a rumble, carrying an authority she could feel more than hear.

"Some women, too." She forced a laugh, feeling her throat tighten. Life hadn't been fair to either sex, and she knew it.

She took a deep breath. "Tell me what I need to know about you."

Julian shrugged, guiding his mount up a small slope until they stopped beneath a huge, ancient tree, its dark-foliaged boughs heavy with shade. Behind them, the vivid green mountains clawed at the sky. When she turned to face the view, Aurelia's breath caught in her throat.

Spread before them lay a panorama of pure, sun-drenched colour—the bold green of plantations, the softer silvery shades of palm forests along the shore, and the brilliant turquoise of the lagoon, fringed by the white lashing surf of the reef. Beyond that, the Pacific stretched in an endless curve, its intense emerald waters protective yet wild, a reminder of the untamed world she had stumbled into.

Yet danger lurked in its limitless expanse.

"I was born here twenty-nine years ago," Julian said, not looking at her. "I expect to die here."

The simplicity of the sentence, delivered with calm certainty, seemed to define him. A man of the world yet rooted to this island, bound to its lush fertility and its merciless cyclones. There was something magnetic in the way he spoke, as if he had claimed not just this land but everything he looked upon. Aurelia found herself leaning a little closer in the saddle, drawn by the quiet power he radiated.

"I ran wild here until my parents shipped me off to school in Australia, then to university in England and America. The family owns the Blue Diamond mines—one day, they'll pass to me. My degree was in business, but it was the reach of the Internet, the sheer scope of it, that fascinated me far more than traditional commerce. That became my career."

She nodded, absorbing not just the words but the quiet authority that laced them. His company—launched when he was barely out of his teens—was now a formidable force in global information technology. And yet, she sensed that world of algorithms and markets, as impressive as it was, remained secondary to something deeper, something older that pulsed beneath his skin.

"However," he continued, his voice taking on a softened, almost reverent resonance, "this is my true life's work—Kaliah Island and its people. My father isn't ready to relinquish his role as head of the family corporation, and I'm in no hurry to take it. But eventually, the responsibility will fall to me."

Aurelia hesitated, then dared to ask, "Do you want to do that?"

"Wanting doesn't come into it." His gaze stayed anchored to the sweeping horizon beyond the terrace, but the hard set of his jaw betrayed the turmoil beneath. "It's hereditary. My family is the last living link to the ancient chiefs of this island. The role may be mostly ceremonial now, but it still carries weight."

He shifted slightly, nodding toward the panorama before them. "Kaliah Island lies at the heart of the great prehistoric sailing routes—east to west, north to south." His voice deepened, smooth and confident. "For centuries, my ancestors traded along those paths.

Fought on them. Explored them. We islanders pride ourselves on our openness to new ideas."

His shoulder brushed hers—barely a touch, more a whisper of proximity—yet it sent a shiver spiralling through her. Nothing overt. No reaching hand. No calculated seduction. Just the weight of his presence, the electric awareness his nearness stirred in her body. Heat climbed her spine. A fluttering ache pulled tight beneath her ribs. It felt almost like fear… except it throbbed with something far more thrilling.

She met his eyes. Those translucent, polar-sea eyes caught hers and held her still, breathless. A slow, sensuous charge passed between them, as undeniable as it was unwanted. And yet—she knew exactly who ignited it.

All her senses sharpened to him. The brush of the breeze felt more intimate, the scents richer, the sunlight hotter, as if her body had been recalibrated around Julian Kingsley's presence. Her pulse thundered in her ears.

"We'd better head back," he said abruptly, as though the small crack he'd allowed into his armour disturbed him. "We've stayed long enough."

She nodded and turned her mount, pretending to admire the view while her mind raced. So, this—this intoxicating, consuming pull—was sexual attraction. She barely knew him, yet she had stepped into his impossible charade without hesitation. Was it compassion for the woman he didn't want? Or was it something darker—some unspoken desire to stay close to him, to bask in the heat and authority he radiated so effortlessly?

The thought made her stomach twist. Was she being foolish?

Through her lashes, she watched him ride ahead, seated on his big gelding with absolute ease. Controlled. Commanding. Self-assured. Was every aspect of his life handled with that same unforgiving mastery—every decision, every confrontation, every… intimate encounter? Heat rushed through her, and she tightened her grip on the reins to keep her reaction contained. Her mother certainly hadn't envisioned this when she planned a relaxing holiday on Kaliah Island.

Julian slowed, waiting for her to catch up. "We can ride back along the beach if you like," he said, frowning slightly. "But you've caught some sun. Do you need sunscreen?"

"No, thanks, I'm covered," she replied, though she was grateful for the pause—grateful for the moment to steady herself. "And yes, I'd love the beach."

"No mad galloping," he said, a wisp of dry humour threading his voice.

"I've never been into mad," she said lightly. "I was always the one checking things were safe before I did them."

Even as she said it, she knew she was lying. Today, she was anything but cautious.

Julian reached into his shirt pocket and tossed her a small tube. "Sunscreen first."

She caught it, the plastic warm from his body. As she spread it over her arms and shoulders, she told herself the heat was from the sun... not from him. But the tiny tremor down her spine betrayed her.

She capped the tube and held it out to him. His fingers closed over hers—firm, warm, deliberate. The jolt that shot through her was instantaneous, visceral. Her horse shifted, startled by the abrupt tension.

"Steady," she murmured, calming it.

Julian still didn't release her.

He looked down at their joined hands—and something shifted in his expression, quick and dangerous. A thought crossed his mind with startling clarity: he wanted her. Not the convenient stranger for the sake of a fabricated engagement. Not the woman he'd taken responsibility for. Her. Aurelia.

And he disliked the realization with an intensity that almost shook him.

He'd always been in command of himself—his emotions, his impulses, the entire landscape of his internal world. But this... this sudden, unwelcome pull toward her... this he could not explain, could not control, and could not seem to stop.

Abruptly, he drew back and indicated a narrow trail leading toward the water. "The sea is that way."

His voice was steady. Controlled. But Aurelia felt the shift all the same—the charged silence humming between them.

He was fighting something.

So was she.

Aurelia followed in silence, sensing a subtle shift between them. The camaraderie of earlier had evaporated, replaced by a quiet barrier that stung in a way she couldn't name. The ride along the beach should have been magical, but although they cantered rather than galloped, she suspected the pace was deliberate—an unspoken way to keep conversation at bay.

Back at the house, Julian said with his customary courtesy, "I suggest you rest after lunch. Our guests will begin arriving at seven."

"I'll be ready," she replied, her tone bright despite the lingering tension.

Shortly after, the hairdresser arrived, accompanied by an assistant. "Our cosmetics specialist," she said, making exaggerated clucking noises as she examined Aurelia's freshly trimmed tresses. "My friend thought you might like a sample of our range."

"I can't afford any cosmetics," Aurelia said firmly.

The women blinked but quickly reassured her. "We offer a complimentary consultation—that's our policy. What you choose to do afterward is entirely up to you."

Aurelia hesitated, but their insistence left her little room to protest.

"So that is settled," the hairdresser said once Aurelia relented. "Now, about your hair…"

They discussed the final cut, Aurelia's sudden, defiant suggestion for short hair vetoed on the spot.

"Apart from it being a crime against whatever gene gave you that fabulous hair, it wouldn't suit you," the hairdresser said firmly. "Your eyes, mouth, and skin would compete for attention, and that wouldn't work. I suggest a gentle curl, softly pulled back to complement your features. Here, I'll show you."

Aurelia couldn't deny the logic—nor could she help marvel at the transformation.

When her reflection appeared after they applied subtle cosmetics scented with exotic tropical flowers, she felt momentarily startled. Her eyes seemed larger, bluer; lashes previously too pale were now darker and defined without appearing artificial. The effect was delicate, enhancing her natural beauty rather than masking it. She'd have loved to purchase the products, but their quality whispered of a price far beyond her means.

"They're made on the island using traditional recipes and scents," the assistant said with pride. "My cousin manages the production. Initially, we sold only to tourists, but the business is expanding to North America and Australia. Mr Kingsley—Mr Julian—thinks Asia will be our biggest market next."

"You've done a wonderful job," Aurelia said, smiling at both women, inwardly hoping they didn't expect a tip. Fortunately, Kaliah Island seemed like Australia in that regard—tipping wasn't customary. "Thank you so much for everything."

After the two women left, Aurelia lingered in front of the mirror, studying her reflection a moment longer before turning away in embarrassment. It was ridiculous to be so impressed by the skill of a cosmetician and some truly exquisite products—she couldn't afford them, and that was that.

But when she moved to change, she froze, astounded. Rack upon rack of outfits filled the room. Every garment she had tried that morning—not only the ones she'd chosen, but every outfit that had suited her perfectly—was there, waiting.

Frowning, she lifted the skirt of a silk chiffon evening dress in the softest apricot. It had looked divine on her, but she'd discarded it, thinking she didn't need more than one outfit for after dark. The silk slipped like water through her fingers, and her frown deepened. Turning to a large chest of drawers, she paused again, biting her lip as she took in the drawer full of subtly shimmering lingerie. Clearly, the boutique owner had misunderstood. Well, she decided, it would have to go.

Halfway down the hall, however, she collided with Litia, who carried a bag of sophisticated blues and greens—the very cosmetics Aurelia had just rejected.

"Oh, no!" Aurelia exclaimed, stopping in her tracks. "There's been some mistake—I didn't buy these!"

"Mr. Kingsley says they are for you," the housekeeper replied, her polite smile vanishing.

"No," Aurelia insisted, flustered but determined. "I haven't bought them."

"But—"

"It's all right, Litia."

The cool, commanding voice of Julian Kingsley cut through the tension like a blade. Both women fell silent, and Aurelia's heart leapt into the familiar flip before settling into a faster, more uneven rhythm.

He held out a hand, and Litia relinquished the bag with a small bow. "Thanks," he said, waiting until she'd gone before adding, with polite authority, "Come into my office."

Fuming, Aurelia followed him, and the moment the door closed she demanded, "Did you buy these?"

"Yes." His long-fingered hand lifted to flick a lock of hair from her flushed face. "Stop going off the deep end. You're reinforcing a stereotype."

"That's ridiculous!" she shot back, her voice sharp, tinged with the nervous thrill of being this close to him. "You don't know anything about me. And anyway, hair colour has nothing to do with temperament! My mother was a redhead, and she had the most even temper of anyone I've ever known."

"Did she?" His tone was dry, amused. "I thought red hair was genetically linked to a hair-trigger temper."

The hint of teasing in his voice made her pulse speed. She drew in a calming breath. "I didn't buy these cosmetics, and I—"

"Why?"

Aurelia blinked, distracted by the piercing intensity of his gaze. "What?"

"Why didn't you buy them?" he asked evenly.

"Because I don't need them," she said, her voice firmer than she intended. She swallowed and tried again, forcing a reasonable tone. "And I don't need the extra clothes that have magically appeared in my wardrobe."

He shrugged, his expression an unshakable mask. "I can afford them. And as you're here because I asked you to stay, and you're participating in this charade for my sake, it's up to me to bear the cost."

"It's the principle of the thing," she muttered through gritted teeth, aware of his dark, amused eyes studying her like a cat assessing a new toy. She knew she was losing this fight—he had more money, more power, and more control than she could hope to match. And behind that compelling mask, she sensed he was savouring it.

Aurelia felt the gulf between them widen, uncrossable, and it scared her. Yet at the same time, a shiver of anticipation ran through her—a dangerous, exciting thrill at the thought of what "services" might be implied by her presence here.

She drew in another breath, attempting calm. "I don't want the clothes or the cosmetics. I know you're trying to help, but I feel—"

"Bought?" Julian supplied, his voice smooth, deliberate, brushing against her awareness in a way that made her stomach flutter.

Chapter Six

Aurelia flinched, her gaze snapping up to meet his. He didn't look amused now; those angular features were carved into a forbidding mask.

"I suppose so," she muttered, cringing inwardly. *How idiotic am I being?*

"And you're afraid I might demand to be recompensed?" Julian asked, his voice level but carrying a disturbing undertone beneath the cool disdain.

Colour flamed through her. "No!" She tried to retrieve some dignity but only managed a breathless rush of words: "I just don't like being dependent on you."

"Dependent?" His tone rang with irony. "I suspect that's only part of it. Do you honestly think I'd go to such elaborate lengths just to get you to stay in my house and—presumably—under my power?"

Put like that, her hazy suspicions sounded utterly absurd. He was far too experienced—he must know she found him attractive. She practically turned pink every time he came near her. But he didn't need to drag her feelings into the open and bathe them in cruel clarity, exposing her embarrassment for his inspection.

Lifting her chin with what pride she could muster, she said, "No. I don't."

He leaned back, inspecting her, the curve of his smile arrogantly assured. "Then what exactly is your problem?"

That maddening heat scorched her cheekbones. "I'm not a charity case or a Cinderella," she said tightly. "I don't need all those clothes."

"Then don't use them," he replied, allowing a thread of impatience to roughen his voice.

"That's not the point." Her hands balled. "I know I agreed to this, but I'm starting to think it's not a good idea."

"You gave me your word," he said, the steel in his tone unmistakable.

Aurelia shot him a startled glance. Her spine stiffened when she saw the narrowing of his eyes, his lips flattening into that hard, uncompromising line. He looked…dangerous. Intimidating. Exactly the sort of man whose focus could burn you alive.

"And now I'm reconsidering," she flashed, indignation flaring. "I agreed to a—a charade, not a complete forfeiture of autonomy!"

Julian lifted his shoulders in that quick, inherently Gallic shrug. "I can't force you," he said, the cynicism unmasked.

The heat drained from her cheeks, leaving her lightheaded. He'd expected this, she realised—expected her to agree then retreat. And beneath his calm, she sensed the faintest edge of contempt. It stung more than she cared to admit.

"Yes, well..." she managed, weakly attempting composure. "I won't wear those clothes."

"Cutting off your nose to spite your face again?" he said lightly, the smile not reaching those cool, hard eyes. He had clearly disengaged. "Do whatever you like with them— they're there if you need them. So are the cosmetics." His gaze swept her flushed face and tense posture, lingering a moment too long. "If you want to appear au naturel, by all means do so."

And then, drawled with wicked provocation. "Well...perhaps not entirely. My male guests would likely be delighted if you attended dinner in the nude, but I'd prefer you didn't."

Her breath caught—half fury, half something much more dangerous.

He held her gaze several seconds longer, then added with a faintly satirical curve of his lips, "Unless, of course, you intend it for my sole delectation."

Her pulse lurched.

"But whatever you choose," he finished, "keep the clothes. And the cosmetics."

"I don't want them," she burst out fiercely. "That's what this is about! I don't need payment. And while I did agree to this charade, I can't pretend it isn't...too close to lying. And lying—even for a noble reason—is still lying."

His brows drew together. "If you want to back out, that's fine. I don't want you compromising your principles."

Balked, she stared at him. The silence thickened, heavy and intimate, pressing in on her until she finally muttered, "You'd make this much easier if you threatened me."

He arched a sardonic brow. "So, you'd give in to threats?"

"No," she admitted, frustrated, "but then I could summon up righteous indignation and storm off and feel noble about it. As it is..." She exhaled shakily. "I keep thinking about that poor girl who believes she's going to be your wife. You're probably right— the kindest way to let her down is to pretend we're..."

Her voice failed.

"Lovers," he supplied laconically. "Or if that's too much—would-be lovers. Or even soon-to-be lovers. I don't care."

He held her gaze for several long, charged moments.

"Let's just take it as it comes. Don't imply anything. Don't lie. Just…blush enchantingly whenever I speak to you, and everyone will draw their own conclusions—without either of us saying a word."

At the mention of her ever-present blushes, her cheeks flamed once more. She clapped her hands over them and muttered in deep mortification, "One of these days I'm going to learn to control this—or die trying."

"Why?" Julian's voice was easy, amused. "You blush beautifully. Besides, I believe the tendency fades with experience… sophistication."

All pretence of dignity gone, she scowled at him. "Thank you. Do you happen to have any women's magazines lying around with pictures of what Julian Kingsley's girlfriend would wear to an intimate dinner for twenty?"

His smile widened, tilting into a laugh that made her stomach flutter. "No, you witch," he said, mock exasperated. "Just wear what you like—something floaty, light, shortish. Tonight's dinner is for a small trade delegation from Australia, here to talk us into letting them prospect for minerals in the mountains. So, prepare to be bored."

"Yes… all right."

But it wasn't all right. He'd had his way with almost indecent ease, and somehow, in doing so, made her acutely conscious of him—and of her own helpless reactions—more than ever before. Julian Kingsley was magnetic, and she was perilously close to realising she might be… infatuated. Telling herself that you couldn't fall in love so quickly did nothing; her brain knew it was absurd, but her body betrayed her, responding to every thought of him with a heat that made her pulse race.

She chose the silk chiffon in apricot, allowing the fabric to skim her skin in airy layers, but ignored the cosmetics at first. That is, until she caught sight of herself in the mirror and froze. Her face looked startlingly bare; at the very least, makeup might camouflage her traitorous blushes.

With a hesitant sigh, she unearthed the cosmetics and carefully followed the instructions she'd been given earlier. It took patience, a steady hand, and a few stifled groans of frustration, but in the end she inspected her reflection with cautious satisfaction.

"Well… perhaps a bit better than all right," she muttered to the reflection, sternly quelling the thrill of vanity that rose unbidden.

After all, the guests were from the mineral industry. Surely, they'd be nothing but middle-aged men with weathered faces.

Wrong.

The first person to arrive was young, tall, and stunning, with a mane of artfully highlighted blonde hair. She greeted Julian with such obvious familiarity that her delight was almost tangible—embracing him warmly, her laughter ringing in the air. He returned her greeting with practiced charm, holding her at arm's length after kissing her on both cheeks, and whispered something that made her laugh, blush, and pat his cheek in response.

Only then did she turn to Aurelia. The blonde looked her over, slightly puzzled, and said, "I thought you were married—oh, sorry, wrong woman!"

Presumably, she meant the mysterious Jessica.

At that moment Aurelia was devoutly thankful to the woman who'd chosen her clothes and to Julian for insisting she accept the cosmetics. They were armour—shielding her from the nervous awkwardness that threatened to unravel her all evening.

Armour she desperately needed, although Julian offered unobtrusive but steady support, a quiet presence at her elbow as she navigated the complex dance of conversation and pleasantries. Surprisingly, she even enjoyed the dinner, though later she realised she could barely remember what she had eaten.

Her dinner partner, the mining magnate, and the most important man in the delegation, proved unexpectedly engaging. He spoke of the Outback with a poet's passion, of red dirt and endless skies, of heat that burned the skin and wind that carved the landscape.

"People underestimate the desert," he said, swirling his wine thoughtfully. "They think it's harsh and unforgiving, but it teaches patience. Resilience. And it gives you perspective—you learn to respect forces you can't control."

Aurelia found herself leaning in slightly. "And yet you made a fortune there. You must have been brave—or reckless."

"Perhaps a little of both," he admitted with a wry smile. "There's a rhythm to it, though. You adapt or you fail. Mostly I adapt."

She smiled, genuinely interested, and Julian's eyes flicked to her over his glass. He didn't interrupt or comment, but he watched—observing the subtle way she animated herself when engaged in conversation, the way her hands moved lightly on the table, the soft catch of her breath as she laughed. Every movement seemed amplified, charged, drawing his attention like an invisible thread.

"Tell me, Miss Carmichael," the magnate continued, leaning forward slightly, "how does a young woman from Tasmania end up here in the Pacific, amidst palm forests and turquoise lagoons?"

Aurelia hesitated, then allowed a small shrug. "A holiday, at first. Circumstances changed, and well…here I am."

Julian's dark eyes flicked to her again. There was amusement there, and something else—something quieter, more predatory. He noticed the way she tensed when she felt his gaze, the faint flush that touched her neck, the small, graceful tilt of her shoulders as she settled back in her chair. He made no move to interfere, letting her charm work its magic, yet always keeping her subtly within his orbit.

"I've read about Tasmania," her partner said, a hint of curiosity in his tone. "Rugged, beautiful… almost like the Outback's gentler cousin."

"Yes, exactly," Aurelia said, warming to the topic. "Small towns, big landscapes, people used to living close to the earth."

He smiled at her, and something in his gaze was respectful, yet attentive in a way that made her pulse quicken. "It sounds idyllic in a way we forget to appreciate in the city."

Julian leaned back slightly, a faint smile tugging at the corner of his mouth. He noted her ease growing as the conversation progressed, yet also the way her attention still flicked to him every so often. Not overtly, but in tiny, telling ways—her glance at his hand resting on the table, the slight pause in her speech when he looked her way. He didn't speak; he simply watched, a constant, magnetic presence at the edge of her awareness.

Aurelia found herself laughing at a dry joke he made about navigating bureaucracy in the mining world, her voice lighter than it had been all evening. Julian's eyes darkened subtly, taking in the delicate arch of her neck and the gentle curl of her hair. He felt the familiar pull of desire, controlled but insistent, a thread running beneath his measured observation.

When the last of the guests departed and the room fell quiet, Aurelia turned to Julian, formally grateful yet still flushed from the tension and conversation. "Thank you. You certainly know how to give a dinner party."

"You seemed to enjoy yourself," he said lightly, the corners of his mouth lifting. "Perhaps I should tell you that your dinner partner is very happily married."

Shock and indignation shot through her. "It's not necessary," she said with a bite. "He's old enough to be my father."

Julian raised a black brow, devastating in its simplicity. "Is that important?"

Goaded, she snapped, "Possibly not to your blonde friend, but it is to me."

He leaned back, a cool menace in his tone, eyes narrowing. "I was jealous," he said simply.

"Jealous?" She stared at him, her breath catching. She coloured, letting her lashes fall in a shiver of frustration. "Neither of us have any right to—to feel anything. Particularly not that," she murmured, turning abruptly as if to escape the intensity in his gaze.

He touched her bare shoulder, and Aurelia froze, breath catching in her throat. No, she thought, looking straight ahead. Tonight, he wore a magnificent tropical dinner jacket that clung perfectly to his masculine waist, the lean strength of his hips beneath it accentuated with an effortless elegance. It should have looked theatrical, but Julian carried it with natural, magnetic authority.

She tried frantically to marshal her thoughts, but her eyes had already betrayed her, fixating on the tanned column of his throat, the elegant curve of his jaw now shaded by a faint, rough stubble—and that mouth…

God, how had she managed to keep her gaze from it for so long?

His lips quirked into a faint, knowing smile. "So why did we both feel it?" His deep, velvety voice brushed against her, teasing and warm, and it unlocked a torrent of sensation that pulsed through her from head to toe.

Aurelia's throat went dry. His hand tightened slightly on her shoulder, then relaxed, the lingering pressure leaving a trail of heat searing down her arm.

"You smell like the sea," he murmured, close enough that the faintest warmth of his breath brushed her ear. "And frangipani. And when you smile—did you know you have a dimple in your left cheek? Infuriatingly elusive, but it adds something wicked, playful. Were you always mischievous, Aurelia?"

"I… I don't know," she croaked, her voice barely audible. There was a subtle accent, a husky rhythm to the way he said her name, and her body responded without consent.

She tried to think, tried to organise her swirling senses, but he was doing nothing overtly, only talking, resting his hand on her shoulder—but the touch was a caress, deliberate and electric, as though her skin held some secret delight meant only for him.

Tension coiled tight in her stomach, spreading through her limbs in waves of delicious torment. If something didn't break this magnetic stand-off soon, she feared she would combust—either out of sheer desire or reckless daring.

His hand lifted slightly, brushing along her collarbone, and she dared to think she might be able to breathe if she stepped back—but she couldn't move.

A single, lean finger drifted to her cheek, resting just above her lips. "Here," he said, his tone grave, yet threaded with a raw, intimate heat that sent a shiver rippling through her.

"What?" she whispered, already trembling.

"I think the dimple is just here."

His lips followed the path of his finger, pressing a soft, tantalising kiss to the spot. His hand slid across her shoulder again, brushing her arm, teasing her, leaving trails of fire in its wake. Her heart hammered against her ribs; her pulse thundered in her ears.

"And perhaps… here," he murmured, lowering his head slightly, letting the next kiss graze closer to her lips.

Desire exploded inside her, a wildfire of need and exquisite anticipation. Her body stiffened, her chin lifting almost instinctively, and the kiss brushed the corner of her mouth, teasing, demanding, promising more without a word.

Aurelia shivered, caught in the delicious torment of proximity, her breath shallow, her mind dizzy with the potent mix of longing and restraint. Julian's presence was intoxicating, his touch searing, and she realised, with both fear and thrill, that she was utterly, helplessly undone.

On a rough, urgent note, Julian breathed her name as though it were a sacred invocation and claimed her mouth in a kiss that seared every nerve in her body. His lips were firm, warm, and insistent, exploring hers with a deliberate intensity that made every thought vanish from her mind, leaving only raw, unfiltered sensation. Aurelia moaned, melting against him, her body going soft and pliant under his lean, taut strength as he drew her close, moulding her against his chest.

A low, urgent sound escaped her lips when he lifted his mouth, part plea, part surrender, and she knew he understood it perfectly. He tilted her back against him, his arms tightening in a possessive, almost predatory embrace, and kissed her again—this time deeper, more demanding. She opened to him without hesitation, every nerve alight, her body thrumming in response as if it recognised a fire it had longed for.

A surge of reckless craving roared between them, mirrored in the taut power of his body and the growing intensity of his kiss. Heat pooled low in her belly, rising with every press of his mouth, every brush of his hands. Her pulse skyrocketed; the ache between her thighs whispered of desires she had never allowed herself to name. She almost cried out in frustrated longing when he pulled back, a flash of restraint in his eyes that only stoked her hunger further.

He drew a sharp, deep breath and spoke, his voice low, husky, and rougher than she had ever heard it. "That may well be the biggest mistake I've ever made."

"Yes," she admitted, trembling with the echo of their closeness, the taste of him still lingering on her lips.

"Do you regret it?"

A subtle tightening in his arms hinted at his own turmoil. "No," she said with a boldness she hadn't expected, "although I probably will in the morning."

"You and me both." He let out a quiet, almost private laugh as he eased his hold on her.

The fire in her veins dimmed abruptly, replaced by the chill of sudden distance. Cold and self-conscious, Aurelia hugged herself, aware of the desperate, needy expression she must wear, and let her arms drop in reluctant surrender.

"I didn't intend this to happen," he said abruptly, his voice steady but carrying an edge that made her ache again.

"Neither did I," she whispered, voice small. "Is… is this normal?"

He closed his eyes for a brief moment, as though considering the question. When they opened again, his gaze was clear and precise. "No. Though it's not abnormal either. Basic biology, really."

"Genes?" she murmured, understanding too well the implication—and why he emphasised it, as though warning her not to indulge in foolish thoughts of love.

His smile was dry, tinged with irony. "Exactly. Science calls it attraction. Nothing more. Our bodies simply… recognise potential. Potential to make… excellent children."

Aurelia's cheeks flamed. The thought of bearing Julian's child sent a jolt of heat through her core, igniting a fragile, almost forbidden part of her she had never known. She forced herself to look away, her eyes tracing anything but him—the subtle rise of colour along his cheekbones, the faintly swollen curve of his lips that had shown her a taste of ecstasy, the piercing clarity of his gaze that seemed to catalogue her every reaction.

Her body still hummed with the memory of him, the lingering warmth of his arms, the intoxicating brush of his mouth, and she realised with both fear and longing how completely he had unsettled her—mind, heart, and body alike.

Julian murmured something under his breath in the local language, his voice low, almost reverent. She stared at him, and he looked up, his face composed, though a flicker of restraint shadowed his eyes. "I'm sorry," he said evenly. "I had no intention of touching you. I won't do it again—unless it's absolutely necessary, in public."

"In public?" Her voice was sharp, betraying a flush she struggled to hide.

"To maintain the charade," he explained, his tone clipped but calm. "We may need to exchange the occasional… significant glance. Possibly even a light—but controlled— caress from time to time."

When she stared, incredulous and a little scandalised, his smile was humourless, the faintest shadow of wry acknowledgment curling his lips.

"Don't worry. I can restrain myself. Lust is rarely a spectator sport, and I have no intention of making it one."

The casual dismissal of the ache she had felt moments ago stung, yet there was something in his controlled, almost imperious calm that made her nod, unwillingly conceding the point.

He shifted slightly, the lean strength of his frame restrained yet palpable even at a distance. "Are you all right for the picnic tomorrow?"

"Yes," she murmured, though her body still remembered the heat of his nearness. "As right as I'll ever be."

Chapter Seven

The picnic was to be held at the Kingsley's private holiday island. Informal, supposedly simple—fishing for those who wanted, a swim in the lagoon, a casual lunch. But to Aurelia, it felt like sailing into uncharted waters, where the danger wasn't the tide or the sun, but the magnetic pull of the man beside her and the carefully contained fire between them.

Even in his careful restraint, Julian radiated a power that made her skin tingle. She knew he was holding himself back, yet every subtle shift, every controlled brush of his shoulder or glance that lingered just a moment too long, left her thinking of what might happen if that restraint faltered.

"Hey, this is fabulous!" The blonde woman who'd embraced Julian so heartily the night before stretched languorously on the white lounger, tilting her face toward a sky the brazen blue of a polished sapphire. Her gaze flicked to Aurelia, and a faintly envious smile curved her lips. "Lucky you," she purred.

Aurelia returned a polite, controlled smile. "It's glorious, isn't it?"

"So is its owner," the woman—Prudence—said, her tone cool, almost teasing. "You know, I wouldn't have pegged you as Julian's type."

"The world's full of surprises," Aurelia replied, shrugging lightly. She kept her voice calm, dismissive, though her pulse stirred at the subtle edge in Prudence's tone. Astonishment, she knew instinctively, would read as weakness.

"Where did you meet him?" Prudence asked, leaning back on her elbows.

"At a party," Aurelia said vaguely, letting the words float past her lips with casual detachment.

Prudence sat up, deliberately slow, and began applying sunscreen in long, languid strokes. "I don't blame you for being circumspect," she said, her voice soft but edged with malice. "He hates publicity. And maybe you are his type—he does like redheads. Is your hair natural?"

The words hit her like a pinprick. "Every last little wave," she said before she could stop herself. "Why? Did you think it was a wig?"

"The colour," Prudence said crisply. "You remind me a lot of one of his previous lovers—Jenny… no, Jessica something. Pretty, model type, dabbled in acting. Lots of charm but not a brain in her head. He soon got tired of her."

Aurelia's lips tightened. The implication was plain. She kept her expression neutral, forcing herself to breathe evenly.

Before she could reply, Prudence's tone shifted to playful charm. "Hello, Julian. What a fabulous place."

Fabulous, Aurelia thought, went out in the eighties, surely? She couldn't resist a small mental scoff. Julian's lips twitched, and she realised he'd noticed the jab. How did she know? Something about the slight curve of his mouth when he said, "I'm glad you like it."

His attention shifted, subtle yet deliberate, toward her. "How long is it since you put on sunscreen?"

"About half an hour," she said. "It's supposed to last two hours."

"The tropical sun is harsh on skin as delicate as yours," he said, settling beside her on the lounger. His presence was magnetic, the faint warmth radiating off him setting her pulse just a touch faster. "Turn your back—I'll make sure it's covered properly."

Prudence arched an eyebrow. "Would you like me to go?"

Julian raised his brows, his voice light but firm. "Why?" He held out his hand for the bottle of sunscreen, the deep timbre of his tone carrying a quiet authority.

Aurelia handed it over, relieved. Julian's influence was subtle but absolute; one lift of his brow or a barely perceptible intonation in his voice could sway more than threats ever could.

Prudence shrugged, her expression carefree. "Oh, I just thought you might need some privacy."

Julian let the silence stretch just a heartbeat too long before answering, "No."

That was that. Prudence, defeated without any more words, gave a languid wave to someone down the beach, slid on her sunglasses, and reclined once more.

Aurelia shivered, the sudden coolness betraying her nerves despite the sun's heat. Julian's hands were on her back, moving the warm sunscreen across her skin with measured care, spreading it in slow, deliberate strokes. The sensation—the warmth of his touch, the smooth glide of his hands—sent a ripple of awareness through her.

She kept her breathing even, but every brush of his fingers against her skin seemed charged, an unspoken electricity humming between them. The world had narrowed to Julian's presence, the curve of his hands, the quiet heat pressing through the small of her back, leaving her heart in perilous rhythm.

She could feel the edge of his cold anger radiating off him like a storm about to break, and she wondered what Prudence had done to provoke it. To make an impression? Possibly. If so, it had spectacularly backfired—unless Julian would rather be dealing with the other woman and was furious that he had to maintain the charade with her instead.

Who cared? she thought bluntly. He'd orchestrated this situation himself. If he wanted to bed the luscious executive, with her outdated slang and shameless forwardness, he had only himself to blame that he couldn't.

Even as his hands moved with skill and precision, there was nothing sensual about his ministrations. Not for him, anyway. He was performing a task, executing it efficiently, while she, in contrast, was ablaze. Every nerve-ending thrummed with molten tension, every small stroke of his hands sending rivulets of fire racing along her skin. Her breath came fast, her chest rising and falling as she fought to fix her unseeing eyes on the swimmers in the lagoon, trying to quell the tide of desire threatening to drown her.

Until a sudden movement caught her attention. "Julian!" she cried sharply.

His hand froze immediately, following her gaze. "What—?" He swore under his breath, leaping to his feet in a single, lithe motion.

Aurelia shot from the lounger, running across the white sand and diving into the crystalline water. She kept him in sight as he surged ahead, slicing through the lagoon with lethal efficiency until he reached deeper water, where he plunged beneath the surface.

The clarity of the lagoon spared her precious seconds. By the time she arrived, Julian had already wrestled the struggling swimmer to the surface, his arms controlling her with ruthless precision, keeping her head well above water while she coughed violently, sputtering and choking.

"I can do this," Aurelia panted, her arms steady despite the rush of adrenaline. "We need a boat out here."

Julian's sharp gaze cut into her. "Can you keep her upright?"

"Yes."

"Show me."

Sliding her arm around the woman in the classic lifesaving hold, Aurelia felt a surge of relief as the swimmer's panic began to ease. The blue-tinged lips and ragged breathing reassured her that she was doing it correctly.

"Good girl," Julian said briefly, his voice taut with approval. Then he turned sharply to the distant shore. "Where the hell is the boat?"

The engines roared in response, approaching rapidly. Julian's hand rose in a command so precise it stopped the craft instantly.

"All right?" he asked Aurelia.

She nodded, a faint, proud smile curving her lips. "The West Coast Beaches junior lifesavers would be proud of me," she said lightly, though the woman in her arms was choking back tears.

Julian's eyes softened just a fraction. "I'm proud of you," he said, and then, with a powerful, fluid motion, he swam to the idling dinghy, hauling himself aboard with a swoosh that nearly capsized it.

He guided the boat back to them, where he and a crew member helped the coughing swimmer aboard. Then Julian bent over, his hands strong and unyielding as he lifted Aurelia from the water. For a breathtaking instant, she was held against his sleek, taut body, the heat of him searing through her drenched clothes, heart racing in tandem with his steady strength.

"Are you all right?" he demanded, his eyes half-closed, piercing, searching. "No after-effects? No exhaustion?"

Surprised by the intensity in his gaze—and the lingering warmth of his body—she managed a steady voice. "No. I'm fine. Just a bit puffed. I haven't been swimming recently."

Her body, however, betrayed her, reacting in strange, unfamiliar ways to the close, magnetic embrace. "Truly," she added, forcing herself to sound calm, "I'm fully recovered from my faint."

"Collapse." Julian's lips curved, half in satisfaction, half in that quiet authority she'd learned to recognise. "Good. Let's get ashore."

He released her with a swift, firm hug, leaving her heart hammering, her skin tingling long after the heat of his body had faded.

Back on the beach, the other guests had gathered in a loose cluster just above the wave line, their chatter muted by the rush of the lagoon.

"We'll use one of the loungers as a stretcher to carry her up to the house," Julian said, nodding toward Aurelia. "We'll need you."

The holiday house was small, sparsely furnished, clearly designed for brief stays. The four men who had carried the still-weeping woman set the lounger down carefully in the shade of the terrace and lingered awkwardly, unsure how to proceed.

Aurelia addressed one of them firmly. "Can you find and bring her clothes?" Then, looking at the others, she added, "Thank you so much. I'll come down and let you know when she's ready for visitors."

Once they left, the woman sank back against the lounger, sobs wracking her slight frame. "I don't know why I'm crying!"

"Shock," Aurelia said robustly. "I've been there. I know how it feels. What you need is a warm shower—"

"Some brandy first," Julian interjected, appearing from the house with a small glass. The corners of his mouth lifted in a swift, challenging grin that made Aurelia's pulse flicker. He held the glass out to the woman. "Here, Ms Baxter. Drink it down—even if you hate it."

"I do hate it," the woman admitted, taking the glass with trembling hands. "But I certainly need something." She drained it in one shuddering swallow, then lay back on the lounger. "Stupid," she murmured. "I really thought I was going to drown. I swam out to look at the coral, and cramps hit both legs at once. I've never had it before."

"How do you feel now?" Aurelia asked, leaning closer.

"Better. I only went under twice—Julian dragged me up the second time. I might have gone under again, but I don't think so. I didn't think anyone could see me, and the waves on the reef would've drowned any cry for help."

"Aurelia saw you," Julian said quietly. "I've checked with the hospital on the mainland. They agree you should be seen as soon as possible. A chopper is on its way." He ignored her instant objection. "Sorry, but that's island policy. There's a risk of complications unless proper care is taken." He smiled gently at the woman's woeful expression, and even Aurelia felt the familiar tug of his presence. "I don't think anything's wrong, but a night in hospital will reassure everyone that you're fine."

The woman's shoulders slumped, and she closed her eyes. "I feel so stupid."

"Cramps happen to anyone," Aurelia said, offering a small, reassuring smile. "Would you like me to come with you?"

"I—no," the woman said, her voice faint. "You're needed here."

Julian's gaze flicked to Aurelia. "I'll manage without her," he said easily.

"I'll just get our bags," she said firmly. "I refuse to take my first helicopter flight in a bikini."

His eyes darkened with amusement—or something more dangerous—but he called sharply to one of the staff. The chopper arrived moments later, its rotor blades chopping the tropical air into a rhythmic roar. Julian's voice rang over the sound.

"Thank you for this. I've arranged with my PA to handle the paperwork, but Ms Baxter is still shaken. I think she'd like you with her until she's seen a doctor."

"I'll be fine," Aurelia said briskly. "You can't go, and no one else has offered." She already knew the disorientation of waking up in a strange place, wondering what had happened.

"She's a senior executive from one of the big Australian companies. She's alone," Julian added, his tone precise.

Then, to her astonishment, he bent and kissed her—firm, commanding, possessive. His arms tightened around her as if to stake his claim, his mouth claiming hers with a pressure that left her breathless and trembling.

Flushed and dizzy, Aurelia hurried into the chopper. As it lifted, she caught sight of the reason for his final embrace—a woman standing at the edge of the pad, eyes hungry, mouth set in determination. Prudence. Aurelia's stomach sank; she knew the blonde would try again, and perhaps more boldly this time.

Yet Julian's hand brushing hers before the chopper rose offered a flicker of reassurance—and a reminder that, for now, she was the one he'd claimed.

Chapter Eight

Some hours later, Aurelia's attention was drawn to a nurse who appeared in the doorway of the private room, waving a mobile phone.

Startled, Aurelia raised her brows and pointed to her chest. The nurse nodded vigorously. It had to be Julian. Her mouth went suddenly dry. Rising from her seat beside the sleeping woman's bed, she crossed the room in a light, uncertain hurry.

"Mr. Julian Kingsley," the nurse mouthed, exhaling in mild amusement as she held out the phone.

Handling it as though it were a live wire, Aurelia lifted the receiver. "Hello?"

"Ah, Aurelia." His voice was cool, almost impersonal, as if he were speaking to his PA—but it sent a jolt straight through her chest. Her pulse sped. "How is Ms. Baxter?"

"She's sleeping. The tests showed no damage, and there are no signs of complications, but the doctors want her to stay overnight." Her own voice sounded foreign to her, almost hoarse, and her heart raced faster.

"I suspected as much. The chopper is on standby if you want to return."

So, this was how the very rich lived—every resource waiting at their command. Aurelia glanced at her watch. "You're leaving for home soon, aren't you?"

"I'll collect you myself, then. Don't leave the hospital until I come."

His tone was casual, but a subtle undercurrent vibrated beneath the words, brushing her nerves like electricity. "Why?"

A pause so slight she wondered if she'd imagined it. Then he said, "Because the last time you were released on your own, you collapsed. Humour me, all right?"

Aurelia swallowed hard. "Okay," she said tautly. "I'll stay put."

"Thank you," he said. "See you soon."

She replaced the phone, her fingers lingering over it for a heartbeat, before moving toward the door. Outside, a tall islander stood silently at attention. His respectful smile made her heart jump—security, she realised, and a reminder of how seriously Julian protected those around him. She returned the smile with a flicker of nervous amusement and headed toward the nurses' station.

"All right?" the nurse asked, looking up from her papers. Aurelia nodded. "Mr. Kingsley wanted to know how Ms. Baxter is."

"She'll be fine," the nurse replied, professional yet warm, eyes twinkling with curiosity. "He's a good man, Julian Kingsley… and yes, very sexy. You look a bit stiff—did you drag her out?"

"Helped," Aurelia admitted with a faint shrug.

"You look like you need a shower," the nurse said, nodding down the corridor. "It's well past patient showering time, but—"

"Will that be all right?" Aurelia asked uncertainly, used to her mother's hospital's rigid rules.

"Of course!" The nurse grinned. "The Kingsley's fund this hospital. There's a big charity do coming up for a cancer ward, so a little extra water and electricity for you won't matter." She leaned closer with a conspiratorial gleam. "Are you keeping up your fluids?"

"How did—?" Aurelia stopped. Of course, everyone on the island would know she'd fainted so dramatically in front of Julian's car. And if not, they certainly knew she'd been living in his house.

The nurse laughed lightly. "Oh, like any small community, we keep tabs. Don't worry—we'll make sure some lime juice reaches Ms. Baxter's room for you. Keep drinking; we wouldn't want Mr. Julian mad at us for neglecting you."

The power of the Kingsley name hit her in full force. Not just here, on their home turf, but everywhere, she realised. Julian was sought after across the globe.

The shower was bliss. The iced lime juice in the ward afterward was a small triumph. Not quite as pleasant was the doctor insisting on checking her over as well, finally concluding, "You're young and healthy. In good shape. Rest every afternoon, and—"

"Keep drinking," Aurelia interrupted with a faint smile. "Thanks for everything."

Afterward, she rejoined Sue Baxter, who dozed and murmured intermittently. Aurelia passed the time with a few magazines, grateful that none mentioned Julian, though his beautiful sisters featured in one, their elegant lives chronicled in a society piece about an aristocratic ball.

Eventually, the private room door opened, revealing Julian—big, capable, and impeccably in command—accompanied by the hospital superintendent.

The next ten minutes passed in a flurry of thanks from Sue; her expressions of gratitude punctuated with polite laughter and a few tears.

Finally, Sue leaned back, exhaling. "You've done enough now—off you go, Aurelia. Have some fun. I'm so sorry for spoiling your day!"

"Please don't say that," Aurelia replied, bending to brush a kiss across her cheek. "I'm glad you're feeling better."

"Just relax and let us take care of you," Julian said, his tone smooth and authoritative. "Someone will be here in the morning, and if the doctor agrees, you'll be taken back to Australia in the afternoon. All you have to do is recover."

"My boss will want to thank you," Sue said weakly, lashes drifting down. "And so will I—once whatever they've given me wears off enough to keep my eyes open for more than five minutes!"

Outside, Aurelia waited as Julian conferred briefly with the superintendent. The tall islander security guard fell in step beside them as they descended in the lift to the car park beneath the modern building.

A young journalist lingered near the exit; his earnest expression tinged with nervousness. He stepped forward cautiously, and Julian's brow darkened, though he listened patiently to the man's request for information.

"One of my guests experienced cramp while swimming and had to be airlifted back to the hospital," Julian said smoothly, his voice controlled but firm. "She's fine now. Miss Carmichael rescued her and stayed with her until she was comfortable."

The reporter's gaze flicked to Aurelia, uncertain, hesitant. "You…are a lifeguard, Miss?" he asked.

"I trained with a surf lifesavers' club growing up in Australia," she said carefully, aware of Julian's calculating eyes on her. "But Mr. Kingsley was first to her side. All I did was help him."

The journalist brightened and ventured, "If I could have a photograph…?" The faint hope in his voice made Aurelia suppress a smile.

Julian's shrug was casual, almost dismissive. "If you want one." He stepped aside and posed with her against the plain hospital wall, the perfect picture of composed elegance. The reporter left, satisfied.

The car had darkened windows. As they drove off, Aurelia glanced at Julian. "If that's the local paparazzi, you breed reporters differently on Kaliah Island."

"Don't be fooled," Julian replied, voice low and measured. "He's clever, persistent. The fact that he was waiting for us makes me wonder what he's heard."

She studied him. His expression was sharp, unreadable, every line of his face tense with analysis, like a predator calculating his next move. Her curiosity edged toward caution.

"What he's heard? Do you mean about the mineral exploration?" she asked.

"Not necessarily," he said, his attention momentarily elsewhere, fingers drumming lightly on the car door. Then, as if remembering her presence, his gaze snapped to hers. "I have a hunch," he added, the hint of a smile—warm, magnetic, infuriating—curling his lips. It was the kind of smile that made her stomach tighten and sent shivers through her body without a single touch.

It wasn't fair. He could unsettle her so completely with nothing more than a glance, a tilt of his head, the subtle power in the inflection of his voice.

Determined to hold her ground, Aurelia met his gaze directly. "I wouldn't have thought you dealt in hunches. Logic seems more your style."

"My father has a saying," he replied smoothly, eyes still on the road. "'When logic fails, follow your instinct.'"

"And does logic often fail?" she asked, her tone light but probing.

"Very rarely," he said, giving a faint shrug, "but when it does, I follow his advice. So far, it's worked." His dark eyes lingered on her a fraction too long, sharp with unspoken meaning. Then, more formally, he added, "Thank you for everything you did this afternoon."

"You've already thanked me and so has Sue. It was nothing," Aurelia said, careful to keep her voice steady. "Someone had to stay with her. If you'd gone, I'd have been lost among all those people."

Julian's lips quirked at the corner, a subtle acknowledgment that contained far more than mere gratitude. Aurelia felt it—a quiet, electrifying current that raced along her nerves—and forced herself to look out the window, though the knowledge of his gaze lingered, inescapable.

He studied her face in a long, slow survey that sent little shivers across her skin. His unusually grey eyes were almost translucent, yet she felt certain they could see straight through her. "You'd have coped," he said finally. "You have a definite talent for organisation and quick thinking."

A rush of pleasure coloured her cheeks. Flippantly, she said, "When I leave, I might ask you for a reference saying just that."

His lashes drooped, giving him an unexpected softness. "Why the reference?"

"I have to find a job."

"Is it likely to be difficult?"

"No."

The truth was simple: her old fast-food job was waiting, or she could do the work her mother's illness had prepared her for—rest home duties or nursing training. One day she'd finish her degree and find a position that would pay off the student loan she'd have to increase.

"You're not telling me the truth," he said shrewdly. Before she could respond, his hand lifted to her chin, tilting her face so he could inspect it closely.

Thoughts scattered through her mind like startled birds. Her eyes flicked to his mouth—cruelly beautiful, sculpted to seduce and command—and her pulse surged. Her lips parted into a single word. "Don't."

When he continued to hold her gaze, drawing some unspoken power from her hesitation, she whispered, "Please."

Julian let her go, his hand falling to his thigh, clenched briefly into a fist. Then, his voice low and harsh, he said, "You pack a hell of a punch, Aurelia."

She swallowed, tongue dry. "So do you," she admitted, the truth bitter and urgent, and scrambled for another topic, desperate to break the crackling tension between them.

Through the window, she realised the car had passed the gates of his parents' house. She let out a relieved breath. "You said your parents were away. Are they on holiday?"

"Having another honeymoon," he said smoothly, the corners of his mouth twitching in a way that told her he knew exactly what she was thinking.

She laughed, a little cracked. "Sounds romantic."

"They're a very romantic couple," he said coolly. "A testament that two strong-willed people can live happily together."

"Some people have all the luck," she said flippantly.

"Luck?" He considered the word carefully. "Perhaps they met at the right time. But after that, it isn't luck that makes a marriage last."

Did he believe in the romantic ideal? If his parents were still lovers after all these years, perhaps he did—and perhaps she might too, if she hadn't seen firsthand how marriages could shatter, leaving nothing but shards behind. She remembered her father, desperate to pursue passion without hurting her mother, and the memory made her chest ache.

"Good for them," she said brightly as the car drew up to the porticoed entrance.

Inside, he said, "The charity dinner I mentioned is here tomorrow night, followed by an after-dinner dance at a mystery venue. Wear something elegant, with sparkles."

"Is there anything I can do to help?" she asked tentatively.

"I shouldn't think so." He scrutinised her closely. "How are you feeling now?"

"Fine," she said, a little blankly. "I seem fully recovered from dehydration. Just a bit tired. The doctor may have overreacted when she said I shouldn't go home yet."

He shrugged, grey eyes still piercing her. "I don't think so. Tonight, have dinner in your room and go to bed early. Tomorrow will be long, though we can come home if you get tired."

He added casually, yet with subtle authority, "Jasmine and her grandfather are arriving mid-morning, bringing another couple—friends of mine—with them."

The second couple of friends turned out to be very well known—Jeremy was another tech billionaire and his wife. Aurelia felt her pulse spike when Julian introduced them. A fleeting moment of panic passed, but after a few minutes of conversation, she settled.

They were enchanting. The wife, Louise, was tall, pale as porcelain, with black hair that fell in a sleek, glossy sheet over her shoulders, and eyes like silver crystals that caught the sunlight and seemed to see everything at once. Her husband, taller still, had the effortless elegance of a man born to the Mediterranean sun; his tawny skin and sharp features were softened by the warmth in his amber eyes, which carried both intelligence and a quiet humour.

"You're from Tasmania?" Louise asked, her voice lilting with curiosity and genuine enthusiasm. "Oh, it's gorgeous. I've spent such lovely holidays there. Do you go to the mainland much?"

"No, this is actually my first holiday," Aurelia replied cautiously, aware of her own nervousness. Louise's gaze lingered on her with an amiable interest that was both flattering and slightly intimidating.

Her smile broadened, warm and effortless. "My sister loves Australia, too. How are you enjoying Kaliah Island?"

"Who wouldn't?" Aurelia said, relaxing slightly and allowing a hint of her own excitement to show. "It's my first visit to the tropics, and it's even more beautiful than the photographs. The water—the colours! —it's like nothing I've ever seen."

"Isn't it just!" Louise agreed, though her smile flickered briefly, a subtle hesitation Aurelia caught instinctively. Jeremy was immediately at her side, his tall frame slightly angled protectively, one hand brushing lightly against hers in a courteous, almost imperceptible way. The sight made Aurelia's stomach twist with a mixture of admiration and envy at the couple's easy intimacy.

Julian, as always, seemed unshakable. He addressed the couple with effortless charm. "I'll show you to your room." Then his gaze swept back to Aurelia—slow, deliberate, and utterly unnerving. The faint curve of his lips—part smile, part challenge—sent a shiver down her spine. "Perhaps you could order tea for us all on the terrace," he said, his voice smooth and calm, yet threaded with an intimacy that made her pulse stumble.

Aurelia forced herself to nod, struggling to keep her composure. Every glance from Julian pressed against her self-control like a quiet, tantalising weight, quickening her heartbeat and stirring a flutter deep in her stomach. She smiled demurely, masking the heat rising in her cheeks, and let him turn back to the couple, leaving her to orchestrate the tea service with trembling fingers and a startling awareness of every movement, every subtle nuance in the room.

Swallowing, she realised she would be left to entertain an elderly Frenchman, keen-eyed and perceptive, and his granddaughter—a striking young woman whose aristocratic hauteur barely concealed a flicker of irritation.

Guiding them to the terrace, Aurelia seated them with all the poise she could summon, chastising herself inwardly. Damn Julian and his effortless assumption that the world bent to his will—and damn herself even more, for letting him override her sensible reservations so completely.

Fortunately, both Jasmine and her grandfather were charming, and conversation flowed with ease, though restrained, until the others returned—minus the Louise, who had decided to rest until lunchtime.

Pregnant? Aurelia's mind skittered there briefly, and she felt a pang of longing she tried hard to suppress. She forced herself to focus on the guests, to steady her fluttering heart.

Lunch passed pleasantly, though afterwards, alone in her room, Aurelia allowed herself a small, guilty sigh. Jeremy and Louise were subtly affectionate, their connection burning like a slow, smouldering fire. It was foolish—and ungracious—to envy them, particularly since such relationships were rare, exceptions rather than the rule, at least according to the gossip columns.

She banished the envy and refocused on herself, preparing for the night ahead. The thought of dancing with Julian made her skin heat and her pulse race, a decadent thrill that curled inside her and tempted her lips into a dangerous, anticipatory smile. Wonderful and terrifying—she had to ensure he never glimpsed just how much she ached for it.

A knock at the door broke her reverie. The maid appeared; face creased with worry.

"What is it?" Aurelia asked.

"I'm sorry, miss. I can't find Mr. Julian, and the tuna hasn't arrived for dinner, and the cook is furious."

"Julian's gone riding with Jeremy," Aurelia said briskly. "All right. I'll come along."

Apparently, the essential ingredient for the dinner—the specially caught and sliced tuna—hadn't arrived, and no one could tell the chef where it was.

"It has to be marinated in lime!" he bellowed. "If it doesn't get here soon, it will be ruined!"

Aurelia held up a hand, firm. "It won't be ruined. You've prepared countless meals. I'm confident you can improvise another starter, one worthy of this dinner."

He pouted, theatrically aghast. "But everything—the wine, the menu—was carefully designed to harmonise perfectly. Any change, any deviation, and the whole exquisite edifice collapses."

Aurelia let her brows lift ever so slightly. "So, you're telling me you can't produce another starter that's just as suitable?"

"Of course I'm not," he said explosively, "but Mr Kingsley will need to choose another wine—and it must be chilled."

"I'll make sure he knows the problem the moment he returns from the stables," Aurelia said, keeping her tone soothing. "What suggestions do you have for an emergency starter?"

He frowned, rattling off several alternatives. Sensing that any hesitation on her part would be disastrous, Aurelia settled on the one dish she recognised. "The onion tart."

He shrugged, clearly handing all responsibility over to her. "So be it," he said, turning away to bark commands at the kitchen staff in the island tongue.

Hoping fervently, she hadn't made matters worse, Aurelia slipped out of the kitchen. The space had been a revelation—huge, ultra-modern, air-conditioned, and clearly designed with staff comfort in mind. Julian evidently understood the value of looking after his team.

She found the housekeeper, Litia, efficiently supervising the setting of a table on the terrace. After a brief explanation, Litia nodded. "I'll leave a message for Julian at the stables, of course."

No other emergencies arose, and Aurelia assumed the cook had managed the rest.

Later, dressed for dinner, she emerged feeling extraordinarily glamorous in a silky camisole gown that matched her skin. She'd fretted over how closely the ivory silk clung to her curves and whether the neckline revealed too much, but after testing several alternatives, she'd settled on this one—it would move seamlessly from dinner to dance floor.

Passing Julian's bedroom, the door opened, and he appeared, darkly handsome in evening attire.

Her heart leapt.

"I hear you handled an emergency," he said, his gaze traveling over her in a way that sent delicious shivers through her.

She laughed, breathy and low, horrified at the sensual edge in her own voice. "I think your cook just needed reassurance because the tuna hadn't arrived."

"Litia said you handled him like a pro—put him on his mettle and then chose the dish he's famous for."

"Did I?" she laughed again, more naturally this time. "Lucky break, really. It was the only one I recognised."

"All he wanted," Julian said, his voice smooth yet threaded with a subtle, intoxicating awareness, "was to have his dilemma acknowledged—and to be challenged to work a miracle. You read him perfectly."

"Good thing he didn't need real help," Aurelia said lightly. "I know nothing of haute cuisine—just plain farmhouse fare."

Together, they moved into the reception room overlooking the lagoon and western horizon. Julian's eyes darkened as they swept over her. "You look exquisite," he said, "but you need something more. Come with me."

"I'm fine," she replied, though her pulse betrayed her.

"Every other woman here," he said, voice low and certain, "will have jewellery. Serious pieces."

She shook her head. "I don't own any, and I couldn't wear anything of your mother's." For once, she wasn't going to be dressed to satisfy his pride.

"I'm not giving you my mother's," he said curtly. "I have some from my great-grandmother and a few I've acquired myself—we mine blue diamonds here; in case you didn't know. Tonight, we need to convince everyone our relationship is serious enough for me to part with them."

When she bit her lip, he added impatiently, "Don't be silly, Aurelia. Think of them as a prop in a play."

"Do you always get your own way?" she asked, a hint of defiance in her tone.

"Usually," he said straight-faced. "Being the only boy in the family will do that. My sisters spoiled me."

Not just his sisters, she thought wryly, as he led her into a small strongroom off his office. Probably every woman who met him had a strong inclination to spoil him in various ways.

Including her.

And she was being ridiculous; the blue diamonds were just a prop. Yet, with a panicky intake of breath, she realised she wanted anything he gave her to mean something.

This was getting out of hand. She'd always noticed him as a man, but that searing kiss had awakened every dormant part of her. Now, every glance, every thought of him stirred a fierce, secret hunger that threatened to consume her self-control.

She had to stop it—right now.

Chapter Nine

Tensely, Aurelia watched Julian open the safe and extract a handful of jewel cases. He flicked up the lids of two and brought them across. "Which do you like best?"

Afraid he might catch the slightest hesitation in her eyes, she forced her gaze on the treasures before her. Both were breathtaking. One was a string of flawless blue diamonds, each one shimmering as if it held the ocean within. The other was simpler, yet no less captivating: a single, tear-shaped blue diamond suspended from a delicate gold chain, its diamond-studded clasp catching the light like a fleeting star.

"They're the same colour as your eyes," Julian murmured. "The pendant... I think it will sit better in the neckline of your dress." He snapped the other box shut and returned it to the safe.

"Turn around," he commanded.

Obeying, Aurelia felt his presence draw close behind her. Julian brushed her fiery hair aside, studying the delicate nape of her neck with a rare, protective intensity. Not that she was defenceless—competent, clever, quick-witted—but there was something about her that made him want to guard her, to claim just a fraction of this moment.

He dropped the pendant around her throat, fastening the clasp with deliberate care, his fingers lingering a heartbeat too long against her skin. The faint, natural perfume she wore curled through him, a subtle, intoxicating signal he recognised instinctively. Not that he was thinking about babies... but desire? That had been intruding on his thoughts far too often since he'd met her.

Usually, he could master himself.

Frowning slightly, he secured the clasp, noting the faint flush that warmed her cheeks. He brushed the bright sweep of her hair back over it, his voice calm, measured, but threaded with something deeper: "There."

He stepped back, letting her turn so he could see the effect. Her blush had deepened, her slight inexperience only heightening the allure. Against his better judgment, a vivid image flared in his mind: Aurelia, wearing only the Kaliah Heart, sprawled across white sheets, her blue eyes heavy-lidded, lips swollen from his kisses, hair spilling across his chest like fire, every curve of her body flushed from his touch.

He released her, keeping his voice clipped, controlled: "Perfect. There are earrings, too."

She shook her head, eyes cooler than her flushed skin, lips pressed in a line. "That would be overkill," she said succinctly, then walked from the strongroom without another word.

For reasons he couldn't explain, it irritated him that she didn't check herself in a mirror. Shoulders straight, she moved with the quiet poise of someone completely unaware of her effect. Julian followed, his gaze lingering on her as they entered the main reception, drawn to Jasmine's voice somewhere beyond, desire and restrained hunger shimmering just beneath his calm exterior.

When Julian noticed the subtle stiffening of Aurelia's body, that odd surge of protectiveness flared again. He rested a hand lightly in the small of her back and said crisply, "You look exquisite. And you have excellent manners and a talent for coping. As my indomitable French great-grandmother used to say in such moments—en avant!"

Forward. Supported by the warmth in his voice and the subtle pressure of his hand, Aurelia turned her head and smiled at him. He was heartbreakingly attractive: the intimate, conspiratorial curl of his lips implying complicity, the arrogant lines of his face set off by the perfection of his tailoring and the gleaming white shirt beneath his dinner jacket.

For a taut second, his gaze lingered on her mouth before he commanded, "Just smile, Aurelia. That's all you need to do."

"Be a good little decoration, you mean?" she shot back.

He grinned, a flash of amusement in his eyes. "You're very decorative, yes, but no. There's something about your smile that makes people instinctively trust you. In fact," his eyes glittered with mischief, "that smile could make you the perfect con artist."

Startled, she stared at him before spluttering into laughter. "You certainly know how to give with one hand and take away with the other!"

When Jasmine and her grandfather arrived, they found their host and his presumed mistress laughing together. Aurelia couldn't help wondering if Julian had deliberately teased her to create just that sense of spurious intimacy. Probably.

The evening unfurled like a blooming flower. She was introduced to a fascinating mixture of islanders and global visitors—names she recognised from the financial press, gossip columns, and film reviews. She might have dreaded being dismissed as Julian's latest inamorata, but his unspoken authority ensured that her supposed position in his life earned her respect.

At one point, she spoke to a native film star whose latest blockbuster had revealed both his talent and his sculpted physique; he turned out to be a cousin of Julian's. He confessed a dream of one day playing Othello. Moments later, she found herself discussing literature with the head of a major investment firm and his wife.

She kept a discreet eye on the guests, ensuring no one was left alone. It wasn't onerous; they were a close-knit group. Even Jasmine seemed to forget her initial shock at finding another woman in residence, laughing easily as she engaged in flirtatious banter with the actor.

Instinctively, Aurelia scanned for Jasmine's grandfather. He was watching his granddaughter with a furrowed brow. Their eyes met briefly, and his frown deepened. Concern prickled her; she turned back to the woman she was conversing with.

Almost immediately, Julian joined them. He made no overt displays of affection, but his presence radiated a magnetic sexual tension. A fleeting touch, a subtle, proprietary brush of his hand—he could command an aura of intimacy without saying a word.

And when their eyes met, no one in the room could miss the sizzle. With Julian, it was calculated; for Aurelia, her responses were dangerously real. Wildfire sensations roared through her at every deliberate, steel-grey glance. She no longer cared about the guests, only that Julian might believe her composure matched his own.

After half an hour, he murmured, "Dinner's ready."

"With or without tuna, I wonder?" she teased.

He took her hand, pressing a light kiss to her palm and folding her fingers over it as though to keep the kiss safe. "Help me get them to the table," he said, voice low and private, and Aurelia's pulse caught at the intimacy of the simple gesture.

Rivulets of fire coursed through every nerve. The clatter of conversation faded into a dull hum; she stared up into his eyes, half-closed, gleaming with desire and impossible intensity.

Then he released her hand and said, "That should convince anyone who wasn't already persuaded. You're doing wonders, Aurelia."

She forced a faint, measured smile, hoping he couldn't see the bitter chagrin that pricked at her. "So are you," she said numbly.

The reminder stung. All of this—the glances, the touches, the laughter—was a performance, a masque for an audience. She respected Julian's chivalry, his careful regard for those who mattered to him, but he wasn't the one who would pay the cost. That burden, she realised with a pang, was hers alone. The masquerade was likely to claim her heart.

Dinner was served on the terrace. Litia and her team had risen splendidly to the occasion, transforming the table into a riot of Pacifica extravagance: lush bunches of flowers, tropical fruits, flickering candles casting playful shadows, and wineglasses and silverware that caught the light in dazzling glints. The fragrance of night-blooming flowers wove through the warm evening air, intoxicating in its languid, sensual allure. A fountain whispered nearby, glinting in the subdued light that fell over great glossy leaves. Above it all, the moon rose, huge and golden, hanging in a cloudless sky where unfamiliar stars mingled with familiar constellations.

Julian did not place her at the hostess's position at the far end of the table; that honour was reserved for Louise. Instead, Aurelia found herself at his right hand, close enough to feel the subtle warmth of his presence, aware of the magnetic pull between them.

The dinner was already a triumph. Yet despite the laughter and clinking glasses, she had never felt so achingly alone. Her gaze fell on the tuna, miraculously arrived and marinated just so in lime, chilli, and tomatoes. Meeting Julian's eyes, she laughed silently at their shared unspoken triumph, and her heart constricted in a tight knot of pleasure mingled with foreboding.

Her emotions surged—a seething, tumbling chaos of anticipation, excitement, and reckless longing. She was acutely aware of the discreet eyes watching them, yet in full knowledge of the likely consequence—heartbreak—she made a bold, defiant choice. This once, she would allow herself to savour the moment, unguarded, unhedged by fear. After all, broken hearts did mend. Even her mother had found a form of happiness after betrayal, though had never been able to love another man. But still, life moved on.

"So, it arrived in time," Julian murmured, his voice low and intimate.

She smiled, a radiant flare lighting her face, and welcomed the quick narrowing of his eyes. "Thank heavens. Does he… do this sort of thing often?"

"He's difficult," Julian said with a shrug, his tone casual but precise. "He knows his worth—people have tried to lure him away for years. He doesn't really like the tropics, you know. Every so often he talks about opening a café in Provence."

Aurelia swallowed her first mouthful, savouring the flavours. "He's a genius," she said on a sigh of pure delight. "Geniuses are allowed their tantrums, I suppose."

"Well, you managed his superbly," Julian said, a hint of amusement in his eyes. "I've said before, you have a talent for coping."

She forced a smile, wishing her skills could be in sparkling conversation or elegant hosting rather than managing a man's whims. "It wasn't really a problem. He just wanted to vent—and for someone else to take responsibility."

Julian's eyes flickered with something like respect. "You don't miss much. That's why the little café in Provence will never tempt him—he doesn't like responsibility. You, however, seem to handle it effortlessly."

"It's easy when it's not really my affair," she said coolly, grounding herself in the temporary nature of her role.

He inclined his head slightly. "Possibly. Yet you showed no hesitation helping me with Sue Baxter. She sends her regards and thanks, by the way. Her company is exceedingly grateful—there's even a gift on the way."

Aurelia frowned. "I did no more than anyone else would have done," she said crisply. "I don't want anything for simple human decency."

"I suggested the surf lifesaving club," Julian said, one brow lifting just so, "and I think they're doing something about that. But Sue wanted a more personal expression of her thanks as well."

Aurelia met his gaze, feeling the magnetic pull of the evening—the heat of his attention, the quiet weight of his claim—and the risk that every fleeting moment of pleasure came at the price of her heart.

Without waiting for a response, he turned to the woman at his other side, leaving Aurelia feeling both sidelined and curiously exposed. Oddly, though, she wasn't anxious the way she had been on the beach. Whether it was the silk of her gown, the exquisite blue diamond resting against her throat, or simply Julian's proximity, she felt… steadier, more able to handle the situation.

"How long have you known Julian?" the man beside her asked, his tone friendly and warm.

Wishing he'd chosen a less perilous topic, she smiled lightly. "Not very long."

"But long enough?"

He was older than Julian, she judged, and clearly inclined to kindness, his eyes assessing her with quiet approval.

"Yes," she admitted, feeling a flush creep up her neck. "Are you from Kaliah Island?"

"Born and bred," he replied. "I grew up with him here. He was a tough kid—rode any horse, surfed any wave, jumped off cliffs into the sea. Keeping up with him was exhausting for the rest of us. I think his mother often wondered what she'd brought into the world."

Aurelia kept her eyes carefully elsewhere. "I can imagine," she murmured demurely.

"He learned to control those daredevil impulses, though. A Kingsley trait—self-discipline runs deep. But those were glorious times." He glanced down at the gem resting against her throat. "I see you're wearing the Kaliah Heart."

"The—oh, the pendant?" she said, suddenly aware of its weight and brilliance.

"That's the one. Beyond price—utterly flawless. The Kaliah Heart. There's a legend around it."

"Legends go with treasures, I suppose?" she murmured.

"Absolutely," he said with a grin. "Julian bought the Heart. I knew he had it set as a pendant, but I don't think anyone—his mother, his sisters—has ever worn it."

Her companion leaned closer and began to explain. "Long before the Kingsley's arrived, Kaliah Island was whispered about among Pacific sailors as a jewel of the sea, a place where the sky kissed the ocean and the sands shimmered like starlight."

"The first Kaliah Blue was discovered by Sebastian Kingsley, Julian's great-grandfather, on a night when a violent storm tore across the island. Lightning split the volcanic cliffs, revealing a hidden cavern deep within. There, amid jagged obsidian rocks, he found a single diamond unlike anything the world had seen—a deep, ocean-blue gem that seemed to hold the tides within its depths, glowing softly even in darkness. They named it the Kaliah Heart."

"Legend has it the storm itself forged the diamond, and that the stone carries the island's spirit: fierce, untamed, and eternally loyal to its discoverer. Locals whispered that the Kaliah Heart would bring fortune only to those with courage, honour, and respect for the island—a protector rather than a mere owner."

"From that day forward, every Kaliah Blue has been mined with care, each stone considered a legacy of the first, a symbol of responsibility, resilience, and the Kingsley's bond to the island. Julian, as the current steward, often touches the first gem in the family vault, a reminder that wealth is nothing without the honour of guardianship— and, as the legend hints, love often follows those worthy of the Kaliah Heart."

Aurelia felt the subtle press of its significance. This was what Julian had meant when he said he wanted everyone to see the relationship as serious. The blue diamond wasn't just decoration—it was a statement. The rare gem resting against her skin made her feel elevated, claimed—a prop, yes, but one branded with a quiet possessiveness she could feel even in Julian's absent gaze.

Her companion leaned closer, curiosity glinting in his eyes. "What did he tell you about the local gems—the blue diamonds of Kaliah Island?"

"Not much," she admitted.

"They're utterly unique. Only on this island—nowhere else."

"Nowhere in the world?" she asked, incredulous.

"Nowhere," he said with a sly glint. "That makes the blue diamonds enormously valuable. Yours is the most valuable there is."

Aurelia nodded, feeling the weight of the pendant anew—a strange, luxurious mixture of pride, wonder, and something almost like a branded claim pressing lightly against her skin.

"The Kaliah Heart," she murmured.

He leaned a fraction closer, his voice low enough to brush against her awareness. "Blue diamonds with that clarity, that brilliant glow… they're meant for women with a certain skin tone. Luckily for you, you have it."

Heat crept up her neck at the compliment, but he didn't stop there. His gaze held hers, teasing, playful. "I must say… the way that blue diamond rests against your skin, it's almost distracting. You've turned a museum-worthy treasure into something… dangerously alive."

Intrigued despite herself, she asked more questions about the blue diamond industry, leaning in slightly to keep her composure.

He took her interest as an invitation and waxed eloquent, clearly enjoying the sound of his own voice. "I run the local end of it. The advances we've made in mining, safety, and marketing are considerable, but of course, the real wonder is the blue diamonds themselves. Each one is a miracle, unpredictable, and—" he paused, letting his eyes linger on her just long enough to make her pulse stutter, "—each blue diamond is a story, waiting for the right owner to bring it to life."

Aurelia forced a polite smile, flattered and unnervingly aware of the subtle, lingering flirtation. Every word, every glance seemed to brush against something more than just curiosity about blue diamonds.

When she turned back to Julian, her gaze collided with eyes burnished like tempered steel, cold and sharp, yet with a flash of blue fire flickering beneath the surface. Her chest tightened, her heart curling into a small, constricted knot—but she met his formidable stare with a level glance, lifting her brows just enough to mask the flutter inside.

His smile was cool, cynical, edged with something that made her pulse stutter. "Enjoying yourself?"

"Very much," she said, forcing a tight smile. "I've just been hearing about your adventurous childhood. Your parents must have been grateful when you finally grew up still in one piece."

"My mother was," he replied smoothly. "My father… apparently just as reckless." His gaze flicked down to the blue diamond at her throat, sharp and assessing. "And what else have you learned?"

"That this pretty thing is rare and very precious," she said lightly.

"Very suitable," he murmured, the flat, lethal edge of his voice contradicting the compliment, sending a shiver curling through her.

What the hell had gotten into him? Her cheeks warmed, and she drew a steadying breath, replying sweetly, "How kind of you."

Julian laughed, and before she could react, his hand covered hers on the table. Shocked by the public intimacy, she tried to pull away, but his fingers tightened just enough to hold her in place. His gaze remained imperious, cool, leaving no doubt that the release would come only at his discretion.

When he finally withdrew his hand, his voice softened slightly but retained a dangerous edge. "Did he happen to mention that I have a nasty temper?"

"No, but I know now," she said, keeping her tone sweet, refusing to show even the slightest intimidation.

His laughter came then, effortless, and genuine, and something inside her melted. Her chest felt hollow in the best and worst ways. She realised, with slow, shocking certainty, that it was too late to guard her heart—it was already compromised, dangerously so.

When Julian's expression sobered, she asked quietly, "What was that all about?"

"I think it must be that emotion we're not supposed to feel," he said, eyes dark and unreadable, the faintest curve of amusement—and perhaps something sharper—playing across his face. Jealousy, maybe. Aurelia's skin prickled at the thought, but before she could dwell on it, he had already returned his attention to his companion, leaving the moment charged, ephemeral, and searingly memorable.

In the car on the way to the after-dinner function, Louise leaned back with a satisfied sigh. "Julian, that was a fabulous meal. And such fun! What a brilliant way to raise money for charity—a dinner with good friends in the most romantic place in the world."

"I'm glad you enjoyed it," Julian said dryly, "and we have Aurelia to thank for saving it from disaster."

Aurelia protested with a quick shake of her head. "Nonsense!"

But Louise wouldn't let it drop. Her laughter rang through the car as she pressed for details, and Julian indulged her, recounting the incident with effortless charm.

Her husband, Jeremy, leaned forward, curiosity twinkling in his tawny eyes. "Where are we going?"

"It's a deep, dark secret," Julian said lightly, a teasing glint in his eye. "On Kaliah Island? Don't expect us to believe that—you know everything that happens here."

"I've been sworn to discretion," Julian added with a smile. "You'll just have to wait until we get there. It's not far now."

Louise tried again, coaxing, but Julian refused to budge. "It's a surprise," he said, adding, "If I told you, I'd be hung, drawn, and quartered by the committee of women who've worked so hard to make the evening a success."

"You're afraid of a committee?" Louise laughed.

"You don't know these women," Julian replied cheerfully. "You'll just have to wait until we get there."

When they arrived, Aurelia's breath caught. A pavilion opened onto a pristine beach, built and decorated for the occasion. The dance floor was veiled by flowing white silk walls, looped with garlands of golden-hearted frangipani and hibiscus. Candlelight shimmered across the tables set under the stars, and a band tuned for the hundred or so guests brought from across the island. The lagoon gleamed in the moonlight, warm and inviting.

Louise turned to Aurelia, eyes sparkling. "We can get our makeup touched up in that tent over there. Coming?"

"Yes," Aurelia said, captivated. The glimpse into this intimate world of the very powerful made her pulse quicken.

Inside the tent, several women from a renowned cosmetics firm worked their magic. One attended to Louise, while another guided Aurelia into a chair. "With skin like yours, you don't need much, but let's bring out the blue in your eyes," she said with a smile.

"Not blue eyeshadow, please!" Aurelia protested, laughing.

The woman chuckled. "No blue eyeshadow, I promise." She worked expertly for several minutes, then held up a mirror. "There."

Aurelia stared, speechless. Her lips glowed in a coral shade she never would have dared to wear—yet it complemented her hair perfectly. And her eyes… they were bluer than she'd ever seen them, the deep, mysterious blue of a wild ocean, magnified and luminous, impossible to look away from.

"How did you do that?" she asked in awe.

"Come to the salon one day and I'll show you," the woman replied, brushing aside her thanks and moving on to the next eager guest.

Louise was waiting, her own transformation dazzling. "Aren't they clever?"

"She said she could teach me," Aurelia admitted, immediately wishing she hadn't; it made her feel slightly naive, out of place among such polished sophistication.

Louise smiled and linked her arm with Aurelia's. "Then let her. Makeup is fun. Now, where are our men?" Taller than Aurelia, she scanned the crowd. "Ah, here they come."

The two men materialised through the throng, cutting through the crowd with effortless authority, and heads turned instinctively as they passed. For the first time in her life Aurelia felt the unmistakable stab of female envy directed at her—sharp, shimmering, and dangerously flattering. A forbidden excitement unfurled low in her belly, loosening the tight knot of anticipation in her chest.

Soon there would be dancing…

She accepted a glass of champagne and took a small, steadying sip, letting the bubbles dissolve across her tongue as she let her gaze drift across the lantern-lit pavilion.

"What are you thinking?" Julian's voice brushed her ear, meant for her alone.

"That it looks like a film set," she said honestly before she could censor herself.

His smile deepened, edged with irony. "With us as the extras?"

She nodded. "It's so… everything's perfect. Like a romantic fantasy."

"Good," he said. "The committee who organised it worked extremely hard to make it exactly that. Our table's over here."

Music swelled behind them as the band struck its first chord. The MC stepped into the circle of candlelight at the centre of the dance floor, welcoming everyone and announcing the extraordinary amount of money raised. Applause rang out, spirited and sincere. Then— "The first dance," the MC declared, making a sly joke about the contrast between the old European waltz and this tropical dreamscape.

Aurelia kept her eyes fixed on the empty dance floor as the opening bars unfurled, shimmering and romantic.

"May I have this dance?" Julian asked, his tone formal, his gaze anything but.

She tried for airy composure. The result was a thin, breathless, "Of course."

His hand found the small of her back—cool, assured, proprietary—and guided her into the soft gold of the lights.

Thank goodness for those high-school midwinter ball lessons. She wasn't an expert, but at least she knew how to waltz. Julian, however… Julian moved like a man born to music and control, his body effortlessly translating rhythm into grace.

After only a few steps he murmured, "We're supposed to be lovers—soon, if not already. I'm afraid you won't convince anyone if you insist on staying a polite three inches away from me."

His smile teased. His metallic eyes commanded.

Heat flooded her skin. Reluctantly, shakily, she eased closer, until the hard, elegant line of him aligned with her own body. His arm tightened, lowering her fully into the circle of his strength.

She kept her gaze fixed firmly on the buttons of his white dress shirt, determined not to drown in the sensuous shivers that rippled through her whenever he moved. His body's warmth, the subtle play of muscle beneath fabric, the faint scent of clean skin and something darker, masculine, intoxicating—it all worked a spell older than language.

He bent his head to speak, his breath feathering across the delicate shell of her ear. The sensation arrowed through her, sharp and dazzling, nearly stealing her footing.

"I hope you're looking soulful," he murmured.

She managed, in a brittle attempt at humour, "I don't think I can quite manage soulful. Would languishing do?"

Amusement roughened his voice. "No… too Victorian. And you aren't the languishing or soulful sort. Perhaps we should stick to something safer. Talk to one another like sensible beings." A slight, wicked pause. "Have you enjoyed the evening so far?"

Sensible?

Impossible.

Not when a divine recklessness was surging through her, smashing her inhibitions to splinters.

So, she found him devastatingly attractive—thousands of other women did, too. *Why should she be any different?* Recognising it didn't mean surrendering to it. And wanting him—aching for him—didn't mean she was falling in love.

She reminded herself fiercely: she'd only known Julian a few days. Desire wasn't destiny. Hunger wasn't commitment. Hormones had a way of dressing themselves up in pretty illusions—longing, yearning, need—but beneath the ribbons and sparkle, it was all the same primal chemistry.

She could control it.

She had to.

She would.

Or at least… she would try.

Chapter Ten

"I'm enjoying the evening very much," Aurelia said sedately. "It's a wonderful way to raise money for charity. Everyone seems to be having a lovely time."

Julian's arm flexed as they pivoted gracefully, a smooth turn that drew her even closer than before. The fleeting brush of his body against hers sent another hot, dizzying shiver skittering up her spine, stealing her breath, and scattering her thoughts like startled birds.

"I don't think *lovely* is the right word for us at the moment," he said thoughtfully, as though they were discussing some minor point of policy rather than the fact that her entire nervous system had become one throbbing pulse of awareness.

His hand slid fractionally lower on her back—an adjustment so small it could have been accidental, except it absolutely wasn't. The new angle pressed her more completely against the firm, lithe strength of him. Every shift of muscle, every measured step, translated directly into her body as a shock of sensual electricity.

With that same calm, evaluating tone he added, "*Stimulated* might be the right word. Or perhaps *aware*—extremely aware. Your hand is trembling."

Aurelia swallowed, amazed her throat still worked, and looked down at the treacherous hand resting against his upper arm. She'd been trying to pretend she didn't notice how hard the muscles beneath his jacket were—like wrought iron wrapped in silk—but now there was no point pretending anything.

She forced her fingers straight. "I'm scared," she whispered thinly.

"What of?" His voice changed—no teasing now. Steel. Command. Absolute certainty. "You're completely safe, Aurelia."

"From—this?" she faltered.

He didn't pretend ignorance. "Yes," he said crisply. "You're safe from this. I don't do casual affairs, and I have no respect for people who do. I'm attracted to you—obviously. And it's equally obvious that you feel the same but don't want to act on it. I respect that."

She should have felt relief. Instead, a hollow, aching disappointment opened in her chest.

Collecting herself, she said, "I didn't think you were going to… leap on me or anything, but—"

"You wondered," he supplied smoothly when her tongue tied itself in knots. "You don't strike me as particularly experienced. Or is it that you've had some bad experiences?"

"No," she said, uneasy and mortified. Apart from harmless schoolgirl crushes, she'd had no experience at all. And she was perilously close to confessing things she'd never said aloud.

She clamped her lips shut—but instinct rushed in, foolish and honest. "I do trust you," she said quietly.

"I'm glad," he murmured. "Then trust me further and rest your head on my chest."

When she obeyed, he bent his head until his breath warmed her temple, his lips so close that her skin tingled in anticipation of a kiss he wasn't going to give.

"Nobody can hear us," he said softly. "And it looks good."

Looks good.

She nearly groaned. She was burning from the inside out, trembling in his arms, while he was cool enough to talk about appearances.

A camera flash blinked from the corner of the pavilion. Aurelia stiffened. "I didn't realise there would be photographers here."

"Some people enjoy seeing themselves in magazines," he said, the cool aloofness in his tone making it clear he was not one of them.

Aurelia followed his gaze to a woman capturing the crowd. Julian added, "She has strict instructions—no shots of anyone dancing, and only with permission. And the magazine is donating a hefty sum to charity."

"So, everyone wins," Aurelia said. "From your tone, I gather you didn't want them here."

"They leave a bad taste," he said, each word honed with contempt. "I've been burned too often by magazines that survive on innuendo. And people believe it." His lip curled faintly. "If I'd slept with a fraction of the women I've been linked with, I'd be dead of exhaustion. Apart from anything else—I'm too busy."

"So," she said lightly, "you won't be selling the rights to your wedding to one of them."

His eyes glinted. "Believe it. When I marry, it will be here—where I can control the exposure." A pause, then more quietly, "And when I decide to marry, I want what my parents have. A partnership built on absolute trust."

"You're lucky," she said bleakly, trying to ignore the molten swell of feeling rising inside her—dangerous, uncontrollable, like a fire burning deep beneath the earth. "My parents taught me that marriages fall apart—and that children can be used as weapons."

Julian lifted his head and looked down at the bright crown of her hair. Her dossier had been brief but stark: a blameless, tightly circumscribed life shaped by responsibilities far heavier than any twenty-five-year-old should have carried. A father who'd vanished to New Zealand to avoid support; a divorce so bitter it had left her wary of relationships; a year at university spent studying and caring for her increasingly ill mother; and then the long vigil until her mother's death. No lovers. No wild years. No freedom.

Was she a virgin?

A fierce, low surge of desire tightened every muscle in his body. He suppressed it with a silent oath. Hell. He was turning into a satyr. He had always steered well clear of innocents, preferring lovers who understood the arrangement—fidelity for the duration, generosity, honesty, and good sex. Most of them were still his friends.

"That's tough," he said quietly. "Divorce is hell but using children as weapons is inexcusable. They need to know they matter."

"I'm over it now." She hesitated, then tilted her head, her voice deceptively mild. "Tell me—who is Jessica? I asked before, but you managed to avoid answering."

Julian thought briefly of the message he'd been handed as they'd left the house—Jessica's name scrawled in a flourish he knew all too well. "She's an old friend," he said, keeping his tone deliberately neutral, "who happens to have hair the same colour as yours. Only hers isn't natural."

Aurelia looked up at him, brows lifted, a glint of feline mockery turning her blue eyes strangely, disarmingly seductive. "What makes you think mine is?"

"The way you blush," he said dryly. "You couldn't fake that if you tried."

Sure enough, colour flared along her exquisite cheekbones. She sighed. "It's the bane of my life. Were you expecting her to visit you? Is that why your driver took me to your house when I fainted?"

"Collapsed," he corrected, almost absently. "And no—I wasn't expecting her."

"But...?"

He didn't want Jessica intruding on this moment. Or on Aurelia. Or on the strange, unsettling knot of tension tightening between them. He chose the bare minimum of truth. "But nothing. There's a superficial resemblance, that's all. My driver's never seen her in person, so he made an honest mistake." His mouth curved faintly. "He would have picked you up and brought you home regardless."

She absorbed that, then said, "Does everything that happens on Kaliah Island land on your doorstep?"

"Not when my father's here," he said evenly.

She'd pulled away from him again—just subtly enough that no one watching could see it, but he felt the withdrawal instantly. It irritated him more than it should have.

So, he countered it deliberately.

Sliding his hand more firmly around her waist, he drew her closer again, bending his head until only she could see the steely intent behind his lashes. She stiffened for a heartbeat, then softened against him, her body fitting to his with unconscious trust.

She felt right there. Alarmingly right.

Julian allowed himself one slow breath, then nodded to Jeremy across the dance floor, all cool aristocratic composure while internally, a far less controlled pulse beat through him.

Aurelia was fighting back a sharp, frightening pang of jealousy. What was Julian's connection to this Jessica woman? Past lovers? Almost certainly. The thought sliced through her far more deeply than she expected.

She followed him through a particularly intricate turn, but her composure felt perilously thin. The music soared to its triumphant finish, applause broke out, and couples drifted from the floor in a glittering swirl.

After that she danced with several of the other men in their party, sat out the more energetic numbers with Louise—who proved to be warmly amusing—and then shared more dances with Julian, each one a masterclass in elegant make-believe. They played their parts flawlessly: his light, proprietary touches; her responding blushes; the simmering chemistry that wasn't entirely an act.

She pretended not to look when he danced with Jasmine—but she noticed everything. The girl's gaze clung to Julian with unmistakable possessiveness, her expression tightening when he smiled down at Aurelia later.

A little while after, Aurelia slipped into the ladies' room and found Jasmine already there. The girl's reflection in the mirror was lovely and aristocratic—until she turned, eyes gleaming with something sharper.

"I hope you are enjoying yourself," Jasmine said graciously.

"Very much," Aurelia replied, summoning a polite smile.

Jasmine's brows rose. "You are not his usual sort of woman." Her lips curved, feline and knowing. "Do you realise he is using you?"

Aurelia hadn't expected such a direct hit. She turned on the tap, letting cold water drift over her wrists while she gathered her composure. "My relationship with Julian is nobody's business but ours."

Jasmine stiffened. "You are wrong. I am telling you this because I like you." Her tone suggested the opposite. "But if you hope this little liaison is more than a temporary amusement, you will be disappointed. Eventually Julian and I are to be married. Did you know that?"

Aurelia lifted her head slowly. "Do you really think Julian would flaunt a lover in front of the woman he's supposedly engaged to?"

A delicate shrug—very French, very dismissive. "You are a romantic, so naturally you don't understand our ways. This marriage has been arranged for years. It is a matter of honour between our families—and, of course, business. My dowry is my grandfather's company. Julian already runs it, but once we marry it becomes his. He is more French than English in these matters."

Aurelia shut off the tap and said neutrally, "It sounds… pragmatic."

It also sounded chillingly plausible. Julian had mentioned nothing about business ties or dynastic alliances. And she had agreed to his charade with absurd ease—because she trusted him.

But why, she reasoned rapidly, *would he entangle her in this reckless deception if he intended to marry Jasmine?* That would make him the worst kind of man.

Or perhaps she simply didn't know him at all.

Jasmine reapplied her lipstick, her voice smooth as silk. "We are pragmatic. It will be a good marriage. No divorce. Our children will have stability. Of course, he will always enjoy chasing little redheads—and yes, I may mind a little, though I know such… adventures mean nothing." Her eyes gleamed triumphantly. "You have no chance of marrying him. He is a Kingsley. His great-grandmother was of the old French aristocracy. He knows what is due his position."

Her tone made it brutally clear: *And it isn't some insignificant Australian with no money, no name, and no lineage.*

Aurelia's spine stiffened, heat pricking her eyes—not with tears, but fury.

Thank God Louise arrived then, cutting off Jasmine's smug declaration with warm greetings and drawing Aurelia away.

But the damage was done. A sour, unsettling taste lingered in Aurelia's mouth long after she returned to the dance floor. Especially when she saw Jasmine laughing and flirting effortlessly with the film star, looking far from heartbroken or betrayed.

The insinuation twisted inside her like a blade, making her wonder—*what, exactly, had she stepped into?*

Apart from that, the evening was pure enchantment. Aurelia looked around, thinking wryly that no cliché had been forgotten: the moon hung in unblemished glory over the island, rollers thundered softly against the reef, and the intoxicating perfumes of the tropics mingled in the warm night air.

Supper was served on the beach, a magnificent spread of local and imported delicacies, champagne flowing freely. After dinner, a group of Kaliah Island youths performed for them—beginning with a fiery war challenge, torches stabbing the night, and ending in a wild, sensuous hula that set the guests murmuring in admiration and surprise.

Heated applause followed the performers as they disappeared into the darkness, and the band struck up again. Julian extended his hand to Aurelia. "What do you think of our dancers?"

"They are gorgeous—and they dance brilliantly." She stepped into his arms with a newfound confidence. The lights had dimmed, and couples drifted across the sand in slow, easy steps. "The challenge was thrilling, and the hula… exquisite."

"You understand Fijian, I gather?" he asked, eyebrow quirked.

Her glance registered surprise, and he added, "I think you and Jeremy were probably the only off-islanders who caught the parody, the playful exaggeration tourists expect. I saw you laugh at one bit."

"I have a working knowledge of Fijian," she admitted, "and while it differs from Kaliah Island, I can usually pick up the gist. So yes, I got some of the jokes. Can you speak it?"

"Of course," he said, tone lightly amused. "My sisters and I grew up trilingual—French with our great-grandmother, the local tongue with everyone else, and English with our parents."

"You were fortunate."

His wide shoulder shrugged beneath her hand. "Children absorb languages quickly. My mother insisted we stick to one at a time; otherwise, we'd mix them up. Start a conversation in one language, you had to finish in it. Made life simpler."

"You have two sisters, right?"

He didn't pause, but she sensed his reluctance. "Yes. One older, one younger."

"Do they live here?"

"One is in Paris, the other in New York."

Lightly rebuffed, she said, "I'd have loved siblings."

"We get on well," he replied simply, and Aurelia felt a pang of envy at that calm confidence.

He steered the conversation away. "You mentioned your father has another family in New Zealand?"

"I don't even know where they are," she said evenly. "When my parents divorced, he told me if I stayed with my mother, I'd never see him again. I stayed. The only reason I know about his other child is that he wrote to my mother after the divorce—he and his new partner had a son."

Julian's mouth hardened. "Do you have any other relatives—cousins?"

"In England. We exchange Christmas cards."

He hugged her briefly—a swift, protective contraction of his arms with no sexual implication, yet it touched her deeply. Julian had everything—wealth, influence, family, physical perfection—yet he could still understand the lonely ache of having no one.

Aurelia felt a quiver in the air, as if something deep had shifted between them. His gaze lingered on her mouth, darkening, before flicking back up to meet hers. For several slow, intoxicating moments, they moved together, lost in the dance—until a raucous male voice shattered the spell.

"Hey, Julian, mate! Get off the floor if you don't want to dance!"

A tall, balding man grinned at them openly, and Aurelia's cheeks flamed. His partner waved sympathetically, a faint envy in her smile. Julian chuckled and drew Aurelia close, guiding her away.

After a few steps, he murmured, "Time to go home, I think."

Aurelia nodded, her voice carefully neutral. "Louise will be pleased. She hasn't joined the last two dances—she looks tired."

Julian shot her a sharp glance but let it pass. "Probably just jet lagged."

No one objected when the guests began to leave. Jasmine, glancing back at the film star with a hint of regret, climbed into the second car with her grandfather, the chauffeur closing the door behind them.

Julian drove through the hushed night. Words were unnecessary as the road wound beneath swaying palms along the coastline, then climbed over a spur of the central mountains before descending into the bay where his house sprawled among lush, exotic gardens.

Aurelia gazed absently at the moonlight, every sense taut with a restless, useless anticipation she could not quell. Julian wasn't going to make love to her—not with the house still full of guests.

"Tired?" His voice broke the silence, calm and measured.

"A bit," she admitted, her tone soft. "It's been… fabulous, in the true sense—like stepping into a fairytale." Only, she thought wryly, the princes in those stories were bloodless compared to Julian.

"I've enjoyed it too," he said casually, the sort of words he probably spoke after any social evening. Still, she clung to them in her heart, treasuring their simplicity.

Back at the house, Jeremy and Louise retired to their room. Aurelia lingered with Julian until the second car had deposited its passengers, then murmured her goodnights.

Once in her bedroom, she crossed to the dressing table and caught sight of herself in the mirror. Reckless, she thought, warily, all blue, mysterious eyes and a sultry, inviting mouth. The makeup had done its work—she could hardly deny it.

Her gaze fell on the fabulous blue diamond pendant Julian had lent her. She bit her lip and lifted it, hesitating for a moment as the gold and diamonds glinted coolly, while the blue diamond lay warm in her palm, its brilliance, flawless, almost like the ocean itself.

Another memory, she thought, quietly aching.

The responsibility of keeping the pendant overnight seemed too much, so she held it carefully and opened her door. Down the corridor, Julian and Jeremy were still deep in conversation.

Though she had been silent, both men turned the instant she appeared. She swallowed. On their faces was the same intensity—focused, predatory almost, like two warriors consulting on tactics.

After a brief, low-voiced exchange, Julian's attention snapped to her. He strode toward her, while Jeremy returned to the bedroom he shared with his wife.

Julian's eyes never left her as they closed the distance. There was no frown, but the keen burnished intensity in his gaze made the air around him feel charged, and she shivered despite the warmth.

Holding out the pendant, she said, "You'd better lock it up."

He took it from her, scanning her face with a fleeting, calculating look. "All right?"

"Yes," she said abruptly, stepping back and closing the door behind her, wondering bleakly whether any other woman had ever shut the door in his face. Probably not, she thought starkly, peeling off the silk dress. Like all the other clothes she had worn here, it would stay behind when she left Kaliah Island.

She was just stepping out of the bathroom when the door opened again. Julian slipped inside, moving with the silent, predatory grace of a large cat. He stopped when he saw her, the door clicking softly closed behind him.

"I did knock," he said abruptly, voice low. "I didn't realise you were in the shower."

Shocked into silence, Aurelia watched him with wide, startled eyes. Against Julian's commanding black-and-white presence, she felt utterly exposed in her camisole and matching shorts, achingly vulnerable, her pulse hammering at her throat. Her gaze darted for her wrap, but it was in the wardrobe, and she wasn't about to cross the room in such flimsy garments.

"We need to talk," Julian said curtly.

She swallowed. "About what?"

"Something that's come up." His mouth compressed, shadows flickering across the angular line of his jaw. "Where's your dressing gown?"

"In the wardrobe. Shut your eyes."

He raised a brow but obeyed, and she hurried across the room, pulling on the crisp cotton gown. Tying the belt tightly, she asked, "Is this about Jasmine?"

Julian's eyes were piercing, uncomfortably intent. "Why?"

"Because if it is, you should know what she said to me tonight."

His frown deepened as she hastily recounted the younger woman's words. When she finished, he said without inflection, "I wonder if that's what her grandfather's told her."

"Is it true?"

Her heartbeat skittered as she waited for his answer. It wasn't quite the reassurance she'd hoped for. "I bought everything from him two years ago," he said evenly.

He continued, harsh and precise: "He didn't sell his interests as a sweetener for a marriage deal. It was purely business. Jasmine's father died young, and she's more artistic than businesslike. He did suggest marriage early on, but I told him I wasn't interested."

Pushing her hair back, Aurelia asked, "Then why does Jasmine believe she's practically engaged to you?"

Too late, she realised she sounded possessive and added hastily, "I think she really believes it, Julian. I don't know her, of course, but either it's a fantasy she's convinced herself will come true—or something she's been told."

"Not by me." Julian's tone dripped scorn. "I've just endured a somewhat embarrassing attempt on her part to seduce me."

Aurelia felt a violent urge to pull the French girl's hair out and send her packing. She said woodenly, "I see."

"I didn't realise things had gone this far," he continued, frowning. "They leave tomorrow morning with Louise and Jeremy, but I'll handle it before they go."

"How?"

His gaze swept over her, implacable and unwavering. "First of all, I'll spend the night in here," he said evenly, daring her to object. "That will convince her grandfather, if not her, that she has no hope. He's a man of the old school—he knows I wouldn't flaunt a mistress if I were planning to marry his granddaughter."

Aurelia's stomach dropped, a tangle of heady fear and anticipation. His flinty expression made it clear: she had no choice. She would be sharing the room.

Fighting back a fragile, excited thrill, she asked, "And will he believe she has no hope?"

"I imagine so. I've already made it clear to her that I play no part in her future. By tomorrow, her grandfather will understand it too."

A shiver ran through her at his cold, ruthless tone. Yet, logically, it was kinder to quash Jasmine's fantasy before it went further.

She pressed, making a final stand. "She told me she wouldn't care if you still chased redheads."

"Did she?" Julian's tone was ice. "I find that insulting. When I marry, I want a wife who loves me enough to be jealous."

Surrendering, Aurelia muttered bitterly, "Heaven preserve me from dominating men."

"And me from recalcitrant women." A glint of amusement appeared in his eyes. "Take off your wrap and get into bed. Don't worry—I won't take advantage. I prefer my women willing."

Oh, she was willing enough—but not like this, she realised with a rush of confused, forbidden heat. She tried once more. "How will she know you've spent the night here?"

His brow lifted in sardonic amusement. "I'll bet that within twenty minutes there'll be a tap on the door, and she'll appear, ready to ask charmingly for some feminine item she's forgotten. Just in case she comes sooner rather than later, get into bed."

Aurelia obeyed, wondering how on earth she'd let herself land in such a ridiculous predicament.

But as she hauled the covers up, she realised he was moving toward her. She froze, her eyes widening in disbelief. Surely, he wasn't… No…

Yet he kept coming. When he reached the other side of the bed and pulled back the bedclothes, she bolted upright, indignation flaming. "You said you wouldn't—"

"And I'll keep that promise," he interrupted between strong white teeth, his tone laced with exasperation. "But if Jasmine arrives, I need to make it absolutely clear that I've actually been in this bed with you. Ideally," he added with a wry glint, "the bedclothes would be in tatters, and we'd be lying in each other's arms in naked abandon—but somehow, I don't see that happening, do you?"

Chapter Eleven

Colour scorched Aurelia's skin. She could have shrunk into a heap of embarrassment, but a stubborn pride kept her upright.

"No, I thought not," Julian said, his voice silky and precise, sending a shiver racing down her spine. He sounded dangerous—and she didn't blame him. After all, none of this was his fault, just as it wasn't hers.

He continued with sardonic ease, "So if you fear contamination by being in bed with me—even with my clothes on—you'd better hop out for the five or ten seconds it'll take me to rumple the pillow and the sheets."

"Oh, all right!" Humiliated, she scrambled out, snatching her wrap to sling around her shoulders.

From beneath her lashes, she watched him lower himself onto the bed, stretching out full length. Her throat went dry at the effortless power in his body beneath the crisp white shirt and narrow black trousers. Lord, he was big. Even dancing hadn't prepared her for the sheer physical presence he radiated. Little needles of sensation pricked at her, and a suspicious, electric warmth blossomed between her thighs.

He shifted his dark head on the pillows, leaving a perfect indentation.

Pulling her mind from the hypnotic contrast of his black hair against the white linen, Aurelia managed a crooked smile. "It's just as well you know more about this sort of thing than I do."

"Sex?" His cynical smile acknowledged her start.

"Yes," she admitted sharply.

He said nothing further, and the silence stretched taut, charged with unspoken words and simmering emotion.

Finally, he rose and surveyed the imprint his body left on the bed. "All right, you can get back in now," he said, striding with that swift, noiseless, panther-like gait to the window.

Aurelia slipped back under the sheets, the linen carrying the faint, earthy scent of him—a subtle, intoxicating hint of strength and potency.

"What happens now?" she asked, careful not to glance at the side of the room where he had disappeared. She caught a flicker of movement and suspected he was undressing. A wave of hot desire coiled low in her belly, making her shift uneasily.

"I'll strip and lie down on the sofa," he said. "Don't worry, it won't be long before she comes."

"You seem very confident about Jasmine if you think she'll do this," Aurelia said cautiously.

He laughed, low and cynical. "I know a fair amount about women. When she knocks, I'll come across and get in beside you."

Her heart jumped into her throat. She concentrated on steadying her breathing, imagining he'd gone to sleep. Snoring would make him ordinary—she could handle ordinary.

Frowning, she tried to think of home, of her life back in Australia, but the thought seemed distant and unreal. Forbidden imaginings crept in. *What sort of lover was Julian?* Superb, of course.

Suddenly, an idea struck her, and she sat up. "Julian, what about—?"

The words died on her lips as he instantly switched on the lamp and stood. Golden light spilled across his shoulders, highlighting the sculpted muscles and sleek skin. Heat stole her thoughts; dry-mouthed and dazed, she noted the pattern of hair across his bronze torso.

"What about—?" he prompted, brusque and commanding.

A knock on the door jolted them both into silence. Heart hammering in her chest, Aurelia froze, staring at the hard, uncompromising determination etched across Julian's face. She gasped as he picked up his shirt and tossed it carelessly onto the floor beside the bed.

Without a word, he closed the distance, hauling her into his arms and kissing her with a heat that sent her pulse spiralling out of control. The bed shifted beneath them, a pillow tumbling to the floor as he half-fell over her, his body pressing hers into the mattress.

Their passion was at its peak when the door swung open.

"I—I am so sorry, but—" Jasmine's voice faltered.

Julian lifted his head, eyes sharp and assessing, then rose to his feet with the authority of a predator in control. "What is it?" he demanded. Silence followed. His gaze sharpened. "Is something the matter, Jasmine? Your grandfather?"

Aurelia sat up, flushed and breathless, aware of the stormy scrutiny now trained on her. The intruder's gaze swept from Julian's handsome, controlled visage to Aurelia— blushing, embarrassed, and very clearly caught in the aftermath of their kiss.

A strange admiration flickered through Aurelia for the girl's audacity—until the words struck.

"Slut! Whore!" Jasmine hissed, launching into a low, furious tirade in French.

Julian's voice snapped across the room like a whip. "I won't ask why you feel entitled to walk into someone else's room uninvited. Go. Now."

Jasmine's face fell, the veneer of sophistication crumbling to reveal raw, youthful vulnerability. "I—I just wanted to…" she stammered.

With cold, disciplined force, Julian cut her off. "I don't know how you convinced yourself there's any connection between us, but it ends here. When the time comes, I will choose my own wife. Do you understand me?"

The girl nodded, voice tight. "I—I am sorry."

"No more interviews with magazines implying a secret engagement. No more sly tips to gossip columnists."

Colour flooded Jasmine's cheeks. "No… no more," she whispered, and, swallowing hard, she turned and fled, leaving the room charged with silence and the faint scent of tension.

Aurelia didn't blame her. Julian in a temper—even one so finely controlled—was formidable, almost terrifying. But she couldn't let Jasmine go like that and bolted off the bed.

"Don't follow her," Julian said, closing the door behind them, a trace of ruefulness softening his otherwise severe expression. "I feel like someone who's just pulled the wings off a butterfly, but she'll need time to herself—not your company."

"Perhaps Louise—?" Aurelia ventured. His brows lifted sharply.

"Your compassion is admirable but misplaced. Louise is probably sound asleep by now. Jasmine—well, for all her flaws, she has pride and guts. She'll deal with it herself. Wouldn't you?"

Aurelia shivered. "Yes," she admitted. "Though I'm older than she is."

"Probably not as experienced," he murmured, eyes lowering to study her with that detached, commanding calm. "I'm sorry you had to witness that. I was cruel, but I needed to make it crystal clear she's been spinning moonbeams."

"It's all right," she said, awkwardly, though adrenaline still coursed through her veins, setting her senses alight. The lingering scent of him—the subtle, masculine heat— twisted her thoughts. And the memory of his mouth on hers, the weight of his body against hers… it made her pulse quicken.

"When I asked you to do this," he continued, voice low, deliberate, "I hoped I was anticipating something that might not even exist. I had no idea it had become such a problem, or that she'd be so persistent."

"Do you think you've ended it?"

He shrugged, the light catching the wide, tanned planes of his shoulders. Her fingertips tingled, and only the sheerest exercise of will stopped her from leaning forward, pressing her lips to the smooth skin of his chest, drawing him back onto the bed to finish what they'd started.

"I hope so," he said finally. "I'll speak to her grandfather tomorrow, just in case he's been feeding her these ideas."

Aurelia nodded, staring straight ahead. "Right. Now, as that's done, you might as well go back to your own room," she said brightly, though the brittle words threatened to fracture under the heat in the room.

"Sorry," he said coolly. "But just in case, I'm staying here."

She swung around, eyes wide, cheeks flushed, the camisole clinging to her breasts. "No!" she said explosively. "I don't want you—"

He studied her with narrowed, intent eyes, a smile creeping across his face—half scorn, half hunger. "Don't lie to me, Aurelia," he murmured. "You're scared, but you want me. Just as I want you."

A lean fingertip traced along her collarbone, lingering as he watched the flicker in her expression shift—fear softening into a slow, dawning desire mirrored in her blue eyes and the gentle curve of her mouth.

"Whoever named you Aurelia should have chosen Calypso," he murmured, voice low, restrained, almost reverent. "It means Greek nymph—temptation, desire at sea. And you… you are both tempting and desirable. Your skin… it's more beautiful than the blue diamond you wore tonight—warm, fine, smooth as silk. Did you know all night I've been thinking of you… and the diamonds around your neck?"

She drew a sharp, startled breath. "You were?"

"Yes," he said, voice deliberate, thick with heat, "you, naked in my bed… wearing only the Kaliah Heart."

He shouldn't be doing this. Shouldn't be teasing her with the slow, tantalising words, the silken brush of his fingers, the relentless hunger that had shadowed him since the moment he'd first seen her.

Julian had never made love to a woman who hadn't made it unmistakably clear she wanted him. He had avoided virgins, and the inexperienced. But now something far stronger than caution or restraint drove him—a raw, insatiable appetite that stripped away every ounce of self-control.

It took all his will to close his eyes and murmur, "Tell me to leave."

She remained perfectly still, the seconds stretching into a suspended eternity. When he opened his eyes, he caught the conflict in her gaze. His voice dropped, rough with emotion he no longer tried to hide. "It's all right. I had no right to place this burden on you."

Her lips parted slightly. "If I said go… would you?"

"Yes," he said, quiet, steady, absolute.

Another pause. Aurelia's breath trembled, but her eyes held his—searching for certainty, for truth, for him. Slowly, deliberately, she nodded, the decision settling deep in her bones. "I want you to stay."

She leaned forward, pressing a kiss over his heart—a kiss potent as a spell, sweet as longing, scorching as restrained fire. Julian went utterly still beneath her lips, every nerve alight, every instinct screaming to possess, protect, and savour this fragile, perfect moment.

And in that charged, suspended beat, Aurelia realised something that thrilled and terrified her all at once: she was entirely his, even before he had touched her—and she would give herself willingly.

Every muscle in her body coiled with anticipation, the air between them charged, brittle, alive. Julian's hand rose—firm, unyielding—curling beneath her chin as he tilted her face up to his. His metallic eyes swept over her slowly, relentlessly, as though he were peeling back every layer she'd ever worn until only the truth remained. There was no cruelty in him—only need. Verification. A final, silent test of her resolve.

When he spoke, his voice was low, almost gentle—yet edged with steel. A challenge.

"Are you sure?"

The question sliced through the last of her hesitation, sharp as a blade. Aurelia felt the weight of his scrutiny settle over her like heat, burning away every doubt, she might have had. Her resolve crystallised—clear, fierce, immovable. Whatever dawn might bring, whatever consequences waited outside this room… she knew what she wanted.

She knew who she loved.

She would always love him.

Her answer was barely a whisper yet rang with absolute certainty.

"Yes, Julian. I want you."

He went still.

For a breath.

Then another.

He didn't move—didn't even seem to breathe. He simply held her gaze, and in that suspended moment something inside him shifted. The cool, controlled smile he always wore slipped away, replaced by something darker, deeper—dangerously intimate.

Hunger.

Reverence.

Possession.

Time seemed to slow.

For a long, heated moment, they simply stared—two breaths, two heartbeats, two bodies trembling on the same precipice. Then she nodded, slowly, irrevocably. The mirrored tension in his body reassured her—he was balancing on the same edge, fighting the same fire.

Julian's fingers slid into the soft waves of her hair at the nape of her neck, his touch gentle but electric. Her breath hitched. Her wide, luminous eyes—shimmering with anticipation, trust, surrender—held him captive.

His other hand rose to cradle her cheek. His thumb traced the curve of her skin with exquisite care, tilting her head with a tenderness that made her chest tighten painfully.

And then—

he kissed her.

The world fell away.

It started soft—an exploration, a tasting, a question. But the tenderness dissolved quickly beneath a surge of heat neither could contain. The kiss deepened, sharpened, flared into something fierce and consuming. Julian pulled her closer, his arms banding around her, moulding her against him as though he needed the reassurance of every heartbeat, every breath she gave him.

"You feel so right in my arms," he murmured, voice low, reverent.

Aurelia melted into the heat of him—mind, heart, soul surrendering in a way that felt carved into her very being. Her hands slid over the broad planes of his chest, clutching him, learning him. She rose onto her toes, chasing his mouth, his breath, his need. When her fingers threaded into the thick, dark strands at his nape, a low, unrestrained shiver rumbled through him.

She had been kissed before.

But never like this.

Never with a hunger that tasted like devotion.

Never with a passion that left her trembling, breathless, undone.

"Julian…" His name escaped her in a broken whisper against his lips.

He answered with a kiss that stole what remained of her breath.

His mouth moved to her jaw, her throat, each brush of lips sending shivering sparks down her spine. She arched instinctively, offering more, craving more, her pulse hammering wildly beneath his touch.

He lifted her—effortless, sure—and carried her toward the bed. She felt the strength in every step, the steady heat of his body pressed along hers, the quiet authority that had always thrilled her.

When he lowered her onto the sheets, his eyes swept over her with a reverence so intense it made her tremble. His touch was purposeful, unhurried, as he slid the strap of her camisole from her shoulder… then the other. The fabric slipped down her skin in a soft whisper, pooling at her waist like silk giving up its last defence.

"Beautiful," he murmured—voice thick, roughened, worshipful.

The single word vibrated through her, sinking deep, awakening a molten tension that curled low in her belly and spread like heat on a rising tide.

His hands traced her curves—slow, mapping, memorising—as though committing her to memory with every deliberate pass. Each touch ignited sparks that rippled across her nerves in dizzying waves. Heat unfurled inside her, a wildfire she could neither contain nor disguise. A soft, startled sound escaped her, her body arching instinctively into him, craving more of the connection only he could give.

Her fingers drifted up his arms, over his shoulders, sliding along the warm, taut lines of his body. Every inch of him was power—coiled, controlled, barely restrained. She felt it in the tight cadence of his breathing, in the subtle tension in his muscles, in the faint tremor of his touch as he fought the urge to rush… to take her too quickly… to give in to everything he felt.

Something shifted in her eyes—boldness warring with vulnerability, want trembling against fear.

He saw it.

And he broke.

He kissed her—hard and sudden—his mouth claiming hers in a fierce, consuming press. His teeth grazed her lower lip, a feral edge threaded through the hunger, a question and a demand wrapped in one explosive touch.

"You want me as much as I want you?" His voice was a rasp against her mouth, raw with need.

Heat—scorching, undeniable—rushed through her. She blushed scarlet, breath catching as her hands lowered to her lap before sliding back up to clutch at him, trembling but sure. "Yes," she whispered, the word barely formed, yet absolute.

His lips followed the bloom of heat across her cheekbones, down the delicate line of her jaw. He pressed feather-light kisses along her skin, one after another, dissolving every coherent thought she had left. Her body melted helplessly against his, every nerve alive, every inch of her acutely attuned to the exquisite torment of him—his mouth, his hands, the heat of his breath ghosting over her bare skin.

He drew back just enough to meet her eyes, a wicked curve pulling at his mouth. "I didn't know you coloured all over," he murmured, his voice warm and amused, threaded with something darker. Before she could form a reply, he lowered his head again with deliberate, devastating intent.

His lips brushed her collarbone—soft, teasing—then pressed again, slower, deeper. Each kiss lingered in the hollow above her heart as though he were imprinting himself there, claiming her inch by inch. Gentle… yet irrevocable.

When his mouth skimmed the delicate shell of her ear, a sharp, helpless shiver shot through her, stealing her breath and scattering her thoughts like dust.

Aurelia's breath faltered.

Her world narrowed to a single, glittering point of heat—

him.

Only him.

This moment.

This undeniable, overwhelming pull that seized her with merciless precision.

And in that breathless, suspended second, clarity flooded her—a soft, aching truth that settled inside her chest:

This night would mark her forever.

A strangled cry escaped her when he cupped her breast, his palm hot and commanding against her sensitised skin. He groaned low—an animal sound—his thumb flicking over her hardened peak, once… then again when she arched helplessly into his touch. Their mouths collided, fusing in a kiss that was deep and consuming, a kiss that stripped her down to nothing but sensation. Tongues tangling, breath mingling, they devoured each other until the world outside their bodies ceased to exist.

His hands explored her with purpose—learning her contours, mapping her with reverence and hunger. He slid her silky shorts down her thighs, slow enough to be deliberate, fast enough to make her gasp, baring her completely to him. When he found the soft, silken curve of her thigh, he stroked upward with excruciating slowness, igniting a molten rush of heat between her legs.

Then he tore his lips from hers only to drag them down her body in a scorching trail that felt like worship and possession all at once. His mouth closed around one taut nipple, his tongue flicking, teasing, tormenting before he sucked deeply, pulling a broken moan from her lips.

Her fingers tangled in his hair, pulling, guiding, needing. Her breath came in ragged, uneven bursts as he moved lower—down the flat plane of her stomach, his lips and tongue tracing every inch as though nothing about her was too small to revere.

He eased her thighs apart, palms wide and steady, and reached between them. She gasped when his fingertip slid through her slick heat—stroking, circling, coaxing more from her with wicked skill. Kneeling between her open legs on the bed, he lowered his head.

And then he tasted her.

Pleasure detonated inside her—sharp, bright, volcanic. Her hips jerked beneath him, shuddering uncontrollably. He held her steady, his tongue swirling through her wetness, savouring every sound she couldn't hold back.

Then he devoured her—tongue stroking, circling, teasing the tight bud of her pleasure until she writhed beneath him, sobbing his name like a prayer and a plea. When he slid a long, masculine finger inside her, she nearly broke. She was tight—so tight—her muscles gripping him with desperate greed. He withdrew slowly, unbearably slowly, then thrust in again, establishing a torturous rhythm that dragged her higher… higher… until she was hanging on the precipice of pure oblivion.

"Oh… Julian, please." Her voice splintered, fractured with need and surrender.

He groaned against her, the vibration sparking another wild jolt through her. "You're incredible," he whispered, breath warm and sinful against her fevered skin.

Tremors racked her body. Her back arched off the bed, bowing toward his mouth as she held her breath, eyes squeezed shut, lips parted in a soundless plea. His tongue flattened, stroking her with its full, rough width—relentless, devastating—then softened, flicking delicately at her swollen bud, teasing her closer to the brink.

Her entire body tightened—arching, trembling—

—and then she shattered with a scream of unrestrained ecstasy.

Another cry tore from her as wave after wave crashed through her, each one more overwhelming than the last. He held her through it, mouth tender but unyielding, drawing out every last trembling pulse until she collapsed beneath him, wholly undone, shaking and beautifully ruined.

Slowly, reverently, Julian kissed his way back up her body, tracing every dip and curve with a devotion that made her chest ache. He hovered over her once more, his weight settling between her parted thighs, the hard, heavy press of his arousal nudging intimately against her softness.

Their eyes met—hot, dark, knowing.

No words were needed.

He wanted her.

She needed him.

And neither of them would deny it any longer.

Breathless, cheeks flushed a delicate rose, she lifted her gaze to his—bright, vulnerable, still dazed from the force of what he'd just given her. "That was... amazing," she whispered, her voice trembling, soft but earnest, every syllable betraying the fire still coursing through her veins.

"Sometimes," he said quietly, a raw edge cutting against the calm he fought to maintain, "the first time can hurt. I didn't want that for you. I wanted you to feel pleasure first."

Her blush deepened, blooming down her neck, but she didn't look away. If anything, she held his gaze harder, gripped by the intensity burning in his eyes. "How did you know it would be the first time for me?" she murmured—half shy, half teasing, completely unguarded. His slight, knowing smile made her blush throb even hotter. "Was it that obvious?"

His laugh rumbled low, deep, and throaty—so sensual it vibrated through her entire body like a caress. "Only to a man who was paying very, very close attention," he murmured, leaning in.

Then he kissed her—slow at first, soft enough to be reverent, then deepening with a rising hunger that curled her toes and made her breath catch. His mouth moved over hers, coaxing her lips to part, tasting her with aching thoroughness, as though he'd never get his fill. His lips traced the delicate curve of her jaw, then the graceful line of her throat, lingering at the flutter of her pulse. Each touch tightened something deep inside her—something tender and desperate and newly awakened.

Her body no longer felt like her own. It moved against his without her permission, drawn to him instinctively, surrendering to the pull of him. She arched into him, welcoming every spark he fed into her, every shiver he summoned, every breathless gasp he stole. She followed the rhythm of his touch, opened to him completely—utterly—without one shred of restraint.

And he met her with equal force. Equal hunger. Equal need.

Surrender had never felt so inevitable… or so profoundly right.

Julian's fingers explored her again—slow, deliberate strokes that traced the lines of her body as though he were memorising her. Teasing, building tension, circling closer and closer until a single, daring motion inside her sparked a new torrent of pleasure. She gasped, hips rising sharply, hands clawing at his shoulders as waves of delight rippled through her.

He rose over her, braced above her, gaze locked onto hers with a heat that made her tremble.

"This might hurt," he warned, voice rough, low, frayed at the edges.

"I don't care," she moaned, pulling him closer, her whole body offering itself without hesitation, without fear. Heart and soul laid bare for him.

A guttural sound tore from his chest as he aligned with her, the slick heat of her body welcoming him, beckoning him forward. In one powerful, fluid motion, he entered her—seamless, overwhelming, electric. The initial burn flared sharp and bright… then melted almost instantly into a wild, exquisite pleasure that pulsed through her entire body, stealing every thought she might've had.

He thrust again… then again… each movement skimming the razor-thin edge of control. She cried out beneath him, her body tightening, nails sinking into his skin—sharp, desperate, claiming. He froze for a single beat, muscles quivering as he fought the primal urge to give in too quickly.

Slow down.

Feel her.

Make her fall apart for him.

He eased back, then drove into her slowly—deliberately—letting her feel every inch of him, every powerful stroke carving pleasure through her body. Her breaths broke in soft, frantic pants. Her hips rose to meet him, urging him deeper, begging without words for more.

Then she shattered—harder this time—her cry slicing through the air and through him.

"Julian…"

Hearing his name like that—raw, breathless, drenched in pleasure—nearly destroyed him.

He felt her clench around him, tight and urgent and impossibly greedy, dragging him into the same explosive free-fall. Their mouths crashed together, ravenous, helpless, their kiss a frantic tangle of heat and need. She moved beneath him like she was made for him, like she wanted him with the same fierce desperation burning in his blood.

Her release detonated through her, white-hot, pulsing around him—pulling, milking, demanding every last drop of him.

"Aurelia—" His voice broke into a guttural groan against her throat as his control shattered. His hands clamped onto her hips, holding her tight to him as he buried himself to the hilt, surrendering to the rush that ripped through him. Her hot, silken tightness dragged him over the edge, pulling him past reason.

A primal, ragged growl tore from his chest as he spilled into her, shuddering violently, every breath stolen by the sheer ferocity of it. He stayed there, locked deep inside her, chest pressed to hers, heartbeat hammering in sync with hers.

Nothing had ever felt like this.

Nothing had ever undone him like she did.

And as he held her—still trembling, breathless, utterly entwined—he knew with devastating certainty:

He wasn't walking away from this woman.

Not now.

Not ever.

Slowly—deliberately—his tension eased. His body softened over hers, settling with a delicious, heavy weight that pressed her into the mattress in the best possible way. His breath felt warm and uneven against her neck, stirring the damp strands of hair clinging to her skin. For a long, blissful stretch, neither of them moved. Time stilled. The world outside faded to nothing. There was only the quiet rise and fall of his breathing, the strong, grounding thud of his heartbeat pressed intimately against her own, and the lingering aftershocks trembling through her limbs like tiny sparks.

Wrapped securely in the fortress of his arms, her cheek resting against the smooth, heated skin of his chest, she felt the last ripples of her climax drifting through her—slow, languid, intoxicating. Her body softened against him, boneless and sated, but beneath the serenity a small ache unfurled—an ache she couldn't hide from herself. Longing, tender and insistent, brushed through her like a breath of cold air.

She was under no illusions.

This—whatever *this* was—could never mean as much to him as it did to her.

She knew that. And yet… her heart betrayed her anyway.

When he lifted onto his elbows, she released a soft, helpless sound—half regret, half plea—before she could swallow it back. The kind of sound that revealed far too much. If he noticed, he didn't comment. Instead, he shifted and rolled onto his back, drawing her with him as though it were instinct, as though he couldn't bear to break the contact. She ended up sprawled over him; her body draped across his like a warm, pliant blanket.

His arm curved around her waist, firm and protective, banishing the fleeting chill that had brushed her heart.

Pressed against him, she felt the powerful, steady rise and fall of his chest beneath her palms. She felt the muted strength in every breath he took, the raw, masculine heat radiating from every inch of him. Her cheek settled just above his heart, and as the deep, rhythmic thud resonated through her ear, her own pulse slowed, aligning with his in a quiet, intimate cadence.

His voice rumbled against her temple, low and velvety, the kind of sound that could unravel a woman with its softness alone. "No pain, I hope?"

"None worth mentioning," she murmured, a tiny yawn slipping through the words despite her best effort to contain it. Her limbs were heavy, warm, liquid with exhaustion and contentment. Another yawn fluttered past her lashes, her eyes blinking slower. "Thank you."

The words were fragile, blurred by sleepiness and something gentler—something that felt dangerously close to wonder. Gratitude. Awe. Maybe even more.

He shifted beneath her, his hand flexing at her waist, tightening his hold as though he felt her slipping into dreams. "No, Aurelia," he said quietly, his voice warm enough to brush against her soul. "Thank you."

The words wrapped around her like a second blanket—thick, cocooning, impossibly tender.

He reached out with his free hand, the mattress dipping beneath the movement, and flicked off the lamp.

Darkness swept over the room, soft and absolute.

She didn't even feel herself fall.

One heartbeat she was aware of his chest beneath her cheek, the strong rhythm anchoring her to him…

The next, she slipped under entirely.

Sleep claimed her in a deep, engulfing wave—like sinking into warm black water—held safely, securely, completely in the unbreakable circle of Julian's arms.

Chapter Twelve

It was Julian's voice that yanked her from the haze of sleep. Shock jolted her upright, heart hammering, breath catching. For a moment, she feared Jasmine had intruded again—but when she lifted herself on an elbow, she saw Julian at the foot of the bed, naked, lamplight gilding the planes of his body in bronze and gold. He wasn't speaking to her.

He was on his phone.

And he was furious.

Every line of his face was carved in dark, uncompromising angles; black brows drawn into a single, lethal slash. His muscles tensed, coiled, radiating authority and danger.

"Are you sure?" he demanded, crisp, clipped, controlled. Then, with a snap of rage, "Damn it all to hell!"

Cold rippled through her. She pulled the sheet over her bare chest, suddenly small, exposed, invisible. His gaze flicked toward her—brief, assessing, impersonal—before returning to the phone. The tenderness of last night seemed erased, leaving only a distant, untouchable man whose presence now reminded her how irrelevant she was to his storm of business and control.

"Do that," he said, low and commanding. "I'll see to things this end."

He snapped the phone shut and turned to her, face cold, distant. "I have a problem," he said flatly. "You're going back to Australia."

Her stomach lurched. "What—what do you mean?" Her voice was tiny, fragile. The intimacy they had shared, the closeness, the whispered promises—they all felt erased in an instant. Only this measured, brusque man remained.

"Get dressed. I'll explain on the way to the airport."

Her lips trembled. "All right," she whispered, though her limbs refused to obey.

He exhaled sharply. "Get up, Aurelia."

"Not with you looking," she muttered, humiliation curling in her chest.

His brows rose, sharp and unyielding. "Far too late for regrets," he said curtly, his voice a blade. "And you don't have the time. I want you off the island as quickly as possible."

The words hit like stones in her chest. Regret. He regretted nothing—but that meant everything they had shared meant nothing to him. Her chest tightened, a hollow ache spreading through her.

When his phone rang again, he turned away without another glance, leaving her staring at the floor, heart pounding, mind spinning.

Finally, trembling, she slid from the bed. Each step toward the bathroom felt unreal, as if she were moving through fog. She gathered clean clothes, showered quickly, her movements mechanical, her mind suspended in disbelief. Dressing, she pulled the fabric over herself like armour, trying to reconstruct the version of herself that could face the day—or whatever remained of it.

When she emerged, Julian was gone. The housekeeper, yawning, folded clothes into a case. Aurelia's eyes fell to the ruined bed. Shame should have burned—but heartbreak eclipsed it entirely.

"I won't need those. Just leave them, please," she said, voice hollow, controlled.

Litia hesitated. "But Julian told me—"

Aurelia shrugged, feeling absurdly small. Clothes didn't matter; her entire world had just shifted beneath her. "I won't be taking them," she said quietly, a fragile ember of defiance flickering beneath the heartbreak.

Julian reappeared in the doorway, composed, immaculate, jaw tight with a tension that spoke of barely contained fury—or was it disappointment? —and a cold distance that cut straight to her chest. "Come and have something to eat. Coffee," he said, clipped, controlled.

Startled, Aurelia glanced at the windows—still night, still dark. Her stomach churned at the thought of food, but she needed something to anchor herself. Coffee. She needed coffee.

A tray waited in his study. The sandwiches sat untouched; she reached for the steaming mug, letting the bitterness bite at her tongue. She clung to it like a lifeline, hoping the heat and caffeine could burn through the weight pressing on her chest.

Julian folded his arms, the authoritative presence filling the small space. "I'm sorry about this," he said. "I'm sending you back to Australia. An emergency has come up."

Her throat tightened. Any protest might betray the raw ache twisting in her chest. "It's all right," she said, voice brisk, brittle. "Really."

He frowned, sharp and uncompromising. She flinched. "It is not," he said curtly. "I don't want to send you away—and after what's just happened, even less so."

Her composure faltered. A tremor ran through her hands as she lifted one toward her coffee cup, the gesture pitifully small. "Look—let's just leave it at that, okay? What happened… it was great. No one could have had a better first time. Thank you." Her words sounded hollow even to her own ears. She poured extra milk into the coffee and gulped quickly, hoping the warmth and caffeine could cut through the ache inside her.

"Aurelia," he said, voice taut, brittle, carrying the authority she had always feared—but now desperately needed. "I'm not sending you away because we made love."

Her heart faltered, but the words offered no comfort. "Then why?" she whispered, voice trembling despite herself.

He hesitated only a moment, then spoke with the uncompromising certainty that left no room for argument. "Listen to me. This is important. When you land in Australia, my man will take you to my penthouse in Sydney. I want you to stay there until I come and tell you it's safe."

Her numbness wavered and broke, leaving a hollow pit in her chest. She stared at him, incredulous. "You don't need to do that—I can find somewhere to stay."

"I'm not offering hospitality out of kindness," he said, taut, controlled, every word measured.

She swallowed hard. "Then why?"

"Because you'll be safe there."

The words hit her like a thunderclap. Her grip on the coffee mug tightened, knuckles whitening. Her eyes widened, luminous and terrified.

"Safe?" she breathed. "What… what on earth do you mean?"

And suddenly—the heartbreak, the fear, the longing, the shame—they collided in a single, icy wave, leaving her reeling with the piercing knowledge that nothing would ever be simple with him again.

Julian had already decided how to break it to her. After a quick glance at his watch, he poured himself another cup of coffee, leaving it untouched on the table. His gaze fixed on her—sharp, unflinching, uncompromising.

"Because I've just been told that a man has got onto Kaliah Island," he said, voice low, measured, "someone who quite possibly intends to kill you."

The words hit like ice. Her face drained of colour, yet her indomitable spirit kept her upright. Eyes locked on his, she whispered, trembling, "What?" Then, before he could speak, she steadied her voice. "Why?"

Julian chose each word deliberately. "You wanted to know who Jessica is. She was once close to me. We parted, and six months ago she married. The day before you fainted in front of my car, she called me. She'd left her husband—apparently convinced he believed she was having an affair with me."

Her mind went blank. Chest tightening, lungs suddenly uncooperative, she barely drew a breath.

"And she said he had beaten her," Julian continued, then, softer but firm, added, "Finish your coffee."

Mechanically, she obeyed, sipping the bitter liquid as a chill raced down her spine.

Julian's tone softened slightly, though his steel-grey gaze remained immovable. "I didn't entirely believe her. She has a flair for dramatics and wanted sympathy. I arranged for her to be taken to a safe house in Switzerland. When she flew to Paris instead, I assumed she'd exaggerated. Then, a couple of days after you arrived, she called again. She'd flown to Kaliah Island—and hoped I'd put her up."

Jessica hadn't sounded very bright, Aurelia thought, shivering. "Why? If he thinks she's having an affair with you, coming here only reinforces his suspicions."

Julian's expression was grim. "She thought she could cover her tracks—but it's almost impossible if the person chasing you has the resources to track you down."

"Don't tell me," Aurelia's voice sharpened with rising fury. "Her husband has the resources."

"He's very rich," Julian confirmed. "I lodged her in a family-owned house in the mountains. Well-guarded, almost impossible to reach unless he hires a helicopter— which he won't be able to do. Unfortunately... you resemble her closely enough to fool anyone who doesn't know her well."

A chill ran down her spine. "So..."

"I assume her husband has discovered someone resembling Jessica has arrived on Kaliah Island," Julian said, voice level but edged with iron. "And if he didn't already know, he would certainly find out after speaking with one or two islanders. They'd mention a woman who looks like Jessica, living in my house—assumed to be my lover."

Aurelia's voice was barely a whisper. "Am I... a decoy?"

Julian's face darkened. "Hell, no!" he barked, then controlled himself, eyes hard and unyielding. "Looking back, I should have taken her story seriously, but it seemed outrageous. I thought she was trying to make him jealous. But he's followed her. Landed here under a false name and passport. I have to assume he believes you are her— and that he's up to no good." He paused, then added crisply, "Or he might just be avoiding the paparazzi. They've worked out they're separated and are trying to locate them."

"Do you believe that?" Aurelia whispered.

"No," Julian said after a long pause. "Jessica is terrified. Convinced he will try to kill her. Which is why you're going back to Australia."

Her mind rebelled. "Surely it would be safer if I stayed… so he can see I'm not her—"

"No," he interrupted, firm, uncompromising. "This has nothing to do with you. You are going back to Australia, and I want your promise: stay in my apartment until I give the all-clear."

Her lips pressed together, resistance crumbling under the weight of love and fear. Unevenly, she whispered, "Yes. Of course. Does Jessica think you're in danger?"

Julian shrugged in that casual, controlled way she had learned to recognise. "She hasn't mentioned it. Anyway, I'm well-protected. But I want you well out of it."

Her heart rebelled, a storm of longing and protest rising within her—but she knew she had no right to demand his presence in Australia. And he wouldn't come. He had spent a lifetime responsible for those in his charge—a deep-seated instinct, woven into his very being.

Once, perhaps, he had loved another. Maybe he still did. Perhaps she had been nothing more than a stand-in—a woman who merely resembled the one he truly loved. The thought cut her with a sharp twist of heartache.

She couldn't stop herself. "What… are you going to do?"

Julian paused, eyes hooded, the faintest shadow of weariness passing over his features. Then he said deliberately, deliberately leaving her in suspense, "I think you'd be safer if you didn't know that."

A new wave of chills followed the first, sharper and more insistent. Aurelia took another cautious sip of coffee, but the warmth that had radiated through her chest with the first swallow had vanished. Carefully, she finished the rest, setting the cup down with deliberate calm. "You're really worried about her safety," she said, her voice steady but carrying an edge of unease. It wasn't a question.

"Yes," Julian admitted, his tone clipped but heavy with concern. "I am worried. My security organisation uncovered an incident in her husband's youth involving the death of a woman. It could be a coincidence, but I don't dare assume it is."

Meeting his hard, unflinching eyes, she said quietly, "I think you're right."

His black brows lifted, and his gaze sharpened as if weighing her very soul. "Just like that?" he asked evenly, but his eyes didn't waver, and Aurelia felt an uncomfortable prickling sensation, as though she were being dissected by a mind both brilliant and relentless.

Trying to temper the defensive note creeping into her voice, she said, "It happened to a friend of mine."

Julian froze, his posture rigid. "What happened to her?"

"She was his high-school girlfriend," Aurelia said, glancing away. "He was jealous— Karen thought it meant he loved her. I did too. But when he realised, she wasn't going to marry him straight out of school, that she was going to university first... he just lost it."

"How?" Julian asked, his voice low, intense.

"He harassed her all through the Christmas holidays," she said, swallowing hard. "He called incessantly, got drunk, blamed her for not loving him enough... said they could get married and live in his parents' granny flat in their backyard. He just wanted to get a job and get married. He couldn't understand why she wanted more than that."

"And then?" Julian prompted, his tone even but taut.

"Her parents sent her away to stay with relatives in New Zealand. She wrote to him from there, saying it was best if they didn't see each other for a while. He didn't seem to care. He didn't try to contact her. Life went on... everyone thought he had just been sulking."

Julian's eyes narrowed slightly, unreadable. "Go on."

"When the semester began, he called her and asked her out. She said no—she'd had time to think about what she truly wanted. But he persuaded her to go for a drive. She trusted him... no one expected..." Her voice faltered. She stared into the coffee, tracing the rim with a finger. Quietly, almost inaudibly, she finished, "Dennis drove her to the beach... and then he shot her in the head and then himself. He left a note. He said he couldn't face life without her, that it was better they go together into the next life."

The room fell silent. Aurelia's hands trembled in her lap, and her eyes glistened.

Julian's large, warm hand closed over hers, steadying, comforting. He pulled her up, letting her lean against him, his solid frame offering the unspoken solace of strength, of safety.

"None of us ever believed Dennis would harm her," she said raggedly. "Not even when he was harassing her. No threats, no warnings... nothing. I'm glad you're taking this seriously. Her husband may not be like Dennis—he might be overreacting—but better to notice, better to act, than to ignore it."

Julian muttered something low under his breath, then his jaw tightened. "I hope I didn't..." His voice cracked slightly before he forced himself to continue. "...upset you. I'm sorry. I had no idea that telling you this would dredge up such painful memories."

"Of course you didn't," Aurelia said, easing from his arms, letting him go. She forced a small, hollow smile. "I still get emotional thinking about Karen... the waste of their lives. But I have made peace with it."

Julian's eyes lingered on her, dark and unreadable, a mixture of regret, concern, and something unspoken swirling beneath the surface. He stayed still for a long moment, as though measuring whether words could ever suffice—or whether his presence alone would have to be enough.

Julian's voice cut through the morning air, sharp and urgent. "I can hear the chopper. We have to go."

"Why aren't we driving?" she asked, her stomach twisting.

He shrugged casually, but she caught the tension in the movement. "The helicopter is faster." Safer, she realised, as they lifted into the sky, the sleeping island shrinking beneath them. No ambushes on narrow, winding roads. Her pulse pounded—not from fear, exactly, but from the helplessness clawing at her chest.

Irrationally, she wanted to stay. To do something, anything, to protect Julian.

How utterly stupid and futile that was.

As they neared the plane—a sleek corporate jet gleaming under the moonlight—Aurelia gripped the armrest, her voice tight with urgency. "Won't you let me stay and be a decoy? If Jessica's husband realised that I'm the person—"

"No." His tone brooked no argument, flat and final.

Her chest tightened. That single word confirmed what she had been afraid to admit: *he wanted her gone.* He wanted to be with Jessica, to make sure the woman he truly loved was safe. She was just a substitute, a placeholder for someone far more important.

She opened her mouth to protest, but his palm covered her hand, firm and unyielding. "No. It's simply not an option. Don't even think of it."

Inside the cabin, she stood still, hollowed out, small and inconsequential. Julian's shadowed gaze fell on her, a quiet intensity that made her stomach twist. "You weren't responsible for your friend Karen's tragedy. Nothing you could have done would have prevented it."

"I know that," she said too quickly, her voice brittle.

"Intellectually, yes, of course you do," he said, low, almost dark. "But when you were telling me about it, you sounded as though you still feel you should have noticed something, anything, that might have changed what happened. Survivors guilt. Useless. Poison."

She swallowed hard, forcing her gaze downward, painfully aware of the truth in his words. "I know," she murmured.

"Do exactly as my security man instructs you," he said, voice firm, clipped, leaving no room for argument. "And don't leave the apartment until I tell you it's safe."

She nodded, though her limbs felt heavy, as if the very air between them had turned to stone. Her eyes followed him as he strode to the door, each step radiating that infuriating, unshakable confidence. No backward glance. No pause. No word of comfort, no gentle touch—nothing to bridge the chasm he'd placed between them.

A hollow ache uncoiled in her chest, tight and relentless. She wanted to reach for him, to pull him back and refuse to let him go—but even imagining that felt impossible, as though he existed on a plane entirely apart from her own fragile, trembling world.

The memory of their closeness—his hands, his lips, the heat of him pressed to her— pounded against the stark cold of his absence. Every step he took toward the door felt like a hammer driving home the truth: Julian Kingsley did not soften, did not linger, did not offer consolation.

And yet... a part of her burned with a stubborn, desperate hope. Maybe, somewhere beneath the flawless control, he cared. Maybe behind that steel façade was a man capable of tenderness—but for now, she was left with only the echo of his authority and the storm of need and longing he had stirred inside her.

When he disappeared through the door, a shiver of emptiness ran through her. She exhaled slowly, trying to gather herself, but the truth was undeniable: he had left, and in doing so, he had left her entirely wanting.

A steward appeared, silent and efficient. "This way, Miss Carmichael."

Her legs felt like lead as she followed, every step a reminder of the widening chasm between her and Julian. The seat on the jet was indulgently plush, the cabin immaculate, but Aurelia noticed none of it. She allowed the steward to tuck her in, fasten the seatbelt, offer food, and drink she refused—and then vanish into the shadows of the cockpit, leaving her utterly alone.

The engines thrummed beneath her, deep and insistent, a vibrating promise of flight, and she pressed her forehead to the cool window, watching Kaliah Island's lights shrink into the night. Her chest ached with fear, longing, and a hollow despair that made each mile feel heavier than the last.

Hours dragged, each one merciless in its silence. Her thoughts clung to Julian—his presence, the island, the dangers lurking in that tropical paradise he called home. She could do nothing, only sit, helpless, suspended in a world that had suddenly lost all meaning. Every heartbeat whispered his name; every nerve throbbed with a desperate wish to protect him, to be near him, even when reason insisted she could not.

She was alone, yes—but her heart remained tethered to him: resilient, stubborn, unyielding. Despite the distance, despite the danger, despite every rational argument she hurled at herself, one truth cut through her with quiet, merciless precision: Julian would go to Jessica. Jessica—the woman he loved. The woman whose shadow Aurelia had unknowingly been living in from the start.

And she… she was merely the echo of something that could never be. A stand-in. A resemblance. A fleeting, foolish interlude in a life infinitely larger than hers.

The ache in her chest sharpened, twisting like a knife. How had she been so reckless, so disastrously hopeful? Falling for the billionaire—her billionaire—was the most foolish thing she had ever done. And yet, she could no more unlove him than she could stop breathing.

That was the cruellest truth of all.

Chapter Thirteen

Three days later, the penthouse phone rang. Aurelia snatched it up, hope flaring painfully—only to freeze at the sound of Julian's voice.

Muted. Bleak. Emotionless.

"What—what's happened?" she asked, gripping the receiver.

He exhaled, the sound faint, almost impatient. "He's dead."

No preamble, no softening. Just flat fact.

"He didn't manage to kill Jessica—that was obviously his intention. She's… shaken." A brief pause. "Emotionally," he clarified, briskly, as though anticipating her alarm. "No, he didn't touch her. And his death was accidental, which simplifies matters."

Aurelia's stomach dropped. "How—how did he die?" Her voice felt thin, brittle.

"He drowned during a swim," Julian said, tone stripped to its bones. "We have boats searching for the body."

"I see." The words scraped out, barely audible. She pressed the receiver harder against her cheek, clinging to the moment even as it hollowed her out.

What now?

She knew.

She would disappear. Quietly. Without fuss. Just as he clearly intended.

"I can't get back to Sydney immediately," Julian went on, his voice clipped, impersonal. "Stay in the penthouse until I contact you again."

She wanted to ask something—anything—but the cold precision in his voice left no room, no foothold, no space for her heart. She swallowed. "I… hope everything works out well for you," she whispered, though the words wavered with emotion she could no longer hide.

"I hope so, too," he said shortly. Then, without hesitation: "I have to go. Take care, Aurelia."

"You, too."

It was all she could manage before the line clicked dead.

She sat there, the receiver lowering slowly from her ear, her hands trembling uncontrollably.

He was gone—

in voice, in presence,

and, worst of all,

in all the ways that mattered.

A couple of hours later, the penthouse phone rang again.

Aurelia flew to it—heart pounding, breath catching—because this time, surely, surely, it would be Julian. She needed his voice like oxygen, needed something—anything— to hold on to.

"Hello?" she breathed.

But the voice that answered wasn't his.

It wasn't even kind.

"Aurelia."

A woman. Cool. Elegant. Edged like glass.

"Yes?" Aurelia whispered, hope splintering into something sharp and trembling.

"This is Jessica Riordan."

Aurelia's heart lurched violently. She had imagined Jessica frightened… fragile… grateful.

But this voice?

This voice could cut marble.

"I—I'm glad you're okay," Aurelia managed, trying and failing to steady her breathing.

"Yes, thank you." Jessica's tone didn't change—still smooth, still indifferent. "I just wanted to tell you… your services are no longer required."

Aurelia went completely still. Her brain simply… stopped.

"I—I'm sorry… what do you mean?"

Jessica exhaled softly, almost bored. "Julian didn't want to tell you. He feels guilty about the whole thing. But really, you've served your purpose. You lured my husband into the open—exactly the way he hoped you would."

Aurelia's heart didn't just drop—it plummeted, smashing into something jagged inside her.

"No," she whispered, gripping the receiver until her fingers throbbed. "No, Julian would never—he wouldn't use me like that."

A soft pause.

And then Jessica laughed.

It wasn't a pleasant laugh. Not amused.

It was a knife.

A clean, cold blade sliding straight between Aurelia's ribs.

"Oh, Aurelia," Jessica murmured, pitying and vicious all at once. "He did. He told me everything. He loves me. He just... lost his head for a moment, that's all. He regrets it now."

A sound escaped Aurelia—somewhere between a gasp and a choke. Her knees buckled, and she braced a hand against the wall to keep upright. The room heaved around her, blurring into meaningless shapes.

Julian's touch, his kiss, his tenderness—

—all of it twisted into humiliation, a cruel illusion she had walked blindly into.

She had been nothing.

A placeholder.

A substitute for the woman he wanted.

Expendable.

Interchangeable.

A mistake.

"I... I see," she forced out, though her voice was a shattered whisper.

"Oh, don't take it personally," Jessica said sweetly, her cruelty coated in honey. "You're not the first woman who's tried to distract him."

And she laughed again—that same brittle, triumphant slice of sound—

before the line went dead.

The receiver slipped from Aurelia's numb fingers, clattering against the polished floor. She stared at it, unable to breathe, unable to swallow, unable to feel anything except the brutal implosion of her own heart.

Then the pain struck.

It hit with such ferocity that she folded where she stood, sinking onto the sofa as if her bones had liquefied. Her breath tore from her in ragged sobs. She pressed her hands to her face, her chest, anything to stop the agony from ripping her apart—but there was no stopping it.

Tears poured down her cheeks. Hot, relentless, unending.

Her shoulders shook. Her throat burned.

The sound of her own grief filled the room—raw, broken, utterly unrestrained.

Julian was gone.

He had chosen Jessica.

And she had been discarded without a second's hesitation.

When the sobs finally ran dry, she felt hollow—scraped out, emptied, barely human. Her entire body ached, her eyes stung, her heart throbbed with a pain so deep it felt carved into her bones.

A cold clarity seeped in, settling like frost.

She couldn't stay here.

Not in this penthouse that still carried the faint echo of his scent.

Not surrounded by every reminder that her love had been foolish, one-sided, doomed from the start.

She had to leave.

Not tomorrow.

Not later.

Now.

Before she shattered again.

Setting her jaw, she scrubbed her face with trembling hands and forced herself into motion. If she kept still, she would fall apart again. Action was the only thing keeping her upright.

The first hurdle was the man assigned to watch over her—the quiet, competent bodyguard who had been her silent shadow for the past three torturous days.

She found him in the dining area, tidying away the breakfast things. "Have you heard from Mr. Kingsley?" she asked, keeping her tone light, almost casual, as though her world hadn't just been ripped in two.

"Yes, I have," he said, looking up at her. His eyes softened with concern the moment he saw her face. "I'm to put myself at your disposal." He hesitated. "Are you quite all right, Miss Carmichael?"

She summoned a thin, brittle smile—the best she could manage. "Yes. Yes, of course. I'm fine." The lie tasted like ash. "This means the danger's passed now, doesn't it? You can go home. You won't miss your daughter's birthday tomorrow after all."

His concern deepened. "Miss—are you sure—"

"Yes," she cut in, forcing a steadiness she didn't feel. "If you give me a contact number, I'll call if I need anything."

It was practical. It was reasonable.

And it would get him out of the way.

The sooner she was alone, the sooner she could disappear—quietly, efficiently, before anyone, especially Julian, decided to come looking.

He hesitated, then said thoughtfully, "I wasn't given explicit clearance to leave you, but… I can't see why I shouldn't take Anita to the zoo. She's been looking forward to it for weeks now."

"Great," Aurelia said, her voice light, but a stab of guilt cut through her relief.

Back in her bedroom, she surveyed the wardrobe Julian had filled with designer clothes and silk lingerie—luxuries she had no use for. Pride rebelled at the thought of wearing them, but necessity won. She packed the barest essentials into the smallest bag she had, items that would carry her through until she could earn her own way.

Stepping into the sitting room, she let her gaze roam over the impeccably furnished space. Like Julian's island home, it was a gilded prison, luxurious yet suffocating. It had driven her nearly mad with uncertainty, with waiting, with longing. Now, though, she didn't have to wonder what he was doing. He was with Jessica—laughing at her naivety, enjoying her affection, fulfilling the life she would never have. Worse, the memory of his hands, his lips—had he imagined Jessica when he made love to her? Nausea twisted in her stomach.

She picked up the newspaper, trying to distract herself. In the world section, a familiar name leapt from the page. Her pulse jumped as she recognised Jessica's husband—a man of prominence and wealth in European circles. Then she saw Jessica, the photograph was black and white, but the resemblance was unmistakable: the same mane of hair, the same features. Few would tell them apart from a distance.

Aurelia blinked fiercely, stanching swift, angry tears, and read the brief item. The man had suffered an accident while on holiday; his body had yet to be recovered. His wife was devastated, staying with friends for the time being.

"Just one friend," she murmured bleakly, giving the newspaper one last glance before setting it aside.

In a way, it confirmed what she had suspected ever since discovering her resemblance to Jessica. Julian's guarded, almost reverent way of speaking about the other woman now made cruel sense.

She walked to the bedroom she'd been given, overlooking the hotel courtyard. The manicured gardens meant nothing to her. She stared at her reflection in the mirror, seeing the remnants of a woman who had once allowed herself to believe in a possibility that was never hers.

Aurelia had been deluded to think Julian could care for her beyond convenience or compassion. *What could she offer him?* She had survived his social whirl, endured his world, yes—but only because he had been there, subtly guiding, supporting, correcting her missteps. Without him, she would have floundered, exposed, a fool. And worse— she would have sullied him with her incompetence.

Her thoughts turned bitterly to his family: tall, aristocratic, impossibly refined. They would never see her as suitable—not for love, not for marriage, not even for companionship. The word love seemed a distant, unattainable star, one she had glimpsed only in fleeting, forbidden moments. And the newspaper article—its crisp, public announcement—had reinforced Jessica's cruel, clinical truth: she had been nothing more than a temporary shadow in Julian's life, a substitute for the woman he truly loved.

Aurelia sat at the small desk, pen trembling in her hand, her heart heavy with a combination of gratitude, shame, and loss. She poured herself into words, every line a quiet act of farewell, every phrase a concession to the reality she could no longer deny.

Dear Mr. Kingsley,

By late afternoon the next day, Aurelia was settling into a modest motel. The place catered to long-term residents rather than tourists—far humbler than the penthouse she had briefly called home—but it marked the first step in reclaiming her life. At least she still had her debit card. Worthless on Kaliah Island, it now provided the small, steady independence she could cling to, enough cash to eat, to sleep under her own roof, and, slowly, to rebuild a life shattered in a matter of hours.

As she unpacked the few belongings she had brought, a hollow ache pressed against her ribs. Every object, every sound in the modest room whispered of what she had lost, of the world she could never return to. Yet beneath the heartbreak, a fragile ember of resolve glimmered: she would survive. She would endure. And perhaps, in time, she would learn to live without him.

She sat on the edge of the bed, exhausted but resolute, tracing her fingers along the hem of her sweater, trying to anchor herself. Julian was gone, Jessica had triumphed, and her heart lay in shards—but she would survive. Somehow, she would rebuild. The world had not broken her entirely, and she still had herself, her wits, and the faint glimmer of stubborn determination that refused to be extinguished.

"What do you mean she's gone?" Julian's voice tore through the humid air of Kaliah Island, sharp, dangerous, leaving no room for hesitation. The words were steel, slicing the night as he glared out over the sleeping island, the waves thrashing against the shore in angry rhythm.

The bodyguard swallowed hard. "Sir… you said the danger had passed. Miss Carmichael insisted I shouldn't miss my daughter's birthday, so I took her to the zoo. When I returned… she was gone. She left a note."

Julian's free hand curled into a fist, knuckles white. "A note? Send me a photo—now," he barked, fumbling for his phone. "Do you have any idea where she could have gone?"

"No, sir. But… she seemed upset the last time I spoke with her," the bodyguard said cautiously.

Julian slammed the phone onto the polished teak table. The crack of impact echoed like a gunshot in the still night, but it did nothing to calm the inferno raging inside him.

She had left. She had actually left.

His mind raced, every memory flashing like fire: the shy smile, the quick glance, the way her hand had brushed his. Every instinctive, fleeting closeness replayed in brutal, excruciating detail. And now she was gone. Alone.

He should have spoken. Should have told her how he felt, admitted what he'd known since the moment she arrived—how impossibly, irreversibly, she had claimed a part of him. Instead, he'd let duty, timing, and fear twist the truth into silence.

His phone buzzed: a message from his security man. Aurelia's letter.

He opened it. Formal. Detached. Every word a dagger. Every sentence a reminder of her absence, of her heartbreak. And then—the last line:

Jessica informed me of the current circumstances, and I wish you and her every happiness in the future.

Julian's vision blurred. His fingers gripped the phone until his nails bit into his palm.

Jessica.

The name alone sparked ice and fire in equal measure. The one who had manipulated, schemed, and poisoned the truth from the start. The one desperate to chain him to a past he had long since outgrown. The one who had stolen Aurelia from him with a carefully measured cruelty.

Fury carved every line of his face. Teeth clenched, jaw rigid, heart hammering. He stormed across the room, every step radiating wrath, phone in hand, and slammed it against the balcony railing. With deliberate, brutal precision, he punched in Jessica's number.

Jessica answered on the third ring, her voice a silken ribbon of composure—too smooth, too rehearsed. "Julian," she purred, as though she hadn't just hurled a grenade into his life.

"What," Julian said, low and deadly, each syllable forged in restrained violence, "did you tell her?"

A breath. A flicker. Jessica blinked audibly, surprise smothered beneath a practiced veneer. "Tell who—"

"Aurelia," he bit out, her name slicing the air. "What did you tell her about me?"

Silence pooled—thick, suffocating, waiting to break.

When Jessica finally spoke, her voice was delicate, poisonous. "I… only told her the truth."

Julian's jaw flexed, the fury coiling in him tightening like a snare. "The truth?" His voice was glacial, precise. "What truth?"

"That you regretted letting me go," Jessica said sweetly, each word dipped in venom. "That you still love me. That you're only pretending with her—because you're confused. And because I'm the woman you truly want."

Julian's stomach dropped, a tidal surge of disbelief crashing through him.

Jessica pressed on, sensing advantage. "Julian, she's nothing like us. She doesn't understand your world—your expectations, your responsibilities. You need a partner who matches you. Someone polished. Someone capable of standing beside you in every room that matters. Someone who won't embarrass you the moment the stakes rise." Her voice softened, coaxing, seductive. "Someone like me."

He felt sick.

"I could have helped you," she continued, voice thick with self-justified longing. "We were a perfect team once. You know we were. You need strength, sophistication, someone who knows how to navigate power. Aurelia can't give you that. But I can. I always could."

Julian's grip on the phone tightened until his knuckles blanched.

"No," he said flatly, the word lethal in its certainty. "You lied to her. You told her I loved you, knowing it wasn't true."

Jessica laughed—a sharp, brittle sound flaking at the edges. "Oh, Julian, please. You're only helping me because you still care. Because you love me. Why else would you protect me? Why else would you rescue me? No man goes this far unless—"

"Enough," he snapped.

The single word cracked like a gunshot.

"I have told you, repeatedly," he said, voice dropping into cold, controlled finality, "that I do not love you. I have never loved you. Not once. I am helping you because I will not stand by while someone gets hurt—not because of you." His tone hardened, cutting through her illusions with surgical precision. "Do not mistake basic humanity for affection."

Jessica faltered. "Julian… you can't mean that."

"I do." His voice became iron wrapped in velvet. "The only woman I have ever loved is Aurelia."

The confession cut through the space between them with irrevocable force.

Jessica inhaled sharply—a sound halfway between disbelief and devastation. "Julian—"

"No." His refusal sliced cleanly across her protest. "My head of security will be at the house within the hour to escort you off the island. You are not to contact me again. Do you understand?"

A small, broken pause.

"Yes… yes, of course. I—I didn't realise…"

He didn't wait for the rest.

His thumb slammed the screen, ending the call with a hard, decisive snap of sound— sharp as the final stroke of a blade, severing whatever hold she imagined she still had on him.

He swore under his breath, eyes blazing, and dialled Sam immediately.

"Sam."

"Sir?"

"Get Mrs. Riordan off the island. Immediately." His tone left no room for argument, no hint of hesitation.

"Yes, sir."

"Then we're going to Australia," Julian said, jaw tight, eyes cold with urgency. "Miss Carmichael has gone missing."

"What do you mean, sir?" Sam's voice tightened with concern.

"She left. On her own. I don't know where. I intend to find her," Julian said, each word clipped, dangerous, unstoppable.

Sam understood instantly. Ten years of service had taught him Julian's ways—he had never seen him like this: relentless, protective, impossibly focused on one woman. Miss Carmichael was that woman.

Julian's gaze swept over the sunlit expanse of Kaliah Island. Every cliff, lagoon, and shadowed path was etched in his mind—but none of it mattered. His thoughts had honed into a single point: *Where are you, Aurelia?*

Every heartbeat screamed the same truth: he would find her, no matter the cost.

By nightfall, Julian arrived at his parents' home. They had returned from their honeymoon only two days earlier, and he had already told them of his intentions—to marry Aurelia when circumstances allowed. He had admitted, without hesitation, that she was the one woman he could love with all his heart. His parents had rejoiced at the news, yet he had also explained why he had whisked her off the island: to protect her from Eddie Riordan. They had agreed he had done the right thing.

His mother greeted him with a warm kiss, but her eyes immediately caught the tension etched deep into his face. "Hello, sweetheart," she said softly. "Julian… what is it? You look… worried."

"It's Aurelia," he said, voice heavy with urgency and barely contained frustration.

Graham Kingsley entered, brow furrowed, his usual jovial curiosity tempered by unease. "What about her? When are we going to meet this remarkable woman, you plan to marry?"

Julian's shoulders stiffened. His mother's sharp, perceptive gaze searched his face. "Tell us, Julian. What's wrong?"

"She's gone," he said, teeth clenched, every muscle taut with frustration and fear.

"Gone? Gone where?" his father asked, stepping closer, worry shadowing his features.

Julian dragged a trembling hand through his hair, fury and fear tightening every line of his body. "Jessica lied to her," he said, his voice low and dangerous—cold enough to freeze the air in the room. "She told Aurelia that I was in love with her. That I regretted letting her go. That Aurelia was… a mistake."

His mother gasped, her hand flying to her mouth. "Oh, Julian… no."

Shock, grief, and something like maternal outrage flashed in her eyes.

Graham's face hardened, the controlled, formidable patriarch cracking just enough to reveal genuine alarm. "You mean she left because of that?" he demanded. "She believed Jessica?"

Julian's jaw clenched until the muscle jumped. "Yes. Of course she did." His voice dropped, hoarse. "Because I never told her otherwise."

Both his parents stilled.

His mother stepped closer, her voice softer but unyielding. "You never told her how you felt?"

There was disbelief there—gentle but accusing.

Julian exhaled sharply, pacing once before facing them again. "No. I didn't. Not clearly. Not in the way she needed to hear." His hands curled into fists at his sides. "I thought there would be time. I thought she knew."

His mother's eyes filled with pained sympathy—and the slightest hint of reproach. "Oh, Julian… how could she know, if you never said the words?"

He shook his head once, a violent, self-directed gesture. "I was a fool. And now—" His breath caught, raw and unrestrained. "Now she's alone. Hurt. And she thinks I never wanted her."

Graham stepped forward and gripped his son's shoulder, firm, grounding. "Then you fix this," he said, voice steady with Kingsley authority. "Whatever it takes, you find her. You bring her home."

Julian lifted his gaze to the dark windows, the night beyond them a vast, threatening unknown. Determination settled over him like armour—unyielding, absolute.

"I'm going to Australia," he said, voice low with conviction. "I have to find her. I will not lose her. Not now. Not ever."

Chapter Fourteen

"Aurelia, we need to talk."

Aurelia jumped at the sound of her employer's voice behind her. She froze, heart skipping a beat. Without turning, she nodded, forcing her voice to stay steady. "Yes—okay."

"Leave that for a moment and come into the staffroom."

She set down the box of biscuits she'd been stacking on the shelves and rose to her feet. The movement was too sudden; the room swirled around her, and the world pitched alarmingly. She shut her eyes, drawing slow, deliberate breaths until the dizziness eased. Fleeing Sydney for this quiet Queensland town had seemed sensible at the time—a place where no one knew her, where she could melt into the steady rhythm of everyday life, restocking shelves and helping in a small, provincial grocery store. Somewhere anonymous, somewhere she could simply… exist.

In the cluttered staffroom, Kath—the blunt, efficient, middle-aged woman who had hired her—filled the kettle with precise, purposeful movements. The rhythmic clink of metal against ceramic echoed softly in the small space. "I'm assuming you can still drink tea," she said dryly, without even glancing at Aurelia.

"I'm fine," Aurelia protested, though her voice sounded brittle, fragile even to her own ears.

"You're as white as a ghost," Kath said, finally setting the kettle down. She poured the steaming water with brisk, assured movements, the rising steam curling like ghostly fingers through the air. She pushed a mug toward Aurelia. "Who are you hiding from?"

Aurelia recoiled, nearly knocking the mug over. "What… do you mean?" she whispered, panic prickling her chest.

Kath's eyes were steady, sharp, unyielding. "It's obvious something is going on. You're always on edge. And just now, I spoke to a gentleman asking if I had seen a young lady in a photograph. It was you."

Aurelia's throat tightened. Her mind spun, racing. "Who… who was he?" she asked, forcing calm into her voice, though every fibre of her body screamed to run, to vanish.

"A private investigator," Kath said plainly, as though that explained everything. "He said he was looking for you."

The words hit her like a hammer. Her hands gripped the edge of the table until her knuckles ached. She struggled to steady her breathing, to quiet the rising panic.

Someone was looking for her. Someone had tracked her down—here, in this quiet town.

Kath poured herself a cup of tea and leaned back against the counter, eyes never leaving Aurelia. "You can't keep running forever," she said softly, almost gently. Then, tilting her head, she added, "When's the baby due?"

Aurelia blinked, shocked, her thoughts catching in her throat. She hadn't expected that, and for a moment, panic flared that Kath might dismiss her entirely.

"How…?" she whispered.

"I can see the signs, Aurelia," Kath said simply, matter of fact, unflinching.

Aurelia lifted her gaze, managing a ghost of a smile. "Until yesterday… I'd been pretending I wasn't pregnant."

"I know the feeling," Kath said wryly, a faint understanding in her tone. "But burying your head in the sand never helped anyone. Have you told the father?"

Aurelia shook her head. "No."

"Why not?"

"Because… he's involved with someone else," Aurelia said, and the moment the words left her lips, a fresh wave of pain and shame coursed through her. But then thought struck sharply—Julian might not even believe the baby is his, he would insist on a DNA test. When he finds out it is his child, he would insist on taking responsibility.

"Even so," Kath said quietly, "he has a right to know."

Panic hollowed out Aurelia's stomach. "I know," she whispered.

"Could the person looking for you be the father?" Kath asked carefully, her voice measured, probing yet gentle, as though testing the waters of Aurelia's guarded heart.

Aurelia's throat tightened. Her fingers clenched around the mug, leaving crescent-shaped indentations in the ceramic. "Most likely," she admitted, her voice barely above a whisper, trembling with the weight of truth she had long tried to bury.

"Well," Kath said, leaning slightly forward, her sharp eyes never leaving Aurelia's face, "then he would obviously want to know what has happened. He has a right to know, don't you think?"

Aurelia swallowed hard, the knot in her stomach tightening. Every instinct screamed to run, to disappear into the anonymity of this provincial town, but Kath's calm gaze held her in place. The truth settled around her like cold rain: hiding from him would only make matters worse, prolong the inevitable confrontation, and leave her with the gnawing ache of secrecy.

"Tell me honestly," Kath continued, her tone softening, "has he hurt you? Physically? Emotionally? Are you afraid of him?"

Aurelia's eyes widened, shock and disbelief flickering across her features. "No—no, of course not," she said quickly, almost defensively. Her heart pounded at the memory of him—his presence, his hands, his voice. He had never been anything but protective, steadfast, and unyielding in his care. Fear was not the right word. Reverence, longing, confusion—yes. But never fear.

Kath studied her for a long moment, the corners of her mouth tightening with thought. "Well then… why don't you want to be found?" she asked gently but insistently, cutting through the layers of avoidance Aurelia had wrapped around herself.

Aurelia's hands trembled, the mug rattling against the table as if echoing the storm inside her. Her voice came out barely audible, raw, almost confessional. "Because… I love him. And he… he loves someone else."

The words hung in the air like a fragile thread stretched taut between them. Kath didn't flinch, didn't judge; she simply let Aurelia speak her truth. "Ah," she said softly. "That makes it harder, doesn't it? Loving someone who can't—or won't—love you back. But hiding? Running? That won't keep your heart safe. It won't keep him from worrying, and it won't give your child a chance at knowing him either."

Aurelia's throat ached, and tears pricked at the corners of her eyes. She had told no one, not even herself, how much she longed for him, how painfully tethered she was to him even now, across miles and lies and impossible circumstances. Yet Kath's words cut through the panic like a lifeline.

"I… I can't," she whispered, shaking her head. "I can't just walk into his life, tell him everything. He's… he's with someone else. He's happy—or he should be. I have no right…"

"Stop thinking about what you have a right to," Kath said firmly, yet with an undercurrent of compassion. "Think about the truth. About responsibility. About your baby. You can't control his choices, Aurelia, but you can control honesty. And the longer you hide, the harder it becomes for all of you."

Aurelia pressed a hand to her forehead, trying to slow the torrent of thoughts, the ache of longing, the fear of rejection. "I… I don't know if I can," she admitted in a hoarse whisper, voice breaking under the weight of everything she had held inside for months.

Kath reached out, placing a steadying hand over hers. "You can. You're stronger than you think. And he… he's not a man who will turn his back on what's right. Not on the woman he cares about, not on the child he's responsible for. You have to trust that much."

Aurelia's chest tightened, every nerve alive with a mix of fear and hope. She had run, hidden, protected herself from disappointment—and yet, she knew Kath was right. She couldn't run forever. The truth would find its way out, and if she was going to survive this with any semblance of dignity, she had to act.

Taking a shuddering breath, Aurelia nodded faintly, the first spark of resolve igniting in her chest. "I... I'll call him," she said, voice trembling but determined. "I'll... tell him everything."

Kath gave a small, approving nod. "Good. Then do it now. Don't give yourself another night of worry and what-ifs. Call him. Let him know and let this... this waiting end."

Aurelia's hands trembled as she lifted the cheap, portable phone from its cradle. Her pulse hammered against her temples, each beat a reminder of the life growing inside her—and the man who did not know. Every digit she pressed felt impossibly heavy, as if she were imprinting her fears into the keys themselves. By the time the call began to ring, her breath was already thin and unsteady.

The only number she had was the penthouse. The one she had fled. The one that held every answer she had been too afraid to seek.

Six weeks had stretched between then and now—six weeks of silence, of hollow days, of nights spent listening to a heartbeat that was not her own. Six weeks of wondering whether she had meant anything to him at all... or whether she had been nothing more than a mistake he was grateful to forget.

The line clicked.

"Kingsley residence."

It was Sam. Calm. Controlled. But beneath the polished professionalism, she heard it— alertness. Concern.

Her throat went dry. "Sam?" she breathed, barely able to force the word out.

On the other end, Sam's eyes narrowed as he took in the scene before him, his instincts screaming. Julian had been searching for Aurelia Carmichael for six long, torturous weeks—weeks that had stretched every boundary of patience and control he had ever possessed. And Sam had never seen his always-in-command, unflappable employer like this: restless, tense, consumed with a need that bordered on desperation. Julian's composure, the ironclad mask he wore to command empires and enforce order, had cracked—exposed in glimpses of raw, unguarded obsession.

Sam's grip tightened on the phone. He could hear the tremor in her voice, and he knew Julian would move mountains to reach her. The thought tightened his chest, a mix of professional duty and something closer to fear. Julian Kingsley needed her, and no one—not even Sam—had ever witnessed the lengths he would go when it came to the woman who had quietly, irrevocably claimed his heart.

There was a pause. Then his voice sharpened with unmistakable recognition. "Miss Carmichael?" He sounded like a man who had just spotted smoke on the horizon.

"Yes," she whispered, fumbling the receiver as her heart pounded so hard she could feel each beat in her fingertips.

"Hold on, Miss. I'll get Mr. Kingsley."

Those few seconds stretched brutally—thin, taut, agonising. The small room around her seemed to close in, as if the air thickened with every silent heartbeat. *What if he refused? What if he didn't care? What if he had already moved on—married, committed, gone?*

Then—

"Aurelia?"

Her breath caught. The sound of her name in his voice unravelled her. Low. Precise. Edged with something that sounded like restraint pushed to breaking. She felt that single word all the way through her—an ache, a memory, a wound.

Her lips parted, and despite her best efforts at composure, his name slipped out in a trembling whisper.

"Julian…"

She hadn't meant for it to sound like a confession. But it did. It held everything she had tried to bury: the longing, the fear, the hurt, the love she had no right to feel—and yet couldn't silence.

He inhaled sharply. Just a breath. But it told her everything.

"Aurelia…" His voice was low, rough, and frayed around the edges. "Where… where are you?"

The question struck her like a physical blow.

"In—Queensland," she managed. Her voice cracked, her shame and exhaustion bleeding through every syllable. She clutched the phone with both hands as though it were the only solid thing in the room.

A beat. Not long—but long enough for her stomach to twist.

"Is someone there with you?" he asked, clipped and alert. Protective in a way that made her throat tighten.

"Yes. My employer."

His tone changed instantly. Steeled. Commanding. "Put them on."

Aurelia swallowed hard and handed the phone to Kath, whose eyes widened in surprise but took it without hesitation.

"Hello?" Kath said, wary.

There was a pause—then her expression shifted into something startled and sharply respectful. "Yes, Mr. Kingsley. She's safe with me. Yes, she works here." Another beat, then her eyebrows shot upward. "No, she won't go anywhere. I'll make sure of it." A pause. "Of course. I understand."

Kath gave the address, sounding suddenly as if she were speaking to royalty. When she handed the phone back, her expression held an astonished sort of awe.

"He wants you," she murmured.

Aurelia took the phone with shaking fingers. Her mouth felt chalk-dry.

"Julian?" she whispered.

"Aurelia." His voice—God, that voice—rolled through her, low and urgent and barely controlled, as if he were speaking through clenched teeth. "Listen to me. You stay where you are. Do you understand? Don't move. Don't leave. I need your word."

Her breath stuttered. Her knees felt weak. Everything inside her—fear, longing, the tiny heartbeat she carried—pulled tight and trembling.

"Yes," she whispered. "I—I promise."

Silence followed. Not empty—charged. Heavy. Full of something that made her chest burn.

Then his voice came again, raw, and unguarded in a way she had never heard from him.

"Aurelia... hold on. I'm coming to you."

Her heart lurched violently, a painful swell of relief and terror and hope surging through her. Her fingers tightened around the receiver until it creaked. Tears burned fiercely in her eyes, but she refused to let them fall—not yet.

He was coming.

For her.

After everything—after the distance, the silence, the impossible gulf between their worlds—

He was coming.

And for the first time in weeks, she felt something fragile and incandescent break open inside her.

Hope.

Her knees threatened to give way, and she pressed her hand to the edge of the table, grounding herself. Kath stepped closer, steadying her with a firm, warm hand on her arm.

"He's coming, then?" Kath asked gently, her eyes wide with awe and disbelief. "Julian Kingsley? The Kaliah Island Kingsley's?"

Aurelia nodded, barely able to speak. "Yes..." Her voice was nothing more than a trembling sigh.

Kath gave a low whistle, shaking her head in quiet amazement. "Well... he'll be here within a couple of hours; you can be certain of that."

Aurelia nodded again, her body trembling, her heart still hammering so fiercely it felt as if it might burst. She pressed the phone to her chest, closing her eyes, and let herself imagine the impossible: Julian, finally, coming for her—through every obstacle, every lie, every danger.

Yes. He was coming.

But that didn't mean anything. Not really.

Aurelia's pulse fluttered wildly, that awful combination of longing and dread tangling in her chest. He could be coming because he felt something... or simply because she had walked out of his penthouse like a fool and he wanted to make sure she hadn't collapsed somewhere. Julian Kingsley was a man who took responsibility seriously. Duty came before everything else—including, she suspected, his own happiness.

Aurelia prayed she would not see Jessica. She couldn't bear it. Not today. Not when she was already stretched thin with worry and morning sickness and that piercing, impossible love that refused to die no matter how firmly she tried to starve it.

But she had to tell him about the baby.

Her hand drifted to her stomach, fragile protectiveness curling through her like a whisper. The baby. Julian's baby.

Her throat tightened as if someone had tied a silk ribbon around it and slowly pulled.

He had a right to know.

Even if knowing would change nothing for her. Even if it cost her the last pieces of her heart.

The moment the line went dead, Julian stood frozen, the phone still clutched in his hand, his pulse hammering so violently he could feel it in his teeth.

Aurelia's voice—thin, trembling, afraid—echoed through him like a blade.

"Julian…"

"Yes… I—I promise."

God. He'd heard fear in people before—rage, pain, panic—but the sound of her fear, directed at him, because of him, carved straight through his chest.

He dragged a breath into his lungs—sharp, unsteady, almost painful.

Six weeks.

Six long, blistering, gut-wrenching weeks he had searched for her, waking and sleeping with the same questions grinding through him like stone:

Where is she?

Is she safe?

Does she hate me?

He'd scoured the entire country, called in favours from people who normally demanded ministers or heads of state before even returning a message. His staff had never seen him like this—relentless, unshaven, sleepless, consumed. The press whispered about his "uncharacteristic disappearance from society." His father had stepped in to manage the corporation, while his parents watched their son unravel over a woman, they now understood he could not bear to live without.

He didn't care.

He hadn't cared about anything except finding her.

And now—now he had finally heard her voice again.

Fragile. Uncertain. Holding herself together by what sounded like the last thread she possessed.

His throat closed.

He lifted his gaze to Sam's expectant face.

"Organise the jet. We're going to Queensland," Julian said, the words flint-sharp. "I want to leave the moment I step on board."

Sam was already dialling, already moving. By the time they reached the front of Kingsley Tower, a car waited for them—engine running, door open. Sam slid in beside him, posture straight, eyes hard with the quiet concern of a man who had witnessed every step of Julian's unravelling.

"We're going to get her?" he asked.

Julian swallowed, hard. "Yes."

Relief flickered across Sam's face—but he didn't smile. He'd seen too much of the torment, the sleepless nights, the frantic dead ends. He'd watched Julian Kingsley— always controlled, always unshakable—come terrifyingly close to breaking.

"Is she safe?" Sam pressed.

"For now." Julian raked a hand through his hair, adrenaline twisting everything inside him too tightly. "But she sounded… terrified, Sam. Exhausted. Alone. And I let her be alone for weeks." His voice roughened, the truth scraping raw. "I'm the one who drove her away."

Sam didn't contradict or comfort him. It wasn't his way. Julian didn't want comfort. Only action. Only her.

Losing Aurelia had nearly broken him.

Hearing her voice today had snapped something back into place and set something else ablaze inside him all at once.

Aurelia Carmichael was not a responsibility. Not a duty.

She was—*God help him*—his.

And he was going to her.

To fight for her.

To finally give her the truth he should have told her from the very beginning.

He loved her.

When the plane door sealed shut behind him and the engines roared to life, Julian strapped himself into his seat and exhaled a single, fierce vow into the charged silence:

"Hold on, Aurelia. I'm coming. And this time… I'm not letting anything tear you away from me."

Not fear.

Not lies.

Not Jessica.

Not even fate itself.

Nothing.

Because now that he finally understood the truth burning inside him—

Aurelia wasn't just the woman he loved.

She was the woman he would cross oceans for, challenge nations for—

the woman he would break himself for if that's what it took.

And this time, he intended to bring her home.

A little over two hours later, a sleek black limousine slid to the curb outside the shop, its glossy surface catching the sunlight like a warning. Aurelia flinched, as though the vehicle itself were a judgment rendered.

Kath leaned in, voice low and sharp. "Tell me—has he ever hurt you? In any way? I need the truth." Her eyes searched Aurelia's, fierce and unwavering.

Aurelia shook her head, almost violently. "I swear on my mother's memory, he hasn't. Never." Her throat tightened. "It's just… I love him. And he doesn't love me. He's with someone else."

Kath's expression softened, a flash of warmth amid her usual pragmatism. "Oh, sweetheart… don't give up yet." She angled her chin toward the street. Julian was striding toward them, every step purposeful, every muscle coiled, his eyes sweeping the space as if searching for the one thing that truly mattered. "You are a good woman, Aurelia. And he wants you—whatever he thinks right now, you've got a hold on him. You can build from that."

Aurelia wanted more than a foothold. She wanted his heart—whole, uncompromised, hers—and nothing less. The thought tightened in her chest like a vice.

Then Julian was inside. His gaze found her immediately, and the world seemed to tilt. The tension in his shoulders dropped, his breath came a little faster, and relief softened the hard lines of his face.

"Aurelia," he breathed, crossing the shop in three long, determined strides. He wrapped her in his arms without hesitation. "Thank God. I've been worried sick."

Her pulse skyrocketed. Relief, heat, disbelief—all collided in a dizzying rush. She pressed into him instinctively, inhaling the warm, steady scent of him. For the first time in days, she felt anchored. Alive.

He pulled back just enough to study her face, eyes sharp yet softened by concern. "What the hell have you been doing to yourself?" His voice was low, almost reverent, threaded with exasperation. "You look… wrecked."

"Maybe worry and exhaustion had something to do with it," Kath muttered dryly.

Julian shot her a lightning-fast glare. "What's she been doing?"

"Working. And fretting," Kath said. "Mostly fretting."

"I'm fine," Aurelia whispered—but her words cracked under the storm of his gaze. The raw mix of fury, protectiveness, and love in his expression stole her voice.

Then Julian tilted the corner of his mouth in that infuriating, small smile—one that softened the edges of everything around him. Even Kath blinked, caught off guard by its warmth.

"Thank you for taking her in," he said, his tone shifting to quiet, steady appreciation. "She won't be returning to work, but if I can help you find someone—"

"That's thoughtful, but unnecessary," Kath interjected, flustered despite herself. "Just… take care of her."

"I will," Julian said, and Aurelia felt the weight of the promise in his voice, sharp and intimate, stirring something deep inside her. Her throat burned, her chest swelled, and for the first time in weeks, the world felt like it had tilted back into place—because he was here, and he was hers to hold—for a little while at least.

Chapter Fifteen

Ten minutes later, Aurelia sat beside him in the back of the hire car. An hour after that, she was on his private jet, Sydney-bound—her life tilting as efficiently and coldly as the aircraft banking through the clouds. She barely spoke, too overwhelmed, too uncertain—about his intentions, about Jessica, about how to confess the tiny heartbeat growing inside her.

Julian's arm was always around her—once in the limousine, again on the jet—clinging as though the mere act of letting go would make her vanish forever. She didn't dare lean fully into him. Hope was a fragile, dangerous thing.

Was he happy to see her? Or just relieved she hadn't plunged off some invisible cliff? And Jessica… was she waiting in Sydney? Would Julian push Aurelia back into the penthouse as if she were merely a complication to manage?

By the time they landed, her thoughts were a storm she couldn't still. Courage scraped itself together inside her.

"I can't go to your penthouse," she whispered.

Julian's gaze snapped to her, brow tightening, jaw clenched. "Why?"

"I can't… Jessica," she admitted softly, the name tasting like defeat.

"Aurelia, listen to me—" he began, but the car was already pulling up to the building's private entrance.

She inhaled, bracing for the doors to open—

A sudden, violent crack split the night.

Glass exploded into a glittering storm.

A searing heat tore across her temple. In a single heartbeat, it felt as though molten metal had been poured through her skull. Blood welled hot and immediate, slicking her fingers before she even registered the pain.

The world lurched sideways, reduced to the vivid smear of red on her palm and Julian's eyes—wide, unflinching, and utterly terrified.

"Julian…" she whispered, barely audible.

Darkness slammed into her like a collapsing wall.

All hell erupted outside the limousine.

Julian lunged over her, pressing his hands against the wound. Blood seeped through his fingers, staining his cuffs crimson, but he didn't care. His voice—raw, ragged, barely controlled—shattered the chaos around them.

"Don't... don't you dare leave me, Aurelia! Don't you dare!" His hands shook violently, pressing desperately against her head, as though sheer force could keep her alive. "Open your eyes! Look at me! Please, look at me!"

Sam was already out of the vehicle, gun drawn, shouting, "GET DOWN!"

Gunfire erupted. The back window shattered completely under Eddie Riordan's shots. Julian threw himself fully over Aurelia, his body a shield, every muscle taut, every heartbeat pounding in terror.

Two sharp, decisive cracks echoed. Sam's bullets struck true, dropping Eddie hard onto the pavement. But Julian didn't breathe. He didn't move. All that existed was Aurelia, bleeding, and unconscious against him.

"Aurelia—" His voice broke, raw with panic. "Stay with me! Don't leave me! You hear me?"

Her head lolled against his shoulder, blood still oozing, her skin ghostly in the dim light. Julian pressed harder, fighting the flow with trembling hands, sheer desperation coursing through every nerve.

The rear door swung open, cold air and chaos flooding in.

"Mr. Kingsley—are you okay?" Sam demanded, breathless, scanning the scene.

Julian didn't look at him. "Don't... don't worry about me! Aurelia's been hit!" His voice cracked, a high-pitched tremor slicing through the night.

Sam's face hardened. He barked into his phone with ruthless efficiency: "Yes, gunshot wound—female, mid-twenties. She's unconscious, bleeding heavily. We're outside Kingsley Tower private entrance—send police and paramedics. Now!"

Julian's chest heaved. Every second she stayed unconscious felt like an eternity. He pressed his hands harder, whispering her name over and over, each syllable raw, frantic, pleading—terrified that if she left him even for a heartbeat, it would be forever.

Movement swelled around them. People spilled out of nearby cars and from the security desk, drawn to the scene by the sound of gunfire and the shattered limousine windows. Voices rose in a panicked chorus—gasps, questions, someone crying, someone shouting that they'd seen the shooter fire his weapon. A security guard attempted to push the crowd back, yelling for space, for calm, for distance.

Julian couldn't hear any of it. The world had narrowed to the lifeless slump of Aurelia's body against his chest and the terrifying silence where her voice should have been.

"Aurelia, please," he murmured, brushing hair back from her blood-matted temple with a shaking hand. "Stay with me. I'm right here. Stay with me."

She didn't move. Her lashes didn't flutter. Her breathing—God, was she even breathing?

For a split second he thought the world stopped.

Then—

"Ambulance! They're here!" someone shouted.

Red and blue lights strobed against the glossy entrance of the tower. The sirens—loud now, overwhelming—cut through the crowd as paramedics rushed toward the limousine, equipment bags in hand.

"Step back, sir. We've got her."

But Julian didn't loosen his grip until a paramedic physically guided his blood-soaked hand away.

He tried to stand and nearly buckled. He steadied himself on the doorframe, face white, eyes wild.

As the paramedics slid their hands beneath Aurelia, fitting a collar around her neck and lifting her onto a board, Julian's heart hammered in his throat.

"I'm coming with her," he said hoarsely. "I'm not leaving her. She's not—she can't—"

Words failed him entirely.

They loaded her into the ambulance, attaching monitors, cutting open her sleeve, checking her pulse, applying pressure with professional force where his desperate hands had failed.

"BP dropping—let's move!" one paramedic snapped.

Julian climbed in immediately, ignoring protocol, ignoring Sam's attempts to talk to him. His entire body trembled as he watched them work on Aurelia, watched the rise, and fall of her chest, faint and fragile, watched the blood that continued to seep through the bandages.

"Aurelia," he whispered again, barely audible over the engine starting and the paramedic's rapid orders. "Stay with me. Please... stay with me."

Sam watched Julian climb into the back of the ambulance without hesitation, the doors slamming shut behind him with a finality that made Sam's chest tighten. For a moment, he simply stood there, heart hammering, adrenaline screaming through his veins. Then training snapped back into place.

He yanked his phone from his pocket and called another bodyguard.

"Get to St Vincent's—now," Sam barked, voice sharp, clipped. "Kingsley's already en route with Miss Carmichael. I need eyes on them the second they arrive."

"Yes, sir," came the reply, and the line went dead.

Police sirens converged, officers spilling onto the scene, shouting orders, taking statements. Sam knew he couldn't leave yet—not until the scene was secured, not until he'd accounted for shots fired, an attempted assassination, and a civilian injured. But there was one call that had to come first.

He dialled Graham Kingsley.

Graham answered on the second ring. "Sam?" A beat, then the chaos bled through the line. "What the hell is going on?"

Sam drew a steadying breath. "Sir… there's been an incident. Miss Carmichael has been shot. The shooter was Eddie Riordan."

A harsh, disbelieving curse erupted. "What? I thought he was dead."

"He is now, sir," Sam said grimly. "But until ten minutes ago, he was very much alive."

A sharp gasp, the clatter of someone moving quickly, and then a voice—refined, panicked, trembling. Heidi Kingsley.

"Graham—what did he say? Sam, is Julian hurt? Is Aurelia—oh God, is she alive?"

Sam's tone softened just enough to keep calm from fraying entirely. "Mrs. Kingsley, Julian is unharmed. Miss Carmichael is alive but unconscious, and she's lost a significant amount of blood. They're en route to St Vincent's. The paramedics are working on her."

Through the phone, he heard Graham bark precise orders—someone to prepare the car, someone to ready the jet, another to call the hospital. Even shaken, Graham Kingsley was a man of action, steel, and instinct.

Then Graham's voice dropped, low and unsteady in a way Sam had rarely heard. "Tell Julian we're coming. He's not alone in this. Neither is she."

Heidi's voice broke through again, trembling but resolute. "Sam, keep us updated every five minutes. Every five. We're leaving now."

"Yes, ma'am," Sam replied.

"We'll be there as soon as we can," she continued, voice breaking with both fear and determination. "Make sure Julian stays with her. Don't let him out of that hospital."

"I won't, ma'am," Sam assured her.

He hung up, the weight of responsibility settling over him like armour—solid, cold, unyielding. The ambulance had already vanished into the night, swallowed by traffic and sirens, carrying Julian and the woman he had thrown himself over without hesitation. The woman he held as if losing her would mean the end of him.

Sam's jaw tightened. There was no room for error now. No room for anything except keeping Julian and Aurelia alive—and together.

Police lights strobed across the street, casting blue, and red flashes over the ruined limousine. The back window was blown out entirely. Glass glittered across the pavement like frost. Uniformed officers were shouting instructions, cordoning off the area, pushing back the small crowd that had gathered—curious, frightened, murmuring in disbelief.

Multiple voices clamoured for answers.

"Was anyone else hit?"

"Who fired the shots?"

"Is that Julian Kingsley's car?"

"Did you see the shooter?"

Sam ignored the noise. He had been in enough high-threat situations to shut the world out when he needed to.

He squared his shoulders. Focused. Calculated.

He knew exactly what time it was and what it meant. Mr and Mrs Kingsley—Graham and Heidi—were still on Kaliah Island. Even travelling by private jet, they were at least three hours away from Sydney. Three hours in which Julian would be terrified and furious and barely holding it together. Three hours in which Aurelia's life would hang in the balance.

Three hours Sam would need to manage alone.

He exhaled once, controlled, and steady.

First step: give his statement.

Second: secure the scene, cooperate with forensics, hand over his and Eddie Riordan's weapon.

Third: ensure the building's security was tightened to lockdown-level protocols.

And only then—only then—would he head to the hospital.

Because tonight wasn't over.

Not by a long shot.

And Sam intended to be exactly where Julian needed him the moment everything began to unravel.

The ambulance roared through the streets of Sydney, tyres splashing through puddles from an earlier rain. Red and blue lights streaked past buildings, reflecting off wet asphalt, and sirens screamed in a relentless wail that seemed almost in sync with Julian's racing heartbeat.

Inside, the paramedics moved with practiced precision, checking monitors, adjusting oxygen masks, and preparing an IV line. Aurelia lay still on the stretcher, her head cushioned, hair matted with blood, her face pale under the harsh interior lights. Each breath she took was shallow, fragile, and Julian's fingers refused to release hers.

"She looks stable for now," one paramedic said, voice clipped but calm. "Vitals are steady. The bullet only grazed her skull. No penetration. No internal injury."

Julian's eyes burned with a mixture of relief and panic. "Only grazed her?" His voice was tight, almost breaking. "Then… why isn't she awake?" His hands clenched around hers like a lifeline. "Why isn't she opening her eyes?"

The paramedics exchanged a glance. "Shock, blood loss, trauma… her body's protecting itself. She's unconscious to stabilise her brain. That's a good sign," one of them explained. "She's alive, sir. That's what matters. Stay with her."

Julian nodded stiffly, unwilling to tear his gaze from her pale, serene face. "I—I'm right here, Aurelia," he whispered, pressing his forehead lightly against the side of her temple. "You hear me? You're going to be okay. Don't you dare leave me."

The streets blurred past in a streak of colour and sound. Every bump in the road made his stomach drop, every screech of tires behind another car jolt his panic. His mind refused to quiet, running through worst-case scenarios in rapid-fire succession.

Then, in the distance, the lights of St Vincent's Hospital came into view. The ambulance neared the entrance, and the back doors were flung open even before they stopped. Nurses and doctors rushed toward them, equipment already in hand, voices shouting instructions that cut through the wail of the siren.

"Move her quickly!" one paramedic shouted. "Trauma bay is ready!"

The team lifted Aurelia from the stretcher with swift, precise movements, hands steady despite the urgency. Julian followed immediately, fingers still entwined with hers, body bent protectively over hers as if even the slightest separation might tear her from him. The fluorescent lights of the hospital cut through the ambulance doors, harsh and stark, illuminating every strand of matted hair, every smear of blood, and the delicate, shallow rise and fall of her chest.

A nurse stepped forward, placing a firm hand on Julian's arm. "Sir, you can't go any further. We'll call you as soon as we've assessed her."

Julian froze, panic coiling in his chest like a living thing. "No," he said hoarsely, voice breaking. "I—I need to stay with her. She—she can't be alone."

The nurse's eyes were calm but unyielding. "She won't be alone. The doctor and the team will be with her every second. We need you to stay here. You'll see her as soon as it's safe."

Julian's hand clenched around air for a moment, then reluctantly let go. His fingers itched for contact as he watched the paramedics wheel her into the emergency department. Each step they took seemed unbearably slow, each flash of their movements magnifying his helplessness. He sank into a chair in the waiting area, his hands clasped tightly together, the minutes stretching impossibly long.

Time lost all meaning. The constant beeping of monitors and distant echoes of hospital activity became a blur. Julian's mind replayed the image of her lying limp in his arms— hair matted with blood, face pale, chest rising and falling in fragile, shallow rhythm. He couldn't bear to imagine her not waking.

It felt like hours before a doctor finally approached, clipboard in hand, expression serious but controlled. Julian rose immediately, heart hammering. "Mr. Kingsley?" the doctor said.

"Yes," Julian breathed, voice tight. "How… how is she?"

The doctor took a deep breath. "Aurelia Carmichael sustained a scalp graze from a bullet. The projectile did not penetrate the skull, and there's no internal brain injury. Right now, she's unconscious due to a combination of shock and the blood loss. Her vitals are stable, but she's fragile, and we need to monitor her very closely before we attempt to wake her."

Julian swallowed hard, gripping the edge of his chair. "How long... how long will she be like this?"

The doctor hesitated, then gave a careful answer. "It's difficult to say exactly. Each person responds differently. Some patients regain consciousness within an hour or two, others longer. The important thing is that she's alive and her brain isn't damaged. Right now, we're keeping her sedated lightly and observing her neurological responses. She may drift in and out for several hours before fully waking."

Julian's chest tightened. "So, she could be... hours?"

"Yes," the doctor said gently. "And it's essential she remains calm and still. Any sudden movement or stress could worsen the bleeding. We're doing everything we can to support her."

Julian's hands twitched, clenched together as he took a deep breath. "I—I just... I need to be with her."

The doctor nodded. "You'll be allowed as soon as we get her settled in a room. Right now, you need to stay here. We'll call you the moment you can see her or if anything changes."

Julian sank back into the chair, fists still tight, eyes fixed on the double doors of the trauma bay. He felt as if every tick of the clock stretched into eternity. Hours—or what felt like hours—stretched before him, each second a torment of hope and fear.

Soon after, Julian was finally allowed to sit with Aurelia. He took her hand in his, holding it as if the mere touch could anchor her to life. Nurses moved efficiently around them, checking monitors, adjusting IVs, and keeping her head elevated just so. Her pulse was steady—weak but rhythmic. Her breaths were shallow, even, each one a fragile whisper of life. She lay serene, almost delicate, and Julian's chest ached with a sharp, relentless worry.

He leaned closer, brushing strands of blood mattered hair from her serene face, whispering her name over and over, soft, and desperate. "Aurelia... please... stay with me... don't leave me..."

The doctor's words echoed in his mind: she was alive. She was safe. But the waiting— the long, torturous, fragile waiting—was only beginning. Every second stretched into a lifetime, each tick of the clock a reminder of how little control he had.

The door opened quietly, and Sam stepped in. He nodded briefly to the bodyguard discreetly stationed in the corner, then left Sam and Julian alone in the room with Aurelia.

"How is she?" Sam asked, his voice low and steady, though edged with concern.

Julian's gaze remained locked on her pale, serene face, following every shallow breath, every delicate rise and fall of her chest.

"She… the bullet only grazed her," Julian said, voice tight with relief and lingering fear. "Thank God. But she could stay unconscious for a couple more hours. Shock, blood loss… it's all standard. She's stable, but delicate." He exhaled slowly, squeezing her hand gently, as if his touch could anchor her to life.

"That's… positive," Sam said, relief softening his tone, though his eyes never left Julian.

Julian finally lifted his gaze to Sam, every muscle in his body taut, the question burning through him like wildfire. "Who was the shooter?"

"Eddie Riordan," Sam said grimly, his voice steady but heavy.

Julian's eyes went wide, disbelief and rage colliding. "What… he was supposed to be dead."

"He is now," Sam replied evenly. "But it seems he faked his death to get close to you, to make you lower your guard. The police think he's been stalking you, waiting for Mrs. Riordan to appear. And when he saw you with Miss Carmichael… he obviously mistook her for Mrs. Riordan."

Julian's jaw clenched so tightly it ached. The old anger, the fury he had buried beneath discipline and control, flared to life, coiling like fire in his chest. His mind went back— once again—to Jessica, to the lies she had whispered to Aurelia, the deceit that had almost destroyed everything. How she had manipulated them, how she had driven a wedge between him and the one woman he could never stop thinking about… and now, even with Aurelia lying unconscious before him, that bitter, burning ache of guilt and fury returned, sharper than ever. He had allowed another woman's schemes to endanger Aurelia. Almost cost her life.

Never again.

He exhaled, slow and deliberate, forcing the fury into a focused edge. Every thought narrowed, every instinct honed to the fragile, trembling life in front of him. Her pulse. Her breath. The warmth of her skin beneath his hands. Everything else—anger, fear, the world outside—dissolved. There was only her. And he would not let anything—or anyone—take her from him.

Aurelia's fingers twitched slightly in his, and Julian's heart caught, hope sparking like a fragile flame. He whispered again, almost to himself this time, "Stay with me, Aurelia… just a little longer… please."

Outside the room, Sam's eyes scanned the corridor, ever vigilant, while inside, Julian remained tethered to her by a single, desperate hand, unwilling to leave her side for even a second.

Chapter Sixteen

Aurelia's eyelids felt impossibly heavy, weighed down as if by invisible chains. The world around her was muted, distant, blurred at the edges—a haze she could not pierce. She was aware of warmth, of a steady pressure, and of a heartbeat beneath her fingers. Slow, insistent, familiar. Her mind hovered between dream and waking, tethered only by that rhythm.

Voices drifted first, soft, and indistinct, carrying through the fog of her consciousness. She tried to open her eyes, but they refused.

"I love her…" The voice was rough, raw, laden with aching desperation. Her chest tightened. That voice—*Julian.*

Who… does he love? Her mind whispered.

"I know you do, sweetheart. The doctors said she should wake soon," another voice answered, calm and gentle, but firm. Warm. Maternal. Aurelia's heart caught—*his mother.*

"I just need to see her… to look at her, to tell her Jessica lied and what I feel…" Julian's words broke slightly, brittle with vulnerability she hadn't imagined he could show.

"You will, son. She's recovering. Give it time," a deep, steady voice replied, authoritative but comforting—*his father.*

A flicker of awareness stirred in her chest, a faint flutter that coaxed her back from the darkness. The voices anchored her, tugging her slowly toward the surface. She tried again, forcing a blink—and this time, a sliver of light cut through the fog. Shapes began to form, colours blurring, movement flickering—but it was Julian's voice, urgent and insistent, that pulled her fully into the present.

"Julian…" The soft female voice prompted, gentle and coaxing.

Her lips felt parched, her throat raw. A weak whisper escaped: "Julian…"

In an instant, he was at her side, grasping her hand with a fierce tenderness, relief flooding every syllable. "Aurelia… thank God."

She blinked again, slow, and tentative, taking in the sterile brightness, the faint antiseptic scent, the soft pressure of his hand cradling hers. Her mind was still hazy, fragments of fear and confusion colliding with the overwhelming warmth of his presence.

"What…" she whispered, voice trembling, her head pounding. "My head…"

Julian pressed his lips lightly to her forehead, brushing stubborn strands of matted hair from her face. His voice, low and urgent, enveloped her: "Shh… don't speak yet. You're safe. I'm here. All of it—we'll talk when you're strong enough."

Even in her haze, Aurelia felt the unshakable certainty in his tone, the raw, unrelenting promise: she was not alone. She was not abandoned. For the first time in what felt like forever, she let herself sink into the fragile, trembling comfort of that truth.

His parents excused themselves quietly, promising to return later, leaving Julian entirely at her side. Exhaustion pressed against her eyelids, pulling her toward the dark again, but the steady, insistent thrum of his heartbeat beneath her fingers tethered her to the waking world.

"You're going to be okay," Julian murmured, his voice soft, almost a vow. "I promise."

Aurelia clung to that sound, letting it anchor her, letting it remind her that, for now, she was alive—and not alone.

Aurelia's eyes fluttered open again, the light sharper now, stabbing at her senses. Every sound seemed amplified—the distant beeping of monitors, the muted chatter of nurses, Julian's steady breathing at her side. She forced herself to focus, and slowly the world grew clearer: white walls, bright lamps, soft footsteps, the sharp scent of antiseptic.

But through it all, Julian's face remained the sharpest image—close, impossibly real, etched with a raw, exhausted relief that made her chest tighten.

He squeezed her hand gently, grounding her. His expression was a mixture of fear, relief, and something fiercer—an intensity she'd never seen so naked on his face. "There you are," he whispered, voice low and hoarse. "You scared the hell out of me."

Her lips parted, but only a dry rasp came out. "Water…"

Julian immediately reached for the plastic cup with a straw. "Here," he murmured, guiding it to her mouth. She sipped, the cool liquid easing her throat. "Thank you."

"How are you feeling?" Julian asked quietly, brushing his thumb over the back of her hand.

"My head…" she whispered, wincing at the pressure pulsing behind her temple. "What happened…?"

Julian hesitated—just for a heartbeat—before answering carefully, "You were shot."

She blinked, confusion tightening her features. "Shot…? Who would want to shoot me?"

"It wasn't meant for you," he said softly. "Aurelia, the bullet—"

But before he could finish, something inside her snapped into focus. A memory. A truth. A jolt of terror that hit her harder than the pain in her skull.

The baby.

Her breath hitched. Her eyes flew wide. Panic surged through her like electricity.

"My baby—Julian—the baby—"

Her heart slammed violently against her ribs. The monitor erupted in sharp, frantic beeps. Aurelia's chest heaved, her fingers clawing desperately for Julian's hand, her vision narrowing to the red and gold blur of fear.

Within seconds, nurses rushed in, a doctor trailing behind them, hands already moving to assess her.

"Miss Carmichael, you need to breathe," the doctor urged, calm but firm. "Slow, deep breaths. Panic will make this worse."

Julian leaned over her, his grip on her shoulders gentle but unrelenting. "Aurelia… look at me," he said, voice low, trembling. "Breathe. You need to calm down. I'm right here."

But she shook violently, eyes wild, breath shallow and jagged.

"The baby—" she gasped, voice breaking. "The baby—please—"

Julian froze, horror and confusion warring across his face. "Baby?" he echoed, turning to the doctor. "Aurelia—what baby?"

Her chest heaved, heart hammering like a drum. Tears spilled over her lashes as terror clawed up her throat.

"Our baby," she whispered, voice fractured and raw. "Julian… I'm pregnant."

The words hit him like a blow. His jaw slackened. His hands tightened around hers until the skin whitened.

"What…?" His voice was barely audible. "Aurelia… you're… pregnant?"

She nodded, trembling, tears streaming freely. "Please—please, I need to know the baby's okay—"

The monitor's frantic beeps spiked, echoing her panic. The doctor stepped forward, voice brisk but steady.

"Aurelia, you must stay calm. We cannot let your blood pressure rise any further."

A nurse pressed a cool hand to her arm. "Miss Carmichael, we'll do an ultrasound immediately. Deep breaths… slow, steady."

But she could barely inhale. Fear strangled every attempt.

"Please—I can't lose the baby… please—"

Julian's face went pale; every line carved with terror. He gripped her hand with a vice-like intensity. "Aurelia," he said, voice rough, breaking, "look at me. Right now."

She forced her gaze to his, trembling, vision blurring.

He leaned closer, pressing his forehead to hers, anchoring her to the moment. "You're not losing anyone. Not if I have anything to say about it." His voice cracked, raw with emotion. "I swear it."

The doctor nodded sharply to the nurses. "Portable machine, now."

They moved with practiced speed—wheeling the device close, snapping on gloves, dimming the lights. Julian stayed by her side, holding her hand so tightly her fingers ached.

Aurelia's breath trembled. "Julian… what if… what if the baby—"

"Don't," he hissed fiercely. "Don't even finish that sentence."

The obstetric registrar entering briskly, clipboard in hand.

"Miss Carmichael, we understand that you're early in your pregnancy. We'll examine the uterus, check for internal bleeding, and locate the heartbeat if possible. Stay as still and calm as you can."

Aurelia whimpered, voice barely audible. "Please… just tell me my baby's alive…"

Julian's grip tightened again. "She means everything to me," he said quietly, jaw tight, eyes blazing at the doctor. "Tell me they're both safe. Both of them."

The tension hung thick in the room. Every second stretched, every beep and shuffle magnified, until all that mattered was her—and the tiny life growing inside her.

The doctor nodded gently. "We're going to do everything we can."

The gel was cold against Aurelia's abdomen, the contact pulling a sharp gasp from her lips. Julian winced as though he felt it himself.

The probe pressed lightly. The machine hummed to life.

Black and grey images flickered across the screen—waves, shadows, a blurred universe of shapes Aurelia didn't understand. She held her breath, eyes darting between the monitor and the doctor's face, searching for any sign of hope.

Seconds passed like hours.

The doctor's eyes narrowed in concentration.

Aurelia gripped Julian's hand so tightly his fingers throbbed.

"Please..." she whispered, voice thin and breaking. "Please..."

And then—

The doctor inhaled softly.

Julian snapped upright. "What? What is it?"

The doctor adjusted the angle, quiet, focused...

Then she turned the screen slightly, her expression easing.

"I see a gestational sac... and..."

Aurelia couldn't breathe. Julian leaned in, every muscle coiled.

"...there," the doctor whispered, pointing. "A flicker."

Julian swallowed hard. "What does that mean?"

The doctor smiled gently. "It's the heartbeat."

Aurelia sobbed—a sound of pure, shuddering relief. Her hand jumped to her mouth as tears broke free. Julian bowed his head over her other hand, shoulders shaking once before he pressed a trembling kiss to her knuckles.

"The pregnancy looks stable," the doctor continued softly. "No signs of trauma. No internal bleeding. You'll need monitoring for twelve to twenty-four hours, but right now... your baby is okay."

Aurelia cried harder—soft, gasping tears of shock and gratitude.

Julian lifted his head, his eyes bright and wet, voice hoarse. "Thank God... Aurelia, thank God."

He leaned down, pressing his forehead to hers, his thumb brushing her cheek as if she were something fragile and miraculous.

"You're safe," he whispered. "Both of you. I'm not letting anything happen to you ever again."

And for the first time since she'd felt that searing heat across her temple, Aurelia allowed herself to fully believe it—

They were going to be all right.

The room slowly quieted after the ultrasound team left. The lights softened, the machines steadied into calm, rhythmic beeps, and for the first time since she'd been wheeled in, Aurelia felt the world ease its grip on her.

Julian hadn't moved from her side—not when the doctors left, not when the nurses quietly stepped out, not even when Sam murmured, "I'll be outside if you need anything," and closed the door behind him.

And now it was just the two of them.

Aurelia and Julian.

Silence and heartbeats.

Pain and relief.

And something deeper pulsing between them than either had dared to name.

Aurelia lay back against the pillows, still pale, still exhausted, but calmer now. Safe. Grounded. The gel from the scan cooled on her skin beneath the hospital gown, but Julian's hand—warm, steady, wrapped around hers—kept her anchored.

He hadn't let go for even a second.

She turned her head slightly, finding him watching her with an expression she didn't recognise at first—raw, stripped of all his usual composure. His eyes were still damp, lingering traces of tears clinging to his lashes.

"Julian..." she whispered.

He didn't speak right away. Instead, he reached out and gently brushed a stray lock of hair from her forehead, careful not to touch the bandage that covered her wound. His hand trembled just a little.

"You almost died," he said softly, as if the words themselves hurt him. "You were bleeding... in my arms... and I—" His voice cracked, and he had to look away for a moment. "I thought I was going to lose you."

Aurelia's breath caught. She squeezed his hand even though her strength barely allowed it.

"You didn't," she whispered. "I'm here."

"That's the only thing keeping me sane right now," Julian murmured.

Silence settled again, warm, and fragile.

Aurelia swallowed, her throat still tight from emotion. "I'm sorry I scared you."

He huffed a breath, half a laugh, half disbelief. "You're sorry? Aurelia, sweetheart—" He leaned closer, eyes fierce. "You were shot. The only thing I care about is that you're alive."

Her lips trembled—not from fear now, but from the way he said it. With such depth. Such certainty.

Then Julian took a slow breath, and something shifted in his eyes. As if he was gathering courage for something he'd carried too long.

"Aurelia," he said quietly, thumb tracing slow circles against her knuckles. "There's something I need to say. Something I should have told you long before now."

Her heartbeat fluttered—not from panic this time, but anticipation. "Julian…?"

He lifted her hand to his chest, pressing it over his heart, letting her feel the rapid, uneven rhythm beneath her palm.

"I love you."

The words fell between them like a confession and a vow all at once—raw, unguarded, unmistakably true.

Aurelia froze. The world stilled.

Her breath caught as if her lungs forgot how to work.

Julian swallowed, voice roughening. "I love you, Aurelia Carmichael. I've loved you longer than I knew how to admit. And today—watching you bleed, not knowing if you'd ever open your eyes again—it nearly destroyed me."

Her eyes stung, tears rising too fast for her to stop them.

"No—you can't… Jessica—" she whispered, her voice breaking.

"She lied," Julian said, the words hard and absolute, leaving no room for doubt. "She never meant anything to me. Not then, not now. And because of her, you walked out believing you were second to someone who was never even part of my life anymore." His jaw flexed, grief and fury warring in his eyes. "That's on me. I should have shut her out completely. I should have made it clear that the only reason I helped her was because I couldn't stand by and watch someone get hurt. But you—" His voice fractured. "You were the one who got hurt. Because of her. Because I didn't protect you. I should have—"

"Julian," she breathed, tears sliding down her temples, her heart twisting at the raw torment in his face. "Please don't blame yourself."

"How can I not?" His voice was hoarse, thick with fear that had nowhere else to go. "You were almost taken from me today. You. And our baby."

Her fingers lifted, trembling, finding the front of his shirt. She curled them into the fabric, grounding them both. "But I wasn't," she whispered, her voice fierce in its softness. "I'm here. And the baby is okay."

Julian released a shuddering breath, something inside him breaking open as he lowered his head. The kiss he pressed to her forehead was trembling, reverent—almost worshipful. It sank into her, warm and aching and everything she had ever hoped he would feel.

"I love you," he whispered again, as if he needed the words to imprint into her skin, her soul. "You and our baby… you're everything. You have been for a long time."

Aurelia's tears spilled freely now, unstoppable. Her voice came out as the faintest breath, fragile and certain all at once.

"I love you too."

Julian exhaled—shuddering, relieved, undone. He lowered his forehead to hers, closing his eyes as if memorising the moment, the closeness, the miracle of her survival.

"Then I'm never letting you go again," he murmured.

And in that quiet hospital room, surrounded by the soft hum of machines and the faint scent of antiseptic, Aurelia finally felt truly safe—wrapped in Julian's presence, his love, and the fragile but powerful promise of a future she had never dared to hope for.

A soft knock came at the door.

Julian lifted his head from where it rested against Aurelia's, his fingers instinctively tightening around hers. He straightened slightly, brushing his thumb over her knuckles in quiet reassurance.

"Come in," he said softly.

The door opened, and Graham and Heidi Kingsley stepped inside.

They looked older than they had hours ago—not in years, but in gravity. Worry had carved itself into their expressions. Heidi moved first, her eyes immediately finding Aurelia, her hand fluttering to her chest in visible relief.

"Oh, thank God," she breathed, voice tremulous. "You're awake."

Graham stood behind his wife, tall and imposing as always, but even he couldn't disguise the strain around his eyes. He cleared his throat, the sound rough.

Aurelia instinctively tried to sit up, but Julian gently pressed a hand to her shoulder. "Easy," he murmured. "No sudden movements."

Heidi stepped closer, eyes glistening as she took in the bandage at Aurelia's temple, the dryness of her lips, the faint tremor in her breath.

"Aurelia, darling," she whispered, reaching out as if afraid to touch her too suddenly. "We were terrified. Julian called us—well, Sam did—but we got on the plane as soon as we could."

Aurelia offered a weak smile. Her voice was thin, scratchy. "I'm… okay. Just a bit sore."

Heidi's voice broke. "You were shot."

Aurelia swallowed. "Yes… but the doctor said—it was only a graze."

Graham stepped forward, his normally stern expression softened. He rested a solid, reassuring hand on Julian's shoulder before turning to Aurelia.

"You gave us all a hell of a scare," he said gruffly, though warmth laced his tone. "How are you really feeling?"

Aurelia hesitated. Julian answered for her, his voice quiet but firm. "She's going to be okay. It'll take time, but she's strong."

Heidi took Aurelia's other hand delicately, careful not to disturb the IV. "You poor thing… we are so relieved you're safe." She glanced at Julian, emotion tight in her voice.

Heidi smiled softly at the two of them, noticing how tightly their hands were woven together. "We were here earlier; we wanted you and Julian to talk.

Julian didn't say anything. He didn't need to. His thumb continued to brush slow circles over Aurelia's knuckles.

Then, after Heidi released Aurelia's hand, it drifted almost unconsciously to rest over her lower abdomen. Heidi's eyes widened, a spark of surprise and gentle, delighted suspicion flickering across her face.

"Is everything… all right?" Heidi asked carefully, her voice gentle but probing. "With the baby?"

Aurelia froze, her pulse stuttering in her chest. Beside her, Julian went completely still, the sudden tension in his body taut and unmistakable.

Graham's brows lifted in surprise, his gaze flicking between his son and Aurelia. "Baby?" he repeated, curiosity mingling with concern.

Aurelia's stomach tightened at the weight of the word, the secret she had been carrying now exposed in the quiet, expectant room.

Aurelia swallowed. Julian gave her a reassuring smile. "Yes," he said quietly. "The baby's fine."

Heidi's hands flew to her mouth. Tears welled, and her breath caught in a soft gasp. "Oh… oh my goodness, Aurelia… Julian…"

Graham blinked hard, the corners of his eyes damp. "Well," he rumbled, voice thick, "that is… remarkable news." He cleared his throat again, trying unsuccessfully to hide his emotion. "Congratulations, you two."

Julian looked down at Aurelia—his expression soft, reverent, overwhelmed—and lifted her hand to his lips, pressing a silent kiss to her knuckles.

Heidi swiped quickly at the corner of her eye. "You're both safe… and now this. Another grandchild." She gave Aurelia a watery smile. "Sweetheart, you have no idea how happy that makes us."

Aurelia felt her own tears returning, but this time they weren't born of fear—they were warm, quiet, full of a belonging she hadn't dared imagine.

Julian slipped his arm around her shoulders, easing her gently into him. "She needs rest," he said softly, protective as ever.

Aurelia looked at Heidi. "Would you do me a favour?"

Heidi nodded quickly. "Of course. Anything."

"Take Julian with you."

Julian protested immediately. "No."

Aurelia's voice was soft but firm. "Yes. You've been here for hours. You need rest."

"I don't want to leave you," Julian murmured.

Aurelia took both his hands in hers. "Please. Go. Hopefully, I can leave tomorrow."

Heidi smiled, a gentle coax. "Come on, Julian. You don't want to upset her, do you?"

Julian hesitated, then reluctantly stood. He bent down and pressed a soft kiss to Aurelia's lips. "I love you," he whispered.

"I love you too," she murmured back.

Graham stepped forward, placing a surprisingly gentle hand over Aurelia's. "You're family now," he said simply. "We've got you."

Aurelia's throat tightened. She whispered, "Thank you."

Heidi kissed Aurelia's forehead lightly. "We'll let you rest."

As Julian and his parents quietly slipped out, closing the door with soft care, Aurelia felt her exhaustion return—but wrapped now in warmth, not fear.

Chapter Seventeen

After a night of deep, restorative sleep, Aurelia stirred, blinking against the soft morning light streaming through the blinds. Her hand instinctively found Julian's, warm and steady beside her.

"Morning, sleepyhead," he murmured, his voice low and rough with sleep, a teasing edge in the softness.

Still drowsy, she yawned, curling her fingers around his. "Morning... you're here early," she mumbled, her voice thick with sleep.

Her blue eyes sharpened as she studied him, a hint of concern creeping in. "Did you... sleep at all?"

Julian gave a small, rueful smile, the corners of his lips twitching. "Not much," he admitted, brushing a strand of hair from her forehead with exquisite gentleness. "But I couldn't stay away."

Aurelia's heart tightened. She reached up, cupping his cheek. "Julian, I'm okay. You need to stop worrying."

His expression hardened—not with anger, but with a fierce, aching protectiveness. "That's never going to happen," he said quietly. "I put you in danger, Aurelia. Because of me you could have been killed." His voice roughened, a whisper of guilt threading through it. "I'll never forgive myself for that."

"Julian," she whispered, sliding her hand to rest over his heart. "Please. Stop." Her voice softened, steadied. "I wasn't killed. I'm still here. With you."

Her gaze held his, full of warmth and a fragile certainty. "And knowing that you love me... that's all I need right now."

Something in him broke then—some strained, rigid line of fear and remorse snapping under the weight of relief. His breath left him in a quiet shudder as he pulled her into his arms, pressing his forehead to hers, as though anchoring himself in the undeniable truth of her presence.

He eased back into the chair, still holding her hand, fingers interlacing with hers. "My parents left this morning," he said softly, a faint smile tugging at his lips. "They asked me to tell you to get better and come home soon."

Aurelia smiled, a warm, shy curve of her lips. "Your parents are... lovely." Her eyes flicked down, voice dropping almost to a whisper. "I didn't think... I didn't think they would like me."

"Why would you think that?" Julian asked, concern knitting his brow as he studied her face.

"Because... I really have nothing to offer you," she admitted, the words raw and hesitant.

Julian's eyes widened in disbelief, a sharp edge of incredulity in his voice. "That's not true," he said firmly, shaking his head. "You're beautiful, smart... and there isn't a part of you I don't admire. You have more to give than you'll ever know, Aurelia. And believe me—you've already given me everything."

Her cheeks warmed at his words, her pulse fluttering like a trapped bird. She searched his eyes, longing for the certainty she needed, and found it mirrored back at her—steady, unwavering, unshakable.

"Are you... upset about the baby?" she asked cautiously, her voice barely above a whisper, uncertainty threading through every word.

Julian's gaze softened, and he shook his head, a small, rueful smile tugging at his lips. "Upset? Aurelia, when you told me yesterday that you were pregnant... I won't lie; I was shocked. For a split second, my mind raced." He reached out, brushing a strand of hair from her face, his touch gentle and grounding. "But then... it hit me. A wave of happiness, stronger than anything I've felt in a long time. I can't wait to meet our baby, to hold them, to watch them grow. And more than that... I can't wait to do it with you."

Aurelia felt tears prick at the corners of her eyes, a trembling warmth and relief flooding through her. His certainty, his love, and his quiet excitement for the future wrapped around her like a protective cloak, dissolving the lingering doubts and fears she hadn't even realised she'd been carrying.

"I'm sorry I ran," she whispered, her voice thick with regret. "When Jessica called me at the penthouse... I couldn't stay and see you with her. I didn't know what else to do."

Julian cupped her face in his hands, thumbs brushing softly against her cheeks, anchoring her with the weight of his presence. "I know why you did it, Aurelia," he said, his voice low, steady, unwavering. "I understand. But promise me... promise me you will never do it again. I love you, and we need to face everything together—even when it gets hard."

A soft shiver ran through her as she nodded, pressing her forehead to his. "I promise," she murmured. "I won't ever run from you again."

Julian's lips curved into a small, fierce smile, and he leaned down, kissing her with a tenderness that still carried the edge of his possessive need. "Good," he said softly against her mouth. "Because I'm not letting you go—not ever."

Moments later, Dr. Moreno entered, a nurse following close behind, charts in hand. His expression was calm and measured, radiating quiet authority and reassurance. With deliberate clarity, he began going over the instructions, each word precise and steady, leaving no room for confusion:

"No bending or sudden movements. No washing your hair for another 48 hours. Take pain medication as prescribed. Return immediately if headaches worsen, nausea develops, or your vision blurs. Follow-up appointment in three days, and staples removed in seven to ten days."

Aurelia nodded, absorbing the instructions, though Julian seemed to memorize every word, his jaw tight with vigilance.

"Her body went through shock," Dr. Moreno added, eyes flicking to Julian with quiet understanding. "She'll be tired, emotional, and sore for a few days. A little dizziness is normal. Rest is the best medicine."

"Rest," Julian repeated, the word rolling off his tongue like a solemn vow.

The doctor turned back to Aurelia. "You've healed remarkably well so far. You can go home once you feel steady enough to get dressed. But no rushing—take your time."

After the doctor and nurse left, Julian reached for the bag of clothes he had brought for her, pausing mid-motion as he looked at her.

"I'll help you," he said softly—not a question, but a certainty.

Aurelia's cheeks warmed, a flutter she couldn't suppress. "Julian… I can dress myself."

"You can," he agreed, voice gentle but unwavering, "but you don't have to."

His tenderness unsettled her, stirring something raw and fragile she wasn't yet ready to examine.

"All right," she conceded softly, a quiet surrender.

Julian helped her sit up slowly, hands warm and steady against her back, grounding her with each slight wobble. Even the smallest movement made her head swim, but he waited patiently, unhurried, as if time itself had bent around them.

When she was finally ready, he helped her to her feet. She swayed instantly, and his arms closed around her in an unyielding, protective embrace.

"I've got you," he murmured, voice low, grounding. "Just lean on me."

And she did.

Aurelia dressed slowly in the loose, comfortable clothes Julian had brought, each garment a reminder of his thoughtfulness. He stayed close—not hovering, not intrusive—just a quiet, unwavering presence, a fortress around her fragility.

Once she was ready, he lifted her overnight bag over his shoulder and extended his hand.

"Ready to go home?"

She hesitated, not from fear, but from the vulnerability that still clung to her like a shadow.

Then she looked at him—at the sincerity, the tenderness, the fierce relief still etched across his face—and her heart steadied.

"Yes," she whispered. "Take me home."

Julian intertwined his fingers with hers, the contact grounding them both, and led her out of the room slowly, deliberately, as though guiding something infinitely precious.

For the first time since waking to pain and fear, Aurelia allowed herself to believe: home was no longer just a place.

It was a person.

Julian escorted her back to the penthouse, and the next seven days unfolded in a tender rhythm—healing, quiet routine, and a slow-burning longing neither of them bothered to hide. At night, he held her close, adjusting pillows, blankets, and even himself to ensure she was comfortable, safe, and cherished. During the day, when he retreated to his study to handle work he could no longer ignore, Sam stayed by her side.

To her surprise, Julian's head of security was easy to talk to—dryly funny, perceptive, and unfailingly loyal. He shared small pieces of his life, stories of his siblings, and the occasional anecdote about Julian that made her laugh until her head throbbed, and she had to cradle her temples, smiling through the sting. She had never imagined she'd feel so at home in a place that wasn't hers.

That afternoon, her staples were finally removed. The doctor was pleased—impressed, even—and assured her the wound would heal cleanly. With her hair down, the injury disappeared completely. She could resume all normal activities, he'd said, as long as she exercised basic caution.

Back at the penthouse, Aurelia and Sam drifted toward the living room while Julian vanished into his office with the purposeful stride of a man settling into work he didn't want to do. Aurelia was halfway through laughing at a particularly outrageous story from Julian's childhood—something involving a dirt bike, a dare, and a furious grandmother—when Julian appeared in the doorway.

He leaned a shoulder against the frame, arms crossed, eyes narrowed in mock suspicion.

"Do I have anything to worry about?" he asked dryly.

Aurelia extended her hand toward him without hesitation. He crossed the room immediately, taking her fingers in his warm, steady grip.

"Never," she said, her smile soft but certain.

Sam let out a low chuckle as he headed toward the hallway. "Of course not," he said over his shoulder. "But I still think Miss Carmichael is more than you deserve, sir."

He disappeared before Julian could retort, laughter echoing faintly behind him.

Julian sank onto the sofa beside her, his presence grounding, his gaze warm. He brushed a strand of hair from her cheek and pressed a lingering kiss to her lips.

"He's not wrong," he murmured against her mouth, his voice a velvet rumble.

When he pulled back, concern flickered through his eyes.

"How's the dizziness?"

Aurelia gave a small, amused shrug. "As long as I don't stand up too fast, it's manageable."

Julian nodded, though the tension didn't fully leave his jaw. He kept hold of her hand, his thumb tracing slow, soothing circles over her knuckles—a gesture both protective and deeply intimate.

"I just want to make sure you're truly okay," he said quietly. "Not just pretending you're fine so you don't worry me."

She leaned into him, resting her head against the hard, warm line of his shoulder. The steady rhythm of his heartbeat anchored her in a way that felt shockingly, beautifully right.

"I know," she whispered. "And I do feel okay. But more than that..." She exhaled, letting the truth slip free. "I feel cared for. In a way I haven't felt in a long time."

"Good. Do you know how much I love you?" he asked, his voice low, molten, and impossibly intimate.

"Yes," she breathed back. "And I love you just as much."

"I think I must have loved you the first time I saw you," he said, a tremor of vulnerability threading through his normally controlled tone. "You were sleeping—pale, still, hair wild around your face—and then you opened your eyes... blue, clear, alive. I thought... hell. What is this? I wanted you from that moment."

Her heart stuttered. "I love you," she whispered, devotion spilling from her in fragile, fervent waves. "Completely. Utterly. Forever. I think I started falling the moment I saw you looking down at me. Living with you made me happy... and the more I got to know you, the more I... just fell. All the way."

He smiled softly at first, then with a warmth that pierced straight through her.

"Do you remember our first ride?" he asked quietly. "When we stopped to look down at the view... and I held your hand?"

The memory hit her like sunlight breaking through clouds. She nodded, breath catching.

"I just stared at our hands," he murmured, gaze locking on hers as though he could still see that moment in the space between them. "And I realised—suddenly, absurdly, irrevocably—I love this woman."

Her lips parted. "But that was only the third or fourth day after we met. You barely saw me for more than a few minutes each morning and night. How could you possibly—"

"I know." A rough, humourless laugh escaped him. "I didn't want to fall in love that quickly. I fought it. I told myself it was irrational, irresponsible, impossible. I wanted you—but loving you that much, that fast..." He shook his head, the memory darkening his eyes. "It terrified me."

She blinked, startled. "You're serious?"

His gaze sharpened, flame-bright. "Aurelia... by then I had carried you to bed. I knew exactly how your body fit against mine. I'd seen your temper—fiery as your hair—and your courage, your kindness. I knew your smile could undo me. I knew your skin was meant to be kissed, and your mind..." He exhaled slowly, voice raw with recollection. "Your mind fascinated me. Intelligent. Loyal. Thoughtful. I knew enough."

Heat raced across her cheeks. "You couldn't have—"

"And that you blush charmingly," he added, eyes glittering with wicked amusement.

Her colour deepened, burning. "I can't help it," she admitted, helpless.

"I hope you'll still blush for me forty years from now," he murmured, pressing a reverent kiss to the top of her head, tenderness folding into the warmth of his lips.

He drew back just enough to lift her hand gently, as if it were the most fragile treasure in existence. Then, from his lap, he revealed a small velvet box.

Her breath caught.

He opened it slowly. Inside rested a large Kaliah blue diamond, its colour the deep, mesmerising blue of the island's waters, cradled in a halo of smaller diamonds that shimmered like captured starlight—a promise forged in fire and light.

His voice dropped low, husky, carrying an intimacy that made her pulse stutter and her breath catch. "Aurelia… will you marry me?"

She froze, wide-eyed, the world narrowing until nothing existed but him and the glittering jewel in his hand. "W… what did you say?" she whispered, her voice trembling with disbelief and something dangerously close to hope.

He smiled that slow, devastating smile that always made her knees weak. "I asked if you would marry me. I want us. Always. You, me… our future. Our family."

Tears welled and shimmered on her lashes. "Julian…" Her voice broke. "I love you. I always have."

His own breath caught. "And I love you." Deliberate. Certain. A vow folded into a confession.

He slipped the ring onto her finger, diamonds nestling perfectly against her skin, as if it had always belonged there.

"This isn't just a promise of marriage, Aurelia," he murmured, voice low, molten. "It's a promise I'll always be here. For you. For us. For our baby."

Her chest swelled, her heart stretching until it felt too large for her ribs. She gazed at the ring, then back into his polar-sea eyes—the same eyes that had undone her from the start.

"I'll marry you," she whispered, a radiant smile breaking through her tears. "Yes, Julian. Yes."

His hands framed her face, thumbs brushing away the tears he had caused—and healed—in the same heartbeat. He kissed her—soft, reverent, sealing their promises… before pulling her close, deepening the kiss with all the fierce, pent-up longing of the last seven weeks.

"Julian…?"

"Yes," he murmured, drawing back just enough to meet her gaze.

They hadn't been intimate yet. Julian had waited, wanting her fully healed, fully ready. Now, with the doctor's blessing, she gave him a look that was at once wicked, serious, and entirely sensual.

"If you don't make love to me right now, I think I might go out of my mind," she whispered, her voice trembling with need and desire.

A slow, dangerous smile curved his lips. Without hesitation, he lifted her into his arms as though she weighed nothing. Her arms went instinctively around his neck as he captured her mouth again, kissing her with urgent, consuming heat.

He carried her to their bedroom, closing the door behind them with a decisive click.

They shed their clothes quickly, kissing between every garment tugged loose and dropped to the floor. Each brush of lips made their hands more desperate, more hungry, until finally they stood before each other—bare, breathless, trembling with anticipation.

Gently, almost reverently, Julian lifted her into his arms. He lowered himself onto the bed, positioning her astride him, her knees bracketing his hips, her body hovering over his but not yet joined. His palms slid up the long, graceful lines of her thighs, along her waist, over the curve of her ribs. Slowly. Softly. As though memorising her with every lingering stroke.

"Mine at last," he murmured against her skin, voice rough and thick with awe. The words seared her as deeply as his touch.

Her hands explored him in return—the heat of his chest, the sculpted strength of his abdomen, the powerful breadth of his shoulders. When he cupped her breasts, brushing his thumbs over her tight, aching nipples, her breath shuddered. He teased the tender pink tips with feather-light strokes, watching her part her lips in a silent gasp that shot straight to his core.

Julian pulled her closer, his mouth closing around her nipple, drawing her deep into the warm, wet heat of his lips. She cried out softly, pleasure snapping down her spine like a live wire. The tension inside her coiled low and tight, building with every slow pull of his mouth. Then he moved to her other breast, squeezing the soft weight in his palm as he suckled the hard, throbbing peak until she was shaking above him, fingers buried in his hair.

When he lifted his head to claim her mouth again, his kiss was hungry, devouring. His hands slid over her shoulders, into her hair, down the elegant line of her back. She reached between them, gently wrapping her fingers around the thick, hot length of him. Aligning their bodies, she held his gaze—dark, blazing, desperate—before slowly lowering herself onto him, taking him inch by exquisite inch.

A strangled sound broke from his throat as her warmth closed around him. She sat poised above him, her breasts swaying softly, her breath trembling, and he looked up at her as though she were a vision he had waited a lifetime to touch.

She began to ride him—slow at first, rolling her hips in smooth, deliberate strokes that drew a deep, guttural moan from his chest. Then faster. Harder. Her lips parted, her expression luminous with pleasure, eyes fluttering shut as she lost herself in the rhythm of them. She gripped his shoulders, pushing herself down onto him again and again, deeper, harder—

Her body fractured first. She screamed his name, pleasure ripping through her in shuddering waves.

A raw, answering growl tore from him. In a swift, powerful motion, he flipped her onto her back, bracing himself above her.

Holding himself, he rubbed the slick, sensitive tip of his arousal against her throbbing entrance. She moaned—helpless, needy. And when he could resist no longer, he thrust into her hard, burying himself to the hilt. The shock of pleasure stole his breath.

Propped on his arms, he drove into her again, deeper, his groan low and hoarse. The sensation—the heat, the tightness, the way she clenched around him—sent pleasure spiralling through him so intensely his muscles trembled.

He thrust again, and again, riding the razor's edge of control.

Then she cried out with fresh ecstasy, her body tightening around his length, fingernails digging into his skin as she shattered beneath him. He squeezed his eyes shut, fighting the tidal wave of release threatening to take him.

His pace slowed—long, slow strokes that made her gasp with each deep thrust. She felt every inch of him claiming her, filling her, drawing her higher until her breath came in desperate, broken pants.

Thrusting. Deep. Unhurried. Devastating.

She came again, trembling violently around him.

"Julian."

His control snapped.

Julian's rhythm broke into desperate, powerful movements as he thrust into her welcoming body, pleasure surging hot and unstoppable through him. With a deep, guttural groan torn from his very core, he shattered—hard, fierce, undone—spilling himself inside her in pulsing waves as he buried himself to the deepest point he could reach.

A final tremor tore through him as he collapsed against her, breath ragged, heart pounding, still buried deep inside her, still shaking from the force of everything she made him feel. He lowered his head and captured her mouth in a kiss—hard, hungry, overflowing with passion, wonder, and devotion.

"I love you, Aurelia," he whispered against her lips, his voice thick with emotion. "I will always love you."

Her fingers traced the muscles of his back, curling over his shoulders, tender and possessive all at once. "I love you too, Julian. Always."

He rested his forehead against hers, their breaths mingling, their bodies still joined, their hearts beating in perfect, fragile rhythm. And in that quiet, breathless space, they both knew—whatever shadows waited beyond this room, whatever battles or burdens the future held—they would face them side by side.

This man.

This love.

This unshakable certainty.

It was the beginning of forever.

Epilogue

The late-afternoon sun spilled across the sweeping gardens of Helen's Greenwich estate, gilding everything in a soft, honeyed glow. Laughter rang out from the backyard where a troop of clowns juggled and blew enormous bubbles, children darting across the grass in shrieking excitement. The air carried the scent of fresh-cut lawn, birthday cake, and warm summer light.

Aurelia sat beneath the shade of a wide white umbrella, Clair asleep against her chest, tiny breaths puffing against her collarbone. Her daughter's soft, feathery curls—her curls—tickled her chin. Nearby, Julian stood beside his father and brother-in-law, watching the children with that protective, amused intensity that never quite left him.

Sarah dropped into the chair beside her, handing her a cool drink before leaning in with a conspiratorial grin.

"William is growing like a weed," Sarah said. "And he looks so much like Julian it's scary."

Aurelia's gaze drifted across the lawn. Her almost five-year-old—tall for his age, all quick feet, and long limbs—was racing after a wobbling bubble with two cousins, shouting orders as if commanding a miniature army.

A warm laugh slipped from her. "He does, doesn't he?"

Sarah brushed a gentle hand over the sleeping baby's back, Clair shifting but never waking.

"Well," Sarah said, "luckily Clair looks like you. With that beautiful fuzzy hair and those big blue eyes."

"I just hope she doesn't blush like I do," Aurelia murmured, cheeks already heating.

Sarah snorted. "Are you kidding? Julian is hoping she will."

Aurelia laughed helplessly, burying her face for a moment in Clair's curls.

"You've made my brother so happy," Sarah added, softer now. "He used to be so stern. So serious. Like feelings were optional."

"Oh, he still is." Aurelia lifted her brows. "Especially when he wants his way."

A burst of laughter sounded behind them.

Helen and Heidi strolled over with plates of cake, both grinning.

"Oh, Aurelia," Helen said, handing her a slice, "the whole family knows you can twist him around your little finger."

Aurelia flushed instantly, rosy colour sweeping up her cheeks.

"See?" Sarah crowed. "There's the proof."

Helen added, laughing, "Honestly, the way he looks at you? He was finished from day one."

Aurelia parted her lips—ready with a modest objection—but the words dissolved the moment her eyes found Julian across the lawn.

He had turned toward her.

Even from a distance, even amid the chaos of balloons and clowns and flying sugar-hyped children, his gaze softened the instant it landed on her—warm, intent, unmistakably his. A private smile curved his mouth.

Her heart gave a helpless, tender flip.

She smiled back.

Around them, her sisters-in-law—and Julian's mother—exchanged knowing looks, their laughter soft and conspiratorial as Aurelia flushed all the way to the roots of her hair. No matter how many years passed, she still blushed like sunrise whenever Julian looked at her that way.

They had married just four weeks after his proposal—inside the small cathedral on Kaliah Island, where nearly the entire island turned out to celebrate them, lining the streets as they walked out as husband and wife. And Aurelia hadn't stopped smiling since. Happiness had settled into her like breath—steady, natural, effortless. She loved Julian to distraction, and he loved her with a devotion so deep it still stole her breath.

William had arrived a week early—strong, perfect, already with his father's steel-grey eyes and determined spirit. And now Clair, nearly one, was a miracle wrapped in soft curls and long lashes, a joy that completed the family they'd built with tender swiftness and absolute certainty.

Aurelia looked down at the warm little bundle in her arms, then across the yard where William tore past in a spray of bubbles, and finally at Julian—her husband—watching them all with quiet, satisfied contentment.

Her heart overflowed.

This life, this love, this family…

It was more than she had ever dreamed.

Julian crossed the lawn toward them, hands in his pockets, shirt open at the neck, the faintest smile tugging his mouth as he navigated children and toppled balloon animals. William barrelled into his leg mid-run; Julian caught him without missing a step, ruffled his hair, and sent him racing away with a laughing shout.

When he reached the umbrella, his entire expression softened. He bent to kiss Clair's head, then brushed a tender kiss to Aurelia's temple, lingering as though that one simple touch steadied him.

"Are my mother and sisters behaving?" he murmured.

"No," Aurelia teased.

The women cackled in unison.

Julian sank into the chair beside her and wrapped an arm around her shoulders with affectionate possession, drawing her in so naturally it felt like breathing. Clair sighed in her sleep, and Julian's big, warm hand settled protectively across their daughter's back.

For a moment, the entire garden blurred into soft colour and distant laughter, leaving only this:

His family.

His wife.

His children.

His happiness.

Aurelia turned her face into his shoulder, smiling against the crisp cotton of his shirt.

"Thank you for making me so happy," she whispered.

Julian pressed his lips to her hair. "I should be thanking you."

Her breath caught.

Helen made a dramatic swooning sound. "Julian, stop being so disgustingly perfect."

He shot her a glare; the sisters and mother dissolved into laughter.

But Aurelia didn't laugh.

She looked up at him—really looked—and saw everything she had always seen from the beginning: strength, tenderness, devotion, a love that had only deepened with time.

She threaded her fingers through his.

Whatever storms came—on the island, in New York, across oceans—they would meet them together.

And here, in the golden light of a family gathering, with their son laughing in the sun and their daughter warm against her heart, Aurelia understood completely:

She was home.

He was home.

And she had fallen for the billionaire—completely, irrevocably, and forever.

The End

Until You Loved Me

Alison Reid

A complete standalone romance

Previously published individually

Chapter One

It was raining at the funeral—not a downpour, but a steady, mournful drizzle, as though the sky itself grieved in silence. A soft patter on umbrellas and wet leaves filled the air. Someone stepped beside Grace and held an umbrella over her, but she scarcely noticed. Her eyes were dry; her tears had been spent. Now she stood hollowed out by sorrow, her mind numbed by the cold, quiet horror of grief.

The minister's voice droned on, reciting words that held no meaning for her. Hollow condolences. Rituals. Her father was dead, his final days shadowed by scandal, and nothing spoken here could touch the ache left behind.

How many people among the gathered crowd were thinking of it—the scandal? How many so-called friends and business partners were waiting for tomorrow's headlines with veiled curiosity? She lifted her chin slowly and swept her gaze across the mourners, her pale face composed with delicate defiance.

Grief, to Grace, was private. Her tears had been shed alone, far from watching eyes. Now, only pride remained. Most looked away. A few met her gaze briefly but faltered, their eyes dropping before the fierce dignity blazing from her beautiful face. All but one.

John Sneddon.

He stood apart from the rest, yet seemed to dominate the entire gathering, his height giving him a quiet command. Even without moving, he was a presence—unshakable, arrogant, unsmiling. His dark eyes held hers with cool indifference, no apology, no discomfort. Just that impenetrable stare she had come to fear.

He was almost dangerously imposing—broad-shouldered, immaculately dressed, his dark hair glistening with rain, his expression unreadable. There was something cold and perfect about him, as if he'd been carved from marble. Those eyes—deep, hypnotic brown—seemed to see everything yet revealed nothing. She knew them too well. They made you feel like you could fall in and never find your way back out.

Was he waiting for her to break? To collapse under the weight of loss? She didn't know. But she could feel his gaze like a hand around her throat.

The minister moved in front of her again, breaking the strange, magnetic pull.

He spoke gently. "Miss Lewis... I didn't really know your father..." His voice was kind, tentative, searching for some word that might soothe. He saw the bleakness in her eyes, the silence that wasn't strength but devastation.

"I knew him," she said. Her voice was flat, stripped of life. Final.

He tried again. "If you need help…advice—"

"She has help."

The interruption came from behind her, deep and authoritative. John Sneddon's voice cut through the rain like steel. He stepped beside her with deliberate ease, claiming space, commanding attention. "It's kind of you, of course," he added smoothly, "but I'll be handling Miss Lewis's affairs. There's no need for concern."

Grace turned her face up to his, stunned by his nearness. He stood too close, overwhelming her with his size, his power, his sheer presence. There was something almost primal in the force of him—as if the very air shifted to make room for him. She felt stripped bare, exposed, a flicker of helplessness coursing through her.

It was as if he controlled the very air she breathed.

Words rose in her throat—protest, defiance—but they died before reaching her lips.

"I'll take you home, Grace," he said quietly. His hand closed around her arm—firm, possessive—and with that single touch, he turned her away from the grave, his authority wrapping around her like a storm cloud.

"I—I can't…" Her voice trembled, and she glanced back, pain and disbelief flickering across her pale features. But he urged her forward, relentless.

"He's gone, Grace. You have to leave. Time will dull the sharpest edge."

She stopped walking, turning her face to his. "How would you know?" she whispered bitterly. "You're like granite—unfeeling, hard. Who have you ever loved?"

Though she kept her voice low for the sake of the onlookers, the rising bitterness in her tone cut through him like a blade. He heard it all too clearly.

"Rage at me if you need to. I can take it," he said coolly. "But keep that face composed and your voice down until we're clear. The press hounds are out. Two photographers are in the trees."

His grip tightened—unmistakable steel beneath the calm warning. She didn't need to ask how he knew. She had already spotted one of them, half-hidden behind a rain-slicked hedge. She was Grace Lewis, heiress to a disgraced legacy, and fair game to the vultures.

She inhaled deeply, steadying herself. Her head lifted once more, her face calm and statuesque, the picture of control.

"Good girl," he murmured close to her ear. "Just hold that a little longer."

He didn't glance at the waiting car or acknowledge the chauffeur. With one silent wave, he dismissed the man entirely. Grace noticed the sleek black Mercedes parked beside the gate—a vehicle that hadn't been there earlier. She frowned faintly. Had he ordered someone to move? Of course he had. He was John Sneddon—decisive, commanding, impossibly self-assured. Dominant, virile, and cold as obsidian.

Without a word, he opened the car door and helped her inside, the warmth and luxury of the leather interior wrapping around her like a shield. He joined her, started the engine, and within seconds they were gliding away, his eyes sharp in the rear-view mirror.

Grace turned just in time to catch the sudden burst of movement—photographers scrambling to get one last shot, lenses flashing, too late.

"They'll be at the house soon enough," she said with a tired sigh, resting her head back against the seat.

"Not with the gates locked," he replied flatly.

She lifted her head, frowning. "I can't lock the gates. People will come—family friends, neighbours. They'll expect…a drink, a few words. Condolences."

"Prying," he corrected, voice dipped in disdain. "They won't be coming. I cancelled all that."

"You did what?" she said sharply, sitting up to face him. But his expression didn't shift.

"I spoke to those who mattered. The people who were truly your father's friends understand your need for privacy. They know what the press is capable of—and they support the decision. The rest don't matter. No one is setting foot inside Rosewood except you and me."

He didn't wait for her response.

"As for the gates," he added, "I brought two of the site men with me. The paparazzi won't get in."

She understood what he meant the moment they turned into the long, tree-lined drive. Two men stood by the gate—broad-shouldered, silent, unmistakably capable. They were workers from his firm, the kind who didn't flinch from confrontation. One of them swung the iron gate shut behind them, and the dull metallic clang echoed like the closing of a chapter.

Final. Inescapable.

Just like everything else.

"A few more enemies made," she said dryly, her tone brittle.

He glanced at her, his dark eyes unreadable. "Enemies don't bother me. I grew up in a tough world, Miss Lewis. Right now, be grateful for it. Good breeding doesn't count for much in the jungle."

"You mean I'm spoiled? Childish? Soft to the core?"

He gave a derisive snort. "A social success, certainly. But in the real world? Lightweight." His gaze flicked to her, cool and assessing. "You have two things going for you. You're beautiful, and your father loved you. He was my friend. I'll protect what I can."

"I don't need—" she began hotly.

But, as usual, he cut across her without missing a beat.

"You don't need the help of a tough nobody who clawed his way out of the gutter?" he said, his voice steeped in sarcasm. "Don't overplay your hand too early, Grace. Learn some caution. The party's over."

There was something in his voice—something final, unsettling—that chilled her more than the rain. She turned her head sharply to study him, sudden alarm prickling her skin.

His face was as unreadable as ever, eyes fixed on the road ahead, lips drawn in a line of hard resolve. Ruthless. That was the word whispered so often about him, and she didn't doubt it for a second.

John Sneddon had always unsettled her. Her father had welcomed him into Rosewood, held him in great esteem, even affection. But Grace had often struggled to stay composed in his presence, her skin prickling whenever he entered a room. Only her devotion to her father—and her duty as hostess—had kept her seated at those dinners, masking the discomfort in her eyes with practiced smiles.

It was the power that frightened her—coiled, controlled, but unmistakable. His eyes, dark and focused, made her feel transparent. Vulnerable. He was a man wrapped in polish, but beneath the civilised surface she sensed something raw, something dangerous. A predator in a tailored suit.

Everyone knew he was brilliant. A visionary engineer. Tireless, relentless, unnervingly intuitive when it came to business. He'd built an empire through sheer will. But to Grace, he was less man and more myth—untamed, like a jungle cat prowling just beneath a civilised veneer. Cross him, and you wouldn't even see the strike before it landed.

She could still hear her father's voice, indulgent and amused when she'd once dared to confess her unease.

'Darling, John's an educated man. Don't mistake his background for ignorance. He won scholarships from the time he could walk, and he's worked damned hard every day since. There were no private schools or tennis club parties for him. No silver spoon. Probably not much of a childhood at all. But he was a first-class rugby player—could've gone pro from what I hear.'

'And I suppose you hear that from him?'

'Don't be scathing, Grace, love.' Brian Lewis had chuckled softly. *'John never talks about himself. He doesn't need to. He works too hard to waste breath on bragging. I'm grateful he came into the firm. He didn't have to.'*

No, he hadn't needed to. John Sneddon already owned a civil engineering empire that seemed to stretch across continents. He had built it from nothing—brick by brick, deal by deal—and was already wealthy long before he ever cast his calculating eye on Lewis Engineering.

When he did, it had felt less like a partnership and more like a quiet, surgical conquest.

Now the company was called Sneddon-Lewis—an elegant compromise, her father had said. It sounded better that way. More balanced. But Grace knew better. John Sneddon had poured money into the firm, yes, but with it came control. Not a takeover, not in name—but everyone knew who was at the helm. He hadn't devoured the company. He had annexed it. Absorbed it. And there was never a moment's doubt as to who held the reins.

She had resented him from the start.

Lewis Engineering had been in her family for generations—solid, respected, steady. It had never needed rescuing, not in her eyes. Grace had grown up in a world of comfort and unquestioned privilege. Wealth had been the air she breathed. She had never imagined it could end.

And then John Sneddon had arrived. Like a shadow that stretched too far. Cold. Polished. Uncompromising. His presence had darkened the edges of her world, a stark reminder that there were wolves beyond the gates.

Her father had loved her too much to make her work. Grace had never been expected to do anything but be charming, graceful, decorative. And John Sneddon—he had always despised that. She had seen it in his eyes from the very beginning. That quiet contempt. That flicker of disdain for her soft, pampered life.

She had also learned, very early, who truly commanded the room. It wasn't her father—not anymore. One glance from John could make seasoned men scramble for footing, their confidence withering under his cool, deliberate stare. He had power, and he wielded it without apology. She found him terrifying. She found him terrifying now.

And yet—beneath the fear—there was also a grudging flicker of gratitude. He was shielding her from the press, from the gawkers, from the circling vultures. For now, at least, he was her barrier against a world she had never been trained to face.

Perhaps tomorrow she would find the strength to take it all in. To face the truth.

Her father had lost everything.

Just before his death, he had told her—quietly, ashamed. There had been another life, one he had kept hidden from her: a yacht, long absences, women, gambling. The debts had consumed everything. The only asset left was his share in the firm, and even that wouldn't cover what he owed. Rosewood would have to be sold, but the sale wouldn't be enough. Not really. Not even close.

She had nothing now. Nothing but her pride, and her bitterness.

Because John Sneddon must have known. He had to. And he had said nothing. Had done nothing. He had waited—patient, cold, calculating—like a predator biding his time.

And now, in the aftermath, he dared to call her father his friend.

Chapter Two

The car glided to a halt in front of the house, its engine humming one last breath before falling silent. Grace stepped out into the soft drizzle, the rain beading in her hair and soaking into her coat, but she barely noticed. She stood motionless, staring up at the house as though imprinting it on her soul—because soon, far too soon, it would be nothing more than memory.

Rosewood had always been the cornerstone of her life. It stood proudly atop the hill, regal and unmoving, the view behind it sweeping wide like something out of a dream. The house itself was grand—almost austere—yet softened by decades of Virginia creeper that trailed along its stone façade, giving it a weathered beauty, a warmth that belied its size.

She had never lived anywhere else. Not once. And the thought of leaving was unbearable. It felt like tearing out a part of herself, something deep-rooted and irreplaceable. Losing Rosewood would be the final blow—and she didn't know if she could withstand it.

She had forgotten that John Sneddon was standing beside her until his voice broke the silence.

"You love this house, don't you?"

"Yes," she said softly. "I've never known another home. And now I have to let it go."

"That's your choice," he replied, his tone cool, almost indifferent. He reached for her arm and guided her gently but firmly up the stone steps toward the door.

"I wish it were that simple," she said with a faint, humourless laugh. "I'd keep it even if I had to live in one room and eat twice a week. Everything good that ever happened to me happened inside these walls. When Rosewood goes, it'll take all of it with it. Even the memories."

"Memories live in the mind," he said, unflinching.

"Is that why you're so cold?" she shot back, bitterness flaring. She hadn't meant to say it—not aloud—but the grief in her chest was twisting into something sharper, something cruel. "Sorry," she added quickly, the fight draining from her as fast as it had come. "That was idiotic. Forget it. Nothing could hurt you. You're invincible, aren't you?"

He glanced at her then, that strange, unsettling half-smile curling at the corner of his mouth. It wasn't friendly. It never was. It hinted at secrets; at thoughts she couldn't guess—thoughts she wasn't sure she wanted to.

"Is that how you see me?" he murmured. "Invincible?"

"I don't see you at all, Mr. Sneddon. I don't think of you."

His smile deepened, though it never reached his eyes. "How comforting that must be—for you. Now let's get out of the rain."

His hand tightened slightly on her arm, the suggestion layered with something firmer than courtesy, and she found herself led forward before she could protest.

The heavy front door opened into the echoing quiet of the hall. Jenny appeared at once, emerging from the shadows like a ghost of the old life, her face pale and drawn, her grey hair pulled back too tightly, as always. She had been with them for as long as Grace could remember. More than staff. She had helped raise her. Watched her grow. And now she, too, would have to leave.

It was clear she had been crying—her eyes were red, her expression raw.

Without hesitation, Grace crossed the hall and wrapped her arms around her.

"Just you and I now, Jenny," she whispered, the tears catching in her throat.

Jenny hugged her tightly. "Aye, love. We'd best face it. We'll have to find ourselves another roof soon enough."

There had never been secrets between them. Jenny was more than a housekeeper—she had been a mother when Grace's own had passed too young to remember.

"I'll look for a flat," Grace muttered. "Something small, somewhere we can both squeeze into. I don't know how we'll manage your wages, though..."

"You hush about that," Jenny said briskly, though her voice trembled at the edges. "I'll find work. We'll get by. We've got each other, haven't we?"

"Oh, Jenny..." Grace's voice broke, and the tears she'd been holding back slipped down her cheeks. "As if I'd ever let you." She clung tighter to the woman who had been her anchor for so many years, grief swelling until it felt like it might drown her.

John Sneddon cut in with quiet impatience.

"Make us some tea, Jen. We'll be in the study."

His tone was clipped, unsmiling—but Jenny gave him the same fond, lopsided smile she always had. He was the only one who ever called her Jen, and she'd always taken it as a mark of respect. She liked him, even if Grace didn't. She had never understood Grace's hostility toward the man. To her, John Sneddon was impressive—self-made, smart, and possessed of the kind of unyielding grit that only those who had known hardship truly recognised. She admired that in him.

Jenny nodded and moved off without hesitation.

"It's not the study," Grace said sharply as the older woman disappeared down the corridor. "It was my father's study. And right now, I don't want to go in there."

"If it weren't necessary, I wouldn't suggest it," John replied evenly. "But we need privacy. There are things to discuss."

"Privacy? From Jenny? She's the only person left in this house who actually cares what happens to me. She already knows everything."

"Not everything." His gaze locked onto hers—dark, unreadable. "There are things you may not want her to know."

Grace opened her mouth to protest again, but he cut her off with a single, dispassionate command.

"Dry your eyes."

And just like that, he turned and walked away.

She stared after him, her fists clenched at her sides. It was infuriating. There was no longer any reason for him to be here. She had needed his help—yes—but that moment had passed. This was her house now. Her father was gone, and John Sneddon had no right to insert himself into her grief, no matter how grand his intentions.

He had never been welcome here—not in her heart.

She marched after him, ready to tell him so. Ready to tell him to get out.

But the words didn't come.

Something about the way he stood in the study—still, silent, gazing out the tall windows at the rain-drenched gardens and the dimming sky—stilled her tongue.

He looked carved from shadow and strength. Unmovable. And yet... weary, too.

She caught herself watching him. Not just with resentment or suspicion this time—but with an unfamiliar curiosity. For all his polished suits and sharp intellect, there was something untamed beneath his surface. Something she'd always sensed and instinctively recoiled from.

But now, in the hush of her father's study, in the fading light, she saw more than just the relentless force of him. She saw his presence. His dark, commanding beauty. The air around him almost seemed to shift with his intensity.

He wasn't merely powerful. He was magnetic.

And for the first time, Grace felt it fully.

The danger.

The allure.

The man.

Plenty of women had tried to catch John Sneddon's eye over the years. Grace had always thought they were mad. He was too hard, too cold—too dangerous.

But now, for a fleeting second, she saw him as they did.

She wondered how he behaved with people he liked. He had liked her father—called him a friend. They'd shared laughs, exchanged quiet words. That had always unsettled her, seeing John so near to her world, woven into her life without her consent. It had made him feel too close. And closeness with John Sneddon felt like standing on the edge of a cliff, the wind pulling at your balance.

He suddenly turned, sharply, catching her gaze. His dark eyes swept over her, unreadable but intense, lingering on the delicate lines of her face. Her honey-brown hair was twisted back too tightly on her head, emphasising the fragile curve of her neck. Her skin was pale, her expression drawn. But her eyes—those remarkable violet eyes flecked with gold—seemed enormous now, luminous with sorrow and exhaustion.

"You need to eat," he said abruptly, his brows drawing together.

"I couldn't," she murmured, her voice fraying.

"For how long?" His gaze swept down her slender frame, all sharp angles, and too much fragility. "Another few days like this and you'll vanish."

She sank into the nearest chair, fingers rising to her temples as she closed her eyes. The headache behind them was relentless.

"I need an aspirin more than food," she muttered, just as he strode from the room without a word. The abruptness of it startled her—and then amused her, in a grim, tired way. Of course. Imagine telling John Sneddon you had a headache. It was like confessing to a bruised ego in the middle of a war.

Jenny appeared with the tea, but John returned right behind her, and Jenny wisely retreated without a word.

"Take these." He startled her by placing two tablets gently into her hand. She looked up, wary, eyes slitted with pain.

"What are they?"

"Perfectly safe," he said gruffly. "Not poison. Jenny gave them to me from her cabinet when I mentioned your headache."

He poured the tea, set it beside her, and added flatly, "Take them."

She murmured a quiet thank you and did as he asked, suddenly feeling foolish for her earlier suspicion. But that was part of John Sneddon's danger—you never knew what he would do next.

Without warning, he leaned forward and tugged the band from her hair. The soft curtain of honey-brown tumbled around her shoulders. He frowned.

"Screwing your hair up like that doesn't help. You look like you're punishing yourself."

She reached up instinctively to smooth it back, but his voice cut in—sharp, commanding.

"Leave it."

Startled, her hand dropped.

"Drink your tea," he added, tone still clipped. "Then we'll talk."

"Talk about what?" she snapped. "I know everything. Daddy explained it all before he died. There's nothing more you can tell me. I've lost everything, and that's the end of it."

He regarded her with that unsettling stillness of his. "Well, you're not a little rich girl anymore," he said bluntly. "That's a fact."

"And you think I care?" she flared, rising suddenly to her feet. "He's gone! My father's gone, and nothing—not you, not this house, not even Rosewood—can replace him!"

She turned away, shoulders curling inward as she broke again, the sobs rising before she could stop them. The grief poured out of her—raw, unfiltered, ugly—and she barely registered his movement until he was there, wrapping her in arms like steel.

She didn't think. Didn't pull away. It didn't matter who he was, or what he had done, or what she thought of him. She needed something solid. And he was solid—immovable, warm, a wall of strength that held her up when everything else had fallen.

For a few precious minutes, she sobbed into his chest, all the anguish she had tried to hold back breaking free at last. He didn't speak. He didn't try to soothe. He just held her—still and steady, letting her fall apart in his arms.

Then, as the storm ebbed, she stirred—humiliation creeping into the silence that followed.

"I—I'm sorry…" she whispered, fingers curling into the fabric of his shirt as she instinctively tried to pull away.

"Don't be," he said quietly. "It's part of healing."

He looked down at her, his arms still resting loosely around her, and she felt as though she'd been pinned in place—like a butterfly caught beneath glass. He had never touched her before, not even in passing, save for that one distant handshake the first time her father had brought him home. Now, the heat of him, the sheer strength of his body, made her achingly aware of her own fragility. She couldn't move—wouldn't move—unless he let her go. Strange feelings danced along her skin, unfamiliar and unwelcome.

"How old are you, Grace?" he asked suddenly.

"Twenty-four."

His mouth curved, but the expression wasn't a smile. It was dry, ironic. "Twenty-four. In the world I came from, you'd be fifteen, maybe sixteen, if you were lucky enough to look as untouched as you do. My mother died at thirty-nine. She looked like she was sixty."

He released her then, stepping away, and she wrapped her arms around herself, cold in the absence of his warmth. Her eyes followed him, wide and glistening, her heart still thudding unevenly.

"How old were you?" she asked softly.

"Nineteen. I was already at university. I never went back." His voice was flat, clipped. "No siblings, so there was no reason to."

"Your father…?"

"A drunk. And a bully. Well-practiced at both."

Her breath caught. "I—I'm sorry."

He turned to her, expression unreadable—his features hard, but not angry. Just impenetrable. "Are you?" he asked, not unkindly, but with a hint of challenge. "I wouldn't waste your pity, Grace. That chapter's long closed. I barely remember it now. Your tears must've stirred something, that's all. Ordinarily, I don't have much patience with tears."

"You didn't have to stay and watch mine," she said, defensive now, her cheeks heating.

"They were for a man I respected. A man I called a friend. That makes them forgivable. And besides," he added, his tone turning pragmatic, "your father was my partner. That means I have a certain responsibility where you're concerned."

He sat down, a commanding presence even in repose, and gestured to the chair opposite with a firm tilt of his hand. "Sit down. Finish your tea. We need to talk."

She hesitated, then lowered herself stiffly into the chair, smoothing her hair back with nervous fingers. Everything inside her felt tight, brittle—like glass under pressure.

"What could we possibly have to talk about?" she asked, her voice low, tight.

"We've managed well enough so far," he said, with the ghost of a smile. "More words than you've spoken to me in the two years I've known you."

"So what?" she muttered, eyes downcast. "They're said now."

"But we're not finished." His voice was cool, resolute. "We're here to discuss you."

Chapter Three

"Me?" She looked up sharply, the violet in her eyes darkening with emotion. "I'm nothing to you. No responsibility at all. I'm not some child who needs looking after. And in any case, my father was only your partner in Sneddon-Lewis—just a pen stroke in your vast portfolio."

Her voice trembled on a note of bitterness, and she didn't care that he'd hear it. Even now, even with everything gone, she resented that name—Sneddon-Lewis. It was her father's firm. Generations of it. And now it bore someone else's name first, someone who had absorbed it into his empire with terrifying ease.

If her bitterness registered, he gave no sign. He merely leaned back, stretching out those long, powerful legs and watching her from under hooded lids. He looked perfectly at ease, a study in control, while she sat bolt upright, every muscle taut, every nerve on edge.

His eyes moved over her with quiet intensity, noting every flicker of emotion, every sign of strain. And when the corner of his mouth lifted—just slightly—it wasn't with warmth. It was amusement. Amusement at her, at the way she sat there rigid with fury and helplessness, yet still visibly caught in the force of his presence.

She hated that he knew it. Hated even more that she felt it.

"What are your plans?" he asked, calm, detached.

She wanted to snap at him—to tell him to stay out of her life—but she didn't. He had been her father's partner. And regardless of how she felt about him, there was no denying that when the Lewis half of the firm was sold off, John Sneddon would be left holding all the cards. He already owned most of the company. The rest had just been a formality.

"I'll stay at Rosewood until the house is sold—or until someone tells me I can't." She lifted her shoulders in a weary shrug. "In the meantime, I'll start looking for a flat. Something small but big enough for Jenny and me. It'll have to be in London… I won't be able to afford too many train fares, not for a while."

She gave a little half-laugh, soft and bitter. "Not that I have the faintest idea how long it'll take before things start getting sorted. I mean…"

"You mean you've never had to deal with anything sordid before," he said, flatly.

Her head came up like he'd struck her. "Did you expect me to have experience with this kind of thing?" Her voice sharpened. "I thought I was just a lightweight, remember?"

Her face flushed, her anger surfacing in waves, but he didn't rise to it. He merely watched her, steady and unreadable.

"You're not involved in anything, Grace," he said coolly. "The press is just flailing around, trying to stir up scandal because my name is linked to the company. If it had only been your father's, his death would have passed with a few polite notices. But now…" He gave a faint shrug. "Now there's a scent of blood. A few days of wild headlines, maybe some colourful speculation. A woman or two willing to sell their story. But that's it."

She blinked. "What are you saying?" He wasn't a man to speak lightly. If he was claiming everything was resolved… she didn't understand how. Or why.

He waved one hand dismissively, as if it were already old news. "Weeks before he died, your father asked to see me. And Dennis—your solicitor. We met; we talked. We made a deal."

Her heart began to pound. "A… a deal?"

He nodded. "On the day he died, it was finalised. I bought out your father's share of the firm. It's done. The cheques went out immediately. There are no debts now."

She stared at him. "But… even that wouldn't have been enough."

"I also bought the house," he said evenly. "Rosewood is mine."

The words hit like a slap. She shot to her feet, fury flooding her body in a searing wave. "So, you did it. You finally got everything."

Her face went bloodless, the words spilling out like poison. "The moment I saw you, I knew you were dangerous. I warned him. He wouldn't listen. You must've known what was happening, seen the signs. But you just waited—calm, patient—until the perfect moment to strike. Now he's dead, and you've got it all."

She was shaking, barely aware of what she was saying until she saw the flicker of something shift in his face—something hard and savage. He rose slowly to his full, imposing height, and when his eyes met hers, they were glacial.

"Be very careful how you speak to me, Miss Lewis," he said, his voice dangerously low. "I don't indulge hysteria."

He stepped toward her, towering now, radiating fury barely held in check. "What exactly did I do? Did I buy that damned yacht—Fantasea? Did I take him to every casino along the Riviera? Did I supply the women?"

Grace recoiled, her anger splintering into something rawer. Her face twisted with grief as she turned away, but he wasn't finished. His hand gripped her shoulders, not gently, and spun her back to face him.

"Yes. That's what stings the most, doesn't it? The women."

Her voice was a whisper. "My mother was beautiful…"

"Like you," he rasped. "I know. Brian kept her photograph in every place he touched—a shrine, almost."

He strode to the desk, yanked open the top drawer, and pulled out the silver-framed portrait. He thrust it into her hands, the image as familiar as her own face—Marie, smiling softly, her honey-brown hair shining like Grace's.

"Marie," he said hoarsely. "I knew her. Through him. She never left him, not really. She died, yes—but not to him. Every time he looked at you, he saw her. That kind of love… it's a life sentence."

Grace clutched the frame, barely breathing. "Then why the others?" she asked, her voice breaking. "Why betray her like that?"

He exhaled, sharp with frustration, his tone rough. "Because it was easier than grief. They were nothing. An anaesthetic. There was only ever *her*. And *you*. I imagine seeing you every day—so like her—was both a comfort and a slow torture. Eventually, something inside him must have… snapped."

For a moment, the room was silent, her breath the only sound as she stared at the photo. But he turned back, all impatience and steel once more.

"This isn't getting us anywhere. Your father didn't even realise how sick he was until it was almost too late. And when he did, he panicked—for *you*. That's what the deal was really about."

She looked up, still dazed, as he continued.

"I agreed to three conditions. One, the firm retains its name—Sneddon-Lewis. Two, you have access to Rosewood for as long as you wish."

She laughed bitterly. "As if I'd want that." Her voice trembled with a mixture of shame and defiance. "You've taken everything. I've gone from ease to… this. I'm nothing. Don't pretend I have choices."

Her pride stung more than her losses. The thought of staying under his roof, his protection, was unbearable.

"I'll leave tomorrow," she finished stiffly.

He didn't flinch. Didn't rise to her emotion. Just gave a shrug, cold and unreadable. "As I told you when we arrived—it's up to you."

"So… what's the last condition?" Grace's voice was tight with pride, though every instinct screamed at her to run. Instead, she lifted her chin and held his gaze. "I might as well know the full extent of the deal."

John's expression didn't shift. His voice came cool and clipped.

"That condition depends on you. He wanted a future for you—a secure one. I agreed… to marry you."

The words hit like a hammer, so blunt and devoid of feeling that for a moment she just blinked at him, stunned.

"You… what?" she whispered, her voice barely audible. "You agreed… to…?"

"It suited him. And it suits me," he said with the same cold detachment. "It gave him peace at the end, and I have no particular objection."

The blood drained from her face. Horror and disbelief surged through her like ice water. She stepped back instinctively, her legs suddenly boneless. "No…" The word barely passed her lips before her knees buckled and everything slipped away.

When consciousness returned, she was lying on the settee, disoriented and faintly humiliated. The scent of leather and brandy hung in the air. John was seated beside her, watching her like a hawk. His dark eyes were unreadable—too calm.

"Well," he said dryly, "neat performance. No wailing, no hysterics. Just a tidy faint. Very efficient. I might try it myself at the next tense board meeting."

His sarcasm struck a nerve, but she was still too dazed to respond.

"Not that I'm shocked," he went on, his tone sharpening. "You look like you've been living on crumbs. If you'd eaten a decent meal today, you might've stayed upright."

He rose and poured a small measure of brandy, returning to offer it to her. She didn't move. Couldn't.

"For God's sake, take it," he snapped. "I promise it won't poison you. I've no interest in your demise. Inconvenient as that would be."

The glass trembled violently as she took it, so much so that he exhaled with visible impatience and reached out, steadying both her hand and the glass as he helped her drink.

"You don't have to…" she murmured, embarrassed.

"I don't have to do anything," he said curtly. "Theoretically, I could throw you out and persuade Jenny to stay on. She's far less dramatic."

"Please," she said faintly, "be serious."

She reached to steady herself, her fingers brushing his hand without thought. At the contact, his eyes flicked downward, sharp, and focused. She snatched her hand back like she'd been burned.

"I'd like to get up," she said stiffly, trying to recover her composure.

"As you wish," he said, rising. "But I'm warning you—sit still if you don't want to end up on the floor again. You're still badly shaken."

"Are you really surprised?" she shot back, swinging her legs to the floor but not rising, her voice sharper now, regaining some fire.

He gave a short, hard laugh. "No. But I'm a little surprised you didn't faint the moment I walked into the church. I've seen less overwrought heroines in Gothic novels."

That did it.

"You're impossible," she snapped, her hands clenched in her lap. "You sit there and talk about marriage as if it's some business merger. No feeling. No consideration. Just—terms and conditions."

"It was your father's dying wish," he reminded her flatly. "And I don't recall offering romance, Miss Lewis. This isn't a fairy tale."

She stared at him, her breath catching, voice low and shaking. "No. It's a nightmare."

He didn't flinch. "That's why I didn't try easing you into it. You'd have rejected the idea out of hand. I'm not under any illusions about how you see me—you've spent two years making that perfectly clear. I'm not your kind of man, and I never will be."

"Then why even bring it up?" Her voice cracked. "What's the point if you already know I'd never agree?"

"Because I gave my word," he said, steel underlying his calm. "And as I mentioned—right before your rather theatrical collapse—it suits me just fine."

"How?" she shot back. "I don't like you. I never have. Why would I ever say yes?"

He turned on her so fast she flinched, and the flash of annoyance in his eyes darkened into something more dangerous.

"I'm thirty-five," he bit out. "I'm successful. I'm wealthy. I'm not married—by choice—and I intend to make Rosewood my home. It's always appealed to me.

Naturally, I need a hostess, and I've seen you in action. Graceful, poised. No one could do it better."

Her laugh was brittle, almost panicked. "You can't be serious. People don't marry for reasons like that."

"No," he agreed coldly. "They marry for love. Like your father married Marie. Love—the eternal promise. Except it never is. People lie. They cheat. They change. I've had a hard start in life, Miss Lewis. I don't intend to have a hard end. This is a business arrangement. Nothing more."

He leaned in slightly, his voice a whip of ice. "No love. No grief. I want a beautiful wife who appreciates beautiful things. Who understands the value of wealth because she's been raised with it. In return, you'll have everything. Comfort. Security. My name—*but not me.*"

Her temper snapped. "I don't want you!" she flared. "I disliked you the moment I met you."

"Why?"

The question was so quiet, so sudden, that it caught her off guard.

"I—" She faltered. "How can you explain something like that? It was instinctive. I saw you... and I knew."

"Knew what?" His eyes pinned her. "That I'm a *tough nobody*? I've heard it before."

"No," she said, flushing. "I never thought that."

"Then what?"

"You're dangerous." Her voice trembled despite her effort to steady it. "I saw it in you the first time we met. And I see it now."

He moved closer, deliberately, and her breath hitched. He was too close, too composed. The air between them thrummed.

"Danger?" he murmured. "Or just a challenge you don't know how to face?"

He reached out and, to her shock, brushed his knuckle down her cheek. She stiffened.

"You really are unworldly, Grace," he said, almost amused. "Your imagination runs wild."

"I have a strong sense of self-preservation," she snapped, jerking her face away.

His soft laugh unsettled her even more, and she flushed scarlet.

"I don't want to talk about this," she said stiffly. "Not now. Not with you. And in any case…" Her eyes narrowed. "What about Miss Peterson—your…?"

"Mistress?" he offered smoothly, without a flicker of shame. "Don't be afraid to say it. Harsh words don't hurt Rita."

Chapter Four

Grace hadn't expected John's mistress to be fragile—and Rita Peterson certainly wasn't. The press had followed her rise with breathless admiration: founder of a boutique empire expanding nationwide, she was sleek, stylish, and sharp as a blade. A high-gloss symbol of success. Grace doubted anything could touch her, let alone hurt her.

"I'm not trying to damage her," she said quietly. "Or anyone else. I just want to wake up and find this is all some hideous dream."

John suddenly turned on her, his voice cutting and impatient. "No wonder your father was panicked. You're completely out of touch with reality. Do you even hear yourself? What do you think you're going to do? You've never worked a single day. You're planning to rent some rundown flat in a forgotten corner of London and fill it with mismatched junk shop bargains?"

"There's furniture here—" she began.

"Yes, and it's mine," he cut in coolly. "You were right. Selling Rosewood wouldn't have covered the debts. So, I bought everything—house, land, and contents. The antiques tipped the scales just enough to break even."

Her voice dropped to a whisper. "So, I have nothing."

He turned back, eyes blazing. "You have your clothes. Assuming you can find a flat big enough to house your wardrobe and your pride."

"You don't know anything about my wardrobe or my life," she snapped, resentment rising.

One dark brow arched. "I know enough. I've seen your name in the society columns. Theatre galas, charity balls, late-night dinners with the usual pedigreed companions. You've lived a charmed life, Grace. You really think you're going to hack it on your own in the real world? You? In a poky flat? With a job?" He gave a cold, incredulous laugh. "What would you even do? You've been trained to look lovely and pour wine with a smile. That's not survival—it's packaging. A lamb in the wolves' den. And worse than that—"

He stopped abruptly, but the implication hung between them.

She flushed. "You have no right to assume—"

"I don't have to assume," he said smoothly, his mouth curving with dry amusement. "You say you see danger when you look at me. I see innocence when I look at you. You wear it like a second skin. And in any case, your reputation is spotless. Your father saw to that."

He studied her face, his gaze unsettlingly intense.

"You've hardly lived at all, have you? Brian kept you in a glass case like a precious relic. A living echo of Marie. When things got too much, he ran—yachts, casinos, women—knowing you'd be here, untouched, waiting in the safety he created. He didn't plan for your future, Grace. He never taught you how to stand on your own."

Her throat tightened. "You despised him," she said hoarsely. "Didn't you?"

John shook his head slowly, still watching her. "No. I respected him. But I think—deep down—he knew I'd step in when it counted."

His voice lowered, but the steel in it remained. "Because I always intended to marry you. From the very first moment I saw you."

For a long moment, Grace simply stared at him, the blood draining from her face. Was this the danger she'd sensed all along? Was this why his dark eyes had always lingered on her in this very house? Not desire—calculation. Strategy. She had never trusted him, and now she understood why. This wasn't kindness. It was control—quietly, elegantly tightening around her like a silk noose.

She straightened her spine, clinging to the only weapon she had left.

"Thank you," she said calmly, her voice quiet but steady. "I know you're only being… generous. Though I doubt it comes naturally to you. For some reason, you promised my father you'd marry me, and now you're trying to make it sound palatable. You don't have to. I'll manage. Jenny will be with me, and—"

He sank into the armchair opposite and began to laugh. Not a cold or mocking sound, but a genuine, deep laugh that startled her. It transformed him—made him human. Even handsome. She blinked, unnerved by the change.

"You're priceless, Grace Lewis," he said, his dark eyes alight with wry amusement. "Alice in Wonderland, stranded in the real world."

"I was only thanking you for your… effort," she said stiffly, but it only seemed to amuse him more.

"And then she drew on her gloves and swept nobly out," he murmured. "You really are a rare creature."

His voice dropped, low and certain now, all amusement edged with something harder. "I need a wife, Grace. And I chose you a long time ago—two years, to be exact. You're everything I want. Beautiful, poised, intelligent. You have dignity in spades, and charm enough to disarm royalty. This isn't some last-minute decision. I told your father about it over a year ago."

Grace blinked. "You—what?"

John's expression turned dry. "He wasn't thrilled. In fact, he delivered a rather kind but firm reminder of the Lewis lineage. Self-made men, he said, don't often marry into families that trace their roots to landed gentry. He gave me a brief tour of your family tree and made it politely clear I wasn't on it."

There was a flicker of something behind his eyes—resentment? Wounded pride?

"Of course, there was also Lord William— *'dear Bill'*, as your father called him. I believe Brian might have let you go to a title. But me? I didn't warrant much consideration. He dismissed the idea... then. But he remembered it at the end, when he realised what he was leaving you to face."

Grace's throat tightened. "And you just waited?"

"I didn't forget," he said evenly. "Because I always intended to marry you. With or without your father's blessing."

For a long moment, Grace simply stared at him. There was something unreadable flickering behind his eyes, something darker than amusement but just as deliberate. He had never spoken this much to her before—never hinted at any desire to marry her. So, what was this really? What game was he playing?

"You're making this up," she said hotly. "Just minutes ago, you told me you needed a hostess, and you made your views on love perfectly clear."

His mouth curved faintly. "Do you love me?"

The question hit her like a slap. "Don't be absurd! I don't even *like* you. I've made that more than clear."

"Exactly," he said, leaning back, his tone maddeningly calm. "So, let's be sensible. I've told you why I need a wife. You're ideal—gracious, well-bred, presentable in every way. You need the kind of life you were raised in, and I can give it to you. You can't survive without me, Grace."

She stiffened. "You have an extraordinarily high opinion of yourself, Mr. Sneddon— and an even lower one of me. Just because I've lived a life of comfort doesn't mean I'm incapable of standing on my own two feet. I'm not some helpless Edwardian debutante in need of rescuing."

That earned her a slow, lazy smile that made her feel as though he saw straight through her bravado.

"Helpless debutante isn't quite right," he murmured. "More like a museum piece— something rare, delicate, lovely, and completely impractical. You've been protected all your life, Grace. Your father's love, Jenny's care—it's left you entirely unprepared for reality. But I'm offering you a return to safety. Familiar comforts. Even Jen would thank me."

Grace's chin lifted proudly. "I don't need saving. And I certainly won't become some gilded ornament in a house I no longer own. I won't play hostess with a wedding ring on one finger and a leash on the other."

"It's not a leash," he said with calm precision. "It's a proposal. A practical, binding arrangement. I am a very wealthy man, even without Lewis Engineering. I've built an empire. I need an heir."

She rose slowly to her feet, unsteady beneath the weight of his words. He stood too, watching her with that unreadable intensity, and suddenly the air between them seemed to pulse.

"You said… you said there would be no love," she whispered. "You said you'd never feel what my father felt."

For the first time, the conversation felt real—stripped of its ironic tone, raw and frightening. There was something new in his expression, something unsettling. He wasn't mocking anymore.

"And I won't," he said flatly. "I don't believe in love. Not the consuming, foolish kind. I watched it destroy my mother. And I watched your father die with his heart still wrapped around a ghost. I won't be broken like that."

"My mother died," Grace said softly. "She didn't mean to leave him."

"No, but she did," he said bitterly. "And it hollowed him out. Took everything from him—and from you, too. I won't give a woman the power to destroy me like that. Love is a risk I don't intend to take."

Grace drew in a shaky breath. "Then go back to Rita. You already have someone who suits you—sharp, successful, selfish."

"She was enough," he said. "Until now."

His voice deepened, grew quieter—but more dangerous. "Now I want more. I want this house. I want you in it, exactly as I first saw you—graceful, untouchable. I want all that cool, golden beauty you try so hard to hide. I want a child with purple eyes and honey-brown hair. I want *you*, Grace."

She gave a small, shocked cry and turned to flee, but he caught her by the waist and spun her back, locking her tightly against him. One strong arm banded around her while the other plunged into her hair, forcing her to look at him.

"I could make you want me," he said darkly, his voice low and rough. "I could hold you until that virginal fear vanished—until you forgot what it meant to be untouched. And I wouldn't need love for that."

She flinched, her breath catching, but he didn't release her.

"You don't know anything about men. Brian made sure of it. He kept you in a glass case, pristine and untouchable, too afraid to let the world near you. Even at the end, he handed you to me thinking I'd treat you the same way—like one of his antiques. Safe. Unsullied. Locked away in your childhood bedroom, admired from a distance like some porcelain heirloom. If he'd had the slightest idea what I really wanted—" His voice grew harder. "—he would've left you with nothing rather than give you to me."

"You hated him," she whispered, shaking in his hold.

"No," he said harshly. "I knew him."

"No. I knew him." Her voice broke and the words collapsed into sobs—raw, helpless, and impossible to hold back. "Today I buried him…"

He made a sound in his throat—part frustration, part something softer—and then, without another word, he swept her into his arms. Her weight was nothing to him, and he carried her with effortless strength through the door.

"Jenny!" he barked.

The housekeeper appeared almost instantly, her face still streaked with tears. She took one look at Grace's crumpled form and moved quickly.

"Take her to bed," he said curtly. "She's finished for tonight."

He carried Grace up the sweeping staircase, her sobs muffled against his chest as she tried to collect herself. Jenny hurried ahead, pushing open the door to Grace's room and turning down the sheets with shaking hands.

At the threshold, he paused. His face was unreadable now, his eyes dark and hard.

"Give her a minute to settle, then feed her," he said, his voice clipped and controlled. "She's not to sleep without eating. One more day like this and she'll end up in hospital."

Seeing him standing at the top of the stairs in her house, issuing orders like he belonged there—it struck Grace like a physical blow. He did belong now. He owned everything. He controlled everything. And she… she was just a guest in her own life.

She said nothing as Jenny helped her undress, her mind spinning. He was rocking the very foundations of her world. She had to get away from him. Run—disappear— anything not to see him again.

But it wasn't that simple.

Jenny returned with a tray—soup, scrambled eggs on toast, and a pot of tea. Grace was still absentmindedly toying with the fork when a knock sounded, followed instantly by the door swinging open.

John walked in as though he had every right.

"This is my room for now," she said sharply, pulling the sheet higher. "Unless, of course, you plan to throw me out tonight?"

"Stop talking nonsense," he said tersely, striding over. "You know damn well I'm not letting you leave this house."

He glanced at the tray.

"Well, you've shifted it around a bit. At least the soup's gone. That's something. Another day like today and hospital won't be optional—it'll be necessary."

"What I do is absolutely none of your concern!" she snapped, her voice tight. His presence made her feel cornered, claustrophobic. Her body screamed at her to fight back, but she was too raw, too bone-weary to summon the strength.

"Everything you do is my concern," he said flatly.

He took the tray, set it on the small table beside her bed, then sat down on the edge of the mattress. Instinctively, she pulled away from him, clutching the sheet tighter.

"Will you please go?" Her voice trembled despite her effort to sound firm. Her skin burned under his gaze. "You're frightening me."

"For God's sake, stop looking at me like I'm going to assault you," he growled. "Do you honestly think I'd force myself on you and tell Jenny to look the other way? I don't need to use force."

"I'm sure you don't," she flung back, flushed, and furious. "The tabloids have been generous with the details of your exploits. If I didn't know your dating history, I'd have to be blind—or illiterate."

His mouth curled into a mocking smile. "You read all that, did you?"

"I didn't have to read anything. It was everywhere. And Miss Peterson's arrival was followed by a neat little retrospective—every woman in your wake."

His eyes glittered with sardonic amusement. "You could've turned the page."

"I wasn't interested!" she insisted. "But some things are hard to miss."

He leaned back slightly, studying her, and the smile on his lips was razor-edged. "Don't believe everything you read. Some women are only too eager to have their names linked with mine. They think it'll elevate them. That's usually when I end things."

"Everybody knows you're cold-blooded."

"The press does love its labels." His tone was dry. "Though the ladies rarely seem to mind. Or do you think it's just the money?"

"Obviously," she lied.

She knew perfectly well it wasn't just his money. Women didn't trail after John Sneddon because of his wealth—though he had plenty of that. It was something far more elemental. He was dangerous. Commanding. A frightening, magnetic pull wrapped in cool self-assurance and unapologetic masculinity. Until today, Grace had kept him at arm's length—turning away when he entered a room, steering clear of his gaze, deliberately evading him at every event held at Rosewood. She'd kept her distance, aloof and self-contained.

But tonight, he hadn't let her.

Tonight, he had cornered her. Stripped her emotional armour. Forced her to see him—and feel him—and now she was terrified, not of his power, but of the man beneath it.

"You're staring at me," he said quietly, almost amused. "Looking for clues? Trying to see what's real beneath the money?"

"You're being despicable," she whispered, her voice trembling. "You've got me at a disadvantage and you're using it to show me exactly who you are."

"No," he replied, the amusement fading from his voice. "You still don't know who I am."

His gaze dropped, slowly, deliberately. She was grateful the white satin of her nightdress was modest and opaque, but it didn't stop him from finding the frantic pulse beating at the base of her throat. His dark eyes glinted as if the sight pleased him. The corners of his mouth curved.

"Virginal," he murmured. "Of course you'd sleep in white."

"Please… go away." Her voice was barely audible, thick with dread and confusion. "You shouldn't be up here."

"I've wanted to be up here for a long time." He didn't move. "Frightened little Grace. You've been locked in a glass cage all your life. Safe. Untouched. Brian thought he was protecting you, but he was just making sure you never really lived."

His words hit like a slap, and all the grief she'd been holding inside broke through. The air in the room shifted. With him standing so close, the world felt electric… but just beyond the door, the world had gone silent.

"I'll never see him again," she whispered, eyes closing as hot tears slipped from beneath her lashes.

"He sees you."

The words struck her like a physical blow. From him, of all people—it was utterly unexpected. She opened her eyes in disbelief and found him watching her with a gaze so deep, so unwavering, it left her breathless. Her vision blurred, purple irises flecked with gold, shining with hurt. And still, he looked. And still, she couldn't look away.

"Suppose I promised to make you happy?" he said softly.

"You couldn't," she choked out. "I hate you. You forced your way into my life. You've taken everything. How could you make anyone happy? You're not even real. You're just… raw power in a suit."

His expression didn't change, but his eyes darkened with something she couldn't quite name. Slowly, he reached for her, his fingers brushing the base of her throat, right where her pulse thundered beneath her skin. It was a quiet, claiming touch, as if he could read every thought she tried to hide.

"Then I won't promise anything," he said quietly. "I'll just wait."

She flinched.

"I've waited two years already, Grace. And I'll wait longer. You'll come to me—not because I take what I want, but because you'll need what I give."

He stood, his presence still wrapping around her like heat.

"In the meantime, I'll make my own arrangements. I'm staying at Rosewood tonight— if that meets with your approval. The security team will remain on the gates until morning. The Press won't get through, but I don't trust them not to try. You're safe."

With that, he walked to the door and opened it.

"Go to sleep, Grace. Nothing will disturb you."

The door clicked shut.

But she just sat there, staring at it. The room still echoed with his voice. His will. His presence.

Everything would disturb her. He disturbed her.

She turned out the lamp and lay down, pulling the sheet up to her chin. Her body was still. Her mind was chaos.

And sleep was very, very far away.

"Oh, Daddy… *Daddy, why?*" she whispered brokenly into the darkness.

Whatever he had done—however tangled his choices—she couldn't bring herself to blame him. Her heart simply wouldn't allow it. He was gone, and in his place stood a man of steel and shadow, a man who now held the reins of her life with effortless power.

John Sneddon.

It was his fault, her pain existed. All of it. The pressure, the confusion, the sense of drowning in a world she no longer recognised. And yet… she didn't know how to fight him. She didn't even know if she could.

Her slender arm slipped from beneath the covers, reaching blindly for the photograph on the bedside table. She didn't need to switch on the lamp. Even in the dark, she knew her mother's face by heart—the soft, serene smile… the cascade of honey-brown hair… the delicate beauty frozen in time.

Was that what she had become? A living echo of a woman long gone.

A china doll, just as he'd said.

The thought struck something deep, something raw. Was she nothing more than a memory wrapped in silk and sorrow? A fragile tribute preserved for a grieving man.

Tears slipped silently from the corners of her eyes, trailing across her cheeks and soaking into the pillow. She pressed the frame gently to her chest, curled around it as if it could shield her from what lay ahead.

And somewhere between heartache and exhaustion, she finally drifted into a restless sleep, her mother's smile the last thing she saw behind her eyes.

Chapter Five

The sound of voices woke Grace early the next morning. She pushed back the covers and crossed to the window, squinting down at the front of the house. A black car was parked at the steps, and four hard-faced men were talking to John.

The sight only tightened the knot already lodged in her chest. It wasn't just the press anymore. The whole house felt under siege—and so did she.

John stood apart from the others, dressed in a perfectly cut dark suit, the image of urbane control. Hands shoved into his pockets, jacket pushed back, one lean, brown hand sliced decisively through the air as he spoke. The men nodded, clearly receiving instructions. Orders. He was organising security. But more than that—Grace had the sickening feeling he was organising her too.

She dressed quickly and headed downstairs, urgency propelling her. She needed to act before more of his plans became irreversible. For two years she'd avoided John Sneddon—dodging him at the office, retreating at home—but now there was no escape. He was everywhere. Everything.

She heard voices in the kitchen and turned away from them, too tightly strung to face anyone just yet. The door to the dining room was open. She slipped inside and sat down, pouring tea from a freshly steeped pot and taking a slice of toast from the waiting rack.

"Good—you're up. I wanted to see you before I leave for the city."

John entered with brisk energy and moved easily to the sideboard, glancing at her in passing. "The day guards are here. Jenny's feeding the night crew now, and I'll drive them back to London on my way in. The press is still camped at the gates, so don't leave the grounds. Better still—don't leave the house. Jenny tells me the pantry's well-stocked."

"I doubt I'll go anywhere today," Grace murmured, her tone edged with weariness. "But I can't just stay here hiding forever. I owe it to my father to—"

"You owe nothing to anyone now," he cut in coldly. "You're free to make your own decisions. But be smart, Grace. Wait a day. By this evening, everyone in the city will know who's running Sneddon-Lewis, and no one will challenge me. I'll issue a statement; the share price will stabilise, and the bloodlust will wane. Give the hounds time to lose interest. No one expects you to re-emerge on day one."

She inhaled deeply and met his gaze. "Very well. I'll stay today. But tomorrow I need to start looking for a flat."

"You don't need to do anything of the kind," he said sharply. "You have full use of this house, and you know it."

"I'm not staying here with you," she snapped, colour rushing to her cheeks.

"I don't recall suggesting that." He gave her a dry look. "I already have one mistress, as you so kindly reminded me. For now, I'll be in my flat. You, on the other hand, need to eat more than scraps if you plan to survive."

"I've got nothing to think about," she said with brittle defiance. But his unwavering stare made her drop her gaze.

"I want to marry you, Grace," he said quietly. "I made myself clear last night. Until you decide, this house is yours. I'll stay in London."

"I see," she said coolly. "So, Rosewood is now a grace-and-favour residence?"

"Until I lose patience—or you fall out of favour," he shot back. "Meanwhile, you're safe."

"Safe?" she flared. "I'm under siege! I can't step outside without cameras clicking, and I have no money. There's Jenny to think about, and yes, I'll need to buy more of my *'bird seed'*, as you put it. If you think I'm going to let you keep us—"

"I pay the bills because I own the house," he said evenly. "Jenny stays, paid by me, and as for you—I can afford you, Grace. Easily."

She surged to her feet, mortified. "Don't you dare speak of me like that!"

But before she could storm out, he was on his feet, already beside her.

"Sit down," he ordered with cool authority. "All of this is nonsense, and you know it."

She stood frozen under the heat of his gaze, trembling. His voice softened.

"I intend to marry you," he said again. "I've fought for everything I've got in this life. It didn't come easy. But once you learn how to win, it becomes second nature. Now there's only one thing missing. You. You're the jewel in the crown, Grace. A gracious, well-bred wife—the final piece that tells me I've made it. When I have you, the past can finally stay in the past."

"You've already made it," she whispered, lips trembling. "You have nothing left to prove—"

"Only to myself," he said.

He turned to leave but paused at the door.

"And you?" he asked, glancing back. "What did you plan to do with your life? You have no qualifications. No degree. No career. You were never even allowed to go to university—your father wouldn't risk losing you. In spite of your intelligence, you're completely untrained. You don't belong behind a desk or in a bedsit. You belong here. And you know it."

It hit Grace like a raw lash—sharp and merciless—because it was almost true. The realisation surged through her, swift and overwhelming. Her father had quietly steered her away from every ambition she'd ever expressed, and she, blinded by love and loyalty, had never fought him on it.

But the anger that bubbled up now had nothing to do with her father. It was all for John Sneddon.

"Do you own my car too?" she snapped as he reached for the door. The question stopped him cold.

He turned, his jaw tight, his eyes glittering with temper. "No, I do not own your car," he said curtly. "Nor your clothes or your jewellery. I only own what your father wanted me to—because he made a deal. I didn't ask for any of it."

"And I was part of that deal," she flared. "You think you bought me."

His eyes narrowed. "Without you, there would have been no deal at all. But I didn't buy you, Grace. Buying objects is easy. Buying people? That's filth. I'm not in that business. I gave my word that I'd protect you—and I keep my word. I want to marry you. I'll wait. For a while."

She lifted her chin, fury blazing in her eyes. "And while you wait, I get to live in this house and pay no bills? Is that the arrangement?"

"Correct," he said evenly, "for as long as I have patience, or until you fall out of favour."

Her mouth parted in disbelief. "Oh, how generous," she breathed. "Well, then, Mr. Sneddon—let's make a deal of our own. If I can trust you to play fair."

His brows lifted slightly, the curve of his mouth mocking but intrigued. "My business reputation is spotless," he replied smoothly. "What kind of deal are you proposing, Miss Lewis—assuming you have something to offer other than your beautiful body?"

Her cheeks flamed, but she didn't back down. "You think I'm nothing but a useless doll—my father's pampered legacy. Maybe you're right. But you fought your way up from nothing using your brain and grit. Give me the same chance."

He stopped walking and turned slowly back, that unblinking gaze settling on her face like a heat lamp. "Go on," he said, his voice quiet and low.

The words almost choked her. The idea had barely taken shape in her mind, but now that it had surfaced, it seemed her only path forward. "Teach me the business," she said breathlessly. "Sneddon-Lewis. Let me prove I can learn. That I can do more than play hostess."

"You?" His tone was more incredulous than insulting. "You've no qualifications."

"I—I do," she said hastily. "At least, I've had some training. I did a business course in secret. I passed—with honours, actually. Daddy didn't know. Not until afterwards."

His gaze sharpened, brows arching with something close to amusement. "You deceived him?"

She swallowed. "Yes. He wasn't pleased. He forbade me from taking a job. But I didn't forget what I learned. I still remember most of it."

He studied her, eyes gleaming with the thrill of the unexpected. "So. You've got rusty skills and no experience. You've lied to your father and now you want me to train you?"

"I don't want to work under you," she rushed out. "Just—somewhere in the company. Accounts, planning, admin—anything."

He said nothing for a long moment, just kept watching her until she wanted to squirm.

"And if you fail?" he asked quietly.

"Then I'll marry you," she said, voice small but firm.

He stilled. Then he tilted his head, watching her as if he'd just uncovered a rare gem buried in dust. "A deal, then," he said at last. "If you fail, you keep your end of the bargain."

He reached for her chin, tilting her face up. "A deal with the devil, Grace?"

"I—I'll keep my word," she whispered.

"You will, angel," he said softly, almost reverently. Then, with a flash of that disarming smile, he added, "And I'll keep mine. A duel it is—winner takes all."

She drew a shaky breath. "I'll need time."

"You have it," he said, his tone turning lightly ironic. "I always play fair. Today is the fifth of September. You'll start with accounts—David Prescott knows his department and he can teach you... about the business, that is." His mouth quirked. "We'll assess your progress at Christmas."

He leaned forward unexpectedly and brushed a kiss across her lips. It was light, brief, but it scorched like fire. "The bargain is sealed," he murmured and turned to leave.

At the door he paused, casting her a long, dark glance. "And if you decide to call it off early?"

She hesitated. "Then what?"

"You marry me, of course," he said, his smile turning wolfish, a challenge glinting in his eyes. "Though I suspect you're secretly plotting to outmanoeuvre me. Just don't get too confident. I don't lose."

Grace lifted her chin, her voice cool but trembling slightly. "Then you're already at a disadvantage. I won't fail—because I have no intention of marrying a man who doesn't love me."

He stepped closer, the smirk playing on his lips. "We'll see."

And then he was gone, leaving her standing there, her lips tingling, her pulse unsteady, her thoughts scattered like petals in a storm.

He was right. He wasn't easily defeated.

But she wasn't the naïve girl everyone underestimated. Not anymore.

Not if she had anything to say about it.

In the meantime, she had the deal—and she meant to work at it with everything she had. When she succeeds, she will secure a job elsewhere, something real and lasting. Then Jenny wouldn't have to worry about a roof over her head or a salary. Grace was determined to win, not to become the final flourish in John Sneddon's ascent—a well-bred wife to erase his less-than-aristocratic beginnings.

When she entered the kitchen, Jenny was bustling around as usual, though there was a faintly dazed expression on her face. The men had left, and she was clearing away their breakfast. For a moment she said nothing, but then turned, her stance resolute, her tone brisk—Jenny never let things stew.

"Mr Sneddon told me he's bought Rosewood."

It wasn't a question. She clearly took John Sneddon at his word—without hesitation or doubt. This was simply her way of letting Grace know she was up to speed.

"He has," Grace replied, voice cool. "Lock, stock, and barrel. Every stick of furniture. Probably even the pans in your kitchen. Like the ads say— *'contents included'.*"

Jenny didn't flinch. "Well, it's a relief, really. It could have gone to strangers. I love this house."

"You don't think Mr Sneddon's a stranger?" Grace asked, arching a brow.

Jenny gave her a withering look. "I think he's a gentleman—a fine one. Strong. Caring. No matter what the papers say. You only have to look at the mess we're in and how he's handled it. If he hadn't stepped in, we'd be under siege. The Press wouldn't think twice about hounding us. Those men on the gate? I'm making them lunch. One of them is coming back at twelve. I was so upset last night; I didn't even think to offer a cup of tea."

"I'll clear the breakfast table," Grace murmured, eager for an excuse to leave. She'd had enough of hearing about what a paragon John Sneddon was.

Jenny paused with her hands in soapy water, glancing back at her. "I hear we're staying on here?"

"For now," Grace muttered, inching toward the door. Her cheeks were already starting to burn.

"How long is *for now*?"

Grace exhaled slowly. Might as well get it over with.

"Until I make it clear to him that I have no intention of marrying him."

Jenny froze, then turned slowly, her expression shifting from stern housekeeper to delighted matchmaker. "He's asked you?" Her voice was soft with something dangerously close to joy. "I knew he would one day. I've seen the way he watches you, even if you haven't. Last night he was asking me what you'd eaten—if I could tempt you with anything. He was worried. Genuinely worried. So... when are you going to marry him?"

"Never," Grace said firmly.

Jenny blinked. "Never?"

"I'm staying here for now because we need the time. I've made an arrangement—I'm going to train in the business. If I do well, I'll find a proper job elsewhere. One with better pay. Then Jenny—" her voice gentled slightly "—you won't have to worry about anything."

Jenny looked scandalised. "You're deceiving him?" she asked, outraged. From anyone else it might have sounded like a moral stance, but coming from Jenny—who would lie outright for those she loved—it was a sign of just how highly she rated John Sneddon.

"I'm not deceiving him," Grace said dryly. "You can't deceive a man like that. I told him everything. If I can't learn the business, I marry him. He thinks I'm useless."

Jenny snorted. "He's humouring you. That's what he's doing. And mark my words—if you don't stop this nonsense, you'll lose him."

"I wish I could," Grace muttered. "I wish I'd never met him."

Jenny, clearly unmoved, turned back to her washing-up. "I'm getting two daily helps," she announced with pride.

Grace stopped mid-stride. "What?"

"Mr Sneddon thinks this house is too much for me at my age. Two women starting next week."

"I always help," Grace snapped, spinning around.

Jenny didn't even flinch. "You're not to," she said briskly. "He says you need to relax. That you're too uptight. Said it would be best to wait until the Press clear off—daily helps talk."

Grace stood glaring at her back for a long second, furious and flustered—but Jenny just kept washing up, already moving on. She had passed along her information, drawn out what she wanted, and now she was simply the housekeeper again.

Grace stormed out, feeling a flush of heat rise to her face that had nothing to do with the kitchen stove.

Mr Sneddon says *this*; Mr Sneddon says *that*! If Jenny mentioned his name one more time, Grace thought she might scream. He had said the Press could get in where water couldn't seep—but he wasn't much better himself. He'd insinuated his way into every corner of her life, smooth as smoke and just as impossible to catch. For two pins, she'd pack her things and leave Jenny to fend for herself.

She stormed upstairs, but the moment she reached her room, the fire in her chest faltered. She crossed to the window and looked out.

The gates were locked. Two of John's men leaned against the stone pillars, talking like they were on a leisurely break. But just beyond the iron bars, a mob clustered—camera lenses glinting, faces eager, hungry. The paparazzi. It was easy to forget they were there—until you looked. Then the siege was impossible to ignore.

She let out a long breath, half anger, half resignation. If not for the muscle at the gate, those people would be on the front steps by now, camped on the lawn, sticking lenses through the windows. She had to admit it: John had done what no one else could. He'd drawn a line they wouldn't cross.

She hoped he had issued his statement already. With any luck, tomorrow would see them gone. But the thought only made her more restless, more uneasy.

He was everywhere. Surrounding her. Trapping her.

She wrapped her arms around herself and stared out at the trees beyond the chaos. How had it come to this? How had she ended up so tangled in John Sneddon's world that she could hardly breathe without his permission?

It felt as if some dark net had been cast over her—deliberate, invisible, and impossibly tight.

For the first time in her life, she would have to fight—for herself, for her future, for the kind of love she knew she deserved.

Because no matter how tempting his offer, or how determined he was to have her…

She would never settle for a loveless marriage.

Not now.

Not ever.

Chapter Six

Her mobile buzzed on the nightstand just as dusk unfurled across the garden, painting the sky in rose-gold and deepening blue. She picked it up without checking the screen—somehow, she already knew.

John.

His voice came through the line, low and steady. "Go to your window."

She blinked, heart suddenly pounding. "What?"

"Now," he said gently. "You should be able to see the gates from there."

"I'm already in my room," she said warily, rising to look. "What am I looking for?"

"A lack of interest," he replied dryly. "I'd be surprised if anyone's still loitering around."

She parted the curtain and looked out. The driveway was quiet. The men from the firm lounged by the gates, playing cards under the security lights. But the crowd—the press, the cameras, the chaos—had vanished.

"They're gone," she told him quietly.

He made a sound of satisfaction. "Good. I've sent a night team down anyway, just in case. But I doubt anyone will bother us again."

"D-did you issue a statement?"

There was a pause, and then that dark, familiar laugh that always seemed to go right through her.

"Yes, I issued a statement," he said. "To the media, we are now officially boring. Still, I suggest you don't read the papers for a few days. Not everything will have been—contained."

"You mean… the women?" she asked hesitantly.

His tone shifted, became clipped. "Yes. There'll be rumours. Ignore them. Remember your father as you knew him."

"I do." The words were no more than a whisper, but he heard them. She could hear his sigh on the line—equal parts frustration and something softer.

"Learn to live, Grace. You're bright. Beautiful."

"I—I'm going to live," she said, her voice trembling. "I have to defeat you."

He laughed again, and she could suddenly picture him—leaning back, dark eyes gleaming, too confident by half. It sent a strange, heated ripple through her that made her press a hand to her chest.

"I can accept any challenge," he said. "And if it helps to pull you out of that little shell, then it's already worth it. But I still intend to win."

"So do I."

"Maybe," he said with maddening amusement, "you'll change your mind about the goal before Christmas."

She didn't answer, and he let the silence stretch before speaking again, low, and smooth.

"You do realise," he said, "that if I'm to teach you about the firm, I'll have to see a great deal more of you than before."

"You said I'd learn from the departments," she replied quickly, her throat tight.

"And so you will. But the drive of Sneddon-Lewis comes from the top. From me. There's no point pretending otherwise. If you're serious, you'll need to learn to coordinate everything—just as I do. Which means you'll be in and out of my office daily. Like it or not, you'll be living in my pocket."

Grace was silent. She hadn't thought that far ahead. Hadn't imagined what it would feel like to be under his gaze every day.

"When you're nervous," he said softly, "you stammer a little. Did you know that?"

She flinched, her voice sharp with panic. "Do you want to come down here? Is that what you're really saying?"

"I could," he said, amused. "But I did promise to stay in my flat while you're at Rosewood."

"You said—until we're married. And that's not going to happen."

"Don't sound so frantic, my angel. I'm not about to pounce on you."

"I can guarantee that," she snapped. "And I am not your angel!"

"You will be," he said with quiet certainty. "At least, you'll look like one, standing beside me at Rosewood, welcoming our guests."

The image struck her like a bolt—elegant, serene, his wife in name and presence. The very thought made her heart lurch.

She ended the call with a sharp tap of her thumb and dropped the phone onto the bed.

She could still see it—that picture he painted. The terrifying part was that it wasn't quite as horrifying as it had once seemed. That was the real danger.

John Sneddon wasn't sneaking into her life.

He was marching in, doors thrown wide—and she didn't know how to stop him. But she had to try.

Grace didn't begin work until the following week. In the meantime, autumn returned in full, cloaking the world in crisp air and golden light that stretched gently into the early evenings. The leaves turned burnished shades of amber and rust, and the chill in the breeze hinted at the season's quiet descent.

She spent as much time outdoors as she could, walking beneath the changing trees or simply sitting still, letting the hush of nature wrap around her like a balm. In that solitude, she found space to breathe—to grieve honestly, without interruption. And in the rustling leaves and fading warmth, she began the slow, painful process of accepting a truth she could no longer outrun. She was on her own now. Truly, completely alone.

Her father was gone—no longer there to coax a smile from her, to tease her gently over breakfast, to spoil her without apology, or to quietly bully her when he thought she needed direction. That last truth she could finally admit to herself, though she would never have confessed it to John Sneddon. Not in a thousand years.

With the arrival of two robust and efficient daily helps, there was little left for her to do inside the house, and she was still too wary to stray far beyond the grounds. The thought of bumping into someone from the past, someone who might offer sympathy—or worse, curious pity—was more than she could bear. So, she kept to the gardens, reading in the shade or walking aimlessly among the roses, letting the sun warm her skin and the silence soothe her frayed nerves. Slowly, she began to heal.

And yet, traitorously, her mind kept circling back to the same thought: *Would I have recovered so quickly if John Sneddon hadn't come into my life with such ruthless force?*

When the first day of work finally arrived, Grace was more nervous than she had anticipated. For all her cultivated poise and years of moving in privileged circles, she had never earned her own living. She'd assumed she could fake her way through this new role with a cool smile and a steady voice—but as she approached the gleaming tower that housed Sneddon-Lewis, her confidence faltered.

The building loomed, a striking testament to modern power—glass and steel soaring upwards, light catching on sharp angles, reflecting the sharp edges of the man who now ran it. Grace had been here before, to visit her father. But this time everything felt different. This time she wasn't the daughter of Brian Lewis. She was Grace Lewis, alone, and under scrutiny.

People noticed her the moment she walked through the glass doors. Of course they did. They knew who she was. But the looks she received weren't merely curious—they were measured, uncertain. She no longer belonged to the old order. She had stepped into his domain now, and it pulsed with drive and energy, ambition humming in the walls. Lewis's quiet, familial charm was gone. The warmth had been replaced by something far more dangerous—efficiency, control, momentum.

For a moment she stood in the centre of the vast foyer, frozen.

Then John appeared, cutting through the space like a shadow with purpose. Impeccably dressed, calm as ever, he crossed to her with that smooth authority she had come to both resent and—deep down—lean on. He didn't give her time to think. With the ease of someone used to command, he took her firmly by the arm and swept her forward into her new reality.

He introduced her to the accounts department as if she were any other new hire—no special treatment, no fanfare. But his tone, his presence, sent a very clear message to the room: *she may be starting at the bottom, but she's under my protection.*

They didn't question it. Many of them had known Grace since she was a little girl with ribbons in her hair, visiting her father's office after school. Some looked at her with sympathy—they all knew about Brian Lewis; the city had whispered every detail. But Grace didn't want sympathy. She didn't want softness.

She was here to prove herself.

To John.

To herself.

She settled at her desk with a calm determination that surprised even her. And as the day unfolded, something unfamiliar stirred inside her—not fear, not grief, but something fierce and new.

Resolve.

She was enjoying herself. For the first time in days—perhaps weeks—Grace felt purposeful, absorbed in the figures and reports in front of her. She lost track of time completely, the hum of conversation around her fading into background noise as she worked. The unfamiliar satisfaction of doing something meaningful, something real, lifted her out of her own grief and worry.

Then, just before lunch, the atmosphere changed.

John walked into the department without ceremony. He said nothing until he reached her desk, and even then, his expression was unreadable. He gestured silently for her to follow. She obeyed, conscious of curious glances as she walked beside him to the lift.

Only when they were alone, gliding upward, did he speak.

"I'm taking you to lunch," he said curtly.

"There's no need. I've already started to eat," she replied, keeping her voice brisk. The nerves that had plagued her earlier had all but vanished; now she was almost buoyant with the thrill of finally doing something on her own.

"I assumed as much." His eyes swept over her with quiet intensity, and she felt her newfound enthusiasm falter. "I've noticed the tan—and the few added pounds. They suit you." His tone was casual, but the look in his eyes made her skin prickle. "But that's not the point. I'm simply taking you to lunch."

"Do I have to go?"

One dark brow lifted. "No. You can refuse, make a scene if you like. I'm not your father—I don't expect gentle obedience. Kick and scream all you like. I'll still win, in the end."

"We were talking about lunch, not anything else," Grace said tightly, her cheeks flaming.

"So we were," he agreed, with a faint, mocking smile. "Have lunch with me, Miss Lewis?"

"If you insist, Mr Sneddon," she said with a touch of derision, lifting her chin. If he could play games, so could she. But the thought of Christmas and his so-called assessment tugged at the back of her mind. She had so little time. *Would he extend it? Or was this part of his endgame?*

"You stare at me a lot," he said suddenly, voice low, almost amused. "You may not realise it, but you do. For the past couple of years, you made yourself invisible—slipping out of rooms before I arrived, avoiding my eyes. Now, though… you study me with terrifying focus. If you want to know something, Grace, just ask. I'm not that difficult to read."

"I wasn't trying to read you," she snapped. "I was trying to make you disappear. Unfortunately, despite long nights of practice, I seem to have failed. You're still very much here."

He chuckled—slow and deep—his dark eyes glinting with satisfaction. "Then give it up. While you're trying to wish me away, I'm wishing myself closer. I suspect we're cancelling each other out—call it the magnet principle. Let me win, Grace. We'll both enjoy it more."

His words echoed in her mind as they stepped into the foyer, and she hated the heat that spread across her face. She hoped the receptionist assumed he was simply reprimanding her for a poor morning's performance. *Did she really stare at him?* She supposed it was possible. Most of the women in the building did, after all—how could they not?

There was something about him—dark, commanding, self-assured. A man like John Sneddon didn't need to court attention. It followed him, trailed him like a shadow. If appearances were anything to go by, half the women in the office would have married him on the spot.

But he stalked through their lives like a remote, untouchable god.

In hers, he prowled like a panther.

She remembered the first time she saw him.

It had been at a formal dinner party at Rosewood, months before John Sneddon had taken any noticeable interest in the firm. Her father had been in his element that evening, moving through the room with effortless charm, greeting guests as though he owned not just the house but the world beyond it. Grace had been poised at the top of the grand staircase, her smile bright, her gown softly shimmering in the light, ready to descend and welcome old family friends—when her father's voice rang out from below, calling up to her.

'Grace, darling. There's someone I'd like you to meet.'

He'd said that countless times before, and she'd descended with her usual composed smile—until she saw the man standing beside him.

John Sneddon.

The smile died on her lips.

Something had hit her, low and hard, like the thump of a dropped weight in her chest. Her heart had tilted, panic flaring through her like lightning. She didn't know what it was, but she knew—knew—this man was different. Not just different, but dangerous. There was no warmth in his eyes, only a sharp, glittering watchfulness. Ruthless focus. Cold amusement. And something darker still, something primal.

She had felt threatened, shaken, stripped bare.

He had taken her hand briefly, his politeness impeccable. 'Miss Lewis,' he'd said with a half-bow, releasing her fingers the moment he felt her recoil.

She hadn't settled for the rest of the evening. She had caught herself watching him when she thought he wouldn't notice—only to find his eyes meeting hers, steady and unreadable. She would quickly look away, heart pounding.

Yes. She had stared. Secretly. Often. She had just never imagined he'd noticed.

It was a habit she needed to break. The trouble was, she wasn't always aware she was doing it.

A hard hand suddenly closed around her arm, yanking her back to the pavement just as she was about to step into the flow of lunch-hour traffic.

"Don't throw yourself under a bus," John said calmly, keeping her firmly at his side. "I need you, Grace. My car's here—I didn't use the car park this morning."

"I—I'm sorry. I wasn't paying attention."

"You were miles away." He opened the passenger door of the sleek black Mercedes and helped her inside. "Don't take life so seriously. You might even enjoy it if you loosened up a little."

"That's difficult. I'm under threat."

"Wrong. You're being pursued," he said smoothly, glancing at her with a faint, knowing smile. "Hasn't anyone ever pursued you before?"

"Yes," she replied tartly. "But they didn't tell me upfront that love wasn't on the table."

He arched a brow but let the jab slide. "Hasn't a man ever told you he wanted you?"

Colour rose in her cheeks. She looked down quickly, fingers twisting in her lap. "I—I don't usually invite that kind of... attention."

"Insolence?" he suggested, clearly amused. "Don't stammer. And don't be afraid. You're out to lunch, not standing trial."

She didn't know what to say. His voice had gone gentle, teasing almost, and she was sure he thought her simple-minded. The truth was, no man had ever said he wanted her. She'd been too shy, too sheltered. Her father had kept a close watch—no late nights, no jobs, no risks.

"You just want a well-bred wife and an heir," she said tightly.

"I want you," he said, his voice suddenly quiet and dark. "I want to look up and know you're mine. I want things to remember when I'm not home. None of it has to do with your lineage."

"You know I won't marry you," she whispered, breath catching.

"You don't want to," he corrected softly. "Time will change that."

"You're arrogant. Ruthless. Dangerous."

"Better that than weak and slow," he murmured, one corner of his mouth lifting. He started the car, pulling out into the traffic with ease. "You can't expect me to behave like your well-bred boyfriends. I'm not one of them. I'm leading you gently—for me. Spoiling you, even. Indulging this little plan of yours to *'learn the business'*, though we both know it's just a way to buy time."

"I'm trying," she said, chin lifting. "You think it's some game."

"I think it's charming." His voice was smooth as silk. "And I'll apply real pressure when I grow impatient. But not yet. For now, you're safe. You're standing at the edge of a life you've never lived. I'm letting you dip your toes in the water."

"What is this to you?" she asked, her voice low but intense. "Why me? Why pick me?"

He shot her a sideways glance, and the smile he gave was slow, self-assured, infuriating.

"Look in the mirror," he said, voice low and infuriatingly calm. "A golden virgin with violet eyes. Of course you're the one. You even shout quietly."

Grace gritted her teeth as he chuckled, maddeningly unaffected.

"Oh, I see," she snapped. "You want a passionate mistress and a meek little wife."

His mouth twitched. "Well, it keeps life interesting."

Her eyes narrowed. "So, the mistress stays once you're married? Does that mean I'm free to take a lover too?"

His expression darkened instantly. "No. No one else will ever touch you."

She lifted her chin, fire dancing in her eyes. "We'll see about that."

A thick silence crackled between them, charged and defiant.

Then, coolly, he said, "Are we done sparring? We've arrived."

The car slowed to a stop in front of Bejarano's. This was clearly no casual lunch. No cheese sandwich in sight.

It was warm inside—elegant, expensive—and the subtle hush of wealth hung in the air like expensive perfume. Grace hesitated just inside the door, suddenly uneasy. She'd never been here before, but the type of people who did come here were exactly the ones who knew her father. The idea of being recognised, of her presence being questioned, made her almost afraid to look around.

"Your table, Mr Sneddon."

The maître d' appeared like a conjurer, all obsequious charm, and polished manners, nearly bowing as he gestured them forward. As they began to walk through the crowded restaurant, Grace was aware of eyes turning toward them—some curious, some speculative, all watching.

She edged instinctively closer to John.

"Relax," he murmured, taking her arm and tucking her firmly into his side. "No one's going to ask you to wash dishes."

"Easy for you to say," she replied under her breath.

"Chin up, Grace. Look the world in the face."

"Even when it's staring at me?" she asked tightly.

He gave a low chuckle. "I hate to disappoint you, child, but they're not looking at you."

"They've seen your horns, then?" she retorted, surprising even herself with the sass in her voice. She was trembling—but somehow the banter helped her find balance.

He gave a soft, wicked laugh. "That's better. No, they haven't seen my horns. They've heard about my latest conquest."

Her eyes widened. "Me?"

He looked down at her like the devil himself. "Such vanity, Miss Lewis. No. Not you. I just finalised the Felton Corporation acquisition last night. The city knows today."

She barely noticed the waiter helping her into her seat, too stunned by his words.

"B-but that's textiles," she said. "What's that got to do with civil engineering?"

"So, the birdseed hasn't damaged your brain." His tone was teasing, but with an edge. "Yes. It's textiles. I've dabbled in plenty of sectors over the years. Felton put up a fight. They lost."

"Naturally," she murmured. "I wonder you even bother with engineering. You seem far more at home in a war zone."

"Back to the gutter, are we?" His eyes gleamed with amused challenge. "I am an engineer, Miss Lewis. That's why I bother. It may not be my only interest, but it's still my main one—especially now." That last part was said softer, with deliberate weight.

He leaned back in his chair, sardonic and sure of himself, scanning the menu like a man with all the time in the world.

"Want me to order for you? I know what you like."

She frowned. "How could you possibly know that?"

"You forget," he said, looking up, "while you were busy stealing glances at me at Rosewood, I was watching you too. I wasn't quite so discreet about it, but I doubt you noticed. I saw what you liked. What you barely touched. What made your face light up."

He paused, and the mischief in his eyes deepened.

"You don't like steak, but you love chicken. You adore strawberries but won't touch the cream. You drink champagne when offered, prefer white dry wine, and sometimes sneak a sweet liqueur when you think no one's watching. You always eat your soup— and you never, ever spill it."

She had been staring at him, wide-eyed, but now she burst into unexpected laughter— light and unguarded, the first time she'd laughed in his presence.

His expression changed subtly. Something darkly appreciative stirred behind his eyes.

"Laughter lights up your face," he said softly. "Turns your eyes into jewels. You're a beautiful woman, Grace."

His voice was velvet, and his gaze was so intent she had to drop her eyes in self-defence. But even with her eyes closed, she could feel him—could hear the echo of that voice in the back of her mind.

"One day," he murmured, "you won't be able to hide from me. One day soon, I'll know every thought in your head. Every secret. Every inch of your body."

"Please," she whispered, barely audible. "You know I won't marry you. I can't marry a man that doesn't love me. I'll leave if I have to. Go away."

His hand reached across the table and gently closed over hers. Firm. Possessive.

"Don't you mean—run away?" he asked quietly. "Face me, Grace. Fight me."

"I—I c-can't." She forced herself to meet his gaze, and it was like diving into the ocean—dark, fathomless, impossible to escape. "Are you just trying to fix me? Toughen me up?"

He didn't answer directly. Just shook his head, smiling slightly, maddeningly confident.

"Don't stammer," he said gently.

It was said with unexpected softness, and she swallowed hard. She didn't pull her hand away.

She didn't quite know how.

Chapter Seven

They had nearly finished their meal when Grace looked up—and froze.

A woman was bearing down on their table with the kind of unapologetic purpose that made heads turn. Bearing down was the only way to describe it, and Grace knew instantly who it was. She'd seen Rita Peterson in glossy magazine spreads and snappy television interviews—lauded by the media as a self-made powerhouse.

But to Grace, it was no mystery. Rita was cut from the same steel as John: ruthless, focused, and fiercely determined to win.

Even from a distance, she radiated a kind of charged energy, as if her ambition created its own gravitational pull. The black hair slicked back into a tight chignon, the sharp-shouldered blazer over tailored trousers, and those glacial blue eyes—all part of an image that had been honed to intimidate.

"Darling!" Rita's voice exploded across the room like a firework, and John looked up in clear surprise.

"Rita? I didn't know you were dining here."

"I'm not," she said breezily, already pulling up a chair. "But I'll have a coffee with you—that's all I've time for. I rang your office, and they said you were here. I had to let you know I can make it tonight after all. I was terrified you might've made other plans." Her eyes flicked to Grace—sweeping her up, assessing her... then dismissing her.

"No other arrangements," John murmured, signalling the waiter. "Although you're lucky you arrived—I might have asked Grace."

He made the introductions with casual ease, and Rita's perfectly arched brows lifted slightly at Grace's surname.

"Lewis? Oh, that Lewis. I do hope you've recovered from the whole ordeal, Miss Lewis. The press can be so cruel when they smell scandal."

"They never bothered me, Miss Peterson," Grace said evenly. "I didn't speak to a single journalist. There wasn't anything worth reporting, really."

"Really?" Rita tilted her head, her expression oozing false innocence. "Oh, I know it was all hushed up, but—"

"Perhaps you could hush up, Rita," John interjected smoothly, his voice quiet but edged like a razor. "Grace is still grieving her father."

Rita gave a saccharine smile that didn't reach her eyes. "Of course. So tragic. And I suppose, having been close to your father, John's keeping you under his wing for a while?"

It was the pointed stress on close that did it. Grace felt her cheeks heat. The implication, the thinly veiled condescension, the casual claim of ownership—it all rankled. And beneath it, a sting: had John spoken to Rita about her?

She smiled sweetly.

"John's been wonderful. I honestly don't know what I would've done without him these last couple of weeks," she said brightly. "I'm staying at his house, actually. He even makes sure I eat. You must come down one evening. We'll have dinner."

The effect was instant. Rita's expression didn't change much—but her eyes did. Shock. Fury. Possession wounded.

John didn't bat an eye.

"That's an excellent idea," he said smoothly. "Come tomorrow night, Rita. Seven o'clock. We'll give you a tour before dinner."

He was enjoying this, Grace realised. Thoroughly.

Rita drained her coffee in silence and left with barely concealed fury.

Grace turned on him the moment she was gone.

"I'm supposed to have Rosewood to myself until Christmas," she hissed. "I never invited you to dinner."

"You invited Rita. Would you rather face her alone?" His tone was maddeningly calm. "You caught her off guard just now—she was pressed for time. But don't count on escaping so easily next time."

"I doubt I'll see her again," Grace snapped.

"Oh, you will." He leaned back, watching her with cool amusement. "Tomorrow night, dinner at my house. Your suggestion, after all."

"I hate you more by the minute," she said coldly.

"And I want you more by the second." His voice dropped an octave. "Anger suits you. Adds fire to an already fascinating equation. And—worth noting—you didn't stammer once. Let's remember that."

"You can't come to dinner," she said tightly, but his expression only grew more insufferable.

"I'll be there," he said. "In fact, I think I'll stay the night. Don't bother preparing—I'll let Jen know."

"Her name is Jenny!" Grace snapped.

"She prefers Jen. Relax a little—you might find out all sorts of lovely things."

"From you?" she asked scornfully.

But her bravado wavered as his smile faded. The mockery dropped away. What remained was worse: intensity. Dark, deliberate, and without softness.

"You know better than that," he said quietly. "I'm not 'nice', Grace. Nothing I do is out of kindness. Everything I do for you—*everything*—is just marking time. Waiting until I own you."

"Y-you won't own me. No one can *own* someone."

Gone was the teasing man. In his place was something far more formidable—calculated power cloaked in patience.

"What should I say to that?" he asked, eyes steady. "Maybe nothing. You're necessary to my plans. And I want you. That makes you inevitable."

Later, Grace would wonder if John had truly meant it—his threat to come to Rosewood. Maybe it had been a game, just another of his tactics to keep her off balance. But she should have known better.

He stayed out all that afternoon and well into the next day. She tried not to watch the clock, tried not to hope—or dread. But when she returned home, Jenny greeted her with a pleased smile.

"Mr Sneddon called. He'll be joining us for dinner—and staying the night," she added, clearly delighted. "He even requested the menu!"

Jenny listed the dishes, and Grace recognised more than a few of her favourites. She should have expected it. She wondered if he would bring champagne just to make a point.

He did.

She was halfway up the stairs, on her way to change, when the front door swung open and John walked in as if he owned the place—two bottles of champagne tucked under one arm, a bouquet of roses in the other. Grace froze mid-step, her hand tightening on the railing.

He saw her and smiled.

"Champagne and roses," he announced lightly. "I ordered a bright moon, but they couldn't deliver on such short notice."

"How disappointing for Miss Peterson," Grace said sweetly, her tone laced with sarcasm. "Never mind—we'll light candles instead."

He came toward her and stopped just beneath where she stood, his gaze meeting hers as if he had all the time in the world. She stood still, poised for flight—but unable to move.

"The roses are for you," he said.

"Why?" Her voice was sharp, the question flung at him like a challenge—partly because of the roses, but mostly because of the way he looked at her. His gaze held hers effortlessly, that dark magnetism cloaking him like a second skin.

"Why?" he echoed. "You're my bride-to-be. I know we agreed not to talk about it seriously—*yet*—but surely, I can bring you flowers. Note the restraint. Pink, not red."

"In case Miss Peterson saw them and got suspicious?"

"In case you misunderstood," he replied smoothly. "Pink suits a virgin bride. More delicate. Less presumptuous. Besides—Rita won't see them, will she? You'll put them in your room. Right by the bed."

"I'll put them in the bin. Right by the back door," she snapped.

"No, you won't, angel," he said softly. "You're far too soft-hearted for that."

Grace turned sharply and climbed the stairs without another word, feeling his eyes on her all the way up. And of course, she wouldn't throw the roses out. He knew that. He always seemed to know exactly how far he could push her—how deeply he'd gotten under her skin, no matter how hard she tried to keep him out.

In her room, she stood for several minutes, torn.

Should she wear jeans and a sweater to show him just how unimpressed she was? Or should she dress for the occasion—to remind him that she wasn't some meek little shadow, grateful for his attention?

In the end, pride won out.

She chose black.

A cocktail dress with fine bootlace straps that crossed over her pale, bare shoulders. It hugged her frame without apology, simple and elegant, allowing her honey-brown hair to shine in contrast. She took her time getting ready, pretending she wasn't doing it for him.

But she was.

And deep down, she knew exactly why.

Rita Peterson had rattled her. She shouldn't have cared—should have laughed off the power games of a woman who wore ambition like perfume. But Rita's presence lingered. Her boutiques catered to the elite; the sort of places Grace had only ever walked past. Rita had clawed her way to wealth and influence, and she clearly hadn't hesitated to step over people to get there.

Grace had no illusions about the kind of woman she was up against.

Still, it wasn't Rita who frightened her most—it was the way she herself had felt at the mention of John's mistress. The slow twist in her stomach, the flare of something far too close to jealousy. It terrified her.

Why should she care?

With a bit of luck, she'd be gone from all of this soon. Free of John Sneddon. Free of this house. Free of the pull he had on her—if she could just keep herself from falling any deeper.

And yet… even as she stared at her reflection, her thoughts weren't on escape.

They were on him.

She was still contemplating her reflection in the mirror, fidgeting with a curl of hair, when a knock came at her door. She frowned, hoping Jenny hadn't burned the dinner.

"Come in, Jenny," she called.

But it wasn't Jenny.

John opened the door and walked in as though it belonged to him.

"You can't come in here!" Her voice came out high and tight—shock stiffening every part of her. Was there no part of her life he wouldn't invade?

"You invited me," he said mildly. "I distinctly heard you."

"I—I thought it was Jenny. Will you please leave now?"

He stepped further into the room with that soundless grace of his, moving like a shadow. Like a predator.

"I brought you something," he said, his voice softer now.

"I don't want it." She spun away from him instinctively, but she wasn't fast enough. His fingers wrapped firmly around her wrist, turning her gently but decisively back toward him.

"You don't even know what it is," he said, almost exasperated. "Stop being foolish, Grace. I'm not here to seduce you. Just stand still for a minute. I want you to wear this."

Before she could protest, he'd turned her toward the mirror and reached around her neck. She felt the cool weight of metal and jewels settle against her collarbones—saw it at the same time she felt it. A necklace, delicate but unmistakably expensive. Amethysts and diamonds glinted in a vintage setting that caught the light with quiet elegance.

She stared. He said nothing, just stood behind her in silence as they both watched her reflection.

"I… I can't accept this," she whispered. "It looks real."

"It is real," he said simply. "I want you to have it. It brings out the violet in your eyes. I've never seen eyes like yours before. I saw the necklace this afternoon and thought of you."

"Please don't do this," she said, her voice catching. "You're putting me in an impossible position."

"Why?" His hands settled at her waist, warm and sure. "I'm a wealthy man. You please me. I want to see you wearing something that's mine."

"But I—I—"

"Don't stammer," he said, almost gently. His hands slid slowly up her arms, brushing her bare shoulders, his touch sending tingles over her skin. "There's no trick, Grace. No scheme. It's just a necklace."

"You're trying to make Miss Peterson jealous," she said, grasping at logic—at anything to help steady her.

His laugh was quiet and low, curling around her spine like smoke.

"No such thing," he murmured. "I just want to look across the table tonight and see you wearing something I gave you."

He leaned down and pressed a kiss to her bare shoulder. It was light—barely there—but it scorched her.

Then, without another word, he turned and left the room.

Grace stood frozen, staring at herself in the mirror.

The necklace had changed her.

A moment ago, she'd been a well-dressed girl—nervous but presentable. Now… now she looked expensive. Polished. Like someone else entirely.

But it wasn't just the necklace. Her eyes sparkled unnaturally. Her cheeks were flushed. She looked as if she were glowing.

Because of him.

She gritted her teeth, quickly applied fresh lipstick, and combed her hair again with trembling fingers. Somehow, she would have to get through the evening. Somehow, she would have to face Rita Peterson.

Before, she had believed it was possible. Now, she wasn't so sure.

Rita proved to be far more glamorous than Grace remembered. Gone was the icy businesswoman with sharp edges and cold ambition. Tonight, she was all silk and suggestion, dressed for John—not for fashion. And she looked it.

Her dark hair was loose and gleaming, falling artfully around her shoulders. She wore a flowing kaftan in red and gold, her lipstick a perfect match, her gold eyeshadow shimmering in the candlelight. Every detail screamed intention.

It was too much for Jenny, who served the meal with tight lips and spent as little time in the room as possible. But when she did glance at Grace, her eyes were full of unspoken warnings: *Take action or lose him.*

As if that weren't enough, Rita's gaze never left her for long—cool blue eyes tracking her, judging, waiting for signs of weakness. And John? He said almost nothing, just sat there watching Grace with that faintly amused look that made her feel more exposed than ever.

Halfway through the meal, Rita finally said, "That's a very fine necklace, Grace. Worth copying, I'd say. I can picture it against a sharp little suit—classic lines."

John lifted his wineglass. "Are you branching into jewellery now?"

"Why not?" Rita said, shrugging one shoulder. "Costume jewellery's booming. A nice return on investment. I've been thinking of launching a small collection—limited pieces, very selective stockists. It's all about exclusivity now, darling."

She turned her gaze on Grace. "That one looks authentic. Where did you find it? I could use a few good places to shop."

It was the perfect cue. All Grace had to say was John gave it to me—simple, direct, true. But her mouth wouldn't form the words. Her nerves had turned to glass. She wanted nothing more than to be out of this glittering cage of a room.

"As a matter of fact," John said smoothly, "I bought it for Grace."

He smiled, not at Rita, but at Grace. "She has violet eyes. Very rare. The necklace suits her, though I can't quite explain why."

"Embarrasses her, I should think," Rita replied coolly, eyes flicking to Grace's flushed cheeks. "Honestly, John, what a thing to do—just springing something like that on her. You do realise how compromising that is?"

"I didn't spring it on her," he said mildly. "I fastened it around her neck. She understands."

"She should," Grace said suddenly, trying to find her footing. "John was my father's friend. He's... helping me get back on my feet."

"How unusually benevolent of him," Rita murmured, her smile as hard as her eyes. "I've never known him to be so avuncular before. But then... you do have that wounded-bird look."

"Feeble," Grace replied sweetly, fire now burning beneath her quiet words. "It's the age gap, I imagine. That's why he's so avuncular."

John only smiled—sardonic and unreadable—but Rita stiffened ever so slightly. She'd heard the bite under Grace's softness. After that, she barely acknowledged her presence.

John didn't intervene. He simply watched Grace, his gaze unreadable, as though assessing how much polish she needed before she was fully his.

And Grace? She sat silent and simmering.

This wasn't her home anymore. It was John Sneddon's house now—his crystal, his silver, his rules.

And the worst part was... part of her had known it the moment he fastened that necklace around her neck.

Chapter Eight

By the time Rita finally tore herself away at ten o'clock, Grace was on the verge of screaming. Her patience had frayed to a thread, and when John rose to escort their guest to the door, Grace flatly refused to follow. She stayed rooted to her chair, her face like stone.

Let him play the gentleman.

She couldn't even retreat to her bedroom—not while they were murmuring in the hall. Murmuring! One stolen glance had been more than enough—Rita's arms were looped lazily around John's neck, her body pressed far too close. Grace fled into the drawing room before she had to see more, the bile rising thick and bitter in her throat.

It was a long time before she heard the quiet sound of his return. She looked up, prepared to see lipstick smeared across his mouth or collar—but there was nothing. He looked infuriatingly composed.

He met her mutinous stare in silence.

"I'm going to bed," she snapped, rising and moving toward the door.

"Does that require a comment?" His voice was bland, faintly amused. "Unless you're inviting me, which I doubt."

"I can do without remarks like that, thank you," she shot back, whirling on him. "I've just spent the most tedious evening of my life, and it's drained me more than a week of formal balls. I'd have thought Miss Peterson would be exhausted too—so much venom, so carefully dressed in ice. No doubt she'll need to be up by five just to fuel her next attack on the world."

"She thrives on early mornings," John said, the corner of his mouth twitching. "And venom. She's got the energy for both. Besides, she drives a Ferrari."

Of course she did. She probably had a satellite dish, an iPad, and a bathroom that looked like the control deck of a spaceship. No doubt she would glide into it, emerge twenty minutes later scented with Givenchy and glowing with weaponised beauty—without lifting a perfectly manicured finger.

"Well, she's not at all pleased about this," Grace said, gesturing at the necklace still glittering at her throat.

"No?" John gave her a sideways glance. "I hadn't noticed. Doesn't matter. Let her guess. She needs to be reminded she's not invincible." He stepped closer. "She'll learn soon enough exactly where she stands. It's mistress or nothing—once I marry you."

Grace inhaled sharply. "Pigs might fly!" she flared, flinging the words at him before sweeping out of the room.

It was unbelievable—this entire situation. She should have laughed in his face and walked out the moment he first suggested anything so outrageous. Looking back now, with the haze of grief beginning to lift, she couldn't fathom why she hadn't left the morning after her father's funeral.

But she couldn't. Fear whispered the small voice in her mind. Not just grief—fear. She hadn't known how to go on. And John… John had been a wall she could lean against. Someone who didn't flinch. Someone who faced things.

But *that* time had passed.

Jenny was settled here—she'd stay, Grace was certain. That left only herself to worry about. And she could manage. She would sell some jewellery, for one thing. Her mind had been too numb before to think of it.

She stripped off the evening's clothes, showered, then paced the bedroom in her silken negligee, nerves thrumming like exposed wires.

How much would she get?

Crossing to the wall, she slid aside a framed Degas print, revealing the small wall safe behind it. Her hands were steady as she spun the dial and opened the door. One by one, she laid the velvet boxes out on the dressing table.

The jewellery sparkled in the lamplight—diamonds, emeralds, sapphires, pearls. So many pieces. Her father had lavished them on her, trying to keep her safely encased in the life he'd built—an elegant cage.

Tears burned suddenly behind her eyes.

It had been terrible for both of them. He had never recovered from losing her mother, and she… she had never been allowed to grow beyond that loss. A china doll in a glass cabinet.

She lifted a diamond bracelet from the box, turning it so the facets caught the lamplight. Could she really sell these? Could she let go of the only tangible remnants of a time when life had felt safe, cherished? Many of the pieces had belonged to her mother. Each one was a fragment of memory—her father fastening a clasp with careful hands, the warmth in his eyes as he saw her wear it, the quiet pride in his smile.

No. Not yet.

With a sigh, she set the bracelet back among the velvet-lined treasures, closing the lid as if sealing away a part of herself. She knew she would have to sell them eventually— it was her only real source of income apart from the small wage she earned at the firm.

But first she needed time. More experience. She would learn as much as she could, make her own way. And maybe, someday, meet a man who loved her completely—a man who would never glance at another woman, let alone keep a mistress under the same sky as his wife.

The thought tightened something in her chest.

Tonight, had unsettled her more than she wanted to admit. For the first time, the truth settled over her like cold rain: none of this—these jewels, this house, this life—was truly hers. Not anymore. She'd been living inside a dream she'd known since childhood, but the dream had ended.

The house belonged to John.

So did the power.

So did the future.

And if she wasn't careful… she might belong to him, too.

The thought jolted her.

To be swept up in those arms… to feel the strength of that hard, commanding body close around her… A flicker of heat stirred low inside, so sudden it shocked her. She pressed her hands to her face, horrified by her own reaction.

No. That's not what I want.

But Rita's sleek, knowing face rose unbidden in her mind—cool, polished, the perfect match for a man like John. That was his world: sharp, powerful people who knew what they wanted and took it without hesitation. He and Rita spoke the same language. They were forged from the same steel.

When Grace married, it would be to a man who couldn't imagine looking at another woman, let alone flaunt a mistress before his wife. Anything else would be degrading.

And what am I? she wondered bitterly.

Certainly not his equal.

Not yet.

It was nearly midnight, and sleep showed no sign of coming. Grace turned onto her side again, her limbs tangled in the sheets, her mind whirling in tight, relentless circles. With a frustrated sigh, she sat up. Better to get up and break the loop—make a cup of tea, clear her head.

She reached for her negligee, fingers brushing the cool satin before slipping it from its hook. For a moment, she hesitated. The garment was more ornament than clothing—sheer lace and whisper-soft fabric that offered no real warmth against the chill in the air. But warmth wasn't what she needed. The house lay in deep silence, shadows pooling in the corners. She would not wake anyone.

John would be asleep by now—undoubtedly at ease, his conscience untroubled after an evening spent parading between his intended bride and his mistress at the same table, baiting her with a calculated smile, all for his own amusement.

The thought made her lips tighten. She had never had to fight anyone in her life, and now that she was being forced to, it infuriated her. Not that he saw her as any kind of worthy adversary. No, he was simply waiting for her to exhaust herself. Watching with that infuriating amusement of his while she flailed like a moth in a jar.

Well, she wouldn't.

Tonight, had done something to her. It had shifted something deep inside—solidified what she already suspected. Not that she'd ever truly been uncertain; she'd always known exactly what life with John Sneddon would look like. Days laced with subtle mockery. Evenings where she'd be the perfect hostess on his arm, porcelain smile in place, every word measured, every gesture flawless. The immaculate china doll.

And all the while, she would try not to think about where he'd be on the nights she wasn't at his side—or with whom. Her mind recoiled from imagining it too closely. Yet the thought of being in his arms, of that dark intensity focused entirely on her, made her tremble—not from cold, but from something far more dangerous.

The house was cloaked in darkness as she padded quietly downstairs, her bare feet silent on the polished steps. She didn't turn on any lights until she reached the kitchen, navigating by the faint glow from the landing above. Once she stepped into the familiar warmth of the kitchen and flicked on the overhead light, she exhaled a breath she hadn't realised she was holding.

Safe, she thought. But the thought didn't bring comfort.

She had lived in this house all her life. It had always been a haven. And now—now it felt like someone else's domain.

John's.

It was disorienting.

She moved automatically, filling the kettle, setting a teacup on the bench. Her hands moved with practised ease, but her mind was in turmoil. It would be so easy to blame John for the way everything had changed. But the truth was harder.

He didn't bring danger. He just uncovered it.

She had been sleepwalking through life—cocooned, indulged, and ultimately stagnant. A rich girl with nothing to do except play at happiness. Looking back, she hadn't truly enjoyed any of it. She was too intelligent for the shallow life she'd led, too aware of the emptiness beneath the glitter. There had been a gnawing boredom, a quiet dissatisfaction she'd never dared name.

John, for all his arrogance, had shattered that illusion. He had forced her to see herself—and the world—clearly. And perhaps, in some twisted way, he had brought security too. Not comfort. Not safety. But something solid to hold onto in the middle of the storm.

If he had simply told her he'd keep an eye on her until she could find her feet, she might have accepted it gratefully—even foolishly. But he hadn't. He wanted ownership, not guardianship. He was offering her the same deal her father had once provided: luxury, protection… and control. In return, she would surrender everything else—her freedom, her independence, herself.

Not anymore. She was finally free from the cage, and she had no intentions of being caught again.

She poured the hot tea into the cup and carried it to the table, her thoughts circling darker and deeper than ever before. *Was she truly afraid of John?* Or was she afraid of what he saw in her—what he drew out of her, whether she liked it or not?

Am I afraid of him—or of becoming someone she could love?

The door creaked open behind her.

She gasped, the sound catching in her throat, and spun around with a soft cry. Startled, the hot tea sloshed over the rim of the cup, scalding her wrist. She winced and set it down quickly, the pain barely registering over the sudden rush of adrenaline.

He stood in the doorway.

John.

Of course it was him.

And Grace felt the world tilt again—quietly, dangerously.

"What the hell are you doing now?" he demanded, striding across the kitchen in two long steps. He seized her arm, not roughly, but with enough force to make her stumble, and dragged her toward the sink. "I should hire a keeper for you—and give him a detailed list of your daily disasters!"

"I'm perfectly capable of looking after myself," Grace snapped, twisting in his grip. "And I'm free to wander where I please, thank you very much."

"With your keeper," he finished darkly. "Honestly, I'm amazed you managed the stairs without breaking your neck." He shoved her wrist beneath the running cold water, his jaw clenched, his eyes furious.

"Ow! My arm's going numb!"

"To match your head," he shot back. "Hold still. The cold will take the sting out."

"Wonderful! I'll be sure to remember that when I'm being treated for frostbite. This water is freezing!"

He glared at her, but after a few seconds released her arm and tossed her a towel. Then he stood back, studying her with an intensity that made her skin prickle.

"What are you doing, wandering around after midnight?"

"I couldn't sleep," she muttered. "I came down for tea."

"Well, that I understand," he said dryly. His mouth curved with something like a smirk. "You're too old to be sleeping alone."

Her face flamed. "You have no right to speak to me like that."

"I'm not claiming rights," he murmured, eyes glinting. "Just experience. A beautiful woman like you should have been married by now."

"Maybe you're right," she snapped, clutching the towel to her chest like a shield. She turned toward the door, her tea forgotten, her pride flaring. "First thing tomorrow, I'll start looking."

She'd expected a sarcastic quip. What she got instead was movement—a flash of motion—and then he was in front of her, blocking the door. Before she could react, his arms closed around her, turning her and holding her fast.

"Start thinking like that," he growled, his voice low and dangerous, "and you'll find out what real danger feels like."

"If you think I'd cast my eye around your office—"

"As if you'd be that foolish." His arms held her with calm, almost careless strength. "If you had, I'd have known. I see everything you do, Grace. I've been watching you for two years."

"Of course you have," she flung back, still fighting his grip, her anger surging again. "You'd recognise a lover instantly—experience does give a man perspective, doesn't it?"

"I've never claimed to be a saint." His voice lowered, but the tension in his body eased, his hold softening. "I've never played Sir Galahad. But I want you, Grace. I've wanted you—more than I've ever wanted anything."

She stilled, the breath catching in her throat.

"Maybe you're just a dream," he went on, voice quiet and rough-edged, "but I still want to keep the dream. I remember the first time I saw you—drifting down that staircase in gold silk, lit from within, walking like you belonged to no one. I didn't want you walking to some sleek, overbred boyfriend. I wanted you walking to me."

She stared up at him, frozen.

"Your father hadn't introduced us yet. But I saw you—and I knew. The dream started then. And one day, you will walk to me, Grace."

His voice had dropped to a velvet murmur, dangerous in its gentleness. The fire in his eyes held her captive. She couldn't look away.

Just for that moment, she stopped fighting. Something shifted in her chest—some small, trembling thread of resistance snapping loose. The thought of him watching her— longing for her in silence—should have unnerved her. Normally, it would have.

But not now.

Not with his eyes burning like that.

Not when her pulse was skipping like this.

And not when the idea thrilled her more than she wanted to admit.

"Grace?"

She didn't move.

She stood frozen, breath shallow, eyes wide—but her body betrayed her silence, leaning just slightly into the heat of him. His voice came again, lower this time, a murmur shaped in her name as he drew her closer. She offered no resistance. His hands, sure and steady, began to move along her back—soothing, coaxing—through the satin of her nightgown, leaving trails of fire in their wake.

He had never touched her like this before.

Never dared.

There had been others—boys, a few men—but none had ever gotten close. She had always kept control, repelling their advances with careful smiles and cool distance. They hadn't mattered.

But now… now she was caught. Spellbound.

Drawn to a man whose strength pulsed just beneath the surface, whose touch was possessive without being forceful. His fingers slid beneath her hair, finding the sensitive hollow at the nape of her neck. He massaged it gently, making her knees threaten to buckle, her thoughts spiral into nothingness.

Her usual defence rose like a reflex.

"D-don't," she breathed, the word barely formed.

"I won't hurt you, Grace," he said thickly.

His voice was dark velvet, frayed at the edges. And for a dangerous moment, she didn't want to pull away. She wanted to stay right where she was, wrapped in his warmth, cradled by his strength. The way his hand stroked her neck sent tremors through her, made her feel seen… claimed.

But there was something else in him too—something wild, something dangerous.

His eyes were too intense. His arm had tightened, just slightly. And with a rush of panic, she tore herself away, stumbling back, breathless. She stared at him, not with horror of him—but of herself. Because she had wanted that kiss. She had craved it. She had imagined what it would feel like to be truly taken into his arms, to feel his mouth against hers. And the real danger wasn't him—it was her own longing.

For a heartbeat he stood there, still as stone, his dark eyes narrowed. Then the dazed look cleared and gave way to sharp, glittering fury.

"You really think I'm a bastard, don't you?" he snapped. "I could be the richest man in the world, and you still wouldn't look at me as anything but the villain. You're wound tighter than a drum, and everything's black or white. And I'm always black, aren't I?"

"I—it wasn't because—I didn't mean—" she stammered, ashamed and trembling.

"For God's sake, stop shaking and go to bed," he growled, turning away sharply, the line of his shoulder's rigid with frustration.

She stood there, helpless, watching the raw tension in his frame—his hands clenched, his back stiff. The air still hummed with the heat between them, but now it was scorched with anger. Her own body trembled with aftershocks—of fear, of desire, of shame.

He was the storm she'd never been taught to weather. The dark waves that could drown her. And if she gave in, even once, she wouldn't survive. She would become something hollow, voiceless—while he returned to women like Rita Peterson without a second thought.

She fled. Up the stairs, to her room. And for the first time in her life, she locked the door.

She lay awake for hours, staring into the darkness, every nerve alight. But she never heard him come to bed.

By morning, he was gone.

Whether he had left in the night or risen before dawn, she didn't know. Maybe he'd gone to Rita. The thought stabbed deeper than she'd expected—and it only hardened her resolve to never marry him.

She dressed with cool efficiency, drank strong coffee, and drove to London with more determination than she had ever felt. She was done being his little dream girl. She would face him coldly, steel in her spine.

But he wasn't there.

She heard—second hand—that he'd flown out to America. He hadn't even stopped by the office.

The news hit her harder than it should have.

She sat numbly at her desk, trying to focus, but her thoughts felt dull and hollow. At lunch, she wandered into a nearby restaurant, still half-lost in the fog of disappointment, as if she'd been left behind by a storm that had wrecked her world—and disappeared without a trace.

Chapter Nine

She chose an old haunt; a cosy Italian restaurant tucked away in a quiet corner near the park—a place she used to frequent with friends. That, in itself, felt significant. Those friends were gone now. Vanished. Not with a dramatic exit, but with silence and absence.

She had followed John's advice after her father's death, staying away from the papers, refusing to read the stories she knew had been written. But she hadn't needed headlines to see the damage. Jenny's tight-lipped expressions and scandalised glances had told her everything. The gossip had run its course, loud and brutal for a week, and then died down—leaving only the quiet, cold judgement in its wake.

The whispers had touched everything—her father's financial chaos, his secretive lifestyle, the collapse of trust in the firm. The city had speculated with cruel enthusiasm. And now Grace had no invitations, no phone calls, no friendly texts suggesting matinees or cocktails. She hadn't realised how thoroughly society could withdraw until it left her standing in silence.

And John… John was all she had left.

The thought tightened like a thread in her chest.

She cursed her own foolishness for choosing this place today, knowing it would remind her of things she didn't want to feel. That regret deepened when, not long after she ordered, a familiar figure strolled in—the easy gait and confident smile impossible to mistake.

Sean Austin.

She stiffened instinctively. He'd once been a regular part of her life, taking her out for dinners and walks before his firm posted him overseas. Australia, she remembered. From the look of him, he'd just come back. Tan deepened by the sun, fair hair lighter, blue eyes almost too bright.

Maybe he hadn't seen her. She lowered her eyes quickly to her plate, praying he wouldn't notice her. She didn't want to watch his expression change—to see the moment recognition gave way to discomfort.

"Grace?"

Too late.

His voice was warm, familiar, and before she could think of a graceful way to flee, he was striding to her table.

"What's this? Dining alone?" His grin was quick and easy. "Answer fast—I'm about to join you."

For a moment she just stared at him, and then warmth broke over her like sunlight through fog. It was so unexpectedly kind—to be treated like a human being again. Not a scandal. Not a fallen heiress. Not a pawn in John's game.

"Sean," she said with a genuine smile. "Oh, do sit down. It's been ages."

"One year, one week, and three days," he said with mock precision, sliding into the seat opposite. "I'm on leave. Two months—less the one week and three days I've already wasted on family lunches and bad airline food."

She laughed softly, surprised by how easy it was to fall into step with him again. His tan suited him. It made his hair look almost white-gold, and his blue eyes even more startling.

"Life clearly agrees with you," she said. "You look…"

"Brash?" he suggested, flashing her that same grin. "Don't be fooled. I still get nervous around you. Always did. I'm just hanging on to my pride."

Once, words like that would have made her squirm. But not anymore. Too much had changed. She didn't feel untouchable now—she just felt alone. And that shift, that quiet loss of innocence, stunned her.

Sean noticed it too.

"How are you, really?" he asked, more serious now. "I heard about your father. I'm sorry, Grace."

"Perhaps you didn't hear everything," she said quietly, her eyes on the rim of her glass.

"I think I did." He shrugged gently. "But I liked him. Even if he did look at me like I was about to elope with you at any moment. Can't say I didn't think about it."

His smile was wistful, kind. Not mocking. And she found herself smiling back, even as something small and bruised stirred in her chest.

"How are you managing?" he asked.

"I work at the firm now."

That seemed to take him aback. His brows lifted, and she saw the flicker of surprise before he could hide it. She braced herself.

"Well, I wasn't exactly left in luxury," she said, aiming for lightness but hearing the edge in her own voice.

He reached across the table and took her hand, his grip firm, almost protective.

"Do you hate it?" he asked softly.

"Not at all," she replied—and realised, as she said it, that it was true. "I think I… I actually like it. It's a kind of freedom."

Freedom within walls, perhaps. But freedom all the same. She was starting, piece by piece, to live again.

Sean gave a low laugh, eyes dancing. "That's you all over, Grace. Quiet rebellion in pearls and silk. I should've seen it coming."

She laughed too, grateful he didn't push further, grateful for the easy way he moved on, letting her breathe.

They were talking like old friends, laughter lingering between them, when Grace felt it—that prickling sensation along her spine. The unmistakable feeling of being watched. It grew so strong she had to glance over her shoulder.

John.

Her breath caught.

He was seated at a corner table with Rita Peterson, and the shock of seeing him—when she had been so sure he was across the Atlantic—drained the colour from her face. Her stomach twisted, and the tentative confidence she'd been nurturing evaporated in an instant.

What was he doing here?

Had he come back early? Had he followed her?

She hadn't noticed anyone when she arrived. But then, she'd been too preoccupied— regretting the decision to eat here almost the moment she walked in, her head down, trying not to draw attention.

Sean, watching her, followed the direction of her gaze. His expression darkened, and he gave a small grunt of annoyance.

"Still staring at you, is he?"

"Staring?" she echoed, dragging her eyes back to Sean. His blue eyes were now slightly narrowed, his easy charm replaced with a flicker of irritation.

"He always did. One of the things that used to drive me mad whenever I came to Rosewood—Sneddon was always there, lurking like some overzealous bodyguard.

Watching you like a hawk. If you'd shown the slightest interest in him, I'd have gone up in flames."

"With what right?" she asked lightly, the edge of mischief in her voice belying the sharp unease curling through her.

Across the room, John was saying something to Rita. She looked delighted. John's smile—a rare thing under any circumstances—was disarmingly intimate. Something inside Grace clenched, and without thinking, she leaned a little closer to Sean.

It was petty, she knew. But suddenly, she wanted John to see her. Wanted to remind him she wasn't a possession to be set aside until convenient.

"No right," Sean said quietly, his voice softening. "Just hope. I was starting to think I was getting somewhere with you, right before I was shipped off."

His hand moved, covering hers on the table. The gesture was gentle but undeniably intimate. She should have pulled away—but she didn't.

"It's only for three years, Grace. I've already done one. After that, I'll be based back in London."

"And miss Australia?" she asked quickly, trying to deflect. She could feel a familiar tightness rising—an old instinct to retreat.

Sean gave a short laugh, his expression turning wry. "I thought you'd changed. But you haven't, have you? Still the same Grace—always one foot behind the door, always holding people at arm's length."

She flinched a little because he wasn't wrong.

"Let's compromise," he offered, leaning in slightly, his tone light but deliberate. "While I'm here, go out with me. No promises. No pressure. If you don't hate it... who knows?"

Grace opened her mouth to reply—probably to say no. But then she looked past him. John was still with Rita, still smiling that smile. Her blood stirred with something hot and sharp—anger, perhaps. Or humiliation. Or worse, longing.

"I'd like that," she said, meeting Sean's eyes with a smile she had to force only slightly. "Actually... I missed you, Sean."

His face lit up in a way that made her stomach twist again, but for a different reason. He looked so genuinely pleased. And for a moment, she hated the part of herself that might be using him.

Too late to backtrack now.

He insisted on escorting her outside, his hand lightly on her elbow as if it had always belonged there. When the taxi pulled up, he held the door with quiet gallantry and helped her in.

"I'll call you at work tomorrow," he said. And before she could react, he leaned in and kissed her—quickly, confidently, his lips brushing hers with a certainty that left her momentarily stunned.

He drew back with a grin. "See? Not so scary."

She couldn't find words. Not because the kiss had been unwelcome—only because somewhere, across a candlelit room, she had felt John watching.

And the thought of that made her feel cold and warm all at once.

When the taxi pulled up outside the Sneddon-Lewis building, a sleek black Mercedes glided in behind it. Grace's breath caught as John stepped out before she'd even reached for her purse.

Without a word, he strode over, paid the fare, and dismissed the driver with a curt nod.

"Get in the car," he ordered, his hand closing around her arm with the familiar, unyielding grip.

"I should be back at my desk. I—"

"You should be doing as you're told," he cut in, pushing her firmly into the warm cocoon of the Mercedes and sliding in beside her. "The boss is right here. If anyone has a problem with that, they can take it up with me."

His tone left no room for argument, but she tried anyway.

"That was completely unnecessary—"

"Who was your lunchtime companion?" he asked coolly, not bothering to hide the sharpness beneath his words.

Grace bristled. "An old friend. And I don't see—"

"No old friends, Grace." His hand caught her chin and turned her to face him, his fingers hard and unforgiving. "I've given you plenty of space, plenty of rope, but men weren't part of the bargain. You're marrying me. That means no competition."

"I am not marrying you," she bit out. "Sean and I have known each other for years. We were seeing each other before he was posted to Australia."

"Yes, I remember now—Austin." His jaw tightened. "You went out with him more than anyone else. I didn't like it then, and I like it even less now. Drop him—or he'll find himself posted to the moon."

Her breath hitched. "You have no authority over Sean's life!"

"I have considerable influence in the business world," he said flatly. "And there are plenty of executives who still owe me favours. Drop him—or he'll be packing again."

"You… you can't do this to me—"

"I can, and I will," he said, his voice low and dangerous. "I'm letting you play your little games, but don't mistake it for freedom. You're mine, Grace. Don't forget it."

He suddenly yanked her toward him and crushed his mouth to hers in a hard, possessive kiss. It wasn't tenderness—it was a declaration. She struggled, weakly, caught off guard by the intensity of it. The kiss ended as abruptly as it began, but the imprint of it lingered—rage, power, desire.

She was still dazed when he yanked open the car door and gestured sharply for her to get out.

"I'm going back to the States," he snapped, his voice cold and hard. "Enjoy your little games while you can. But forget Austin. I'll be back."

Her eyes blazed with defiance. "I can see whoever I choose. And I have no intention of marrying an unfaithful man—remember, you said it was time I got married."

His jaw clenched, anger flashing in his eyes, but without another word, he slammed the door, started the engine, and roared away into the traffic.

She stood trembling on the pavement, watching the black car vanish, her mind reeling.

She didn't know who was winning anymore. She wasn't even sure what game she was playing.

What was supposed to happen at Christmas? That had always been the end point, hadn't it? But now the lines were blurred. One thing was certain—she needed to be gone by then. Secure. Independent. Jenny safe at Rosewood.

But how had she let it come to this?

A month later, Grace found herself summoned to work directly with John.

He was cold. Remote. All trace of the possessive fury he had shown that day had vanished, replaced with a professionalism so icy it left her floundering. He treated her as though there had never been a private understanding between them—as though they were strangers. Business associates. Nothing more.

She had thrown herself into the work with relentless determination. John demanded weekly progress updates, sometimes daily, and she delivered them without fail. The pressure was unrelenting.

People had started to talk—but not aloud. There were glances, hushed conversations, and silent speculation. *Was she being groomed for something higher? Or was this punishment?*

No one dared ask. But quietly, Grace sensed sympathy around her—colleagues who offered soft smiles or kind words in passing. It helped, a little.

But nothing about John helped.

Since returning from America, he had maintained an impenetrable distance. No warmth, no smiles. Only terse instructions and cool dismissals.

In just a month, she had been rotated through two departments. Everyone saw she was being tested. Some admired her resolve. Others pitied her.

As for John—he gave away nothing.

And Grace, who once believed she had some control, was starting to wonder if she had ever had any at all.

The summons to John's office sent a ripple of unease down Grace's spine. When she stepped inside, he was already deep in conversation on the phone. Without so much as a glance in her direction, he waved her to a chair and continued speaking, his tone clipped and authoritative.

She sat silently, hands folded in her lap, eyes drawn to him against her will. As always.

His dark hair resisted the strict grooming he imposed on it, hinting at a natural wave just barely contained. His lashes, thick and dark, shielded the intensity of his eyes. He was making rapid notes while speaking, utterly absorbed, as though she had ceased to exist the moment she entered the room.

Then, abruptly, he finished the call, tossed down his pen, and looked straight at her.

"You're moving up here," he announced.

Her heart stumbled. "I'm not ready."

The moment the words left her mouth, she regretted them. His eyes darkened with a flash of anger, though his voice remained controlled.

"I'm ready," he said sharply. "I want you where I can see you. If this game is to be played according to the rules, I'd better start teaching you what those rules are. Starting tomorrow, you'll be my personal assistant."

Grace blinked. "Me?"

It was so far beyond what she'd imagined—she hadn't even considered the possibility. Her voice faltered. "I—I wouldn't know where to begin. I've only been—"

John stood abruptly, exuding that familiar, commanding presence that reduced her to a jittery novice.

"You've worked in two departments," he interrupted, flipping open her file and dropping it onto the desk. "You've done exceptionally well in both. Everyone who's worked with you has been impressed. Your typing is excellent, and your computer skills have improved remarkably." He looked up at her, a flicker of amusement crossing his face. "Honestly, I never realised how much that business course had done for you. I knew you were intelligent, but I didn't even think you could type."

"I took extra classes," she admitted, straightening slightly. "Typing, computer programming… I kept it quiet. My father didn't know either."

He narrowed his eyes, considering her. For a long moment, he said nothing. Then he dropped the file and leaned against the desk, looking down at her with an inscrutable expression.

"You wanted a chance," he said. "You asked to learn the business, and I agreed to play fair. This is me, keeping that promise. Let's see how you manage as my personal assistant."

Grace's pulse kicked up. "What exactly would I have to do?"

It was terrifying and exhilarating all at once. For the first time in her life, real responsibility was within reach. But the phrase *play fair* made her uneasy. She hadn't exactly been honest—at least not about Sean. She and Sean had been out several times since John's trip to America. And today, in fact, they had lunch plans.

"What will you have to do?" John echoed, a gleam of dark humour in his eyes. "Everything, Miss Lewis. Be assured, you'll earn your keep. And if it gets too hard, don't forget—I once offered to keep you."

Before she could respond, a knock at the door broke the tension. Arthur Watkins stepped in, looking unusually grim.

"Can I see you, John?"

John nodded once, then turned to Grace.

"There's an office already prepared for you," he said briskly. "First door on the left after mine. Move in now. I'll see you later."

Arthur gave her a sympathetic nod as she hurried out.

A personal assistant. It still didn't feel real.

But the truth was if she managed this—even for a few months—it would open doors. Personal Assistant to the Managing Director would look impressive on any future job application. She just had to keep calm. Stay focused. Control the shaking in her hands.

And stop letting him get under her skin.

She had just settled into her new office and taken her first sip of coffee when the intercom buzzed.

"Bring your coffee in here, Grace," came John's cold voice.

She didn't. She left the cup on the desk and went at once.

Inside, John and Arthur Watkins were hunched over a table covered in blueprints. They barely looked up.

"Trouble at the Westfield Block," John growled. "We're going there now. You're coming with us."

The Westfield site. Grace winced. It would be freezing out there—wind off the river and November biting at her bones. She also needed to cancel her lunch with Sean, and she wasn't sure when she'd get the chance.

"I'll get my coat," she murmured, only half-masking her reluctance.

John's eyes flicked to hers, sharp and suspicious, but Arthur offered a kinder look.

"It's cold out there," he said, giving her a rueful smile and casting a sidelong glance at John.

"She can wrap up warm," John replied curtly. "Bring a clipboard. You're taking notes."

She could tell from the look on Arthur's face that her presence on the site was completely unnecessary. Whatever had sparked this outing, it had little to do with her role and everything to do with John. She must have angered him somehow. And this— dragging her into the bitter cold—felt like punishment.

The moment she reached the privacy of her new office; she lunged for her phone.

"Sean, I can't make lunch," she blurted as soon as he picked up.

"Oh?" he replied lightly, but there was a teasing edge in his tone. "Gone off me already?"

There was something possessive in his amusement, a lazy assumption that made her pause. But she didn't have time to untangle that particular thread.

"I've been sent out to one of the sites," she explained quickly.

"What? In this weather?" His voice sharpened with concern. "Grace, it's freezing. What are you going out there for? You're not an engineer—and you're definitely not a builder."

"I'm a personal assistant," she said, sharper than she meant to. "I've been promoted."

There was a pause.

"Whose personal assistant?" he asked quietly—far too quietly.

"John's, of course." Her voice lifted almost without her knowing it, touched with a flush of pride. There was a hum of excitement she couldn't suppress—and Sean heard it.

His reaction was instant.

"What's his game?" he snapped. "Grace, come on. You'll never be a personal assistant in that kind of world—not unless he's playing you."

She froze. For a moment, she didn't even know how to respond. It wasn't just the insult—it was the way he'd said it. As if she were nothing more than a decorative distraction, a child playing dress-up in someone else's world. She had changed— grown—but Sean hadn't noticed.

"I know more than you think," she replied, her voice cold. "But that's not why I called. I only wanted to let you know I have to cancel."

"Grace, wait—I didn't mean—" His tone shifted, contrite, but she cut him off.

"I'll be in touch later," she said quickly. "Goodbye, Sean."

She hung up.

And turned to find John standing in the doorway.

His expression was thunderous. But—more terrifying than anything—he said nothing at all.

She slipped on her coat in silence, picked up her clipboard and bag, and was halfway past him when he growled, "Bring a scarf."

She didn't dare look at him.

She spent the next fifteen minutes half-jogging to keep up with his long strides on the way to the car and again at the construction site. The air was knife-sharp with cold, and Grace quickly discovered that muddy ground and deep, rain-slick trenches did nothing to ease the chill. She wrapped her coat tight around her and accepted the hard hat John handed her without a word. It did nothing for the cold, but it was regulation.

John barked orders. She took notes with numb fingers. He didn't look at her, didn't soften once. Whatever mood he was in, it had calcified into pure steel.

After a while, it was as though she ceased to exist for him. She wasn't a person, not even an employee. She was simply… there. An afterthought. A shadow.

He had brought her out here to make a point—and she understood it, loud and clear.

She didn't belong.

Not in his world. Not in his business. Not anywhere but by his side—as his polished hostess, the bearer of his name, the mother of his child.

The thought hit her like a blade: a child. His child.

Her steps faltered.

A dark-haired child with his eyes. She could see it too clearly, and the image twisted something inside her. It was too much—too close to something she hadn't allowed herself to feel.

She couldn't bear to look at him anymore. Not now.

She drifted back from the group, needing space. Not just to breathe, but to escape the painful tenderness she hadn't expected to feel. It was bitter. And sweet. And dangerous.

She was so wrapped in her thoughts—so turned inward—that she stopped paying attention.

The ground underfoot was treacherous with muck and puddles. She didn't even register the tarpaulin or the narrow plank laid across it until she was already stepping onto it, her mind still full of John and that imagined child.

She heard someone shout—maybe more than one voice—but too late.

The plank tilted beneath her foot.

The world reeled.

And then she was falling—helplessly, head over heels, down into the open trench below.

Chapter Ten

For a long moment, Grace couldn't move.

She lay sprawled on her back, half-submerged in cold, clinging mud, the breath knocked clean out of her. Rainwater trickled into her hair, seeping through her clothes, numbing her limbs. She could hear voices shouting—but they were distant, muffled, like echoes through glass.

Then John appeared above her, sliding down into the trench with a furious grace. His immaculate suit was instantly ruined—soaked, plastered in sludge—but he didn't even seem to notice. He dropped to his knees in the muck beside her.

"Grace." His voice was tight with fear. "Are you all right?" He cradled her head in his hands, brushing wet hair away from her eyes. "Did you hit your head? Your back— can you move it?"

She blinked up at him, dazed, trying to focus. Only now did she grasp where she'd landed—how close she had come to real danger. The trench stretched long and deep, a skeleton of heavy pipes laid end to end. By some stroke of sheer luck, she'd fallen just wide of them. A few feet to the right and...

Her blood ran colder.

"I—I missed them," she whispered, her voice shaking. "I didn't hit anything." But the adrenaline was leaving her now, and her body sagged. Trembling, she gave in to the need for warmth, for safety, and buried her face against the soaked lapel of his jacket. She didn't care if he liked it or not.

"Get a ladder down here!" John's voice cracked like a whip above them, sharp with command. He didn't take his arms from around her, didn't stop supporting her head as he shouted up to the men leaning over the edge of the trench. "She's conscious but I want her out—now."

He was holding her too tightly for her to move, but she didn't want to. She couldn't. Her limbs felt boneless, her mind foggy. All she could do was lean into him while he guided her up the rungs of the ladder, his body braced behind hers protectively.

By the time they reached the surface, she was shivering violently.

He wrapped his coat around her the moment they were free of the trench, shielding her from the wind. His own clothes were plastered with mud, his hair wet and dark, but there was only one thing in his eyes: fury.

At her? At himself?

She wasn't sure.

He carried her to the car and set her gently in the passenger seat, the heat already blasting. His jaw was clenched; his expression carved from stone.

Arthur jogged up just as John was about to slam the door shut.

"What about—?"

"Do as you damn well like!" John snapped, then let out a hiss of breath and dragged a hand through his soaked hair. "No—wait. I'll try to come back."

He got in and drove fast—*too fast*—his grip rigid on the wheel.

Grace shrank a little in the seat, unable to stop shaking. She felt cold all the way through, the kind of cold that came from more than the weather. She'd been stupid. She could have been badly hurt. And John… John looked like a man trying not to explode.

She didn't dare speak, not at first.

But when the silence grew too heavy to bear, she summoned the breath to ask, quietly, "Where are we going?"

"My flat," he snapped. "It's either that or the hospital. If you're in one piece, I need to get back to work."

The sharpness in his voice stung, but she didn't argue. He was right. She was filthy, drenched, and trembling uncontrollably. And John—John looked like a storm barely held back by willpower alone. He wasn't in any shape to go back to the office either.

They looked, she realised bleakly, like survivors of some disaster—dragged from the wreckage, covered in mud and bruises.

And worst of all, she knew the disaster had been her fault.

John ushered her inside without a word, and Grace was grateful the street was nearly empty. This was clearly an exclusive part of the city—quiet, discreet, expensive. The sort of place where residents didn't expect to see two figures soaked to the skin and streaked with mud entering through polished doors.

Even in her dazed state, she could sense the luxury all around her. Everything breathed wealth—cool, understated, effortless. The gleaming floors, the high ceilings, the art on the walls. She didn't have the energy to take it all in, but she felt it.

"Go have a shower," John said curtly, his eyes flicking to the puddle growing around her feet on the gleaming floor. "Guest room is down there. I'll use my own."

His tone was clipped, his expression unreadable. He simply pointed to a doorway, and she turned without protest, still faintly staggering from the shock.

"Can you manage?" he asked, his voice tight as he stepped toward her again. "Is anything hurting you?"

He took her arms and gently turned her, searching for signs of injury, but his grip wasn't as careful as before—it bordered on rough.

"I can manage." Her voice was low. She couldn't meet his eyes. If anything had been truly wounded, it was her pride—and something else she didn't want to name. His cold detachment stung more than the bruises she'd acquired. She had nearly been killed. Surely that should have warranted more than a reprimand dressed in concern.

He was treating her like an inconvenience. And for some reason, that hurt far more than it should.

She lifted her chin and looked up at him. Her eyes were dark with pain—not physical, but emotional—and he stilled under the weight of it. His jaw flexed. His hands tightened on her arms.

"Look, just get your shower, and then…" He faltered. Her gaze didn't waver, and for a beat, he seemed lost.

"Oh, hell," he muttered. "What am I going to do with you?"

Before she could respond, he swept her off her feet and carried her through to the guest room, kicking open the bathroom door and setting her gently on the tiles. She stood numbly as he turned on the shower, adjusting the temperature.

She barely noticed when he slipped off her mud-caked jacket and laid it over the edge of the tub. But when his fingers reached for the buttons of her blouse, awareness returned in a sharp rush.

"John!" Her voice cracked with shock. Her cheeks flushed, and the wounded misery in her expression turned to something closer to reprimand.

He didn't flinch.

"What do you expect me to do—stand here and watch you shiver?"

"I… I can manage."

He studied her face for a long, weighted moment, then gave a sharp nod. "Call me if you can't."

For a heartbeat, it looked as though he might argue. But at last, with a muttered curse under his breath, he turned and left, the door closing behind him with a soft click.

Grace stood motionless for several seconds, listening to the silence, trying to push through the fog in her head.

Then, slowly, she peeled off the rest of her wet clothes and stepped beneath the stream of hot water. It stung her chilled skin at first, but gradually the heat seeped in, thawing her, driving out the bone-deep cold. She scrubbed herself clean with mechanical movements, her fingers trembling as they worked shampoo through her hair until it gleamed like honey once more.

She found a couple of bruises on her cheekbone and a scraped leg, but nothing worse. She had been incredibly lucky. Still, the shaking wouldn't stop. Even wrapped in warmth, with water cascading over her shoulders, there was something inside her that refused to be soothed.

And then she realised—she had nothing to wear.

Not a single dry thing. No clothes, no towel she could call her own, and a man on the other side of the door who terrified her in a way she didn't yet understand.

Grace turned in dismay, reality crashing down on her like cold water. Her clothes— soaked, filthy, unwearable—were piled in a sodden heap on the tiled floor. Her tights and underwear were just as ruined, clinging with mud. With no other option, she rinsed them in the sink as best she could, then hesitated before cracking open the door.

"John?"

There was no answer.

Clutching the towel tightly around herself, she stepped out cautiously, calling his name again. He appeared so suddenly—so fast and imposing—that it made her dizzy.

"What is it?" His voice was sharp, already laced with concern.

He was freshly showered and barefoot, his dark hair damp, droplets still clinging to his temples. A crisp new suit hung from his shoulders—except he hadn't yet finished dressing. His shirt was unbuttoned to the waist, revealing a bronzed chest dusted with dark hair, every inch of him lean and powerful. Grace's breath hitched in her throat.

She took a step back, gripping the towel as if it were armour. But it wasn't her fall that left her unsteady now—it was him.

"I—I haven't got anything to wear."

She couldn't tear her eyes away. The way his body moved. The way he looked at her— steady, direct, unblinking. Her face flamed as heat rushed into her cheeks, mortified by both her situation and her reaction.

"I didn't forget," he said quietly, his eyes lingering on her flushed face. "I've sent your things out to be cleaned. But it doesn't matter right now. You're staying here tonight."

She blinked. "You made up the bed?"

"In the guest room," he said, tone clipped. "While you were in the shower."

Grace's heart sank. The sight of the neatly made bed, the fluffed pillows, the fresh sheets—it made her feel caged. Panic stirred in her chest. She couldn't sleep here. Not under the same roof. Not this close. Not when every breath around him left her shaken.

"I want to leave," she said quickly, her voice tight and brittle.

He moved toward her slowly, deliberately—like a tiger circling its prey. "You're going to bed. You've had a shock, Grace. You're in no condition to do anything else."

"I know how I feel," she snapped. "And you are not trapping me here!"

She was trembling, and not from fear. It was something more dangerous—an unfamiliar, rising heat she couldn't name. Her eyes flicked to his chest again before she forced herself to look away. She wanted to touch him. To know what his skin felt like. And the very thought terrified her.

"Trapping you?" His voice hardened, cutting through her denial. "You nearly died today. If that's the kind of judgment you've got, then maybe we should forget the deal and just announce the damn wedding."

His cold words jolted her like a slap.

"There isn't going to be a wedding!" she cried. "When I marry, it won't be you!"

She was shouting now, retreating from him as if space could protect her from the chaos inside her. He was furious, and she could see it in the tight lines of his jaw, the glitter of scorn in his eyes.

"You're planning to marry Austin?" he sneered. "Better think again. He couldn't afford the box your earrings came in."

That stopped her dead.

So that's what he thought of her.

A useless little rich girl with nothing to offer but a name, clinging to a man for money. Not like Rita Peterson, all sleek confidence and sophistication. Just Grace. Silly, helpless Grace.

Something snapped.

"You think all I care about is money. I don't give a damn about money." She lunged at him, embarrassment forgotten. Furious and wounded, she slammed her open palms against his chest, desperate to push him away, to wipe the disdain from his face.

But he caught her effortlessly, trapping her in his arms. Her feet lifted off the ground as she struggled, fists pounding uselessly against him, legs thrashing in frustration.

"Put me down!" she shouted, breath ragged. "I hate you! I've always hated you!"

Her voice cracked on the last word, tears blurring her vision. He must have heard them, because he lowered her gently, holding her at arm's length, his face grim.

"Stop it, Grace," he said quietly. "You've had a nasty fall. This won't help."

"Nothing helps!" she sobbed. "I'm leaving, do you hear me? I'm leaving this flat, and then I'm leaving the firm. I don't know why I ever made that stupid deal! Jenny doesn't need me. I can sell my jewellery. I'll find a flat—I don't need you!"

She sank to her knees, clutching the towel around her body like a lifeline, shaking with sobs. She was ashamed—humiliated. She could almost hear him thinking how pathetic she was, how childish. Rita would never fall apart like this.

He didn't speak.

Instead, he crouched down and gathered her into his arms again, lifting her easily. She didn't resist. The fight had gone out of her. Her body ached and her tears flowed freely.

"Let go, Grace," he murmured, voice low and tight. "Stop fighting everything."

She turned her face into his shoulder, unable to answer. But her heart broke a little more when he spoke again.

"It always has to be you, doesn't it?" she whispered bitterly. "I can't win. I don't even know what I'm fighting anymore."

His lips twisted, and for once his voice lacked its usual steel.

"Maybe it's me," he said. "Maybe it's always been me. You hate me, I know that. And if I had any sense, I'd let you go. But I can't. I want you, Grace. In any way I can have you."

He carried her back to the bed, gently setting her down.

"Roll out of that wet towel," he said, his voice low. "And snuggle down."

She didn't move. She couldn't.

She looked up at him, eyes brimming, heart pounding, and realised—she wasn't sure she wanted to run anymore.

He laid her gently on the bed, and though her hands trembled, Grace managed to wriggle free of the damp towel, slipping beneath the sheets and tugging them up to her neck. She was still crying softly, her breath hitching in small gasps as she turned her face away. The towel landed with a soft thud on a nearby chair.

He turned back to her. "What's this—cowardice?" His voice was quiet, but there was an edge to it. "Don't you care to go on shouting at me?"

She opened her eyes slowly, and he was standing there, tall, and still, watching her with unreadable intensity.

"Let's go back to that fall," he said. "Where do you hurt?"

She hesitated. "All over."

"That's not helpful," he said, and reaching down, he tilted her chin, forcing her to meet his gaze. "Where particularly?"

"There's no one place," she whispered. "I think I'm just... shocked. Th-that's why I..."

"That's why you reminded me how much you hate me?" he asked, a faint smile curving his lips, though his eyes didn't match it. "Yes. I got the message."

She couldn't hold his gaze. Her defiance had drained away, leaving her raw and vulnerable.

"I'm grateful," she said shakily. "You didn't have to take care of me. You didn't have to make this deal. I was never your responsibility and—"

"But you are, Grace." His voice dropped, softer now, more dangerous. "I'm going to marry you."

He sat beside her on the bed, so close that she could feel the heat of his body. Panic fluttered inside her.

"There's nothing to talk about," she said quickly. She would have moved, but she was painfully aware of how exposed she was beneath the sheet. Every small shift made the fabric cling more tightly to her skin—and she saw the way his eyes tracked those movements. "Can't you just... go? Take my clothes to be cleaned? Go back to the site, or—or something?"

"Leave you here?" He shook his head slowly. "No, Grace. I'm done letting you hide. It's time you woke up. And I'm going to be the one who does it."

He leaned in slightly. "Maybe if I'd had a different beginning, I could've stood back, let you date Austin, smiled politely at the wedding. Maybe I could've played those harmless little games men like him play."

His hand moved, light as a whisper, settling against the sheet where it covered her breast. She gasped, frozen. Her heart pounded in her chest like a drum.

"But I didn't have that kind of beginning," he said. "I had to fight for everything I ever wanted. And now… I want you."

He didn't move. Just watched her. Waiting. Holding her eyes with his. She should have pushed his hand away. She knew that. But the thought barely formed before it dissolved. Her mind was a storm, a whirl of confusion, but underneath it was something hotter, sharper. It surged through her like lightning.

"Do you like this?" he asked softly.

She didn't answer. Couldn't. Her breath hitched again. Her lips parted, instinctively, as if seeking something just out of reach. Her eyes—wide, dark, uncertain—were fixed on his.

He moved his hand slightly, a gentle coaxing pressure through the thin sheet. A flush of heat swept up her neck, blooming across her cheeks. Her tongue darted out to moisten her lips without thinking, and his gaze followed it, hungry and possessive.

"Does Austin touch you?" His voice was darker now, rougher. "Do you let him hold you? Kiss you?"

Her thoughts scattered like leaves in the wind. She should have answered, should have lied, should have reminded him that he had no right to ask. But all of that seemed so far away. Her body was responding before her mind could catch up, surrendering inch by inch to the overwhelming nearness of him.

His other hand stroked back her damp hair, tenderly, and her lips trembled under the weight of unsaid things—longing, confusion, fear.

Then he reached for her and gathered her into his arms.

She didn't resist.

The solid strength of him enveloped her, his shirt cool against her bare skin, his scent—a mix of soap, clean linen, and something darker—filling her senses. She melted against him, boneless and breathless, lost in the warmth and certainty of his hold.

"You're mine, Grace," he said thickly. "I'm tired of this game."

She could hardly breathe. Her thoughts were unravelling, one after another, until all that remained was sensation. His kiss claimed her—hungry, deep, and demanding. Her fingers threaded into his damp hair, her lips answering his with instinctive need.

He was drowning her in velvet shadows, in heat and want and the impossible feeling of being utterly seen.

"Let me look at you," he whispered, his voice rough with restraint.

It wasn't a question. It was a command laced with reverence.

But Grace couldn't think, couldn't answer. She had already surrendered—in her heart, in her trembling limbs, in the tears that had dried unnoticed on her cheeks. All her fear had been a mask. All her hatred, a defence.

Maybe this was what she had been running from all along.

Chapter Eleven

John drew the sheet down with slow deliberation, uncovering her inch by inch. The look in his eyes was not crude or mocking, but something deeper—almost reverent. Grace shivered as his dark head dipped, and he took one rose-tipped nipple into the warm heat of his mouth.

A frantic moan escaped her lips, her fingers clutching his shoulders as if to anchor herself against the storm he was stirring inside her. He looked up at her briefly, eyes glittering with heat, then shrugged out of his shirt and tossed it aside.

"Touch me," he said thickly. "Touch me, Grace."

She hesitated—unsure, inexperienced. But he didn't wait. He gathered her close again, pressing her bare breasts against the hard plane of his chest. She gasped at the sensation, the delicious ache in her body intensifying as he moved her against him. His hand slid slowly down her back, tracing each vertebra with exquisite care, until she melted into him, her own hands finding their way to his warm, bronzed shoulders, to the powerful lines of his neck.

The contact seemed to ignite something deep inside him. He pulled the sheet away completely and eased her into his arms, stretching out beside her on the bed. His mouth claimed hers in a kiss that was wild and searching, and she felt as if she were floating—adrift in a world where only sensation mattered.

His hands were everywhere—stroking, exploring, learning her body. Each touch sent sparks across her skin. Her mind was a blur, filled with nothing but the sound of his breath and the pounding of her heart. She whimpered into his mouth, uncertain and overwhelmed, but when she tried to speak, he only kissed her deeper, his arm slipping beneath her, cradling her head as if she were something fragile and precious.

Her thoughts scattered. A slow, burning heat flooded her entire body, beginning in her toes and climbing upward until she was trembling with a need she didn't understand. She had no idea where this would lead—only that she didn't want it to stop.

It felt like a drug, like something her body had been aching for without her knowing it. She clung to him with a kind of desperation, her lips fusing to his, following where his hands led, responding with a hunger that frightened her.

"Do you want me to take you now?" he murmured roughly, his teeth grazing her bare shoulder in a way that made her cry out softly.

She was beyond thought, beyond words. She wanted all of him. She wanted to feel the weight of him, the heat of him. She wanted to belong to him, just for this one moment—maybe forever.

Her hand moved to his waist without her even realising it, her fingers slipping beneath the waistband of his trousers. He inhaled sharply and pulled her closer, crushing her to him until there was no space left between them.

"Is that an answer?" he asked, his voice husky, brushing his lips against hers. "Do you want me to stay? To make you mine completely?"

"Yes," she breathed. "Yes."

She had forgotten everything—who he was, what he represented, her pride, her self-respect. None of it mattered. The only thing that mattered was the storm inside her, and the man who had set it free.

Her surrender—trembling, urgent—was the final thread snapping. He rolled onto his back, dragging her with him, guiding her astride him, his hands shaping her hips, his expression dark and intense.

"God, I want you," he said raggedly. "But you're still shaken. You're not even fully aware of what you're doing—and I can't take you like this."

She cupped his face with both hands, seeking his mouth again, her eyes wide and desperate.

"John—please—"

"No." His voice cracked with restraint. He shifted her gently off him, lowering her to the cool sheets again, and hovered over her, his breath uneven. "I haven't forgotten how you feel about me, Grace. I won't let you wake up tomorrow saying I took advantage of you—used you when you were too shaken to resist. When I make love to you, it's going to be when you're strong enough to know what you want. When you look at me and choose me."

He let his hand drift slowly down her body, claiming every inch with his eyes. "At least now you know what it will be like," he added, his voice low with promise.

She reached out instinctively, clutching at his hand, his name a broken sound in her throat.

"I know," he said hoarsely. "You're hurting. But marry me, Grace, and you won't have to hurt anymore."

But she wouldn't—not when she knew she wouldn't be the only woman in his life.

John had made it painfully clear that his desire wasn't love—it was possession. He would have her… until he didn't. Until someone like Rita summoned him away. And when he grew tired of her, she'd become exactly what he'd always believed: fragile, decorative, and easily discarded.

She turned away, dragging the sheet over her body, shame washing over her in hot waves.

"It's too late, angel," he said behind her, his voice grating. "I know what you look like now. I know how you respond."

"You don't," she whispered, throat raw. "Any experienced man could've done that to me."

He gave a humourless laugh. "And more," he said derisively.

He crossed the room, retrieved his shirt, and began buttoning it up with slow precision. She kept her eyes tightly shut, praying he would leave.

"You'd better open your eyes," he said after a beat, his tone laced with amusement. "You'll have to face me sometime. Might as well be now. Or do you plan to stay there, hiding, when I bring your clothes back?"

Her eyes snapped open, blazing with humiliation and anger. Her cheeks were crimson.

"I probably won't be here," she snapped. "I expect Miss Peterson leaves clothes here. When you've gone, I'll borrow something and call a taxi."

He laughed, a low, amused sound that made her seethe.

"You're welcome to try," he said lazily. "Search every drawer. Every cupboard. For each item you find, I'll give you a hundred pounds."

"Only that?" she flared. "You really are cheap as well as impossible."

"Marry me," he said quietly. "And I'll give you everything. Anything you dream of— I'll make it real."

"How could you?" Her voice cracked. "I'll be dreaming of Sean."

His expression changed instantly—darkening with something far more dangerous than anger. She clutched the sheets tighter around her, her heart stammering in her chest. Whatever he'd been about to say... he swallowed it.

"I don't think so," he said softly, with devastating certainty. "From now on, you'll be dreaming of me—and of what nearly happened here tonight."

He leaned closer, his eyes narrowed with dangerous satisfaction. "And Grace... if I ever believed that Austin had done more than hold your hand, you wouldn't be lying there now, giving me attitude. You'd be on your knees, begging me to let you go."

He walked out, the door clicking softly behind him, and Grace flung herself off the bed, dragging the sheet with her and wrapping it tightly around her body. She began yanking open drawers with furious determination. She had to get out of here. She couldn't very well leave in wet underwear and nothing else.

John walked back in moments later, adjusting his tie, his gaze resting on her with exasperated amusement.

"Save yourself the trouble," he advised coolly. "There's nothing here for a woman to wear. Besides, you're supposed to be having a nap, remember?"

"I don't need one, and I don't need—" Grace spun around, forgetting the awkward length of the sheet. It tangled around her legs, and she fell in a graceless heap to the floor, making his brows rise in astonishment.

"I'm never quite sure whether you're mad or not," he muttered, striding forward and lifting her effortlessly to her feet. Before she could protest, he had unwound the sheet and began to straighten the bed with infuriating calm.

"Stop it!" she cried, snatching up the damp towel and managing to wrap it around herself just in time. He turned to face her grimly, advancing when she tried to back away.

"Don't touch me!"

"Only for medicinal purposes," he said smoothly. "Think of me as a concerned keeper."

Before she could mount a proper defence, he'd swept the towel away and deposited her back on the bed with infuriating ease, delivering a light slap to her bottom as she scrambled to recover the sheet. The gesture was so unexpected, so shockingly familiar, it stilled her anger for a moment. Like a lover, she thought dazedly.

She stared up at him, wide-eyed. His expression softened into something close to regret.

"I'm sorry," he murmured. "Not about the slap," he added dryly when she blinked in surprise. "I'm sorry I made you go to the site. It was cold, miserable, and unnecessary. I should've had more sense."

"Then why did you make me go?" she asked quietly, watching him finish dressing—tightening his tie, slipping into his jacket—as if this were a scene from a life they shared.

"So, you wouldn't keep your lunchtime date," he said, his tone rueful. "Pathetic, isn't it?"

He gave her a crooked smile but didn't wait for a reply. With his usual air of command, he walked out, giving brisk instructions as he went.

"Get some sleep. I put your phone next to the bed. I'll call before I collect you. No idea how long these miracle dry-cleaning people take."

She stared after him, the door closing quietly behind him. Alone now, she lay back, pulling the sheet over herself. Her thoughts spun, uninvited and unwelcome.

Everything about him should have terrified her—the way he commanded, the way he touched, the way he looked at her. But it didn't. It stirred something reckless, something exhilarating.

She turned on her side, eyes fluttering closed, shocked by how quickly sleep crept in. She could still feel the strength of his arms, the imprint of his mouth. Her breasts still ached with remembered pleasure, but she didn't regret any of it—only trembled with excitement and a warmth she had never known before.

She must not fall in love with him.

That was the last thought she had before sleep took her.

As far as John was concerned, the incident at the flat might never have happened. In the days that followed, he gave no sign—by look or word—that it had meant anything. He buried himself in work, dividing his time between the office and the sites, and she followed his lead, unsure whether to be relieved or hurt.

Had it been real?

Her breath still caught when their eyes met, and a flicker of heat whispered through her blood. That alone told her it hadn't been imagined. But to John, it had been no more than a passing desire—easily dismissed. The realisation both dismayed and enraged her.

Christmas loomed ever closer. The calendar on his desk marked its approach with relentless clarity. Jenny's attempts to drum up festive cheer only added to the pressure.

"It won't be the same without Mr Lewis," Jenny sighed one afternoon. "And now there'll be no friends to fill the house."

"What friends?" Grace asked bitterly. "They vanished the minute the money did. I can do without that sort of loyalty."

"Well, Christmas is going to be quiet," Jenny said mournfully. "Maybe Mr Sneddon will join us?"

"He'll have other plans," Grace said quickly. "I'll probably stay in London and spend it with Sean. He's going back to Australia after Christmas."

"That leaves me, I suppose?" Jenny sniffed.

"Oh, Jenny, I'm sorry," Grace said at once. "Of course I wouldn't leave you. We'll have our own Christmas. Just the two of us."

Privately, Grace would have skipped Christmas altogether if not for Jenny. And John. The thought of the reckoning ahead made her stomach twist.

She buried herself in work. She did everything John asked, followed every instruction, absorbing everything like a sponge. She still saw Sean—brief, occasional lunches, and the odd late night in London—but she had never invited him to Rosewood.

It wasn't just that John might turn up unexpectedly. It was more than that.

It felt wrong.

Still, Sean had noticed the distance.

"Why don't I come down to Rosewood for the weekend?" he suggested one lunch hour. "We barely see each other. A weekend together might help us move forward."

It would bring things to a head, all right.

She could just imagine John's reaction. No, it was too risky. And too confusing.

"I can't invite you," she said awkwardly. "It's not possible."

"Why not?" Sean frowned. "You think I'd jump you the second I arrived? I've never touched you without permission, Grace. Jenny's still there, isn't she?"

"Yes, but that's not the point. It's not about you. It's—" She hesitated. "I haven't told you something."

Sean's expression tightened.

"I'm living at Rosewood," she said evenly. "But only until Christmas. It's not mine anymore. John bought it after my father died. I didn't have anywhere else to go, so he let me stay. That's all."

"With him?" Sean's voice was sharp.

"No! John lives in London. He just—he offered the house until I could sort things out. After Christmas, I'll be leaving."

"That's what this is all about? You're living in his house because he was feeling charitable?"

"Sort of. He arranged it with my father. It had to be sold anyway."

"I see." Sean's tone was heavy with disbelief. "He wanted the house—and you."

"Of course not!" she snapped, flushing. "Don't be ridiculous."

"I'm not. I'm a man, Grace. I've seen the way he looks at you. He's been undressing you with his eyes for two years."

"You're imagining things. He has… intense eyes. He looks at everyone like that."

"No. He doesn't."

"I don't want to talk about this. I have to get back."

She stood quickly, gathering her things, but Sean caught her arm.

"You're playing with fire, Grace," he said grimly. "And you're going to get burned."

She pulled away, shaken—and not just because of Sean's warning. It was the truth she didn't want to face; he was right. She already had been.

Burned—by John Sneddon.

John didn't look pleased when she returned. She was nearly half an hour late, and she could feel the weight of his gaze as she crossed the gleaming foyer toward the lift. He was already waiting there, and as she approached, he glanced meaningfully at his watch.

"Rather a long lunch break, Miss Lewis," he said coolly. "Am I to assume you're trying to irritate me on purpose?"

"I'm not," she replied, breathless from hurrying. "I couldn't get away."

"You were being held too tightly?" His voice was low, deceptively calm, but the confined space of the lift made him feel overwhelming—far too tall, too close, too perceptive. "I seem to recall advising you to end things with that particular admirer."

"Well, I didn't choose to obey," she snapped, turning on him. "And don't bother with threats. His leave's almost over."

"Threats?" His brows lifted. "What need have I for threats? I can afford to be magnanimous—we're nearly there."

"There?" She blinked up at him as the lift chimed and the doors slid open. There was something unsettling in the way he looked at her—dark amusement, veiled promise. She stepped out quickly, her heels clicking on the polished floor.

"Christmas, Miss Lewis," he said smoothly. "We reassess your progress then, if I remember correctly."

There was something ominous in the way he said it, and Grace was grateful to finally reach her room and shut the door behind her.

Christmas—just a few short weeks away—and she still had no idea what would happen when it arrived. But one thing was certain: she had enough experience now to find another job. She'd started selling her jewellery, and her bank account was steadily growing. Soon, all this would be over, and she could move on with the rest of her life—without John.

Chapter Twelve

Grace hadn't fully recovered from the emotional storm when John rang for her. She went to his office with unsteady steps, her mind still fogged—only to find him standing by his desk, arms crossed, his expression a storm of exasperation and something deeper.

"You're really learning, aren't you?" he said abruptly, his gaze locking with hers. "Once upon a time, I thought butter wouldn't melt in your mouth. But now—every day, I discover something new."

She froze. His tone wasn't amused—it was too edged for that—but there was something else behind his words. A kind of grudging fascination.

"First, I find out you go wild in my arms and beg to be possessed," he continued, his voice low and biting. "Now I learn you're remarkably devious."

Devious? She blinked, momentarily confused. But his earlier words—*wild in his arms*—were enough to silence her. Had he discovered her plan? Had he found out she'd been selling her jewellery?

He let the silence hang for a beat, then added coolly, "I just had a phone call from your admirer. Apparently, I'm a treacherous friend who stole your home and plans to fire you next month."

"Sean?" Her voice came out in a whisper of disbelief. "He called you?"

He gave a shrug, but his lips quirked slightly. "You have other admirers I don't know about?" he asked, mockingly. "In this case, it was Austin. Very noble. He's determined not to let you suffer. He intends to marry you and take you off to... wherever his next assignment is."

Her face must have shown too much—shock, regret, or guilt—because his eyes narrowed slightly.

"No need to look so stricken," he said dryly. "I reassured him of your probable survival. And I turned him down on your behalf."

Her head jerked up. "What?"

"I explained he couldn't marry you," John said, stepping closer. "Because you're marrying me."

"I am not—" she began, but he didn't let her finish. He reached for her and drew her hard against him.

"You mean to live with me?" His voice dropped to a murmur. "No, Grace. That's not what I want. I refuse to be your lover."

"You won't be anything," she snapped, struggling. "I will never marry you."

He didn't release her. His arms held her firmly, implacably. "You're not free, Grace," he said, his voice dark. "You know it. Just admit it."

His fingers brushed along her cheek, lingering at her jaw. "You've changed, my love. You've come alive. And you want me. That changes everything."

"I don't want you."

"No?" He captured her lips in a fierce, unrelenting kiss. His arms closed around her, pressing her tight against the heat and strength of his body. She could feel the hard wall of muscle against her trembling softness—and a wave of longing surged through her, fierce and unstoppable.

Her hands rose slowly, hesitantly—then with quiet surrender, they slid around his neck.

His knee shifted, parting her thighs, drawing her even closer. She felt the triumph pulsing in him—but strangely, it didn't matter. She wanted to be here. Wanted him.

"I like you better without clothes," he murmured against her mouth, his voice thick with desire. "I'm not waiting much longer, Grace."

His arousal pressed hot and insistent against her, and she shivered, caught in a rush of sensation as his mouth devoured hers. His hands roamed over her with knowing precision—cupping her breasts, stroking the curve of her hips, sliding along her thighs. She moaned, arching into him, surrendering to the searing heat of his touch.

His hands gripped her with desperate strength, and he broke the kiss to look down at her, breathing raggedly.

"How much of this do you think I can take?" he demanded hoarsely. "You're not a child—you know what you're doing to me. Marry me, Grace. Now. Stop hiding from it, from me."

She could only stare, dazed, trembling, her lips parted from his kiss.

"If you want to go on working, do it. If you want independence, fine. But marry me before I go mad with wanting you."

Grace had no idea what she would have said. She was too overwhelmed—too flushed with desire, too caught in the shimmering heat between them. At that moment, she might have promised him anything.

But she never got the chance.

The door burst open without so much as a knock, and there stood Rita Peterson, her expression a polished mask of mockery—though her eyes betrayed something harsher. Beneath the gloss of amusement, there was fire. Rage. Jealousy.

"John, darling! Do you ever stop?" Rita's voice dripped sweet poison. "I never realised your mentoring style was so… hands-on. Is this part of your recovery plan for the little ingénue?"

Grace felt John stiffen, his muscles tensing against her. But he didn't let her go—not entirely. His hand, still pressed against her side, brushed against her breast again, as if he couldn't—or wouldn't—break contact. Even now, desire still arced between them.

Grace was shocked to find she could face Rita without flinching. But John—John couldn't seem to let her go. And Rita saw everything.

"Try making an appointment next time you want to see me," John said coolly, his tone edged with ice. "That way you won't be so shocked."

"Shocked?" Rita's laughter was brittle. "Please. I know you too well. There's always another woman waiting in the wings. This one just seems a bit tame."

"She's not tame enough," John said, his voice turning hard. "She refuses to marry me. I'm persuading her."

Grace froze.

It was as if a statue cracked and crumbled before her eyes. Rita stared at him, speechless for once, her elegant composure faltering. All the bite drained from her, and for a flickering moment she looked… wounded.

Then she turned, sharply.

"Give in, Grace," she snapped, her voice sharp with venom. "He always gets what he wants. But don't think it's about love. He's never offered marriage before—so there must be a reason. He never does anything without one."

The door slammed behind her, the sound echoing like a verdict.

Grace was shaking from head to toe. She stared at John as if seeing him for the first time—and not in a flattering light. Her voice trembled when she finally spoke.

"Why did you tell her that?"

He met her gaze, unflinching. "Why not? It's the truth."

He moved away then, circling back behind his desk, as if the distance would cool the air between them.

"Don't worry—Rita won't spread the news. She has her own game, and she's more persistent than most."

"I don't care what she says," Grace whispered. "I'm not going to marry you."

"Time will tell," he said, and there was an edge to his voice now—tight and brittle. "A few minutes ago, wedding bells were the last thing on my mind."

He raked a hand through his hair, jaw tense.

"We both know where this is going. Now get the hell out of here, Grace, before I decide to start all over again."

But he didn't pursue her. Not then. Despite the heat in his voice and the fire in his eyes, John didn't push. Instead, he stepped back and gave her space, as though letting the moment fade into something quieter. Something strategic.

In the days that followed, he seemed to settle into an odd kind of normalcy, and Grace—still shaken—allowed herself to breathe. But she was never truly relaxed. There was always tension when he was near, something unspoken straining between them.

From the moment she'd met him, she'd felt it: a sense of inevitability. Of destiny. John had cast some invisible thread between them and now she understood why it had always felt like he was just waiting—waiting to reel her in.

She'd feared that thread for good reason. Because she wanted him, too. Even if she hadn't known it, or couldn't admit it, she felt it now in every glance, every charged silence, every brush of his fingers that lingered just a second too long.

Yet something had shifted.

He was still her boss, yes—but he was something else now, too. A challenger. A teacher. And, in some strange way, a friend.

For the first time in her life, she was proud of herself. Really proud. She was no longer just Grace Lewis, the sheltered daughter of a powerful man. She was a capable woman, trusted with real work, responsibilities, decisions.

John had made that happen.

She wasn't naïve about why she'd risen so fast—he'd brought her close because he wanted her close. But she wasn't floundering. She was doing the job—and doing it well. She'd surprised him. She saw it in the narrow-eyed way he watched her when she kept pace, anticipated needs, solved problems before he had to ask.

That small flicker of approval gave her a secret thrill. Her eyes sparkled now when they worked together over plans and details. She was confident, collected. Comfortable. Almost.

Only when their eyes met—when silence fell too suddenly—did the deeper current break the surface. Desire never quite left the room. And when it surged, John would crush it swiftly with a sharp, dry comment or a biting joke that left her laughing, confused, and aching all at once.

He was infuriating.

He was brilliant.

He was dangerous.

And he was the best boss she'd ever had.

Sean never called again.

Apparently, he had decided she was utterly deceitful. The realisation left a low thrum of guilt beneath her calm exterior—but, if she was honest, she was relieved. He had already left by the time the feeling fully settled, and with that came an unexpected sense of freedom.

Rita didn't return to the office either, though Grace had little doubt she and John were still in contact. The prospect of a wife on the horizon wouldn't faze Rita in the slightest. If anything, it might only increase her interest.

On Friday morning, John announced that he'd be out of the office for the day. He left behind a detailed list of instructions—none of which intimidated her anymore. What she couldn't manage, however, was the sudden emptiness she felt knowing she wouldn't see him until Monday.

"I'm going to check on that new stretch of road off the motorway," he informed her, shrugging on his coat. "If they take much longer, we'll be in breach of contract. They need a shot in the arm."

There was no doubt they'd get it—John Sneddon in person was motivation enough for anyone. Grace nodded but avoided his eyes. She was afraid her face might betray too much. She'd been watching him closely all morning, storing up the sight of him like it might have to last her days.

"If anything happens, call me," he said after a pause, watching her more intently than she liked.

"Anything like what?" she asked, turning back to meet his gaze with forced composure.

"One never knows," he murmured with that familiar thread of mockery. "We're living in interesting times, after all."

Then he turned to go, and Grace's eyes followed him once again—obsessively, helplessly. He seemed to be growing his hair out slightly. It suited him. No matter how late he worked or how hard the day had been, he never looked tired. That, she supposed, was part of his power: the aura of invincibility.

What would it be like, she wondered suddenly, to be married to him? To welcome him home at night, talk over their days by the fire, share something that wasn't always shadowed by tension or unfinished sentences?

As if sensing her thoughts, John paused at the door and glanced back. His dark eyes glittered as they caught the expression on her face.

"If you're not careful," he said softly, "you'll get to like me. Added to desire, that could prove... problematic."

Colour flared in her cheeks, but she couldn't look away. He smiled faintly and added, "Don't forget who is boss while I'm gone."

The door closed behind him, and Grace stood still for several seconds, his last words spinning in her mind.

Had he meant she was the boss while he was out? Did he really trust her that much now?

It seemed so. She intercepted all his calls, organised his meetings, managed the chaos of his schedule—and people were starting to ask her opinion. For the first time in her life, her opinion actually mattered.

Until John, no one had ever cared what she thought.

Jenny had run the household, and her father had run everything else. Grace had simply floated between the two, orchestrating dinner parties and ensuring things ran smoothly. It had been expected of her, just part of the scenery. If she were being honest, she might have made a better housekeeper than executive assistant—at least, when she first arrived.

But John had changed that.

He had taught her—pushed her, challenged her—and she'd learned fast. It hadn't just been her own stubborn pride pushing her forward. More than anything, it was his praise she craved.

She was getting to like him. More than like him. She was teetering on the edge of loving him, and with desire already burning between them, that was dangerous.

A problem, as he'd called it.

But it was a problem she would keep entirely to herself. John must never know. The thought of him discovering her feelings left her unsettled, almost sick with vulnerability.

And yet, what disturbed her most was how hollow she felt when he wasn't near. It was as if she couldn't fully breathe without the sound of his voice or the weight of his presence.

This couldn't continue.

John was holding himself back, keeping control with an iron grip, and she didn't know how much longer either of them could pretend they were just employer and assistant.

By Monday, Grace was pale and listless, a small, persistent ache twisting in her lower side and never quite letting go. It had been coming and going since her father's death—something she'd chalked up to nerves—but now she wasn't so sure. Maybe it was the fall at the site. A pulled muscle? Something deeper?

Whatever it was, it left her drained and unsettled. Still, she pushed herself through the morning, clinging to routine like a lifeline.

John wasn't in the office, and there was no message from him. By mid-morning, the phone lines were buzzing relentlessly, and Grace barely had time to breathe. She managed everything with a quiet efficiency that surprised even her—but she couldn't shake the sinking feeling inside.

He appeared around ten, slipping in so quietly she only realised he'd arrived when he cut into one of her calls and took over. The abruptness of it rankled—far more than it should have.

She'd wanted him to come to her office first. She'd wanted acknowledgment. And when it didn't come, she felt foolishly dismissed. Left out. Ridiculous, yes—but the hurt lingered.

When he finally sauntered into her office, she sat perfectly still, back straight and pale, trying to mask the heat of emotion rising inside her. All of it—jealousy, frustration, pain—was neatly disguised under cool civility.

"I'll take you to lunch," he offered lightly when she glanced up and quickly looked away.

"I'm not very hungry. Thank you."

"What's wrong with you?" He pushed off from where he leaned against the doorframe and crossed to her desk, studying her intently.

"Nothing. I've just been busy. The phones haven't stopped—"

"And you resented being thrown in the deep end?" he asked, cutting her off with a trace of amusement. "I had things to do."

"I'm sure you did," she replied tightly. "You're the boss. You don't have to explain yourself to anyone."

After longing for him all weekend, now she couldn't bear to look at him. Everything hurt more when he was close.

"So, you are angry with me," he murmured, clearly satisfied by the fact. "Come out to lunch like a good girl and I'll make it up to you."

"You're treating me like a child," she snapped, the words slipping out before she could stop them.

His eyes sparkled with that dangerous, infuriating amusement. "What else do you imagine you are, sweetheart?"

The word stunned her. He'd never called her that before. She should have dismissed it as teasing, but it twisted something deep inside her—because she wanted him to mean it. She wanted sweetness, affection. And to him, it was only a joke.

A shudder ran through her, and he noticed.

"You're pale again. Tell me what's wrong."

"Absolutely nothing."

"Grace." The warning note in his voice made her lift her head. His hand came out, swift and sure, tipping her chin so she couldn't look away.

"I'm taking you to the doctor. He's in this morning."

"Just leave me alone!" Her voice broke. "You can't treat me like a fool one minute and then—and then—"

"Make love to you the next?" he finished, low and rough. "I want to look after you."

"Why?"

The question hung between them. It was the kind of thing he usually asked, sharp and unexpected, and it clearly caught him off guard.

His eyes darkened as they swept over her pale, drawn face. "Because—hell! Suit yourself." His voice turned bitter. "I'm never short of a lunchtime companion anyway."

He turned and walked out without another word.

As far as Grace was concerned, that was the end of the day.

He avoided her completely for the rest of the week. By Friday, she'd stopped hoping to see him and instead fell into a quiet state of resignation. When the phone rang and it was Rita asking to speak to John, something in her chest seemed to splinter. It wasn't over between them—whatever it was. And suddenly the days stretched ahead like a bleak, empty plain.

At the end of that day, John walked into her office without warning. He stopped abruptly when he saw her, then closed the door behind him and crossed the room in two strides.

"What's wrong?" he demanded. "Don't put me off this time. I haven't seen you for days, and you look ghastly."

"Surely you don't imagine it's because I've been missing you?" she murmured, too hurt to hold back the sharpness.

"I have no such illusions," he snapped. "In the normal course of events, I doubt you'd even look twice at me. I'm fully aware that I'm taking advantage of your insecurity. What did you expect?"

His bluntness cut deeper than she thought it would. Her face went even paler.

"You're white as a sheet." He was beside her in an instant. "I'm taking you home."

"No. I'm fine." Her voice was sharp, too defensive.

"Very well," he said coldly. "But I am your boss, and there's one thing I can insist on: you're finished for the day. I want you out of here. Right now."

She stood slowly and began gathering her things, but he didn't move. He just watched her, eyes dark with something unreadable.

She winced suddenly, a bolt of pain tightening her features.

He was at her side before she could hide it.

"Forget this," he muttered. "You're coming in my car. And if you argue," he added, voice low and furious, "I'll carry you to the elevator and across the lobby. Argue your way out of that, Miss Lewis."

"My car—"

"Damn your car! Don't test me."

She could tell from his voice that he meant it—and somehow, she didn't want to fight him anymore. She wanted… comfort. The warmth of his presence. Something to hold her up, even for a little while.

When he opened the door, she didn't say a word. She simply walked through it, grateful for the steadiness of his steps beside her. Because suddenly, she wasn't at all sure she'd have made it out on her own.

Chapter Thirteen

The pain was no longer coming in waves—it was constant now, sharp, and all-consuming, stealing her breath and blotting out everything else. Grace sat stiffly in the passenger seat, her arms wrapped tightly around her middle, teeth clenched against the moan that wanted to escape. She didn't speak. Neither did John. But the speed of the car spoke for him, rising steadily as they tore through the streets toward Rosewood.

When they finally arrived, he barely waited for the car to stop before he was out and opening her door. He didn't ask if she could walk—he simply offered his arm, and she took it without a word. Inside the house, his voice cut through the stillness like a blade.

"Jenny! She needs to lie down. Now."

Grace didn't argue. For once, she welcomed his take-charge tone. She was too exhausted, too wrung out to summon any pride. She made it upstairs and into her room, sinking onto the edge of the bed, trying to undress but her hands wouldn't work properly. She had to sit to pull at the buttons of her blouse, and even that felt like too much.

Jenny arrived moments later, her face pale with concern.

"The doctor is on his way," she said gently, helping Grace out of her clothes with surprisingly tender hands. "I don't know what's happened to you so suddenly. You were looking so well lately. I thought Mr. Sneddon was working wonders."

Grace ignored the comment, too tired to snap back. She shook her head slowly.

"A doctor? I don't need a doctor. You shouldn't have called him, Jenny. He's going to think I'm being hysterical over a stomach ache."

"Mr. Sneddon called him," Jenny replied pointedly. "And good on him, too. If it is just a stomach bug, at least we'll know. But between the pain and the vomiting, something's not right."

Grace opened her mouth to argue—wanted to say that she hadn't even eaten lunch, and if it was food poisoning, then Jenny's breakfast was the culprit—but the pain surged again. She groaned and staggered toward the bathroom, barely making it before she was sick once more. This time, when she came back, she was trembling from head to toe.

By the time the doctor arrived, she was lying still and white beneath the covers, only half-aware of his presence.

After a brisk examination, he straightened with a frown.

"Appendicitis," he announced. "She needs hospital care immediately."

Grace blinked at him. Dr. Hollings had known her since childhood, and he wasn't prone to overreaction. That alone frightened her more than anything else.

Jenny began to fuss, wringing her hands. "Oh dear—oh my. Hospital? Should I call an ambulance?"

"I'll take her," John said, his voice clipped. "I'll get her there faster."

The doctor raised a brow at his tone. "The anxious fiancé," he murmured with dry amusement, clearly misreading the relationship. "Just don't break the speed limit, son. She needs to get there in one piece. I'll call ahead to the hospital—she'll need to go into surgery as soon as possible."

Grace felt a ripple of concern at the doctor's words. So did John—she saw it in the way he looked at her, more worried than she had ever seen him. But there was no comfort in that gaze. She knew, with a bitter twist of thought, that it wasn't love—he simply didn't want her dying before he could put a ring on her finger.

"Pack her bag, Jenny," John said briskly. "I'm taking her myself."

Dr. Hollings merely nodded in approval. As he left to notify the hospital, John turned back to her.

"No arguments?" he asked, his tone unexpectedly soft.

"No," she murmured, closing her eyes briefly. "I don't think I could, even if I wanted to."

"We're in agreement, then," he said. "I didn't care for the anxious fiancé bit. I was half-waiting for him to call me 'boy.' That would've been the last straw."

She made a faint sound—half laugh, half gasp. He handed her the dressing gown and helped her into it with surprising gentleness.

"Thank you for…" she began.

"Bossing you about?" he finished, one brow arched. "I told you—I plan on keeping that up. Excellent practice."

She shook her head faintly. "John… I can't marry you," she whispered, the words frayed with effort and pain.

His face darkened—but before he could speak, her body gave way.

"Grace—?"

The last thing she saw was the flash of alarm in his eyes before her knees buckled. He caught her in a single, swift motion, scooping her into his arms with a muttered curse.

She was weightless in his hold, her head lolling against his shoulder, her breathing shallow… fading.

"I've got you," he murmured, his voice raw and urgent. "Damn it, Grace… I've got you."

But her eyes had already closed.

"Still feeling woozy?" The nurse glanced down at Grace with a professional smile that didn't quite reach her eyes. "It'll wear off soon. These little ops are barely a hiccup nowadays—no pain at all."

Grace resisted the urge to ask whether she'd recently had her own appendix removed. The nurse had the warmth of a vending machine and the kind of authority that suggested reprisals would follow any sarcasm. Instead, she forced a faint smile. The nurse patted her hand as if Grace were a particularly slow child.

"That's better. No self-pity on my ward, Miss Lewis. The anaesthetic can linger, especially after a late-night procedure. But by lunchtime, you'll be bouncing out of bed."

With a nod and a brisk clip of her heels, she was gone—radiating smug good health. Grace watched her go, amused in spite of herself. She half expected to be handed a mop and told to polish the floor by tea. A quiet giggle escaped her, but even that small effort sent a bolt of pain slicing through her side. She turned her face into the pillow, grimacing.

Two weeks to the deadline.

She wondered what he was doing. It was Saturday—the office would be closed. Was he at his flat? The image came easily, uninvited: John, tall and casually elegant, a drink in hand, framed by the sleek lines of his living room. But then—inevitably—Rita Peterson swept into the picture like a shadow, and with her came a sharper pain than anything the surgery had caused.

Her thoughts drifted, restless and unwelcome. What was she thinking? John Sneddon was never alone. She'd known it from the start—the champagne parties, the poised, polished women who floated through his world as if they belonged there. Getting along with him now didn't change what he was. Or what she was.

Jealousy. The word stopped her cold. Was that what this was?

No. She couldn't allow herself that weakness. Not about him. There would always be another woman. He had practically told her so.

She was slipping into an uneasy sleep when he arrived. It wasn't visiting hours, but Grace doubted anyone would dare try to stop him. The ward was quiet, the other beds empty, but he still paused at the doorway as if irritated by the room's existence before striding to her side.

He looked down at her, his gaze sharp and intent. "How do you feel?"

"All right," she rasped. "According to the nurse, it doesn't hurt a bit."

His mouth curved in a faint, unwilling smile as he sat carefully on the edge of her bed.

"They told me you hadn't come a moment too soon—any longer and it could have been much worse," he said grimly. "A week here, then proper rest."

"You enquired, of course?" she murmured, torn between resentment and reluctant gratitude.

"I did," he replied simply, a wry glint in his eyes. "Someone had to. Left to yourself, you'd have waited until the thing burst."

Guilt prickled, but before she could murmur a thanks or an apology, he changed tack.

"What are you doing about Christmas?"

The question caught her off guard. It had been the same thought gnawing at her only moments earlier. She hesitated.

"Resting, I suppose. Jenny and I were going to attempt some sort of festive effort, but now…" She shrugged slightly. "I imagine it'll just be a fire, a quiet dinner."

"Spend Christmas with me."

She looked up sharply, blinking. For a heartbeat, his expression was unexpectedly raw—almost vulnerable. It disappeared as quickly as it came, but it stopped her sharp retort.

"I… I'm not really up to parties. And I can't leave Jenny. Besides—"

"Besides, you've got better things to do than waste time on me," he said, finishing for her.

"I wasn't going to say that." She frowned. "You just surprised me."

"Did I?" He stood, restless, pacing to the window and back. "God, I wish Christmas had never been invented. The last couple of years were bearable—when I spent them at your house."

"It was miserable," Grace said quietly. "We missed my mother. But you… I assumed you went to every party in town."

"Oh, I did," he muttered. "And counted the hours until I could decently appear at your house again—without making it obvious I was forcing my way in."

"I didn't know you liked Rosewood that much," she said awkwardly. "No wonder you were glad to buy it."

"I wanted to see you." He swung back toward her, his eyes dark and intense. "I'm obsessed with you, Grace. Didn't you know?"

Her breath caught. The heat rushed to her cheeks, but she lifted her chin stubbornly.

"I'm sure Rita would've been more than willing—"

"Oh, stop it, for God's sake." He sat down again, took her hand in his, and held it firmly. "I wanted you from the moment I saw you. It doesn't take much for a dream to become an obsession. And frankly, behaving like a smitten teenager doesn't suit me at all."

"John…"

"Don't say no before you've even thought about it," he said quietly. "I'm not inviting you to some cramped London flat. Before you came waltzing into my life with that cool little smile, I used to spend Christmas in Bahamas.

My aunt has a villa there. You'd like her—she was my mother's sister. She can't manage English winters anymore. Come with me. Bring Jenny. Rest, recover, and breathe for a while."

"I can't. What would people think?"

"They can think whatever the hell they like. Your friends will understand."

"What friends, they've all but disappeared," Grace admitted, a little ruefully. "But still…"

"Grace." His grip tightened slightly, and just like that, she knew she would say yes. If only to see him every day. If only to keep Rita Peterson far, far away.

"I'll ask Jenny."

"Then you're as good as there," he said, satisfied, his shoulders finally relaxing. "She's putty in my hands."

"We'll see about that," Grace said with mock defiance. But a smile tugged at the corner of her lips. He looked down, caught her eye, and lifted her hand to his mouth, brushing it with a gentle kiss.

"What does it matter? Once we're married, she can look after both of us." He rose and headed for the door, glancing back with a faint smile. "I'll take care of the jet."

"I haven't said yes," she called after him—but he glanced over his shoulder with a knowing look.

"You're ill, Grace. Trapped. Nowhere to run. It's the perfect time to negotiate. I'm learning."

As he reached the door, the nurse came in—and her briskness vanished like steam. Her cheeks flushed as John smiled at her, all charm and effortless persuasion.

"Nurse. I'd like Miss Lewis moved to a private room. Things were a bit rushed last night, but I've sorted the paperwork."

"I'll stay here," Grace said, louder than she intended. The deep breath it required sent a shock of pain through her chest. She winced, clutching her side.

"Please move her as soon as possible," John said calmly, without even glancing her way.

"At once, Mr. Sneddon."

They were talking over her—about her—as if she weren't there at all. Grace could feel the reins tightening. One crack in her defences, and John had stepped in, taken over.

He would never speak to Rita like this, she thought bitterly. He wouldn't dare override her.

She shifted against the pillow in frustration, forgetting the fresh stitches and earning another stab of pain for her trouble. Tears sprang to her eyes. She bit down on her lip to muffle the moan.

John turned instantly, eyes narrowing, voice like velvet laced with steel.

"Miss Lewis is in pain, nurse. I don't expect that in this enlightened age."

"Of course not. I'll fetch something immediately."

"Very kind," he said, in a tone that sounded like both a compliment and a warning. Then, without another glance, he walked out.

Grace stared after him as the nurse fussed around the bedside with renewed briskness, her expression pinched. Clearly, she'd heard the threat too—and Grace had no doubt she'd be punished for it. Probably with a needle instead of a pill.

She sighed and let her head sink back into the pillow.

Maybe it would just be easier to give in.

The worst part was—she already missed him.

"Is Mr. Sneddon your fiancé?" the nurse asked, her tone dry but edged with curiosity.

"In a peculiar sort of way," Grace replied wearily, shifting slightly on the pillow. In truth, he was. He intended to marry her. He gave orders as though the contract were already signed. Only the ring was missing—though, at times, it felt like the one in her nose was firmly in place.

The nurse gave a small, knowing sniff. "Well, he must love you very much. The way he looks at you—like he'd take on the whole world if it so much as made you frown."

Grace didn't answer. Her chest tightened with something that wasn't quite pain.

Love?

No. He'd told her himself—coolly, decisively—that it wasn't about love. She was convenient. Suitable. Safe.

And yet, her heart betrayed her by leaping at every look, every touch, every carefully disguised act of concern.

She closed her eyes. Convenient or not, she was falling for a man who had no intention of falling with her.

Chapter Fourteen

Grace flew out to the Bahamas with John two days before Christmas.

Jenny had been positively bubbling with enthusiasm when John had brought Grace home and mentioned the trip—so much so that Grace hadn't even tried to argue her way out of it. But later, in a complete about face that left her reeling, Jenny declared that she was *'far too wary'* and *'much too sensible'* to fly.

She made her announcement over tea, folding her arms with the serene satisfaction of someone who'd just revealed a masterstroke.

"I'll be spending Christmas with my married brother," she said lightly. "It's been years since I've seen him."

Grace blinked. "You knew you were going to do this!" she accused, stunned by the sudden reversal.

Jenny met her glare with a perfectly bland expression. "I might have had an idea," she admitted smoothly. "I wasn't going to go off and leave you by yourself, now, was I? I never have done, have I? But another thing—" her voice turned prim— "Mr. Sneddon tells me his Aunt Harriet is his only relative. It's time you met her, seeing as you're going to be part of the family."

Grace's protest froze on her lips. *Part of the family.*

"I am not going to be one of the family," she snapped—but unfortunately, John chose that exact moment to pull up. Jenny's knowing sniff said it all, and Grace, swallowing her irritation, let the conversation die.

John glanced between them, raising a brow. "Unfortunate timing," he murmured, but his amused expression told Grace he had expected Jenny's retreat all along. Perhaps he'd even planned it with her.

Everyone else seemed free to follow their own inclinations—except me, she thought bitterly.

Now, seated beside him in the plush cabin of his private jet, she stared out at the endless stretch of sky and mused on just how completely John Sneddon had altered the course of her life.

Once, she'd been cold and guarded, certain of her hatred—convinced her fear was of him.

But now she realised her fear had never been of John. It had been of herself.

Because she was starting to get used to this—being swept into his world, wrapped in his presence, caught in the current of his relentless will.

She knew what he was. Ruthless. Calculated. A man who had chosen her with cool determination. She knew all about his past affairs, his appetite for control, and she knew—oh, how she knew—that he didn't love her. He'd told her so.

And still… here she was.

They were bound together by an unwilling magnetism neither of them seemed able to resist.

She glanced sideways. John was watching her again, that ever-present gleam of triumph in his eyes. It had been there since they boarded the jet—a spark of anticipation, a quiet, almost physical thrill that radiated off him in waves.

He was exhilarated. For the next week, she would be his. Entirely.

"How are you feeling?" he asked, voice low, eyes possessive.

She shouldn't have felt anything—but she did.

A tremor ran through her at the note in his voice, and she hated herself for the way it thrilled her. I must be losing my mind, she thought. She wanted to belong to him. Not just in words—but in body, in spirit, in every way a woman could belong to a man.

"I'm feeling fine," she said stiffly. "You know that already. The doctor said I'd be back to normal in a week. It's been nearly three."

"I'm glad," he murmured—and the faint smirk curling his lips made her flush. There was no misreading that tone. He wasn't thinking about her appendix.

She turned her face away, flustered. "Tell me about your aunt," she said quickly, needing to talk, to ground herself in something ordinary.

John didn't move. The heavy, sensual tension between them still pulsed like a low current in the air—but his expression softened.

"Harriet?" he said. "She's a dear. My mother's side were wealthy, old-money types. When she married my father, they never recovered from the shock. He was a labourer—came to do some work on the estate. They met. She fell in love. Married him in secret and left everything behind.

"She vanished from their world—and for a long time, they didn't even know I existed."

Grace turned slowly to him. "How did they find out?"

His voice changed, deepened. That old bitterness crept in, the one that always came when he spoke of his past. She regretted asking immediately.

"When she died," he said quietly, "I went looking for them. I was angry—too angry. I blamed them for not rescuing her, for letting her suffer alone. But there was only one uncle left by then, and Harriet. She told me the truth. All of it. And since then, I've kept her close. She reminds me of my mother—the way she would've looked if she'd lived."

Grace felt a tightness in her throat. "I hope I won't be intruding. If you usually spend Christmas with her—"

"I used to," he said, turning his head. "Until I met you."

Her heart stumbled.

"I spent the week after Christmas with her last year. Once the excuse to come to your house evaporated with the season, I gave Harriet a few days. But you're not intruding, Grace. She's expecting you."

Grace looked at him, and for a moment, she didn't know whether she was walking into a holiday… or deeper into his life than she'd ever meant to go.

There was something so inevitable in the way he spoke of her.

He hadn't come to her house to propose or negotiate—he'd come simply to look at her. And probably, if he hadn't liked what he'd seen, he would never have bothered to take over her father's company. That single visit had changed the course of her life.

If he'd walked away, she would still be the girl she had always been—shy, hesitant, existing quietly in her father's shadow. And Rosewood? It would have slipped into the hands of strangers, the way so many old homes did.

The realisation deepened the strange, persistent sense of destiny that had taken root in her since John Sneddon entered her world.

"What have you told your aunt?" she asked quietly, glancing across at him. Her voice was tentative, almost fragile.

His lips curved slightly, eyes glinting with faint amusement. "I told her that—with any luck—you'll marry me." He kept his eyes on the view beyond the jet's windows. "I didn't have to make any promises about the sleeping arrangements. She's too old-fashioned to imagine anything else."

"So am I," Grace muttered, turning to stare out the window, her cheeks flushing hot.

John reached over and covered her trembling hand with his own.

"For what it's worth, so am I," he said gently. "I don't want to seduce you, Grace. I want to marry you. Besides, you're still recovering from surgery."

"I am not," she snapped, tossing her head and glaring at him. "I'm perfectly fine."

He looked at her then, his eyes dancing with mischief.

"All right," he said with mock seriousness. "So, you want me to seduce you. I'll think about it—but don't get your hopes up."

"John!" she gasped, scandalised—but the laughter bubbling in his chest was infectious, and his teasing was far too gentle to take seriously.

Then, without warning, he lifted her hand and brushed his lips across her knuckles—a gesture so unexpectedly tender it stole her breath.

"Relax," he murmured. "I'm teasing."

She leaned back, heart pounding, trying to obey. But her nerves were a mess of contradictions—tense, trembling, thrilled.

He traced slow, thoughtful fingers over the back of her hand, as though memorising the feel of her.

"I don't know what's happening to me," he said after a moment, his voice low and raw with truth. "I like you, Grace Lewis. And if I didn't want you so damn much, I think I'd make you my best friend."

He couldn't have said anything that would have touched her more. She made no move to pull her hand away.

He had given her more than just a place in his life—he'd given her purpose, confidence, fire.

She loved him. That truth settled inside her with quiet finality.

No use pretending anymore. John Sneddon had become the centre of her world. And the thought of losing him… of going back to a life without him…

It was simply too bleak to bear.

The warm, golden air enveloped them as they stepped off the jet. Grace tilted her face to the sun like a cat basking in a patch of light. The tension that had gripped her during the flight melted away beneath the radiant heat and gentle sea breeze.

Aunt Harriet had arranged for her car to be waiting, and within minutes they were cruising along the island roads. The convertible's top was down, and the soft wind whipped Grace's hair from her face as palm trees blurred past.

She felt free. Happy. Suspended in a dream.

And though John had no idea, she felt completely at one with him.

After a while, he steered the car off the main road and down a narrow track that led to a secluded inlet. Towering rocks jutted from a sapphire-blue sea, the waves curling in white ribbons around their base. It was breathtaking—raw, untouched beauty—and Grace sat in silent awe as he cut the engine.

He didn't speak. He let her absorb it, his profile still and unreadable beside her.

"Can you see the sea from your aunt's villa?" she asked at last, turning toward him with shining eyes.

He was watching her, not the view. Watching her as if she were the remarkable thing.

He nodded slowly. "Yes."

She waited, sensing something else behind his quiet. He didn't speak again until her questioning gaze compelled him.

"I want to ask you something," he said at last. "I know I'm dropping it on you, and I fully expect you to say no."

"What is it?" she asked softly. The warmth between them made his hesitation feel strange—uncharacteristic.

"Harriet and I... we're all we've got. She's my only family. Her health isn't what it was—that's why she lives here. She's sharp, she reads the papers, she sees the headlines. She wants me to settle down." He hesitated, then let out a breath of frustration. "I want to make her happy. While we're here, Grace... I want you to wear my ring. Just while we're with her. Let her believe we're already engaged."

She blinked, stunned—not by the request, but by the unsteady note in his voice. John Sneddon, uncertain? Almost pleading?

"It would be a lie," she said slowly. "If you care about her, how can you let her believe something that isn't true?"

His face darkened. The flash of temper returned to his eyes.

"As far as I know, this might be her last Christmas. Who can predict anything? I do intend to marry you, Grace. This just moves things forward a little. If you don't want to do it as a kindness—then consider it a trade."

"A trade?"

"I gave you until Christmas to prove yourself. And after the hospital, I'm willing to extend that deadline another three months. All I'm asking in return is a bit of harmless theatre. I want a fiancée to show off. Just for Harriet."

"John, you're talking like I've already agreed to marry you," she protested. "You said there'd be an assessment at Christmas—I didn't even know what that meant!"

"We'll discuss that when we get back to England," he said tightly. "Right now, I'm asking for a small favour. What do you say? Are you too scared?"

"I'm not scared! I just…" She pressed her hands to her face, torn. "As usual, you've got me all twisted around. If I say no and something happens to her, I'll feel awful. But if she turns out to be fine, then I'll be tangled up in this lie. No wonder people are scared of you, John Sneddon."

"Are you?" he asked quietly.

She dropped her hands and met his gaze head-on. "No. I never have been."

And it was true. She had never feared him—only her own reaction to him.

"You said you hated me," he said. "Do you still?"

She opened her mouth to say yes. She wanted to. It would be simpler. But the words wouldn't come.

Because she didn't hate him.

He stirred her. Made her feel things that unsettled and excited her. Sometimes she even had a foolish urge to protect him, as if he needed it.

"No, I don't hate you," she said at last, her voice soft. "How could I? You've been good to me."

"Have I?" he said with a wry smile. "I'm sure I never meant to be."

She gave a long sigh, then held out her hand. "Fine. Let's get it over with—before my conscience gets the better of me. But if she's fit as a fiddle, you'll regret this."

"Threats?" His eyes gleamed with sudden amusement. "We're making progress. Where's the cool, distant moon-maiden?"

"I worked her out of my system." Her eyes sparkled and he smiled, and her heart flipped wildly in her chest.

"Maybe it's because you're free now, Grace. For the first time in your life, you can say what you feel—without guilt."

"I can manage without you," she said archly, enjoying this rare sense of equality. "I'm an experienced personal assistant now. I could get a better job."

"Please don't," he replied, with mock gravity. "I'd never find anything again without you."

Suddenly, they were smiling at each other—and then he brought out the ring.

A large, dark sapphire encircled by diamonds nestled in the velvet box like something out of a fairytale. Grace watched, almost mesmerised, as John slipped it onto her finger. It felt real. Too real. As though he had just proposed in this breathtakingly romantic place and she had said yes.

The emotion was overwhelming. One moment she had been laughing, and the next she was struggling not to cry. The ring glittered on her hand like a symbol of something she could never have. It was all for the comfort of an old woman. Grace didn't know whether she was a wicked accomplice in the deception or merely a pawn in some dark, strategic game John was playing. No doubt she could keep the ring—if she gave in and married him. But she would never have John. He had told her that from the very beginning, and she believed him.

"Tears?" he asked softly, tilting her chin to study her face. His eyes caught the shimmer in hers. "It's an emotional moment, getting engaged."

"I'm not engaged," she said quickly, blinking back the tears. "It's just to show your aunt. It's not real."

"We can make it real, Grace. Any time you say the word, we can make it very real."

"I don't want to, thank you," she replied, her voice unsteady.

He slid his arms around her, drawing her close. "You'll never get away from me, Grace. You're under my skin. In my bloodstream. I want you, and I'm going to marry you."

Her protest was silenced by his mouth. She never got the words out. His lips caught hers, stealing her breath, drawing her into the fire she'd fought so hard to resist. Her body responded before her mind could rebel. Desire had been simmering between them for too long.

"No, John…" she gasped, trying to push away. She knew her own vulnerability—knew she had to stop this before it consumed her. But he was already following her retreat, gently catching her fingers, brushing his lips across them in a slow, sensuous trail. His tongue circled each one, his mouth capturing the finger that bore his ring, sucking softly, rhythmically. Erotic. Intimate. Dangerous.

A cry escaped her lips—small, helpless, completely betrayed by her body. Every defence shattered into pieces. He gathered her close again, his kiss this time deeper, more demanding. One hand cupped the swell of her breast, fingers kneading gently, knowingly.

"You like this," he whispered against her lips. "We both know that. You like it when I touch you here. It sets your heart racing."

His fingers coaxed her, finding the erect peak and teasing it until white-hot pleasure coursed through her. She burned for him. She ached. She wanted.

"I want to see you again," he murmured. "To feel your skin against mine."

"You promised…" she whispered, sobbing her need and her resistance in the same breath.

"I said I didn't approve," he said hoarsely. "But I can't promise not to take you, Grace. You've haunted me for more than two years. And soon, you'll be mine."

His lips found hers again—fierce, demanding—and she gave in, surrendering to the storm. His hands slipped the buttons of her dress open with practiced urgency, sliding inside to cup her bare breast. The sensation was almost too much, too raw, and she whimpered, a small sound of protest.

Instantly, he stilled.

"I'm hurting you," he said, his voice rough with restraint. "I don't want to. Forgive me."

That was her undoing.

Gentleness from John Sneddon was her greatest weakness. He caressed her with such aching tenderness that her body arched toward him instinctively, seeking more. His lips took hers again, slow now, devastating in their intimacy.

Her dress slid lower, and his hand moved to her stomach, spreading wide and heavy over the place where her ache pulsed strongest. She moved against him, helpless, caught in the whirlwind of a desire she barely understood. His touch was a promise and a threat.

But then he stopped.

"No, Grace," he whispered, voice thick with longing. "Not like this. I won't take you here. When I make love to you, you'll be my wife."

And suddenly she was crying, her body shaking with the shame of how easily she had given in. She had wanted him—wanted everything—and she hadn't even tried to stop herself.

He held her close, rocking her gently, stroking her hair until her sobs quieted.

"Marry me, Grace," he said, brushing the last tears from her cheeks. "Don't fight this anymore. You know what's between us is inevitable."

"If I left, you'd find someone else," she choked, turning her face from him. "Another woman. A lover. You told me yourself; I'm just one of many."

He cupped her chin, forcing her to meet his gaze. "Jealous?" he asked softly, a glint in his eye.

"What do I have to be jealous about?" she said bitterly. "To be jealous, I'd have to care. And I don't."

His face shut down instantly, turning to stone. He released her and leaned forward to start the car.

"That makes us even, then," he said coldly. "You're wearing my ring as a favour. I've extended your time as another favour."

"And what happens when I run out of time and still refuse to marry you?" she asked, heart aching at the distance between them. "I've held up my end. I've learned the business. By spring, I'll be indispensable."

"No one is indispensable," he replied icily. "If I looked around, I'd find another suitable bride. Someone beautiful. Well-bred."

"Then why all this?" she asked, shaken to the core. "Why go through this charade if you could have anyone?"

"I want you," he said flatly, eyes never leaving the road. "I saw you, I decided, and I planned. That's how I operate."

"A takeover bid," she muttered. "An addition to your portfolio."

He gave a short, humourless laugh. "Perhaps. But if that's all this was, I could have had you ten minutes ago."

The truth of it silenced her. She looked into the mirror, wiping at the tears that lingered. She was about to meet his aunt, a supposedly happy fiancée. But she felt like a fraud. At this moment, she wasn't sure she could fool anyone—not even a child.

The Bahamas stretched around them in hues of turquoise and green, a glittering paradise. Grace tried to gather herself.

There were over a hundred and fifty islets and inlets in the Bahamas, but she knew Aunt Harriet's villa by the sea was their destination. From the high road, she saw rooftops glinting white in the sun and walls tinted the palest pink. John pointed to one set back behind tall greenery, its manicured lawn sloping to the silver sand. It looked idyllic. Peaceful.

But inside the car, tension crackled.

John barely spoke, his jaw tight, his profile unreadable. The fragile truce between them had shattered again, leaving only the brittle shell of what might have been. Grace's courage, so recently burning bright, flickered weakly in the silence.

Soon, she would have to smile. Soon, she would have to play the role of a devoted fiancée. But all she felt was dread. Because right now, she was more lost than ever—and John Sneddon, the man who held her heart without knowing it, was once again a stranger beside her.

Chapter Fifteen

On the quiet, winding road that led to the villa, John eased the car to a stop and turned toward her, his gaze steady and unreadable.

Grace didn't look at him. If he started another confrontation now, she might actually scream—and show up at Aunt Harriet's front door in the midst of a hysterical breakdown.

"Perhaps a truce is in order," he said at last, his voice low but edged with authority.

She kept her face turned stubbornly toward the window. "I didn't realise we were at war."

"There'll be a battle," he replied tersely, "until you're in my arms all night." A pause. "But since that isn't happening—*yet*—we need a civilised arrangement. I won't raise my voice if you can manage to look less like a prisoner and more like my fiancée."

His imperious tone snapped her head around, her eyes blazing.

"Shout at me? Just try it, and I'll be on the first plane out of here," she snapped. "And let me remind you, Mr. Sneddon, I'm perfectly capable of managing without you."

Her fury drew a reluctant smile from his otherwise hard mouth. But he wasn't backing down.

"In a few minutes," he said coolly, "you'll be meeting my aunt. No threats. No arguments. Please behave yourself."

"I was brought up with excellent manners," Grace replied stiffly, refusing to soften. "I said I'd play the part while we're here, and I will. But only in public."

"Agreed." He studied her with narrowed eyes. "How do I explain your present... miserable condition?"

"You can say I'm a poor traveller. And then, of course, there's my operation," she added, her tone edged with sarcasm.

"Ah, yes," he murmured dryly. "Subterfuge seems to come quite naturally to you. I should have realised after the Austin episode. Let's continue, then. You look as though you're in desperate need of rest."

"Well, that should break the ice nicely," Grace said tartly. "Hello, Aunt Harriet—here's my weak-kneed fiancée. I would have brought my very powerful lover, but she was busy demolishing a few walls."

His mouth twitched. "I'm really beginning to think you are jealous."

"Let's get one thing straight—I'm not jealous," she shot back. "I'm disgusted that you could ask a woman to marry you in one breath and, in the next, tell her you're keeping your mistress."

A flicker of unease passed through his eyes, there and gone in an instant. Maybe she imagined it.

"Let's just get on with it," she muttered. "I need to practice my smile. And don't speak again—you'll only ruin the effect."

Maybe they could fool Aunt Harriet after all. He didn't reply—just shifted the car into gear, the silence between them as taut as wire.

Grace turned her head away, fixing her gaze on the lush scenery beyond the window. She would have to be careful—especially when it came to her remarks about Rita Peterson. John was too perceptive, and jealousy... well, it wasn't as easy to disguise as she'd thought.

His aunt was a complete shock.

Grace had imagined someone very different—some worn-out woman living on the edges of John's success. She'd unconsciously pictured a tired, careworn soul in frumpy clothes, perhaps a leftover image from how she'd imagined John's mother: someone drudging through life, badly used and quietly fading.

Harriet Sneddon was none of those things.

Though there was a slight frailty in her step, everything else about her radiated aristocratic command. She was tall, willowy, and blue-eyed, with a regal bearing that made her seem as formidable as John himself. Her voice was light but authoritative, and her slender hands—blue-veined and elegant—were covered in dazzling rings. She looked like a woman who had lived a full life on her own terms, not one who'd been rescued by a successful nephew.

There was nothing browbeaten about her.

And she adored John. That was instantly clear. She swept him into a hug as soon as he stepped from the car, her eyes shining with fondness before turning to Grace with an amused and curious light.

"So, this is Grace?" she said, grinning like a delighted conspirator. "This is the woman who's going to save you from the black pit, is she? My dear, I'm thrilled. It's high time this rogue was tamed."

"I'm already tamed," John said smoothly, lifting Grace's hand to display the ring glittering on her finger.

His arm slipped firmly, possessively, around her waist, and his aunt leaned in to kiss both of Grace's cheeks. Warmly. Kindly. As though she truly believed this engagement was real.

"So, you agreed," Harriet said softly, her eyes full of meaning. "I had hoped you would. But then, John usually gets what he wants—though I did wonder if it would be quite so easy with someone he actually cared about." She gave Grace a teasing look. "He didn't order you to become engaged, I trust?"

"No," Grace said evenly, managing a small smile. "It was… a mutual agreement."

"She had a rough flight," John interjected before more questions could follow. "Let's show her to her room."

It was the best thing he could have said. Grace had taken an instant liking to Aunt Harriet—and the guilt hit her like a wave, warm and shameful. She felt it colour her cheeks. This woman wasn't some deluded fool. She was sharp, clever, kind—and Grace was here under false pretences.

"Of course, dear. But do let her meet Sharon first." Harriet turned as a woman entered the room and smiled. "Grace, this is my nurse, Miss Wright—but she won't mind if you call her Sharon. She's been with me nearly five years."

Grace turned with a smile that faltered almost immediately.

Miss Wright looked more like a runway model than a nurse. She was around thirty, tall and strikingly slim, with a curtain of rich auburn hair and the kind of classic bone structure that belonged in glossy magazines. And her face lit up like a chandelier the moment her eyes landed on John.

Grace remembered that he'd visited the Bahamas every year—possibly more than once—and from the look on Sharon's face, they were well acquainted.

The dismay struck hard. Of course she was beautiful. Every woman in the Sneddon-Lewis building had seemed half in love with him. It was only natural that Sharon Wright would be no different. But seeing it so blatantly—right in front of her—was something else entirely.

"Oh, John! How lovely to see you again," Sharon gushed, her voice soft and honeyed. She moved toward him with theatrical delight, her hips swaying, her entire body language that of a woman expecting a warm—and possibly intimate—welcome.

Grace turned away sharply. If he kissed her, she didn't want to see it. She couldn't.

But he didn't. He merely gave Sharon one of his signature smiles—charming, flattering, and impersonal.

"Sharon. You're more beautiful than ever."

Grace clenched her jaw. She waited for Sharon's inevitable reply—and wasn't disappointed.

"It's the excitement of seeing you, John."

Harriet stepped in quickly, her expression pinching with faint disapproval.

"And this," she said firmly, "is his fiancée, Sharon. They're engaged. Isn't she lovely?"

"Lovely to look at," Sharon agreed, her smile tight. Her gaze flicked over Grace with practiced appraisal.

"And delightful to know," John added smoothly, pulling Grace closer with a possessive arm around her waist. "You'll help me keep an eye on her, won't you? She's just had an appendix operation."

"I'm perfectly recovered," Grace said quickly, her voice sharper than intended. The last thing she wanted was to be sent to bed by Sharon Wright while John basked in the sun and Harriet took her afternoon nap. She could already picture Sharon in her designer swimsuit, conveniently close to John—offering to rub sunscreen on his back.

No. She wasn't going to let that happen.

Not without a fight.

Her room faced the sea.

Harriet led her along the wide hallway while John stayed behind to collect the bags from the car. The scent of salt and frangipani drifted in on the breeze as they stepped inside, the doors already open to a stone balcony that framed the ocean like a painting.

From the window, they could see him. Sharon Wright had followed him out, and they were standing close beside the car—laughing. Laughing in the kind of easy, familiar way John never laughed with her.

Grace felt the sharp twist of something she didn't want to name, and Harriet must have sensed it too. She spoke briskly, her tone just a shade too bright.

"I had to leave my car at the airport for John," she said, steering Grace away from the view. "Visitors aren't allowed to hire vehicles here—not without special permits. Of course, John could easily manage it if he wanted to…"

Grace understood the tactic instantly. Harriet was distracting her—deliberately guiding her away from the scene outside, from the woman standing far too close to John. And Grace appreciated it more than she could say.

"It's a beautiful room," she said softly. "Thank you for letting me stay."

"My dear, I'm just so glad you're here," Harriet replied, her voice warm with affection. "John means everything to me. I never had children of my own, you see. And I can tell he loves you. It's written all over him. I want you to come here as often as you like."

She patted Grace's arm, and Grace had to fight the sudden urge to confess everything. This woman was kind, perceptive, and clearly not strong—at least that part of John's story hadn't been a lie. But the rest? This arrangement, this engagement—it wasn't built on truth. And the deception felt heavier by the moment.

"I'll let John bring your bags up," Harriet added, glancing toward the door. "But when he's not hovering, you and I must have a proper little chat."

That had a worrying ring to it.

Grace managed a smile, but as Harriet left, her heart gave a hard, unsteady thump.

She turned back to the window and stood there, unmoving, her gaze on the glittering turquoise water. It was safer to look at the horizon than at John. She needed a moment to recover—from Sharon's perfect red smile, from her own dismay, from the jealousy that had flared up so easily, so stupidly.

The truth was, John rarely laughed with her. He teased, he commanded, he kissed— but he didn't laugh. And she wasn't sure what that meant.

She heard him before she saw him—the creak of the door, the soft thud of a suitcase being placed on the polished floor. Still, she didn't turn. She couldn't. She felt too raw, too exposed. And John had always been too perceptive, always able to read her with alarming accuracy.

"Is something wrong, Grace?" he asked quietly. His voice was calm, but alert. "You look… strained. You've lost weight again too. Maybe I should tie you down in case of strong winds."

She said nothing.

He crossed the room and gently turned her to face him, tipping her chin up with one hand. His eyes scanned her face, their expression unreadable.

"What do you think of Harriet?" he asked.

"I liked her at once. She's… unexpected."

He smiled faintly. "Because of my background?"

"Stop putting words in my mouth," Grace replied, her tone sharp with frustration. "You've got this fixation with your past. No wonder you're so hard sometimes. It isn't natural—constantly dragging the weight of it behind you."

"The only fixation I have," he murmured, pulling her closer, "is you. And that feels very natural to me."

Before she could reply, his lips found hers—light at first, then deepening with slow, consuming intent. His arms gathered her close, fitting her against the length of him like something inevitable. Her resistance, as always, collapsed like a house of cards. Her arms slid around his neck, her fingers threading into his hair, and when he opened his mouth over hers, she welcomed him without hesitation.

When he lifted his head, she was trembling.

John looked down at her with an intensity that stole her breath.

"Grace…" he began.

"Shall I unpack for you, John?"

Sharon Wright was already in the doorway as she spoke, perfectly poised, as if she had every right to be there. Grace flinched and instinctively pulled away from John, her face burning—not with embarrassment, but with a fury that threatened to boil over. How many more women were going to come charging into the room as if they belonged to him?

John didn't miss a beat. "No, thank you, Sharon," he said smoothly. "I'll take care of it myself—once Grace is settled. She needs rest. I'll meet you on the veranda shortly. You can bring me up to date then."

Sharon's lips curved—not in disappointment, but in a slow, knowing smile of triumph. Then she turned and walked away with deliberate grace, as if she already knew the story wasn't over.

Another woman. Another obstacle. Another reminder that Grace wasn't the first and would never be the only.

Grace's voice was tight with frustration. "How exactly do you plan to keep this farce alive when your old flame is lurking behind every door? Miss Wright is going to trail after you like some elegant ghost. It's going to be like dancing a waltz—with three people."

John's expression didn't shift, but his eyes locked on hers. "I seem to recall calling you my friend," he said quietly. "Or does that title now belong solely to Sharon?"

Grace's eyes flashed. "Don't twist my words. I know exactly what Sharon is—and so do you. And as for being your friend, I'm not. I'm here because we struck a bargain. That's all."

He stepped closer, his gaze darkening. "Is it?"

"Of course it is," she snapped. "Don't pretend otherwise."

"Then tell me why," he said, his voice low and dangerous, "you melt every time I touch you."

She couldn't answer, not truthfully. Instead, she lashed out with brittle defiance.

"Sheer feminine instinct," she said with cutting scorn. "Any man with enough experience could do the same. You're not special, John—just… practiced. You parade your conquests in front of me often enough for me to know that."

The moment the words left her mouth, she regretted them.

His hands closed around her shoulders, not gently. Fury lit his face, deeper and colder than hers. For a breathless second, she saw something elemental in him—something untamed and dangerous.

Then he let her go as abruptly as he'd grabbed her, the colour draining from her cheeks.

"I'll see you later," he said, voice clipped. At the door, he glanced back with a dark curl to his mouth. "Thank you for keeping your voice down. If you ever feel the need to scream at me again, I suggest we take a walk on the beach."

And then he was gone.

Grace moved to the window, her chest tight, her fingers clenched. She wasn't surprised when she saw him almost immediately below, stepping onto the sand with Sharon beside him. He offered her his hand. She took it. And moments later, her arm curled possessively through his.

They were laughing.

Grace turned away from the window.

What was the point of it all?

What exactly was she hoping for? He had told her plainly—he didn't love her. And he probably never would. This—watching him laugh with other women, seeing them cling to him, knowing they had once shared something she never would—this would be her life with John. A life of quiet torment. A life of wondering.

If she ever gave in to that fierce, aching urge to marry him, this would be her daily truth: jealousy like a stone in her chest, longing twisted into pain. To love a man like John Sneddon was to share him—and she couldn't do it.

She loved him. God help her, she did. But she couldn't marry a man whose heart she didn't own.

Somewhere deep inside, she knew she would have to walk away—and soon.

After Christmas, she would leave. That had always been the plan. She had sold her jewellery—some for a surprisingly good price—the only piece she'd kept was the necklace John had given her. And she'd been quietly saving every pound she earned. It would be enough. Enough to start again. Enough to stay free.

Because staying here, pretending, hoping… was too dangerous. John was becoming harder and harder to resist. The touch of his hands, the pull of his mouth, the sheer force of his presence—it was all eroding her will. And if she wasn't careful, she would fall so deeply she wouldn't be able to climb out again.

Yes, she had his ring. But she'd never have his heart.

Grace slipped off her dress and lay down on the cool bed, her limbs leaden, her chest tight. It wasn't the long journey that had worn her out—it was the constant emotional strain. The push and pull of want and fear. The exhausting dance of pretending not to care.

She closed her eyes.

And somewhere between sorrow and exhaustion, between a love that hurt and a lie she couldn't keep living, Grace drifted into sleep.

Chapter Sixteen

Dinner was difficult—mostly because Sharon joined them.

There was nothing unusual about her presence, of course. Miss Wright was more than a nurse; she was a kind of companion to Harriet, and it would have seemed strange if she hadn't been treated like one of the family. Still, her presence cast a long shadow across the table, and Grace couldn't pretend it didn't unsettle her.

She asked herself, honestly, whether she would have liked Sharon if John hadn't been involved. The answer came swiftly: *no.* There was something too polished, too knowing about the woman—something that reminded her far too much of Rita. Perhaps John had a type: glamorous, glossy, confident women brimming with energy and ambition.

Grace, by contrast, felt like a ghost at the table.

She tried to keep the conversation going, but it was a struggle. Sharon's attention never wavered from John, and what was worse—he talked back. Easily. Comfortably. As if their rapport had long since been established. Grace found herself largely left to Harriet's company while Sharon and John exchanged remarks, smiles, and the occasional shared glance that made her stomach knot.

"John was telling me about your beautiful house—Rosewood, isn't it?" Harriet said kindly, trying to draw Grace out.

"Yes," Grace replied, managing a smile. "It's beautiful. But it's not mine anymore. John bought it when my father died."

"I don't suppose it matters really, does it?" Harriet asked gently. "I imagine you'll live there once you're married?"

The question threw Grace. She opened her mouth, caught between a lie and the truth—but John, as ever, was one step ahead.

"Yes," he said smoothly. "We'll live there. That's the only reason I bought the house. Grace would simply fade away without Rosewood. Her life revolves around it."

His tone was casual, but there was an edge to it—an undercurrent of possession or resentment—that Harriet missed. Grace didn't. Neither, it seemed, did Sharon. Her eyes flicked between them, sharp with interest.

"I shall come to England for the wedding," Harriet said warmly. "When is it?"

"Grace hasn't set a date yet," John answered blandly. "But don't worry—we'll let you know in good time."

"Maybe you should hurry her along," Harriet said with a teasing smile. "She might change her mind if you leave it too long."

"She won't," John murmured, his dark gaze fixed on Grace. "I've got her securely trapped… haven't I, love?"

Grace's cheeks burned. She looked down at her ring as it caught the light—mocking her with its brilliance. "Well, that's one way of putting it," she said lightly. "Besides, I have to think of the scandal if I walked away. The great John Sneddon… jilted. I doubt the world would recover."

John smiled then—one of those slow, unreadable smiles that to an outsider might have looked affectionate. But Grace saw it clearly. It was a warning.

He wasn't going to let her go easily.

And when the time finally came for her to walk away, she knew—it would cost her.

Later, they gathered on the veranda. John kept the conversation light for his aunt's sake, his voice relaxed, his posture casual—but Grace noticed how carefully measured it all was. Sharon Wright hovered nearby with a hopeful smile that practically begged for an invitation.

"Do join us, Sharon," Harriet said with her usual gracious warmth. That was all the encouragement needed. Sharon moved quickly, smiling a little too brightly at John as she claimed the seat beside him.

It didn't sit well with Harriet. Grace could see it in the way her expression cooled slightly, the way her fingers tapped against the armrest. Having coaxed John to the point of engagement, she clearly expected the next step—marriage—and she wasn't pleased by any woman attempting to insert herself now. Still, her gaze kept drifting toward Sharon's laughing face, and she grew less engaged in the conversation Grace tried to maintain.

Grace felt like she was sitting on a powder keg, and after a few minutes, she stood abruptly. "I think I'll go in."

But John caught her wrist before she could step away. "Walk on the beach?" he asked, gently enough to calm Harriet's watching eyes.

"If you like," Grace murmured.

She didn't. Not really. She didn't want to be alone with him—not when her heart was tangled up in ways she couldn't untangle. But what choice did she have? He was orchestrating this entire performance, and from the look on Harriet's face, it was working.

His grip on her wrist didn't loosen as they walked away. Instead, his fingers slid down to lace through hers, warm and sure, as if the act were entirely natural. Grace was aware of eyes following them as they left the veranda and wasn't at all surprised when Harriet's pleased voice floated behind them.

"They're so close. You can see it. I never thought it would happen to John. I can't tell you how happy I am."

Grace didn't catch Sharon's reply—but she could imagine it. Polite. Predictable. Hollow.

Once they were far enough from the others, she gently pulled her hand free. Not because she wanted to. But because she did.

He said nothing, only strolled quietly beside her, stooping now and then to collect flat pebbles from the sand. One by one, he flicked them into the sea, watching as they skipped lightly across the surface like sparks of silver in the dark water.

"Bet you can't do this," he murmured, not looking at her.

"You'd win that bet. I used to try when I was younger—until my arm felt like it was going to fall off."

She found herself smiling despite herself and paused to watch the pebbles skimming like dragonflies over the water.

"Want to try again?" he asked, offering her a perfectly flat stone.

"No, thank you." She drew her hand back as though the pebble might burn her.

"We need to pass the time," he said lazily. "Harriet's expecting some romantic interlude. Of course, unless you have a better idea…"

He didn't leave room for argument, and reluctantly, she took a stone. Her attempt was pitiful—it plopped straight into the water without a single bounce.

"Wrong action," John said smoothly, handing her another. "You're overthinking it. You have to relax the movement. It's supposed to feel easy."

"It's stupid."

"Then why are you annoyed?" His voice had a trace of amusement. "Trying to be someone you're not is exhausting."

"I'm not trying to be anyone," she snapped. "Who would I be imitating?"

"Me," he said softly.

She turned sharply, but he was already beside her, lifting her arm gently. "You're not made of hard edges, Grace. But you keep trying to get the better of me—just to prove something. Probably to yourself."

He adjusted her wrist and leaned closer. "Let's stay in the present. Back like this… turn, and release."

The stone danced across the water, graceful and weightless. For a moment, Grace forgot herself—forgot the tension and the heat inside her—and simply watched the ripple it left behind.

And then she realised how close John was. His hand still rested lightly on her arm. His breath brushed her temple. She turned toward him, and that was her mistake.

The look in his eyes told her everything: he'd disarmed her again—and he knew it.

"You might be a late achiever," he murmured, his mouth curving. "But we can't spend the rest of our lives throwing pebbles. When will you belong to me, Grace?"

"I never will."

She tried to move, but his arm came around her waist, firm and inevitable. His hand tilted her chin up, his other arm drawing her against his chest.

Too close. Too familiar. Too much.

And yet, she didn't pull away.

He didn't answer. He simply kissed her—slowly, deeply—his mouth claiming hers with a certainty that shattered her resistance. The quiet beach disappeared. The world narrowed to the feel of his arms around her, the strength of his body anchoring hers. When she finally gave in, it was like falling—helpless and breathless—into something inevitable. She clung to his lips as if she needed him to breathe.

He drew back slightly, his hands still framing her face, his voice a velvet murmur against her mouth. "How long do you think you can hold out against me?"

The taunting intimacy of his tone cut through the fog of sensation. Grace stiffened, snapping back to herself, the spell broken.

Without a word, she wrenched free and fled up the beach, her heart pounding in her chest like a warning. She didn't stop running until she reached the edge of the veranda, her breath coming fast, her lips still tingling from his.

John could make her do anything.

She hated that truth—hated how close she'd come to melting in his arms again, how dangerously close she was to giving him everything he wanted.

She paused just outside, forcing herself to breathe. She couldn't charge back in like this. Harriet would see straight through her, and Grace didn't need another sharp pair of eyes cataloguing her emotional unravelling. It was nearly dark now, and the villa lights had come on inside. Thankfully, they'd all gone in. No one was watching.

Grace sank down onto the veranda steps, her body thrumming with frustration, desire, and something more dangerous—*hope*. That had to be crushed.

She sat very still, trying to quiet the wild rhythm of her heart. But even in the darkness, even with the sound of the sea behind her, she could still feel his kiss.

She didn't hear him at first. One moment she was alone—and the next, he was there, emerging from the shadows like some mythic figure drawn straight from the night. She looked up at him, and her voice shook when she spoke.

"Why are you doing this to me?" she asked, barely more than a whisper. "You have no right—"

"Right?" he cut in, his voice rough, laced with something darker. "I've never claimed the right to anything. What I have—what I've always had—are responsibilities. I'll carry them more easily once you're mine."

He stepped closer, his eyes unreadable in the dusk. "And as for kissing you?" His voice dropped, low and steady. "I like it. You're kissable, Grace. And a lot more besides."

He reached down and took her arm—not roughly, but firmly—pulling her to her feet.

"Come on," he said, his tone clipped. "Let's go inside and bring this day to an end. I'm tired."

So was she. But as she followed him in, Grace knew her exhaustion wasn't from the travel or the heat. It was from trying—and failing—to guard her heart from the one man who already owned it.

They ate Christmas lunch on the veranda and later drifted down to the beach where the soft hush of waves and the gold-brushed sea should have made the afternoon idyllic. But Grace couldn't enjoy any of it. Not with Sharon Wright lounging beside them like some sleek, bronzed ornament in a black bikini, and not with John stretched out just feet away, laughing at something Sharon had said, his smile slow and effortless.

Grace tried not to look. Tried not to listen. But every time Sharon tossed her head or gave John that bright, possessive smile, Grace felt it—like a tiny knife sliding under her skin. And worse, she saw the way his eyes sometimes flicked toward Sharon, amused, indulgent. A man used to being adored.

The worst of it was, he didn't have to do anything. Just lying there, long limbs and sun-drenched skin, his presence radiated that effortless magnetism she'd once tried so hard to ignore. His sensuality was a force of nature; one he didn't even bother to wield. It simply…existed.

She should have stayed in England. She had no business being here—playing the dutiful fiancée in a sunlit drama where everyone else seemed to know their part. There was no future with John, she knew that. And most of the ache she carried, she knew, came from one thing.

Jealousy.

She didn't want to feel it. It humiliated her. But here it was—tight in her chest, bitter on her tongue.

Of course he'd chosen Sharon himself. Handpicked her to entertain him during the quieter moments of his visit with Aunt Harriet. He couldn't even go a few days without some woman orbiting him. Grace turned her head to glance at him again and then immediately looked away. She understood why they came so easily, why they stayed. Even his silence could seduce.

She was wearing her bikini, too—but unlike Sharon, she'd swathed herself in an ankle-length beach-wrap, unwilling to give John the satisfaction of seeing her exposed. She didn't want those cool, cynical eyes raking over her like she was just another contender.

He glanced over with a glint of amusement, clearly reading her. Of course, he understood exactly why she'd covered up.

"That's a lovely wrap," Harriet remarked, glancing up from her knitting. "That blue really suits you. It's the same colour as your eyes."

"They're purple," John said smoothly, not even looking at her. "Purple with gold flecks."

The quiet certainty of it landed like a pebble in still water. He didn't glance her way, didn't smile. It was an offhand statement, yet it rang with familiarity. Intimacy. As though he'd memorised her eyes and hadn't forgotten a thing.

Grace felt heat flood her cheeks. Sharon cast her a sharp look, the smile slipping from her lips for just a second. Even Harriet seemed pleased, returning to her knitting with a contented little smile.

Of course, she thinks it's all going well, Grace thought. It was a good thing John wasn't leaving the performance up to her. She could barely look at him anymore—could barely speak without giving herself away. It was beginning to hurt too much.

She closed her eyes, letting the sun press against her face, trying to sink into silence—until John's voice jolted her.

"I'm taking Grace sailing for a few hours. Will you feel neglected?"

Grace's eyes flew open. He was standing over Harriet now, his posture casual, his voice lazy—but there was something too smooth about it. Harriet looked up at him and smiled serenely.

"How can I be neglected, John, when Sharon's here? Run along. I know Grace will enjoy it."

Grace blinked. If she hadn't been feeling equal parts dread and longing at the thought of being alone with him, she might have laughed. Harriet was subtle, but not subtle enough. That was a clear warning shot. Miss Wright wasn't invited.

"Right," John said with satisfaction. "That leaves me with a clear conscience." He held out his hand to Grace. "Come along, love."

"I should change—put on trousers or something…"

He raised a brow. "You expecting a gale force wind?" The corners of his mouth curled. "You'll be fine as you are. We're not rowing across the Atlantic."

Before she could argue, he took her hand—warm, firm—and led her toward the boathouse at the edge of the water. Grace felt the weight of Sharon's gaze on her back, sharp as needles.

"Don't struggle," John said under his breath. "Just come along nicely. We're being watched."

"I noticed," she said through clenched teeth. "Feeling guilty about abandoning Sharon?"

He shrugged. "Not especially. I wanted you to myself. That's why you're here."

Her breath caught. "She's the one you brought out here, not me."

"She's the one who tagged along. Persistent type. Don't let it bother you."

"Why should it?" Grace snapped, her voice tight. "She's nothing to me. And neither are you."

He chuckled softly. "Well said. Sounds like you've been practising."

She pulled her hand away, glaring. "So, since we're nothing to each other, why don't we just turn around?"

"Because I've got something to show you," he said, eyes gleaming. "And I don't feel like sharing."

The boat was a sleek, mid-sized cabin cruiser, its white hull gleaming under the blazing Caribbean sun. Grace had never stepped foot on a boat before, and as it skimmed effortlessly across the shimmering water, a thrill of excitement swept through her, momentarily chasing away the heaviness that had haunted her all day.

With the same confident skill, he applied to everything else, John took the helm like he'd been born to it, hands steady on the wheel, eyes fixed ahead.

"Where are we going?" she shouted over the thrum of the engine.

He didn't look at her, just nodded toward the emerald silhouette of an island that was growing rapidly on the horizon. "There. It's quiet—secluded. Perfect for swimming. Much more peaceful than where Harriet built her villa."

He cut the engine, and the boat drifted in, the only sounds now the gentle slap of water against the hull and the cry of distant seabirds. Grace stood, holding the rail, her eyes sweeping over the golden crescent of beach and the thick fringe of trees that swayed almost to the shoreline.

"It looks private," she said quietly. "I don't like trespassing."

John raised an eyebrow. "Do you imagine I do? It's amazing how we always come back to my unsavoury beginnings. I haven't stolen apples in years, Grace. These days, I'm almost respectable. Especially on dark nights."

His sarcasm cut through the fragile peace that had begun to settle over her, and the excitement drained away. She turned her face from him, unwilling to argue. Now that they were alone, truly alone, there was a dangerous intensity about him—and she suddenly wished she'd stayed behind, claimed tiredness, anything to avoid this. But refusing John Sneddon never seemed to make a difference. He got what he wanted.

"This place is mine," he added curtly, as though sensing her unease. "I bought it years ago but never built. I usually stay at Harriet's when I'm here. More company."

More Sharon, Grace thought bitterly, biting her lip. The idea of him spending time here with that woman made something inside her twist, and the perfect beach lost all appeal.

She sat on the deck, legs curled beneath her, refusing to swim—even when John disappeared below and returned wearing nothing but black swim trunks that clung to his lean hips. Without a word, he dove into the water in one smooth motion.

The sun blazed down. The sea sparkled like sapphires scattered across silk. Grace longed to shed her wrap and dive in too, but she didn't move. Not with him watching her like that. There was something almost taunting in his gaze, as if he knew exactly what she wanted and enjoyed keeping her on edge.

For a while, she just watched him. He swam in long, strong strokes, circling the boat with ease, predator-smooth, as though keeping her contained within a private world only he controlled. When he finally dove beneath the surface, she felt a rush of relief, the weight of his dark eyes lifted.

But he didn't return to the boat.

When he resurfaced, he was already halfway to shore, cutting through the water with powerful strokes, leaving her behind without so much as a glance.

Annoyance surged in her chest. She knew she'd been sulking, sitting there like some brooding child, refusing to play along—but this? This was a dismissal. A reprimand. And she wasn't having it.

She stood and unwrapped herself, pausing just a moment in the dark blue bikini she'd deliberately kept hidden all afternoon. Then, with defiance burning through her veins, she dived cleanly into the sea.

The water was warm and crystalline. She surfaced beside the boat and began swimming, diving beneath the surface, trying to forget John—trying to enjoy herself. To prove that she wasn't just the sheltered, breakable girl he seemed to see.

But she wasn't like John. She wasn't strong, and a recent hospital stay had left her weaker than she cared to admit. She surfaced again and looked back. The boat seemed a long way off. Too far.

How had she gotten so far out?

She tried to calm herself, to slow her breathing—but panic was rising fast. Her arms felt like lead, her legs weak. She tried to float, but her body sank, and she broke the surface again, coughing, flailing.

Inside her, something cracked wide open.

She couldn't make it to the boat. She couldn't reach the shore.

"John…" The cry slipped from her lips, soft and torn, barely more than a whisper. Was that her voice—thin, frightened?

Was this how it would end—quietly, carelessly, beneath the sunlit surface of an endless sea?

And would he care?

Would he even know?

The thought sliced through her. In that moment—stripped of pride, of performance—she knew the truth.

If she lost John, there would be no joy left in anything. Life would go on, of course—quiet, orderly, unremarkable—but drained of colour, like winter without end. Yet she had already made her decision. She would walk away, no matter how much it tore at her. Even if her heart shattered in the process.

Because loving him wasn't enough.

Not when he would never love her back.

Not when he had told her so—with words, with silences, with every kiss that only ever took and never gave.

It would hurt. God, it would destroy her.

But she would do it anyway.

Because staying… would hurt even more.

But perhaps she wouldn't have to worry about leaving—or about John—because as she slipped beneath the water again, she knew she no longer had the strength to surface.

Chapter Seventeen

Just as the warm water swallowed her for the last time, muffling the world, she felt a sudden, fierce grip seize her arm.

"Grace!"

John's voice cut through the silence, raw and desperate. His hands were steady and strong, pulling her upward, breaking through the surface with a gasp of air.

She choked and coughed, clinging to him as his eyes blazed—wild, a storm of fear and something deeper, something she hadn't dared to hope for.

Then his face darkened, thunderous, and carved with fury, but his grip never wavered. He flipped her onto her back and began towing her powerfully toward the shore.

She didn't fight. She couldn't.

In those terrifying minutes, she lived a lifetime—and died a little. And deep within that quiet, desperate place inside, she finally faced the truth of her own heart.

"What the hell were you doing?" His voice lashed across her the moment his feet touched sand. He scooped her into his arms and carried her up the beach, lowering her gently before kneeling beside her, searching her pale face with blistering intensity.

"I thought… I thought I was strong enough to…"

The words broke off as tears slipped unbidden down her cheeks, carving silver tracks across her skin.

But his face only darkened. "Well?" His tone was still unforgiving, taut with the effort of controlling the emotion beneath. "When I left you, you were sitting calmly on deck. Then you're gone—and when I spot you, you're diving and thrashing like you've lost your mind. I didn't even know you could swim. Damn it, Grace! I thought you'd fallen overboard and were drowning."

"I didn't know it would be so hard…" Her voice shook. "It's been so long since I swam. And you—" she glanced away "—you seemed occupied."

His expression shifted then, the edge of fury softening, replaced by something quieter, heavier. "I was on the beach. Down there." He gestured vaguely behind him, but she didn't have the energy to look. "I was thinking about where I'd build."

"You left me." The accusation slipped out—a plaintive, broken whisper—and immediately, she regretted it.

"I didn't leave you," he said softly. "I thought you didn't want to come. You looked so damned remote, wrapped up in that cover-up like a nun at a baptism. I got frustrated. I thought I had everything under control. Thought you were under control."

"You could have told me," she snapped, trying to sit up, anger now overriding shame. "Maybe I wanted to go with you—maybe I wanted to see too!"

He reached out and pushed her gently but firmly back down. "I didn't think you cared," he said, voice low, raw. "Sometimes I just can't go on looking at you, Grace. I want you too much. And when I can't have you—when you keep yourself just out of reach— I have to move, do something. If there'd been tools on that beach, I swear I'd have started building the damned house right then, just to stop thinking about you."

He stood and brushed the sand from her legs with a tenderness that contradicted the storm between them.

"Come on. Let's get you back."

Grace didn't want to move. A languid sleepiness overtook her, her limbs heavy, her lashes brushing sun-warmed cheeks where a hint of colour had returned. The sun was already drying her skin and her damp bikini, and the soft sand beneath her felt impossibly luxurious. She turned onto her side and let her head rest on her arm.

"Just give me a minute," she murmured drowsily.

"You can't sleep here—you'll burn," John warned, his voice roughened by a mix of concern and frustration.

"Just a minute… please," she whispered, already halfway lost to the pull of sleep.

He sighed, and his voice dropped into a reluctant gentleness. "How can I refuse such weary pleading? A minute, then. I'll go fetch the dinghy. But stay here—this time, I mean it. If you've moved when I get back…"

"I couldn't if I tried." Her lips curved into a blissful smile as she gave herself over to the warmth, the exhaustion, and the quiet. He lingered just long enough to study her face, then turned and dove into the sea.

She must have fallen asleep instantly. She never heard the outboard motor when John returned. The first thing she knew, he was beside her again, kneeling in the sand and gently shaking her shoulder.

"Wake up, Grace. We're going back to the boat."

She blinked up at him, disoriented. "Have we been here long?"

"Hardly. Just a few minutes," he said, lifting her to her feet. "And already you've forgotten where you are."

"I haven't forgotten. We're on your island. I'm just tired… because I was stupid. I wore myself out. Next time—"

"There won't be a next time." His voice cut clean through her excuse. "After today's performance, I'll make sure you stick to things you're actually suited for. Evening gowns. Cocktail parties. Not open water."

With that cool remark, he turned and strode away, leaving her to follow alone.

She hesitated, stung. So now he was too annoyed even to walk beside her? Fine. She didn't need him. Except… she did.

The sun felt hotter now, the sand deeper and harder to walk through. Her legs dragged beneath her as a slow, creeping weakness spread through her body—a mix of adrenaline drain and something less tangible. She was in love. Hopelessly. Foolishly. And she would never, ever tell him. Not when he saw her as nothing more than a complication.

But then the world tilted.

She stumbled, the ground swaying, and sank to her knees. Dizziness rushed over her, making her press her hands to her face as if to steady the horizon. The bright sky, the heat, the shimmering sand—it all spun around her like a carousel.

"Grace?"

He was suddenly there again, his shadow falling across her, his voice sharp with alarm.

She looked up at him—those strong legs, that tanned, powerful body—and then moaned, covering her eyes. "I don't know what's wrong. Everything's spinning."

He crouched instantly beside her. "Lie back. Just for a minute. You've overdone it."

She obeyed, shielding her eyes from the glare. "I suppose it's the exercise. I'm not really… fit."

When she opened her eyes again, he was still watching her, his brow furrowed with concern and something else—anger, maybe. Not at her. At himself.

"You do the most ridiculous things," he muttered. "Did you really have to throw yourself into the water like that? Trying to prove you're as strong as me?"

Annoyance flared in her, cutting through the haze. She sat up, glaring at him. "I wasn't trying to prove anything. You left me, John. You just—walked off. What was I supposed to do? Sit and twiddle my thumbs like a good little girl while you vanished into the jungle?"

His expression shifted, softened. "So, you did want to be with me." His voice dropped, quiet and insistent. "You care about me."

"I do not," she shot back, but the flush creeping over her face betrayed her. "I would've been annoyed no matter who it was. I'm not used to being taken somewhere and then abandoned. Your company was… acceptable. I was willing to overlook who you are."

With a swift, fluid motion, he stood and scooped her into his arms.

"My poor, reckless little maniac." His tone was half-scolding, half-affectionate. "Let's get you on board. You need a drink. The sun's cooked you more than you realise."

"You think I'm delirious just because I don't care about you?" she challenged, her voice unsteady—because now that he was holding her, his skin hot against hers, her flimsy bikini no barrier at all, the trembling started again.

He didn't look down at her. He didn't need to.

"You do care, Grace. I'm not blind. I can feel it—you're shaking."

"It's shock."

"Little fool," he muttered. But there was no heat in the words. Only something quieter, something that made her heart ache.

He waded into the sea with her in his arms and gently set her into the waiting dinghy. His voice was low when he spoke again, a soft growl that seemed to come from somewhere deep inside.

"I'm not so easy to lose. And I have no intention of letting you go."

On the boat, John poured her a tall glass of something cold and held it out. Grace took it with both hands, drinking almost greedily, the chill a balm to her dry throat and overheated nerves.

"You probably swallowed half the bay," he remarked, watching her closely. "And most of the beach is stuck to you. You need a shower."

"When I get back to the villa," she said coolly, proud of the crisp firmness in her voice—even if she couldn't quite hear the tremor running beneath it.

"You'll get it here." He nodded toward a sliding door. "Shower's through there. I need one too—and if you hesitate much longer, I might just join you."

It was the kind of threat that wasn't a threat at all—low, teasing, and far too effective. Grace obeyed without another word, slipping inside and letting the cool water ease her tension. As the spray washed over her skin, some of the tightness in her chest began to unwind.

She slid one arm out through the narrow gap in the door. "My robe," she called lightly.

John placed it in her hand. "Pass me the bikini. I'll dry it."

She stepped out a moment later, wrapped tightly in the soft robe, her hair dripping down her back. With a flicker of reluctance, she handed him the two flimsy pieces. He was already in a robe himself, and she stood near the vanity, combing the salt from her damp hair as he stepped out to peg the bikinis up in the sun.

"Peculiar flags," he said wryly. "Let's hope Harriet doesn't have her binoculars out."

Grace flushed, but he spared her further embarrassment by heading straight for the shower. She walked quietly out of the cabin and back into the open air, where the sunlight glinted across the waves. She didn't want the sun just now. She wanted… something she couldn't quite name. Something warm and dangerous and already too close.

She sank down onto the long padded bench, leaned her head back, and closed her eyes.

"Sleeping again?" John's voice came above her moments later. He stood towelling his dark hair, his robe clinging to the lines of his body.

"No. I was thinking. I feel… odd."

"In pain?"

"Of course not." She gave him a small, dry smile. "Unless you count my pride."

He didn't smile back. "I was thinking about your operation."

"For heaven's sake, John. I told you—I'm fine. Even the doctor agrees. If I weren't, do you think I could've dived off a boat and swum around like…like—"

"Like someone in despair?" he cut in quietly. "You thought I'd lost interest in you."

Her breath caught. "I thought you were just being your usual angry self. That's different."

"It would be—if that were the truth." He came to sit beside her, much too close. "You care about me, Grace. Admit it."

"I don't," she denied quickly, her voice shaking as she tried to rise. "I won't do this, John. It's too dangerous."

But his hands were already on her shoulders, firm and warm, anchoring her in place. She looked up—and into his eyes. There was no teasing there now. Just raw, searching intensity.

"Yes, you do care," he said quietly. "And you don't have to keep punishing yourself for it. I'm here."

Then he leaned down, brushing against her, and she could hardly breathe. Her mind screamed for space, for sense, but her body ached for what it had already chosen.

"Don't, John," she whispered, her voice breaking. "Don't do this to me. Why do you keep—?"

"Because I want you. And you want me too."

"I don't—" But her denial was a whisper against his lips before he kissed her—deeply, possessively—as if to silence every doubt she'd ever had.

The tears came instantly, welling up and spilling over. He lifted his head just enough to see them, then cupped her face gently, his thumbs brushing her damp cheeks.

"Shh, Grace," he murmured, his voice tender and urgent. "Shh."

He kissed her again—softer this time, then with increasing hunger. Her lips responded instinctively, no longer afraid, only open. She wasn't running anymore.

"Darling," he breathed against her mouth, "this is sheer necessity."

And when he pulled her closer, her arms slipped around him easily, instinctively—her gasp soft, broken, a pure note of surrender. Her heart was open now, wide, and defenceless, and John was already inside it, like a truth she could no longer deny.

He lifted her in his arms and carried her to the bunk, as if she weighed nothing at all. It would always be like this with John. The fight would leave her the moment he touched her. If he'd touched her two years ago, everything might have happened then. It was inevitable.

He laid her down gently, then followed her down, the solid heat of his body pressing into hers. She felt the restless strength in him, the taut line of his hips shifting against her with unmistakable urgency. Her arms locked around his neck, and even through the barrier of their robes, she felt the hard arousal of his body, unmistakable and thrilling.

Her own body surged toward his with eager delight, moulding to him mindlessly. The pressure of his thighs against hers sent shimmering bursts of pleasure up her spine. She arched into him, needing to be closer, needing him.

He groaned low in his throat and came down harder, the scent of soap on his skin blending with the deeper, darker musk of desire.

"John…" Her voice was a breathless whisper as she tilted her head back, already lost to him. His mouth found the long curve of her throat, then sought lower, searching for her breast beneath the thick fabric.

It was too much—too much between them—and in a fit of wild impatience, she tossed her head from side to side, moaning softly. Her whispers turned to gasps when he pulled the robe aside and his mouth found her, hot and unrelenting. His tongue circled her nipple, and the sensation made her cry out, her fingers clawing at his shoulders as waves of aching need coursed through her.

"I want you against me," he said thickly, his voice rough with need. "I want nothing at all between us."

He stripped off his robe and then hers, his gaze flaring as it moved over her body. His fingers curved around the fullness of her breast, reverent, possessive.

"Tell me now I can't have you," he whispered hoarsely. "Because if you don't, this doesn't stop. You know that."

"I know," she whispered, the words torn from her in a long, trembling sigh.

His face darkened, need sharpening the lines of it, his knee slipping between her legs as if his body had taken over.

"I want you now," he growled, raw and almost savage.

Desire exploded between them like flame to dry tinder. His lips found hers again, fierce, and hungry, and his hands moved over her with utter, claiming possession. She was his—he knew it, and so did she. Her body welcomed him, opened to him, adored him.

His eyes devoured her—lingering on her breasts, her parted lips, her face so open and vulnerable.

"At this moment I could devour you," he murmured. "I want to see you carrying my child."

The words struck her like a slap. Her breath caught—joy vanishing in a heartbeat. His voice had sounded so final, so intentional.

And suddenly it came rushing back—his original proposal. A wife to complete his empire. A child to inherit his wealth. A future shaped entirely on his terms.

Her heart constricted.

What about her? What about love? The child would never be hers—not really. John would mould it in his image: sharp, invulnerable, brilliant. And the women? They'd continue, always. Because John Sneddon loved no one. Cared for no one. Least of all her.

He was still watching her. He saw the change in her eyes, saw the light die there, even as the hunger in his own remained fierce and unrelenting.

"Grace," he rasped—but it was too late.

She knew what had to happen. If she didn't fight now, in the only way she could, there would be no going back. If he held her again—if he made love to her—she would lose herself. And John would never release what he possessed.

"I can't stop you, John," she said softly, her voice trembling but clear. "You can make me want you. We both know that. But whatever happens—afterwards—I'll never marry you. I want you to understand that."

She would remember his expression for the rest of her life. The sudden stillness. The raw disbelief. His face went pale, and his eyes turned black—not with desire now, but with something colder. He didn't speak. He didn't argue.

He simply sat up, pulled on his robe, and tossed hers toward her.

Then he left.

A moment later, he came back, threw her bikini onto the bunk without a word, and walked out to start the engine.

Chapter Eighteen

Somehow, while Grace had been getting dressed, her bikini now dry, John had already changed. She found him at the helm, composed, silent. As they cruised back to the villa, she sat quietly on the deck, eyes on the horizon. She didn't try to speak. She didn't see the point. She knew John too well by now. Whatever had existed between them was over. Completely.

It was John who broke the silence—just as the landing-stage came into view.

"Why, Grace?"

His voice was rough, stripped of his usual control.

She didn't answer. She didn't dare meet his eyes. Instead, she fussed with the belt of her wrap, pulling it tighter, her fingers fumbling for time. For distance.

"Look at me, Grace. Damn you, look at me!" he rasped, thick with emotion.

Still, she kept her head bowed. "I don't want to, John," she whispered. "I don't even want to look at myself. I feel… cheap."

The word landed like a slap.

"What?" His voice was stunned—appalled and ferocious in the same breath. She knew it would be. That was why she hadn't wanted to say it.

But now she looked up, forcing her features into composure, into steadiness.

"I can't help how I feel, John," she said calmly, too calmly. "I feel cheap—whether I should or not."

He didn't reply. Not a word. But when they docked, his hand closed around her arm like iron, and he marched her across the sand, his face white with fury. He didn't loosen his grip until they reached the sunlit terrace, where Aunt Harriet sat smiling at the sea.

"Grace, dear, are you alright?" Harriet asked, concerned, turning at once to Grace's pale, shuttered face.

"She's tired," John cut in before Grace could answer. "I think it's the sun."

"Yes… I'll go lie down for a while," Grace added quickly, her voice faint but steady. She didn't wait for Harriet to offer help or suggest Sharon follow. She just needed to get away—from John, from his furious silence, from the heat that had nothing to do with the weather.

His rage clung to him like a storm cloud.

When John came to her room later, she didn't move. She lay motionless on the bed, eyes closed, feigning sleep. Cowardly, perhaps—but necessary. She couldn't face him. She wasn't ready. John didn't forgive easily, and apologies only made her feel more vulnerable, more helpless.

He came in, stood over her for a moment, then spoke in a low, tight voice.

"I know you're not asleep."

She didn't answer.

"No matter," he said with dark finality. "Harriet and the staff won't let you starve or waste away. I'm going out."

A pause.

"I'm going out with Sharon."

Her eyes flew open.

"I suggest you do," she said coolly, her voice sharp with wounded pride. "You shouldn't be in here anyway. Think what your aunt would say."

"I'm past caring what people think," he muttered, his voice raw. "I only know what I think. And what I know is this—you want me. You care about me. But you'd rather die than admit it."

His eyes were blazing now. "What is it, Grace? Is this some princess-and-the-stable-boy fantasy? You're afraid I'll embarrass you in public? Afraid I'll use the wrong fork or eat peas off my knife? Don't worry. I manage just fine. Even if I do make you feel cheap."

"That's not what I meant—"

"Spare me." His voice cracked, all control gone. "You've made yourself perfectly clear. Again, and again. I have no illusions left about what you think of me."

And then he turned, walked out, and closed the door behind him with quiet finality.

He simply walked out, leaving Grace lying there, staring at the closed door. It had never once occurred to her that he would take it like this—so cold, so final. She had chosen the worst possible way to try and free herself from this tangled mess. Did he really believe she thought marrying him was beneath her? Would she have to confess she loved him just to make any of this make sense?

His world was crowded with women—one practically living under the same roof—and yet, somehow, he wanted her.

Maybe now he'd ignore her completely. She had no idea how she would bear that. When she said she felt cheap, it was because she knew she would be just one more woman among many—and that thought was degrading.

To protect herself, she had lashed out and wounded John, but the contempt in his voice burned as fiercely as his kisses had. Meanwhile, Sharon Wright would be smiling up at him in his arms. What would Aunt Harriet think now? After all the careful pretence about the engagement, he was showing unmistakably that he didn't care at all. Was she going to be the one left to explain?

She couldn't stay at Rosewood—not now, not anymore. The time had come to stand on her own two feet, to break free of the past—and of John.

She didn't stay in bed. It felt too miserable to shrink away while Harriet sat alone downstairs. Waiting to hear the car leave, she finally got dressed and went to find his aunt.

"Why, Grace! Should you be up already?" Harriet's concern was genuine, and it warmed Grace more than she expected. "John thought you'd be resting."

"I'm all right," Grace assured her. "I brought this on myself. I haven't taken any real exercise in ages, then I jumped into the sea and swam like a lunatic. I suppose I deserved it."

"Well, I'm surprised John allowed that," Harriet said sharply. "He usually has more common sense than that."

"He does—when he's here." Grace glanced at Harriet, who waited patiently for more. "John left me alone for a while. I wanted to swim and… I overestimated myself." She gave a wry little smile. "He wasn't exactly pleased when he found out."

"I can imagine," Harriet chuckled, shaking her head. "That explains the scowls I saw earlier. I thought for a moment…"

She looked at Grace thoughtfully. "I suppose I've always expected the worst. I never thought John would marry. He's strong and successful, yes, but there's a vulnerable side to him, too—a wide streak of it. His childhood was difficult."

Grace met her gaze. "He told me some of it—about his mother. Not much, but enough to understand."

"She wasn't a battered wife, Grace." Harriet's lips tightened. "That cruelty was reserved for John. Sometimes I struggle to forgive Marion for leaving the family—for leaving John—but he understands. She loved her husband enough to forgive his violence, and she loved John enough to let him build his shell of protection. I always imagined that if John loved anyone, it would be me—since I resemble my sister so much. When you came with him, I was overjoyed. That's the greatest understatement I've made this year."

Grace's eyes drifted to her clenched fists. The picture of John she'd held—the invincible, polished man—was breaking apart. She saw now the frightened, dark-haired boy who had been bruised and left to fend for himself. She understood the women he sought, the fierce demands of desire, the desperate need to guard himself. John dared not love.

"Have I upset you?" Harriet's gentle voice drew Grace from her thoughts. She looked up, tears threatening.

"No. I understand now."

"Because he never speaks of love?" Harriet's gaze was sharp and knowing. "I've watched you both closely. I know his attitude."

"He says he needs me." Without anyone else to confide in—not a mother, not a friend—Grace felt almost desperate for support. Harriet slid closer and covered Grace's hand with her own.

"Perhaps that's as close to a confession of love as John will ever come," she said softly. "I've known him since he was nineteen. It took him a long time to say anything at all. In all these years, I've never heard him speak of need."

Grace whispered, "I don't even know what kind of need it is. John wants to marry me, yet there are other women. Even now, he's gone off with Miss Wright to—"

"Indeed, he has not!" Harriet's eyes widened in surprise, then twinkled with amusement. "That's what he told you? I thought I heard him dole out some of his biting remarks earlier. I've seen him in action over the years." She stood and rang for tea. Her eyes sparkled. "John's gone to fetch something for me. Miss Wright left to visit friends—going the opposite way. She did consider ditching him when she found out you were indisposed, but John in a bad mood is hardly the most encouraging companion."

The news lifted Grace's spirits in a way that felt almost absurd. She knew there was always something between John and Sharon—and nothing could erase Rita Peterson from the equation. Still, she couldn't deny that life felt a little brighter, a little less heavy.

"I have to be honest with you," she said, meeting Harriet's gaze. "I'm not sure I can marry him if I'm not the only woman in his bed."

Harriet looked at her thoughtfully, then patted her hand gently. "I understand. I wouldn't expect you to."

When John came in later, his scowl made it clear his irritation hadn't softened enough to fool his aunt—though Harriet was far from easily fooled, as Grace had learned.

"You do realise, John, that we'll have the usual gathering tonight?" Harriet said, watching them both with a knowing look.

"I expect so," John replied curtly.

"We usually have friends over on Christmas evening," Harriet explained to Grace. "A few drinks, a get-together to make up for the absence of a tree and pretty baubles. Presents are generally exchanged just before everyone arrives."

Grace carefully avoided John's gaze, memories flooding back of past Christmases—the carefully chosen gifts John had brought her, and her own equally deliberate refusal to buy for him. This year, though, she'd given it serious thought. He'd been kind, helpful, and she'd enjoyed searching for something he might truly want.

It hadn't been easy—there wasn't much he didn't already have—but her brief time at his flat had sparked an idea. Now, tucked safely away in her luggage, was the gift she hoped mattered most. Knowing more about him now made it feel terribly important to give.

Sharon returned before the evening, and Grace went to her room to prepare, choosing a dark blue chiffon dress with a round neckline and long sleeves. The full, flowing skirt swayed over a satin sheath beneath. Normally, it would have made her feel glamorous, but tonight nerves tangled her thoughts. She feared facing John and pretending at some loving facade in front of others.

In the long drawing-room overlooking the sea, Sharon was already there—and so was John. Grace's heart sank. Sharon Wright had undeniable glamour; in a tight, white dress, she looked nothing like a nurse. For a moment, Grace faltered under their simultaneous gazes.

"Champagne, Grace?" John asked, crossing the room with a glass. "We have our little toast before the hordes arrive."

"Not hordes, please, John," Harriet laughed, stepping in. "I couldn't cope with hordes, and the buffet wouldn't stretch that far. Just a few friends, Grace. Don't let him intimidate you."

"How could I?" Grace replied dryly. "I'm an accomplished hostess, remember. Used to running a huge house, handling everything from business lunches to week-long parties. I even run John's office now, quite efficiently. Don't let my delicate looks fool you—I can cope with anything, including him."

Her backhanded compliment didn't sit well with Sharon, whose vision of a wishy-washy fiancée seemed abruptly deflated. Harriet, however, was amused—especially since it came with more accusation than praise.

"Present time!" Harriet announced, with the glee of a child. "I love this part best of all."

She sank onto the settee amid the scattered gifts as the two servants brought in theirs, grinning widely. John looked surprised when Grace excused herself to fetch gifts—a perfume for Sharon and a stunning piece of costume jewellery for Harriet.

"I couldn't afford diamonds," Grace smiled as Harriet pinned the brooch to her dress.

"My dear, it's beautiful. How did you know what to choose?"

"I guessed John would have an elegant aunt," Grace admitted, watching John closely. No doubt he thought it sarcasm.

Then, nervously, she gave him his gift—a flat, carefully wrapped package she had dreaded damaging or being forced to reveal.

His face was stunning—stunned almost—as he held it. For a long moment, he didn't open it.

"For me, Grace? You carried this all the way here?"

Her throat tightened, nearly bringing tears to her eyes. She trembled, fearing she'd overdone it or reminded him of her previous refusal to give him anything at all.

"I had to. I knew there wouldn't be time once we arrived." Her voice was steady, though she hoped it disguised her nerves.

As he unwrapped it, all eyes turned to them. Grace felt like a child offering an aloof headmaster an apple.

It was a beautiful Monet print, expertly framed. John stared at it, and Grace's cheeks flushed with anxiety.

"Don't you like it?" she asked, meeting his glittering, narrowed eyes.

His aunt rose, eager to see. "It's beautiful, Grace! This must be quite valuable."

"It took some effort to find the right colours. But if John doesn't like it…"

"I do." His gaze searched her face, seeking something she wasn't ready to reveal. "I suppose you've already picked the perfect spot for it at your place."

"No," Grace said softly. "It's for your flat. Maybe the hall?"

"Or over the bed," he suggested with a low smile.

"Thank you."

Right there, before Harriet's delighted smile and Sharon's hard eyes, John slid an arm around Grace and kissed her thoroughly. The tension in him was palpable, and Grace longed to wrap her arms around him—to beg forgiveness without words.

John slipped a delicate bracelet onto Grace's wrist to match the necklace he had already given her. She was so stunned by her own success as an unexpectedly capable Father Christmas that she barely noticed what the others received. Throughout the evening, she felt his watchful eyes on her every move—an unspoken tether she neither resisted nor questioned.

Soon after the gifts were exchanged, a lively party of friends arrived—young and old alike—and the engagement was celebrated with warm laughter and champagne, though a few younger men openly voiced their disappointment.

"Come for some fresh air." John's invitation was more an order than a request, and when Grace found herself nearly cornered by an overly admiring guest, his stiff glare silenced any protest. In seconds, they were outside, standing at the far end of the cool veranda.

"We can't just stay out here," Grace said quickly, wary of the intensity in his gaze and still overwhelmed by the evening's whirlwind.

"I don't like people pawing at you," he muttered, his voice low and fierce. "It kills my Christmas spirit."

"Surely I deserve the same freedoms you enjoy in this modern world?" Grace replied quietly, meeting his eyes. "You've been surrounded by women all evening—Sharon practically had you hemmed in at one point."

He laughed, dark eyes sparkling as he swung her gently toward him. "I hope you realise what that tells me. We're both watching, both jealous."

"Of course I'm not," Grace lied with a playful smile, hiding the truth she'd gleaned from his aunt's candid words. She wasn't about to show John how deeply he already had her.

"We won't argue," he said, pulling her close, satisfaction curling his lips when she made no move to break free. "But I have an indelicate question," he confessed softly. "Curiosity's killing me. How did you afford that Monet print?"

"It wasn't very expensive," she replied, shrugging.

"Grace," he warned, voice gentle but firm, "I'm no fool. I recognise value. Last I heard, you were barely making ends meet, considering a cheap flat. And now you've come up with a costly gift. How?"

"I sold a ring my father gave me," she admitted, then quickly added, "I have no place to wear those things any longer."

He didn't know she'd sold more than just a ring—all her jewellery had quietly disappeared, little sacrifices for a future she was determined to build soon.

"I wanted to get you a Christmas present. So…" She lowered her gaze. "I saw the print and…"

"I'll have to do something about the lies you tell," he said, tightening his hold on her, locking eyes with hers. "You catch fire when I hold you. You sacrifice for me and still say you don't care?"

Denial was useless. She was still raw from how she'd hurt him earlier, and the weight of it pressed down on her. She rested her cheek against his chest, hiding from his intense gaze.

"I do care. I can't help it. But I won't marry you, John. Not with all those women…"

He murmured, "Have we reached the stage of discussion?"

"What is there to discuss? I even understand."

"Do you, Grace? I wonder how much." He tilted her face to his and kissed her gently— soft and soul-melting. If they were alone, she would have surrendered completely, but the party's noise surrounded them, and at that moment, Harriet appeared.

"Oh! I'm sorry, John. I didn't mean to intrude."

Her eyes sparkled with mischief, making it clear she wanted to check on them—and all embarrassment fled from Grace. John, however, was unruffled. Holding Grace firmly, he turned to his aunt.

"We're going home, Harriet. Tomorrow."

"All right, dear. I'm sure you'll be back soon. But come inside now and help out— once Grace catches her breath."

Harriet disappeared back inside, and John tilted Grace's face toward the moonlight.

"Come back to London with me," he whispered. "We can't talk here. Harriet's like Cupid—I want you all to myself."

"All right." She knew exactly what she was agreeing to—and it no longer mattered. She already knew what had to be done.

She loved John. Leaving him would break her, but there was no other way.

Chapter Nineteen

They returned to London to find the cold waiting for them like a punishment. The biting wind cut through her coat as soon as they stepped off the plane. The Bahamas, with its golden warmth and sun-soaked days, might as well have been another lifetime. Overhead, the sky hung low and threatening, the same leaden grey it had been when they'd left.

John drove straight to his apartment. There was still time to make the journey to Rosewood, but he didn't suggest it. Instead, he glanced at her face and said, "Just a discussion, nothing more. I'm not planning a seduction scene, Grace. I'll give you lunch, and then I'll drive you home."

She nodded, grateful for the clarity, even if her chest was tightening with dread. Jenny's not back at Rosewood yet. She wasn't due back until tomorrow. It was hard to keep track of who was loyal to whom anymore—when it came to John, everyone seemed to fall into silent agreement.

John's phone rang insistently as they walked into the apartment. He answered with visible irritation, but as the call continued, his entire expression changed—tightening, sharpening.

"When?" he barked, already moving.

Even before he ended the call, Grace could tell something was wrong. His face said everything.

"I have to go," he said flatly. "Get the jet ready for Madrid."

"What happened?" she asked, already reaching for her own phone as he strode toward his bedroom, shedding his coat and unbuttoning his shirt.

"The development we're building on the east coast—suddenly we've lost planning permission. The thing's halfway completed and they're threatening to force a teardown. It's insane. Bureaucracy gone wild. Clearly a mistake, but I've got to handle it myself."

He disappeared into the room, already switching modes—no longer the man who'd kissed her on a moonlit veranda, but the executive ready for battle.

She set everything in motion—the jet, the flight plan, the car at the other end. John Sneddon never delayed, never delegated what truly mattered. And he wouldn't take her with him. She knew that, too.

When he re-emerged, changed, and packed, she told him the jet would be ready in an hour.

"Do you want to stay here until I get back?" he asked casually. She shook her head. He didn't notice the weight in her silence; his mind was already elsewhere. He didn't know this would be the last time he saw her.

This was her chance—a clean break. Jenny wouldn't be back until the following day. She could slip away without confrontation, without begging, without giving him the chance to persuade her and unravel her resolve all over again. She would leave him a letter—something final.

"All right," he said, distracted. "Take the Mercedes. I'll collect it later."

The casual offer gave her courage. Slowly, she reached for the engagement ring and slid it from her finger.

"Where should I leave this?" she asked, trying to sound practical. The ache in her chest made it almost impossible to breathe.

John glanced at her, expression unreadable. "How about back on your finger?"

"I can't wear it, John. It was for your aunt. And she's not here anymore."

He turned away with a tight exhale. "Leave it on the desk, then."

Her mouth parted in disbelief. "Just on the desk? It's valuable."

"Not unless you're wearing it," he snapped. "Otherwise, it's just a piece of metal."

He took the ring from her hand and dropped it onto the desk with barely a look, already consumed by the crisis. "Let's go."

They were barely in the car before they were heading out again. She drove him to the airport in silence.

"How long do you think you'll be gone?"

"God knows. I'll let you know," he said, pressing the spare apartment key into her palm. "Take this."

"I don't need it. I'm not—"

"Take it," he growled, then turned and walked away without another word.

Grace sat behind the wheel for a long moment, frozen in place. Then, without looking back, she slipped the car into reverse and pulled away from the terminal. The jet hangars faded in the rearview mirror, their steel outlines blurring through the sting in her eyes. She turned onto the motorway and headed toward Rosewood.

With every mile, her heart cracked a little more.

The estate was silent when she arrived—too silent. The kind that pressed in on her, heavy and absolute. There was no warmth left in the place. She moved quickly, afraid that if she paused even once, she might lose her nerve.

She packed what she could into two suitcases, leaving her mobile phone neatly on the bed with the necklace and bracelet John had given her. She wouldn't call Jenny. Not yet. Not until she was gone, far enough away that John couldn't trace her. Not until it was too late for him to stop her.

She returned to his apartment in her own car, leaving the Mercedes parked in the driveway at Rosewood like one final act of refusal. By the time she reached the city, night had fully descended, draping everything in icy shadows and brittle silence.

She let herself in quietly. The apartment was still, untouched since they'd left it that morning. His presence lingered everywhere—in the scent of leather and sandalwood, in the shirts still hanging in the wardrobe, in the echo of his voice that seemed to cling to the walls.

Grace slipped into his bedroom and lowered herself onto the bed they had never shared—and never would. She curled into his pillow, wrapping her arms around it like it could hold her back. The sheets still smelled faintly of him. She closed her eyes and let the tears come, quietly, without protest.

By morning, she was hollowed out and calm.

She rose, washed her face, and walked to his desk. The engagement ring still sat where he had left it, glinting faintly in the early light. Untouched. Waiting.

She stared at it for a long moment, then reached for a pen.

She took a deep breath, steadying her hand—and began to write.

Dear John,

First—thank you. After my father died, I was lost. I didn't know who I was or where I was meant to go. You stepped into that void—not gently, not easily, but completely. You changed everything. You gave me shelter, direction, and something far more dangerous: hope.

You told me more than once that you would never love me. I heard you, even when I pretended not to. But the heart doesn't listen to reason, and somewhere along the way, mine stopped belonging to me. I did the foolish thing—I fell in love with you.

And now, it's tearing me apart to walk away.

I know you'll think I'm being dramatic. Maybe I am. But I can't marry a man who doesn't love me. I can't share my life with someone whose heart is still scattered—across the past, across other women, across choices I was never part of.

I couldn't say it that day on the boat—not properly. I told you I felt cheap. But it wasn't because of what happened between us, and it had nothing to do with your past. It was because I knew, in that moment, I was just one of many. And I can't be that, John. I won't survive it.

If you care for me at all, even a little, I beg you—don't come after me. Don't try to find me. Let me go. Because staying would have destroyed me more than leaving ever could.

You would have given me your ring, your name, your protection. But never your heart. And I love you too much to settle for anything less. Choose someone else—you have so many to choose from.

Please, forgive me.

—Grace

She folded the letter slowly, her fingers trembling, and placed the engagement ring on top—its sapphire glinting faintly in the morning light. For a moment, she just stood there, letting her eyes take in every detail of the apartment that had briefly felt like a home. Then, without a word, she turned, closed the door quietly behind her, and slid the key beneath it.

As she stepped into the hallway, the apartment phone began to ring—sharp, insistent, echoing through the silence like a final plea.

She didn't go back.

Sliding into the driver's seat, Grace gripped the wheel, her knuckles white as tears slid unchecked down her cheeks. She started the engine with a trembling hand, the soft purr of it swallowed by the rush in her ears. The streets shimmered through her tears, lights and shapes running together in a blur of colour and shadow.

She stopped only once—at an ATM—to withdraw as much cash as she could. Then she drove on, leaving London in the rearview, its skyline dissolving into the dark.

Ahead lay Birmingham. She didn't know what waited for her there—only that she needed a job, something steady, something real. Something that might hold her together when nothing else could.

But mostly, she just needed to begin again—somewhere John Sneddon would never think to look.

John was pacing again.

The floor of the Madrid hotel suite had worn a groove beneath his shoes, and the phone at his ear crackled with yet another unanswered call. Grace's mobile. Again.

He ended the call with a muttered curse and checked the time—twenty-nine hours since he'd left London. It should've been a quick trip, but local authorities were proving impossible. No one wanted to take responsibility for the planning mix-up, and he was battling bureaucracy with both hands tied.

But it wasn't the stalled project that made his jaw clench. It was the silence.

He had called Grace's mobile more times than he could count. He'd rung his apartment. Nothing. No answer at Rosewood, either.

He tried Rosewood again now, leaning over the desk and bracing one hand on the surface like he could physically will her to pick up. This time, after three rings, someone answered.

"Rosewood Estate. Jenny speaking."

Relief surged, mingled instantly with tension. "Jenny, thank God. It's John."

"Oh! Hello, Mr. Sneddon. I only just got back an hour ago. Everything all right?"

"No. Is Grace there?"

There was a pause.

"No, sir. I haven't seen her. Your car's here, but hers is gone."

A beat of silence—then a cold shiver slid down John's spine.

"Jenny… check her room," he said, his voice dropping into something low and dangerous.

"Of course. Hold on."

The line went quiet, the wait stretching taut as wire. He could hear the faint sound of footsteps, then the click of a door. Another pause.

When Jenny spoke again, her voice was softer, almost reluctant.

"Some of her clothes are gone. And… her phone's here, Mr. Sneddon. It's on the bed. With a necklace and bracelet."

John went utterly still.

Beyond the hotel window, the rooftops of Madrid blurred into nothing. Only one thought cut through the roar in his head—hard, final, brutal.

She was gone.

She had told him she wouldn't marry him. That she would leave. And he hadn't listened—because he thought she was bluffing. Too sheltered. Too dependent to survive without him.

He had been wrong.

John didn't speak.

Not right away.

His hand tightened around the phone, the knuckles white, his breath shallow and hard in his throat. Jenny's voice came faintly from the other end, hesitant.

"Mr. Sneddon? Are you still there?"

He closed his eyes.

"Yes." His voice was hoarse. He cleared it and tried again. "Yes, I'm here."

"She must've gone somewhere," Jenny said softly, clearly trying to be reassuring. "Maybe just for a bit. A break. She's been under so much strain— She wouldn't leave without telling me. Not like this. Not Grace."

John said nothing.

He didn't blame her.

Because the truth was staring him straight in the face. She had left. And she hadn't just left—she was trying to vanish. Quietly, deliberately. She'd taken her things, abandoned her phone, left his car in the driveway like an afterthought.

He hadn't even kissed her goodbye. He was too preoccupied with the Madrid problem.

"Mr. Sneddon?" Jenny again. "Is there anything you want me to do?"

He didn't answer. Couldn't.

He'd built an empire by staying in control, by making decisions without blinking. But this—this was different. It didn't just unnerve him. It unmade him.

He had told her he would never love her.

But that had been a lie.

A desperate, foolish lie born out of fear—because the truth had terrified him far more than the idea of losing her.

He'd been in love with her from the very beginning.

From the first time he'd seen her—wide-eyed, too innocent for her own good, walking along side her father at the airport like she didn't quite belong—she had disarmed him. And nothing had been the same since.

He hadn't wanted to love her. God knew he'd tried not to.

He paraded other women in front of her hoping to make her jealous enough to stay. It was the only way he knew how to fight for her without admitting how much she meant.

And when that hadn't worked, he'd pushed harder, cornered her with logic and pride and wounded emotion, until she'd finally agreed to marry him.

But now…

She was gone.

No goodbye.

And for the first time in years, John Sneddon—who could track assets across continents and make governments bend—stood completely powerless.

Because the one person he couldn't afford to lose had disappeared.

And he had no idea where to begin looking.

"Mr. Sneddon?"

He exhaled, forced composure back into his voice.

"Thank you, Jenny," he said tightly. "If she contacts you, call me immediately. I don't care what time it is."

"I will. Of course."

He hung up.

The moment the line went dead, John turned and struck the edge of the desk with the flat of his palm—once, hard. The pain barely registered. He pressed both hands down against the wood and stared at nothing for a long time.

Then, slowly, he lowered his head, his shoulders bowing as if under a weight he couldn't name.

His aunt's voice came back to him, sharp with quiet warning. '*Don't take her for granted John.*' She had pulled him aside before they'd left, her eyes fierce. '*That sweet woman in there won't stand for it. I saw her face when you flirted with Sharon—it was breaking her. You need to make her believe she's the only one.*'

And now Grace was gone.

For the first time in years, John Sneddon had no move to make, no strategy to play. The board was empty.

And he was losing.

Chapter Twenty

Grace drove north through the endless stretch of motorway, the London skyline shrinking in her rearview mirror until it was swallowed by the winter mist. She barely noticed the road signs flashing by. The rain smeared the windshield, blurring her vision—but not enough to hide the truth of what she'd done.

She had left him.

By the time she reached Birmingham, her shoulders were tight with fatigue and her heart felt like a hollow echo inside her chest. The city was unfamiliar—bustling and grey, full of noise and strangers. It was exactly what she needed.

She found a flat just outside the city centre. Small, worn around the edges, with a faulty boiler and a stain on the ceiling she didn't have the energy to care about. The landlord gave her the keys without ceremony. No questions, no warm welcome. Just a few forms and a muttered warning about the meter running out if she didn't top it up.

She parked the car on the street and sat for a moment behind the wheel, gripping the steering wheel as if it could anchor her to something real.

She had driven away from the only home she had ever known.

From the only man she had ever loved.

She rested her forehead against the steering wheel and breathed through the ache in her chest. She thought she was doing the right thing—she knew she was. She couldn't marry a man who didn't love her, not truly. Not the way she loved him. Being with him but never really having him… it would have destroyed her.

Still, leaving him felt like cutting her own heart out.

Eventually, she made herself move. She grabbed her suitcases, walked up the narrow stairs, and unlocked the flat. The space was cold and smelled faintly of mildew, but it was hers. Temporary. Anonymous. A place to hide.

She didn't unpack. She didn't eat. She simply sat on the edge of the narrow bed, staring at the blank wall, and let the tears come—silent, steady, unstoppable.

Tomorrow, she would look for work. An office job, something that paid just enough to keep her afloat.

Tomorrow, she would try to feel human again.

But tonight, she would mourn the man she loved—and the life she couldn't have.

John unlocked the apartment door and pushed it open with the weariness of a man who hadn't slept properly in days. The Madrid trip had dragged on longer than expected. The planning fiasco was still unresolved, but he'd handed it off to his legal team—he couldn't focus, couldn't breathe properly, not when Grace wasn't answering her phone.

He dropped his overnight bag by the door and called her name.

"Grace?"

Silence.

The place felt… empty. Not just unoccupied. Hollow.

He walked through the apartment, tension tightening with every step. Her coat wasn't on the hook. Her bag wasn't on the sideboard. He glanced into the bedroom, already dreading what he wouldn't find—and felt his chest clamp at the sight.

Her scent still lingered faintly in the room. She had been here. Recently.

His eyes landed on the desk.

There it was—the engagement ring, gleaming like ice in the early afternoon light.

Beneath it, a folded note. His name in her handwriting.

He reached for it slowly, as if the paper might vanish the moment he touched it. He unfolded the letter, eyes scanning the first few lines—and then he sat down heavily in the chair, the weight of it all pressing him down.

Dear John…

Thank you…

You changed everything…

You would never love me…

I fell in love with you…

It's tearing me apart to walk away…

I can't marry a man who doesn't love me…

One of many…

He read it once. Then again. Each sentence hit like a blade, and he didn't realise his hand was trembling until he set the note down.

She had left him.

Not in anger. Not in spite.

But because she loved him.

And because he had made her believe he would never love her back.

He leaned forward, bracing his elbows on the desk and burying his face in his hands. For a long time, he didn't move.

He had told her he'd never love her—thinking he was protecting them both. But all he'd done was drive her away.

The ring sat between his hands, a symbol of everything he could've had and everything he'd thrown away.

He whispered her name into the quiet. "Grace…"

But she wasn't there. And he had no idea where to begin looking.

A week had passed since Grace slipped away from the world she'd known—since she'd left John, the ring, the pain. Birmingham was grey, a bit noisy, but it gave her what she needed most: anonymity and distraction.

Her small flat on the edge of the city centre. It wasn't much—barely two rooms and the walls were paper thin—but it was hers. Quiet, plain, manageable. The job came next: a receptionist position at a local real estate office just off the high street. It was routine work—answering phones, typing up listings, printing brochures—but the people were kind and didn't ask questions she couldn't answer.

It wasn't anything like working for John, and that was exactly the point.

That afternoon, she was walking home as dusk rolled in, the wind tugging at her coat. Her bag was heavy with groceries and the heel of her boot pinched slightly, but the motion of walking helped settle the ache that never quite left her chest.

Then she heard it—her name.

"Grace?"

She froze.

The voice was familiar, too familiar.

She turned slowly.

Sean.

He stood only a few feet away, looking startled and slightly winded, as if he couldn't quite believe she was real.

"Sean," she said softly, her own surprise catching in her throat. "What are you doing here?"

"What the hell are you doing here?" he shot back, stepping closer, his expression a jolt of shock and concern. "I'm visiting my mum—she lives in Birmingham. She had a heart attack."

She nodded faintly. "Oh... I'm sorry, Sean. Is she okay?"

"She's recovering." His gaze sharpened. "Why are you here?"

"I live here now. I found a job at a real estate office—it's just a short walk from my flat."

He paused, studying her more closely. The playful glint she remembered was gone, replaced by something far more serious. His eyes swept over her face, her frame, registering the changes—subtle, but impossible to miss.

"You don't look well," he said quietly. "You've lost weight. A lot of it."

Grace straightened her spine, forcing steadiness she didn't feel. "I'm fine. Really. I can take care of myself now. It's time I stood on my own two feet."

"Does John know you're here?"

"No." The word came too fast. "And I'd appreciate it if you didn't tell him."

Sean exhaled slowly, shaking his head. "He should be taking care of you. He said he would."

"I'm not his responsibility," she replied, barely above a whisper.

He watched her for a long moment, as though debating whether to push. Then, half to himself, he muttered, "I never liked the way he looked at you—like you already belonged to him, but he didn't have the guts to admit it. Still… he told me he was marrying you. I believed him."

Grace said nothing. There was nothing she could say.

"I'm glad you're okay," he said at last. "If you ever need anything—"

"I won't," she interrupted gently. "But thank you. And I hope your mother gets better."

He gave a short nod, though his eyes lingered on her, troubled and searching, as if trying to read what she wouldn't give away. Then he stepped aside, letting her pass.

Grace walked away without looking back, her throat tight, her heart heavier with every step.

She hadn't lied—she was surviving.

But fine?

No. She wasn't fine at all.

John sat in his office, staring out at the London skyline, but he saw nothing.

Ten days. Ten long days since Grace had vanished from his life, leaving only a letter and an empty silence that hollowed him out more with each passing hour.

The private investigators had found nothing. No transactions except for the large withdrawal the day after he had left London. No contact. No trail.

It was like she'd never existed.

He hadn't slept. Not properly. He hadn't eaten unless someone forced a tray in front of him. And still, he couldn't focus on anything but the memory of her voice, her scent, her eyes just before she left.

Then, from beyond the office door, he heard a commotion.

"You can't just storm in there!"

"I don't give a damn."

John's head snapped toward the door just as it flew open and Sean charged inside, anger burning in his face.

Karen stood frozen. "I tried to stop him—"

"It's fine, Karen," John said quietly. "Leave us."

She hesitated, then slipped out, closing the door behind her.

Sean didn't wait. He slammed his hand on John's desk, fire in his eyes.

"You bastard."

John looked up, startled. "Good morning to you too."

"You told me you'd take care of her," Sean said, his voice tight with rage. "You promised me she'd be safe with you. So, tell me—what the hell happened?"

John pushed back from his desk and stood, jaw tightening. "Don't come in here throwing accusations—"

"She looks awful," Sean cut in, fists clenched at his sides. "Like she hasn't eaten in weeks. Like she's barely holding herself together."

John's eyes snapped to his. "You saw her?"

Sean hesitated. "Yeah. Two days ago."

John's voice dropped, raw and desperate. "Where, Sean? Tell me—please."

Sean shook his head and turned away. "She didn't want you to know."

"Where is she?" John's voice cracked, the words torn from his throat. "Is she okay."

Sean swore under his breath, dragging a hand through his hair. "She's not okay," he said finally. "I ran into her on the street. She looked… wrecked. Thin. Hollow-eyed. She said she was working and living in a flat. She deserves better."

John stumbled back a step, as if the words had struck him physically. The room tilted for a moment.

She was out there. Alone. Hurting. And hiding.

"Please," he whispered. "I need to find her. I have to. I can't stand knowing she's out there thinking I never—thinking I never—" His voice faltered. "Please, Sean. If you ever trusted me with anything, let it be this."

Sean turned slowly. His expression was torn, a war between loyalty and guilt.

"She asked me not to tell you," he said. "She obviously doesn't want you to know."

John's eyes burned, but he refused to let the tears fall. "I can't breathe without her. I can't sleep. I can't think. And every hour that passes, knowing she's hurting because of me, is—" He broke off, swallowing hard. "Just give me something. I swear, I won't hurt her."

Sean's gaze was steady. "Will you help her?"

"I promise."

Silence stretched between them before Sean finally exhaled. "She's in Birmingham. Works at a real estate office. That's all I know."

John closed his eyes. Relief hit him like a wave—swift, staggering—followed by a grief that hollowed him out.

"Thank you," he whispered, his voice rough and unsteady. "God... thank you."

John didn't waste a second. The moment Sean walked out of his office; he picked up his phone and called his head of security.

"I need a car. Now. Birmingham."

Within thirty minutes, a sleek, black chauffeured car pulled up in front of his building. He slid into the back seat, jaw tight, heart pounding.

"Birmingham," he told the driver. "And don't spare the speed."

As the car cut through the traffic, John sat forward, tablet in hand, searching. Real estate agencies. Every single one in the Birmingham area. Big ones. Boutique ones. Temporary offices. Chains. Independents. He didn't care how long it took—he would go door to door if he had to.

She was there. Somewhere.

He scanned every website, every team photo, every 'Meet Our Agents' page, desperate for a glimpse of her. Nothing. Not yet.

But she was there. Sean had seen her.

The guilt twisted in his gut with every mile. He'd let her down in the worst possible way. Pushed her too far. Tried to control something so delicate it had shattered in his hands. All his pride, all his careful manipulation—what had it earned him?

A cold, empty apartment. A ring on a desk. And a memory of a woman who felt like she belonged in his arms.

"Are we close?" he asked sharply.

"Another fifteen minutes, sir."

Fifteen minutes. And then he'd begin.

He would knock on every office door in the city if he had to. Grace might not want to be found, but he wasn't going to stop—not until she looked him in the eyes and told him to leave. Until then, he'd search.

She had walked away because she thought he didn't love her.

And God help him; he had to convince her she was wrong.

Chapter Twenty-One

Grace was seated behind the front desk, her fingers flying across the keyboard as she typed in a message from a call she'd just taken. The office was quiet except for the soft hum of conversation in the back and the occasional ring of the phone.

The bell above the door chimed.

She didn't look up. "Just a moment," she called politely, eyes still on the screen, trying to finish logging the client request before she lost her train of thought.

From across the room, she heard Marissa, one of the senior agents, get up from her desk. Her voice drifted over, flirtatious, and syrupy sweet.

"Oh, can I help you?"

A pause.

Then a deep, unmistakable voice cut through the room.

"No."

It was just one word—but it stopped Grace cold.

Her fingers froze on the keyboard. Her heart lurched painfully in her chest. Slowly, disbelieving, she lifted her head—

And saw him.

John.

Standing in the doorway, his towering frame backlit by the soft grey light spilling through the glass. His coat was still buttoned; his eyes locked on her like he'd just found water in the desert. He looked tired. Strained. Desperate.

Grace's breath caught. For a moment, neither of them moved.

Marissa blinked and glanced between them, her flirty expression fading into mild confusion. "I'll... leave you two, then," she murmured and slipped away.

Grace stood, her knees shaking slightly.

"What are you doing here?" Her voice was barely more than a whisper.

John stepped closer, slowly, like approaching a frightened animal.

"Looking for you," he said, and in his voice was everything—regret, longing, and something dangerously close to heartbreak.

"I've been looking for you every day."

Tears welled in Grace's eyes before she could stop them. She blinked hard, but one slid down her cheek anyway.

"You need to leave, John," she said softly, her voice trembling. "Please."

John's jaw tightened. He took another step toward her, but she held up a hand, palm shaking.

"No. Don't," she whispered, trying to breathe past the ache in her chest. "You shouldn't have come."

"I had to," he said, his voice low, rough. "You disappeared, Grace. I couldn't sleep. I couldn't think. I didn't even know if you were safe."

"I'm safe," she said. "I'm fine."

"You're not," he said gently. "You're thinner. Your eyes look haunted. Sean told me—"

"You shouldn't have spoken to Sean," she cut in, voice rising just slightly, brittle with emotion. "He had no right to tell you anything."

"I begged him," John admitted, stepping closer again. "I was losing my mind."

Grace's chin trembled as she fought the wave of emotion rising inside her. "Well, you found me. You've done what you came for. Now you can go."

"I didn't come to check a box, Grace," John said, his voice low and aching. "We need to talk. Please."

She shook her head. "Go and talk to Rita. Or Sharon. Or any one of your other women. I'm not one of them." Her voice cracked on the last word, and she hated how much it gave her away.

John flinched as though she'd struck him. "You were never one of them."

"Grace…" Marissa, the senior agent at the office, stepped out from behind the reception desk, eyeing the scene with concern. "Maybe you should leave for the day."

"I don't—"

"Thank you," John said smoothly, cutting her off with a faint smile in Marissa's direction.

Grace stared at him, stunned by his audacity.

Marissa turned to her gently. "You're shaking, Grace. Just go home. We've got everything here."

"I can't—"

"I insist," Marissa said softly, but firmly. "Take the rest of the day. Get some air."

Grace hesitated, pride and pain tangling inside her like thorns. But the weight of John's presence—his eyes searching hers, his face carved with emotion—was too much to bear.

She nodded stiffly, her movements mechanical, as she picked up her purse and walked around the counter, head held high despite the tears threatening to spill. She didn't look at him. She couldn't. If she did, she'd break.

John followed a step behind, silent, and solemn. At the door, he reached past her and held it open, the gesture tender, almost reverent.

"I don't want to talk to you," she whispered, stepping out into the grey afternoon light.

"You don't have to talk," he murmured behind her. "Just… let me do the talking. Come with me. Just hear me out."

She turned slightly, eyes glistening with pain. "I can't do this, John. Not again."

He stepped closer, his fingers lightly brushing hers before taking her hands gently in his. "Please," he said softly. "Just come with me. Listen to what I have to say. If after that, you still want to walk away, I'll take you home myself. No questions, no arguments."

She shook her head, disbelief flickering in her eyes. "I don't believe you. You'll just tell me you want me, and that I have to marry you."

"I won't. I just need to tell you the truth. Then you can leave."

"You promise?" Her voice was almost inaudible.

"I swear."

She nodded slowly.

Without another word, he guided her to the sleek black car waiting at the curb. A uniformed driver opened the door as John gave a quiet instruction: "The Grand Hotel, please."

Grace slid into the car, her heart thudding, her breath catching.

She didn't know what he was going to say.

But she knew it had the power to change everything.

Grace sat rigidly in the car, her arms folded tightly across her body, her gaze fixed on the window as the city blurred past. Her reflection in the glass looked pale, strained, unfamiliar. She didn't speak, and neither did John. The silence between them was thick with everything unsaid.

When they arrived at the hotel, the driver opened the door, and John stepped out first. He turned and offered her his hand. She hesitated, then placed hers lightly in his, more out of necessity than trust.

He led her into the lobby and up to the penthouse suite. Every step felt heavier than the last.

Inside, the space was airy and luxurious, all quiet elegance and sweeping views of Birmingham through the floor-to-ceiling windows. Grace walked automatically toward them, drawn to the glass as if the world outside might offer a steadier view than the storm swirling inside her.

Behind her, she heard the soft click of the door closing.

"Would you like something to drink?" John asked gently, his voice careful—too careful.

"No, thank you." She kept her eyes on the skyline, arms folded, posture defensive.

He watched her for a moment, then gestured toward the plush seating area. "Please… sit with me."

She didn't move. Not right away.

When she finally turned, her expression was guarded, chin tilted high. But something in John's eyes—raw, unshielded—softened her resolve. Slowly, she crossed the room and sat on the very edge of the sofa, her hands clenched in her lap, her entire body humming with tension.

John took the seat across from her, not too close.

He looked at her like she was a ghost—someone lost, someone cherished.

He exhaled and ran a hand through his hair. "I don't know where to start."

"Then don't," she said quietly. "We could skip this. You've found me. I'll go now."

But she didn't stand.

Neither did he.

And somewhere between the quiet of the room and the beating of two bruised hearts… the truth waited.

John drew in a slow breath, steadying himself. Then, quietly, he began.

"Do you remember the first time we saw each other?"

His voice was low, roughened by emotion.

Grace turned her head toward him, surprised. "Yes… I was coming down the stairs at Rosewood," she said softly, recalling the awkward, charged moment.

But he shook his head, a faint, rueful smile touching his lips. "No. That wasn't the first time I saw you."

Her brows pulled together. "What do you mean?"

"I was about to board a flight to New York," he said, his eyes holding hers. "And I saw you. At Heathrow. You were there waiting for your father—he'd just landed, and the way you ran into his arms…" His voice caught slightly. "It was like time stopped. I remember thinking I'd never seen a smile like that in my life."

He paused, his jaw tightening. "I never got on that flight."

Grace's eyes widened. "You didn't?"

"No." He hesitated, then added, "I followed you."

"You what?"

"I followed you and your father. All the way home." He looked a little sheepish now, but unrepentant. "I stayed back. Went down into the village, asked around. Found out Brian Lewis of Lewis Engineering lived at the old house. And that he had a daughter named Grace."

She stared at him, stunned. "So, none of this was coincidence?"

He shook his head slowly. "No. Not a bit of it. The only thing that was accidental was seeing you that day. But once I had…" He exhaled. "I couldn't leave it to chance. I'd fallen in love, Grace. Hard. And it hurt in ways I didn't even understand. You were like a wound that refused to heal."

Her throat tightened. "You told me you didn't believe in love. That you'd never fall in love."

He looked away, the smile fading. "I lied. I was protecting myself. Trying to control something that had already taken hold of me." His voice deepened. "And then when we finally did meet, you looked at me like you hated me."

She dropped her gaze. "I didn't hate you," she whispered. "You scared me."

He gently lifted her chin, making her meet his eyes. "I never wanted to scare you. But you looked through me that day—as if I didn't matter."

"It wasn't you," she said softly. "It was how you made me feel. I didn't know you, but you already felt like something I'd never recover from."

He nodded slowly. "But I knew you. From the first moment. I knew you were going to ruin me. And you did."

Her eyes filled with tears. "You fell in love…" she echoed, struggling to process it. "With me?"

"Utterly," he said simply. "Hopelessly. And every day without you has been hell."

Grace swallowed hard. "Really?" she asked, her voice brittle and laced with disbelief.

He reached for her hands and pressed them to his lips. The kiss was tender, reverent. "I don't want to spend another day without you."

She shook her head slowly, painfully. "I can't, John. I can't share you. It would destroy me."

"There's no one else, Grace," he said firmly. "Not since the moment I saw you."

"But you told me…" she faltered, "you told me Rita was your mistress."

He exhaled, regret shadowing his face. "I told you that to make you jealous. I thought… maybe if you were jealous, you'd start to see me as something more than a cold, untouchable man. Maybe you'd care."

She pulled her hands back, folding them tightly in her lap. "It worked," she said softly. "I cared so much it nearly broke me."

John's voice dropped, raw with remorse. "I've made every mistake a man can make with a woman he loves. But it always came back to one thing—I wanted you too much. I didn't know how to be honest about it."

"Why?" she asked, her voice breaking. "Why not just tell me?"

He looked at her, eyes bare. "Because love makes fools out of men who've never needed anything. And I needed you so badly it scared the hell out of me."

Silence stretched between them. Thick. Honest. Painful.

Then, barely above a whisper, she asked, "And now?"

He leaned forward, cupping her face gently. "Now, I'll tell you every day if you'll let me. I love you, Grace. No lies. No more distance. Just you. Only you."

Tears slipped quietly down her cheeks.

"Come home," he whispered. "Or let me build a new one with you—anywhere you want."

Her breath caught. "You'd do that for me?"

"I'd do anything for you." His voice cracked with raw emotion. "I've loved you from the moment I saw you over two years ago—and it's only grown stronger."

She looked sceptical, searching his eyes. Then, slowly, she saw the vulnerability there—and dared to hope it was real.

They sat like that, locked in silent understanding, until a single tear slid from her lashes.

"I love you too, John."

He exhaled a breath that was half relief, half awe. Rising to his feet, his hands cradled her face as if she were the most precious thing in the world.

"Marry me," he said, his voice hoarse. "Please… put me out of my misery."

"Yes, John," she whispered. "If you still want me."

He let out a raw, broken laugh, one hand reaching up to brush back her hair. "If I want you? I've wanted you from the moment I saw you. I've waited, longed, ached—until I wasn't sure I'd survive it."

She flung her arms around his neck, her kisses wild and tearful against his cheeks, his lips. "Don't ever leave me again, John. I love you. I want forever with you."

He let out a breathless, joy-filled laugh, pulling her tightly into his chest. "Grace… my Grace. I've waited so long for you to say that. I need you."

"I need you too," she whispered.

Without another word, John swept her into his arms, cradling her as if she were something breakable, beloved, and utterly irreplaceable. He carried her toward the bedroom with the sure, quiet urgency of a man who had waited too long.

At the edge of the bed, he set her gently on her feet. For a long, charged moment, he simply looked at her. Then, slowly, his hand found the zipper of her woollen dress. He pulled it down, the sound impossibly loud in the hush of the room. The fabric slid from her shoulders, pooling at her feet in silence.

She stood trembling before him, clothed now only in delicate white lace. Her body was almost fragile in its softness, her bra a whisper of a thing that barely concealed her. Her nipples showed dark and aching beneath the lace, and John's jaw clenched as his gaze devoured her.

"You're so beautiful, Grace," he said hoarsely. "I can't believe you're finally mine."

Her hand moved up his chest, tentative but certain. "I want to be yours. Forever," she breathed. "Please, John."

His hands came up, reverent and slow, tracing the nape of her neck, then sweeping down the elegant line of her shoulders to the soft curve of her breasts. He was watching his own hands as if they didn't belong to him, mesmerised by the feel of her, the rise and fall of her breath.

She stood motionless under his touch, her breathing shallow and fast, her lips slightly parted as she tried to steady herself.

"I want you," he said, the words raw and urgent. "Now. Be mine, Grace. And I'll never let you go."

"I don't want you to," she whispered against his lips. "I don't ever want to let go."

His breath hitched, sharp in his throat. "In my heart, you've always been mine. But each time I see you like this, it's like the first time all over again."

She gasped softly as he pulled her close, his hands restless, roaming, reverent. He buried his face in her hair, breathing her in as though he could anchor himself in her scent. Her heartbeat felt like a thunderstorm against his chest.

When he finally let her lean back to look into her eyes, she was trembling—shaken by the force of emotion and need crashing inside her. Her gaze locked with his, wide and shining, her lips parted as if caught mid-breath.

He was being careful, painfully so. Not rushing. Not demanding. Just holding her like she was everything.

But Grace felt like she would shatter from the sheer weight of wanting.

She pressed closer, her body seeking his with a feverish desperation. And when he gathered her fully into his arms again, holding her tight until their breaths merged into one, she felt her resolve dissolve in the heat between them.

His gaze dropped, lingering on the swell of her breasts, and something inside him broke. Whatever restraint he had left snapped like a bowstring.

He crushed his mouth to hers, a groan rising deep in his chest as he kissed her—wild, desperate, aching. His tongue swept into her mouth, claiming and pleading all at once, as though trying to drink down everything she offered and more.

And she gave—everything. Every trembling breath. Every hidden hope. Every secret she'd locked behind her ribs. She gave him everything.

Because she was his. Because he was hers.

And tonight, there would be no more walls. Only truth. Only surrender. Only love.

Chapter Twenty-Two

He lifted her into his arms and laid her gently on the bed, as though she were the most precious thing he had ever held. His gaze never left her—not for a heartbeat—as he stripped off his clothes with swift, practiced movements. Then, bare before her, he came to her side, the heat of his body warming the space between them.

"I'll be careful, sweetheart," he whispered thickly, voice raw with emotion. "I'll never hurt you again, darling." His tone was dark velvet—possessive, reverent, thick with aching desire. He tilted her face up, his eyes locking with hers as his hands slid slowly over her trembling form. "My beautiful Grace…"

Words melted away as his lips captured hers, full and deep, silencing the space between them. His arms wrapped around her with a kind of desperate hunger, fingers tracing the line of her spine until she arched into him, helpless against the fire building between them.

Magic. That was the only word for it. Magic and love, engulfing her, claiming her.

He was everything—perfect and powerful, intoxicating like a dream she'd always known, even before she met him. With her eyes closed, she could still see him. She had always seen him—always seen this. Her future had worn his face.

Her arms curled around his neck in pure surrender, her thoughts dissolving into nothing but the need to be close to him, to feel him, to finally belong to him in every way. He let out a low, broken sound of longing, his mouth moving along her neck in breathless, reverent kisses, his control trembling beneath the surface.

His lips were like warm honey, soft and addictive, as he kissed her again and again, until she couldn't breathe without him. Her arms clung to him, drawing him closer, anchoring him to her as if her heart couldn't survive even an inch of distance.

"Say it," he murmured hoarsely, his mouth brushing her cheek. "Grace… say it again."

She opened her eyes, drowning in the depth of his gaze. "I love you," she whispered. "I want you."

"God, I want you too." His mouth covered hers in a kiss that was both fire and silk—urgent and tender, desperate and slow. A groan escaped his throat, deep and raw. "God, Grace…"

Her skin flamed beneath his touch, every nerve alive as his hands explored her with reverence and need. The press of his palm, the graze of his fingertips—it all set her ablaze. She moaned softly, her own hands sliding over him, marvelling at the heat and strength of his body, the rough silk of his skin against hers.

"Touch me, sweetheart," he breathed thickly. "Show me how much you want this... how much you want me."

She did.

With her hands, with her mouth, with every breath she took, she told him what words could never fully express.

That she was his.

That she had always been his.

That she would never want anyone else.

He worshipped her—with his hands, his mouth, his body—every touch a vow, every kiss a promise. He moved with reverence, as though memorising the very shape of her, learning her with aching devotion.

He slid the delicate lace of her underwear down her hips slowly, his breath catching as he took in the full beauty of her, exposed and trembling beneath him.

"You're so beautiful," he whispered against the heat of her skin, his lips brushing the sensitive hollow of her thigh.

He took his time, mapping her with lips and tongue and fingertips, drawing sighs and moans from her lips until her breath was ragged and her body taut with need. When she shattered, it was with a desperate cry—an overwhelming wave of pleasure that left her trembling, gasping for breath, her fingers tangled in his hair as if he were the only thing anchoring her to earth.

Only then did he rise above her, his gaze full of awe and restraint, his body straining with need but his touch still gentle.

"It might hurt a little," he said softly, brushing her hair back from her damp forehead. "But I'll be careful, sweetheart. I swear I'll take care of you."

"I trust you, John. Take me... please."

Her words were a whisper of surrender, and something inside him fractured—cracked open by the way she looked at him, by the courage it took for her to say those words. He leaned down and kissed her, slowly, reverently, his lips lingering over hers like he was trying to memorise the taste of her breath.

Then, with exquisite care, he eased into her—inch by aching inch. Her body tensed beneath him, and he stilled, his lips never leaving hers, his fingers brushing her hair back from her face.

"You feel like heaven," he whispered against her mouth. "Just breathe, sweetheart. I've got you."

She nodded, tears springing to her eyes not from pain, but from the overwhelming closeness—the sense of finally, fully belonging.

He began to move slowly, barely withdrawing before sliding deeper, coaxing her body to relax around him. Her arms wrapped tightly around his shoulders, her legs curling around his hips as she began to meet his rhythm, her breath catching on every thrust.

The burn turned to warmth, then to something sweeter—deeper.

He worshipped her, body and soul, his hands caressing every inch of her skin, his mouth trailing kisses along her jaw, her throat, the hollow of her collarbone. When his lips closed over her breast, she arched into him with a soft, desperate moan, her fingers buried in his hair.

"You're so beautiful," he murmured against her skin. "Every part of you. Mine."

She whimpered as he filled her again, deeper this time, and she clung to him, her body rising to meet his in an instinctive, hungry rhythm. Pleasure shimmered beneath the surface—growing, building, until it consumed her, wave after wave of blinding sensation that shook her from the inside out.

"John!" she cried, her head thrown back, eyes wide and unseeing as release claimed her.

He stilled for a moment, holding her through it, kissing away her cries as if they were sacred. Then he began to move again, no longer holding back, his control fraying as her name fell from his lips like a broken prayer.

"Grace… God, Grace… I love you so much."

His rhythm turned urgent, hungry, and she met him with the same wild, aching need. They clung to each other, bodies slick with heat and devotion, until he surged forward one last time and let go, groaning her name like it was salvation.

They lay tangled in each other, limbs entwined, hearts still racing as the world fell quiet around them.

He brushed her damp hair back and kissed her temple, his voice hoarse and unsteady. "I'll never leave you, Grace. You're everything."

She turned her face toward his, eyes still shining. "And you're mine, John. Always."

He held her tighter, as if he could fold her into his soul and never let go.

But one time wasn't enough.

Not for him.

Not even close.

John lay beside her in the hush that followed, his chest rising and falling as if he'd run a great distance. But even as her breath evened out and her body relaxed into his, he knew he hadn't had enough. Could never have enough.

Not of her skin, her scent, the way she whispered his name like it meant something sacred.

She shifted slightly, curling closer to him, her lashes still damp, her lips swollen from his kisses. And the sight of her—naked, open, utterly his—undid him all over again.

He traced a slow line down her back with the tips of his fingers. "Grace," he said softly, his voice thick, "I'm not finished with you."

She stirred against him, a smile teasing at the corner of her mouth. "I didn't think you were."

"I could spend the rest of my life memorising every inch of you," he murmured, pressing a kiss to her shoulder. "And I still wouldn't be satisfied."

She turned toward him, her eyes meeting his, still dark with desire. "Then don't stop," she whispered, threading her fingers into his hair. "I don't want you to."

Something raw moved across his face—hunger, worship, and something deeper than both. Without another word, he rolled her gently beneath him, cradling her as if she were something precious, and kissed her like a man starved.

He didn't rush.

This time was different—slower, deeper. As if he were learning her all over again.

Every sigh, every shiver, every whispered plea.

He worshipped her body with his hands, his mouth, the reverence in his eyes. As if she was not just a woman but his woman—his home, his redemption, his future.

And when he joined with her again, it wasn't just about need.

It was love.

Fierce, desperate, all-consuming love.

And Grace gave herself to it—gave herself to him—completely.

Because once wasn't enough for her either.

Not with John.

Not now.

Not ever.

Sometime later, as the soft hush of the suite wrapped around them, John stirred beside her. Grace lay still, her body curved into his, her fingers lightly resting on his chest. She turned her head slightly, her voice hesitant in the quiet.

"John?" she whispered.

He opened his eyes at once, alert to her tone. "Yes, sweetheart?"

"Can I ask you something?"

He brushed a strand of hair from her cheek. "Of course. Anything."

She hesitated, her voice barely audible. "Did you know... about what my father was doing?"

His body went still. Then he gathered her gently against him, kissing her fingers as he held her hand in his.

"I did," he said softly.

Her breath caught, but she didn't pull away.

"I found out a few months before he passed," he continued, his voice low and weighted with regret. "About the debts. The shady deals. His drinking. I tried to talk to him, Grace, but by then... he was locked in. Hell-bent on his own path, and nothing I said made a difference."

Grace's eyes shimmered, the ache of betrayal resurfacing. "Why didn't you tell me?"

"Because it would've broken your heart," he murmured, his thumb stroking over her knuckles. "And I couldn't do that to you. I thought if I stayed close, I could soften the blow when it finally came."

She closed her eyes and pressed her face against his chest.

"I hated you for a little while," she admitted quietly.

"I know," he said. "I hated myself too."

He kissed the crown of her head, then sat up and swung his legs over the side of the bed.

"You look like you're fading away," he said gently, glancing over his shoulder at her. "I'm going to order room service."

She smiled faintly, the tension in her easing a little. "That actually sounds amazing."

She hadn't eaten much since coming to Birmingham. Now, for the first time in days, she was genuinely hungry.

They ate curled up together on the sofa, sharing bites from silver-domed trays while wrapped in one of the suite's thick blankets. The quiet intimacy of it—laughing over strawberries, sipping tea, stealing soft kisses between bites—felt like something out of another life. A better one.

And then, finally, they dressed.

"Let's go get your things," John said, his hand firm at her back as they stepped into the lift. "You're not spending another night in that place."

Grace didn't protest.

But when they arrived at the run-down walk-up where she'd been staying, John's face darkened.

The peeling paint. The flickering stairwell light. The damp chill that clung to the air.

He was silent as they climbed the stairs, his jaw set hard, his hand tightening around hers.

"Grace..." he said quietly, as she unlocked the door to the cramped flat, "you were living here?"

She gave a small nod, embarrassed.

He stepped inside behind her, surveying the stained carpet, the barely functioning heater, the sagging sofa bed.

"This is unacceptable," he said, his voice low and tense. "You should never have had to stay in a place like this."

"I didn't plan to be here long," she said softly. "I just... didn't know where else to go."

He turned to her then, eyes dark with something fierce—not anger, but something far more potent. Protectiveness. Devotion. A need to shelter her from every harsh corner of the world.

"You'll never go without again, Grace," he said, his voice low and resolute. "Not while I'm breathing. I promise you that."

She stepped closer, her hand finding his chest, her voice trembling but sure.

"I don't need possessions, John. I don't care about money or anything else."

Her eyes found his, shining with unguarded emotion.

"All I want is *you.*"

His breath hitched, just slightly, like her words had struck some place raw inside him. Then he pulled her into his arms, holding her like she was the only thing that had ever mattered.

"You have me," he whispered into her hair, his voice rough with emotion. "Every part of me. For as long as you'll let me stay."

She tilted her face up to his, her eyes shining with love, her smile soft and certain.

"Forever won't be long enough," she whispered back. "But it's a start."

Epilogue

The spring sun filtered through the ancient oak trees, casting soft, dappled shadows across the manicured gardens of Rosewood. The house stood just as it had when Grace was a girl—elegant, timeless, full of memory. Today, it was dressed in flowers and ribbons, the air rich with wisteria and fresh-cut roses, the grounds alive with quiet celebration.

It was Grace's twenty-fifth birthday.

John had planned everything in secret—an intimate surprise party, just close friends, and family. Nothing lavish, just thoughtful. Meaningful. Just like him.

They had married two weeks after their reconciliation. He'd offered her a grand wedding at any destination in the world, but she had simply smiled and said all she wanted was to be Mrs. John Sneddon—as soon as humanly possible. And so, they'd wed quietly in the rose garden behind Rosewood, with Harriet's tears, Jenny's blessing, and the sweetest winter breeze weaving through her veil.

In the six months since, John had done everything he could to make her happy. He'd tracked down and bought back every last piece of her mother's jewellery—the ones Grace had once sold in desperation. He surprised her with books she'd loved as a child, remembered the smallest stories she told him, held her every night like she was something sacred.

But today, Grace held a secret of her own—one she knew would bring him joy. Something he'd wanted more than anything.

She stood alone now at the stone balustrade just outside the drawing room, her fingers splayed on the sun-warmed stone. Her gaze wandered across the lawn to the hills beyond, where soft green rolled into a pale blue sky. A breeze toyed with a lock of her hair, carrying the scent of wisteria and sunlight.

Behind her, laughter spilled out through open windows. Harriet was charming the guests with one of her dramatic stories. Somewhere in the kitchen, Jenny was locked in a passionate debate with a caterer over the proper way to slice strawberries. Glasses clinked. The piano in the sitting room played something quiet and lovely.

And then she heard them.

Footsteps.

The rhythm of them, the quiet weight, was as familiar as her own heartbeat.

John.

His arms slid gently around her waist from behind, drawing her close against him. His chin found her shoulder, and his lips pressed a kiss just beneath it.

"Why are you out here all alone?" he murmured, his breath warm against her skin.

She smiled, leaning back into him. "Just needed a minute."

"You're not thinking of running again, I hope."

She let out a soft laugh. "Not a chance. You're stuck with me."

"I was stuck from the moment I saw you in that airport," he said quietly, his voice thick with memory. "You just didn't know it yet."

She turned in his arms to face him, her eyes glowing with tenderness. "I love you," she whispered. "More than I ever thought was possible."

He kissed her then—slowly, deeply—like the world might stop for them and wouldn't dare rush them.

When they pulled apart, he brushed a lock of hair from her cheek and smiled. "Happy birthday, my love."

"Thank you," she said, her voice a soft murmur. "The party's beautiful. But if I'm honest…"

"Hmm?" His brows lifted.

"I wish we were alone."

He tilted his head, intrigued. "Why?"

Grace took his hand, placed it over her heart.

"Because there's something I need to tell you," she said, her voice trembling slightly. "And I don't think I can wait a minute longer."

John's fingers curled around hers, warm and sure.

"And what might that be, Mrs. Sneddon?" he asked, his voice low and playful.

Grace laughed, her smile lighting up her whole face. "I like the sound of that."

"So do I," he murmured, brushing his lips over her knuckles. Then her expression shifted—softer now, more serious.

Her gaze searched his. "What can I do to make *you* happy, John?"

He looked at her for a long moment, the breeze lifting strands of her hair, the late afternoon sun gilding her in gold. His answer was quiet but firm, spoken like a vow.

"You make me happy just by being here with me. That's all I'll ever need."

Her breath caught. "Really?"

"Grace," he said, drawing her closer, "you could never do more for me than just love me. I don't need grand gestures. I just need you. Your laugh in the morning. Your hand in mine. Your voice when you say my name. That's happiness."

She blinked back tears, her fingers tightening around his.

"Good," she whispered. "Because I have something to tell you. Something I've been waiting for the right moment to say."

His eyes sharpened, the playful smile fading into something far deeper. "Tell me."

She guided his hand lower, to the soft swell just beneath her waist—subtle, barely there, but growing. Her heart thundered in her chest.

"I'm pregnant, John."

For a moment, he simply stared. No sound. No movement. Just the wild, stunned joy beginning to blaze in his eyes.

Then he exhaled like a man who'd been holding his breath for a lifetime, and pulled her into his arms, lifting her clean off the ground as he buried his face in her neck.

"Oh, Grace," he breathed. "You've just made me happier than I thought possible."

She laughed, tears of relief and joy slipping down her cheeks.

"I was hoping you'd say that."

He kissed her again, fierce and tender, holding her as if the whole world had been waiting for this moment to arrive.

And maybe it had.

They stood together for a long moment in the golden hush of spring, wrapped in each other's arms, hearts full.

Then Grace leaned back, her eyes shining with mischief and tenderness.

"Let's keep it just ours… for a little while," she whispered. "Just you and me."

John nodded, his hand drifting once more over her belly in silent wonder. "Our secret," he agreed. "But it's the best one I've ever been part of."

Fingers entwined, they turned back toward the house—toward the voices, the music, the warmth of family and friends waiting inside. The great doors of Rosewood stood open, spilling light and laughter into the garden.

And as they crossed the threshold together—heart to heart, hand in hand—Grace knew something with absolute certainty.

She had finally come home.

Not just to Rosewood.

But to love.

To him.

To the life that had waited for her...

Until she loved him.

The End

Vows of Vengeance

Alison Reid

A complete standalone romance

Previously published individually

Chapter One

Angela watched her father with a tightening dread as he paced the length of his study, back and forth like a caged predator. The Persian rug muffled his steps, but every turn was sharp, every pivot a jolt of barely contained rage. His broad shoulders, once square and commanding, were hunched now, his breath coming in ragged bursts. The veins at his temples stood out against skin flushed a furious red. He looked less like the titan who had built an empire and more like a man driving himself toward collapse.

Her heart clenched. He was killing himself with this fear—this obsession—and she could do nothing to stop it.

At first, she had dismissed his dread as paranoia, the fevered imaginings of a man who had fought too long and trusted too little. But four years had taught her otherwise. His terror had roots, deep and poisoned. Lincoln Spokes had vowed to destroy Marsden Enterprises, and he was keeping that vow with cold, methodical cruelty.

It wasn't a swift strike—it was a slow, merciless strangulation. Piece by piece, Lincoln had dismantled them, a master at a chessboard tightening his trap with elegant precision. Each move was deliberate, inevitable. Angela could still see his eyes—those icy grey eyes—haunting her like some unfeeling deity, orchestrating their ruin without lifting a finger.

"Five years," Kurt Marsden muttered at last. He stopped mid-stride, his voice a low growl ripped raw by bitterness. His gaze flicked to her where she stood by his desk, hands knotted helplessly. "Five years to the day. He promised me—promised—and last night the stock was suspended." He gave a jagged, broken laugh that held no humour. "By tonight, liquidation. Everything gone. Everything."

He turned to the tall windows and stared out at the manicured garden below—the garden he had once stood in proudly when this house was first built nearly two decades ago. Then, it had been a monument to triumph, a declaration that he had arrived. Now it was only another possession fated to fall with the rest. How long before even the roof over their heads was gone?

Angela's throat closed, the ache of despair choking her breath. She had tried—God knew she had tried—to shield him, to take the weight on her own shoulders. But she had been powerless against Lincoln Spokes. Worse than powerless—she had been a pawn in his hands, a weapon wielded against the very man she loved most.

Her father's once-straight back sagged beneath an invisible burden. His hair, nearly white now, bore testimony to years of unrelenting battle. He had fought, yes—but Lincoln had known he would. He had planned for it, counted on it. And so, he had tightened the noose slowly, with merciless patience, until resistance itself became torture.

The final blow would fall today, and Lincoln would not even dignify it with his presence. Angela could picture him too clearly—seated in his glass tower, his name emblazoned across the skyline, receiving the news with no more than a flicker of satisfaction. He would crumple the report in those long, ruthless fingers, discard it, and move on—his vengeance achieved.

Angela's heart broke as she looked at her father. He was already fading, hollowed out by years of attrition. Tomorrow's headlines would not only announce the end of Marsden Enterprises; they would announce the end of him.

He had already handed the reins to her—not formally, but by absence. He had not crossed the threshold of his empire in months. Every crisis, every boardroom clash, every futile skirmish for survival had fallen squarely to her. One day in that office, one face-to-face confrontation with ruin, might kill him outright.

"I'll have to go," she said softly, her voice steadier than she felt. "Today of all days, I should be there."

"There'll be no miracle, Angela." His reply was flat, bitter. His eyes stayed fixed on the garden, but she saw the reflection of his anguish in the glass. "Miracles are for Lincoln Spokes. He doesn't leave any for the rest of us. There's nothing you can do."

"I know," she whispered. Her chin lifted, stubborn even through the ache in her chest. "But I'll still be there."

She left before he could answer.

Outside, the morning sun blazed too brightly, careless, and cruel against the shadows inside their house. Her father remained at the window, a solitary silhouette, rigid and unmoving. He didn't even glance down as she slid into her car.

It would take a miracle to save them—and miracles, Angela knew too well, were not gifts. Not when Lincoln Spokes was involved. He manufactured miracles only for himself—and twisted them into nightmares for everyone else.

Angela carried the scars to prove it.

"The sharp click of her heels echoed like gunfire as she crossed the marble lobby of Marsden Enterprises. Maria Belle looked up the instant Angela pushed through the revolving doors; her lined face already creased with worry.

"You've got two meetings this morning," Maria announced briskly, though her voice carried an edge of protectiveness. "Jenkins' manager is coming in after lunch, and the bank called—sending a man this afternoon. And the phone—" she lifted a page-long list of names, each one scrawled in Maria's precise hand "—it hasn't stopped all morning."

"Are you surprised?" Angela leaned against the desk, scanning the names with a weariness that seemed etched into her very bones.

Maria's face softened. She had served as Kurt Marsden's secretary for twenty years, had seen victories and defeats both, but this defeat was different. This one was final. Everyone knew it. It was only a matter of waiting for the axe to fall.

Angela caught her expression and forced a faint smile. "Thank you, Maria. Soon it won't matter. We'll just be another casualty in the business pages."

"There's nothing you can do?" Maria's voice dropped, hushed, almost fearful—as if even speaking hope aloud might tempt fate's wrath.

Angela tilted her head, her dark eyes flashing with bitter humour. "I could stand on the roof and scream. Maybe throw a chair through a few windows. Care to help?"

It startled a laugh out of both of them, quick and fragile, but real. Even at the edge of ruin, people could still laugh. Angela straightened and walked down the long corridor toward her office, the defiant rhythm of her heels echoing against the silence.

Maria watched her go, her heart twisting. Seven years ago, Angela had walked in here for the first time—glossy black hair, bright eager smile, a girl untouched by the weight of empire. That brightness hadn't left her completely, but now it burned under strain, bowed by burdens no young woman should bear. Kurt should have been here, shielding her, fighting to the bitter end. Instead, Angela carried it alone.

The shrill ring of the phone shattered Maria's thoughts. She snatched it up, her tone clipped, her expression hard. "There will be no statement to the media today. No, the chairman is not available." She slammed the receiver down, her lips pressed into a thin, angry line. Vultures. That's all they were. If she could do nothing else, she would guard Angela from them. It was the last loyalty she had to give.

Behind the heavy door of her office, Angela sagged into the chair. Her father's name still gleamed in gold letters on the outer door—**Kurt Marsden, Chairman**—but it was hers now in every way that mattered. Hers to hold. Hers to lose.

She closed her eyes. Every conversation, every meeting was the same. Suppliers clawing for security. Banks tightening the noose. The stock suspended. End of story.

And yet… a flicker of relief whispered through her. Perhaps the slow death was worse than the end.

Her gaze fell on her hands, pale and steady despite the storm inside her. The faint glimmer of the wedding band caught her attention. A cruel, silent reminder. She had never taken it off. It wasn't a token of love—it was a brand. A brand that bound her, body, and soul, to the man who was destroying them.

Lincoln Spokes.

Angela's breath hitched. She had been powerless against him all these years, but not today. Not anymore.

She reached for the phone, her voice crisp, cutting through hesitation. "Maria. Cancel my appointments for the day. I have something to do."

A pause. Then Maria's anxious voice: "Are you going to see—? Shall I come with you?"

"You can't do anything," Angela said sharply, then softened, her words edged with steel. "And neither can I. But I'll settle this today. I won't win—" her voice hardened, her eyes glittering with defiance "—but I'll be damned if I go down whimpering."

Maria's laugh was short, almost fierce. "That's my girl. Leave the office to me. And... let me know if—"

"It will be bad news," Angela cut her off, her voice brittle, glass-edged. "But at least it will be news. We've died slowly long enough."

She slipped out the back, moving fast. If reporters were camped at the front, they would wait in vain. She had no more words for them. No more silence, either.

The Uber dropped her across from a building that dominated the street, a tower of glass and stone that dwarfed its neighbours. The name blazed above the entrance in six-foot gold letters, bright enough to sear her eyes.

Spokes.

One word. One man. A monument to vengeance.

Angela clenched her teeth and strode across the street. The glass doors whispered open, spilling her into a foyer of polished marble and chrome. She did not pause.

"I wish to see Mr. Spokes."

Her voice carried across the hushed reception, calm, unwavering. The young woman behind the desk blinked, startled.

"Unless you have an appointment—"

"I don't." Angela's gaze did not waver. "But I intend to see him. Call his office."

"I'm sorry, that's—"

Angela was already walking. The receptionist darted forward, but the elevator doors closed before she could stop her.

When they opened on the third floor, Angela stepped out to find the woman flushed and breathless, clearly having raced the stairs to intercept her.

"You cannot see Mr. Spokes!" the girl panted, panic edging her voice.

Angela smiled, cool and sharp. "Yes, I can. I don't need an appointment. I'm his wife."

The words dropped like a stone in the silence.

Two men turned at once from outside a vast office door. One—tall, dark-haired, impeccably dressed—locked eyes with her. For a heartbeat, his mouth hardened, his gaze steely. Then, almost imperceptibly, the corners of his lips twitched, a slow, teasing smile forming, and something flickered in his eyes—wanting, sharp and unmistakable, before he regained his composure.

"Hello, Angela," Lincoln Spokes said softly. His voice was velvet over steel. "Come right in."

He dismissed his companion with a flick of his hand, silenced the flustered receptionist with a single cutting glance, and gestured her inside with smooth authority. Angela walked past him without faltering, chin lifted high, her heartbeat a wild hammer in her chest. He closed the door, and the sound was final, sealing them in.

"So," he said, crossing to his desk with measured grace, "what can I do for you, Angela?"

"Nothing." The word spat from her lips like poison. "I'm not in the habit of begging."

His eyes glinted with amusement. "No. You've changed. The shy girl is gone. An efficient, professional woman now." His gaze sharpened, voice dropping to a silken murmur. "I've kept my eyes on you."

When he turned fully to face her, the impact nearly broke her composure. He was unchanged—and yet utterly different. The same tall, lithe figure, the same dark hair gleaming with vitality. But the warmth, the teasing laughter she remembered, was gone. His grey eyes were as cold as frost. His mouth, once quick to smile, was a firm, merciless line. Handsome, yes—but honed to steel, stripped of humanity.

Angela's breath caught, but she masked it with fury. "All you know about me is the wreckage you've left in your wake."

"There is no wreckage," he replied coldly. "Chaos is not my way. I plan."

"You plan very well," she flung back. "Marsden Enterprises is finished."

"Not quite," he murmured, his eyes locking onto hers with hypnotic intensity. "The firm is still viable."

He lowered himself into his chair with unhurried elegance, gesturing to the seat opposite. It was an invitation to a game he had already won.

"But you're not here to beg. So, tell me, Angela—what do you want?"

"Nothing!" Her fury cracked, raw and trembling. "We surrender. Strike now, make the final cut."

He leaned back, studying her with slow, deliberate appraisal. His gaze traced the fall of her hair, the lines of her suit, the blaze in her eyes. His silence stretched until she wanted to scream.

"You were never included in this," he said at last, voice low.

"No?" Her scorn snapped. "I was a pawn. A weapon. That sounds like inclusion to me. And now? You've won. This will kill my father, Lincoln. That's what you wanted."

"I do not!" His denial tore from him, harsh, unguarded. For one blazing instant, fury flared through his icy composure, his eyes alight like fire over ice. "But if I did, I'd be justified. Kurt Marsden killed my father—and my mother."

Angela gasped, her knees buckling. She sank into the chair, eyes wide with horror.

"No… no, you're lying—"

"Lying?" His laugh was jagged, brittle, like breaking glass. "Ask him, Angela. Ask the great Kurt Marsden why my parents lie in their graves. Remind him of John and Kathleen Spokes—my parents. Did you think I burned your world down because you walked away? Did you imagine you were ever that powerful?"

"No…" Angela whispered, shaking her head violently. "I knew I wasn't important to you. You proved that when you said nothing when I left."

For the briefest moment, a flicker of regret—pain—crossed his features, so fleeting she thought she'd imagined it.

"You would have told me about your parents before. When we were married—you would have—"

"You were never part of this." His gaze was relentless, pinning her in place. "This was always about him. I wanted you—so I took you. And as for our marriage…" His mouth curved into a smile that wasn't a smile. "We are still married. You proved it yourself the moment you walked in and announced it to everyone."

Angela's voice wavered, almost pleading. "My father is not a villain."

"The law will never touch him," Lincoln said coldly. "He was too clever. Too careful. But I never needed the law. Five years, Angela. Promises to keep. Promises fulfilled. And now I have him exactly where I want him—my hands around his throat."

Angela staggered to her feet, trembling. She didn't recognise this man. She had never truly known him. And yet... this was the man she had once loved—helplessly, disastrously.

Fear crashed over her—not for herself, but for her father. Lincoln was far from finished. His vengeance was far from complete.

The room tilted, her world spinning. With one final, horrified glance at him, Angela collapsed, fainting into darkness.

Chapter Two

When Angela came round, she found herself cradled against Lincoln's chest, his arms hard and unyielding, as if iron had been forged into flesh. The sharp scent of his cologne—woody, dark, threaded with the faintest spice—filled her lungs, a fragrance so achingly familiar it jolted through her like a half-forgotten melody. For a disorienting heartbeat, memory and reality blurred. She was back in the days when those arms were sanctuary, not a prison.

But then her senses caught up, and the illusion shattered.

The receptionist hurried breathlessly into the office, her eyes widening at the sight before her.

"She fainted," Lincoln said curtly, his voice clipped with authority, leaving no room for question or interference. "I'll take her to the first aid room."

"I am all right," Angela whispered, her pride stung, though her voice came out frail and strained. "You can put me down now. Thank you."

Lincoln's mouth curved in a hard, humourless line. "Such gentle manners," he muttered with quiet disdain, his eyes narrowing. "You always did have that sweet nature. But you're not all right, Angela. Contrary to popular fiction, people don't faint from disgust or melodrama. You fainted because you're unwell. And you will lie down in the first aid room."

She knew him too well to argue. Resistance would only amuse him—or worse, provoke him. Still, a shiver coursed through her. These were the same arms that had once felt like home, arms she had longed for with every breath. Now their strength only terrified her.

"I can walk," she tried again, her voice thin with stubborn dignity.

He didn't even glance at her. His grip tightened, possessive and inexorable, and with long, purposeful strides he pushed through a side door, carrying her into a small, clinical room that smelled faintly of antiseptic and starch.

The narrow bed gave a protesting creak as he laid her down, his touch brusque but careful, the controlled efficiency of a man who always got what he wanted.

The receptionist swooped in at once, brisk yet oddly tender, her eagerness to serve him filling the air.

"See that she stays here," Lincoln ordered, his tone low, unchallengeable. The young woman nodded, obedience instant, as though hardwired. Angela watched him turn on his heel and stride out without a backward glance, his tall frame radiating cold authority.

"A little rest," the receptionist murmured, kneeling to unfasten Angela's shoes with quick, competent hands. Angela tried to push herself up, but the woman pressed her gently back, firm as steel beneath her politeness.

"Don't worry—he won't contemplate killing you yet." The words slipped out, half-jest, half-warning.

Angela froze, staring, breath caught in disbelief.

"Just rest, Mrs. Spokes," the girl urged, tugging lightly at Angela's jacket until it slipped free. Her voice dropped to an almost pleading note. "It will save a lot of trouble. You do look pale."

Pale. Fainting. Helpless. The words pricked like needles. Angela subsided reluctantly, unease stirring beneath her ribs. How much did they know in these offices? Did whispers about her—Lincoln's estranged wife—already curl through the corridors like smoke? Did they murmur about her father's crumbling empire, slowly being throttled by Lincoln's merciless grip? Her name was already on their lips; what else might they pass from desk to desk?

Soon she was lying beneath cool sheets, clad only in lace bra and panties, the thin coverlet drawn up to her chin. The receptionist sighed with relief, as though accomplishing some dangerous task.

"Just sleep," she said softly. "If you're resting when he returns, he'll be satisfied."

Angela closed her eyes—not from trust, but to shut out the girl's insipid voice. Lincoln wouldn't return; she told herself fiercely. He would already have dismissed the moment of weakness, flicking it from memory like ash from a cigar. Yet even in denial, her body betrayed her. Light-headed, trembling, her hollow stomach twisting, she could not deny the truth. Lincoln had been right. It wasn't melodrama or grief that had felled her—it was simple starvation. She had eaten almost nothing in days. Her body had surrendered when her will refused.

Exhaustion dragged her down, stealing her choice.

When her eyes fluttered open again, the first thing she saw was Lincoln. He stood like a sentinel beside the bed—lean, immovable, grey eyes burning with an intensity that startled her more than his presence itself.

"When did you last eat?" His voice was clipped, frigid. "And don't bother lying. Your skin is nearly translucent. You've lost weight—too much. You're withering."

Angela pushed weakly against the pillows, trying to rise. His hand was there instantly, pressing her back with quiet force.

"Answer me." His tone was low, edged with steel.

"I—I don't know," she faltered. "Yesterday… perhaps lunch. I'm not sure."

His mouth hardened. "You'll eat now."

His arm came around her back, sitting her upright with brisk efficiency. She had no choice, no room to refuse. "Get dressed. Soup is waiting. After starving yourself, it's all your body can manage."

"I don't need your help," Angela snapped, clutching the sheet to her throat like armour. "I can feed myself—in my own time. Leave, and I'll dress."

Lincoln's eyes flashed. His mouth twisted, cruel and beautiful. In a single movement he tore the sheet from her grasp, his voice merciless.

"Get dressed," he snapped, steel in his tone. "Don't play at modesty. I've seen—and touched—every inch of you. You'll eat before you leave this building, Angela. That's not a request.

She lifted her chin, summoning defiance even as her body trembled. "Then watch me," she said, pulling her blouse on with deliberate slowness. "I'll eat—but not because you order it. Because I refuse to let you think I'm weak."

Once she was dressed, she straightened her shoulders and, summoning every ounce of defiance, said, "I'm ready."

He turned, his gaze sweeping over her with a measured, almost predatory appraisal, before he opened the door and led the way.

The dining room was small, luxuriously appointed, hushed as a chapel. A steaming bowl of soup sat waiting, fragrant and simple. Angela's eyes darted around—the thick carpet, the polished wood, the oppressive stillness.

"The executive dining room," Lincoln said, his voice low and grim. "Put in after you fled. Private. Secure. You'll eat here. No interruptions."

Who would dare, she thought bitterly, with him sitting there like judge and executioner?

He seated himself opposite, his gaze never wavering. Her fingers trembled as she lifted the spoon. Her stomach knotted.

"I—I can't," she whispered, the words raw.

"You'll eat," he ordered. "Refuse, and I'll keep you here until you do."

Angela's hand trembled on the spoon, but her voice cut through the silence. "Then you'll starve me and cage me. Congratulations, Lincoln—you'll finally make me what you've always wanted. A prisoner."

His jaw clenched. For a heartbeat, his eyes softened—as though the word prisoner pierced deeper than she knew—before his mask snapped back into place.

"Eat," he cut in, final. His eyes glinted, cruel amusement sparking. "If my presence ruins your appetite, I'll leave the room. But don't think of escape." His smile was cold, razor-sharp. "You announced yourself as my wife in front of half my staff. The whole building is buzzing. If you try to leave, I'll know before you reach the lift."

He rose abruptly, his chair scraping softly against the carpet, and strode out. The door closed with a quiet finality that echoed louder than any slam.

Angela stared after him, her heart thudding. She had thought she was here to confront him. To reclaim something. But she saw it now—she had given him power instead.

She had reminded Lincoln Spokes that she still existed in his world.

And if he could use her, he would.

Turning her attention to the soup, she forced herself to eat. Without his unrelenting gaze upon her, the sharp gnawing of hunger could no longer be ignored. The broth was rich and warming, the rolls soft and fragrant. She buttered one with trembling hands and bit into it hungrily. It was the first real food she had managed in days. She hadn't lied to Lincoln; she truly could not recall when she had last eaten. Her life had blurred into a restless cycle of bitter coffee—morning, noon, and night—and now, at last, her body seized on the nourishment like a drowning woman clinging to driftwood.

When she set her spoon down at last, the door opened again with his usual impeccable timing. Lincoln stepped inside, composed, and deliberate, as though he had been waiting for this exact moment. Angela rose to her feet, summoning defiance like a shield.

"I've eaten—as ordered. And now I'll leave," she said tightly.

"And why not?" Lincoln drawled, the mocking edge in his voice cutting deep. "After all, you've accomplished what you came for."

Her eyes flashed. "What do you mean?" Anger surged hot in her veins. Was he implying she had come here to faint? To wring sympathy from him? The idea was absurd. Lincoln Spokes had no sympathy left in him—certainly not for her.

"You came to announce surrender." His glance was mocking, ironical, and when her cheeks burned, he arched a brow. "Correction—you came to announce your father's surrender."

"My father and I are in this together," she retorted sharply, her voice crisp with pride.

His eyes narrowed, hardening like steel, a dangerous glitter igniting in the cold grey depths.

"Oh, no, you're not," he rasped, the contempt rough in his voice. "You've never been in it. You may have reinvented yourself as a brisk, competent career woman, but believe me, you haven't even scraped the surface of what it means to fight this kind of war. You've never so much as dipped those beautiful toes of yours in the mud."

Her throat tightened. "Not even when I was married to you?" she demanded, each word clipped and fierce.

For a moment, he stared at her with raw hostility, his expression so dark it winded her. Then his lips curved in a slow, cold smile, humourless and cruel.

"Your feet barely touched the floor," he said softly, derisively. "You were in my arms most of the time. Memory can be so… elusive."

The barb struck deep, but before she could recover her voice, he turned and opened the door with a commanding sweep.

"Time to go, Angela," he said, his tone a mixture of dismissal and possession. "This way."

It became clear almost at once that Lincoln had no intention of letting her slip away quietly. He was taking her outside, deliberately, and that meant more time for his cutting remarks. Angela set her lips firmly, her spine rigid, and walked beside him with forced composure. Neither spoke as the lift descended, silence pressing around them like a weight. It was only when he pushed open the glass doors to the street that she thought of escape.

"I didn't bring my car," she said quickly. "I'll call an Uber."

"You won't need one," Lincoln replied implacably, as if the matter were already settled. "I intended to take you back myself."

At that moment, a sleek black Jaguar slid to the curb with effortless precision. A sharp-looking youth sprang out, opened the passenger door with a deferential smile, and within seconds Lincoln was behind the wheel. The movement was so smooth, so practiced, that Angela found herself seated beside him before she could even protest.

"This isn't necessary," she murmured, her voice low but steady.

"I decided it is," Lincoln said softly, his eyes fixed on the road as the Jaguar merged into traffic like a predator slipping through shadows. "It's been nearly five years since I last drove past Marsden's offices. Seeing them again will be… interesting."

"The place will be yours soon," Angela whispered, her throat tightening with emotion.

And then she could say no more. The ache of memory swept over her, stealing her voice. Being in this car with Lincoln was too much. It was the same make, the same sleek leather-and-steel masculinity that clung to him, even the same faint, clean aftershave she had once breathed in with something close to adoration. The scent twisted inside her now, pulling her back into memories she wanted desperately to bury—like a pressed flower whose fragrance lingered long after the bloom was gone.

"I don't want the place," Lincoln rasped suddenly, his voice rough as gravel. "I want the man. And I've almost got him."

"You've already got him," Angela whispered hoarsely. "If you could only see him now—"

"I've no desire to see him!" Lincoln cut in savagely. His hands tightened on the wheel, knuckles whitening, and she darted a frightened glance at his hard profile. His jaw was granite, his eyes glinting with a fury that chilled her like lightning against her skin. She turned away swiftly, staring down at her clenched hands, trying to keep her breathing steady.

No words would change him. She knew that now. His hatred of Marsden was all-consuming, a fire that had burned too long to be extinguished. It had always been there—she had simply been too young, too dazzled, to recognise it.

"Here we are." His voice broke into her thoughts as the Jaguar purred to a halt before the modest Marsden offices. Compared to Spokes' gleaming tower, the building looked small, worn, unremarkable. Lincoln's gaze flicked over it with cool disdain, dismissing it as beneath his notice.

"Thank you," Angela whispered automatically, though the word felt hollow on her tongue. Relief shuddered through her—until his hand closed on her arm. His fingers bit cruelly into the wool of her jacket, pinning her with a grip that was part warning, part punishment.

"Harden up, Angela," he rasped, his grip bruising her arm. "Any other woman would've slapped me by now. But you... you whisper, *'thank you'*. Sweetness doesn't touch me anymore."

She wrenched free, chin high, her voice steel-edged. "Then perhaps you're the one who's hardened too much. Strip me of everything if you like, Lincoln, but you'll never strip me of hope. That's mine—not yours."

For the briefest instant, something flickered in his eyes—pain? Regret? —before he slammed the wall back into place. She flung open the car door, stepping out with swift, sharp resolve, the slam echoing like a gunshot in the quiet street. Without a backward glance, she strode toward the building—her family's pride, soon to be swallowed by Lincoln's empire. Every step was defiance, though her heart thudded painfully in her chest.

She didn't turn, not even once. Long before she reached the steps, the low, predatory purr of the Jaguar drifted behind her, merging seamlessly into traffic. If her words had pricked his temper, his driving betrayed nothing. Lincoln remained, as always: untouchable. Imperious. Cold.

"Did you see him?"

Maria's voice broke across her thoughts as Angela stepped onto her own floor. She was waiting, eyes wide with questions, watching Angela head for her office.

"Yes," Angela said dully. "I told you not to hope. There was nothing to hope for."

"I just thought—because you were with him so long—" Maria faltered, her words hesitant, her face bright with anxious expectation.

"I fainted," Angela muttered, brushing past her. "He brought me back."

"And?" The note of alarm in Maria's voice sharpened at once. The idea of Angela collapsing clearly unsettled her, but Angela had no wish to linger.

"And nothing. It was a courtesy, that's all."

She didn't slow down. She walked past, her eyes fixed straight ahead, and Maria could do nothing but stare after her.

Maria knew the truth—or thought she did. She had been there at the wedding, after all. She had watched the two of them, their union the kind of thing that made strangers catch their breath. Angela, radiant and heartbreakingly young. Lincoln, powerful and protective, his very presence making the air vibrate. Even in a crowded church, they had seemed to exist in a world of their own, wrapped in a glow that had looked, to all who watched, like love.

And yet it had all been smoke. A shimmering illusion. The glow had died; the dream had shattered—and Angela was left to bear the ruin.

Maria clenched her hands at her sides, a fierce anger burning through her helplessness. How did Angela endure it, day after day? How did she still lift her chin, still walk through these halls as if she were not carrying the ashes of her own heart?

Chapter Three

With her appointments cancelled for the rest of the day, Angela found herself adrift, restless in a silence that felt oppressive. It was useless to work at anything—what future could there possibly be when the very foundation beneath her feet was crumbling? Every number on every report was meaningless, every plan hollow. Even if she walked through to another part of the building, she knew the eyes would follow her: anxious, pitying, questioning. People would wonder if she knew something they did not. Some had already left, accepting offers elsewhere, choosing survival over loyalty. Those who remained did so only because of her, their faith in her keeping them tethered. That loyalty was a weight pressing into her chest, a burden she could neither honour nor relieve.

She couldn't shield them. She couldn't even shield her own father.

And she could not yet go home. If she arrived earlier than expected, the moment her father saw her car his anxiety would ignite—he would know something was wrong, and she could not bear to add to his worry.

Restlessness drove her to pacing. Finally, she decided on coffee, though she doubted she could drink it. The long corridor muffled her footsteps, the thick carpet swallowing sound. This was the executive wing—quiet now, too quiet. At the far end, through a glass door, lay the open-plan office where Maria had her desk. Once, this place had thrummed with life. It had never matched the sheer opulence of the Spokes building, but it had been vibrant, successful—the air itself scented with money and ambition.

Now, the stillness carried an almost funereal air. The vice-chairman's office stood empty, its blinds drawn, its silence accusatory. He had left at the first opportunity, slipping away before the word "redundant" could be branded across his nameplate. That office had once been intended for Angela. A steppingstone. Her father had made that clear. But she had bypassed it, taking on the role of chairman far too soon—years before her father's retirement, years before she was ready. She had worn the title like armour, but it had always hung too heavy on her slender frame.

The boardroom loomed across the corridor as she returned with her untouched coffee. One glance at the nameplate on the door was enough to make her burn with memory. She turned away quickly, back into her office, shutting the door as though to keep the past from flooding in.

But memory was not so easily locked out.

She could still hear his voice echoing there—the first time she had heard it. Harsh. Cutting. Enough to stop her mid-step, her pulse faltering in her throat. She hadn't had time to retreat to the safety of Maria's chatter or the clamouring telephones beyond. Had she managed it—had she hidden herself in the familiar bustle—he would never have seen her. And if he had never seen her, she would not now be drowning in this guilt that refused to let her breathe.

She had been nineteen then. Slender, willowy, her long black hair a curtain around her pale face, her green eyes unguarded, unworldly. She had been working for her father since leaving school—a path never questioned. Kurt Marsden had always made it clear: she would work for him, then with him, then one day take the firm into her hands. She would be his heir, his legacy. Angela, obedient and soft-spoken, had never thought to defy him.

But even if she had, it would have been useless. Defiance was not something one used on Kurt Marsden. He had clawed his way to the top, a self-made man in property and development, ruthless and relentless. Marsden Enterprises had been built on the sharpness of his eye for opportunity and the iron of his will. He expected the same iron from her. He envisioned a daughter forged into a businesswoman of power, hardened by experience, beginning at the bottom, learning the grind, and rising to the top with scars to prove her worth.

At nineteen, Angela had been at that bottom, and strangely—innocently—she had loved it. She had delighted in the gossip of the outer office, the clatter of keyboards, the scolding but protective oversight of Maria Belle, her father's secretary. She had run errands, lugged heavy files, fetched endless coffees, printed invoices with stiff fingers. She had embraced the work as though it were a game, refusing to think too far ahead to the daunting future her father had mapped for her. She had been happy in her small corner, shielded from responsibility, safe in her youth.

And then—she had met him.

Lincoln Spokes. Thirty-one. Handsome, alarming. A man with sharp edges, with fury burning in his eyes and authority radiating from every line of him. He had been like no one she had ever encountered—harder, darker, more dangerous than her sheltered world had prepared her for. The air between them had cracked like lightning, violent and shocking, even in that accidental moment.

It had been sheer chance. A matter of minutes, perhaps seconds, and their paths might never have crossed.

But they had.

And in that instant, her fate had changed.

If she had slipped away unnoticed, he would never have known her face, her name, her existence. Her life might have remained her own. She would have been safe.

Instead—she had been seen. And nothing had been safe since.

It had been a Monday morning—the kind that always seemed to begin at a run. The week ahead promised endless pressure, and Angela was already behind. The board meeting that afternoon was set, the long polished table gleaming beneath the weight of carefully laid papers and crystal glasses, Maria directing every detail with brisk efficiency. Now Angela hurried through the corridor with an armful of files—too many to carry at once, but there was no time to go back for more. Her own desk still held a mountain of work, and she was determined to finish it before lunch.

The files wobbled precariously, stacked so high she could barely see over them. She pushed her way through the heavy swing-door at the end of the corridor, bracing the weight against her chest. That was when she heard it—the voice.

Harsh. Dark. Furious.

"Keep looking over your shoulder," it bit out, vibrating through the silence like a blade against steel. "Because I'll always be there. And I'll get you. Five years—that's how long it will take. Start counting now, and remember this—your fate, and my promise."

The slam of her father's office door followed a violent crack that echoed down the corridor. Angela flinched, instinctively flattening herself against the wall, the files slipping from her grip. The footsteps that thundered toward her sounded like a storm breaking loose—fast, unstoppable, blinding in their rage.

He didn't even see her. He struck her shoulder as he passed, the jolt sending her stumbling, and the files cascaded to the carpet like a broken pack of cards. Papers scattered everywhere, fluttering across the thick pile, and he kept going, carried forward by sheer fury.

It was only when he reached the far end of the corridor, hand already on the door, that something seemed to pierce through his anger. He stopped. Turned. And saw her.

Angela was on her knees, her slender arms reaching quickly, desperately, trying to bring the files back into some kind of order. She didn't glance up, didn't curse, didn't even frown. She simply worked, intent on the task, as though it were natural for him to sweep through her life like a storm and leave wreckage behind.

Something shifted in his expression. Curiosity, perhaps. Amusement. An unguarded flicker of surprise.

He walked back. Stood over her. For a moment, she felt the weight of him, the force of his presence, before she lifted her eyes.

They were green. Wide. Startled. The clearest, most extraordinary green he had ever seen.

"'I'm sorry," he said at last; his voice softened into something almost rueful. "I was too damned annoyed to see you."

He crouched down beside her, reaching for a file, but she shook her head quickly, a wary smile ghosting her lips.

"It's all right. You can't help, really—they've got to be in order."

"Alphabetical?" His mouth tilted faintly, teasing.

"No, priority," she explained, her voice low. Then, with a faint blush warming her cheeks, she added, "I'm afraid they're private."

There was a brief silence. Her embarrassment at telling him to leave her work alone was plain, written in the delicate flush across her skin. He straightened, studying her from above, his mouth curving with something like amusement.

"Sorry again, in that case." He gave her a short nod, then turned as if to go.

Angela bent quickly to the files, determined not to look up again. Her heart was beating too fast, too loud. He was the most handsome man she had ever seen—how could anyone look so furious one moment and then so unexpectedly gentle the next? His hair was dark, his face deeply tanned, and those eyes—grey, sharp, flashing with something she could not name. Power radiated from him, the kind of authority that filled the air without needing words.

She dared one small glance as he reached the door. He had not left. His hand rested on the handle, but he was still watching her.

"What's your name?" His voice was softer now, though it carried the same command as before.

Angela hesitated only a heartbeat. Telling him seemed the most natural thing in the world.

"Angela. Angela Marsden."

His eyes narrowed, flaring over her in one swift sweep—from the shining black fall of her hair to the soft pink jumper, the dark skirt sprinkled with tiny flowers spreading around her as she knelt. Something in his gaze made her pulse stumble—half alarm, half something she couldn't quite name, a strange thrill that prickled along her skin.

She looked away, her fingers trembling as she gathered another file. He gave a low, quiet laugh, the sound curling down her spine like smoke.

"Goodbye, Angela Marsden."

She didn't have time to answer because, when she looked up, he had already gone. The heavy door at the end of the corridor swung shut with a final thud, and the sound echoed like a sigh of loss. Angela's own sigh followed as she gathered the scattered files into her arms and pushed herself to her feet.

Disappointment settled over her more strongly than it should have. She didn't even know his name, and yet something about the suddenness of his absence left her feeling oddly bereft. She wondered who he was, but knew there was little chance she would find out.

Strangely, she didn't dwell on the words she had overheard as she came through the door—his furious threat, the dark promise hurled at her father. Instead, her mind clung to him—the tall, powerful man whose anger had melted so quickly into warmth when he had spoken to her. She should have been disturbed, even frightened, but she wasn't. She was far too dreamily impressed.

Two days later, she saw him again.

Angela always drove herself to work. Her father insisted it was best to show everyone that being Kurt Marsden's daughter brought no special privileges. She didn't mind; she enjoyed the independence, the small thrill of steering her own car through the city streets, arriving at the office as if she belonged to the world of business in her own right. It gave her a quiet sense of power, though she rarely admitted it.

Still, since Monday, she had caught herself drifting into daydreams, chastising herself whenever his image returned. The grey eyes. The voice that lingered like smoke in her memory. A fantasy, she told herself firmly. Nothing more.

But on Wednesday evening, leaving the building with her bag tucked neatly under her arm, fantasy became reality.

She had barely reached her car when a quiet voice stopped her in her tracks.

"Hello, Angela Marsden."

Her heart lurched violently. That voice. She would have known it anywhere. Slowly, almost unwillingly, she turned.

He was there. Lincoln. Leaning casually against a dark Jaguar, the very image of power and ease, his grey eyes catching the fading light and fixing on her as if she were the only person in the world.

For a moment it was as though she were walking in a dream. She hadn't forgotten him for a single heartbeat since their first encounter, and now—impossibly—he was here.

"Going home?" His eyes swept over her, unhurried, piercing, and Angela felt a rush of gratitude that this was her Wednesday night—her night to go out. She wasn't in her usual office clothes. She was dressed instead in a silk summer suit, green as her eyes, the jacket fitted, the skirt skimming her figure, her heels giving her extra poise. She had chosen it with no one in particular to impress, but now it felt like destiny.

He, too, was impeccably dressed. His suit was superbly tailored, his shirt crisp, his tie knotted with the kind of careless perfection that spoke of both wealth and taste. He looked like a prince—no, more dangerous than that, like some powerful figure who had stepped out of a different world altogether. Tall, lean, and lithe, every movement of his body spoke of controlled strength. Angela's breath caught.

"Don't you answer when a stranger speaks to you?" he asked softly, his voice edged with teasing command. "If you've been warned not to talk to strange men, let me remind you—we've spoken before. I almost knocked you down, remember?"

"I remember," Angela whispered, her cheeks flushing with warmth. His words made her feel suddenly very young, a child almost, and she didn't know where to put her eyes.

"Then let me begin again." He smiled—a slow, devastating smile that seemed to reach right into her. "Are you going home?"

"No," she managed, her voice trembling slightly. "I'm going out. This—this is my night when I stay in town."

"Ah." His gaze sharpened. "You've got a date."

The faintest shadow crossed his expression, a quick flash that made her heart pound harder. Was that disappointment? Panic seized her and she rushed to correct him.

"Not a date exactly. I go out with an old school friend on Wednesdays. We have dinner, sometimes see a film afterward. She's a girl," she added hurriedly, the words tumbling out, desperate that he understood.

For a moment, silence stretched between them, his grey eyes unreadable. Then, softly, almost lazily, he asked:

"What would she do if you didn't turn up?"

"I—I always turn up," Angela faltered. Her heart was racing so fast she felt dizzy. "If for any reason I can't, then I ring her."

"Ring her," Lincoln said quietly. It wasn't a suggestion. It was an order, calm and absolute.

Angela's lips parted in protest. "But—"

"You're going out with me."

He looked at her steadily, unblinking, and Angela bit down harder on her trembling lip, unable to quite believe what was happening. The air between them seemed charged, too thick to breathe. When he moved closer, closing the space with unhurried certainty, she tilted her head back, her voice breaking from her before she lost the courage to use it.

"I don't know you," she whispered, the words a fragile protest.

"I know," he said simply, nodding as though he understood far more than she had spoken. "That's why you're going out with me—unless you don't want to know me."

"I do!" The words escaped her with more urgency than she intended, almost pleading, as though she were afraid he might vanish if she hesitated. There wasn't even a flicker of caution in her heart, no thought of danger, only the sharp fear that he might change his mind and walk away.

Lincoln smiled then, slowly, intimately, the expression deepening the lines of his face. His storm-grey eyes lingered on hers, probing gently, searching her face with a scrutiny that was not harsh but unsettling in its tenderness. Under that gaze she felt stripped bare, as though he saw straight through her practiced composure, straight into the softness of her. Weakness curled through her, warm and strange.

"Then why don't you leave your car here," he said quietly, his voice like velvet over steel. "Come with me now. You can call your friend in the car. After that, dinner. I'll bring you back to your car later."

Angela looked up at him as though caught in a spell, her green eyes wide, her body taut with something she didn't have the words for. She could only nod, too dazed to resist, too enthralled to think.

His hand lifted, unhurried, and his fingers brushed her cheek with a touch so light she might have imagined it. Her skin burned beneath it.

"There's nothing to be afraid of," he murmured.

"All right?"

She nodded again, though inside she knew it wasn't true. There was something to be afraid of—something vast, something she couldn't name. She should have been very much afraid of this man with his quiet authority, his darkly compelling voice, and those startling eyes that seemed to see everything. But she wasn't.

She was bewitched. Helplessly, completely bewitched.

Chapter Four

The shrill ring of the phone dragged Angela back to reality with a jolt, scattering the dreamscape she had been drifting in.

"Barry Windsor on the line for you," Maria announced briskly, connecting the call before Angela had time to brace herself for the shift from reverie to the bleakness of her present.

"How are things?" Barry's voice was warm, steady—so safe, so ordinary—that Angela found herself smiling faintly as she answered.

"Hanging by a thread," she admitted. "And I expect the thread to snap at any moment."

"Well, there's no new word about," he reassured, calm as ever.

"What do you do, Barry?" she asked softly. "Do you wait for the axe to fall—or slide out from under now?"

"You can slide out from under," he told her firmly. "Angela, you're not the one they want. You're only in this position because your father's ill. If Maria Belle had been holding the fort, do you think she'd have been expected to make a last stand?"

"Knowing Maria," Angela mused with a faint smile, "she probably would. But in any case, I carry the name. I'm a Marsden. I can't just hide."

"You're merely a girl," he countered, his frustration bleeding through.

"I'm twenty-four," she said quietly, "and I feel eighty. The girl disappeared—somewhere along the way."

He swore under his breath, the sound sharp and raw through the receiver. For a moment she thought he might leave it there, but then his voice came again, low, and urgent.

"Look, love, I'm flying to Germany in the morning. I may be a week—maybe longer. Let me fix you up with us before I go."

"No, Barry," she said wearily. "I have to stick this out. To the end. But I appreciate—"

"You're not expected to appreciate anything," he interrupted. "I can use you in the firm. You're good. The trouble with you, Angela, is you're too good. Too gentle."

Her teeth caught her lip at that. That was almost word for word what Lincoln had told her earlier that day, only he'd delivered it with icy precision instead of Barry's kindness.

"When I'm back," Barry continued, "I'll phone you at once. In the meantime—"

"I'll keep my back to the wall and my finger on the trigger," Angela cut in, forcing a brittle laugh.

Angela had begun to notice it—small things at first. The way Barry's voice softened when he spoke to her, the way his eyes lingered a fraction too long, the way his protectiveness slipped past the line of friendship into something warmer, something unspoken. She wasn't blind, not entirely. A part of her suspected that if she reached for him, even tentatively, he would be there. But she had no intention of reaching. The thought of stepping into another man's arms was unbearable. Whatever else Lincoln had taken from her, he had stolen her ability to want another man, to trust one. And Barry—kind, dependable Barry—deserved more than to be her substitute for what she had lost.

"Dear, unworldly Angela," Barry murmured over the line, his voice threaded with quiet sorrow. "Nothing stops a wolf. Not this wolf. Lincoln Spokes is power beyond imagining—and you know it." He exhaled then, a sound more resigned than hopeful. "And I won't even be here to offer a shoulder to cry on. Take care."

"I will." She placed the receiver back in its cradle with slow care, then sat staring at it, her smile turning rueful, haunted.

A shoulder to cry on. Yes, she might need one—but it would never be Barry's. It would never be anyone's. Not after Lincoln. Since him, she hadn't wanted another man to care for her. It was too dangerous, too cruel, too unfair—to them and to herself.

And yet... she still dreamed of him.

Even now, she would wake in the night, bewildered, aching, disoriented, her heart convinced that his arm had just slipped from around her waist, that his breath had just warmed her neck, that she had only to turn her head and his mouth would be there, waiting. Too wonderful to be true when it had been hers. Too brutal to be real when it had ended.

She pressed her hands together tightly, as if by sheer force she could still the restless memories, but they came anyway—unbidden, relentless. Lincoln had been both her heaven and her torment. And no one else could ever be allowed to take his place.

When she finally reached home, the same question awaited her, as always.

"Anything new?"

"Nothing."

She wasn't about to tell her father she'd been to Lincoln's office. That revelation would have driven him over the edge—he had always hated Lincoln; with a bitterness she had come to understand only too well. With her appointments cancelled, there was nothing left to discuss, and silence fell.

Once again, Angela was alone.

Kurt Marsden was almost entirely silent through dinner, answering Rita's careful service with little more than a grunt of thanks. Their long-time housekeeper knew—of course she knew; by now everyone did—and each time she came in, her eyes strayed anxiously to Angela's pale face. Even Rita, it seemed, was depending on her. Everyone expected Angela to perform miracles, to hold back the tide. The weight of it pressed on her shoulders until even her own home felt like a cage.

There was nowhere to run. Nowhere to hide. Vulnerability clung to her like a second skin, and helplessness burned like an acid in her veins.

"Something has got to be done!" her father burst out suddenly, his voice rough as gravel as he slammed his cup onto the saucer.

The words shattered the brittle quiet. He pushed back from the table and began to pace, his agitation winding tighter with every step. "There must be some action we can take—something I'm missing. It's never been a problem to get hold of money."

Angela's fingers tightened around her cup, her voice calm but carrying an edge of despair. "No amount of money would match the Spokes Group."

"Money isn't the problem." Kurt wheeled around, his face flushed with anger. "Even without the backing of two powerful banks, Lincoln has millions of his own. And you—" His eyes flared, pinning her like a hawk on prey. "You're entitled to some of that!"

Her breath caught. She knew what was coming, but the words still stung.

"You never divorced him!" he snarled. "If you had, he would have been forced to part with plenty."

Angela sat straighter, her face drained of colour. "I doubt it. In any case, I want nothing from Lincoln. I wouldn't accept even a crust."

"You're too soft!" Kurt spat, his voice sharp enough to cut. "One day, my girl, you'll learn—you have to take what you want! You let him off scot-free!"

Her lashes lowered, shadowing the pain in her eyes. When she spoke, it was little more than a whisper, but it carried across the room with chilling finality.

"I was just glad to survive."

They had circled this argument too many times before, and every word of it was as bitter as gall. The subject was painful, distasteful, and one she refused to relive. When she had walked out on Lincoln, she had severed that life completely, closing the door on it with finality. She had no need of her father's reminders—no fresh tearing at old wounds.

Kurt lapsed back into his usual silence, the heavy kind that pressed down like judgement. Before he could stir it all up again, Angela rose quietly and slipped away to her room. He always managed to make her feel as if she were to blame, as though the ruin of everything could be traced to that single choice—to her marriage. If she had never married Lincoln, her father would have insisted, none of this would have happened.

But it would have. She knew it would have.

She was no longer the naïve girl of nineteen, blind to the shadows behind Lincoln's grey eyes. The memory of his threat from that day five years ago was still etched into her bones, chillingly real. Even when he had been her husband, even when she had lain in his arms, he had been planning her father's destruction.

She lay in bed, too battered by the day to sleep, her mind drifting back—always back—to Lincoln. The man she had faced that morning had been cold, ruthless, stripped of any trace of humanity. Nothing but power. He might keep tearing at them until there was nothing left, until Marsden Enterprises was reduced to dust. Perhaps, with his wealth and influence, he could save the company—but not for them. Never for them. What did he intend? Would he strike like a hawk and seize it outright, or simply stand back and watch them sink quietly into oblivion?

His face hovered in her thoughts, first hard as granite, then softening into the warmth and tenderness he had once shown her. That contrast hurt more than his cruelty. How could she have been so trusting, so blind? From the very beginning she had been under his spell, eager to believe anything, if only it meant being with him.

After that first night, Lincoln had called her every day—never when she was home, always careful, as if he knew even then that secrecy would bind her tighter to him. He had wanted her constantly, drawing her deeper into his world, and Angela had gladly adjusted, staying late in town so she could see him. Her father had made no comment; he hadn't even noticed.

Kurt Marsden never noticed much beyond his own schemes. As long as she was at her desk each morning, he asked no questions. She had been motherless, friendless, a girl adrift with no one to confide in. The fact that she came home late more often than not had raised no suspicion. He simply assumed she was out with friends, and Angela had let him. Deep down she knew—had always known—that if he discovered the truth, his rage would have been volcanic.

So, she kept her silence, burying the unease stirred by their first encounter, the sharp edge of that threat he had hurled on the day they met. It lingered, shadowed in the back of her mind, but she ignored it. How could she resist when she was already drowning, bewitched by the silver-grey of Lincoln's eyes, helpless under the spell of his smile?

At weekends she belonged entirely to Lincoln. They spent long hours walking, driving into the countryside, going to the theatre, dining out. Sometimes he took her to little hidden places where the food was plain but good, sometimes to restaurants so exclusive Angela might have shrunk from them—had it not been for the man across the table. With him there, everything seemed possible. The way he rose to pull out her chair, the light touch of his fingers closing over hers—it all made her feel cherished, chosen.

And yet he held her at arm's length. He treated her with exquisite care, almost as if she were made of glass. She was enthralled, utterly captivated, but bewildered. When she parted from him, she carried away a strange ache—a longing for something she could barely name, something deeper than handholding, more binding than smiles. Sometimes she wanted nothing more than to be caught up, claimed, kissed—but Lincoln never pressed. He never crossed that invisible line.

Still, he could not keep away from her. A day without him seemed impossible, and Angela thrilled at his need of her even while she wished, with a desperate ache, that he would stop holding back. She wanted to be swept away. She wanted to fall.

One Saturday evening he brought her to a restaurant where music spilled into the air, couples drifting around the floor in an elegant rhythm. The sight both fascinated and unnerved her. The idea of being in Lincoln's arms, held close, moving together—it made her tremble. She had dreamed of it since their first meeting, yet now, when it might actually happen, fear and anticipation tangled in her chest.

"Come and dance with me." Lincoln rose as they finished their meal, his eyes smiling as they locked with hers.

Her breath caught. Her legs felt weak, but she stood. He came around the table, his arm slipping with easy authority about her waist, guiding her onto the floor. The first brush of his touch lit a fire inside her. She forgot to think. All that remained was sensation—his body aligned with hers, the contained strength beneath the smooth cloth of his jacket, the heat of his nearness.

She lifted her gaze. His eyes were fixed not on her but beyond, his face drawn taut, almost fierce. Power emanated from him in waves—command, control, mastery—and she felt both awed and small in the presence of it. Then he looked down at her, his silver eyes catching hers, probing, searching every line of her face. Slowly, reluctantly, he smiled, as though yielding something rare. His hand rose and brushed her cheek with a gentleness that stole her breath.

"Angela," he murmured, voice low, roughened. "Beautiful Angela, with hair like a blackbird's wing and eyes like emeralds."

She should have blushed. Once, she would have. But the words melted through her like sunlight breaking into her soul, filling her with something too sweet, too sharp. Delight curled around her insides, making her tremble. She sighed, shivering, trying to breathe again.

His eyes narrowed, his hand capturing hers, drawing it up to rest against the steady thud of his heart. Neither of them smiled now. Neither could look away. The air around them was charged, vibrating with an intensity that left her weak. At last, he bent his head, his cheek brushing her hair.

"Shall we go?" he asked softly.

She could only nod. Words were gone. Something had shifted—something deep, undeniable. Her nerves tingled, her heart raced to the point of pain, and as he led her from the floor, out of the restaurant, his arm firm around her waist, she shivered with the force of it.

Outside, he took her hand again, walking beside her with the same fluid, feline grace she had noticed from the beginning. He seemed untouchable, far above her reach. Tears burned behind her eyes—hot, helpless. It wasn't fair. There would never be another man like Lincoln. Not for her. He would grow tired of her soon, cast her aside. What could an extraordinary man like him want with a nineteen-year-old girl who still trembled at a touch? Surely there were women—sophisticated, worldly women—lined up to claim his attention. Hundreds of them.

And still he chose to be with her.

In the car, Lincoln turned his head to look at her, and Angela quickly averted her face, desperate to hide the foolish tears that still clung stubbornly to her lashes. But his hand came—firm, unyielding—tilting her chin until she had no choice but to meet the piercing demand of his gaze. Her breath caught; she tried to resist, her eyes falling shut in mute defiance.

And then his mouth brushed hers.

It was the faintest touch, almost no more than the warmth of breath passing between them, yet it jolted through her like lightning. Soft, fleeting, more a question than a claim. She gasped at the shock of it, the tiny sound breaking from her before she could smother it.

He felt it—her tremor, the way her body betrayed her—and instead of retreating, he drew her closer. His lips grazed the corner of her mouth with maddening patience, tracing, teasing, hovering as if he meant to torment her with possibilities. Her pulse thundered in her ears, every nerve strung taut, until at last he angled her fully against him and claimed her with a kiss that erased every doubt.

There was nothing tentative now. His mouth was hard, warm, and utterly insistent, a demand that consumed her. She could feel the strain in him, the restraint barely holding as his whole body tensed with the sheer force of it—as though even he hadn't anticipated the violence of his own hunger.

Her response was helpless, innocent, yet fierce in its own right. Pleasure surged through her, raw and dizzying, stripping her of thought. She tilted her face to his with unthinking trust, yielding utterly to him, surrendering in a way she never had to anyone. His taste, his heat, the inexorable pressure of his mouth—she wanted more, needed more, and the realisation terrified her even as it thrilled.

It felt endless, that kiss, as though time itself had bent to hold them in its grip. But when he tore himself away at last, it could only have been seconds. His chest heaved as if he had fought a battle, his eyes closing briefly, as though to master the storm inside him. Angela's entire body shook with aftershocks; she was trembling so violently she could scarcely breathe.

Lincoln looked across at her then, seized her hand and squeezed it with a force that bordered on cruelty—as though anchoring them both, binding her to him by sheer will.

"I'll take you home," he said thickly, his voice roughened by something darker than desire.

"I—I have my car," she managed to whisper.

"You're not fit to drive, Angela. I'll take you."

"It's a long way and—and if my car is here, I'll…" Her voice faltered, her joy spilling into words that tumbled out unchecked. "Tomorrow is Sunday. If you want to see me—"

"You know I want to see you," he cut across her hoarsely, his eyes burning.

"I'll come by train," she rushed on, hardly able to believe her own daring.

"I'll meet you at the station. Ten o'clock. We'll have the whole day."

"I'll tell you where I live—" she began, radiant, almost dizzy with the knowledge that even after kissing her, he wanted more.

But Lincoln only started the engine, his gaze fixed straight ahead. "I know where you live."

And of course he did. She never questioned it. He was Lincoln—perfect, unstoppable, a man who always knew. And she… she worshipped him.

At her door he didn't kiss her again, and Angela was glad. If he had, she would never have been able to make her legs carry her inside.

"Tomorrow. Early." He lifted her hand to his mouth, brushing it with a brief, commanding kiss. His voice was low, threaded with steel and hunger. "I'll be waiting, Angela."

Chapter Five

She couldn't sleep. Her mind was too alive, too full of the memory of Lincoln and the promise of tomorrow. Her father had still been in his study when she slipped past him, murmuring a quiet goodnight. She was thankful he hadn't noticed the car leaving the house—obviously not hers—and he hardly glanced at her. She didn't care. Her heart and mind were caught in a single refrain: Lincoln. Lincoln. Tomorrow, she would see him again—and this time, it would be different.

The next morning, he was waiting as she stepped off the train. The instant their eyes met, his face brightened, and her pulse leapt. His glance swept over her, sharp and appraising, and she felt a thrill at the knowledge that she looked… right. Her summer ensemble—a dark green skirt and matching sleeveless blouse, cinched at the waist with a golden belt—felt as if it had been made for him to notice. Her gold high-heeled sandals completed the outfit, and Lincoln's low laugh made her cheeks warm.

"I see we're not walking," he murmured, amusement in his voice. Angela couldn't help laughing. For the first time, she felt almost equal to him.

She fumbled in her bag, producing a pair of flat sandals and dangling them in front of him. "I'm prepared for anything," she said brightly.

"Are you?" His steady gaze made her blush, and for a moment she felt exposed. Then he held out his hand.

"Let's go," he said quietly. "We'll have to get an early start tonight—tomorrow's a workday. Best not to waste a single moment."

Angela slid into the passenger seat, heart fluttering. "Where are we going?" she asked, her voice soft and eager.

He stared at her for a beat, drinking in her brightness and charm, before answering. "On the river. I've got a boat moored by a small inn a few miles out. We'll have lunch there, then sail away… into the distance."

Angela's heart leapt. She almost hugged herself with delight. He caught her glance, smiling at her excitement.

"I take it you've never been on a boat before?" he teased lightly.

"Not on the Thames," she agreed, tossing her head. "But I've been on a cruise—Jamaica, the Caribbean…"

"Oh, impressive," he mocked softly. "Here, there's only the occasional duck to contend with. Nothing like your worldly sophistication."

"You—" Angela pouted, "—are laughing at me."

"It seems a good idea," he admitted quietly. "You look like an enchanted princess. Laughter is harmless. I think we'll laugh all day."

Angela felt a shiver of awareness. His words, his gaze—they devoured her. The air between them crackled with tension, thrilling and frightening in equal measure. She longed for his touch, and her pulse betrayed her. He knew it. She could feel it in the tight grip of his hand on the wheel, in the set of his jaw, in the quiet intensity radiating from him.

"I'm sorry," she whispered, her voice trembling.

"Can you help it?" he asked darkly, not even pretending ignorance.

"No," she admitted. She wanted him—wanted him to love her, to take her. The ache had been building for days, and it hurt.

"Neither can I," he said quietly. "Perhaps… this should be our last outing."

The words hit her like a shock. Her breath caught, and her cheeks paled.

"Don't leave me, Lincoln," she whispered, desperation spilling from her.

His head whipped toward her. Seeing her pale face, he pulled the car to the side of the busy road and drew her against him. "God! I can't!" he muttered hoarsely, his lips capturing hers in a kiss that seared through her. Heat and electricity raced through her veins as she responded instinctively, lips parting in innocent surrender.

"Not here," he husked, reluctantly breaking away and putting a small distance between them. She blinked up at him, dazed, only to notice the astonished eyes of bystanders. The Jaguar glided smoothly away, sparing her further embarrassment.

"Oh dear," she murmured, her voice trembling.

Lincoln laughed, the tension in his shoulders easing. "Well, at least they didn't stare too closely," he said with a grin. Then, his eyes lanced over her, silver-grey and intense. "Do you still want to go on that boat trip?"

"Yes," she said without hesitation. Fear and caution had no power here—only the magnetic pull of him. She had never felt like this before, and she knew, with a thrill and a shiver, that neither had he. Nothing else mattered.

It was a perfect, sunlit day. They made their way to the small boat moored by the old inn, and Angela slipped off her sandals, eager to climb aboard. The boat was not grand, but it was larger than she had expected, rocking gently on the warm, honey-scented river. She stood on the deck, breathing in the sweet, sun-filled air, and her eyes sparkled with delight.

"It's marvellous!" she exclaimed, her voice ringing with unrestrained excitement. Lincoln looked at her with a rueful half-smile, his grey eyes sweeping over her face like lightning, sharp and assessing.

"You're the easiest girl in the world to please, Angela," he said, amusement lacing his tone as he leapt lightly down to the riverbank.

The note of cynicism she thought she detected in his voice stung. Angela felt a sudden flush of embarrassment, as if her childish enthusiasm had made her ridiculous. Her smile faltered.

"I suppose you're used to more… sophisticated women," she said sharply, trying to mask the hurt that flared in her chest. For a moment, it seemed as if he had found her delight tiresome, and her eyes threatened to fill with tears.

"Very sophisticated women," he replied, mockingly inspecting her flushed face with his piercing gaze, "never show enthusiasm. A little boat like this would bore them senseless."

Angela's soft mouth drooped. She looked away, the day's glow dimming in an instant.

"I can't pretend," she admitted, her voice trembling. "If I like something, I have to show it. Perhaps, one day, I'll learn to curb my childish excitement."

Lincoln's low, dark voice cut through her despondency, warm and commanding, sending a shiver down her spine. "Come here, Angela." Her wide green eyes met his, hesitant and unsure.

"Collect your sandals and come here," he instructed softly. She bent to gather them and stepped to the edge of the boat. He reached for her, hands spanning her tiny waist, lifting her aboard with a gentleness that made her chest ache with pleasure. When she bent down again to fasten her sandals, he held her arm, steadying her. As she straightened, his hands cupped her flushed face, tilting it toward him.

"You're beautiful," he said softly, his fingers brushing back strands of her dark hair, his eyes scanning the luminous sweep of her shoulder and neck. "You're the sweetest girl in the world. If you were one of those sophisticated women… I would be bored senseless."

Angela's heart thumped so violently she could hardly speak. The hurt of moments before melted away beneath the warmth of his gaze. He leaned down, his cool lips brushing hers lightly, a whisper of touch that made her tremble.

"Let's eat," he said quietly, lifting his head. His voice was calm, his movements composed, yet the same taut, thrilling tension from the car surged between them. He turned her toward the inn, sliding an arm possessively around her waist. Angela stiffened instinctively, afraid that if she surrendered fully, she would lose herself in him.

"Don't be afraid of me, Angela," he murmured, bending toward her again.

"I'm not," she whispered, though the truth was more complicated.

"I'll never let anything hurt you," he promised, his breath warm against her cheek as he pulled her closer. "You're precious. I need to care for you. You can come to me with no fear."

His hand shifted from her waist to the back of her neck, fingers tracing a gentle path that made her pulse leap. Angela gave in, leaning against him as they walked, her arm sliding around his waist, and a wave of joy burst inside her when he tightened his hold, holding her as if she were the only thing that mattered in the world.

During the meal, Lincoln put her completely at ease, and by the time they took the boat out, Angela felt free to show her delight in everything around her. They moved slowly down the Thames, gliding through quiet, sunlit waters. She gazed at the grand houses lining the river, their gardens stretching down to the edge of the water. It seemed like paradise, and by the time they were cruising back toward the mooring, Angela was both exhausted and deliriously happy.

Lincoln had been gentle all day. They had lingered on deck, sipping lemonade and talking softly. The sun caressed her skin, its dying rays catching the brilliant green of her eyes, making them sparkle like gems.

"We'll tie up and clear our things," Lincoln announced as they reached the bank. "After that, it's home fast for you."

Angela went into the little cabin to stow away their things, but the glow of the day had dimmed. She didn't want to leave him. Every time she had to say goodbye, it felt harder and harder. When Lincoln jumped back on board, she was standing in the cabin, staring blankly ahead.

"What is it?" His voice was low and quiet as he approached, and Angela hung her head, biting her lip miserably.

"I—I don't want to go," she whispered. "I don't want to leave you."

"You're nineteen," Lincoln reminded her softly, "not one of my many sophisticated women."

"Don't!" she shot back, turning to him, her eyes swimming with emotion. Pain and longing shimmered in their depths. He swore under his breath and drew her into his arms.

"There are no sophisticated women," he muttered unevenly, his lips brushing her hair. "If there were, do you think I'd look at any of them when you were here? I'm trying to keep this light, to protect you."

When her gaze remained fixed on him, green eyes wide and vulnerable, he pulled her closer, his fingers tangling in her shining hair.

"Dear God, Angela!" he said hoarsely. "I want you, and you know it!"

He kissed her then—hard, fast, hungry kisses that parted her lips and set her body aflame. She swayed against him, winding her arms around his waist, and he drew her head to his shoulder. When she lifted her face, desperate for his mouth, he responded with the same fierce intensity.

His hands roamed over her, caressing every curve, sending shivers through her. Her legs threatened to give way, and she sank slightly, trying to hold him with her.

"No!" he gasped, voice ragged. "Let's get out of here." But he didn't release her, keeping his arms tight around her as if the world could not exist between them.

By the time they left the boat and walked along the riverbank, Angela was still trembling from the rush of sensation. Darkness had fallen, and she was grateful for the shadows hiding her flushed face.

"In here," Lincoln said almost harshly, pushing the door of the inn open. They were instantly enveloped by music from hidden speakers, laughter, and loud chatter. The room was dimly lit and crowded.

"Just what we need," he muttered, scanning the space. Most of the people were gathered at the bar. He found a small, shadowed corner where the red-covered benches offered them privacy. "Sit here," he instructed, gesturing to the seat. "I'll get our drinks."

Angela sank gratefully into the seat, though her trembling hadn't lessened. She welcomed the brief moment alone while Lincoln went to the bar. She had always faced life head-on; she had never been allowed to do otherwise. And now, she faced this truth squarely: she was utterly, completely in love with Lincoln. She wanted him as intensely as he wanted her. The realisation was both thrilling and terrifying, a sensation she had never known. She wanted to be with him for the rest of her life, and the thought of him not feeling the same left a hollow ache in her chest.

Lincoln returned, sliding into the seat beside her and handing her a glass of brandy.

"Drink it—Dutch courage," he murmured with a teasing edge. Angela tried to sip the fiery liquid, but it caught in her throat, making her cough. She felt unbearably young, far apart from Lincoln's commanding presence. Her hands shook on the tabletop, and she looked down at them, despair rising. She nearly jumped when one of his strong hands covered both hers, warm and grounding.

"Sweet, sweet Angel," he whispered, leaning forward, his lips tracing her delicate jawline. With a low groan, he set his drink aside and drew closer, his arm encircling her shoulders.

"I give in," he breathed, tilting her chin gently. As her gaze met his burning grey eyes, his lips claimed hers in urgent, possessive desire.

Angela surrendered instantly, her head resting against his shoulder, lips parting willingly. The dim room, the people around them—all of it disappeared. Only Lincoln existed, masterful and intoxicating. And once again, it was he who pulled back, leaving her gasping.

"We have to go," he murmured, his lips brushing her flushed cheeks. "We seem to choose the damnedest places."

He took her hand, guiding her from the bench, and they stepped out into the cool night. Lincoln's hand brushed hers to his lips as they walked toward the car. In the dark, private confines of the Jaguar, he pulled her close, one hand smoothing her hair, the other cupping her cheek.

"What would you say if I asked you to come back to my penthouse with me?" he asked, huskily, his gaze intense and unwavering. The streetlights painted harsh shadows across his face, emphasising the almost rueful twist of his mouth.

Angela's pulse raced, certainty flooding her. "I would say yes," she whispered. "I love you, Lincoln. I don't want to be anywhere except with you."

He groaned softly against her hair. "Why are you so sweet, so beautiful?" he murmured, tilting his head to kiss her very gently. "I never want to let you out of my sight."

"Every time we're together, I try to be sensible," he confessed, "but parting from you is agonising. Don't ever leave me again, Angela."

"I won't," she whispered, and he finally eased her away, starting the car. Angela rested her head against his shoulder, a deep, contented sigh escaping her. From the first moment she had seen him, she had wanted to be in his arms, to surrender herself completely. It was no shock; it was destiny. Her fate. Here, with Lincoln, there was no room for fear, no thought of home or her father. She was exactly where she was meant to be, and she would stay, wholly and entirely, with him.

In his penthouse, Angela's eyes widened with awe. Every corner spoke of elegance and taste, a luxury that left her both dazzled and slightly apprehensive.

"Can I explore?" she whispered, barely daring to look at him. Being here seemed unreal, and the unknown made her pulse quicken.

"No," he said quietly, a note of gentle command in his voice. "You can explore later."

He drew her into his arms, turning her to face him. His hands framed her face, steady and sure. "Don't be afraid of me. I want you, my sweet darling, and I would never hurt you."

The intensity of his gaze, the absolute certainty in his tone, melted Angela. That voice, that strength—it left no room for doubt. She believed him utterly. Lincoln would never harm her.

"Don't ever send me away," she whispered, her eyes locked with his, her breath unsteady.

He pressed her closer, his body a solid wall of heat and strength. "Never in my whole life," he vowed thickly, the words roughened by truth. "I couldn't exist if you weren't beside me."

He led her toward the bedroom; every step charged with the thrum of something uncontainable. When his hands touched her again, they were slow, reverent, undoing each button, sliding each layer from her as though unwrapping the most sacred treasure. Angela's breath quickened. She had never been seen like this, never revealed herself so completely. Yet under his gaze she felt not shame, but wonder.

Her black hair spilled across the pillow like ink against snow, her silken limbs stretched bare before him. His eyes devoured her—hot, fierce, and worshipful. The raw hunger in them made her flush, but it also made her heart soar.

When at last he came to her, drawing her into his arms, Angela released a sigh that seemed pulled from the depths of her soul.

"What is it?" he murmured, his voice husky, thick with restraint.

"I just… belong here," she breathed, her lips curving in a tremulous smile. "It's as if I've always been waiting—and now I know what for."

"Angel." The word was broken from him, almost a groan.

His mouth found hers then, fierce, and consuming, a kiss that exploded through her, shattering thought and leaving only sensation. She clung to him helplessly, trembling beneath the storm of his touch as his hands mapped every curve, his lips following, tasting, worshipping. Her name spilled from her lips in a voice that startled her with its need, raw and aching.

Her hands were restless on him—skimming the breadth of his back, the strength of his shoulders, tangling in his dark hair as if to tether herself to him. Every inch of him was heat and power, every breath stolen between kisses another promise that he was hers as much as she was his.

And then, when he moved to claim her fully, her breath caught. A shuddering cry broke from her as he pressed into her, slow and steady, filling her until she thought she would break with the intensity of it. She parted for him willingly, instinctively, her body opening as her soul had already surrendered.

Her eyes met his—those storm-grey eyes seared into hers—and the world seemed to vanish around them.

"You're mine," he ground out, his face taut with urgent passion. "You belong to me—forever, from this moment on."

"Forever," she whispered, her body arching into his, her heart soaring toward him without hesitation. She believed it utterly.

His rhythm built, each thrust a declaration, each kiss a vow. Pleasure rose in waves, fierce and overwhelming, until she could do nothing but cling to him, lost in the rapture of him, her cries muffled against his throat.

Being with Lincoln wasn't just desire—it was destiny. She had known it from the moment he touched her, felt it in every fibre of her being. And now, as he held her, moved within her, loved her with all the unrelenting force of his will, nothing beyond him seemed to exist.

Chapter Six

It was only the next day that reality intruded—the reality of her father. Lincoln insisted on taking her home early before anyone had left for work.

"He's not going to like this," Angela said, her voice tight with worry.

Lincoln drew her close, his eyes serious, unyielding as steel. "He has no choice. You and I are going to be married. Nothing—and nobody—can stop that. Like it or not, your father has to face it."

Angela's heart fluttered wildly at his words, a dangerous mix of fear and lingering, dreamlike happiness. It was a heady thing, to be chosen by a man like Lincoln, to be claimed with such certainty. His power, his dominance, the sheer inevitability in his tone swept over her like a tide, and she—young, dazzled, desperately in love—let herself be carried along without question.

She didn't notice what was missing. She didn't stop to wonder why there was no declaration of love, no whispered endearments, no gentle vow of devotion. At the time, she had been too blind, too enraptured by the force of him to see what now, years later, seemed so obvious. She had mistaken possession for passion, determination for tenderness.

Now that she was older and wiser, she realised the truth: Lincoln had never said he loved her that day. He had claimed her, certainly. He had decided for both of them. But love? That word had been absent, and she had been too naïve to care. She had been deafened by her own heart, blind to the warning in his silence.

Then, she had only leaned into him, allowing him to guide her into the waiting car. The early morning light slanted across his face, burnishing the hard lines of his jaw, gilding the world in deceptive softness. She braced herself for sharp words, perhaps even unpleasantness from her father—but nothing in her girlish imagination could have prepared her for the battle to come.

From the moment she met Lincoln, she had been consumed by him. Common sense had fled, swept away by a tide of desire, hope, and youthful certainty. But standing later in that room, caught between two titans, their hatred sparking like white-hot flame, she had felt small, powerless, and terribly out of her depth.

It was only with distance and the cruel schooling of time that she saw it clearly: she had walked into that confrontation already defeated, because she had never truly understood what Lincoln was giving—and what he was withholding.

Her father was leaving his study as she entered the hall, Lincoln at her side. Kurt Marsden froze at the sight of them, his gaze locked not on Angela but on Lincoln, his face dark with fury. The hours she had spent away meant nothing to him; she was irrelevant. All that mattered was the storm of anger between them.

"Get out of my house!"

Angela barely recognised the sharp edge in her father's voice as it lashed toward Lincoln.

"Daddy!" she cried, stepping forward, but he ignored her completely.

"Get out!" he repeated, each word like a whip. His eyes swept to Angela, narrowing. "Where the hell have you been?"

"She's been with me," Lincoln said curtly, his voice calm but steel-edged. "We can handle this civilly—or any way you choose. Angela is with me."

Her father's face darkened further, the veins in his forehead standing out as he reached for her arm.

"Go to your room! I'll deal with this," he snapped.

But Lincoln's arm swept around her, shielding her against his chest. "Angela goes with me!" His words, sharp and final, finally cut through her father's rage.

Kurt Marsden's eyes widened as comprehension dawned. "So, this is how you intend to do it," he growled. "You think you can reach me through Angela? Not a good move, Spokes. She doesn't control anything yet. You'll get nothing."

"All I want is Angela," Lincoln said, voice cold and unyielding. "She doesn't even need her clothes from this house. Anything she wants, I'll get for her."

"She's nineteen!" her father bellowed, fury blazing. Angela moved to step toward him, desperate to stop the battle, but Lincoln's arm held her fast.

"She's old enough to know her own mind," he said evenly. "Old enough to marry me. You can come to the wedding, give her your blessing—if you wish. It's up to you."

"You'll get no blessing from me!" Kurt Marsden shouted, hoarse with rage.

Lincoln turned, taking Angela with him. "I want nothing from you," he said, his tone icy. "Nothing you can give matters. Angela is nobody's property. She's outside all this. We simply came to tell you—we're getting married."

They were at the door, and her father hadn't moved a step. Angela looked at him miserably, regret and helplessness in her eyes. She had never had a say in anything; mostly, he ignored her unless it was about work. Now, she felt like nothing more than an object over which men were battling.

Her father misread her glance. A spasm of triumph crossed his face.

"Stay here, Angela," he said more calmly. "You don't know Spokes. He's ruthless—cruel!"

He didn't say he loved her. He didn't even acknowledge that he was her father.

"I have to go with Lincoln," she murmured, voice low and sad. "I want to go with him. I love him. Why does it have to be like this?"

"She'll not marry you!" Kurt Marsden roared, ignoring her entirely. Lincoln glanced at him with cold contempt.

"She's mine already, and she'll stay mine. This is permanent," Lincoln said, his voice steady and unyielding. "My secretary will send you the wedding arrangements. Come, or stay away as you please—but if you fail her..." His tone dropped, dark and threatening. "If you're not there to give her away like any other father, it will be just one more mark against you. I won't forget it."

There was a hardness in his voice Angela had never heard before. For a fleeting moment, Lincoln seemed like another man entirely—powerful, unstoppable. But she didn't have time to dwell on it.

She was already outside the house, in Lincoln's car, the past left behind. Her father made no move to follow, didn't even come to the door. And in Lincoln's arms, Angela felt a comfort she had never known in her life.

Her father had come to the wedding after all. He had given her away, making a great effort to appear normal, though he hadn't spoken to Lincoln or any of the guests on Lincoln's side of the church.

She had told herself it was because he loved her too much to let her down—but now she knew better. Even then, long before Lincoln had begun his ruthless vendetta, Kurt Marsden had feared him.

Angela sighed and turned onto her side, desperately seeking sleep. It was the only escape she had—and even then, she often woke in the middle of the night, reaching for Lincoln, only to remember that he was not there, and never would be again.

Seeing him today had been a mistake. No good could come of it, no help for them. All it had done was stir up bitterness, exposing her as vulnerable as ever. Her fainting spell must have angered Lincoln—and left her feeling utterly foolish. It would have been wiser to lie low, to remain invisible while he carried out his deadly work, as he had done all this time.

The next morning passed with the eerie stillness of expectation. The summons to the bank never came, and the day stretched endlessly in a haze of waiting. For once, nobody was pestering her; her phone barely rang, and by the time Angela was ready to leave the office, unease had replaced any fleeting relief. No news might be good news, but it was unnerving.

Maria caught her eye as she packed her things. There was a hint of worry in her glance.

"What's happening?" she asked, her voice low. "Something dreadful, I expect."

Angela leaned on Maria's desk with a long sigh. "They're probably somewhere plotting the swiftest way to sink us."

Maria shook her head gently. "Never say die."

Angela shrugged, weary beyond argument. "What else is there to say? Nothing happened today, but we all know it will—maybe tomorrow. Certainly tomorrow."

She left the office with that thought gnawing at her. Perhaps by next week there would be no need to come here every day. Perhaps by next week the whole place would belong to Lincoln. The prospect should have been comforting, but it left her drained instead. She was tired, worn out, desperate for a moment when the constant calculation, the careful navigation of threats, would finally end. Then, she could leave it all behind, and Lincoln would vanish from her thoughts—finally. She might take a job with Barry, start again, and escape the shadow of all this.

Maria caught up with her near the car. "Let's go for a coffee," she said, planting herself at Angela's side as if her presence were a shield.

Angela hesitated briefly, then smiled. "All right." Why not? Home promised the usual questions and recriminations. Right now, she wanted nothing more than the comfort of someone else's company.

Settled in a quiet corner of a nearby café, Maria leaned back and confessed softly, "I never expected all this, you know. Not after you married him, anyway."

Angela shook her head glumly. "I can't think why. I was nothing, after all. I still don't really understand it—the enmity, the bitterness. I understand battles in business, but this is personal. Daddy was furious about the wedding, yes, but all this… it's Lincoln. And even before I met him, there was tension, something unspoken. Neither he nor my father ever explained it. After I married Lincoln, I hardly saw Father; it was too traumatic. He'd fire questions at me I couldn't answer."

Maria's gaze softened. "Your father ruined the firm Lincoln's father started."

Angela frowned. "As far as I know, it was all just business."

"Some survive, some go under," Maria replied quietly. "Lincoln's father went under—he even died."

"But that wasn't my father's fault!" Angela protested.

"I've told you everything I know," Maria said steadily. "If I knew more, I'd tell you. You're the one suffering—and all this happened before your time."

Angela's eyes went distant. "I played right into Lincoln's hands."

Maria frowned, her eyes narrowing with quiet conviction. "He loved you."

Angela gave a short, bitter laugh, the sound cutting through the room like glass. "Oh, please. I'm not a child, Maria. I'm not the idiot he thinks I am. Lincoln used me to get at my father. He never intended for us to last. He wouldn't even let me have a baby." Her voice caught, then hardened. "I was a weapon. Nothing more."

Maria studied her for a long moment, the silence almost gentler than words. "Suppose you're wrong?" she asked softly.

Angela's head shook at once, her tone lowering into a flat, wounded murmur. "No. He needed me as a weapon. You've heard of Fiona Martin, haven't you? She was there before my time—and I expect she's still with him. She told me herself they did more than work together."

At the name, her chest tightened, an old ache pressing against her ribs. She tried to bury it, but the memory rose like smoke, inescapable…

She had been blissfully happy a year into their marriage, happier than she had ever believed possible. Lincoln was still brusque, still maddening, but he was hers—and every stolen kiss, every night spent tangled in his arms had convinced her that he did, in his own way, love her. Then came that afternoon in the lobby, after leaving Lincoln's office.

Angela remembered stepping off the lift, her heart light, when she saw Fiona Martin. The woman's beauty was as breathtaking as ever—cool, untouchable, the kind of woman who left perfume and whispers in her wake. Fiona's smile had been sharp when she cornered Angela, her words like poisoned honey. "He'll never give me up, you know. You're just… temporary."

Angela had tried to laugh it off, but by the time Lincoln came home that evening, the poison had already seeped into her veins. He kissed her, unhurried, then pulled back at once, his sharp eyes narrowing. "Something's wrong. What is it?"

Her heart had pounded as she forced the question out. "Is Fiona Martin your mistress?"

The look he gave her—half disbelief, half exasperation—still burned in her mind. "Of course not. Where would you get that idea?"

"From her," Angela whispered.

Lincoln scoffed, his mouth curling in disdain. "That's ridiculous. You must have misunderstood."

"No, Lincoln. I didn't misunderstand." Her voice had cracked then, a mix of fear and fury.

Impatience had sliced across his features, his tone snapping like a whip. "You're being idiotic and childish." With that, he turned away, stripping off his jacket as though dismissing both the question and her with one swift motion. "I'm having a shower."

The memory seared. She remembered standing frozen in the silence after the bathroom door closed, her world tilting. She had packed only what she had brought into the marriage, leaving behind every gift, every gown, every glittering token of his wealth. Within the hour she was gone—back to her father's house, her heart shattered but her pride intact.

And Lincoln had never come for her. Not once. No letter slipped beneath her door, no knock in the dead of night, no whispered vow begging her to return. Not even anger, not even reproach. Just silence. A silence so vast, so deliberate, it drowned out every memory they had shared. To Angela, that silence was louder than any confession. Louder than words of love would have been—because it told her, without mercy, that she had never truly mattered.

The memory slipped away, leaving her drained, her voice little more than a whisper. "He didn't even chase me, Maria. Not once. And that told me everything."

Maria's sigh was heavy with regret, her attempt at unravelling the web of power, ambition, and betrayal having failed. "Not done a lot of good, have I?" she murmured woefully.

Angela managed a faint smile, brittle at the edges. "It would take a miracle."

And there were no miracles. According to her father, at least. Lincoln had the monopoly on those—and he kept them all for himself.

When Angela got home, the coldness of the house hit her anew. It had always been like this, stretching back as far as she could remember. Her mother existed only as a hazy shadow in her mind, and even before her death, her father had been entirely absorbed in his business, leaving nothing else a place in his life.

"I'm back, Rita." Angela poked her head around the kitchen door and found Rita bustling over the stove, the clatter of pans filling the air.

"I won't be long," Rita said comfortably, without looking up. "You're late tonight, but as expected—you're safely in. Your father is in his study, I think."

Angela stiffened. Of course he would be. Going in there was unavoidable; he would expect a rundown of the day's events, even when there was nothing to report. She squared her shoulders and walked across the hall, opening the study door quietly.

At first, she thought the room was empty. She called his name, but no answer came. Angela was just about to leave when she saw him: lying behind his desk, his body oddly still. His feet stuck out, and the moment she ran around, the truth struck her like a physical blow—he had collapsed suddenly, with no warning, unable to alert anyone.

Angela dropped to her knees beside him, pressing a hand to his face. It was icy, damp with sweat; his breathing was erratic, laboured. The reality she had dreaded for weeks had finally come. Her father's heart had failed him. Panic surged through her, and she ran from the room, calling for Rita and then frantically dialling for an ambulance. It might already be too late. His lips were tinged blue; his skin was impossibly cold.

The next hour stretched into what felt like a week. Rita offered no help, frozen in her usual panic. But the ambulance men arrived faster than Angela expected, their calm professionalism only heightening her own terror. Her father had come around during the journey, yet his awareness was fragmented. He recognised nothing fully, not even her.

Chapter Seven

At the hospital, a nurse gently suggested, "You should have someone with you." Angela's thoughts immediately turned to Maria. Barry was in Germany, and even Maria had been out when she needed her most. She phoned, leaving a terse message on her answering machine, then paced the waiting area, unable to eat, her body trembling despite the hospital's warmth. She felt the blow of fate with every tick of the clock. Hope had long since fled, leaving only self-recrimination. She ran over every decision, every misstep of the past weeks, searching for some way to have prevented this.

A strong hand suddenly gripped her arm, pulling her into a chair. The sharp command made her shiver.

"Sit down!"

Angela's eyes widened. "What are you doing here? How did you—?"

"Maria called me," Lincoln said shortly, still keeping her firmly seated. "You left a message on her machine, and she called me. Apparently, I should have anticipated this. I've been condemned without trial by that staunch ally of yours." He watched her with a dark, almost ferocious intensity.

"I never asked her to phone you," Angela whispered, voice breaking. "I called her because... I had no one else, and—"

"Damn you, Angela! You're my wife!" Lincoln's eyes blazed at her. He sat beside her, his hand gripping hers. "Who else would you call but me?"

Angela gave a high, shaky laugh, almost hysterical. "Please! You're the last person I would want here! This is my father! Did you come to witness the final act?"

Lincoln snarled something under his breath, stood abruptly, and began to walk away. Angela's heart leapt in panic. He couldn't leave—not now. She needed him here, even if she hadn't meant the harsh words that had slipped out. It wasn't Lincoln who had caused her father's collapse; it was her father's own reckless drive, his drinking, his obsession with work, the way he had demanded control of everyone and everything. Whatever Lincoln had done, it had not brought this on.

Exhaustion overcame her, and she closed her eyes, bowing her head as weariness sank into her bones. She jumped when Lincoln's strong hand gripped her arm and pulled her to her feet. She couldn't believe it—he had come back.

"Come with me," he ordered grimly, his voice leaving no room for argument. "You need something inside you, and you need to be warm."

"I can't leave—" she protested weakly.

"Yes, you can." His tone was absolute. "Just around the corner is a small place where we can eat and get a drink. I've spoken to the staff. They say it'll be some time before there's any change in your father's condition. I gave them my cell number. They'll call if anything happens. Sitting here worrying does no good, and I will not allow it. You're coming with me."

Protesting was futile with Lincoln. His determination had always carried her along, whether she wanted to go or not, and nothing had changed now. Besides, this was sound common sense, and Angela knew it.

"I'll come," she sighed, and his storm-grey eyes shot a lightning glance at her.

"There was never any doubt about that," he grunted irritably.

Shock, hunger, and the sheer weight of the past few months had left Angela almost numb. Sitting across from Lincoln in the small, dimly lit bar, she finally realised it. She was not fit to cope—not with the crumbling business, not with her father fighting for his life. She simply sat, staring at him as he ordered their drinks and food.

The place was almost empty at this hour; chairs were stacked for closing, and she checked her watch with surprise. Almost ten o'clock. She had been at the hospital for hours without noticing the passage of time. Hours more would likely pass before any news from the intensive care unit where her father lay struggling to survive.

Would he fight? She had once believed in his iron will, but now she wasn't so sure. He had been fading before her eyes for a long time, and she had done nothing.

"I knew this was coming. I should have acted," she muttered to herself.

"What?" Lincoln's voice cut through her thoughts. She looked up at him, dazed and vulnerable.

"I was thinking aloud," she confessed, then, under the weight of his devastating, unrelenting gaze, she dropped her head. "I should have seen this coming. I did see it coming, but I didn't act. I just… let it happen."

"So now you're to blame for his heart attack?" Lincoln's tone was harsh, unforgiving. "What could you have done to prevent it? Kurt Marsden never listened to reason. He considered only his own schemes, his own ambitions."

"You don't know him! You never did!" Angela shot back, the sting of his judgment igniting her.

"I know every last thing about him," Lincoln growled, his voice a low, commanding rumble. "Every detail of his life up to this very moment. When I set my gaze on someone, there isn't much left that remains hidden."

Angela's throat tightened. There was no arguing with him—his certainty was absolute, a force of nature. Yet beneath the anger and commanding presence, she felt a fragile thread of comfort. In the storm of her father's crisis, Lincoln was the only anchor she had.

Angela forced herself to meet his gaze—the cold, unyielding glitter of eyes that had once smiled at her, warmed her, even cared for her. Or had she only imagined that? Had she ever truly known this man? Had she really been his wife in every sense of the word, or just another pawn in his relentless war against her father?

"I wonder how much you learned from me," she murmured shakily, her throat tight. "I must have told you plenty without even knowing it. And now he's dying—"

"And once again, you're taking the blame," Lincoln cut in, sharp with impatience. His mouth twisted in a grim, almost mocking curve. "Or are you shifting it this time? Is it finally my turn? If he hadn't been my target, Kurt Marsden wouldn't be lying in that hospital bed. Is that the way we're settling the score?"

"Who knows what would have happened?" Angela whispered, staring at her trembling hands as if they might steady if she only held them still. "If any of us could see the future, how differently we would act." Her eyes lifted, locking on him. "But not you, Lincoln. You would never have chosen differently, would you?"

His face seemed to blur before her, the room tilting. She blinked rapidly. "This drink… it's gone straight to my head."

"You need food," Lincoln said curtly. The waiter set the plates down at that moment, and when she only looked at hers blankly, he pushed the cutlery into her hands.

"Eat," he ordered, his voice like a whip. "You don't move until I've seen you eat. Sleep comes after—but food first."

"I can't sleep," Angela said, her voice shaking, though she obeyed, forcing bites past the knot in her throat. "I'll just sit on a bench at the hospital and try to rest."

"You'll get into a bed and sleep," Lincoln countered without hesitation. "When you've finished this, you're going to the penthouse."

Her fork froze midway. "What penthouse?" She looked at him, startled, but his expression was steady, almost grim.

"Our penthouse. We've only ever had the one—and it's still there."

"It's yours," she whispered, a faint edge of panic in her tone. "It has nothing to do with me."

He didn't rise to her panic. Instead, he regarded her with unnerving calm. "When you married me, half of everything I had became yours. The penthouse. The house. The company. If you don't want to sleep in my half, then sleep in yours."

"This isn't the time to be amusing," Angela said chokingly, but his only answer was a look of quiet disparagement.

"I'm stating facts, not telling jokes. If you'd divorced me, you'd already be wealthy. If I die first, you'll be rolling in money."

"Stop it!" Angela cried, sharper than she meant, emotion breaking free. "I want nothing of yours. Nothing—and you know that."

"But you'll get it, Angel," he murmured, his tone soft and cutting all at once. "By now, perhaps you're old enough to handle it."

"Then marry again! I'm sure Fiona would be happy to take my place." she blurted, desperation roughening her voice. She wanted this cruel sparring to end, wanted him to stop taunting when her father lay between life and death.

His eyes chilled, but the derision left them. "I have a wife. One catastrophic marriage is more than enough. I don't need another set of chains."

"If my father dies," Angela whispered bitterly, forcing down the last mouthful of food, "then at least one thing will be finished."

Lincoln pushed back his chair with a snap of impatience, and in one movement he was on his feet, pulling her sharply up with him.

"This conversation is over. Now you sleep."

"I will not!" she flared, but the fight in her voice didn't match the weakness in her body. She was swaying, dazed—exhaustion, grief, and the wine tangling together until even standing upright felt impossible. She could have laid her head on the table and slipped instantly into oblivion.

"Walk to the car," Lincoln warned, his voice low, dangerous, "or I'll carry you."

She managed to reach the door, her limbs heavy, every step dragging. The sleek black Jaguar waited outside, its polished lines gleaming like salvation. Wherever Lincoln intended to take her, she would go, because she couldn't stand much longer.

"My father…" she began faintly, but his hand closed firmly around her elbow, guiding her with quiet strength.

"Leave that to me," he said, his voice suddenly rough with something close to promise. "I'll not let you down."

And hazily, as he helped her toward the car, Angela realised with a kind of broken clarity that he never truly had. Not in the ways that mattered. Except, of course, with Fiona Martin. That betrayal still lay like a stone in her chest, hard enough to keep her awake until the penthouse—once thrillingly familiar, once hers—rose before her again.

How many times since she had left him had Lincoln brought Fiona here? The thought twisted like a knife. If Fiona had wanted a baby, would he have refused her too? No—Fiona would never have wanted the burden of children. But she had wanted Lincoln's child. Wanted it so desperately that Angela could still feel the shadow of that rivalry pressing down on her chest.

"Why?" The word broke from her lips, barely a whisper. She stood swaying, drained, as Lincoln closed the door behind them. "Why couldn't I have a baby?"

He turned at once, as if the sound of her voice had struck him, his gaze sharpening when he caught the glimmer of tears on her cheeks. Tears not just of exhaustion, but of regret. If there had been a child, she would have had something—someone—a piece of Lincoln that could never have been taken away.

"You're tired, Angela." His voice was low, rougher than she expected.

"Why?" she whispered again, her eyes clinging to his, hollow with the question that had never left her. "I never understood. I wanted a baby, Lincoln. What harm could it have done? Even if you never meant to stay with me—even if all you wanted was my father—it would have been mine. Something that belonged to us."

His jaw tightened, the hard line of his mouth betraying tension he didn't speak aloud. He moved toward her, unfastening her jacket with deliberate care before tossing it aside on a chair.

"This isn't the time," he said grimly. "You need sleep. Ask me again—another day."

"You're always putting me off," she whispered, staring at him as though she could drag the truth out by sheer force of will. But he only shook his head, steady, unyielding.

"Go to bed, Angela. You know the way."

"I've nothing to sleep in…" The words slipped out, small and uncertain, a last barrier against being dismissed.

"You left everything when you fled," he said, his tone clipped, almost cold. "Including your clothes. They're still here—exactly where you abandoned them. As I recall, you had more than enough nighties."

Her knees felt too weak to move, and for a long moment she simply stared at him. Then, with a sharp exhale of impatience, Lincoln strode forward, lifted her into his arms, and carried her to the bedroom.

He set her down on the bed with the same brisk authority he had always wielded, pulled open a drawer, and tossed a silk nightgown across her lap. His gaze pinned her, dark and warning.

"Undress yourself," he said harshly. "Otherwise, I might just change my mind about that baby."

The words cracked like a whip, half-taunt, half-threat, leaving her too stunned to speak. She watched him stride out and close the door firmly behind him, the echo of his presence lingering long after he was gone.

For a moment she only sat there, numb, staring after him. Sometimes she wondered if she had only dreamed the Lincoln she used to love—the man who had once made her believe she was his world. This man, with his biting words and unreadable eyes, felt like a stranger.

At last, moving as if through water, she slipped into the nightgown. The pillow met her cheek, cool and familiar, and exhaustion claimed her before she could think again. Sleep was a mercy; tonight, it was the only one she had.

Chapter Eight

The next morning Angela awoke to the hushed stillness of the penthouse. For a moment she lay disoriented, staring at the familiar ceiling, her heart hammering as memory returned. This place—once the setting of her happiest dreams—now felt both achingly familiar and frighteningly alien.

She forced herself up, washed, and dressed quickly, determined not to linger. The silence pressed against her ears, and when she discovered she was alone, her unease deepened. No Lincoln. No sign of him at all.

Seizing her chance, she made herself a hasty breakfast, though the cereal turned to paste in her dry mouth. She swallowed a few spoonfuls, her nerves knotting tighter with each bite. She had slept through the night—far too deeply—and dread coiled in her chest at what she might hear from the hospital. Her father. She had to know.

She crossed to her bag, fingers fumbling as she dug for her cell phone. Her hands trembled so badly she could barely hold it steady, the screen blurring through the sting of unshed tears. She was about to press call when the faint click of the door handle froze her.

The door swung open. Lincoln stepped inside. His presence seemed to fill the room instantly, a charged weight pressing against the air. One look at her pale, strained face made his eyes narrow, sharp, and unreadable. He closed the door behind him with a measured, deliberate calm—an action that felt less like courtesy and more like sealing them off from the rest of the world. Then he turned, his gaze locking onto her as if nothing else existed.

"Your father is holding his own."

Angela's breath caught. "How do you know? Did you ring? Why didn't you wake me?"

"To what purpose?" he returned evenly. "They wouldn't have let you see him."

"Of course they will! I'm going there now—at once!" Her voice rose, raw and urgent. She spun toward him, blazing with the conviction that he was once again trying to manipulate her.

"Do so," he said with cold indifference. "But they'll not admit you."

"Oh? And how would you know?" she snapped, her anger brimming over.

His gaze flicked to hers with cutting scepticism. "Because I've already been there."

The words struck like a blow. She froze, her fury dissolving into shock. Lincoln—at the hospital? Visiting her father? Impossible. Unless… unless he had gone to twist the knife further.

"You went to torment a man who may be dying?" she choked, her voice breaking. "You went to gloat?"

Lincoln's head snapped around, fury blazing in his eyes. "How highly you think of me, Angela. How well your father's training took root. Every word from him is gospel, and I—always the villain." His voice hardened, lethal with restrained anger. "Why the hell did you marry me at all?"

The answer escaped her before she could choke it back. "I loved you."

Silence fell, heavy and aching. The words hung between them, fragile and undeniable.

His expression darkened, though some of the raw anger drained away. "Childish fantasy," he muttered, his mouth a hard line. "That's all it ever was."

Angela sank down, trembling, grateful at least that his temper seemed to be ebbing. She had never seen Lincoln's rage fully unleashed—only heard the stories, felt the edge of it in his dealings with others.

"I went to have a word with him," Lincoln said at last, his tone clipped but steadier. His bleak gaze pinned her. "I thought it might help. You may not have noticed, but no one is circling Marsden Enterprises at the moment."

Her pulse stumbled. She had noticed—yesterday. And it had terrified her all the more.

"The bank—" she began, her voice thin.

"I called the dogs off," he cut in curtly. "After you came to me, I reconsidered. I went to the hospital today to deliver the news myself—and to make my offer. I thought it might perk him up. Unfortunately, they wouldn't let me near him."

Angela's throat tightened, her breath quick and shallow. "What offer?"

There was something in his tone, in the cold deliberation of his words, that made her blood run cold. Lincoln never stopped—he only changed direction. If he had abandoned the vendetta, it was only because he had conceived of something more dangerous.

He gestured to a chair, his own body settling into one with calm finality. "Perhaps you'd better sit down. You'll need to."

Dread pressed on her chest, but she obeyed, lowering herself opposite him. Her wide green eyes clung to his, betraying every flicker of fear and confusion.

"What offer?" she whispered again.

"I'm prepared to end this." His voice was level, almost conversational. "I'll make a bid for Marsden Enterprises and ease it into my firm. Or—if he prefers—I'll help rebuild it. Put it back on its feet."

It was impossible. He couldn't mean it. Angela's eyes searched his face desperately, probing for some hidden snare, some cruel trap, but Lincoln's expression remained cool, unreadable. At last, she drew in a long, ragged breath.

"Why?" she whispered. It could not be because she had gone to him, nor out of pity for her father. Lincoln had never been moved by pity. Unless he chose to tell her, she had no hope of understanding. He was colder now, harder—perhaps he always had been. She had simply been too young, too entranced, to see it.

"Not generosity," he said smoothly, "and not from the kindness of my heart." He leaned back in the chair, one long leg crossing elegantly over the other, his mouth curving in a faint, sardonic smile. "There is one condition."

Of course there was. And it would be appalling. Angela's lips parted, but no sound came; she was too afraid to ask.

"I'd be grateful if you would stop looking at me like a frightened rabbit," he drawled, the same sceptical amusement now glinting in his eyes. "The condition is not too terrible, all things considered."

"What things?" Her voice trembled despite her effort to keep it steady.

"I'll admit this much," he said, his tone clipped, deliberate. "My relentless pursuit of your father's firm has played its part in his condition. I never wanted him dead—I told you that before. But even without me, Marsden Enterprises is finished unless someone intervenes. Unless I step in openly, visibly. You need me, Angela. And I'm willing to help."

"But—" she breathed, sensing the sting in the tail, the real cost.

He inclined his head, dark eyes holding hers. "I wish to have my wife back for a few weeks. Nothing arduous. No... marital duties. Merely a front for a necessary trip."

"What?"

Angela rose slowly, gripping the chair for support. Lincoln's gaze followed her, one brow lifting, and in the depths of those astonishing eyes a dangerous spark of mischief danced.

"You're not stupid," he said softly. "You heard me. You understood. I have a trip to make. For a few weeks, I need a wife—in name only. Conveniently, I already have one. What could be simpler?"

Her breath came back in a rush, fury surging to replace shock. "What are you up to now?" she stormed. "Even the sight of you could kill my father. Any hint of such a scheme would finish him! If you must have a companion, then take Fiona Martin!"

"She isn't my wife," Lincoln returned smoothly, his amusement sharpening. "I have a business deal. A very large one—with an American family firm. The man at the head of it has… old-fashioned values. No mistresses. No divorces. He expects to meet my wife. I'm buying him out, Angela. With his company I gain another foothold in the States."

"Then go and buy him out!" she flung at him. "Leave Marsden Enterprises to sink! We've managed perfectly well without you for months."

His gaze cooled. "He doesn't need the money, and there are other buyers circling. Given a choice between my offer—however generous—and that of a solid family man, he'll take the latter. He's peculiar that way."

"This isn't amusing!" she spat. "You're thinking of schemes while my father clings to life. I won't let you near him!"

"You think I owe him favours?" Lincoln's voice cut like a blade, his earlier amusement vanishing. "I made a promise five years ago—and so far, I've kept it. I could take someone else, yes, and risk discovery. But I offer this to you, Angela, because I never vowed to see Kurt Marsden dead. Not despite what he did to my father. And my mother."

"He did nothing!" she cried, her voice breaking with rage. "It was business. That's all it ever was!"

"He's a liar and a cheat." Lincoln surged to his feet, looming over her, his anger vibrating in the air. "Go to the hospital. See for yourself. Then ring me with your decision. The offer expires tonight. Make the deal yourself if you like—without telling him. But if you refuse…" His jaw tightened. "Then I unleash the dogs again."

Angela's hands trembled, her throat raw with unshed tears. The words slipped out before she could stop them, fragile and desperate in the silence that followed her outburst.

"Why did you marry me?"

For a long, breathless moment, he only looked at her. His gaze burned into hers, unreadable, unyielding. Then, with deliberate slowness, he lifted her chin with one imperious finger, tilting her face up until she could not escape him.

"I've told you before," he said, his voice low, threaded with something dark and rough, almost haunted. "Because I wanted you."

And just like that, he was gone. He turned without hesitation, walking out of the penthouse, the quiet echo of his footsteps vanishing into the muted chime of the lift.

Angela stood frozen, her pulse hammering against her ribs. Still no declaration of love. Never love. Just want. Want for possession, want for control. A pawn in his ruthless game of vengeance. That was all she had ever been.

How she wished—achingly, foolishly—that he had said the words just once. At their wedding, when her heart had been full and blind, he had never spoken them. Not once. Passion, yes. Desire, yes. But love? The one thing she had craved most. It had never been given.

And now, older, wiser, she could finally see the truth she had been too young to recognise then: she had mistaken the hunger in his eyes for the devotion she longed for.

He was leaving her space to think, but the very idea made her laugh bitterly. Think? About what? There was no chance she would ever agree to his outrageous plan. She had her own future mapped out, a job waiting with Barry Windsor. Marsden Enterprises could drown in the deep, murky waters where it belonged.

She would never go back to Lincoln—never again. The scars from the last time had not even begun to fade. Yet here, in this penthouse filled with memories of him, the air seemed thick with his presence, and against her will, old longings stirred, threatening to rise from the shadows. She pressed her hands hard against her temples, as though she could drive the weakness from her.

Lincoln had always been what he was now—danger. And she knew, with bone-deep certainty, that no matter how he dressed it up in business, charm, or talk of want, he would always be the greatest danger of all—to her heart.

Angela dressed quickly and ordered an Uber. Perhaps the nurses would turn her away, but she had to see for herself. She would not—could not—take Lincoln's word for anything.

At the hospital, she barely made it past reception before the nurse at the desk blocked her path.

"I'm sorry, Mrs. Stokes. No visitors allowed. Your father is holding his own. The signs are good, but he cannot have visitors. I told your husband the same when he came earlier. If he had passed that message on, it would have spared you the journey."

"He did tell me," Angela said tightly, frustration pricking her. "But surely that doesn't apply to me. I'm Kurt Marsden's daughter—his family. Even if my husband couldn't see him, I have that right."

The nurse only shook her head, her expression firm. Angela was still arguing when the ward sister appeared, her presence instantly more authoritative.

"Your husband was told—" the sister began, but Angela cut across her, her voice trembling with fierce determination.

"I have every right to see my father! You can refuse his son-in-law, but not me. I'm his daughter. I'm next of kin."

The word son-in-law tasted bitter, and she cringed at the sound of it. To Kurt Marsden, Lincoln was the son-in-law from hell. He hadn't acknowledged her marriage when life had been good; he certainly wouldn't now.

The sister studied her face in silence, and something in Angela's pale, desperate features seemed to soften the woman's stance.

"You may look at him through the glass," she conceded at last, though reluctantly. "But you cannot enter the room. And you mustn't try to speak to him—even if he recognises you."

"Is he still unconscious?" Angela whispered.

"Sometimes he wakes," the sister said briskly as she led Angela down the corridor. "Even lucid, at moments. Though it's difficult to make sense of what he says."

They reached the intensive-care unit. The sister motioned her forward, and Angela's breath caught as she stepped up to the wide glass panel. Only one bed was occupied.

She pressed closer to the glass, biting down on her lip in shock. If there had been more patients, she might not have known which one was her father. The man lying in the stark white bed was a stranger—smaller, diminished, his once-commanding face as colourless as his hair. But it wasn't the pallor that undid her.

It was the machinery. The tubes. The endless wires snaking around his frail body. He looked less like a man than a fragile thing kept alive by willpower and machines. For the first time, Angela felt hope crumble.

Her knees buckled, and she swayed until the sister caught her arm.

"This is why we restrict visitors," the woman said gently now. "It's not cruelty, Mrs. Stokes. Some family members can't bear it. Better to wait until he's stronger, until the shock won't scar you as much. Tomorrow, perhaps, or the next day, he may look more himself. Your husband should have prevented you from coming."

"He—he tried," Angela muttered faintly. "He told me I wouldn't be able to see him."

She had distrusted Lincoln—as always. But he could not have known her father would look like this. Would he have tried to stop her if he had known? That, she couldn't answer.

"Has… has my father asked for me?" she asked shakily as the sister guided her back along the corridor.

"Not that I've heard. When he wakes, he grows agitated. He talks about the company. But it's so confused, I can't say what he means."

Angela's mouth twisted bitterly. "I can guess."

Marsden Enterprises. Always Marsden Enterprises. Even with death pressing close, her father's thoughts were chained to his company. Not her. Never her. Her whole life had been proof of it. Her mother had come second, she herself lower still.

If Kurt Marsden fought for life, it would not be for his daughter. It would be for Marsden Enterprises—to keep watch as it slid toward ruin.

Chapter Nine

Angela returned to the penthouse, only realising when she reached the door that she no longer had a key. All those reminders of Lincoln—every token of their marriage—she had thrown away four years ago. For a moment she stood numbly on the step, uncertain what to do, before instinct pushed her to turn away.

The door opened before she could retreat. Lincoln filled the frame, tall and immovable, his expression unreadable. Without a word she brushed past him into the apartment.

"I take it you've been to the hospital?" His voice followed her into the sitting room, edged with suspicion. He leaned against the doorframe, frowning at the bleakness in her face.

"Yes." Her throat tightened. "I saw him. They wouldn't let me at first, but I insisted. They finally let me look through the glass, and I—" Her voice fractured. "I could see… I could see…"

"You little fool." In two strides he was at her side, pressing her firmly into a chair.

Before she could protest, a glass of brandy was in her hand. She swallowed obediently, the burn spreading through her like reluctant warmth. Lincoln hovered above her, then turned away sharply, striding to the window to glare down at the street below.

"What did you gain by this visit, Angela?" His tone was weary, almost accusing.

"I saw him," she whispered, her voice dull with shock.

Lincoln spun round, his grey eyes blazing. "Damn it all, Angela! Why don't you ever listen? Why can't you let me protect you? You walk straight into pain as if you crave it. You're no steadier on this earth than you ever were. God knows how you function in that office. I don't even know how you manage from one hour to the next."

"I'm not the incompetent fool you imagine." The brandy gave her a thin thread of courage, enough to lace her voice with bitterness. She lifted her chin, green eyes sparking. "Thanks to you, I have no choice but to go into the office. It might be running without me now, but it won't for long. There's no one else to take charge—to face things."

"There's nothing to face," Lincoln shot back. "I told you—I called off the pack. Nothing is happening."

"Exactly!" she flared. "No business, no progress—because you interfered. You've strangled every path we had. Nothing and nothing still adds up to nothing!"

"Maria Belle can manage *'nothing'* quite well," he said with biting sarcasm. "And she's not alone in that building. The staff are still working."

"For now! But soon enough they'll be gone too."

"Not if I take the firm under my wing." His voice dropped, quiet and deliberate, and Angela looked away quickly, dread tightening her chest.

She had been turning the thought over ever since leaving the hospital. Her father would not fight for her—he never had, never would. He would fight only for the firm. If Marsden Enterprises collapsed, so would Kurt Marsden's will to live. The truth was brutal, undeniable. Without Lincoln, there would be no company. And without the company, her father would let go.

Lincoln dropped into the chair opposite her; his storm-grey eyes fixed on her downcast face.

"What are his chances?" he asked abruptly, cutting into her spiralling thoughts.

"Not good." Her voice was hollow, her gaze distant. "The sister told me he came round earlier. He never asked for me. He was talking about the firm."

Lincoln's eyes narrowed, a flash of anger tightening his jaw. But when he spoke, his voice was even, controlled. "He would have been half-conscious, rambling. Don't take his words to heart."

"I never expect miracles," she said quietly. "I'm far too ordinary for them. Miracles are for you, Lincoln. You hunt them down and bend them to your will."

Something flickered in his eyes at that—half amusement, half something darker—but he didn't smile. "He's hanging on," he said instead. "It's his nature."

"It always has been," she agreed, her voice heavy with sorrow. "But he's always had something to fight for. Now he doesn't. He won't fight for me."

Her words lit fury across Lincoln's face, his eyes sparking with icy rage. Angela watched him, her heart thundering. Every line of his body radiated power, danger, temptation.

And deep inside, the real question formed—did she have the courage to step back into his world?

For one long, glorious year he had been everything—her lover, her confidant, the axis of her world. When it ended, she thought she would never recover. In truth, she never had. Even now, as she looked at him across the room, memories returned with cruel clarity—secret, painful fragments of laughter and tenderness that haunted her like ghosts. He was still magnificent, still devastatingly powerful. His voice now carried more anger than gentleness, but she could still hear the echoes of the man she had once loved.

"I agree," she said quickly, before fear or pride could silence her.

His gaze sharpened. "To what?" He remained utterly still, watching her with unnerving intensity until her face grew hot, a tide of embarrassment mingling with fright. What if he had only been mocking her? What if he had already changed his mind?

"You… you said you wanted me back for a couple of weeks," she stammered. "To make a bargain with my father."

"So, I did." His voice was low, rough, almost a murmur of smoke. "But I never got to him. And even if I had, it's clear he wouldn't have been capable of striking any bargains."

"Why are you like this?" Angela burst out, her voice tight with sudden anger.

His eyes cooled to steel. "Maybe I was born like this. Or maybe I became this way— driven by circumstances sharper than knives. Whatever the reason, I am what I am now. Fixed. Unyielding."

He leaned back, stretching with lazy arrogance, one ankle crossing over his knee, his gaze half-lidded but piercing. "So, you're prepared to make the bargain yourself? A unilateral decision?"

"I have no choice." Her eyes dropped to her hands, studying the restless movement of her fingers rather than risk the verdict in his. "I have to give my father something to fight for. Otherwise… he won't."

Silence spread between them, thick and heavy. She was beginning to believe he would not answer when suddenly he rose and looked down at her.

"Very well. I accept." His words were clipped, final. "You'll play the part. You'll pretend to be my wife again—"

"I was never pretending!" The words tore from her in a fierce shout, her head snapping up. Her green eyes blazed into his. "The pretence was yours, Lincoln! I never betrayed you. I never had a secret lover. I never set out to hurt anyone you cared about!"

"I believe you," he murmured, but the irony in his tone cut like a blade. "As I understand it, though, you've corrected that oversight since you left me. Barry Windsor, isn't it?"

"Yes!" she lied swiftly, her voice ringing with vehemence. Let him believe it. If he thought she belonged to another man, perhaps he would keep his distance until this charade was over.

"Let me remind you," she added sharply, "Barry and I didn't even know each other when I was married to you."

Lincoln's smile was a cold, dangerous curve. "You're still married to me, sweetheart. Tell him to remember that. Tell him to keep his distance. As far as the world is concerned, we're reconciled—until this is finished. And if one whisper of this arrangement being a sham reaches my American contacts, the entire deal collapses. If my deal collapses, Angela—" his eyes burned into hers, relentless, merciless— "then so does yours."

She rose abruptly and began gathering her things. There was nothing more she could do about her father tonight, and she had no intention of staying here a moment longer.

"Where are you going?" Lincoln's voice snapped across the room, his hand closing round her wrist like a steel trap.

"Home. Where else?" Her tone was cool, brittle as glass. "No doubt you'll inform me when this little farce is to begin. I'll be there, Lincoln. At the starting line, ready and waiting."

"Going back to that house isn't a good idea," he said, quieter now, though no less firm.

Her laugh was short and sharp, edged with scorn. "Don't start, Lincoln. I'm not nineteen anymore, and you're not going to get me under your thumb again. We have a bargain, nothing more. And before it begins, I want proof—something solid, not just your word."

"It's already begun," he murmured, releasing her wrist. His voice was soft, but it carried weight. "It began the moment I called off the bank. You may doubt everything else about me but never doubt this—my word has always been good enough, Angela."

Her anger faltered. For a moment she just stared at him, caught by the truth in those words. Lincoln's word was good enough. It always had been.

"Very well," she conceded stiffly. "But there's no reason for me to remain here tonight."

"We're close to the hospital," he reminded her, his voice low, measured. "If your father wakes and asks for you, you'll be minutes away. And if..." His jaw tightened. "...if anything happens, you'll be on hand."

The brutal honesty of his words struck a raw nerve. She couldn't bear hearing him say what she herself had already feared. Her composure broke.

"You pig!" she cried, flinging herself at him, tears flooding her eyes. Her hands struck at his face, trembling with grief. "That's what you want, isn't it? You're circling like some hunting animal, waiting for him to die!"

Lincoln caught her easily, his grip merciless as he pinned her arms, one hand tangling in her long dark hair to force her head up.

"I am not waiting for him to die!" he roared, his fury blazing. "For God's sake, use your brain! When he collapsed, you had nothing—no one. And you still don't. You have me, Angela. Like it or not, without me you are alone."

The truth hit harder than his hands ever could. The words sank into her like acid, stripping her anger, stripping her fragile dignity. When had she ever truly had anyone? She had never even really had him.

Her resistance drained away, her body sagging in his hold, shoulders trembling beneath his punishing grip, lashes still jewelled with tears.

"All right," she whispered, broken. "I'll stay. But I can't—I can't stay here with you."

"I never thought you would." His voice was cold now, edged with control. "I'll move out. But we'll have an understanding: if anything happens, you call me. Immediately. You may despise me, but you need me."

Her head bowed, hiding her tear-streaked face. "I'll call," she murmured.

"Where will you—"

"I'll be at the house," he cut in tightly. "Our house. Remember, Angel?"

She flinched. "I have the number somewhere," she said quickly, deliberately dodging the weight of his meaning. "If anything happens… I'll be ready when you want me."

In an instant, his arms crushed her to him, his body iron against hers.

"When I want you?" His voice vibrated with vehemence. "Angel, I've always wanted you. Some things don't change, no matter what else in this world does."

His grip was punishing, his grey eyes blazing with anger when she dared to look up. She struggled, fear sparking in her gaze, and he let her go suddenly, shoving her away as self-disgust twisted his features.

"Don't fear me, Angela," he said bitterly, his tone chilled to ice. "Once, you had me chasing you like some idiotic schoolboy. I won't repeat the mistake. This is business, nothing more. When it's finished, you can have the divorce you've so meticulously avoided."

Lincoln walked out, slamming the door behind him, and Angela remained rooted in place, too shaken to think clearly. He was heading to the house—the house she had once helped to furnish and fill with dreams of happiness. How impossibly long ago that seemed now. She sank into a chair, her body trembling with anxiety. Pretending to be a happy wife to Lincoln was going to be far harder than she had imagined. Mostly, she would have to rely on his own acting ability. She would need to consider her clothes, plan her behaviour carefully. Wherever Lincoln went, there was wealth—an opulent world she had known only in fragments.

The thought of the upcoming trip to America only deepened her anxiety. Glamorous people, glittering events—the kind of world he navigated effortlessly—would surround her. And without warning, she was transported back nearly five years, her pulse stinging with an old, familiar ache: jealousy. The mere thought of Lincoln mingling with some sophisticated woman she had never met made her self-confidence falter.

Why did he insist on taking care of her, when it had all been over for four long, weary years? Perhaps it was masculine pride. She was still, in name at least, his wife. In another life, in another set of circumstances, it would have been natural to lean on him. But she could not admit that she longed to; she had borne every burden alone for so long that allowing Lincoln's strength into her life again felt like surrender—an erasure of her hard-won independence.

Meanwhile, Kurt Marsden began to recover. Within days, the hospital called to inform Angela that he was conscious and asking for her. She went immediately, deliberately avoiding any contact with Lincoln.

Her father was weak and frighteningly vulnerable yet awake. He looked as though he might start fighting his way back to life.

"What's happening?" he asked, his voice weak but sharp.

Angela forced a weary smile. He did not mean the personal turmoil she was facing—he could not know the momentous decisions she was preparing to make. His mind was occupied solely with the firm. She settled into the rhythm of familiar explanations, carefully avoiding any mention of Lincoln.

"Nothing much," she said lightly. "Everything seems quiet. The bank has backed off if that's what you mean."

"Why?" He immediately tensed, suspicion flashing in his eyes. Angela hesitated, caught in a dilemma. If she admitted Lincoln had softened, her father would likely not believe it. If she said nothing, he would continue to worry, and any surge of anxiety could send him backward in recovery.

"Well, business is still coming in," she said vaguely. "Perhaps they're having second thoughts."

"Angela, you're hopeless," he snapped. "Banks don't have second thoughts. It's all profit and loss to them, and they saw long ago that we're on the losing side."

He fell silent, thinking, brow furrowed. "There's something peculiar going on," he muttered at last.

Angela noted the tension creeping back into him and considered carefully how to respond. She barely had time to decide when the sister appeared to usher her out—the visit was over, and there was urgent news to share.

"He needs surgery," the sister said once they were in her office. "The surgeon has explained everything to your father. He requires a triple bypass. It's the only path to any sort of normal health. After that, he'll need rest and careful nursing. With luck, you should have him back at home soon."

Angela's heart lurched. "Does he agree to all this?" The thought of such a major operation terrified her. Her father had not even mentioned it; his mind had been entirely occupied with business.

"Yes, he agrees," the sister replied, smiling gently. "He doesn't even seem anxious. I think he just wants to get back to work."

Angela nodded grimly. She knew him well enough to predict that he would take no real precautions—too much stress, too little rest, too many bad habits. Yet he had agreed, decisively and independently—unilaterally, as Lincoln would have said. All she could do now was wait and prepare for the day when her father would return from the brink.

Chapter Ten

It arrived two weeks later. Until then, she had not seen Lincoln. She had promised to contact him if anything happened, but she did not. Seeing him felt too dangerous, and she wanted to keep him out of her life until the last possible moment—until she was forced to act on their agreement.

She saw her father every day, but each conversation was a tightrope. At any moment, he might say something that would compel her to reveal her arrangement with Lincoln.

The night before the operation, however, her father seemed stronger. He questioned her more insistently, probing for news, and Angela decided it was time to take the risk. The thought of returning to his office had sparked a vigour in him she could not ignore; he needed to know there was more hope than the vague notion that the bank might show mercy.

"Lincoln called off the bank," she said quietly, watching for any flicker of disapproval. "He tried to see you, but you were too ill."

At the mention of Lincoln's name, her father's face flushed with colour. Angela grasped his hand anxiously. "It's all right," she assured him. "He didn't want anything to happen to you."

"You believe that?" Her father barked an incredulous laugh. "He always bamboozled you, girl. Had you wound around his finger, and now you're falling for the same old tricks. If the bank stepped back, it's nothing to do with Spokes."

Angela felt a surge of anger—angry at the constant battering of her self-esteem by both Lincoln and her father, angry that she bore the blows and still received no acknowledgment.

"Lincoln called them off," she said steadily. "It's not just the bank—he's stopped all the creditors. Things are in limbo, but at least nothing's getting worse. He did it because… because he has a bargain with me."

"What bargain?" Kurt Marsden leaned forward, eyes narrowing. "What kind of bargain would a man like that make? And even if he did, he'd never honour it."

The word 'honour' lingered uncomfortably on his tongue. Angela looked at him sharply. Despite everything, she trusted Lincoln implicitly—she knew without doubt that he would uphold his word.

"I'm going to America with him when you're better," she said firmly, stopping short of calling herself his wife. "I'm going as… his hostess."

"He has a deal there and he needs me," she explained, her voice quick and urgent. "In return, he'll take Marsden Enterprises under his wing—either buy us out or get it back on its feet to return to us. He'll respect your decisions and make it clear he's involved. It will make us viable again and take all the heat off."

Her father lay back against the pillows, colour fading, eyes narrowing as he assessed her words.

"He wants you back?" he asked at last. Angela shook her head emphatically.

"Definitely not! I wouldn't go if he did want me. It's just a cover for a business deal. Once it's over, he suggests I get a divorce."

Kurt's head snapped up, his gaze piercing. "It must be a significant deal," he probed quietly.

"It is," Angela admitted. "Another foothold in America. He can't risk it falling through. The man involved doesn't like anyone of Lincoln's age to be unattached—he's old-fashioned."

"So, you're going as his wife," her father said flatly, still watching her, without anger or outrage.

"In name only," she assured him quickly. He considered her words thoughtfully.

"We've nothing to lose and everything to gain," he pronounced after a pause, a faint, approving smile lighting his eyes. "Go ahead, Angela. It will lift the firm out of trouble. Good girl."

Her chest sank under the weight of his approval—it reminded her how expendable she often felt. As she rose to leave, he added one more comment that struck deeper than any before:

"You're still his wife, after all."

Yes. It was all right to be Lincoln's wife—if it served Marsden Enterprises. If the bitterness between Lincoln and her father hadn't existed, Kurt Marsden would have welcomed his new son-in-law five years ago with open arms. He would have seen it as a strategic advantage for the firm. That was the unvarnished truth, and Angela left feeling like a mere commodity, shuffled between two powerful men who regarded her only in terms of usefulness, never as a person.

That night, Lincoln phoned. She told him about her father's operation, and there was a long pause on the line.

"It seems to me we had agreed," he said idly, "that if anything happened, you would contact me."

"Nothing happened," Angela said, careful. "I didn't think you wanted to be bothered with every detail."

"What you mean," he grated, "is that you wanted to make damned sure I had no excuse for being anywhere near you. When is this operation taking place?"

"Tomorrow."

Before he could insist on accompanying her to the hospital, she plunged ahead. "I told him... about... our bargain," she said quickly.

"And?"

Lincoln was silent, his voice unreadable even over the phone.

"He seems to think it's a good idea."

A cold, harsh laugh rang out from him, and she tightened her hand on the receiver.

"I can well believe it," he said acidly. "He does realise, I hope, that it will necessitate you being out of the country?"

"I told him all that—but I can't go before the operation."

"Do you think I'd expect you to, Angela?" he murmured, softer now. "I want a happy, smiling wife with me, not some wistful creature looking over her shoulder, bracing for bad news. We can wait until this is over. We'll go as soon as he's safe."

"Thank you," she whispered. For the first time, his laugh was free of anger. She could almost see the sparkle in his grey eyes, and a slow flush warmed her cheeks.

"You're welcome, Mrs. Spokes," he said mockingly. She said nothing, and his voice darkened, familiar and magnetic. "I give up on you, Angel. You'll never toughen up, it seems. I'll probably spend most of my trip to America watching to make sure nobody upsets you."

"I can take care of myself!" she shot back sharply.

"Well," he said, amusement in every note, "we can pretend. As long as I'm right beside you, we can pretend anything."

Angela hung up quickly, cutting off the sound of his voice. The old, familiar shivers ran over her skin. She paced the penthouse, berating herself.

"I will not fall for anything again!" she told herself fiercely. "I will not let Lincoln get to me."

It was a panicked reaction to his voice, just as it had been to his presence before. And who was she fooling? She had avoided calling him to the hospital not because she didn't need his support, but because she felt too vulnerable with him around. Even the way he had grabbed her roughly the last time they'd met lingered in her mind. He was always there—lurking at the edges of her thoughts. The sooner she could be entirely free of him, the safer she would be.

The operation went smoothly, without complication. Apart from his heart condition, her father was still the tough, unyielding man she had always known—the surgeon had assured her of that later. At the last minute, she had called Lincoln to tell him the time of the operation, and when she arrived, he was already there. He had stayed with her throughout the long hours, saying little, but simply being present gave her courage. She could look up and see him scrolling through his phone, wandering the hospital corridors, or watching the activity around them. He was like a rock—immovable, steady, unshakable—and she had never doubted him so completely.

Afterwards, he took her out for a quiet meal. That night, Angela slept more peacefully than she had in months. Lincoln's calm, solid presence had soothed her like a balm; for a short, precious time, she had felt safe.

But the next day, reality intruded. This was it—nothing could delay the arrangement for her trip to America. She had leaned on Lincoln's strength, accepted his help with both the firm and her personal problems. Now she had to pay the price and honour her side of the bargain.

Returning to work could no longer be postponed. The atmosphere in the office was still slightly uneasy, but she could sense that everyone recognised change had arrived.

"Lincoln is helping," she told Maria, deciding honesty was better than secrecy.

"About time, too," Maria sniffed, but it was clear she was delighted. She asked no further questions, and Angela offered no explanations. If Maria chose to imagine a romantic reconciliation, she would discover the truth eventually—it was all business.

"I have to go to America," Angela added, a little distantly. To her surprise, Maria accepted it calmly.

"Things will still be here when you get back," she said comfortably, though Angela could not miss the gleam of satisfaction in her eyes. Maria, it seemed, was just as prone to daydreams about Lincoln as anyone.

"By the way," Maria added as Angela headed toward her office, "Barry Windsor phoned. He's back from Germany sooner than expected."

"Fine," Angela said, smiling faintly as she walked on. Another complication. There was the small matter of his job offer and the larger matter of the lie she had told Lincoln.

But it didn't feel urgent. The two men would never meet, and she would contact Barry when this arrangement with Lincoln was concluded. She had no intention of working under Lincoln's constant supervision, no desire to be tossed about by the whims of her father. If he wanted to try, he was welcome—but she would not let it control her life.

For the first time in months, Angela found herself enjoying the day at work. Something had shifted—a sense of freedom, a weight lifted, whether from the promise of Lincoln taking over the firm or from her renewed determination to stand alone. Either way, it felt good to reclaim a piece of her own life.

She left the office with a small smile. With her father off the danger list, there was no need to linger at the penthouse, and she had her own car. Tonight, she intended to go home, make arrangements with Rita, and bring her fully up to date.

As she approached her car, a horn blared, stopping her in her tracks. Barry had drawn up beside her, the window down, shouting before he even stepped out.

"Angela, love! I'm back! You can stop worrying—rescue is here!"

She laughed, turning toward him, relieved to see his warm eyes and fair hair tousled by the wind. But her laughter faltered when the familiar dark Jaguar slid silently behind Barry's modest car. Lincoln sat inside, icy-eyed, his mouth tight with controlled anger.

Before she could react, Barry leapt from his car and pulled her into a long, unrestrained hug, planting a quick, bold kiss on her lips—a gesture he had never attempted in all the time she had known him.

"I came tearing back from Germany as soon as I could," he said eagerly. "I've been worried about you nonstop. Now we can plan your future."

Angela froze. The dull thud of the Jaguar door signalled Lincoln's silent arrival. He was moving toward them, and she was powerless. All her careful composure from the office had evaporated. Lincoln would see Barry's display of affection and likely take her lie as truth.

"Angela, love?" Barry's voice faltered as he sensed the sudden tension. His boisterous tone carried, and she prayed he hadn't overstepped.

"There's no need to worry," he continued, oblivious, "everything will be fine. The firm can—"

He trailed off, noticing Lincoln now standing before them.

"Angela is overwhelmed," Lincoln said coolly, his voice as icy as his eyes. Barry spun around, stunned.

"However," Lincoln continued, "the firm will not go hang, and my wife will not be going with you. She has a future that does not include you, Mr. Windsor."

"You're back together?" Barry gasped, too stunned to sense the threat in those cold eyes.

"Oh, yes," Lincoln said with biting sarcasm. "Next week, America—a second honeymoon. Don't make the mistake of trying to see her again."

He grabbed Angela's arm, moving her toward the Jaguar before she could protest.

"Let me go!" she said, her voice low with embarrassment.

Lincoln stopped, looking down at her, his anger blazing.

"If I let you go, Angela, I also let the firm go. It will collapse. The bank will seize the valuable parts, and by the time your father leaves the hospital, there won't even be dust left to sweep up."

"You promised!" she cried, fear and anger mingling.

"And I keep my promises," he reminded her sharply. "You struck a bargain alone, and I made it clear: any sign this is a sham, and the deal is off. Moving in with Windsor would be proof enough. Then neither you nor Marsden Enterprises would be of use to me."

"You—misunderstood!" she said urgently. "He didn't mean—he offered me a job! He never—"

Lincoln's stormy eyes pinned her. Fury simmered beneath the surface, and she clenched her hands in anxiety. He studied her hands, then took a deep, controlled breath.

"Very well. We continue—but one false move, Angela, and the deal is off. Any sign of Windsor, and you—and Marsden Enterprises—are on your own."

He began to lead her toward his car again, and she pulled free.

"I have my own car. I'm going home tonight. When you want this to start, you'll let me know. In the meantime, I have arrangements to make—Rita is alone at the house, and I can't leave without preparing things."

"And Windsor?" Lincoln snapped.

"What about him!" she retorted, patience exhausted. "I don't need a third man underfoot. Between you and my father, I have enough trouble. This deal involves me on civilised terms. Understand *'civilised'*, Lincoln?"

He watched her for a moment, his eyes softening slightly.

"So, you've finally grown up, Angela," he said quietly. "Prepared to face the two wolves in your life and hold your ground."

"I just want to see the back of them both!" she flared.

"You were never humble," he mused, touching her face lightly, "just too sweet for your own good. Sweet, sweet Angela. I'll need a lot of convincing that the sweetness has gone."

"It should be easy to prove," she replied tartly, turning away. "Let me know when I'm on duty."

"If you need anything—" he began.

"Space!" she snapped, flashing green eyes.

"You'll get it," Lincoln said, amusement gone from his voice. "When this is over, you'll have the divorce—and all the space you could want."

She marched off, uneasy at the cold fingers of fear Lincoln's words had sent racing through her heart. This should have been the end of him—obliterated from her life— and yet she knew it wasn't. He had always lingered, right at the back of her mind. After this, she would have to banish him completely. Only then could they both be free.

A sudden vision of Fiona Martin made everything click. Now she understood why Lincoln had mentioned divorce. He couldn't tell her outright; she might have refused to go to the States. He couldn't marry Fiona quickly, either—it would probably jeopardise the delicate arrangement he had to keep in place for the man he was dealing with.

Pain tightened her chest. She almost walked past Barry without seeing him, lost in thought. But he was still there, beside his car, and when he touched her arm she spun, meeting his worried eyes.

"Is it true, Angela? Are you two back together again?"

Lies, lies, lies, Angela mourned silently. She longed to tell him the truth, but doing so could ruin everything for her father. Not even the dust would remain to sweep up, as Lincoln had threatened.

"We're going to try," she said carefully, pale, and distant. "I'm sorry about all that, Barry. Lincoln completely misunderstood."

"I hope I haven't messed things up," he said ruefully, noting the tension in the air.

"It's all right," she soothed, forcing a smile. "Lincoln can get very angry over very little. He misread the situation."

"I can understand him being jealous," Barry said wryly.

"I rather put my foot in it myself," Angela admitted. "I was only being my usual blundering self."

"You were simply being kind," he replied softly. "I'd better let you go. Rita's expecting you, and you have a lot to do before you leave for America."

She summoned a brilliant smile and turned toward her car. Lincoln jealous? No. He was simply enraged that his carefully laid plans were threatened. When this was over, he would move on to Fiona Martin without hesitation.

She started the car, swinging out of the parking area, her lips tightening as she saw Lincoln still standing by the Jaguar, eyes watchful. He wasn't taking any chances. If Barry tried to follow, Lincoln would probably ram him off the road.

Her father had been right: the American deal must be extraordinarily important. Lincoln was putting his private life on hold, taking Marsden Enterprises under his wing, and demanding a respectable wife to accompany him. Until she could step clear of both Lincoln and her father, she would never be anything more than a pawn.

Chapter Eleven

Once her father was safely moved to a private convalescent hospital closer to home, Angela faced the moment she had dreaded. Rita would manage the household, friends would visit, and her father would recover under proper care.

"I have to go with Lincoln," she reminded him. "I don't like leaving you alone, but unless I go, the deal falls apart. He's inflexible about these things."

"He must have some flexibility," Kurt Marsden pointed out. "Otherwise, he wouldn't have waited until I was out of hospital. He must care for you, in his own way. Just remember he's very wealthy. Play your cards carefully this time."

Angela's stomach tightened. She was only doing this for her father, yet Lincoln's hold over her was almost mystical. The only way to navigate it was to fight it—and now her father was urging her to cast aside her standards to secure a financial lifeline.

"Waiting was part of the bargain," she said tightly. "He knew I wouldn't go unless I knew you were safe and recovering."

"I've never needed anyone to prop me up," her father snapped. "Help the firm, not hang around here bringing me flowers. Keep your mind on why you're doing this."

"I could hardly forget," she said drily. "I'm going to America to live a lie for as long as Lincoln specifies."

"Hardly a lie," her father said with a knowing smile. "You're acting as his wife. And you are his wife, aren't you? He's got sense after all."

Angela bit back a bitter retort. Lincoln's cunning was matched only by her father's ruthless practicality. She counted for nothing—merely a useful daughter, a virtuous wife. Once, she had longed to do something wild, impulsive, just for herself. Now she was trapped.

But after this... she swore she would change. She would leave her father to his precious firm and Lincoln to his life, as she had first realised five years ago. Lincoln was beyond her, outside her world. It had only ever been a dream.

Lincoln rang a few days later while she was in the office.

The moment had arrived, and her heart thumped alarmingly when he stated, flatly, that they were leaving at the end of the week.

"It gives you three days to complete your preparations," he said, inflexibly. "We fly Saturday afternoon, stopover in New York, then on to California."

Angela's mind instantly conjured images of sun-bronzed women in skimpy bikinis, and any hard-won self-assurance she had cultivated vanished at the thought.

"Why there?" she asked shakily.

Lincoln sounded mildly surprised. "He lives there."

"You mean… we're staying at his house? His home?" Angela's voice caught.

A low growl of exasperation came through the line. "We are not. Hospitality was offered, but I refused."

"Why?" Suspicion trembled in her voice, and Lincoln snapped at her before she could even think it through.

"Not for any devious motives concerning you! This is a business trip, not some furtive, sensual weekend."

"Are we just going for the weekend?" Angela muttered, her face burning.

"We're going for as long as it takes to make the deal. Get a grip on yourself, Angela! I have no intention of demanding my rights as a husband. My interest is purely business, and it will take all your intelligence to play the part of a normal wife without any distractions. I'll collect you Saturday morning."

"It's not necessary. I—" she began, but Lincoln slammed the phone down before she could finish. Angela stared at the receiver, a mix of desperation and relief surging through her. He would come for her, and thank goodness, her father would not be there. They had not met since the wedding five years ago, and the thought of their encounter—despite Lincoln's altered attitude—made her shiver.

"California…" The word floated through her mind as she stood by her desk, thinking frantically about her wardrobe. Would she be smart enough? There would surely be dinner parties, social gatherings. She would be meeting these people in a way that made Lincoln's presence essential.

He had said the man liked things to be homely. What did that even mean? Just because someone's morals were *'homely as apple pie'* did not mean the women would wear gingham dresses and ribbons in their hair. Her only knowledge of California came from films, and the images flashing through her mind left her unnerved.

Angela left the office early, telling Maria she would not return until after her trip.

"Good luck!" Maria said cheerfully. "Have a wonderful time." Angela looked at her as though she were mad.

It would be the most stressful time of her life. She had to perform, and she had never pretended to be anyone other than herself. She would be in close, daily contact with Lincoln. While she trusted his word completely, she did not entirely trust her own emotions. His hold on her had always been powerful; she was not foolish enough to believe she could resist his charm.

She shrugged angrily. What charm? Lincoln still felt he had the right to dictate to her, to lose his temper. If she had possessed even one scrap of common sense, she would have chosen Barry and an easy, amusing life. Barry was light and comforting; Lincoln was raw electricity, a force of nature. Any contact with him made her pulse race—and reminded her just how perilous her task would be.

Over the next two days, Angela fussed endlessly over her possessions. Her father had never stinted on her allowance, even when she was younger, and now, with her own earnings added, she had amassed a wardrobe of expensive clothes. A pang of regret struck her as she thought of the penthouse—beautiful things she had simply walked away from.

When she had been with Lincoln, they had travelled overseas and frequented all the smart London venues. Lincoln had delighted in spoiling her, piling treasures into her arms, relishing the look on her face whenever he returned with something new and glamorous. Glamour was exactly what she needed now.

Sitting on the edge of her bed, she wondered if she had the nerve to raid the penthouse. She had a key; after the fiasco, the first time she had tried to enter, she had wisely stashed a spare in her bag. Lincoln was staying at the house—he wouldn't even notice she had been back until he saw the clothes she wore. His memories would be of Fiona's wardrobe, not hers.

It was that thought that propelled her into action. Why not? The clothes were hers, the jewellery hers. She left in the late afternoon and drove to London to retrieve them.

An unnatural darkness hung over the city as she pulled up outside the building. Black clouds gathered in the sky, and Angela frowned, aware that a downpour could complicate her mission. She dashed up the steps to the door, determined to make this a quick raid. She already knew what she would take.

The silence inside was a little alarming, heavy with memories—every one of them tied to Lincoln. Angela shrugged them off, shedding her coat, and marched to the bedroom with resolve.

The last time she had been here, anxiety about her father had dulled her perception of the place, but now it pressed in on her. The entire penthouse sang of Lincoln. She knew, without being told, that he had spent most of his time here since she had left him four years ago. Perhaps he had lingered out of irritation—the penthouse had been his before they had met—but the home they had built together had always been his in essence.

She quashed maudlin thoughts of any women he might have brought here. This was no time for emotional crises. Besides, there could have been only one, and she already knew who.

Angela strode resolutely to the bedroom; her gaze fixed on the dressing room door that had once been hers. Inside, the huge walk-in wardrobe promised everything she could need. There was no time, no money, and no inclination for an exhausting shopping spree—everything she required was here. All she had to do was collect it and take it home to pack.

At first, it was easy. The dresses, suits, and gowns were still pristine, and Angela began selecting them briskly, piling them at the end of the bed. She had no idea how long they would be away, so each choice had to be carefully considered. Her first, panic-stricken instinct—to scoop up everything and leave—had to be restrained.

After a few moments of thought, she calmed. Occasionally, she tried on a few pieces. Her slender figure had not changed over the past four years, but some outfits now required a subtle adjustment to suit her more subdued appearance. Far from disappointing, the clothes reignited the glow she had once known. Colours lifted her face, and a smile returned as the confidence she had grown into with Lincoln resurfaced. Methodically, she tried everything she had chosen, tossing her original outfit over the back of a chair.

A vague awareness of the rain began to prick at her consciousness. One glance at the window confirmed that it had already begun pounding down. Angela tossed a bright red raincoat onto the growing pile, deciding she would not take chances—even if California might be dry. A small, nervous giggle escaped her, and that was when a sound behind her shattered the fragile calm.

She spun, green eyes wide, to find Lincoln leaning casually against the open bedroom door, his gaze appraising her with dark, slow intensity.

"Don't panic," he warned, his velvet voice low and dangerous. "I thought we were being robbed."

Angela stiffened at the intimate 'we', turning quickly, only to realise she was clad in nothing but silky white panties. She had removed her bra to try on some low-cut gowns and had not bothered to replace it.

"Please... go out and shut the door, Lincoln," she stammered.

"I know what you look like, Angel," he murmured softly. "Every inch. The feel of your skin, the curve of your shoulders, the fall of your hair. I've never forgotten. You'll feel the same if I touch you."

Her breath caught, a rush of fear and excitement tangling in her chest. "Please, Lincoln!"

"I'm not touching you," he reassured her, voice deepening. "Words can't hurt you."

Angela grabbed a dress, holding it in front of her as a shield, but he moved closer, his presence overwhelming.

"Don't hide," he said thickly. "It's too late. I saw you the moment I came in. I knew how I would feel." His warm breath brushed her shoulder, fingers tracing lightly along the curve of her trembling body.

"Do you think I'm made of stone, Angel?"

"I—I didn't know you were here," she gasped. "I didn't think you would come."

"I saw your car," he murmured, hands now moulding her shoulders, pressing just enough to make her quiver. "I wondered what you were up to. I never expected this."

"I… I came for clothes," she whispered, voice shaky.

"Keep talking, Angel," he purred, lips brushing her shoulder. "It's safer."

"I'm going!" she cried, trying to summon steel in her limbs, fighting the pull of his voice and touch.

But he was relentless. The dress she clutched dropped, and his arms encircled her, pressing her back against the searing heat of his body.

"Don't," he husked. "You said that once—don't leave me, Lincoln. And you also said… forever."

His hands moved with deliberate possession, cupping her breasts as his mouth brushed the curve of her neck. Fire raced through her veins, and the sound of his voice slid over her like silk dipped in flame.

"I still want you, Angela. I never stopped."

"It's not fair!" she sobbed, twisting, trying to escape, but his lips followed her jaw, hands tracing every curve. Her body betrayed her, aching with surrender.

"Nothing is fair," he murmured darkly. "This isn't about fairness—it's desire. And it's burning you too, sweet Angela. You want me."

Rain lashed the windows, but the softly lit room felt sealed from time and consequence. Another world, long dreamed of, now consumed her. His voice, his touch, his scent— it was achingly familiar. She had missed him with a hunger that ripped through her defences. A low, broken cry escaped her throat, half anguish, half longing.

Chapter Twelve

When he turned her fully into his arms, she yielded, pressed close, her breath catching in a sob of pleasure as his mouth found hers with devastating force. His lips claimed, his hands searched, and she moved helplessly beneath his mastery, trembling with mounting need. Every nerve was alive, straining toward him, his breath on her neck a flame that ignited all she had buried for four long years.

Her arms rose, twining around his neck, and she abandoned herself to the fierce hunger that had never truly died. Memory exploded into feverish life. The excitement was so sharp it was almost pain, so heady it threatened to sweep her into unconsciousness.

"Lincoln!" she cried, her voice raw with torment and desire.

He held her tight, then lowered her to the bed, sweeping aside the silken garments as though they were nothing. His own clothes followed with impatient hands, his eyes dark and burning.

"I know," he rasped thickly. "It hurts, doesn't it, Angela? Like a hot knife inside. Tell me—does Windsor know what you like? Can he make you shatter in his arms the way I can?"

Before she could speak, before she could deny, his weight pressed against her and her body was already lost—sensitised, desperate, despairing with longing.

"Angela."

He framed her face between strong hands, his body braced on iron forearms, his weight a tantalising threat above her trembling form. His gaze seared into hers—molten, merciless, demanding.

"Do you want me to stop?"

She didn't. Words abandoned her. Her lips quivered, parted, but no sound came. Wide green eyes betrayed everything she fought to hide, and with a desperate tenderness she lifted trembling fingers to his cheek. The simple touch said more than speech ever could.

"Dear heaven," he muttered hoarsely. "Do you even know how you look right now? How much I've wanted you? How obsessed I am with this silken body?"

His mouth descended on hers, fierce and consuming, a kiss that stole breath and reason alike. She yielded instantly, her lips opening beneath his, her body arching into the hard, relentless heat of him with frantic need. The last fragile barrier of cloth slipped away beneath his hands, and then it was skin against skin—hot, raw, unforgettable.

"Lincoln!" Her wild cry broke from her throat, shattering the silence.

His answering laughter was dark and triumphant. "I'm here, my lovely. I know that cry. I remember, Angela."

After that, there were no words—only the fever of his touch, the heat of his body, and the helpless surrender of hers. Every caress, every grip, demanded her complete giving, coaxing out desires she had kept buried, too proud or too frightened to admit. She writhed beneath him, shivering, gasping, pleading in broken breaths, her fingers clutching at him as if anchoring herself to the only certainty in her world.

"Now, my wild little Angel," he groaned, his voice rough with urgency, vibrating through her very core. She sobbed his name, trembling, desperate for him, and he growled in response, deep and satisfied, a sound that filled her with longing and need.

"I want you," she confessed, ragged and raw, the words tearing from her throat like a lifeline.

His lips traced every inch of her—her shoulders, her arms, the hollow of her neck—before descending to her breasts, her stomach, the soft curves of her inner thighs. Every kiss, every lick, inflamed her senses until she was quivering beneath him, her body aflame with the exquisite torment of desire.

"Lincoln… please…" she whimpered, her voice cracking under the weight of the pleasure coursing through her.

She shattered, every cry of rapture filling the room, mingling with the low, relentless rhythm of his heartbeat against hers. Then he rose above her, sliding into her in one smooth, possessive thrust, consuming her entirely. The sensation was fierce, overwhelming, obliterating all thought, all fear—leaving only him, only this fierce, unrelenting connection.

She gasped, clinging to him, lost in the relentless cadence of his body as it mastered hers. The world fractured into shards of light and shadow, passion too sharp to endure, yet too intoxicating to resist. Every nerve was alight, every gasp and moan answered by his own feral hunger.

Her nails raked down his back, her voice a chorus of broken cries, and he caught her face in his hands, claiming her lips with a kiss that felt like it could draw out her very soul. Every movement, every thrust drove her higher, until she trembled and broke, her body convulsing beneath him in a cascade of ecstatic surrender.

"Shh," he murmured, his lips brushing her hair, his voice ragged yet tender, the anchor in the storm of sensation. "It's all right. I'm here sweetheart."

For the first time that night, trembling in his arms, her racing heart finally slowed, her ragged breath settling, and she believed him—believed that in his presence, for this fleeting, furious moment, she was utterly, completely safe.

The sound, the caress, was too familiar—it broke through the haze, dragging her back down to earth. Tremors shook her as reality struck like a blade. Stark grief engulfed her.

What had she done?

What had she allowed to happen?

Lincoln loved her no more now than he ever had. The love had always been hers, all hers, from the beginning. He wanted her—that was all. Desire, not devotion. Possession, not partnership.

The betrayal burned in her chest—not his betrayal, but her own. She had betrayed herself. Every principle she had once clung to, every ounce of dignity she had fought to preserve, lay in pieces at her feet. She had sworn she would hold herself apart, stand strong until the end and build a new life when this was over. But the moment his hands touched her, she had dissolved, crumbling into his arms as though she'd never learned strength at all.

Angela turned from him sharply, forcing her trembling body to sit upright. She reached for her clothes, dragging them close in a desperate effort to shield herself from his nearness.

"You want me to shower with you?" Lincoln drawled lazily behind her, his voice dark and honey-smooth, as though they had simply woken from a night of contented passion.

Her spine stiffened at the seductive sound. "Stop it!" she spat, the bitterness at herself burning like bile in her throat.

"I always did," he murmured, unrepentant. His hand lifted, one indolent finger trailing down her bare spine with deliberate slowness. She shivered before she could stop herself, and his quiet chuckle mocked her weakness.

"You lie, Angela," he added almost conversationally. "Your father lies. So do you. It must run in the family."

Her head whipped around, green eyes flashing like fire. "I don't ever—"

"You do," he cut in, calm, unshakable. His silver gaze pinned her. "Poor Windsor. I destroyed him without cause. No one has touched you since the day you left my arms four years ago."

"Don't fool yourself," she snapped, though her voice faltered as she yanked at her clothes. Every movement seemed clumsy beneath the weight of his gaze. She was painfully aware of him—lying there still, long-limbed, utterly magnificent, and far too relaxed, a slow, mocking smile curving his mouth.

"I'm not fooling myself," he said softly, his tone carrying dangerous certainty. "Angela, I know your body as I know my own. It was mine then, and it's still mine now."

She fumbled for composure, pulling her clothes into place with jerky, angry movements. "I suppose you think that little trick was clever," she hissed, refusing to look at him.

"There was no trick." Amusement laced his voice. "You came to me willingly. I gave as much as you gave."

No. Her heart splintered at the lie. He gave nothing—nothing but desire. His gift was never love.

"Really?" Her voice was brittle, tight as glass.

When at last she was dressed, she turned to face him, her face carefully composed though her pulse was wild. "Well, your cleverness backfired. I don't need these clothes now because I'm not going with you. My father will recover, he'll take back his firm, and I'll find another job. Threaten all you like—it's finished."

Lincoln didn't move. He lounged back against the pillows, an arm resting easily behind his head, one strong leg bent, the very picture of effortless power. His grey eyes glittered with sardonic amusement as they traced over her face.

"Your father will have nothing left to take back," he replied smoothly. "The moment I believe this childish rebellion of yours is real, I'll reactivate everything. For now, my bankers are servicing your debts, keeping your creditors at bay. One flick of my hand, Angela—and Marsden Enterprises is gone. If I let go, the scavengers will be circling before the ink dries."

Her throat closed. "Servicing our debts?" Her voice was strangled. "You can't be—"

"You're unworldly," he mocked gently. "Why do you think your bankers have been so patient? Do you imagine I simply told them to wait, and they obeyed?"

The truth was written on her stricken face, and his smile widened, wolfish. He rolled from the bed with a careless grace, reaching for his shirt.

"Oh, Angel," he said almost tenderly, as though speaking to a child, "if I were half as powerful as you imagine, I'd rule the world."

"I'll have to go with you, won't I?" she whispered miserably, every ounce of strength leaking out of her.

He turned, buttoning his shirt, watching her with eyes that softened almost imperceptibly at her forlorn expression. "I'm afraid so," he said, almost with regret. "Maybe after today, you'll play the part better."

"It will never happen again!" she flung back, sharp with defiance.

His gaze narrowed, piercing. "Never is a very long time. And when the time comes, Angela, you'll forget all about never."

Her cheeks flamed hot. She spun for the door, but his voice halted her.

"Your clothes, Angela. Don't leave them behind. I'd hate for all your ordeal to be wasted."

Taunting again. He knew—knew it hadn't been an ordeal at all. The only pain was this: coming back to reality, to distance, to the aching void after his touch. The only ordeal was losing him.

Silently, she gathered her scattered things. He crossed the room to the wall safe behind the Degas print, pulled out her jewellery case, and set it on the bed.

"You'll need these," he said, quieter now. "There'll be social evenings. You'll want jewellery." He lifted a necklace of emeralds, the stones catching the light. "Take this. It was always my favourite. It matches your eyes."

Her breath hitched. That necklace—his wedding gift, once cherished, like him. She almost snatched it from his hand, shoving it into her bag with a trembling fury. A relic of a past she longed to discard.

She turned away quickly, but desolation washed over her, crushing. She still loved him. God help her, she still loved him. And if he reached for her now, she would fall into his arms without a fight. That truth must never, ever reach him.

She fled before he could see the tears shimmering in her eyes, slamming the door behind her.

The rain had stopped, but the streets glistened. She packed her clothes into the car with rigid precision, not daring a single glance back at the building. If he was watching, she would give him no satisfaction. He had won, and she would not show him how deeply.

Her body ached, the echo of him still alive within her. The longing was there, pulsing steady, undeniable. His knowing grey eyes had seen it, of course—they always saw too much.

And as the engine roared to life, Angela knew she would have to guard herself fiercely on this journey. Because the real danger wasn't Lincoln's threats. It was her own heart.

New York was stifling, the air heavy and close even as twilight crept across the city. The flight had drained her, though they had travelled first class. Comfort meant nothing when every mile had been spent in taut silence, her nerves stretched thin beside Lincoln.

Now, as the car drew up to the hotel and the doorman hurried forward, Angela felt her knees threaten to buckle beneath her.

"Have something to eat in your room, then go straight to bed," Lincoln advised after one searching look at her pale face. His tone was cool, businesslike. "The only reason we're here is because I have a meeting tonight. Otherwise, we'd have gone directly to our destination. Perhaps it's just as well—you look worn out."

"I'm tired," Angela admitted, her voice flat.

Tired didn't begin to cover it. She was crushed, raw, still reeling from the way she had given in to him. Shame prickled at her skin, the gnawing edge of guilt twisting deeper with each hour. And yet, if Lincoln sensed any of it, he gave no sign.

He had spoken little on the flight, not with the icy hostility of old, but with an indifference that was worse. That afternoon—the heat, the hunger, the terrible sweetness of surrender—might never have happened. To him, it seemed, it had left no trace. While she was devastated, he was untouched.

He accompanied her briefly to her room, his eyes flicking over the neat space with swift inspection. "I'll have something sent up," he said. "If you need me, I'm next door—though I'll be out within the hour, and I won't return until late."

A polite nod, the firm click of the door closing behind him, and he was gone.

Angela sat heavily on the edge of the bed, staring at the door long after it had shut. His courtesy, his composure, was perfect—an astonishing lesson in manners that cut her more deeply than cruelty. He might have been speaking to a colleague, a secretary. Not to the woman he had held only a day ago.

Any lingering doubts were finished. Lincoln was a stranger—aloof, unreachable. His lapse into passion had been no more than a man's appetite. She had been used and now discarded.

The shower soothed her body if not her thoughts, and when she emerged, a tray waited neatly on the small table. Under gleaming silver lids were delicate dishes, chosen with exquisite care. Lincoln always knew what to order. He always knew the right gesture. But the note propped against the tray was written in a stranger's hand: Compliments of Mr. Spokes.

Her mouth twisted. How had he registered them? As Mr. and Mrs. Spokes? Did the hotel staff think them a peculiar pair—separate rooms, yet supper sent to his 'wife' with formal compliments? Send something up to my wife, with my compliments. The words might have been absurd if they had not made her feel so unbearably alone.

Her emotions swung like a pendulum—despair, regret, loneliness. Tomorrow loomed like a sentence. Playing his wife would be agony. He would stand close. He would touch her. And she would have to endure it, or the mask would slip. The charade could not fail.

She prayed whoever this man was, the one they were here to impress, would expect only flawless manners, not warmth, not affection. Lincoln could provide the surface with ease. Why, then, had he insisted on dragging her with him? Why not a photograph—proof enough to boast of? Why must she be paraded in person, forced to endure his proximity?

It was cruel. Cruel and calculated. His way of reminding her that he held Marsden Enterprises in a grip that could strangle at will.

Angela forced herself to eat a little, though each bite tasted of ashes. Afterward, she slid beneath the crisp white sheets, curling on her side. Somewhere beyond the tall windows, Lincoln was at play in the world he truly loved—power, games, victories measured in deals struck and empires bent to his will. That was his passion. Not her.

Never her.

Did he love Fiona Martin? The thought sliced through her, though she almost laughed at her own foolishness. If he had truly loved another woman, he would have freed himself long ago.

She pressed her face into the pillow, weary to her bones. Stupid, she told herself. You're grasping at fantasies.

Sleep, she prayed. Sleep was the only escape from tomorrow, from the weeks to come—however long Lincoln chose to hold her prisoner in this sham of a marriage.

The weight pressed harder. Her father, Rita, Maria, the loyal staff who looked to her. Their survival rested on him—and therefore, on her compliance. And as always, the responsibility dragged at her heart like a chain that would never break.

Chapter Thirteen

They arrived in California the next afternoon, and Angela felt almost restored by the change of air and the night's rest. To her surprise, it was Lincoln who looked strained. For the first time she noticed faint lines etching his handsome face, a shadow of fatigue dulling the usual force of his presence. Whatever hour he had returned the previous night, it had clearly cost him.

A long white car waited at the curb, gleaming in the sunlight, and Angela's spirits lifted as she spotted the man standing beside it.

"Here he is," Lincoln murmured, and a moment later she was being introduced.

Gary Carter was well past middle age, his thick hair turned white, but he carried himself with the robust energy of a man far too vital to be thinking of retirement. His smile was broad and guileless, his handshake hearty.

"My wife, Angela," Lincoln said, threading his fingers briefly through hers. "Angel, this is Gary Carter."

She barely had time to respond before Gary swept her into a bear-like embrace.

"The most beautiful thing I've ever seen," he declared, his voice booming with warmth. "You'll forgive my enthusiasm, little lady, but I've heard so much about you from Lincoln. Thought he was exaggerating—but he wasn't."

Angela managed a bright smile, though she was a little dazed. Little lady? She was hardly petite, though compared to Lincoln's towering height—or Gary's overwhelming presence—she supposed she might seem so. Still, his words carried a reassuring weight. If Lincoln had spoken of her often, then their charade gained credibility. His leaving her behind in England would have raised questions.

"Knew his grandpa and his uncle Greg," Gary confided, tucking her arm into his with avuncular warmth as he steered her toward the car. "Never could get him down to my place before now. Big day, this. Just waiting on Paul…" He glanced around, impatience flickering before he added with an apologetic shrug, "My son will be here any second."

He turned back to Lincoln, drawing him into animated conversation, and Angela took the moment to stretch her legs, grateful to breathe freely after the long flight. Her gaze drifted, her mind idling—until Gary's voice rang out, charged with sudden delight.

"There he is! Paul—come meet this delightful creature."

Angela looked up—and went rigid.

The man who approached was nothing like his father. Gary radiated wholesome vitality, but his son exuded something darker, slicker. Paul Carter's pale hair gleamed, brushed back too perfectly from a bronzed, handsome face. His smile was slow, practiced, and his dark eyes—far too dark—fixed on her with unnerving intensity.

"This is Lincoln's wife," Gary announced proudly. "Angela, meet my boy, Paul."

"Well, hello, Angela." His hand closed over hers and lingered, the grip deliberately too long.

Angela forced herself not to recoil, but every nerve in her body prickled. The way he spoke her name carried a faint mockery, a kind of insolent intimacy that made her skin crawl. Out of the corner of her eye, she saw Lincoln stiffen, tension sparking off him like a drawn wire. She understood why.

Paul's gaze didn't waver, and the gleam behind those eyes made her feel cornered. They held the cold, hypnotic pull of a snake, and she thought with a faint shudder: *He has the eyes of a basilisk.*

They were dropped at their hotel, and after the unsettling encounter with Paul Carter, Angela was more than relieved they weren't staying at the Carter estate. The younger Carter was the sort of man she must avoid at all costs. Perhaps he showered every woman with that insolent, predatory attention, but to Angela it felt invasive—almost sordid. A few minutes in his company had been disturbing enough; the thought of living under the same roof, forced into polite silence for the sake of Lincoln's business, would have been intolerable.

"Did Gary Carter book us in here?" she asked as they stepped into the cool, tiled foyer of the whitewashed hotel, its Spanish arches and wrought-iron balconies glowing in the late sun.

"No. I did." Lincoln's voice was clipped.

He was still simmering from their encounter with Gary's son, his irritation running beneath the surface like a taut wire. Angela, sensing his mood, kept her thoughts to herself as they followed the porter up the broad staircase. She had other things to worry about—chiefly, the sleeping arrangements. Here in Carter's territory, appearances mattered. Would Gary expect them to share a double room? The very idea knotted her stomach.

Her anxious glance must have betrayed her because Lincoln's eyes flicked to hers with a sharp edge of annoyance.

"These are your rooms," the porter announced at last, throwing open two polished doors. "There's a connecting balcony."

"Splendid," Lincoln muttered grimly. "I trust it doesn't connect with anyone else."

"You're completely private here, sir."

Angela thought the porter gave them a curious look, but Lincoln ignored it, issuing a brisk order for tea before dismissing the man. Their luggage was placed neatly inside, and for a moment the silence felt heavy, as if the air itself carried Lincoln's disapproval. Angela stood uncertainly by the bed, feeling as though she too had been delivered, neatly labelled, along with her cases.

"Whichever room you want," Lincoln said at last, his tone detached, his gaze coolly impersonal.

"They both seem the same," Angela murmured, trying to match his indifference. "It doesn't matter."

With a curt nod, Lincoln gathered his luggage and disappeared through the adjoining door, leaving her alone. Angela exhaled a long, weary sigh and turned to unpack. If this was how he meant to behave—distant, irritable, almost disdainful—then perhaps Gary Carter would rethink the entire idea of their marriage. For Angela's part, she could only hope so.

Her thoughts strayed uneasily to the woman Gary had married. What sort of wife tolerated such a son? The memory of Paul's dark, watchful eyes made her shudder.

The waiter arrived with a silver tray and laid out the tea on the curved balcony. Angela abandoned her half-unpacked case and stepped into the last warmth of the sun. The little hotel was unlike the towering city blocks she had known in New York—here everything sprawled low and wide, spilling into gardens ablaze with bougainvillea and hibiscus. There was no lift, no chrome, no sterile grandeur. Instead, whitewashed walls glowed beneath red-tiled roofs set at uneven heights, the whole place softened by the lush sweep of greenery. Their rooms, though, were clearly special, perched in a small tower that commanded the heart of the estate.

From the balcony, the view stretched across terraced lawns down to a pale ribbon of sand, the sea beyond shimmering blue-green, tranquil, and endless. Angela stood drinking it in, her heart lightening in spite of herself.

"It's wonderful!" she breathed, turning with shining eyes just as Lincoln stepped out to join her.

For the briefest second, his gaze caught hers, something unreadable flashing across his face before his mouth curved wryly. "It was recommended by someone who comes here often," he said, his voice even, almost dismissive. He seated himself at the wrought-iron table and began to pour the tea without offering her the chance.

Her smile faltered. She recognised that look—the one that reminded her of other times, long ago, when her enthusiasm had made her seem too young, too naïve. Like the day on the Thames, five years ago, when she had glowed with happiness while he had watched with quiet amusement. Now the memory only stung.

She sat opposite him silently, nodding her thanks as he handed her a cup. The shadows of the past pressed close, curbing her delight.

"Tonight, Gary Carter and his wife are dining here with us," Lincoln said at last, his tone clipped, businesslike.

Angela's head lifted sharply. "Paul Carter?"

"I didn't enquire," Lincoln replied, his mouth tightening. "I dealt with Gary alone. I can only hope the younger Carter will find a nightclub to occupy him."

Angela's distaste sharpened her features. "He's got eyes like a snake—a basilisk."

Lincoln's brows lifted faintly. "I've heard basilisks have beautiful eyes," he murmured into his cup.

"Not when they belong to a man," she shot back, disgust plain on her face. "He makes me shudder."

"I can't say he inspires my admiration either," Lincoln admitted, leaning back, one ankle resting over his knee, his long frame radiating controlled impatience.

"He looks like trouble," Angela said quietly. "I will ignore him and perhaps he'll slither back into the grass," she added hopefully.

Lincoln's eyes glinted, a sharp edge to his composure. "I don't ignore pests. I deal with them. But you—" His voice cut, crisp with command. "You'll steer clear of him. Do you hear me?"

Her chin lifted. "It would be nice to know I could slap his face and tell him to crawl back into his hole. But that wouldn't exactly endear you to his father, would it? The deal would be over in a heartbeat."

"You put up with nothing," Lincoln snapped, his eyes blazing like ice. "Not one thing. He acts—and you react. Always. Do you understand me, Angela?"

"I'm not deaf," she answered quickly, her eyes darting around the balcony, relieved to see they were quite alone. His voice had risen, his temper cracking through his veneer of control, and the intensity of it unsettled her.

Lincoln drew a steadying breath and leaned forward, his tone softer, though no less resolute. "Anyway. You'll be with me. I told Gary this was a second honeymoon, and he's delighted with the idea. Which means he'll expect to see us inseparable, heads bent together, very much in love. I'll be keeping you close, Angela. So, you've nothing to fear from his son."

The words were matter-of-fact, but something in the way he said them—low, final, with a note of possession—sent a ripple through her chest, confusing and unwelcome.

Angela forced herself to meet his gaze coolly, quelling the sudden leap of her pulse. "What a good job Gary Carter doesn't know about the two adjoining rooms," she said tartly, words tumbling out more to disguise her fluster than anything else. "When you send my supper up with your compliments, he'll be quite taken aback."

Lincoln's grin spread, his grey eyes dancing with mockery as they lingered on her flushed cheeks.

"It amused me," he confessed easily. "It startled the man at reception too. I was laughing all evening."

Angela frowned. She doubted it. In New York there had been no laughter, no trace of amusement—only the ruthless focus of a man hunting his prey. Lincoln in action was like a tiger, sleek and merciless.

"If you get lonely," he continued in a low, deliberate murmur, "you can always drift along the balcony to me."

"I'd rather drift over the balcony rail," Angela snapped, rising to her feet in defiance before striding toward her own French doors.

"You're telling lies again," Lincoln called softly after her, his gaze following the sway of her figure. "It's a hard habit to break when it runs in the family."

Her shoulders stiffened, but she didn't turn. Once she was beyond his sight her lips drooped, the spark of anger sliding into heaviness. He never forgot, never missed a chance to press the wound. And though she had once sworn by her father's innocence, Lincoln's unflinching conviction—and her own dawning doubts—gnawed at her. She had seen with her own eyes how devious her father could be, and Lincoln's cruel truthfulness made denial harder with each passing day.

Her thoughts circled, dark and uneasy. Why had he helped them? For years he had manoeuvred her family into his grip, tightening it with a strategist's patience, then, at the crucial moment, steadied their sinking fortunes with one ruthless hand. Was it really for the sake of a single American business transaction? Had she not been here beside him, she would never have believed it. Even now, doubt whispered that this was another move in a larger, merciless game of vengeance.

And yet—she had no choice but to go along. Whatever his plans, whatever trap lay ahead, she must walk into it. Worse still, being near him was its own torment. She still loved him, and he only had to lift a finger, and she would come. Whatever happened, she must not let him see it.

Dinner that evening was a relief, if only because Paul Carter did not appear. Gary's wife, Irene, proved to be a plain woman whose hair was dyed such an implausibly dull black that Angela found her eyes drawn to it like iron filings to a magnet. She had to school herself sternly not to stare. Left natural, it would likely have been a soft grey—and kinder.

"Oh, honey, look!" Irene exclaimed to Gary as she met Angela. "A real brunette. Look at that blue-black shine. You just can't get that colour."

Gary chuckled at Angela's flustered silence. "Irene changes her hair as often as she changes her mind. This week she's a brunette. It was red the week before."

"Ash-blonde," Irene corrected primly, jabbing him in the ribs. "Red was last month."

"I lose track," he laughed, and Angela's embarrassment melted into amusement as she joined in their laughter.

Lincoln looked faintly astounded at the exchange, though he covered it smoothly, stepping forward to lead them into dinner—a candlelit veranda overlooking the sea, where shadows and moonlight mingled like secrets waiting to be spoken.

A round table awaited them, glittering with crystal that caught the candlelight in sharp, delicate sparks. A bowl of white roses glowed in the centre, their fragrance mingling with the salt air drifting in from the sea. The veranda's trailing greenery and bursts of brightly coloured potted blooms turned the setting into something intimate, almost enchanted.

"This is really romantic," Irene cooed, leaning toward Gary, who smiled knowingly at her.

"Second honeymoon," he confided in a stage whisper. "We'll have to remember to leave at a respectable hour."

Angela's cheeks burned, her blush blooming like a wild rose. Lincoln stepped behind her, helping her into her chair with exaggerated courtesy. His hands lingered a moment too long on her shoulders, warm and possessive, his touch sending an unmistakable message.

"We've got all the time in the world," he said easily. "The second honeymoon started before we even left England."

Angela's heart lurched. In an instant she was back in the penthouse, in that lamp-lit bedroom, reliving the confusion of passion and pain. She fought the urge to flinch beneath his deliberately taunting hands. Was she expected to play the doting wife—smile sweetly, lower her lashes like some coy bride? Fortunately, her burning cheeks seemed to satisfy him. Lincoln settled opposite her, a complacent curve to his mouth that made her want to throw the roses in his face. Irene and Gary, oblivious, beamed at them both.

Dinner passed without a single mention of business. Gary seemed more interested in recalling the old days, speaking warmly of Lincoln's grandfather and uncle. Angela listened quietly, absorbing pieces of Lincoln's life she had never known. She learned how he had first come to America to attend Harvard, only to stay on afterward, working under the stern tutelage of his grandfather and uncle in the fast, brutal arena of American commerce.

"They were quick on their feet in those days," Gary reminisced, eyes bright. "Your grandpa was a whirlwind right to the end. And your Uncle Greg—same cut of cloth. Between them, there wasn't much they didn't know. To compete with those two, you had to be up before dawn, and even then, you'd still be behind."

Angela's gaze flickered across the table. No wonder he's in a league of his own, she thought with a sinking heart. He had been sharpened like steel by experts, forged in their world. It was hardly surprising that Marsden Enterprises had been slowly strangled into near extinction by his skill and relentless will.

"I couldn't believe it when your Uncle Greg was killed in that car crash so soon after your grandfather passed," Gary went on, shaking his head. "What a tragedy. Everyone expected you to stay here, take the reins. It was a real shock when you went back to England and left things to managers."

Lincoln's expression didn't change. His voice was clipped, almost dismissive. "My roots are there. I never intended to remain in the States."

"Sure," Gary murmured. "Couldn't be expected, I suppose, with your folks in England. Your dad married an Englishwoman, didn't he? Lost track after that. How is he these days?"

"He died."

The words fell cold and flat, like stones into still water. Lincoln offered nothing more. Gary faltered, looking stricken. He murmured his regrets, fumbling for tact.

But it was Angela who felt the real chill, deeper than she expected. She had known already—Maria had told her, and Lincoln himself had revealed as much once, long ago—but the way he said it now, bitter and stripped of all softness, startled her. No sorrow. No warmth. Only ice.

Her heart clenched. The bitterness in his voice was more than grief—it was a wound that had never healed, a promise of vengeance that had calcified with time. He had not forgiven. He had not forgotten. And with Lincoln, that could mean only one thing.

Revenge.

Chapter Fourteen

Whatever calculating game Lincoln was playing, Angela no longer doubted the truth of it: the hand Lincoln had extended to her father's firm was not generosity, but cold iron wrapped in velvet. She was here only because of that hand, gambling everything on his promise, and yet the vendetta simmered on, relentless. It would not stop—not until her father was ruined, perhaps even destroyed.

Lincoln's schemes ran too deep for her to fathom. He moved like a master strategist at a chessboard—every move concealed, every gesture deliberate, every word laced with meaning she could never quite unravel. Even that night in the penthouse—his mouth crushing hers, his body searing heat against her own—had that too been part of his ruthless game? Perhaps. Perhaps not. In the end, it hardly mattered. He had claimed her there as surely as he claimed everything, taken what he wanted and left her with nothing but the bitter certainty that there would be no bright, hopeful future waiting in his shadow.

Escape. The word pulsed in her mind like a forbidden prayer. But escape had no place in Lincoln's world, no room in the labyrinth he had built around her. And if she truly meant to find it—if she dared to dream of freedom—she would have to plan carefully. Methodically. One step at a time. And she would have to do it without Lincoln ever guessing her intentions.

Gary never asked about Lincoln's mother, though Angela braced herself for the question. Her nerves thrummed like taut strings, haunted by the echo of Lincoln's words when she had gone to his office to surrender. *'Remind him about John Spokes and his wife, Kathleen.'* At the time, she had flung the suggestion aside as impossible, outrageous. But now—now a terrible doubt gnawed at her. If her father had been responsible for two deaths… the thought alone filled her with cold horror.

Later, when Gary and Irene finally took their leave, she walked with Lincoln to the car. The night wrapped around them like a velvet cloak—moonlight spilling across the dark sea, the sound of waves rolling onto the sand, froth bubbling and hissing against the shore.

Angela lingered a moment as the car disappeared down the drive, her gaze drawn helplessly to the scene before her. The silvered beach, the restless ocean, the glittering arc of stars—it was all heartbreakingly beautiful, as though mocking the turmoil inside her.

Lincoln's eyes never left her. He watched in silence, his gaze sliding over the delicate line of her figure, the ivory sheen of her dress glowing pale in the moonlight against the glossy darkness of her hair. A dangerous contrast—innocence and temptation bound together in one slender, defiant woman.

"Want to walk on the beach?" he asked quietly.

She did. God, she did—but her nerves were frayed raw. For once, it wasn't the danger of losing herself in Lincoln's arms that unnerved her. It was the coldness in his voice when he had spoken of his father, the bitterness that lingered like poison in the air. She ached to know the truth, yet the thought of asking chilled her to the bone.

"I would, really," she said hesitantly. "You—you don't have to come, though. I can—"

"Don't annoy me, Angela," he cut in sharply, his hand fastening around her arm as he steered her toward the path. "You've been staring at me all evening as though I've grown horns. Did you think I wouldn't notice?"

"I haven't!" she protested, halting to look up at him. But the moonlight betrayed her. With the hotel lights behind them, he seemed taller, darker, the silver in his eyes flashing like steel. Her breath caught as the fierce set of his face loomed above her.

"I told you—I never lie," he grated. "The news of my father's death was no surprise to you. You already knew. So why the look of horror, Angela? Were you braced for me to say how he died? Waiting for me to add— 'at the hands of Angela's father'? Was that it? Were you shrinking from the words before they were even spoken?"

"No! I never thought that!" Her voice shook with indignation. She wrenched her arm free and stormed away, but his footsteps came hard and fast behind her.

"Don't walk away from me!" His voice cracked like a whip. "If you think I'll let you wander this beach alone, forget it." He caught up easily, falling into stride beside her.

Angela shook her head, despair rising thick in her throat. "I didn't want to walk alone, and I never thought you'd mention my father tonight. But whatever happens—whatever is said—it's always my fault. Always on my shoulders." Her lip trembled, and she bit it hard, her words failing.

Lincoln gave a low growl of frustration, then swung her round, gripping her shoulders. "When have I ever laid blame at your feet?" His voice was rough, urgent. "I carried you, protected you, gave you everything I had. Look at me!"

She refused, keeping her gaze lowered until he tilted her chin up, impatience in the motion—only to falter as moonlight revealed her shimmering eyes, her face pale with emotion.

"You little idiot," he muttered hoarsely, pulling her against him. "I never learn. I should just throw you over my shoulder and carry you off."

Warmth surged through her as his hands slid over her back, his head bending, lips brushing along the delicate curve of her jaw.

"I wasn't anxious about you mentioning my father," she whispered, desperate for him to hear. But his focus was elsewhere breathing her in, tightening his arms, drowning in her presence.

"Lincoln."

"Hmm?" His reply was thick, drowsy with desire.

Gathering her courage, she lifted her face. "I didn't think you'd speak of him. I'm learning more every day. Once, I was sure. But now... I don't know what to believe anymore."

His arms dropped. The warmth vanished as he turned away, striding along the sand. She hurried to keep pace.

"You'll hear nothing from me," he said, voice taut. "Not before, not now, not ever. If you're waiting for explanations, you'll wait a lifetime."

"I'm not waiting for anything," she murmured, the words barely audible.

He laughed harshly; a sound stripped of all humour. "No—you never do. You take what's handed to you. You never demand, never claim. Always ready to endure, to settle. You live off scraps."

"And I take yours too," she shot back, her voice sharp with bitterness. "If I'd fought for what I deserved, I wouldn't even be here."

His head snapped toward her, grey eyes blazing with sudden fire. "Then where would you be? With Windsor?"

The words cut deep, sharper than any slap. Her throat tightened, but she forced the retort through trembling lips. "If you think I'm such a fool, so idiotic and childish, then why did you marry me at all? I must have been a chore for you—a burden you had to put up with!"

Angela spun on her heel, fury propelling her across the sand, but her anger faltered almost instantly as her heels sank into the soft grains, making her stumble. She bent down, muttering under her breath as she yanked at her sandals—only to feel herself swept up in one sudden, effortless motion.

"Put me down!" she gasped, thrashing in indignation, but her strength was nothing against his. Her dignity burned, her cheeks hot, while he held her as though she weighed nothing.

"Be quiet, Angel," Lincoln murmured, his voice low, disturbingly tender in contrast to her fury. His gaze softened as it lingered on her face, his words striking with disarming intimacy. "I'll just imagine you're still nineteen, and suddenly it all makes sense again.

Nothing's changed—you still glow with the same innocence, the same purity. To Gary Carter, you must look as though I stole you straight from a convent."

Angela didn't know whether to laugh, cry, or slap him. But as she stole a glance at his face, she saw his wide grin had returned. And against her will, relief washed through her.

Angela slept deeply that night, the sea breeze lifting the gauzy curtains and cooling her skin. For the first time in days, she'd felt soothed. It was later than usual when she finally stirred awake. She hurried out of bed, wondering if Lincoln had already breakfasted.

But when she stepped onto the balcony, there was no sign of him—no clink of china, no deep voice rumbling through the adjoining room. Then, from below, she heard the crunch of tyres on gravel. A car.

Leaning over the rail, she froze as the hotel doors opened. Lincoln appeared, striding to meet the arrival. Angela instinctively drew back, pulse racing, half-expecting Gary Carter. She wasn't dressed to be seen.

The voice that reached her, however, was not masculine. It was female, low and smooth, and it chilled her blood with recognition.

"Well, I'm here, darling, and utterly exhausted."

"You look dazzling as ever," Lincoln replied lightly, amusement threading his voice. "Clearly overnight flights agree with you. You should take them more often."

"Only if you command my presence."

Angela's fingers curled tight around the balcony rail. She knew before she looked, but still she glanced—and her heart cracked all over again. Fiona Martin. Elegant, immaculate, clinging to Lincoln's arm as though she belonged there. He carried her briefcase, while a porter trailed behind with her luggage.

"Thank God you're here," Lincoln murmured, his voice pitched low, but it carried. Angela's breath hitched, humiliation slicing deep.

She had lived this nightmare once. She couldn't live it again. As his mistress or his lawyer, it didn't matter—he had summoned Fiona to his side, and Angela could not bear it. Not when she was here playing out a charade, pretending. Not when Fiona would be through the other side of the connecting door, breakfasting with him, smiling at his side at every function.

Her chest burned with fury as Angela stormed through the French doors and into the bedroom. She yanked open drawers with trembling hands; each fold of fabric shoved into her case a defiant strike against humiliation. She would be gone before lunch—

gone before she had to sit across a table from Lincoln and his lover, swallowing down betrayal with breakfast.

When Lincoln entered minutes later, his pleased, almost smug expression froze. His gaze swept over the half-packed cases; the clothes scattered across the bed. The shift was immediate—his eyes hardened, his jaw turned to stone.

"What the hell do you think you're doing?" His voice was low, lethal, every syllable edged like glass.

"Leaving," she shot back, chin lifted. "The charade is over. Tell Gary Carter I ran off with the hotel manager."

He advanced with the slow, contained menace of a predator, and though instinct screamed for her to retreat, she refused to move. Her emerald eyes locked with his storm-grey ones, fury sparking between them like lightning.

"You'd better explain," he warned, his voice quiet but dangerous, "before I lose my temper."

Her composure snapped. Rage flared bright, feeding on betrayal. "What do you take me for?" she cried. "I was blackmailed into playing this sordid role, and now you've summoned your mistress to join us! How will you explain that to Gary? — *'You've met my wife, Gary, but this is Fiona. She's different. I can't manage without her'.*"

Lincoln's temper flared. "Of course I can't manage without her! She's my company lawyer. I can't close this deal without her."

"Don't insult me!" Angela's voice trembled with outrage. "We have a lawyer too and he doesn't call me *'darling'.*"

"I see," Lincoln said coldly, his lip curling. "You were leaning over the balcony. Spying. Eavesdropping."

"I went to look for you and you weren't there," she shot back. "I kept out of sight because I wasn't dressed. And I didn't expect to find your mistress hanging on your arm!"

"You're not dressed now," he countered silkily, his gaze sliding over her with infuriating deliberation.

Angela ignored the sting, turning back to her suitcase with shaking hands. "I'll be dressed soon enough—once I'm packed and out of this place. Clearly you think I'm too *stupid* to notice this insult. Too *stupid* to care for a child when we were married. Too *stupid* to see through your games."

Lincoln's eyes narrowed, his fury suddenly giving way to something far more dangerous. "You're jealous." His voice was low, satisfied, the words a blade and a caress all at once.

Her hands froze mid-fold.

"If you're only here because I forced you into it," he pressed, stepping closer, his presence overwhelming, "then why react so violently to Fiona's presence?" He gripped her shoulders, forcing her to meet his blazing gaze. "I told you, Angela—she is my lawyer. Nothing more. She's here for business. Not for me."

"Well, count me out of your ridiculous game," Angela snapped, twisting beneath his hands, too hurt, too furious to register the pull of his nearness. "I'm going home. Nothing you say will change my mind."

In one swift motion, Lincoln scooped her into his arms, ignoring her frantic struggles, his hold unyielding.

"I'm done talking," he said grimly, his voice rough as gravel. "Words mean nothing to you. This—you—this is all that's real."

He dropped her onto the bed, pinning her there when she tried to twist away. His gaze bore into hers—dark, mocking, yet hypnotic, as if daring her to deny the fire sparking between them.

"Don't touch me!" Angela warned, her voice shaking.

His lips curved into a cynical, almost playful smile, though his eyes burned with something far more dangerous. "You keep reminding me you wanted a baby," he murmured, fingers tugging loose his tie, unfastening his shirt with deliberate slowness. "Fine. You can have one. Maybe it will give you some sense—keep you out of mischief."

"No!" She pushed at him, panic, and fury warring in her chest.

"Yes, Angel." His voice gentled, though his eyes gleamed with heat. He leaned closer, the warmth of him stealing her breath. "You're jealous. And I'll prove to you—here, now—that Fiona means nothing. She's here, but it's you I want. You I can't let go."

"You don't love me!" The cry tore out of her, raw and trembling.

He lowered his mouth to her throat, his lips grazing the tender line of her skin, sending a shiver through her. "Is that what you want me to say?" he breathed, thick with longing. "Fine—I love you. Does that ease the jealousy, Angel? Does it silence the ghosts?"

"No," she wept, twisting against him. "You don't love me—you never did. She's your mistress! She's always been!"

"You never grew up after all," he whispered, tilting her chin up, capturing her lips in a kiss that was both tender and unrelenting. "But it doesn't matter. You still undo me. You still set me on fire with nothing more than a glance."

His breath fanned hot against her skin. "You smell like morning roses," he murmured, voice husky, reverent. "Delicate, fresh, unforgettable. You've haunted every dream I've ever had."

His mouth claimed hers again, deeper this time, coaxing past her resistance. A soft moan slipped from her throat as instinct betrayed her, her arms winding around his neck, pulling him closer, closer. He broke the kiss only to nip at her lower lip; his demand ragged against her mouth.

"Tell me, Angel. Say it."

Her body quivered beneath him, her lips trembling. "I… I want you," she whispered at last, the confession torn from her.

"And I want you," he growled, rough with need. "I've never stopped. From the first moment I saw you in that pink sweater and black skirt… you've been mine."

Her protest faltered on her lips as his words sank into her. She touched his face with trembling hands, kissed him with desperate urgency, unable to hold back.

He stripped quickly, and she clung to him, lips never leaving his, as if the heat between them was the only truth left in the world. When he returned to her, there was no more resistance. She gave herself to him—body, heart, soul—wrapping herself around him, letting him lead her into a place where pain and longing blurred into an unbearable, consuming fire.

The world dissolved. The storm of desire crashed over them, exploding in a universe of sensation that left her gasping, trembling, undone.

Lincoln held her through it, pulling her tight against him as the aftershocks shuddered through her body. Her soft whimpers cut him to the bone, and he buried his face in her hair, his voice breaking with raw despair.

"Oh, Angel," he whispered hoarsely. "What am I going to do with you? Wanting you is like fighting a war in the dark—endless, hopeless, but I can't stop."

Angela pressed her face into his chest, letting the trembling subside. Her body felt weightless, lifeless almost—yet bound to him, consumed by him. Her heart still wept in silence, but her mind was empty, emptied of everything except the brutal truth. How could she ever truly escape Lincoln?

"Come on," Lincoln murmured, lifting her into his arms and leading her to the shower. She yielded, subdued and obedient, letting him envelop them both in the warm spray. In that moment, she felt utterly lost, a bewildered extension of Lincoln, a helpless captive to his desires. He bent to kiss her, lips brushing hers with a shadow of his own unspoken despair.

Chapter Fifteen

She lingered in the bathroom to dry off, wrapping herself in a white bathrobe. When she emerged, Lincoln was already dressed, her clothes neatly tucked away.

Angela knew she had to leave when they returned. She couldn't live in the same country—let alone the same house—knowing that with one touch, one glance, Lincoln could undo her completely. She deserved more than this. She deserved to be loved without conditions, without cruelty—loved wholly.

"I've ordered breakfast up here for you," he said quietly. "It should be obvious I have to eat with Fiona. We have matters to discuss. And frankly, you'd only be upset if you joined us. I'm not asking you to be part of that."

Angela didn't answer. She sat at the dressing table, drawing the brush slowly through her hair, praying he would leave her in silence, leave her to recover her dignity in her own way.

"I can't keep you out of everything, Angela," he went on, his voice lower now. He stood behind her, eyes fixed on her through the mirror. "Tonight, at Gary's club—she'll be there."

Her gaze lifted, meeting his reflection. The mocking satisfaction she had seen in him before was gone. In its place was only gravity, shadowed and serious. She dropped her eyes quickly, unwilling to search deeper, unwilling to admit that some part of her wanted to understand him. Perhaps she never would.

"I'll cope," she whispered. Her hand moved steadily, the brush sliding through the blue-black fall of her hair, though every stroke felt like a battle. She had to hold herself together—until she could leave. If she stayed, Lincoln would destroy her.

A flicker of pain passed across his face, almost boyish in its suddenness, his eyes lingering on her downcast features, the graceful movement of her hands, the sheen of her hair in the lamplight.

"There'll be a lot of people there," he reminded her, the words softer now, almost apologetic. "It's not going to be an intimate dinner."

"It doesn't matter," she said flatly.

He shrugged, moving toward the door. His hand paused on the handle. "By the way," he murmured, not turning to look at her, "I phoned the hospital this morning. Your father is fine."

The words struck like a gale against calm water. Angela spun, her eyes wide, searching his face. Why had he done that? What did it mean? She couldn't fathom his motive—so she only stared.

His grey eyes hardened instantly, narrowing to icy slits. The fleeting softness vanished as if it had never existed. "Don't even ask!" he snapped, his voice razor-sharp. "I can see your mind working. You're wondering if I called hoping he'd relapsed."

Angela shook her head, her gaze steady, her voice deliberate. "Such a thought never crossed my mind. Don't judge everyone by the cunning of your own mind. Some of us think simply and straightforwardly. I was surprised, that's all. Thank you for phoning. Thank you for telling me. If you think that's the sweet manners of a simpleton, then perhaps you're right. I've already proved what a fool I am this morning—otherwise, I'd be downstairs booking a flight home."

She turned back to the mirror, lifting the dryer with composed hands. The steady hum filled the silence as if nothing had been said.

For a long moment Lincoln simply stood watching her, his expression taut with restraint. The anger drained away, leaving that sombre, brooding shadow she had come to know too well. Without another word, he left the room, the door closing with a muted click behind him.

The moment he was gone, Angela's control broke. She set the dryer down, her head falling into her hands. Her shoulders shook as grief flooded in, unrestrained, unguarded. She wept not only for the morning, not only for her wounded pride—but for the cruellest truth of all.

She still loved him. She loved him more fiercely than she ever had. She had thought nothing could surpass the bright, consuming passion of nineteen, but the years had only honed the yearning sharper, etched him deeper into her heart.

There was no girlish haze now, no illusion. She knew exactly who Lincoln was—hard, ruthless, impossible—and still her heart reached for him, needed him, as if he were carved into her very being. Without him, life stretched ahead like a wasteland of ashes. The faith she had once placed in her father's protection was gone, and with it any illusion of safety.

All that remained was the hollow certainty: when she left, without Lincoln, there would be nothing but emptiness.

After breakfast, Fiona had gone to rest, which, Angela realised, made avoiding her comparatively easy. She gleaned this unwanted information from the talkative waiter who had collected her tray. Lincoln had gone out, too—another fact confirmed by the same source. Left alone, Angela lingered on the balcony, her gaze fixed on the shimmering sea, her mind desperately searching for comfort.

There was none. She wasn't even angry anymore. When another waiter appeared to summon her to lunch, she went downstairs like an obedient shadow, her face an impassive mask. She could not show grief—Lincoln was far too astute to mistake it for anger or outrage.

The meal was silent. She knew she had been summoned merely for appearances. Once again, Lincoln's expression was dark and serious, and after lunch he excused himself, leaving her alone. She did not know whether he was going to Fiona or to his own room, but she could not return upstairs and wait passively for the evening's ordeal to arrive.

Instead, she walked along the sun-baked beach, the breeze lifting her hair and cooling her heated face. Memories attempted to surface, but she suppressed them ruthlessly, forcing her mind blank—focused only on sky, sea, and the people she passed, as if none of them existed. Angela herself seemed to have vanished entirely.

She did not even worry about the dinner at Gary's club that evening. Numbness had taken over, leaving no room for fear or anticipation of seeing Fiona Martin face-to-face.

Returning to the hotel garden, her eyes flicked to the balcony connecting her room to Lincoln's. He stood there, still, and silent, watching her—or at least appearing to. He gave no sign that he saw her, distant, cool, and unreachable.

He was still there when she reached her room. As she stepped in from the corridor, he appeared at the French window.

"Eight o'clock tonight," he stated flatly, eyes fixed on her. She nodded silently, waiting for him to leave.

"Take care in the sun," he muttered when she said nothing. "It's strong—nothing you're used to. If you're going to walk on the beach, wait for it to die down a little."

"I didn't walk for long," Angela said wearily, turning away from his penetrating grey eyes.

"You walked for an hour, back and forth," he corrected, and she spun around, irritation flaring.

"How do you know? Haven't you anything better to do than spy on me? Did you think I would sneak off?"

"I was watching to make sure you were safe," he snapped, anger flashing across his features. "Or maybe I just can't keep my eyes off you." His voice sharpened with fury. "Eight o'clock. Angela."

He walked away, bristling with controlled anger. She collapsed onto the bed, her body aching from weariness. Perhaps she should rest, too. The hours until eight stretched endlessly before her, and sleep seemed the only refuge.

When she awoke, she began her preparations at once, knowing she would need every defence she could summon for the evening. Why hadn't Gary and Lincoln completed the deal? Why weren't the papers already signed? Because Fiona had only just arrived, Angela reminded herself grimly. After that, nothing would shield her—her life with Lincoln, however she tried to deny it, would be over.

She selected a turquoise dress, recently purchased for a dinner with Barry that she had never attended due to work obligations. The colour complemented her black hair perfectly. The dress, off the shoulder and fitted to her slender form, swirled gracefully from the waist down. Angela allowed herself a small thrill of satisfaction—it had not been a gift from Lincoln.

Yet the narrow diamond necklace and matching bracelet he had given her adorned her still. Painful memories flared, but she kept them on, stubbornly. Studying her reflection, she thought she looked too young even in finery. On a rare impulse, she rang reception, inquiring about the hotel hairdresser.

By eight o'clock, Angela was as sophisticated as she could manage. Her hair was swept up into a loose cascade of curls, framing her head in elegant swirls, and her reflection bore the image of a woman ready to face the world—even if her heart remained elsewhere.

Lincoln had rung her room to say he would meet her in the foyer. Angela gathered her gauzy turquoise wrap and descended, heart fluttering. He had apparently not been prepared to escort her, but with Fiona accompanying them, she could not face waiting alone.

The stairs opened into a wide, shallow foyer, brilliantly lit. Angela stepped down, immediately aware of the many eyes on her. Anxiety made her pale, almost ethereal, and she dared only shy glances upward as Lincoln approached. His face was serious, his storm-grey eyes sweeping over her, lingering on every curve, every movement, every curl of her hair.

Her pulse thudded wildly. Raw desire flared from him like silver lightning, and she was certain anyone watching could see it too. There was no love in those eyes, only need—blazing, undeniable, and terrifying.

"Where is she?" Angela asked before he could greet her, eyes darting around the foyer for the woman who would outshine her in every way.

"She's already left," Lincoln said tightly. "Paul Carter asked to escort us, so I sent Fiona ahead and waited for you."

"You let her go with him?" Angela's voice rose with surprise, and he gave a grim smile at her astonishment. It was clear she had expected him to stay near Fiona; equally clear she still believed Fiona to be his mistress.

"She can take care of herself," he said icily. "Fiona doesn't need protection. The younger Carter recognised that immediately. He left in a subdued frame of mind."

"I can take care of myself too," Angela protested, but he took her arm and led her to the waiting Uber, as though reminding her silently that he doubted it.

"We won't be putting that to the test," he murmured sardonically, glancing down at her delicate face and the slender lines of her gown. "Wild obstinacy has never influenced me. You stepped out this morning like a flower fairy from a bright cloud. Fiona could hold her own in a black hole and defeat a magnate. If he tried any tricks with her, he'd be savaged."

Probably, Angela thought grimly. No doubt Fiona and Carter would make a striking pair—but she knew exactly who Fiona would attach herself to the moment they arrived.

Lincoln settled her in the car and ignored her for the journey. Luckily, it was short because his deep silence and controlled expression only heightened her tension. Every touch—every brush of his fingers against hers—had sent shivers of electric desire along her skin. And yet she knew that his longing was not love.

Love was gentle; it forgave. Lincoln would never forgive. His desire, as intense as it was, might one day fade. Perhaps if she had stayed with him, it would have faded already. And she realised, with a mix of dread and longing, that no triumph awaited her here—only the stark, consuming reality of his need, untamed and unyielding.

The club glittered with lights, music swirling into the warm night air. Opulence announced itself at every turn: crystal chandeliers, polished floors, and patrons in gowns and tuxedos that spoke of fortunes few could imagine. The high gates they had passed through clicked shut behind them with the smooth precision of well-oiled mechanisms, sealing them in a world of wealth and power.

Through the doorway, Angela caught the shimmer of sequins and silk, the glint of jewels, and the sparkle of champagne flutes. A wave of relief passed over her—her turquoise gown was perfectly at home amid the expensive elegance. Relief deepened when her gaze found Fiona, already poised and composed at the top of the steps, waiting.

Gary and Paul Carter were there too. Gary came down the steps with his customary warmth.

"You make me glad to be alive," he said, taking her arm gently.

Angela laughed softly, her nerves taut. "I'm not even sure I can stand it." She looked up, catching Irene Carter's gaze, and carefully avoided the others. Tonight, Irene's hair was a striking blonde, and Gary noticed the flicker of astonishment in Angela's eyes.

"A wig, a wig," he muttered, patting her arm. "It's her hobby. She's done this all her life. Supposedly keeps me interested—mostly brings me to the verge of fainting."

Irene grinned at Angela, irrepressible as always. "I decided I couldn't compete with that hair," she explained, nodding toward Angela's shimmering black curls. "I'll go off black. Too easy to spot the difference."

Paul Carter approached, drawn by curiosity and a subtle fascination. "You look…" he murmured, moving closer. "When I met you the other day, I was stunned. Now I'm not even sure you're real."

"She's only real for me," Lincoln said sharply, stepping forward and taking Angela's wrist in a firm, possessive grip. "To anyone else, she's merely an illusion."

The Carters were distracted, conversing with Fiona, giving Paul a moment of boldness. His gaze sharpened. "In other words—hands off," he said, his tone warning, if not entirely polite.

"In plain words," Lincoln replied, icy and precise, "this is my wife."

Paul's usual smirk returned, masking irritation. "Sure," he said lightly. "Did I doubt it? Complimenting a beautiful woman comes naturally, I guess. They usually like it."

"Perhaps not their husbands," Lincoln countered acidly, eyes flicking to Fiona. "I seem to think Miss Martin is your partner this evening."

Paul glanced at Fiona, a wry smile tugging at his lips. "That lady is tough," he commented, and Lincoln guided Angela forward, his hand firm and warm against her back.

"I thought you'd notice," he murmured dryly.

Fiona, watching from a distance, had indeed noticed. She was too far to hear the sharp exchange, but her eyes took in every detail: Angela's flush, Paul Carter's speculative glances, Lincoln's subtle irritation. She drifted toward him, clinging to his arm with practiced ease.

"I thought you'd never get here," she purred in a low, sultry voice. "What odd people. Let's get this deal over with and get back to London."

Angela stiffened, unable to hide it. Lincoln felt the tension, of course, but Fiona seemed oblivious. Oh yes, Angela thought bitterly, Fiona was eager to return to London—but perhaps this voice, this sultry charm, was reserved only for Lincoln.

After that, Gary took over, and the evening relaxed into a more comfortable rhythm. The club was enormous, rivalling anything London had to offer, and even Fiona seemed impressed. Angela observed her discreetly, her attention drawn despite herself.

She had never really studied this woman before, and she had to admit—Fiona Martin was undeniably beautiful. Her hair was sleek and straight, in contrast to the swirling curls that Angela had battled with all her life. The honey-blonde sheen lent Fiona an effortless sophistication Angela felt she could never quite achieve. Her dress—a dark blue silk sheath—clung perfectly to her slim figure. Angela noted that she looked far more like a model or an actress than a lawyer.

It was only Fiona's eyes that betrayed her true nature: icy blue, sharp, and calculating. They flicked toward Angela with a watchful intelligence and a subtle hardness that set her on edge. When Fiona smiled, it was not warm—it was precise, controlled, and almost piercing.

Angela understood immediately: in Lincoln's eyes, Fiona hadn't lost, and her expression made sure Angela knew it too. Every movement, every glance was a quiet challenge, a reminder of her position in this carefully measured game.

Chapter Sixteen

After dinner, the party continued, the music swirling and the lights casting a warm glow over the glittering crowd. There was dancing, but Angela quickly found herself swept up by Gary and Irene, who seemed genuinely delighted to have her in their company. They guided her around to meet other guests, easing her nerves, though all the while she was painfully aware that every moment she spent away from Lincoln played right into Fiona's hands.

Each time she glanced across the room, Lincoln was deep in conversation with Fiona, only moving away when Paul Carter returned from greeting friends and assumed his role as escort to Lincoln's lawyer. Angela couldn't avoid dancing with Lincoln, but he spoke little, his attention elsewhere, and her eyes kept drifting toward Fiona.

She was surprised to notice that Fiona seemed entirely at ease, even enjoying herself as she conversed with Paul Carter. Each time their gaze flicked toward her, her heart skipped a beat. She tried to convince herself that Fiona's attention was on Lincoln, but the icy blue eyes fixed on her with too much intensity for her to be mistaken. There was something under the surface she could not fathom—and it made her uneasy. If Fiona was charming Paul Carter, it was surely to gain some advantage for herself.

Eventually, Angela drifted back to where Gary and Irene were seated, forcing polite conversation while her gaze strayed to the dance floor. Lincoln was dancing with Fiona. She tried not to notice the way Fiona's hand lingered—just a little too long—on his sleeve, but her treacherous eyes betrayed her.

Memories stirred, unwelcome and sharp. After she and Lincoln were married, Fiona had always been there—at dinners, at dances, at every glittering function. Lincoln had often spent more time with her than with Angela, but back then she had never doubted him, never felt threatened. Not until that single, poisonous moment when Fiona had leaned close and whispered that Lincoln would never give her up.

It had been the first crack in her trust. She hadn't wanted to believe Fiona's taunts, hadn't even imagined that an affair could be unfolding right under her nose. But now, watching them together, the memory burned through her with a fresh, raw humiliation.

The final crack had come later, when Lincoln brushed aside her fears with a sharp, scornful retort—childish, idiotic, unworthy of his patience. She remembered staring at him, waiting—aching—for some reassurance, some sign that he loved her. A single word could have steadied her, could have silenced the whispering doubts. But nothing came. Not once had Lincoln ever told her he loved her.

And the silence had said more than words ever could.

She was so lost in the ache of it—so consumed by the past colliding with the present—that she failed to notice Paul Carter striding toward her. His voice broke through her reverie, sharp and insistent.

"Angela," he said, extending a hand. "Dance with me."

He didn't ask politely. With his parents watching, Angela felt she could not refuse. She braced herself for the ordeal, offering a brittle smile that seemed to amuse him in the most irritating way.

"So," he began as they danced away from the others, "you and Lincoln are separated?"

"Of course we're not separated," Angela replied quickly. "Does it look like it?"

Now she understood the whispers she had glimpsed between Fiona and this odious man. Had Fiona really left Paul Carter misinformed about the terms of Gary's insistence on a happily married buyer? Angela was completely on her own, forced to improvise.

"It doesn't look like it," he said sarcastically. "Looks just too good to be true, in fact. I've never met a husband this jealous before."

"Well, I'm sure you must be an expert on husbands," Angela shot back, her sarcasm a fragile shield. "In this case, you've been misinformed."

"I don't think so, babe," he sneered. "Separate rooms mean separated, and according to my sources, you've got the best rooms in the hotel—next door to each other."

"How dare you speak to me like this?" Angela's anger flared, fuelled more by indignation than fear. "Our affairs are none of your concern."

"They would concern my father," Paul murmured slyly, steering her into a shadowed corner, his grip tightening as he pulled her closer—far too close. His breath brushed her cheek, rank with smugness. "Unless, of course, I could be persuaded not to tell him."

Angela recoiled at the heat of his body, wrenching against his hold. "Let me go!" she cried, twisting violently, but his laughter rang out, low and taunting. He only clamped down harder, relishing her struggle.

She fought, desperate, unaware of the figure looming up behind them. The first thing she registered was Paul's sudden cry of pain—the sound sharp and strangled—as Lincoln's hand closed like a steel vice around his neck, jerking him back with lethal precision.

"Didn't I tell you to keep away from my wife?" Lincoln hissed through clenched teeth. "I see words alone don't impress you."

His hand shot to Paul Carter's shoulder, and Angela's eyes widened in horror as she watched the other man begin to buckle, slowly sinking to his knees under Lincoln's unyielding grip. Panic surged through her.

"Lincoln! Please!" she cried, her voice urgent and trembling. She had never seen him like this, and the sheer intensity of his anger made her body shiver. Relief washed over her when Gary appeared, his expression a mix of astonishment and controlled fury.

"What the hell is this?" Gary demanded, his voice cutting through the tension like a knife. Lincoln's grip loosened immediately. Paul Carter staggered upright, clutching his shoulder, his face as pale as chalk, before he pushed past everyone and fled from the club.

Lincoln's gaze snapped to Angela, pulling her close, his arms a shield around her. Then he turned, eyes blazing, to Gary.

"When I see someone manhandle my wife," he said coldly, his voice low and dangerous, "I see red. I don't yet know what this was about, but I will find out. Meanwhile, we're leaving. If this deal is going ahead, Gary, we sign tomorrow morning. Otherwise… forget it. We're going home tomorrow, with or without the deal."

Irene appeared at Angela's side, her gaze falling immediately on the slender arms bruising beneath Lincoln's hold.

"Oh, honey, look!" she whispered sharply to Gary, and the anger drained from his face at the visible evidence.

"I'll take this up with him at home," Gary said, his tone a promise and a warning all at once. "Don't worry about the deal, Lincoln. That young man has a lot of explaining to do."

Lincoln's jaw remained rigid; he barely spared a glance for reassurance. With one firm, protective sweep, he guided Angela toward the exit, his arm locked tightly around her shoulders.

"I'm not worrying about the deal," he ground out, his voice a low growl. "I can take it or leave it. Let me know tomorrow—early."

Angela found herself being led toward the door, the eyes of nearly everyone in the club following them.

"Don't let it embarrass you," Lincoln muttered, his face still etched with fury. Angela felt a sudden, almost hysterical urge to laugh.

"I'm not embarrassed," she whispered, struggling to steady her emotions. "I'm just wondering what that little creep will tell Gary when he gets home. He claimed he knew we were separated."

"Did he?" Lincoln murmured, his tone distant, almost dismissive.

"You're not taking this seriously enough," she shot back, quickening her pace to keep up. "When Gary finds out, the deal will be off."

Lincoln swore under his breath, but it was more a sound of his own frustration than genuine concern about the deal. Angela sank back into the Uber beside him, shaking and drained. The entire evening felt like a disaster.

All the trauma, all the stress, had been for nothing. She had been forced close to Lincoln, forced to confront her love for him once more, only for it to feel useless. She couldn't tell him what she suspected—that Fiona had orchestrated Paul Carter's little provocation—and when they returned to the hotel, Lincoln would demand a full account.

Resting back against the seat, utterly exhausted, she knew she had to hold her thoughts in. If she spoke, Lincoln would assume she was simply jealous, trying to sabotage Fiona.

Back in her room, Lincoln closed the door and turned on her, his expression unreadable but forbidding.

"Word for word!" he ordered, his grey eyes locking onto hers.

"There were few words," Angela said. "He asked me to dance—no, he told me to dance—and then he came straight out with it. He announced that you and I are separated. He even knew about the separate rooms."

"Why didn't you just walk off?" Lincoln grated, his jaw tight, eyes flashing with frustration.

Angela met his gaze, her own fury simmering. "You saw what happened when I tried," she said, lifting her bruised arms, the marks dark against her pale skin. "I could have hit him, but I left the big scene for you."

Lincoln's lips pressed into a hard line. "And what did you expect me to do—laugh it off?" he snarled.

Angela turned away, exhaling sharply, a mixture of exasperation and resignation in her movements. "No. I was glad to see you… but this makes everything awkward. When he faces Gary tonight, he'll spill every scrap he knows—or thinks he knows. That could ruin the deal entirely."

"Damn the deal!" Lincoln muttered under his breath, storming toward the phone with a controlled fury that made the air around him tense. "Get a tray of tea up here—my wife needs it. And make it fast."

When he turned back, the rigid storm in his features had softened slightly, replaced by a sharp, contemplative edge, his eyes scanning her with a mixture of concern and calculation.

"Get into your dressing gown," he suggested, his voice low, deliberate, threaded with a dark, brooding possessiveness. "You'll be far more comfortable."

It seemed like a good idea, and there was always the slim hope that when she emerged from the bathroom, he might be gone. After all, he had left Fiona at the club, and even though that woman could fend off a small army, abandoning a guest was not exactly Lincoln's style.

Angela slipped into the bathroom and carefully removed the beautiful dress, feeling a pang of disappointment that circumstances had not allowed her to wear it properly. She lingered, washing her face and brushing out her hair, but when she returned, Lincoln was still there. He had flung himself into a chair, and the sharp lines of his clever face told her he was thinking hard.

He nodded toward the tray of tea that had already been delivered. "So, Fiona tried to sink the ship. Why not come right out and say it?" he asked, his voice steady but edged with curiosity.

"I'm not competent to speculate on big business deals," Angela replied cautiously. "In any case, he simply said it—according to his information. Maybe it was a waiter. One of them is always gossiping."

"Nice try, Angela," Lincoln drawled, sardonic. "To the best of my knowledge, Snake Eyes hasn't been in this place since we arrived, except to collect Fiona tonight. At that time, he didn't wander far from my icy glare. Nobody spoke to him. I was hard-pressed to speak to him myself."

Angela's lips twitched at the nickname Lincoln had given Paul Carter—it was exactly how she felt about him herself—but she refused to be drawn into any speculation about Fiona.

"Well, I can't see what she could possibly gain," she murmured. "And she has plenty to lose."

"Knowing how your mind works, I won't ask what," he said, irony flickering in his grey eyes. "Drink your tea. I'll get to the bottom of this tomorrow."

"I don't expect there'll be any deal now," Angela sighed. "He's sure to tell Gary what he thinks, even if only to save himself. Add that to the considerable pain he suffered, and it seems to be the end of everything."

"You think I should have walked up and pretended not to notice?" Lincoln asked dryly. Angela shook her head, shuddering at the memory of that unpleasant encounter.

"As to the deal," he continued, "it's not that important. I already have a stake in this country that makes Gary's business look insignificant."

"Then why…?" Angela asked, astonished. He tilted her an amused sideways glance as he walked to the door.

"The machinations of a devious mind," he murmured, pausing to turn back toward her. His gaze darkened, sharp and concerned. "Let me see those arms. He didn't hold back, did he?"

Before she could protest, his hands gently pushed up the sleeves of her dressing gown. His eyes, usually so controlled and unreadable, narrowed with anger as he examined the bruises.

"I should have squeezed his neck a damned sight harder," he muttered, a low growl rumbling in his throat. "Does it hurt?"

Angela shook her head, catching a fleeting glimpse of vulnerability in his storm-grey eyes. For a brief, precious second, the intensity of Lincoln's fury softened—and a small, unbidden smile tugged at her lips.

"Not much. I'll bathe them in cold water," she replied quietly, her voice steady despite the tremor of emotion beneath it.

"Shall I ring down for something? There's an all-night chemist here."

She shook her head, brushing off the offer. "It's all right, Lincoln. Really." Unthinking, almost instinctively, her hand rose to rest against his arm.

He looked down, and the sight of her slender, pale fingers on him seemed to soften something in the rigid lines of his face. Slowly, deliberately, he cupped her cheek, his thumb brushing lightly against her skin before leaning down to press a careful, tender kiss to her lips.

"All right, sweet Angel," he murmured, voice low and guarded, yet laced with a warmth she rarely saw. "If you need me, I'm just next door."

"Aren't you going back for Fiona?" she asked.

He gave that tilted grin again. "I think not. If she gets very uptight about being deserted, she's probably innocent. If she lets it drop, she's most likely guilty."

"You don't know that," Angela reminded him quickly.

"I don't," he agreed quietly. "It's a matter of instinct. And your instincts were always better than mine when it comes to Fiona. What do you think, Angel?"

"How could I know?" she said swiftly.

He studied her steadily. "You watched her all evening. Mischief usually shows itself quite visibly."

He left, and Angela was left to wonder where that left her—and more importantly, where it left Lincoln. Why didn't he seem to care about the deal after dragging her all this way to finalise it? Now he appeared utterly unconcerned, as if he were the one doing Gary a favour.

She gave herself a mental shake. Lincoln's thought processes were impossible to follow, but somewhere along the line, she had clearly missed an important fact. She could only hope they were leaving tomorrow—and that she would not have to endure another encounter with the insufferable Paul Carter.

She turned to bathe her arms. They throbbed in pain, the finger marks darkening with every passing moment. Any sight of them in the morning would undoubtedly reignite Lincoln's fury.

Angela was up early the next day, and there was still no sign of Lincoln. Last night, strangely, had left her feeling more self-assured. He had been protective, unflinchingly so, and there had been no pretence about his anger. It had not been jealousy alone. She decided to wait downstairs, refusing to skulk in her room like a frightened child. If Fiona appeared, she might inadvertently reveal that she had told Paul Carter about the supposed separation.

But there was no sign of Lincoln or Fiona, and Angela felt a small, sinking weight in her chest at their absence. Her informant, the ever-talkative waiter, delivered the news with a brittle smile. She returned a curt nod, irritated at the intrusion—why couldn't people mind their own business? Some things were better left unknown.

"They ate earlier," he said, and she dismissed him without another word.

Later, she went for what would likely be her last walk along the beach. She knew Lincoln too well—he would not linger here now, even if the affair concluded without incident. It was a shame that this beautiful place had only served as a stage for deception, an ordeal she had been forced to endure. A holiday here could have been blissful, but only with Lincoln. Alone, or with anyone else, it held no appeal.

When she returned, he was there again, watching her from the balcony. This time, however, there was no reproach in his gaze, only that distant, inscrutable intensity that always seemed to keep her simultaneously uneasy and captivated.

"We're leaving this morning," he told her as she entered the room.

"I'll be ready." That was all she was prepared to say. She didn't want to know what had happened—or to face the possibility that all the subterfuge, all her misery, had been for nothing.

"We could stay… have a real holiday, if you like," Lincoln said quietly, studying her downcast face. Her head shot up, green eyes wide with surprise.

"A holiday?" she exclaimed. "Oh, Lincoln, don't offer a continuation of a nightmare as if you're doing me a favour. I can't get out of here fast enough. And, whatever happens, I've done my part—don't forget that. It wasn't my fault we ran into a lunatic."

Lincoln's brow darkened at her tone, but he kept his temper and nodded seriously.

"No. It wasn't your fault at all. You played the part perfectly, Angela. You even went above and beyond the call of duty."

His words carried weight, and Angela felt her face flush as he stared at her with that icy intensity.

"So, you'll help Marsden Enterprises?" she pressed, and he turned away, shrugging dismissively.

"I've already said so. I gave you my word. Last night's fiasco wasn't your fault. In any case, it made little difference—though it has left a certain strain between Gary and me. I signed the deal this morning."

"With Fiona?" The words escaped her before she could stop them, and he turned, his expression bleak.

"Naturally, with Fiona. I told you she had to countersign."

"So… she's flying back with us?" Angela asked quietly.

"She's already left. I had a job for her in New York. You and I are going home."

"She won't like being left behind," Angela said, though she immediately regretted sounding foolish.

Lincoln's grey-eyed glare pinned her in place. "What she likes—or doesn't like—is of no importance. If she wants the job, she follows my instructions exactly. She goes where I send her. Pack your clothes, Angela, and don't play out of your league—especially as you refuse to play your ace."

"I don't have an ace," Angela muttered miserably.

"Oh, yes, you do, Angela," he insisted softly, pausing in the doorway to look at her. "The trouble is… you've never recognised it."

Chapter Seventeen

After the golden blaze of California sunshine, London felt grey and joyless. A heavy downpour had left the streets slick and glistening, the city shrouded in damp dusk as their Uber sped through the traffic. Angela watched the blurred lights through the window, her chest tight. Beside her, Lincoln sat silent and rigid, his jaw set, every line of his body taut with thought. She hardly dared breathe, let alone speak, terrified that the wrong word might tip the balance between them.

They had made no plan, but it was inevitable they would return first to the penthouse. Lincoln's car was there; hers was still at her father's house. Home. The word twisted painfully in her mind. The old adage drifted to her unbidden—home is where the heart is. And her heart, foolishly, irrevocably, still belonged to Lincoln. From now on, she could never be content with her father's house. Nor could she stay with Marsden Enterprises once Lincoln returned to his office.

The firm's survival balanced precariously in Lincoln's hands, yet Angela knew her own life could not remain tied to his battles. Whatever the outcome, she had to move on— find another job, another direction, something that belonged to her alone. For a fleeting moment, her thoughts strayed to Barry Windsor. He would undoubtedly offer her a position, though Lincoln's scathing disapproval of Barry still echoed in her mind. Accepting his help might solve her problem, but it would invite trouble for Barry, and Lincoln's wrath was not something to be borne lightly.

No—her escape had to be complete. The thought had already taken root: leaving not just Lincoln, but the country itself. France was too close, too accessible for Lincoln's reach. New Zealand, perhaps—or Australia. Somewhere distant enough that Lincoln's shadow could not stretch across her life, somewhere she might finally breathe without the fear of his hold tightening again.

"Come into the penthouse."

Angela startled, dragged from her thoughts by the sound of Lincoln's deep, unyielding voice. The Uber had halted outside the building, and Lincoln was already thanking the driver, his movements as decisive as ever.

"Is it necessary?" she asked in a low voice, turning away from the driver's curious glance. "Can't you just take me straight home?"

"I want to talk to you," Lincoln said flatly. His cool stare sent the driver scurrying away. Gathering up their luggage with effortless strength, he left Angela only two small bags to carry. "A drink and a few words. Then I'll have you on your way."

Angela nodded, forcing calm. Was this it? Was this where he would finally tell her she was free—that she could pursue the divorce she had once avoided for so long? Or perhaps he meant to dictate new conditions for his aid to Marsden Enterprises.

Whatever the reason, there was no escaping his will; she had no way of getting home without him.

Inside, the penthouse lights banished the dreary gloom of London, but Angela felt another darkness settle over her heart. This might be the last time she would ever stand here, in the place where she had once been deliriously happy—and bitterly unhappy. She could not bear to take a lingering look around. Instead, she remained standing in the middle of the sitting room, her hands clasped loosely before her, her nerves stretched thin.

Lincoln glanced at her, one brow raised in faint scepticism, before pouring himself a drink. He held the glass lazily, then extended another towards her.

"I'd rather have tea," she said evenly.

He shrugged, lowering the glass without protest, though his mouth curved in deliberate provocation. "You know where the kitchen is. It's your kitchen."

Angela felt the sting but refused to react. She turned and went into the kitchen, steadying herself by keeping her hands busy with the simple, homely ritual of making tea. Yet every nerve in her body was straining, attuned to his presence in the next room. Whatever he had to say, she knew it would matter—because Lincoln never spoke or acted without purpose.

When Angela returned, the tea tray balanced in her hands, Lincoln was stretched out in the chair as though it belonged to him—and perhaps it always had. His head rested against the back, eyes closed, his long frame at ease, though the air around him was taut with unspoken thoughts. She set the tray down softly and sat opposite, her every movement careful. She would not prompt him. Not yet.

He looked weary, shadows etched faintly beneath his eyes, his lashes dark against his cheekbones. For the first time in a long while, she saw not the ruthless titan of business but a man carrying something heavy, something private. Did he think of his parents now, she wondered? Did their loss drive him still, feeding that relentless hunger to outwork every competitor, to push beyond human limits? For four years he had seemed unstoppable—superhuman—but at what cost to his heart?

Her chest ached with the old longing. How often had she knelt by him once, laying her head against his knee, secure in the knowledge that he belonged to her as much as she to him? She longed for the right to do it now, but the gulf between them felt impossible to cross.

"What are your plans?"

The grey eyes were open suddenly, piercing her across the room. Angela gave a guilty start, trapped in his scrutiny, before forcing herself to answer.

She couldn't tell him she was planning to vanish completely—not yet. First, she needed a divorce; only then would the break be absolute.

"That depends entirely on how you intend to act," she said steadily, refusing to let her voice falter. "If you come in to take over, I'll brief you until you're satisfied, then I'll step aside. If you'd rather work from the background, I'll stay until my father is strong enough to return. After that, I'll go."

"And go where?" His tone was curt, clipped, as though daring her to answer. "Windsor's."

"I was offered a position there long ago. That's what Barry was discussing with me when—"

"When I tore into him," Lincoln cut in, irritation sparking in his grey eyes as he leaned forward, his gaze sharp as a blade. "You've worked yourself raw these past years. That firm could still be yours if you fought for it. Within months it could be back on its feet. Why throw it away now?"

"Self-preservation," Angela replied evenly, though her pulse hammered in her throat. "I don't want to salvage what's broken. I want a new life—a life that's mine. If I stay, I'll be dragged back into the old chains. I intend to start again, Lincoln—before they close around me."

She drew a sharp breath, making her choice. Better to face it now than suffer in uncertainty. "I'll apply for a divorce, as you once suggested. That can be dealt with immediately, no matter what happens with the firm."

Lincoln leaned back, regarding her with infuriating calm. His tone was quiet, almost bland—yet all the more dangerous for its control.

"I'll oppose any divorce."

Angela's heart jolted to a stop. For a moment she could only stare at him, stunned. "You said—when you attacked Barry—you told me to go ahead, that I should divorce you."

"From time to time, I lose my temper," he replied silkily, every syllable measured. "I'm not angry now. And I repeat—I will oppose any divorce."

"You can't!" Angela burst out, her composure fracturing. "We've been separated for years. Even if you fight it, I can still get one. Next year it will be five years' continuous separation. With or without your consent, the court will grant it. It would be a mere formality."

"I'm quite serious," Lincoln said, eyes narrowing, voice like steel. "And no—it will not be five years. We've been lovers twice in the last week. In the eyes of the law, in the eyes of the world, we are reconciled. There will be no divorce, Angela."

The truth hit like a blade. She remembered—those words whispered in the penthouse, in the hotel—the touch that had set her body alight with longing. Now she saw it with brutal clarity. A tactic. A calculated move in his endless game. Her whole being flared to danger alert. She had fallen for him again, and it had been part of his plan all along.

"It was deliberate," she breathed, her voice shaking. "Even that—you planned even that."

"You helped." His mouth curved wryly, mocking and intimate all at once. "I don't recall you putting up much of a fight. What I do recall is you trembling in my arms as you always did. If it was a plan, then you were a very willing accomplice."

His eyes glittered like tempered steel. "It was no great hardship to want you. I've always wanted you—from the first moment I saw you."

"Take me home!" The words tore out of her, sharp and desperate. She glared at him because glaring was the only weapon left to her. His face revealed nothing—but she knew Lincoln. He never opposed anything calmly. When he said he would resist divorce, he meant it. He always had another plan. Always.

"You can stay here," he countered, his gaze fixed, intent as a blade pressed to her throat. "It's better than that mausoleum you've haunted these last four years. To the world, we're reconciled. Let them go on believing it. Under the circumstances, your father will be delighted."

"What circumstances?" Her voice was tight, brittle.

"Don't be obtuse, Angela," he murmured, rising with deliberate slowness. "I'm supposed to be helping. And sooner or later Kurt Marsden will have to work with me. He'll find it easier to swallow if his rescuer is his son-in-law—happily reunited with his daughter."

Her thoughts scattered like shards of glass. But one thing was certain—he was plotting, weaving fresh mischief. Fear clawed her chest.

"You made a promise," she choked, voice unsteady. "I pretended to reconcile. I kept my part of the bargain. You said you'd save Marsden Enterprises. You gave your word."

"And I'll keep it," he said softly, dangerously. "The trouble is, Angela, that having had you back—even briefly—I want you back permanently. Come back to me, and your father is right off the hook."

"You promised!" Her cry broke raw from her throat. Wide-eyed, desperate. But Lincoln only shrugged, a faint smile tugging his lips.

"I promised to help the firm. I said nothing about setting your father free. I've never had the slightest inclination to do that. There's more than one way to collect a debt— or to exact revenge."

Her blood iced. "What are you going to do?"

Lincoln's smile widened, slow, amused, his handsome face a mask of ironic triumph.

"I see that look again," he drawled. "That old certainty that I'm omnipotent. Perhaps I am. As for what I intend to do…" His eyes gleamed with wicked calculation. "I never show my hand until the moment is right. I've waited a long time, Angela. I can wait longer—unless, of course, you'd rather gamble."

Her heart thudded. Trapped. Always trapped. First by blind love, then by loyalty to her father. And now by Lincoln's cold, relentless snare.

He hadn't asked her back for love. His threat was darker, sharper. A trap dressed as temptation.

"Nice try," she said at last, her scorn ringing clear. She even smiled faintly; a smile of disdain she knew would gall him. "But hard luck. You're counting on my loyalty to my father, on my guilty conscience. You've guessed wrongly this time. I don't feel the same anymore. Once, I would have done anything you asked—just because I was bewitched." She met his gaze squarely, cold fire in her eyes. "But I'm no longer bewitched."

The smile had died on his face, leaving his features stark, stripped of mockery. For the first time, Angela felt a fierce surge of triumph. Once—just once—she would outwit Lincoln. If she could walk away from him without betraying that her love still burned, then she would have won.

"As for my father," she continued, her voice steady in the silence he left, "I don't trust him any more than I trust you. These last weeks have shown me there's little to choose between you. You both use me when it suits your purpose, twisting my life to serve your ends. Neither of you loves me the way I deserve. But not this time. This time, I'm not falling for anything. We'll stick to the bargain as it was set down, and I'll hold you to your word. After that, I'll leave. I'll start again—on my own terms."

Her chin lifted, defiant. "I told you I was tired of being pig-in-the-middle, and I meant it. I'm done accepting scraps from the people who are supposed to care about me. Barry Windsor wants me in his firm, not out of pity or patronage but because he knows my worth. I'm good at what I do, Lincoln, and I intend to prove it in the world—without you, without my father."

For a long moment he said nothing. Then, in a voice so low it slid over her skin like a whisper of smoke, he asked,

"You want me to say I love you?"

Angela turned away, refusing to let the quiet lure of his voice splinter her resolve. She bent to gather her bag and small case, her fingers clenching hard around the handles as if they were her lifeline.

"Don't bother to lie," she said, her tone as flat as steel. "You say you never lie—and it's far too late to begin now. You don't love me. You never did. Even when you asked me to marry you, you didn't say the words. All you cared about was revenge, and I was nothing more than a pawn in your game. Well, I no longer care. All I want is to go home. My part of the bargain is finished. Soon I'll be gone for good, building a new life—one that doesn't have you in it. Maybe one day I'll find a man who will love me the way I deserve. And you can go off with Fiona or find another woman you can belittle, call a fool, and control because you're too afraid to meet your equal."

Her legs trembled with every step as she walked deliberately toward the door, but she lifted her chin, refusing to falter. She had fooled him—at least, she told herself she had. He offered no reply, no sharp retort, no cutting remark. He only rose, silent as stone, picked up her cases, and followed.

And just like that, it was over.

Lincoln never appeared at Marsden Enterprises. When Angela returned the following Monday, the change in the offices was already palpable. Fresh life had been breathed into the place, though from a distance. Lincoln would not cross the threshold of a building he despised, but his influence was unmistakable. The old rhythm was back, the bustle of a company reborn. Relief washed through her—he was keeping his word. Yet the knowledge carried its own sting. Every hum of activity, every sharp exchange of business ideas, reminded her of the day she had first met Lincoln here.

In his place, he had sent one of his most trusted men. Jeff Scott, a seasoned strategist with a formidable mind, was not the sort of man anyone could mistake for avuncular. But he worked side by side with Angela, digging deep into the business, and to her surprise, she found herself growing comfortable under his terse manner. When she offered a sound suggestion, his quick, approving glance told her more than words that Barry had been right—she was good at what she did.

Her father's progress, however, grated. Now that the crisis had passed, he grew more pompous, more insufferable. Though he still hadn't set foot in the offices, he interfered at every turn, questioning her plans, countermanding her decisions, treating her—as always—as if she were a child playing at business.

Fortunately, Jeff had no patience for Kurt Marsden's meddling. He merely grunted at the messages Angela relayed and pressed on in his own way. Reporting to Lincoln every evening, he told her, was the only thing that troubled him. That, more than Marsden's bluster, was the weight he carried.

Angela could only agree. And yet, in a way she could not admit even to herself, she took comfort in it. Lincoln still went over everything. Lincoln still knew. Her cheeks flushed hot whenever she wondered whether Jeff reported her contributions, whether Lincoln was aware of her ideas, her effort, her growing skill.

So, she threw herself headlong into the work. She had no choice. She could not afford the dangerous luxury of brooding on Lincoln. But each night was harder than the one before. She had always missed him. Now, after their trip, the absence was sharper, the silence heavier. She longed for him with an ache that no pride, no bravado, could ease. She wanted his arms, his voice, his strength.

But not without love.

Never again without love.

Chapter Eighteen

One evening the following week, Angela left work early to do some shopping. The days were still warm, yet shorter now, and by the time she emerged with her parcels the shopfronts glowed with light while the sky deepened into indigo twilight.

"Why, it's Lincoln's wife!"

Angela turned sharply from her last-minute window-shopping to find herself confronted—and neatly cornered—by Fiona Martin.

"I hear Marsden Enterprises is thriving again," Fiona continued smoothly before Angela could slip away. "The city is enthralled, holding its breath, so to speak. Of course, now that you're back with Lincoln, everything is explained."

"Is it?" Angela murmured. "So, the city concerns itself with Lincoln's private life as well as his business?"

"Well, he's not just any man, is he?" Fiona's smile was knowing, edged with mockery. "There's always been a kind of morbid interest—ever since his father committed suicide. But even without that, Lincoln is brilliant, magnetic. Naturally, the city watches him."

Angela froze where she stood, her body rigid as stone. The words rang in her head, drowning out the bustle around her. People brushed past, jostling her, but she barely noticed. All she heard, over and over was, *'ever since his father committed suicide'.*

Her voice when it came, was strange, almost unrecognisable. "What do you mean?"

Fiona lifted her perfectly arched brows. "But didn't you know? Everyone knows. That's what brought Lincoln back from America—why he stayed in England instead of returning. He owns far more there than here. And I should know," she added with a frown. "I'm often dispatched to oversee things. I used to fly out with Jeff Scott, though I hear he's now working with you."

Angela's legs felt hollow beneath her. Someone collided with her shoulder, muttering an apology, and she swayed where she stood. Fiona caught her arm with a little tut of impatience.

"You're about to be knocked over. I didn't imagine my little bit of gossip would stun you. I thought Lincoln would have told you." Her smile sharpened. "Come, have a coffee. At least sit down before you faint."

Angela knew she was walking straight into Fiona's hands, but she had no strength to resist. If it were true—if Lincoln's father had taken his own life—then that was the root of everything. The cause of Lincoln's relentless hatred. And it would never end.

"There, that's better." Fiona swept them into a table with a careless grace and gestured imperiously for a waiter. "You do look pale. I would never have told you, but after all—you were Lincoln's wife."

"I am Lincoln's wife," Angela said softly, struggling to muster some defence, however feeble.

But she knew the truth—this was deliberate, calculated. How it served Fiona's purpose she couldn't yet see, but she also knew she could not leave now. For five years she had searched for the truth about Lincoln's vendetta. At last, she was about to hear it.

"Why?" Angela asked quietly. "What drove Lincoln's father to…?"

"He was tricked. Cheated. Ruined." Fiona sipped her coffee delicately, her satisfaction plain. "He was a property dealer—respected, honest. Like Lincoln, his word was his bond. He built the Spokes Group slowly and cleanly, above reproach. There was competition, yes, but he held his own. Until your father."

Angela's breath caught, her heart thudding painfully. Fiona's gaze was cool, deliberate, forcing her to beg for each piece.

"So—what went wrong?"

"Jealousy and greed," Fiona replied. "Some men cannot wait. Some want everything, even what belongs to others. Your father lined up agents to dupe John Spokes into buying worthless land—parcels that would never receive planning consent. The deal was vast, financed with heavy borrowing. And when it collapsed like a house of cards, your father went for the jugular, circling to buy the Spokes Group for a fraction of its worth."

Her eyes gleamed with cruel enjoyment. "That alone might not have driven John Spokes to despair. But he had borrowed money he could not repay, made promises he could not honour. He stood to lose everything—even his home. He drove his car off the Embankment."

"Perhaps… perhaps it was an accident," Angela whispered. She had no strength left even to defend her father, not against Fiona's pitiless gaze.

"That was the verdict," Fiona said scathingly. "But everyone knew better. Suicide meant the insurance money would at least keep his wife safe."

"She died," Angela managed.

"She was already gravely ill," Fiona replied, with cold finality. "Losing John finished her. She followed him within the week. I never saw them again."

"Lincoln was wealthy," Angela said, almost desperately. "He would have helped—"

"Not then. His wealth came later—too late to save the Spokes Group."

"But his grandfather, his uncle—why didn't his father appeal to them?"

"Have you never heard of pride? Honour?" Fiona's contempt was cutting. She gathered her things with sharp movements. "Qualities your father never had—and qualities you seem to lack as well, crawling back to Lincoln. You know he still sees me; you knew it when you were together years ago. I can only assume you've gone back to him, so he'll rescue your father after spending years destroying him. But don't delude yourself. Lincoln will have his revenge. He always does."

"I know that," Angela said, rising unsteadily. "For your information, I haven't gone back to Lincoln. I'm working until Marsden Enterprises is strong again—and then I'll be out of his life. He can see you whenever he wishes."

Fiona's smile was glacial. "We already see each other. But does this mean we can stop hiding?" Her voice carried a precise, cutting edge.

"You have my blessing," Angela replied, quiet but resolute.

"Excellent. I'm tired of sneaking around."

Fiona swept out, her perfume trailing like smoke, leaving the air tainted in her wake. Angela dropped money for the coffee, gathered her bag, and forced herself to stand. Her legs trembled so violently she thought they might give way beneath her.

But the weakness in her body was nothing compared to the icy certainty burrowing into her heart. She understood now—why Lincoln's hatred burned so fiercely, why her father feared him so deeply. Fiona's words might have been barbed for cruelty's sake, yet Angela could hear the ring of truth beneath the venom.

And echoing through her mind, relentless as a curse, came Lincoln's voice from his office:

'Promises to keep, Angela.'

Lincoln's life was built on promises and his father's life had been built on them too. John Spokes had not been able to keep his promises, and the dishonour had served in killing him. Lincoln would keep his promise. This would never end.

She didn't go in to see her father in the hospital. She couldn't face him. She only had a vague idea of what had really happened. Only Lincoln could tell her the complete truth and Angela had the terrible feeling that her father would not even offer excuses. He would say it was business practice.

Perhaps it was but it was discreditable, corrupt, and while at one time she would have staunchly defended him, said it could not possibly be true, she could not do that now because, in her heart she knew it was near enough to the truth. Now it seemed almost like a rough sort of justice that Lincoln had begun his campaign by taking her away from her father.

It had been his first line of attack, his first section and since then he had been steadily wiping Marsden Enterprises out. He had outbid them in every project, used his wealth to squeeze than out of business and had still, with his brilliance, made a profit for his company when profits should have been almost non-existent. He was helping now because he had some terrible plan—something much worse than anything he had done before.

The next day Angela was quiet at the office, weary in body and spirit. Jeff Scott kept glancing at her from the corner of his eye, asking nothing but clearly thinking a great deal. By lunchtime, her restraint snapped. With the small dining room almost deserted, she seized the chance to silence Fiona's cruel words, if only by digging for the truth.

"How long have you been with Lincoln?" she asked when they were seated across from one another.

"Almost six years," Jeff said, setting down his fork. "I joined him soon after he came back from the States. The Spokes Group was practically on its knees back then. Lincoln just threw money and expertise into it and worked harder than any man I've ever seen. I don't know the full story, but I heard the banks were reluctant to back him at first. Then he stormed in and practically dared them not to. He's got enormous holdings in the States." Jeff flushed suddenly and gave her an awkward glance. "I don't know why I'm telling you all this. You're his wife. You probably know far more than I do."

"I don't know much about his father," Angela said carefully. "I only found out yesterday that… there was a suspicion he took his own life."

Jeff frowned, uneasy. "A bad business. There were whispers still going around when I first joined Spokes, but you know how it is—scandal burns hot, then fades. As far as I know, nothing was ever proved."

"No. Of course not," Angela murmured bleakly. But inside, her thoughts twisted like knives. Lincoln had said the law would never catch her father—but he had caught him. That he appeared to let Kurt Marsden go made no sense, unless he was biding his time for a darker, final blow. And that must be why he wanted her back. He wanted her father close, exposed, helpless—just as his own father had been.

That night she went to the private hospital. Kurt was almost ready to come home; the doctors had told her as much. She knew she had to confront him before that day arrived. If Fiona had spoken the truth, Angela would not be there to greet him. He could take back his office, his empire—and face the ruin himself.

He looked well, smiling broadly when she entered, ignoring the fact that she had not come the night before.

"You look tired, Angela," he observed. "Is that husband of yours working you to the bone at the office? They say he's a hard taskmaster."

"He's never set foot inside," she replied steadily. "I work with Jeff Scott. He reports to Lincoln, and things are picking up rapidly. In fact, I don't see how Lincoln is managing it so quickly."

"Probably channelling back the business he stole from us in the first place," her father muttered. "I can't think why he's bothering anyway. There isn't a weak spot in his armour. If there had been, I'd have found it."

"No, he's not weak," Angela said quietly. "Maybe he learned not to be—after his father died."

Her father's head snapped up, his glare hard. "What do you mean? His father wasn't just weak—he was a fool."

"An honourable fool?" Angela asked softly. "Is that how you managed to trick him?"

"I don't know what Spokes has been telling you—"

"I haven't seen Lincoln at all," she cut in, her eyes fixed on his face. "I heard it from another source. Lincoln has never shared the truth of this vendetta with me—and neither have you. So, I'll ask plainly: was it because of you that his father died?"

"I didn't drive his car into the river," Kurt snapped, his face reddening. "He was a fool who trusted too easily and lost his company. What he did after that was his own choice."

"After you left him with nothing," Angela said icily. "Not even his dignity."

Kurt leaned back and gave the cold, cutting laugh she knew too well. "Dignity doesn't pay the bills. Honour doesn't keep a business afloat. He drowned because he was weak. Business is cutthroat, Angela—it's sink or swim. John Spokes trusted the wrong man. That makes him a fool. And you—you're just the same. Too soft to survive. You always were."

"Not anymore." Angela rose, her voice low but steady. "All my life I blamed Lincoln for not loving me back when I loved him so much. But how could he? His whole world had been poisoned—and you were the one who did it. I'm not a fool anymore. I learn fast when I finally know the truth."

"So, what now?" her father demanded scathingly. "Do you go running back to Lincoln Spokes?"

"How can I?" she asked, staring at him as if seeing him for the first time. "I'm the one who loves—Lincoln never did. No, I won't run back to him. I'll walk away from both of you. When you're ready to return to the office, it's still there. But it's your problem, not mine."

"Come back here!" he barked furiously.

Angela turned on her heel and walked out. She had taken all she was ever going to take. There was nowhere she wanted to be but with Lincoln. And now she knew she could never have him.

Nothing else mattered.

Angela did not go into the office the next day. There seemed little point. In truth, there seemed little point in anything at all now that she finally understood. Lincoln had never stopped his vendetta—and he never would. Helping Jeff Scott, working late into the night, offering her ideas with such desperate determination—none of it had been for her father's sake. It had always been for Lincoln, fulfilling his plans, moving at the pace he set, guided by his unseen hand.

And she no longer felt the need to protect her father. She understood him too well now—his cold ambition, his ruthless pride. He had destroyed lives and called it business. He would never change. All she wanted was to leave, to erase the past, to silence every memory. But that was impossible. Not when she loved Lincoln. Not when her heart was chained to him with a bond she could never sever.

So, she spent the day alone, quietly sorting through her belongings, preparing to leave the house that had never truly been home. Each drawer emptied, each folded dress placed into a suitcase, was done with careful precision, as if order could keep the ache from breaking her. She knew she would never come back here. She could not stay, could not face her father each day. Every sight of him would only remind her—of the lies, of the battles, of the man she could not stop loving.

And of the silence in which that love would die.

The next day at the office was her last. Angela knew it before she stepped through the wide swing-doors. The only tug of regret she felt was for Maria and the handful of people who had stood loyally beside her through the bitter struggle with Lincoln.

Maria was away from her desk, and Angela decided the goodbyes could wait. She had no intention of lingering here; there was too much to do at home. If her father returned from the hospital sooner than expected, he would try to force her into staying. She couldn't face another battle with him. By then, she would be gone. Gone for good.

"You're back, Mrs. Spokes." Jeff Scott greeted her warmly as she entered her office. He even smiled. "There was a panic when you didn't turn up yesterday. The whole place seemed to be holding its breath. From what I can tell, the staff rate their chances of survival by your expression when you walk through the door. Strange, isn't it—that the fate of Marsden Enterprises seems to rest on the warmth of one young lady."

It was meant as a compliment, obscure as it was, but it only stung. Her guilty conscience stirred—sharp, relentless—reminding her of what she was about to do. She owed the loyal staff more than this, and yet she was ready to vanish. If even one missed day had caused them to falter, what would her absence now mean?

Her bleak look wiped the smile from his face.

"Are you ill?" he asked quickly. "Can I get you something?"

"No. I'm not ill," she murmured.

Turning to the window, she stared down at the street below. Now or never. If she stayed another day, her father would return, and her resolve would crumble beneath old loyalties. This was her last chance to break free.

"I'm leaving," she said suddenly, swinging round to face him. "You don't need me here. You're running the place for Lincoln, and you're doing it well. The staff will follow you—they're the best, loyal, and hardworking. I've been little more than a mascot. Anything I know, Maria can tell you—she worked with my father for years."

Jeff frowned. "But I thought… Mr. Spokes said you'd be staying. That you'd continue with the firm even after I've finished here."

"No. I never agreed to that," Angela replied firmly. "I promised to stay while you needed me. But the truth is—you don't. And I can't stay. Not now, not with what I know. I'm leaving today."

"Does Mr. Spokes know?" His voice held a note of anxiety.

Angela almost smiled. This clever, formidable man, uneasy at the thought of reporting her departure to Lincoln. "He'll know when you tell him," she said lightly.

"I'll have no choice," Jeff admitted, flushing with embarrassment. "I go over everything with him each evening. The first thing he asks is how you're coping. Even how you look." He cleared his throat, shifting in discomfort. "Not kindly, you understand, but… he asks. He wasn't here last night, so I didn't have to mention you were absent."

"Never mind," Angela said with ironic gentleness. "Now you'll have two reports to deliver. One—that I played truant yesterday. Two—that I walked out today."

"Must you?" he asked quietly.

"I must if I want to survive," she answered, gathering her things into the box she had brought. Her voice was calm, but the weight of her decision pressed down like stone.

Chapter Nineteen

Angela said her goodbyes to the staff, trying to reassure them as best she could. She called a small meeting in the dining room, keeping it as official as possible, outlining that Lincoln Spokes was now guiding Marsden Enterprises toward recovery. The staff already knew Jeff Scott, of course, but Angela's explanation that Lincoln would restore the firm brought a collective, almost audible sigh of relief.

There wasn't a single person present who didn't know Lincoln's formidable reputation, and several also understood why Marsden Enterprises had spiralled into decline. A few looked at her with subtle pity, but at least the immediate pressure was off, and that was enough for now.

Maria lingered behind, watching Angela quietly. When Angela finally stepped aside for a private moment, Maria asked softly, "Has he stopped, Angela?"

Angela exhaled, a small, tight breath. "With the firm, yes. He gave me his word, and that's good enough."

Maria's eyes narrowed slightly. "Then why are you running for cover?" she asked. "And don't tell me you're not. I've watched you fight for this firm. I've seen you nearly break yourself trying. You didn't run then—but now, you're running."

Angela looked down, her fingers twisting together. "I fought because I was angry, and because of loyalty to my father," she admitted slowly. "But there's no anger left, no loyalty that matters anymore. I've learned things I can't ignore. It's better if I just go."

"Where?" Maria pressed. "Will you work for Windsor's?"

"No," Angela said firmly and shook her head, a flicker of relief in her eyes. "That's what I intended... but now I can't. To be perfectly honest, Maria, I don't really know what I'm going to do. I just need to think. I need to get away."

The words *'space'* hovered unspoken on her tongue. She had already said that to Lincoln. Now, she would have all the space she could want, because Lincoln would no longer be part of her life. It would be final. What he might do, she didn't want to know, and she would brace herself for whatever blows the future held.

Once she left, she would sever every remaining tie to Marsden Enterprises. No more pity for her father. Misfortune sometimes struck without reason, but his ruin was a wound of his own making. Whatever consequences Lincoln—or fate itself—chose to deliver, she would no longer shield him from them.

Her first stop was the bank. With steady hands, she closed her account and withdrew her savings. It wasn't a fortune, but it was freedom. Enough to plant new roots, enough to begin again. From there, she went straight to the airline desk and bought the earliest one-way ticket to Australia. No return.

By the time she returned home, night had settled over the city. Her belongings went into suitcases with quick, mechanical efficiency. Rita was away for the day, sparing Angela the web of explanations she would otherwise have to spin. She was grateful. She couldn't bear another set of questions, another reason to doubt. All she wanted was to run—run from the lies, from the weight of her father's failures, from the wreckage Lincoln had carved into her heart.

Distance—that was the only cure. And Australia, vast and unreachably distant, felt wide enough to hold the shattered pieces of her and give her the escape she craved.

On the long drive back into London, the truth settled over her with slow, aching weight: despair didn't absolve her of practicalities. She had nowhere to go. Her flight was tomorrow afternoon—somehow, she had to find a bed for the night.

Turning away from the glittering avenues she knew belonged to Lincoln's world, Angela steered toward a row of modest hotels she had once glimpsed—quiet, unremarkable buildings with peeling paint and narrow, unassuming doorways. No glamour. No glitter. No place Lincoln's friends or colleagues would ever tread.

But she had seen them. She had remembered.

When she had first left him, she had toyed with vanishing entirely—fleeing so far that neither her father nor Lincoln could ever find her. The idea had tempted her endlessly: small, anonymous rooms with curtained windows, offering secrecy, escape, even the promise of reinvention. She could be anyone she chose. No one would question her. And now... she was finally doing it.

She pulled up outside the middle hotel, stepped inside, and her footsteps echoed faintly on scuffed linoleum. A room was available. Later, she would fetch her things from the car. Later, she would turn the key, shut the door against the world, and surrender to sleep.

Tomorrow, she would leave. Tomorrow, she would begin her new life, far from Lincoln, far from her father. Tonight, all she sought was oblivion.

Without pausing, she scrawled her name across the registration card. Only when the ink dried did she realise her mistake. She had not meant to do that. She had meant to choose another name, any name. But there it was, stark in black ink—Angela Spokes.

The sight jolted her. Her heart tripped into panic. But the man behind the desk gave no sign of recognition, no flicker of interest. To him the name meant nothing. Angela exhaled shakily. Outside Lincoln's empire, Spokes was just another name.

She paid in cash—no receipts, no paper trail—and went back out with the porter, a stooped old man whose hand shook faintly on the trolley handle.

"No parking here," he muttered when he caught sight of her car. "It's all right across the road," he explained in a tired, matter-of-fact tone. "After six, before eight in the morning. Later than that you'll have to move it. Best to leave it there for tonight, miss. It's late."

It was.

Almost eleven. The weight of it pressed on her suddenly, explaining the bone-deep weariness that dragged at her limbs. It had been a long day—a cruel day—and now she wanted nothing but to sink into sleep.

She drove across the street, reversing carefully into the narrow gap between two cars. At least it was legal until morning. She shut off the engine and looked up at the hotel. It seemed different now—less like a refuge, more like a cell. What she really wanted, what her body still ached for, was the only place forever denied her: Lincoln's arms, the hard heat of his body, the cool, smiling grey of his eyes.

But that world was gone. Gone forever.

Her own eyes blurred with tears as she opened the door and stepped out, the pavement slick beneath her shoes. She started across the road, head bent. Only when a blinding glare cut through her tears did she look up.

A horn shrieked. An engine roared.

The car came out of the corner too fast, and she was too dazed, too weary to leap aside. The impact caught her on the front wing, flinging her like a broken doll against the line of parked cars. She slid down into the wet darkness of the street, her body crumpling into stillness, her breath stolen, her eyes closing on a silence as complete as sleep.

She never saw the old porter watching her from the hotel doorway, his faded eyes narrowing with concern. Something about her fragility, the way she moved as though carrying an invisible weight, had troubled him from the first moment. When the shriek of brakes split the night, he reacted instinctively.

By the time he reached the edge of the pavement, the street was chaos. The car had screeched to a halt, its headlights glaring like an accusation across the wet road. A young man—hardly more than a boy—was already crouched beside her crumpled body, his face chalk-white, his hands fumbling.

"Come on… please…" he stammered, fingers pressed desperately against her throat, then her wrist, his shoulders jerking with panic when he found no answering beat. He was trembling so violently he could scarcely breathe.

"Leave her!" the porter snapped, his voice unexpectedly sharp and commanding. He shoved the young man aside with surprising strength for one so old. "You've done your worst—don't touch her now."

The boy staggered back, stricken, as the porter sank to his knees beside her. With reverent care, he slipped off his shabby jacket and laid it over her still form, shielding her from the cold night air. His hand trembled as he brushed the dark hair from her face, tucking a strand gently behind her ear.

"Ahh…" His voice cracked, low and rough with grief he hadn't expected to feel. "Such a beautiful little thing… and all alone. Too young, far too young…"

His gnarled hand lingered at her temple, stroking her hair as though he could comfort her even now, while the wail of sirens began to rise in the distance, carrying toward them through the rain.

Lincoln sat in his office, the glow of the laptop spilling a cold, sterile light across his desk. Rows of numbers flickered on the screen, swimming into a blur he couldn't hold steady. He hadn't absorbed a single figure. His mind was elsewhere—where it always was. On her.

Angela. Her pale, stricken face. Her trembling voice. The fleeting brush of her hand that still burned like a phantom weight against his palm.

He had come straight from a punishing meeting outside London, exhaustion grinding through his bones, yet all he could do was wait. Wait for Jeff Scott to check in, to tell him how she was. Jeff had told him in previous meetings that Angela was an exceptional manager, sharper than any man he'd ever worked with, and Lincoln was so proud of her. But that was meaningless.

None of it mattered. The only question that mattered—the only thing that mattered at all—was how is she? Was she still furious, still hurting? How much longer could he endure this iron restraint, keeping himself away from her when every instinct screamed to go back, to hold her, to force her to see the truth?

The thought clenched his chest until he could barely breathe.

When he'd lost her the first time, all those years ago, his pride had destroyed him. She had accused him of an affair—a charge so absurd it had cut deeper than she could have known. Didn't she understand? There had never been another woman, not since the moment he'd first laid eyes on her. He hadn't wanted anyone but Angela. Ever. But she hadn't trusted him. And when she left, first anger, then pride, damnable pride, had chained him in place. He had let her go, refusing to chase after her, convincing himself that if she didn't come back on her own, she wasn't his to claim.

It had been the greatest mistake of his life.

But this time… this time the loss was unbearable. Ten times worse. A hundred. Because this time she hadn't simply walked away in youthful defiance—she had left with her heart in pieces, telling him exactly why she was finished with him.

Her last words still cut through him like a blade:

'You don't love me. You never did. Even when you asked me to marry you, you didn't say the words. All you cared about was revenge, and I was nothing more than a pawn in your game. Well, I no longer care. All I want is to go home. My part of the bargain is finished. Soon I'll be gone for good, building a new life—one that doesn't have you in it. Maybe one day I'll find a man who will love me the way I deserve. And you can go off with Fiona or find another woman you can belittle, call a fool, and control because you're too afraid to meet your equal.'

The words seared into him, echoing in the stillness of his office until he wanted to smash the laptop just to silence them.

The thought of Angela in another man's arms nearly crushed the air from his lungs. His fists clenched on the desk, knuckles blanching, the tendons in his hands straining with the force of it. He had never wanted another woman—not after her. From the first instant he had laid eyes on her, there had only ever been Angela.

Fool that she was. Fool that *he* was. She didn't know. She had never known. Because he had never told her. Never given her the certainty, the security of knowing she was the only one he would ever love.

That was his failure. His silence. His damnable pride. Why had he kept the words locked inside when they burned him night and day? Why had he let her believe she was nothing but a pawn when in truth she was the axis his entire world spun upon? Why had he not fought for her when she left, not stormed after her, not broken down every wall until she understood that he loved her to distraction?

Because he had been a coward in the one thing that truly mattered. Because the only fire that had ever driven him, above all else, had been vengeance—not love, not her.

And now, that mistake was exacting its relentless toll.

The sharp buzz of the intercom yanked him from his torment. He inhaled, forcing his chest to steady, his voice regaining its usual clipped control as he pressed the button.

"Mr. Stokes, Ms. Martin is here to see you."

"Send her in," he said flatly, not lifting his gaze.

He didn't want to see Fiona. She was the spark that had set his marriage on fire, the one he blamed for Angela's doubts. He was certain she had fed Paul Carter insinuations about his and Angela's separation. For what end, he couldn't guess. He had never crossed the line—never laid a finger on her in the way Angela imagined.

Fiona glided in, flawless as ever—hair sleek, dress hugging every curve, confidence dripping like perfume. But instead of taking a seat as she always had, she moved around his desk, leaning in close, pressing herself into his space with an audacity he hadn't seen before. Lincoln's brows shot up. He didn't like it.

If Angela were here, he realised with a flash of irritation, she would see it too—the closeness, the insinuation, the threat to her heart. And he knew all too well how that would twist her doubts into poison.

"I have some good news," she purred, voice honeyed, deliberately teasing.

"What news?" His tone sharpened instantly, instinct warning him.

"Your wife has given us her blessing."

Lincoln's head snapped up, icy disbelief lancing through him. "You saw Angela?" His voice thundered across the desk, low and dangerous.

"Yes," Fiona replied smoothly, her smile feline. "She's finally given in. She told me we can be together now." She leaned closer, lips curving. "So, we no longer need to hide our feelings."

"What?" Lincoln surged to his feet, shock slamming into him like a physical blow. His pulse hammered in his ears.

Fiona blinked, startled by the force of his reaction, but quickly recovered, her smirk sliding back into place. "Oh, come now. You've wanted me for years, Lincoln. Angela always knew it. I didn't want to be the other woman, so I waited. And now she's stepped aside. We don't have to pretend anymore."

For a long, breathless second Lincoln just stared at her, incredulous. Then her words hit, jagged and merciless. He had dismissed Angela's doubts as petty jealousy, dismissed the hurt in her eyes as insecurity. But Fiona's smug admission made everything clear. Angela hadn't been paranoid. She hadn't imagined it. Fiona had fed her lies— poisonous, deliberate, calculated lies.

His blood turned to ice. His wife's pain, her quiet accusations, every tear he had brushed aside—every moment he had told her she was being childish—all of it came roaring back, cutting him to the bone. And now Fiona stood here, bold as brass, twisting the truth to her own ends, gloating over the wreckage.

Chapter Twenty

Lincoln's fists curled, his voice a lethal growl. "Fiona. How long have you been telling my wife these lies?"

"I told her years ago," Fiona said, chin lifting, her eyes glittering with triumph. "The truth—that you would never give me up, that she was only temporary. And I was right. She's gone now."

Lincoln dragged a hand down his face, fury and shame crashing through him in a wave that left him trembling. God, what had Angela endured because of his silence? He hadn't reassured her, hadn't defended her heart, hadn't cut Fiona out when he should have. He'd left his wife exposed to a viper, and Angela—sweet, trusting Angela—had believed the venom.

When he spoke again, his voice was iron. "You've misread everything. There is no us, and there never will be. I have never wanted you, Fiona. You're my lawyer—nothing more."

Her smirk faltered, a crack splitting her composure. "Oh, Lincoln. Don't pretend. Everyone saw it. You spent more time with me than with her—even when she was in the room. She knew. She accepted it. Why fight what's obvious?" She moved closer, sliding her arms around his neck as if claiming what she believed was hers.

Revulsion flared hot and violent. In one swift, brutal motion, Lincoln ripped her hands away and shoved her back. She stumbled, shock flashing across her face before she masked it with hauteur. His eyes blazed, his chest heaving.

"Don't you dare," he snarled. "Don't you ever touch me again. You've lied to my wife. You've sabotaged my marriage. You've twisted her doubts for your own gain. Do you even understand what you've done? Do you realise how deeply you've wounded her—how deeply I wounded her—because I let you anywhere near us?"

Fiona's mask flickered, a tremor of uncertainty cracking her arrogance. "She's gone, Lincoln. She said it herself. You and I—"

"Never!" His roar stopped her cold, reverberating through the office like thunder. "Not now. Not ever. Angela is the only woman I want. The only woman I have ever loved. And if she's left, it's because I was blind, because I failed her, because I let poison like you near her. But I will make it right. I will prove to her that she's, my life. My only."

His grey eyes burned, fury and remorse warring in their depths. "Get out, Fiona. You're finished here. Out of my office. Out of my life."

She hesitated, lips pressed thin, her mask slipping into something raw and ugly. But his glare—merciless, absolute—left no room for argument. With a flick of her hair and a brittle facade of composure, she turned on her heel and swept toward the door.

Lincoln didn't watch her leave. He couldn't. His hands braced on the desk, head bowed, as guilt and determination warred inside him. He had been so certain Angela was wrong, so certain Fiona's presence meant nothing. He had dismissed her fears as irrational jealousy, called her childish, idiotic.

But the truth was like acid now. Angela hadn't been imagining things—she had been drowning in lies he had allowed. Lies he had fed.

He had always been careless with Fiona. Complimenting her in front of Angela as though it meant nothing. Hugging her in greeting, brushing a kiss across her cheek without a thought. Even dancing with her at events when Angela's eyes were on him, trusting, uncertain. He had laughed it off, assured himself Angela was being dramatic. But what else could she have believed, when her husband's arm was around another woman and his lips brushed her skin while his own wife stood watching?

God, what had he done?

Angela's tears, her trembling accusations, the raw ache in her voice—they rang through him now like a death knell. Her voice had begged him for reassurance, and instead of defending her heart, he had let her drown in doubt, abandoned her to the poison Fiona whispered.

His chest tightened until he could barely draw breath.

Only one thought cut through the torment, raw and consuming. He had to find her. He had to prove—no matter what it cost—that she was not a pawn, not a convenience, not a passing desire.

She was his everything. The only woman he had ever loved. And this time, he would fight for her with everything he had.

The intercom buzzed sharply, shattering the silence. "Mr. Stokes, the police are here to see you."

Lincoln's head jerked up, a prickle of unease running through him. The police? His stomach clenched, cold and hard. What could they possibly—

"Send them in," he ordered, forcing his voice into the clipped authority he always commanded, though his chest had tightened like a vice.

Two officers entered, faces grave, their solemnity like a dark omen. One spoke, each word precise, merciless. "Mr. Stokes, we regret to inform you that your wife has been in an accident."

Time stopped.

The words struck with brutal force, shattering through his composure. For a split second, he couldn't breathe. His pulse roared in his ears, drowning out everything but that one devastating truth. *Angela. Accident.* The two words collided in his brain like thunder.

"An… accident?" The question rasped from him, strangled, almost unrecognisable.

The officers gave a slow, grave nod.

Lincoln's vision swam. The floor seemed to tilt beneath him, the world collapsing into a single unbearable thought: *Angela, broken.* Angela, slipping away. His Angela. And he hadn't told her. Not once. Not ever.

Not that he loved her.

He had wasted years hiding behind pride, feeding her insecurities with his silence and with every careless gesture toward Fiona. He had thought there would always be time— time to win her back, time to prove she was his everything. But time had betrayed him.

What if it was already too late?

The control that defined him, the armour he wore in every battle, shattered like glass. All he could see was Angela's face, pale and tear-streaked as she'd hurled her last words at him. All he could hear was her voice, broken and bitter: *'You don't love me. You never did.'*

And God help him if she had died believing it.

His throat closed, his body trembling with a fear he had never known. Deals, empires, fortunes—none of it mattered. None of it could buy him back the one thing he had already thrown away.

Forcing breath through his lungs, he managed, hoarse, urgent, "Where… where is she? Is she—alive?"

The officers exchanged a weighted glance. One of them said carefully, "Sir, you should come immediately. It's critical."

The word carved itself into his chest. *Critical.*

Lincoln surged forward, no longer capable of the cool precision that had defined him all his life. He grabbed his coat with shaking hands, his mind consumed by raw panic. He strode for the door, so fast the officers had to hurry to keep up.

This was it. The moment he had always feared yet never allowed himself to believe possible. He might lose her. Not to pride, not to vengeance, not to lies—

But to death.

And if she slipped away now, without ever hearing the words he should have spoken a thousand times, it would destroy him.

Nothing—no power, no wealth, no empire—could shield him from this truth.

Angela was his whole life.

And if she died, he would never forgive himself.

Lincoln arrived at the hospital not long after Angela had been brought in. Stricken. Devastated. The word *accident* reverberated in his mind, yet he knew—this was no mere mishap. It was the threat of losing her, of being wrenched away from the only woman he had ever truly loved.

The police had insisted on an escort, and every flashing siren, every bend in the road felt like a countdown. He barked at his driver, voice rough, raw with urgency. "The hospital. Now. As fast as you can."

The journey was a blur, the world outside the window nothing but streaks of colour he couldn't focus on. Every second carved into him like a blade, every heartbeat pounding like a war drum in his chest. His fists clenched on his thighs, knuckles bone-white, the tremor of barely contained panic running through him.

The moment Lincoln stepped through the hospital doors, staff converged on him, their movements brisk, efficient, almost rehearsed. They knew who he was. They knew how to move for a man of his stature. But none of it mattered—not the power, not the wealth, not the influence that could command entire boardrooms. None of it could change the brutal truth: *his Angel* was hurt. Precision and protocol meant nothing against the raw terror ripping through his chest, a fear no authority could silence.

"How is she?" His voice cracked, ragged with desperation, as though speaking could make the world right again.

A doctor in green scrubs stepped forward, calm yet carrying the weight of gravity. He glanced at the chart, then back at Lincoln, eyes steady but unreadable.

"She's alive," he said quietly. "But it was very close. Significant injuries—head trauma, fractured ribs, contusions. She's unconscious."

Lincoln felt his knees go weak. Alive—but hanging by a thread. Relief and terror collided, a storm tearing at his chest.

The doctor's tone softened, aware of the man's raw, exposed fear. "We're monitoring her closely. The next twenty-four hours will be critical. Her heart is strong—that's in her favour. But we can't predict how, when, or if she'll wake."

Lincoln swallowed hard, his throat raw, voice hoarse. "Can I see her?"

The doctor paused, studying him, then nodded. "You may. But be prepared—she won't look as you remember. And she won't hear you. Not yet."

Lincoln's chest tightened. The thought of seeing her like that—helpless, fragile—was unbearable. Yet he moved forward, driven by a single, unrelenting force: the desperate need to be near her, to hold her, to do anything to keep her in his world.

Lincoln squared his shoulders, every nerve taut, his jaw set with a fierce, unspoken vow. Not yet was not the same as never. He would not let her go.

The door opened on a hushed, sterile room, the rhythmic beeping of machines the only sound. For a moment Lincoln couldn't move. He had faced hostile boardrooms, political battles, and rivals bent on his ruin without flinching—but this stopped him cold.

Angela lay motionless on the bed, pale as porcelain against the white sheets. Her black hair spilled across the pillow, stark against the bandages at her temple. Tubes and wires tethered her to machines that kept watch over every fragile breath.

He moved forward slowly, as though afraid even the sound of his steps might disturb her. His chest ached at the sight of her bruised face, the faint swelling at her lips, the rise and fall of her chest too shallow, too mechanical. She looked breakable, nothing like the fiery woman who had defied him only days ago.

He reached her side and sat heavily in the chair, his hand hovering before he dared to touch. Finally, he smoothed the hair from her forehead with trembling fingers, his jaw tightening to hold back the storm inside him.

"Angela," he whispered, his voice rough and low. "You don't get to leave me. Not like this."

He bowed his head, pressing his forehead against the back of her hand as though he could will his strength into her fragile body. His voice broke, low and desperate.

"Fight, damn you. You've always fought me—every word, every kiss, every promise. Fight this too."

His fingers tightened around hers, clinging to the faint warmth of her skin. "Don't leave me. You promised me forever. Do you hear me, Angela? Forever." His throat burned, the words tearing out of him before he could stop them. "I love you, Angel. I always have. I always will."

Tears slipped unchecked down his face, falling onto her hand, darkening her pale skin. He bent over her, shattered, his breath uneven as he fought the helpless terror clawing at his chest.

But she gave no answer. Only the monitors replied, steady and merciless, filling the silence with their unfeeling rhythm. And Lincoln—once untouchable, imperious, cold—sat broken beside her, stripped bare by the sight of the only woman he had ever loved, lying silent and still.

Through the swirling mists of pain, voices drifted in and out—distant, indistinct—but one rose above them all. It was close, achingly familiar, the only one she reached for. A husky voice, roughened now with quiet desperation.

'Fight, damn you. Don't leave me. You promised forever. I love you, Angel.'

Other voices intruded—measured, calm, professional. Cool, efficient hands touched her, easing the agony, steadying the chaos. Darkness pulled her under once more, relentless, and absolute.

When she finally surfaced again, the world was gentler, hushed. The harsh glare was gone; the room bathed in dim light that allowed her eyes to open without stabbing pain. A steady warmth anchored her—strong fingers wrapped firmly around hers, tethering her to life.

Her gaze drifted down, blurred with fatigue, and her heart lurched. Lincoln. His dark head rested against her hand, his large frame folded uncomfortably into the hospital chair, yet his grip on her never loosened. Even in sleep, he clung to her, as if letting go would mean losing her forever.

With a trembling effort, she eased her fingers free, her hand rising unsteadily to brush through his hair. The silky strands slid against her skin—brown and gleaming, softening the harsh planes of his face. For the first time she saw him unguarded. Shadows hollowed his eyes, exhaustion carved into his features, stripping him of the ruthless armour he always wore. Vulnerable. Achingly human.

Her chest constricted. How she loved him. How she wished she could be enough for him. But that wish had always been hers alone. Her love was a secret burden, too deep, too dangerous to confess.

"Lincoln…" Her voice was the faintest breath, a whisper woven with longing and sorrow.

His eyes snapped open instantly, storm-grey locking onto hers with raw intensity. He sat upright in a heartbeat, capturing her hand against his cheek as though it was the only thing keeping him alive.

"Angel!" His voice broke, hoarse with relief. "Sweetheart, I'm sorry. I'm so sorry."

Tears pricked her eyes, fragile and helpless against the weight of his tenderness. She gave the barest shake of her head. "It's okay, Lincoln," she whispered, though the words scraped her throat with pain. "None of it was your fault. I know you couldn't forget… or forgive. I understand why you could never love me."

Her lashes fluttered as weakness stole through her, her voice breaking on a sigh. "But it's all right now. You don't have to pretend anymore. I hope you and Fiona are… happy."

Her words pierced him like knives, each syllable a wound he couldn't staunch. His face twisted, torment carving deep lines, his eyes glistening with a sheen of tears he never allowed anyone to see. He reached for her, desperate, but her strength ebbed too fast. With a shuddering exhale, her eyes slipped closed, her body sagging back into the darkness.

"Angela!" His cry was raw, shattering, torn straight from his soul. Panic clawed through him as he gripped her hand tighter, refusing to let her slip away. His forehead pressed desperately against her limp fingers, his voice breaking apart.

"Fiona means nothing to me—nothing! She never has. She never will." His breath came ragged, thick with anguish. "But you—you're everything. I do love you. I've always loved you. God help me, I always will."

The monitors wavered, their rhythm fragile but steady. Nurses burst into the room, quick and efficient, but their eyes flickered with something more as they took in the sight before them.

Lincoln Stokes—the man whose name alone commanded empires, the man whispered about as cold, untouchable, merciless—was bent over his wife's hand, trembling, broken. His lips pressed to her skin, whispering love into the silence, begging the unconscious woman before him to live.

A young nurse faltered mid-step, her eyes widening at the sight. This was the billionaire whose reputation filled boardrooms with fear, and yet here he was—shattered, undone by a slip of a woman lying pale against hospital sheets. The doctor's voice was calm, steady, but quieter than usual as he gave an order to check her vitals. Even he couldn't help glancing at the man bowed so low, as if the weight of the entire world had been torn from beneath him.

No one dared comment. But the air itself seemed to hold its breath. They were witnessing something raw, something few ever saw: a man who had ruled empires, conquered industries, bent rivals to his will—now brought to his knees by love, by fear, by the fragile body of his wife.

Lincoln didn't care who saw. Pride, reputation, power—none of it mattered. His shoulders shook, his voice rasping as he bowed his head over her hand, clinging like a drowning man to the only lifeline he had ever wanted.

"Stay with me, Angel," he whispered, the words breaking on a sob he could no longer contain. "Please… I can't lose you. Not now. Not ever. I can't survive without you."

But she lay still, her silence a knife twisting deeper with every passing second. Only the monitors answered him, their steady rhythm merciless in its indifference, marking time as his heart fractured.

For the first time in his life, Lincoln Stokes was powerless. No fortune could buy her life. No influence could compel her to stay. All he was left with was the raw, unguarded truth of his heart—love laid bare, desperate, clinging to the only woman who could destroy him completely.

When Angela woke again, sunlight streamed gently into the room. Lincoln was still there, his hand wrapped around hers, steady and warm.

"Lincoln…" she whispered, her voice fragile.

His grey eyes met hers, soft yet intense. "Sweetheart."

"Why are you here?" The words cut deeper than she intended, a shadow of guilt in her tone.

"Because I love you," he said simply, conviction steady in every syllable.

It was hard to speak, but she managed softly, "No… Fiona…"

"Fiona means nothing to me, Angel. I have never wanted her, and I never will." His voice was firm, filled with quiet intensity.

"But…"

"No buts," he interrupted gently but decisively. "I do love you, Angela. I've always loved you. Every minute away from you was a minute wasted. I tried to divide my life—one part filled with your sweetness, the other with anger and revenge. I wanted both. I wanted you, and I wanted justice. Living like that could never work, and I was too arrogant to see it. I lost you… and nearly lost you forever."

Angela managed a shaky smile, her fingers curling around his. "It was a stupid accident," she murmured. "I wasn't paying attention. I was unhappy, running away…." She sighed, eyes fluttering closed. "Nobody can really run away, can they?"

Her words were slurred, weak from exhaustion. Lincoln's grip tightened. "Don't leave me, Angel," he pleaded, urgent and raw. "They said you should be all right—but I need to hear it. You promised me once… you said forever."

A faint smile touched her lips, her eyes still closed.

"I'll promise again, Lincoln. Forever. I won't leave you—if you want me."

"I want you," he breathed, voice vibrant and full of life. "I love you, Angela. Whatever it takes, I'll make everything right."

She simply smiled, small and tender. Lincoln lifted her hand to his lips, his voice soft but imploring. "Don't sleep yet, Angel. Just tell me I'm not imagining it. Tell me you love me."

"I love you," she whispered, a hint of mischief and warmth threading through her exhaustion. "I never stopped. Can I go to sleep now, please?"

Lincoln chuckled softly, shaken but relieved. "Such sweet manners," he murmured, brushing a strand of hair from her face. "Sleep now, my angel. I'll be here. Nothing in this world will ever hurt you again."

He stayed with her as the morning light poured in, watching her chest rise and fall gently. His fingers traced the delicate lines of her hand, memorising the warmth he had nearly lost. For a long moment, he simply held her, leaning close enough to catch the faint scent of her hair, the softness of her breath on his cheek.

She stirred slightly, murmuring his name in a half-dreaming whisper, and he pressed a soft kiss to her temple. "I'm right here, Angela. Always," he promised, his voice a vow that would never waver.

Time slowed. Outside, the city moved on, indifferent, but in this quiet hospital room, nothing existed but the two of them—tangled hands, whispered promises, and the steady certainty of love that had survived everything. He leaned back slightly, still holding her hand, and allowed himself a brief moment to feel every fear, every regret, melt into the relief of her presence.

She slept, but he did not. Lincoln watched, vigilant and protective, until the light shifted across the room and he felt the weight of the morning settle softly around them. And in that silence, he swore again that he would never allow anything to come between them—not again.

Chapter Twenty-One

When Angela opened her eyes again, the first thing she saw was Maria. The last trace of severity had softened from her face, replaced by a look Angela had never seen directed at her before—pure relief. Angela tried to lift her head, but the sharp pull of pain stopped her instantly.

"No! Don't move," Maria said quickly, rising to her feet. "You're all bandaged up, Angela. Moving will only hurt you. I'll come where you can see me better."

She circled to the other side of the bed, her movements unusually careful, as though even her presence might cause harm. Angela lifted a trembling hand to her face. Her fingers brushed bare skin. No bandages. But when her hand drifted higher, she felt the thick wrappings around her head.

"You're not scarred, thank God," Maria murmured. She sat gingerly on the edge of the mattress, watching Angela as if any flicker of pain might undo her. "It was your head, your shoulders, and your back that took the worst of it."

Angela's voice was little more than a whisper. "How... how am I?"

Maria covered her hand, her touch unexpectedly gentle. "You'll recover, love. Otherwise, they'd never have let me sneak in to see you. Until today it was only relatives. And that meant Lincoln."

Angela's heart gave a weak, unsteady leap. "Lincoln? He was here. I remember..." The sound of his voice came back to her in flashes—low, desperate, saying words she wasn't sure had been real. Telling her he loved her. Was it true, or just the fevered confusion of pain?

"He's been here for two days," Maria said firmly, as if cutting through Angela's uncertainty. "Never left your side, not once. They all but dragged him out this morning—he hadn't eaten, hadn't slept. He refused to move until the doctor himself told him you were going to be all right. You know what he's like—still the boss, even when he's about to collapse."

Angela's lashes fluttered. "But... how did he even know?"

"The police found him. As soon as they saw your I.D. they went straight to inform him. He's been here ever since."

"The car," Angela whispered faintly. "I remember the car..."

Her eyes were already closing, too heavy to fight. Maria's voice went on, calm and steady, but Angela no longer heard the words. She was searching inwardly, reaching for another voice. Lincoln's voice. The memory of it clung to her like a fragile thread—he had said he loved her. Hadn't he? Could it possibly be true?

But it blurred with the pain, with the haze of dreams and morphine. She couldn't hold onto it. Not yet. With a long, shuddering sigh, Angela let the darkness pull her back under, surrendering to the sleep that the painkillers demanded.

When Angela stirred again, the room was dim, bathed in the muted glow of the bedside lamp. The steady hum of machines filled the silence, each rhythmic beep tethering her to life. Her body felt leaden, her head wrapped in a fog that blurred the line between dream and reality.

She blinked slowly, piecing together fragments—voices, touches, words. Had Lincoln been here? She could almost hear him still, that deep, aching tone breaking in a whisper: *'I love you. I've always loved you.'*

But no—that couldn't be right. That had only been her mind, conjuring comfort from despair. Lincoln Stokes didn't speak words like that. Not to her. Not ever.

Her throat tightened as she shifted her hand against the sheets. The memory was too vivid—the heat of his palm closing around hers, the ragged desperation in his voice. It felt real. Too real. And yet... when she turned her head now, the chair beside her bed was empty.

A hollow ache spread in her chest. She must have dreamed it; she told herself fiercely. Morphine dreams, cruel and mocking. Perhaps he had sat with her—out of duty, out of guilt—but those words... no. Lincoln would never give her what she wanted most. Not when she had already lost him.

Her lashes fluttered shut, but the sting of tears slipped free anyway. How merciless her imagination was, to taunt her with the one thing she could never have.

From the doorway, unseen, Lincoln stood frozen. He drank in the fragile rise and fall of her chest, the delicate tremor of her lashes against pale skin, the faint glimmer of tears she tried in vain to hide. His heart tightened with all he longed to say—the words he had whispered when he thought she could not hear, words that had fallen unheard, lost in silence.

The nurses had handed him her purse, carried in with her belongings. Inside, he found undeniable proof of her intentions: a one-way airline ticket to Australia, a bank cheque made out to her name, and a substantial sum of cash. Every detail confirmed it—Angela was leaving the country. The realisation struck him like a hammer to the chest, and the iron grip of fear and helplessness coiled around him like a vice.

He had hurt her so deeply, so irrevocably, that she was willing to vanish without a word, to flee across the world rather than face him. The thought made his stomach twist, a hollow, sick ache no power, no wealth, no influence could ever ease.

Whispers in the dark weren't enough—not anymore. She deserved more than words spoken to a woman half-conscious, fading. She deserved proof of his truth, manifest in every choice, every action, every breath he had left to give.

"Angela," he said softly, stepping into the room. Her name cracked on his tongue, as though even speaking it might shatter him. He crossed the space slowly, deliberately, and reached for her hand.

Her eyes opened at once, glazed with unshed tears, and when they found his, the raw pain in them nearly drove him to his knees. "Lincoln."

Relief surged through him, yet it broke instantly on the rocks of her anguish. He wrapped her fragile fingers in his, clinging gently but firmly—as though letting go meant losing her forever.

But she flinched, tried to pull away. The rejection cut deeper than any blade, but he couldn't release her. His thumb brushed across her knuckles with aching tenderness. "Sweetheart—"

"No." Her voice cracked, thin but sharp enough to wound. Each syllable cost her strength she didn't have. "Lincoln, just… just go."

He stilled, every muscle locking as though her words had frozen him in place.

"I can't do this anymore," she whispered, her voice frayed with sorrow and shame. Her face turned from him; lashes wet against her cheeks. "I can't be with someone who thinks I'm stupid and childish. I deserve better. Go to Fiona. Be happy with her. That's what you want. That's what you've always wanted. I need to… to move on."

The finality in her voice gutted him. For a heartbeat he couldn't breathe. Couldn't speak. The roaring in his ears drowned out everything but the truth he had denied for too long—he was losing her. For good.

He bent closer, his grip tightening around her fragile hand, desperate, unrelenting. His voice broke from the deepest part of him, hoarse and raw.

"No," he rasped. "Don't you dare believe that. Not for one second. I never wanted Fiona. I never touched her. I never saw her the way I see you."

Her eyes flickered back to his, wide, wounded, glistening with disbelief. Her lips trembled. "She said you did. She said you both already were—"

His jaw clenched hard, the muscles ticking with the effort of restraint, fury at himself and at Fiona burning in his chest. "She lied." The word cracked out of him, sharp as steel, leaving no room for doubt. His voice dropped, stripped bare, every syllable shaking with remorse.

"And I was a fool—God, I was a fool—for letting her lies touch you. For letting you believe, even for a second, that you weren't everything to me. My pride, my silence… I let them destroy us. I should have fought harder. I should have proved every single day that you are not a pawn, not a mistake—you are my life. My everything."

His hand lifted, unsteady, his thumb trembling as it brushed away the lone tear trailing down her cheek. He lingered there, his palm cupping her face as though she were the only thing tethering him to this world. His voice dropped, thick with anguish and devotion.

"Listen to me, Angel. You are my wife. My life. There is no Fiona. There has never been a Fiona. There has only ever been you."

Angela shook her head weakly, as though the weight of hope in his words was too heavy to bear. "I… I want to believe you," she whispered, her voice splintering with pain.

"Then let me make you believe." His forehead lowered until it rested against hers, his breath unsteady, his words fierce. "Not with hollow apologies. Not with empty promises. With every choice I make. Every breath. Every moment I'm given. Let me prove to you, day after day, that you are the only woman I will ever love."

Her tears spilled faster, sliding down into the hollow of her throat, her heart tearing between the scars of betrayal and the desperate ache to trust him again. "You dismissed my fears as idiotic… and childish," she choked out, each word reopening wounds she had tried so hard to close.

Lincoln flinched as though struck, guilt cutting across his features like a blade. His voice cracked, stripped of all pride, bare and broken. "I was wrong. God, I was so wrong. You are the most extraordinary woman I've ever known—the most beautiful soul I will ever meet. And I will spend every day I have left making it up to you. Every hour. Every heartbeat. Until there's not a shadow of doubt left in your heart."

Something in her gave way then—not her strength, but the fragile walls she had built to protect herself from him. With a shuddering sob, Angela reached for him, her hand trembling as it clutched at his shirt, dragging him closer as though she feared he might vanish if she let go.

Lincoln caught her instantly, his hands framing her face, achingly gentle against the bandages yet burning with the desperation of a man who could not survive losing her again. He bent his head, burying his face in her hair, his voice muffled, raw, a vow carved from his very soul.

"I love you, Angel. I swear on my life—you will never doubt me again."

And this time… she didn't push him away.

Her tears soaked into his shirt, but her voice—soft, broken, and true—rose between them, carrying the fragile strength of her heart.

"I love you too."

The next day, Lincoln and Kurt Marsden walked in together, and Angela's stomach tightened like a fist. They hadn't seen each other since the day, nearly five years ago, when she had married Lincoln. To see them side by side now—whether by intention or coincidence—felt like a loaded signal, one that could only end in reckoning.

"How are you, Angela?" her father asked, moving toward her first. Lincoln held back, letting Kurt take the lead, though his storm-grey eyes never wavered from her. Angela felt the familiar pull in her chest, a strange mixture of relief and unease that always came with Lincoln's nearness.

"I feel much better today," she said, forcing steadiness into her voice. Her gaze flickered to Lincoln, and his answering smile—quiet, reassuring—was like an anchor dropped in a storm.

"You gave us a fright," Kurt said gruffly. "I had no idea about the accident until…" His pause was slight, but heavy. "…until Lincoln told me."

The hesitation in his tone revealed more than his words. This was not their first meeting. Lincoln had already stepped into the breach, shaping the ground beneath them with his characteristic authority. Angela saw it in every glance, every restrained gesture.

"Have you been here before?" she asked, her voice tighter than she meant.

"Straight away. That first night," her father admitted. "You were unconscious. I thought…" His voice cracked, the rest left unsaid. To her astonishment, his face—so often set in stone—wavered with raw emotion.

"Well, I'm all right now," she said briskly, and in that moment, Lincoln moved closer, his presence a protective shadow. Her pulse stuttered.

"And you're going to stay all right," he said firmly, his fingers brushing hers in a fleeting, intimate touch. "Soon, I'll have you home. This time, I might just lock you in."

"I won't be going anywhere," Angela whispered. The words slipped out before she could stop them, and for a heartbeat the world narrowed to just him—his nearness, his voice, his unwavering focus.

"I want to give up the firm," Kurt said suddenly, his voice unsteady. "But he won't let me."

"No, I won't," Lincoln said flatly, the protector in him rising again. "What would you do with yourself otherwise? And I'll not have Angela dragged into tedious details."

"Not exactly tedious—" her father began, but Lincoln's sharp look silenced him.

"This is a new beginning. Marsden Enterprises is your company, and you'll continue to run it. I'll help, yes—but the responsibility is yours. One day it will be Angela's. That was always your plan."

"It was," Kurt agreed, regret in his voice. "It's all I have to leave her. I always meant to train her, but… it all fell apart."

"I tore it apart," Lincoln said grimly, no excuses in his tone. "But you can build it again. And Angela doesn't need training—Jeff Scott says she already knows exactly what she's doing."

Angela's throat tightened. "I may not want to go back," she said softly.

Both men turned to her, eyes sharp with concern.

"It's all right," she assured them, forcing calm into her voice. "I'm not clinging to the past, and I'm not bitter. I just… I may want something different. To be Lincoln's wife. To have a family."

Lincoln's gaze softened, fierce and tender at once. "Then the firm will be a legacy for your grandchildren," he said, his smile brushing over her like a vow.

Her father's eyes shone, the hardness in them gentling. "It's something to work for."

Lincoln's hand slid into hers again, this time holding it firmly, a silent promise she could feel down to her bones. Angela met his gaze, her pulse racing. Even here, with her father watching, she felt the truth of it: Lincoln would never let her go again.

Two weeks later, Lincoln came to take her home. He gave her a choice with a small, teasing smile.

"The house or the penthouse?" he asked as he settled her carefully into the car and slid in beside her.

"The penthouse," she said without hesitation. "It all began there. It can start there all over again."

"It never ended," Lincoln said deeply, his eyes tracing the delicate lines of her still-pale face. "When you left me, I stayed at the penthouse all the time. I couldn't bear the house. We had so many plans there… I more or less hid in the penthouse, clinging to every memory of you."

Then, as if the words alone weren't enough, he leaned across and pulled her into his arms, holding her tightly. "God, I love you, Angel!" he murmured, his voice thick with emotion. "You've always been the centre of my life—from the very first moment I saw you."

She tilted her head, her hand brushing over his face, tracing every contour with a quiet reverence. Every unspoken question in her heart seemed answered by the intensity in his eyes.

"There never was Fiona, was there?" she whispered.

Lincoln shook his head, lips twisting ruefully. "No, sweetheart. There was only you—from the moment I met you. There never has been anyone else."

"Nor for me," Angela said firmly, and the warmth in his gaze melted the last of her lingering anxieties.

"I know, sweet Angel," he murmured softly. "In my heart, I've always known. There was only ever you and me, just as it was meant to be."

Later, in the quiet warmth of the bedroom, Angela lay curled against him, her head resting on his shoulder as she looked dreamily around the penthouse—her first home with him.

"You made a miracle for me," she whispered, and Lincoln bent, letting his lips trail lightly across her cheek.

"I can't make miracles, Angel," he said softly. "I can only hold onto the one miracle I've got—a miracle I almost lost because of my bitterness."

"I couldn't blame you," she said gently. "When Fiona told me... I was sure you could never have loved me at all. She even mentioned your father's death—"

"It was an accident, Angela," he interrupted firmly. "Something went wrong with the car. He lost control. He would never have left my mother behind. They loved each other. I always knew it was an accident, but the rumours kept spreading. And I did nothing to stop them. It fed my anger. I thought I could have everything—keep you with me, shield you from the truth, and continue my destruction. Kurt is your father, yes—but I had no pity. No mercy."

"Don't," Angela urged softly. "It's over. He's back at work, and he looks so different now."

"Putting a good mind to straightforward action," Lincoln grunted, a trace of irritation in his voice, though Angela wound her arms around him, softening him instantly.

"Don't be angry," she whispered, and he relaxed, turning toward her, his eyes roaming over her face with gentle intensity.

"I'm not angry. Not ever again," he said softly. "Though it is ironic... if your father had run his business as he is now, I would never have had the chance to crush him."

"Not even you?" Angela teased, her green eyes sparkling with mock innocence.

"Not even me," he growled, tightening his hold on her. "And don't look at me like that—not until you're fully recovered."

"I am!" she protested, and he gave her a rueful smile.

"You're not well enough for me to make love to you," he said, voice low and seductive. "There are no half-measures with you, my love."

"Why did you never let me have a baby?" she asked breathlessly, tilting her head so his smiling lips brushed her skin.

"I thought you might get tired of me," he confessed softly. "You were too young, and I knew it. I couldn't burden you with a child."

"So, it was my youth and your stupidity," Angela teased.

"Fairly accurate," he agreed with a delighted laugh. "But don't get too used to turning that sharp tongue on me. You won't always be too fragile to touch."

Epilogue

14 months later…

Angela knelt beside William Henry Stokes' crib, her eyes drinking in every detail of her eight-week-old son. He was so impossibly small, yet already the axis on which her entire world turned. The rise and fall of his tiny chest, the faint flutter of his lashes, even the way his fist curled in sleep—it all seemed like a miracle she could never tire of watching. Her heart swelled as she bent close, brushing a feather-light kiss across his warm forehead. For that single, suspended moment, nothing beyond this room existed; there was only her and her child, cocooned in a silence broken only by his soft breaths.

At last, she straightened, her steps quiet as she slipped from the nursery. Downstairs, her gaze instinctively sought the window. The sight she was waiting for—Lincoln's car— wasn't there yet, but she didn't need to see it to feel his presence. They had been back at the house for two months now, since William's birth, living in the home they had dreamed of together long before. Outside, the first snow of winter was falling in thick, lazy flakes, blanketing the garden and fields in a soft, brilliant white. The trees and hedges were frosted, and the world seemed hushed and magical. It was almost Christmas—their second together since reconciling—and the Spokes Group had closed for the holiday. She would have him all to herself for a whole week.

Angela returned to the tall evergreen beside the glowing fire, kneeling to adjust the last ornaments, her fingers lingering on a sparkling ribbon. The house was quiet, except for the soft rustle of the housekeeper in the kitchen. Her mind wandered through the happiness of her present life. Lincoln had made things right, just as he had promised. Her father had returned to work a changed man, and while there was still a faint stiffness between Lincoln and Kurt Marsden, both men made every effort to be normal—for her and for William.

She smiled softly, her gaze resting on the twinkling lights. For the first time in years, Angela had no doubts about Lincoln's love. None at all.

The quiet was broken by the sound of footsteps in the hall, and she turned, startled, to see Lincoln standing in the doorway of the drawing room. His eyes were fixed on her, intense and unyielding.

"I didn't hear the car!" she exclaimed, and he shook his head, his gaze never leaving her face.

"I parked around the back. It can stay there for the week—we're not going anywhere. I hope we get snowed in," he said, the corners of his mouth lifting in a rare, private smile.

Angela's cheeks flushed as she realised the slow, heated sweep of his gaze. She swallowed, suddenly aware of how small she seemed beneath his commanding presence.

"I found this when I was clearing the last of my things to bring here," she said softly, kneeling beside the tree again, holding up the black skirt dotted with pink flowers and the pink sweater that hugged her figure. "I thought it might… surprise you."

Lincoln's breath hitched. "You little devil," he murmured, stepping forward. "You knew exactly what it would do to me. It's like seeing you for the first time all over again."

He dropped his briefcase with a soft thud and moved closer. Angela laughed, looking up at him, the warmth in his eyes making her heart flutter.

"I hope this isn't my Christmas present," he said huskily, "because I'll want a lot more than just the sight of you."

Before she could respond, he gently pulled her to her feet. His hands were firm yet tender as he encircled her, holding her close. "It's like going back with no unhappiness in between," he whispered, his face resting against her hair. "If I lost you now, sweetheart… I don't think I could survive it."

"You're never going to lose me," Angela said, wrapping her arms around his neck. "I know you love me. Nothing will ever make me doubt it again."

"I will never give you reason to," he promised, brushing his lips over hers in a soft, lingering kiss before lifting her into his arms. He carried her effortlessly toward the stairs, teasing her with kisses along the way.

"I hope William is settled for a little while," he murmured once they reached their bedroom. "Because I don't need anything else right now—no dinner, no work. I just need you."

They sank into each other, bodies entwined, moving with a closeness that only years of love and reconciliation could bring. When their breathing finally slowed, Lincoln hovered over her, his grey eyes glittering with devotion. Angela lifted a trembling hand to his face.

"I love you," she whispered.

"I love you too," he said, kissing her fingertips, his voice low and unshakable. "I'll never let you doubt it again. I could stay like this forever and never move a muscle."

Angela smiled, her green eyes bright with mischief and warmth. "Maria and my father are coming to dinner," she reminded him.

Lincoln groaned and rolled onto his side, pulling her with him, their laughter and whispered promises filling the room as the snow continued to fall outside. For the first time in a long time, the house was theirs in every sense—full of love, warmth, and the promise of forever.

The first rays of the winter sun filtered through the curtains on Christmas morning, casting a soft golden glow across the room. Angela stirred beneath the warmth of the blankets, her head resting against Lincoln's chest, and for a moment, she simply breathed him in—the steady rhythm of his heartbeat a comfort she had never known she needed so desperately.

A tiny coo drew her attention downward. William Henry was nestled between them, swaddled in a pale blue blanket, his tiny fists curling and uncurling as he stirred awake. Angela's heart swelled, and a smile tugged at her lips as she gently stroked his cheek.

"Good morning, my sweet boy," she whispered. William's little fingers twitched as though responding, and she laughed softly.

Lincoln shifted slightly, lifting his head to peer down at them. "Merry Christmas, my angels," he murmured, brushing a kiss across Angela's temple before kissing William's tiny hand. His grey eyes glittered with adoration, and Angela felt the familiar pull in her chest, a mixture of love, awe, and comfort.

"You two are up early," she said, sitting up and adjusting the blankets around them.

"We couldn't wait," Lincoln said, a mischievous smile tugging at his lips. "Besides…" He leaned closer to William, whispering playfully. "Santa's been very generous this year, but I think we might be the best gift of all."

Angela laughed, her voice soft but full of warmth. "I think William agrees," she said, watching as their son gurgled and kicked gently.

Lincoln's hand found hers, fingers interlacing naturally. "I've never felt more complete," he said quietly. "Everything we've been through… it's all led us here. To this. To you. To him. To us."

Angela rested her head against his shoulder, her eyes drifting to the soft morning light playing across the room. "It feels like a miracle," she whispered. "And I don't ever want to take it for granted."

Lincoln's lips brushed hers in a slow, lingering kiss. "Nor I," he promised, his voice thick with emotion. "Every day with you and William is a gift I'll never squander."

For the next hour, they lingered in the quiet intimacy of their bedroom, talking in soft whispers and laughter, sharing gentle kisses and stolen glances. William gurgled happily between them, and every coo and tiny movement seemed to draw them even closer.

When the house began to stir—the distant clatter from the kitchen and the faint murmur of Maria preparing breakfast—they rose together, Lincoln carrying William in one arm while his other hand held Angela's.

Outside, the snow continued to fall, blanketing the world in perfect white. Inside, the warmth of love, laughter, and family wrapped around them. For the first time in years, Angela knew there were no doubts, no fears—only the certainty of Lincoln's unwavering devotion, their shared future, and the tiny miracle of their son nestled safely in their arms.

Lincoln leaned down to Angela's ear as they reached the breakfast table, his voice a low murmur filled with promise. "This is only the beginning. Our first Christmas as a family, Angel… and it's going to be perfect."

Angela smiled, resting her head on his shoulder as they joined Maria and Kurt, and for the first time, she felt truly home.

The End

Before You Go…

If you fell for these characters and want more love stories filled with emotion, passion, and second chances, my newsletter is where I share them first.

You'll receive:

💕 Early access to new releases

💕 Exclusive reader-only content and extras

👉 **Join my reader list here:** https://alisonreidauthor.com

I'd love to welcome you. 💕

Alison Reid

Thank you for reading Alpha Kings!

If you enjoyed this collection of irresistible alpha heroes, keep an eye out for more upcoming romance collections by Alison Reid, including:

Cautious Hearts - *A Trust-After-Heartbreak Romance Collection*

Dark & Dangerous - *Brooding Heroes Romance Collection*

Final Surrender - *Alpha Heroes Yielding to Love Collection*

Forbidden Hearts - *A Forbidden Love Romance Collection*

Forever Mine - *A Longing-for-Love Romance Collection*

Guarded Hearts - *A Surrender to Love Romance Collection*

Hearts & Secrets - *Small Town Romance Collection*

Hearts in Peril - *A Suspenseful Romance Collection*

Hidden Truths - *A Secret Identity Romance Collection*

Lies & Hearts - *A Lies, Secrets & Betrayal Romance Collection*

Love After Regret - *A Second-Chance Redemption Romance Collection*

Misjudged Hearts - *A Love After Judgement Romance Collection*

Torn Between Hearts - *A Love Triangle Romance Collection*

All of Alison Reid's books feature standalone stories, swoon-worthy heroes, and guaranteed happily-ever-afters.

Books by Alison Reid

A Billionaire for Christmas

A Heart in Florence

After The Storm

Always You

Before I Fell

Before the Thaw

Beneath the Lies

Billionaire Bodyguard

Billionaire Rancher

Blueprints of the Heart

Branlow

Collide

Echoes of Deception

Falling for the Billionaire

Forever Yours

Heart of the Outback

Hearts on the Line

Hidden Gem

Kept Promises

Mended Hearts

Mistaken Hearts

New Year's Eve Kiss

Quiet Danger

Reckless Hearts

Reflections of Deception

Second Glance

Shadows of the Past

Shattered Dreams

Shattered Hope, Stolen Kisses

Still Yours

The Billionaire's Accidental Legacy

The Billionaire's Bargain

The Billionaire's Mistake

The Billionaire's Regret

The Billionaire's Secret Baby

The Billionaire's Unexpected Heir

The Blood Debt

The Playboy's Surrender

The Wrong Sister

Trust in Time

Undercover Billionaire

Until you Loved Me

Vows of Vengeance

Wife in Name Only

Find all my books on Amazon:

https://www.amazon.com/author/alisonreid1970

About the Author

Alison Reid writes contemporary and small-town romance filled with heart, passion, and second-chance love stories. Her novels feature strong heroines, irresistible heroes, and the happily-ever-afters readers adore.

Before turning her love of storytelling into a publishing career, Alison spent thirty-five years working as an engineer—proof that happily-ever-afters can be built as carefully as any blueprint. She began writing as a hobby during the COVID lockdowns and quickly discovered a passion she couldn't ignore.

Alison is happily married, has two grown children, and shares her home with two beautiful dogs who are convinced they deserve to be her main characters. When she's not writing, she enjoys reading, spending time with her family, and imagining new love stories. She hopes her books give readers a few hours of escape, joy, and swoon-worthy romance they won't soon forget.

https://alisonreidauthor.com